Thank you for choosing to celebrate ten years of award-winning romance with Arabesque. In recognition of our literary landmark, last year BET Books launched a special Collector's Series honoring the authors who pioneered African-American romance. With a unique three books-in-one format, each anthology features the most beloved works of the Arabesque imprint.

Sensuous, intriguing, and intense, this special collector's series was launched in 2004 with *First Touch,* which included three of Arabesque's first published novels written by Sandra Kitt, Francis Ray, and Eboni Snoe; it was followed by *Hideaway Saga,* three novels from award-winning author Rochelle Alers; and the third in the series, *Falcon Saga,* by Francis Ray. Last year's series concluded with Brenda Jackson's *Madaris Saga.*

This year we continue the series with Donna Hill's *Courageous Hearts,* the book you are holding, which includes three of this best-selling author's most popular romances—*Temptation, Scandalous* and *Deception.* We invite you to read all of these exceptional works by our renowned authors and hope that you look for upcoming Collector's Series from Felicia Mason, Bette Ford, and Shirley Hailstock.

In addition to recognizing these authors, we would also like to honor the succession of editors—Monica Harris, Karen Thomas, Chandra Taylor, and the current editor, Evette Porter—who have guided the artistic direction of Arabesque during our successful history.

We hope you enjoy these romances. Please give us your feedback at our website at www.bet.com/books.

Sincerely,

Linda Gill
VP and Publisher
BET Books

DONNA HILL

COURAGEOUS HEARTS

BET Publications, LLC
http://www.bet.com
http://www.arabesquebooks.com

ARABESQUE BOOKS are published by

BET Publications, LLC
c/o BET BOOKS
One BET Plaza
1900 W Place NE
Washington, DC 20018-1211

All Kensington Titles, Imprints, and Distributed Lines are available at special quantity discounts for bulk purchases for sales promotions, premiums, fund-raising, and educational or institutional use. Special book excerpts or customized printings can also be created to fit specific needs. For details, write or phone the office of the Kensington special sales manager: Kensington Publishing Corp., 850 Third Avenue, New York, NY 10022, attn: Special Sales Department, Phone: 1-800-221-2647.

ISBN 1-58314-660-1

First Printing: February 2005
10 9 8 7 6 5 4 3 2 1

Printed in the United States of America

Contents

Temptation

PROLOGUE

Fast.

The sleek bronze-toned Mercedes-Benz convertible sped down the black tarred San Francisco freeway. Jordan had purchased the car for her a year ago, to celebrate her twenty-seventh birthday and their fourth wedding anniversary. Just before. . . . Noelle shook her head and stepped on the gas. She wouldn't think about it.

Faster. The turbo charged engine hurtled forward. Her honey-colored hair, fashioned after actress Halle Berry, whipped around her copper-toned face. Maybe if she drove faster she could make the memories rush past like the scenery that graced the precisely manicured lawns. Rush past the incompleteness that was her life, now that Jordan was dead.

She'd allowed herself to be totally transformed by the charismatic Jordan Maxwell. He'd taken a scrawny, uneducated girl from the New Orleans bayou and turned her into one of the most powerful women on the West Coast. She'd come so far from where she'd been, her past was almost a blur. She was in limbo. She could never go back, and the powers that be, would keep her from going forward.

Without thinking, she adjusted the black sunglasses on her nose. The simple gesture had become habitual. The designer accessory had become her signature for nearly a year.

Noelle didn't wear the blacker than black glasses so much for sun, or to hide the tears that so frequently welled up in her eyes. She wore them more to camouflage the emptiness that had taken up residence in the dark brown orbs.

She couldn't let them see the void or the fear that kept her walking the floors at night. There were too many jealous onlookers—so-called friends that couldn't wait to see her fail. She knew that they snickered behind her back and that hurt her more than she'd ever let on. And no one was more outraged at her success than Trent Dixon.

Noelle rounded the hairpin turn with ease and recalled a conversation she'd stumbled upon at a party one night. *It was not only amusing that Jordan hadn't turned his company reins directly over to her, but expected,* she'd overheard. Noelle was an heiress to an empire with no throne. Trent had been with Jordan when he'd hit his first big deal in the Sudan. Trent knew everything there was to know about the import-export business. Noelle supposed that it was only fitting that Trent be handed the reins. As far as she was concerned, Trent Dixon could take the company and go straight to hell.

She'd never had any interest in the import-export business and Jordan was fully aware of that fact. Her views and his remained in opposition throughout their marriage. Nonetheless, she'd continue to receive her share of the profits whether she took over or not. What she really wanted to sink her teeth into was the villa, Liaisons. The villa that Jordan had willed to her. She had plans for that. Big plans. She'd make a name for herself on her own terms, not on Jordan Maxwell's coattails, and certainly not under the tutelage of Trent Dixon. He was the last person she wanted anything to do with.

Every time she thought about Trent Dixon she got a headache. Her body began to overheat and she couldn't think straight. There was no way that she was looking forward to their impending meeting, since their long-distance phone conversations over the past year had been anything but cordial. They had been treading the thin line between chilly politeness and outright sarcasm. Anytime he called to advise her that her signature was required on a document, even over the scratchy phone connection, Noelle could practically taste his indignation all the way from the Sudan. But he would never know how deeply she despised him. There was nothing that he could ever say or do that would make her believe that he didn't have something to do with Jordan's death. And for that she'd never forgive him.

He was scheduled to arrive in the states in two weeks. She'd never met him face to face. For some strange reason the thought of his arrival made her nervous. Because of that, it was more important than ever that Liaisons be perfect when he arrived. There was no one better than Tempest Dailey to pull off that miracle. And she'd done precisely that. The gala opening of Liaisons was scheduled for the following evening.

Tempest and her husband Braxton were two people who had risen above the others and proven themselves to be true friends. Noelle couldn't wait to see Tempest again.

Noelle stepped on the gas while smoothly cutting around a red Porsche. She checked the digital clock on the dash. Twenty minutes before Tempest's plane was to arrive. If she kept up the 85 mph speed, she'd beat the plane with time to spare.

CHAPTER 1

The trill of soft music wafted across the warm San Francisco night. Hundreds of twinkling lights hung from the trees, the balustrades and windows, turning the enormous villa into a fairyland.

Noelle St. James-Maxwell, breathed a sigh of contentment. Everything was exquisite. The caterers had laid out a fare fit for royalty. Every imaginable delicacy was there for the taking. She smiled in satisfaction as she regally strolled across the grounds, nodding and waving, greeting the guests, the curious, the envious.

Noelle couldn't call any of them friends, she thought, ruefully, shaking hands with the president of NBC studios. She knew they'd all come to gawk, to pass their comments, stir more rumors and most of all, to see if the young widow of Jordan Maxwell had what it took to run his empire.

They wanted her to fail, she knew, smiling graciously at the arrival of Whitney and her superstar husband. The circle of elite associates that her late husband surrounded himself with were a tight-knit, cliquish group. They turned their noses up at any who were not one of them. Background, education and family trees were more important than personal substance. Noelle couldn't count a friend among them. The group had yet to adjust to the fact that Jordan Maxwell, owner of one of the largest import-export companies in the U.S., a man who could have any woman he chose, had plucked a no-count waitress from the bowels of the Louisiana swampland and dropped her in their midst. They were still reeling from that indignity five years later.

Jordan had groomed her for a world that she had never fully adjusted to and was never accepted in. Liaisons was her first real attempt at anything independent of Jordan. The thought of failure terrified her, and failure would solidify every negative comment ever said about her. For that reason, she'd never let them see the loneliness or the fear that lived in her soul, visible only through her eyes. For now, the darkness would hide her secret.

But tonight was her success, she thought, shaking off the disturbing thoughts. Liaisons was the culmination of her dreams, a tribute to Jordan, and no one was going to ruin it. Not even Trent Dixon.

"Noelle! Noelle!"

She turned in the direction of the familiar voice, the smile she displayed being genuine for the first time in hours.

"Tempest."

The two women embraced warmly, then quickly stepped back to assess the other.

"That dress is fabulous, girl," Tempest enthused, admiring the silk sheath of champagne gold that seductively stroked Noelle's notorious curves, reaching just above her slender ankles. The daring side split gave a teasing view of a perfect copper leg from ankle to hip.

Her soft creole accent floated through the air. "*Merci.* But of course you have outdone yourself, *chère amie.* Red was always your color."

Tempest smiled at the compliment. With a wicked grin she asked, "What do you wear under something like that?"

Noelle smiled slyly, "Absolutely nothing."

The two women laughed in unison, drawing the attention of one who stood apart from the growing crowd.

Quietly he watched the two beautiful women, but his attention was riveted on Noelle. He'd instantly recognized her. She was more magnificent than any newspaper clipping or photograph, he realized with a jolt that shot straight to his loins.

Her skin brought to mind the tangy taste of cinnamon. The silky head of chestnut hair, begged him to run his fingers through it. Her statuesque form screamed sensuality. Yet she had a presence that demanded respect. She was a woman who could make a man want to keep her in bed and never let her out. By just looking at her, the stirrings of arousal swept through him. He began to imagine what she would feel like moving beneath him.

Damn, man, what the hell are you doing? Fantasizing about making love to your best friend's widow?

He took a quick sip of champagne. In all of the years that he'd worked with Jordan, he'd never met the woman who'd captured the icon's heart. His years of work in the Sudan had kept him out of the States. Now he could see exactly why Jordan had remained so faithful even when he was away from home for months at a time.

Being home again was going to take some getting used to. Especially since he knew he was not welcome here. But he had a job to do. He'd taken an unbreakable oath and he would fulfill Jordan Maxwell's wishes. His beautiful widow would just have to accept that.

As if reading his thoughts, Noelle slowly turned her gaze in his direction. The contact was electrifying. She felt hot and cold at once. His unwavering deep stare seemed to see right through her. The dark eyes were unreadable and she felt naked and vulnerable under their appraisal.

What he saw in her eyes shook him to the marrow of his bones. There in the depths of the nut brown eyes was a haunting loneliness, a well of vulnerability and a compelling pain that made him want to pull her into his arms and make her know that he would make everything right with her world.

Then, as quickly as the force had taken hold of them, the contact was broken when Noelle's attention was diverted by Tempest.

"Noelle? Are you all right? You look like you've been hit by lightning," Tempest said.

Noelle shook her head. "I'm . . . fine." She passed off a weak smile at Tempest, whose eyes turned in the direction of Noelle's gaze.

"Who-is-that?" Tempest asked, admiring the man who defined tall, dark and handsome and made her wish her own gorgeous husband was there to wrap herself around.

"I'm not sure," Noelle answered slowly, noticing that her pulse was racing.

"Well with the vibes that the two of you are giving off, I suggest you find out. Don't you?"

"Maybe later," Noelle answered absently, not trusting the rush of emotions that swirled within her. She expelled a breath. "Where's Braxton?" she asked, needing to change the subject, while forcing calm into her voice.

"I was just thinking the same thing." Tempest checked her watch. Briefly she scanned the blooming crowd, while noticing that the handsome stranger had not taken his eyes off Noelle.

Braxton was not in sight. Tempest frowned. Over the past few months, Braxton's absences and late arrivals had become a bone of contention between them. "He should have been here by now. His flight was scheduled to arrive nearly an hour ago."

"You know how those flights from Morocco can be, *chère.* They're always delayed."

"Hmm. You're probably right. But in the meantime," she added, lowering her gaze to the ground as she spoke, "cutie pie is coming this way."

Noelle angled her head to see him coming toward them. For some inexplicable reason her heart thundered so forcefully she momentarily felt breathless. The closer he came the quicker her pulse galloped.

He didn't just walk, Noelle realized with growing alarm. His every move sizzled, tossing electric sparks in his wake.

Raw was the word that leaped into her brain. Raw, animal sexuality poured from him like sweat after hours of erotic loving. She felt dizzy.

"Good evening ladies." His mellow voice warmed Noelle like brandy in winter. Politely he inclined his head toward Tempest, who smiled knowingly.

"Listen, Noelle, I'm going inside to call the airport. Please excuse me," she said to both. Without another glance she walked up the small incline toward the main entrance.

"I hope it wasn't anything I said," he quipped, flashing a smile that made Noelle's insides quiver.

Smoothly she returned his smile. "I'm sure it wasn't. She's expecting her husband. It seems his plane has been delayed."

"In that case, I feel better." His smile stroked her. "At least about it not being my fault." He made a small show of looking over the grounds, if only to take his mind temporarily off of the face and body that was making him lose his sense of perspective.

In profile, Noelle stole the chance to observe him up close. He had to be over 6'3", she noted, as he stood head and shoulders above her 5'8" height plus heels. His hard muscular body told her that he took care of himself. He had a strong chiseled face of smooth sienna, a well-tended beard that outlined his rugged chin. His eyes were wide and dark, shadowed by thick black lashes and thicker brows. His full, sensuous lips promised unmeasurable pleasure.

He had a real *GQ* look. Even in semicasual attire he gave the impression of power and confidence. He wore a suit of navy linen, that hung loosely on his body, as was the fashion. He chose to wear a V-neck T-shirt of white silk. The low collar entreated her to run her fingers across his chest. She curled them into a fist to quell the urge.

He returned his attention back to her and her flesh warmed under his gaze, shooting flashes of liquid desire to her center. She felt the tips of her breasts ripen under his open perusal, which made her even more self-conscious.

She feels it, too, he realized, her ardor boldly evident through the revealing dress, even as he fought to control the turbulence of passion that raged within him.

He forced his mind to clear. "This is a beautiful place you have. You've done wonders with it."

Noelle's tapered eyebrows arched. "You're familiar with the villa, *monsieur?*"

"Actually," he replied in a confidential tone, "I was with Jordan when he purchased it almost ten years ago. He always had intentions of working on it, but . . ." His sentence drifted off. "I'm glad to see that his very beautiful wife decided to take it over."

His dark eyes held hers a moment too long and Noelle felt lightheaded. *It must be the champagne.*

She cleared her throat. "It seems that you know a great deal about me, *monsieur . . . ?*"

"Noelle! Noelle!"

Noelle turned around to see Braxton and Tempest coming toward her. Her face lit up when she saw Braxton approach. It had been months since she'd last seen him. After the completion of the interior architecture and the landscaping, he'd had to fly off to Morocco.

Now that both of the honored guests were present the official opening of Liaisons could commence.

Braxton embraced her in a warm hug. "It's good to see you again, Noelle. I'm sorry to be so late, but my plane . . ." He gave her that smile that had imprisoned Tempest's heart for life.

Noelle looked at her relieved girlfriend. "I told you," Noelle admonished. She took Braxton's arm and turned back to make introductions.

He was gone. All that remained was his erotic scent that seemed to have seeped into Noelle's pores.

"Oh . . ." she muttered, a bit confused and somewhat embarrassed, looking over the heads of her guests.

"Is something wrong?" Braxton asked.

"No . . . I was just talking with . . ." She expelled a breath. "Never mind." She smiled brightly. "Now that you're here, I can make the announcement to open the house for the tour. That's what's important."

For the next hour, Noelle, Tempest and Braxton were bombarded with congratulations and enthusiastic approval of the three-story villa.

Noelle's jaws began to ache from the continual smile that she had carved on her mouth. But her thoughts were elsewhere. In every free moment, she subtly tried to locate the man whose image she couldn't get off of her mind. He seemed to have vanished, and she didn't even know his name.

"You're completely distracted," Tempest said, surprising Noelle with her nearness.

She laughed, embarrassed. "Is it that obvious?"

"Very." Tempest followed Noelle's gaze. "You're looking for him aren't you?"

Noelle's shoulders slumped. "I am transparent, aren't I?"

"Only to those that know you. So—who is he?"

Noelle turned her palms upward. "I still don't know."

"Excuse me? You mean that the two of you were practically undressing each other on the lawn and you don't know who he is? You're losing your touch."

An underlying sadness scored her voice. "I've had no reason to be interested in a man in a very long time."

"Yes, I know," Tempest said softly, placing a comforting hand on Noelle's bare shoulder, "but you're a healthy, vibrant, beautiful woman. You can't stay in hibernation forever. And you can't use Liaisons to shield yourself from the world."

Noelle's voice quivered. "He's only been gone a year. I . . . I just couldn't . . . He was my life, my world. He . . ."

"He was just a man, Noelle," Tempest said gently. "Just a man. Not the god that everyone, including you, made him out to be. I can't believe that Jordan would want you to remain alone for the rest of your life. He groomed you to be a part of the world, not just the world that he created."

Noelle lowered her eyes, struggling to fight back the tears that burned her eyes and seared her throat.

Her life had changed irrevocably. It was due to Jordan. Everything that she had, what she was, what she thought, was because of Jordan. He'd rescued her, brought new meaning to her life, gave her reason to want to get up everyday.

He'd turned her life around and now he was gone. He'd left her to deal with this evil, hungry world alone. To face his enemies that would just as soon help her as stab her in the back.

Five years ago, sweating in her aunt Chantal's tiny cafe, darting the grubby hands of the male customers she would have never imagined that her life could have ever been any different. Not until the moment that Jordan Maxwell walked into her life. Since that day nothing in her life had ever been the same.

Forever would she recall the way he looked at her when he walked through those doors. . . .

CHAPTER 2

"Noelle! Stop daydreaming," her aunt Chantal ordered. "We have customers."

Chantal wiped her hands on the once-white apron, and shook her head in annoyance.

"For a woman of eighteen, you sometimes act like an *enfant,*" she sputtered, tossing up her hands. "Get your head out of the clouds. There's no knight waiting to rescue a poor orphan girl like you. This is your life, *chère.*"

Chantal marched off toward the kitchen, demanding and instructing all who came in her path.

Noelle sighed deeply, knowing all too well that her aunt was right. This was her life. Here in the bayou of New Orleans, forever at the disposal of someone else.

She knew her aunt meant well, even when her words were harsh. Chantal had immediately taken in Noelle when her mother, Vivian, had died. And Chantal had given her a home. With her father's whereabouts unknown, Chantal became the only family Noelle had. Being Vivian's older sister, Chantal felt it her duty to take in her niece. But not without a price.

Noelle had to drop out of school in order to work in Chantal's cafe. Her aunt felt that an education was a waste of time. Once a person knew how to add, subtract and read the alphabet, school was useless. Common sense and a strong back would be how Noelle would make her way in the world.

Noelle had missed her school years. She missed her friends, she missed her youth. She felt doomed to a life of hard work and poverty.

Many nights she'd lie awake imagining beautiful clothes, a house that didn't always smell of gumbo, and a wonderful husband who adored her. *Dreams.* But her aunt was right. Who would want her? She had nothing and would never *be* anything more than a poor, orphaned waitress.

She pulled her shoulder-length hair behind her ears and walked out of the supply room into the small cafe.

As usual, the dinner crowd had packed the cafe. Although, Chantal's was on the outskirts of the city, patrons came from far and wide to sample the renowned cuisine.

Noelle put on her trained smile and began her routine of checking on customers and seating the incoming diners.

After seating one of her regular customers, she returned to her station at the door, and there stood Jordan Maxwell.

Immediately she knew that this man was different from all of the others. His clothing spoke of wealth, his posture indicated confidence and his smile was warm and inviting, not like the leers that she was used to.

"*Bon soir, monsieur.* May I help you?"

"I hope so," he answered in a voice that vibrated through her like currents on the shore.

She felt suddenly nervous, and childlike under his steady gaze. She lowered her eyes, focusing them on her notepad.

"Will you be dining alone?" Irrationally she hoped that he was.

"Fortunately."

Her head snapped up in question. Her face was hot with embarrassment, as if he'd read her mind. "*Pardon?*"

Jordan chuckled at her discomfiture while enjoying the lilt of her creole accent. "Fortunately, because I hope that you may be able to join me."

"Oh, no, *monsieur,*" she mumbled, both flattered and afraid. Nervously she looked around for her aunt. "That is not possible."

"Maybe not now. But you will. Perhaps next time," he said, fully confident that it would be a reality.

Jordan looked at the lovely young woman and smiled. He was used to having what he wanted and from the moment he set eyes on Noelle, and saw the spark of eager intelligence in her eyes and the pride with which she wore her stained uniform, he determined that she would be his.

"In the meantime, I'd like a table and a bottle of your best wine—to toast the occasion of our meeting."

Noelle felt her heart flutter. She didn't know which way to look. Instead she turned and quickly guided him to a vacant table near the piano.

For the balance of the evening, she consciously avoided going near Jordan's table. But it didn't stop him from following her with his eyes.

Throughout the night, each time that Noelle dared to look in his direction, he raised his glass in a toast. Then, in an instant, without warning, he was gone.

Several months passed and Noelle didn't see Jordan again. But she couldn't seem to forget him or the way he'd made her young heart feel. *Special.* No one had ever done that before. Each time that she strolled through the teeming New Orleans streets, she thought she spotted him in the crowd. At night she dreamed of his face. The strong caramel features, wide dark eyes and hair that reminded her of the first sprinklings of snow.

Then, when she was beginning to believe that seeing him again was an impossibility, he reappeared one steamy night in August.

Noelle saw him standing in the doorway. A flood of heat swept through her and for several moments she stood immobile, unwilling to believe that he had returned. She willed her legs to move.

"You're just as beautiful as I remember," he said, his deep timbre thrilling her.

No one like him had ever called her beautiful. She smiled in response.

Her heart raced. "What brings you back after so long, *monsieur?*"

He took her hand in his. "I thought you'd be ready to have dinner with me now."

Noelle felt her body tremble. She quickly looked around the cafe. She spotted her aunt scowling at her from the rear.

She looked up at him, her eyes begging him to understand. "Please, *monsieur,* my aunt . . ." She looked over her shoulder.

Jordan looked beyond Noelle and spotted Chantal.

"Let's tell your aunt that you'll be leaving." Gently, he pulled Noelle behind him and walked up to Chantal.

That was the last day that Noelle worked in the cafe. Jordan had smoothly convinced Chantal that her niece had the potential to achieve wonderful things, and he was going to be sure that she did. In exchange for Noelle's services, Jordan dutifully sent a very large check to Chantal each month, which seemed to appease her. However, it was difficult for Chantal to believe that a man like Jordan Maxwell could see any value in her meek, little niece. But if he was willing to pay for Noelle's absence, who was she to argue? Perhaps Jordan saw something in Noelle that she, herself, had missed all of these years. She could only hope that Noelle would be happy in her new life.

For a man who had conquered every obstacle in his life, Noelle was a new challenge for Jordan. Somewhere, deep in the recesses of his soul, Jordan saw in her a part of him that was missing. Her naïveté intrigued him. She didn't have a greedy, or pretentious bone in her body. She was unlike any woman he'd ever known. But he knew that in order to fit into his world she would have to be molded as a sculptor models clay into a work of art.

Noelle was instantly caught up in Jordan's vision of what he wanted for her. His dream became hers. She was overwhelmed by his expectations, thrilled at the possibilities yet frightened of the doors that he intended to open for her.

"You have talents that you have yet to discover," he'd said to her. "I intend to bring them to the forefront for all of the world to see."

The first step in her transformation was her education. Jordan hired private tutors to help refine her speech and catch up on her studies. Studies that were conducted in the cozy apartment that he'd selected for Noelle. With that completed, he sent her to the University of Virginia, where she'd met Tempest and Braxton. Her graduate work took place in Europe, Africa, the Orient. She purchased her leather from Italy, her jewels from Africa, her silks from Hong Kong. She visited the finest *haute couture* houses in Paris.

Noelle didn't have time to think about what was happening to her. She felt as though she were in some magical dream world where Jordan was the magician who could make anything happen. But Jordan was a hard taskmaster. "Can't" was not in his vocabulary. He demanded perfection from everyone around him, and accepted no excuses for anything less. He readily used ridicule as a weapon to propel you. Ultimately you produced, if for no other reason than to prove him wrong. In the end, you achieved what you thought was impossible, and secretly you thanked Jordan. He, in turn, received your loyalty.

With no close friends nearby, and her only family hundreds of miles away, Noelle was enveloped in the cocoon that was Jordan Maxwell. She relied on him for everything.

Noelle always felt as if she were in a never-ending dream. She agreed with every suggestion, critical comment or word of effusive praise that Jordan uttered, afraid that if she ever challenged Jordan's wishes, for her, she'd wake up from her dream and find herself back in Chantal's cafe.

Her transformation took five years to complete, and in the fifth year, Jordan married his creation.

Jordan Maxwell had literally swept Noelle off of her feet and into a world that she had only imagined. Only now it was more magnificent than she'd ever dreamed. She was only beginning to see the power that Jordan wielded. With a simple phone call he could have planes, boats, cars at his disposal. With a dash of his signature he could transfer millions of dollars. By simple request, he could secure the company of politicians, diplomats, movie stars. "Everyone has a weakness, Noelle," Jordan often told her. "Find it and you have conquered them."

Her sheltered years in New Orleans had left her naive about the ways of the world. Even her travels across the globe were chaperoned. She never imagined how much subterfuge, envy, and viciousness that existed in Jordan's everyday life and did not believe the rumors of darker dealings.

What she did understand, however, was that she did not truly fit into his world. All of the fine clothes, the culture, the money, the power would not change the fact that she was only a cook from a backwater cafe. And to Jordan's friends and associates, she always would be.

Jordan protected her as much as possible from the gossip. She, in turn, worshipped the ground that he walked on. But deep in her heart, she wondered if Jordan truly loved her. She knew he loved what he could do for her and he loved the person that he'd created. But did he truly love her? She didn't think so.

"I didn't mean to upset you, Noelle," Tempest said softly. She gently stroked her arm, pulling Noelle back from the depths of her memories.

Noelle blinked back the images. She gave Tempest a faltering smile. "I know," she whispered. "These are my ghosts. I'll find a way to banish them. One day." She forced a smile. "In the meantime, I have a half dozen guests that have reservations for the opening weekend. So, shall we get them settled?"

CHAPTER 3

Trent moved like a caged panther around his suite, tossing his belongings around as if they were to be discarded.

Noelle St. James-Maxwell had unnerved him. That's all there was to it. He'd never met a woman capable of doing that to him, especially without even trying.

He blew out an exasperated breath and jammed his hands in his pockets. How in the world was he supposed to accomplish what he'd come to do, if he couldn't be in the same room with her without losing his cool? To compound the problem, once she realized who he was, he was sure she wouldn't come within ten feet of him.

He ran his hand across his bearded chin. Perhaps he could get around that little inconvenience, he thought. At least until he won her confidence.

He stopped pacing. The wheels began to spin. He was sure that he could pull it off. All he needed was a few weeks, two months at best, and his work would be finished.

He strode across the room to the phone and picked up the elaborate Liaisons brochure that had only been distributed to the selected few. He dialed the private number.

The illuminated numbers on the bedside clock, were reflected in Noelle's weary eyes. In little more than an hour the sun would rise across the bay. She hadn't slept more than a few minutes all night.

Instead of succumbing to the fatigue that enveloped her, she tossed and turned, reliving the moment she'd heard of Jordan's death. She never confided her true feelings to anyone about that moment.

She'd always been too ashamed.

No one really knew or understood her relationship with Jordan. On the surface, they appeared to be the fairy tale couple come to life. In a way, they were. They looked great together. Their goals were one. They were perfectly complementary. Yet her life was anything but a fairy tale, it was simply all that she knew.

While she respected and adored Jordan, he left her empty. She was a shell, a product of his creation. She missed something she had no name for and every so often pangs of loneliness would hit her. How many times had she questioned her reasons for remaining with Jordan? How many nights had she spent alone, unfulfilled, but too loyal to her husband to commit the unspeakable? Jordan sensed it too and inexplicably he provoked her, intentionally trying to drive her into another man's arms.

Yet through all of her hurt and loneliness, she understood Jordan like no one else. She saw through the ruthlessness, the drive, to the vulnerable man beneath the facade. And she knew that as long as they remained husband and wife she would stay committed to her wedding vows. Vows that she believed in with all of her heart. "What God has joined together . . ." For that reason, she knew, deep inside, Jordan was grateful for her tenderness and compassion. In turn, he showered her with gifts, cars, jewelry. They traveled, they danced, they met dignitaries, they dined in all of the exotic places across the globe. But they never truly loved. Not in the same sense that a husband and wife loved. More like two dear friends who were truly indebted to each other for their very existence. An existence that was cruelly snatched away from her and she had only one man to blame.

It was nearly noon when Noelle emerged from her room. She'd finally fallen into a deep sleep shortly before sunrise, with dreams filled with vivid images of the man she'd met at the opening. The titillating dreams left her more on edge than before, which only added to her anxiety for having overslept.

She went directly to the lower salon to check the guests who had stayed over. Spotting Liaisons's manager, Gina Nkiru, she quickly crossed the polished marble floor to Gina's desk. As she approached she wondered, once again, why Gina had chosen the hotel industry as a career. With her exquisite streamlined looks and penchant for top of the line clothing, she could have easily been a success in the world of high fashion. Nonetheless, her credentials were above reproach.

Gina's auburn head snapped up from her paperwork when she sensed a presence above her.

"Oh. Good morning, Mrs. Maxwell," Gina beamed. She quickly rose and smoothed her mauve skirt. Gina felt honored to be asked to hold the highest position at Liaisons. Gina's years of work in the hotel industry, working as her father's aide at the embassy of Ghana and her multilingual skills had served her well in vying for this job. But all of her experience could not have prepared her for the mystique of Liaisons. It was something out of the most vivid imagination. She'd lost count of the celebrities and public figures that had graced the building the previous night. To think that many of them would become regular patrons was almost too much for Gina to comprehend.

Gina wished that she could tell her friends and family about everyone that she'd seen. But all employees were bound by legal contract never to divulge that information. That along with her uncompromising professionalism would never allow her to breach a trust.

Anonymity was the big draw of Liaisons. Each and every guest was secure in the knowledge that their identities and their dalliances would remain secret. Hence the name Liaisons. That and the $2,500.00 per night fee and the exclusion of any media, effectively deterred the foolhardy.

Even with that knowledge she was still stunned to be holding a cashier's check for $75,000.00 for the new arrival, Cole Richards.

"How is everything Gina?" Noelle inquired, briefly scanning the guests as they milled about.

"So far, so good, Mrs. Maxwell." She took a peek at the occupancy list that indicated, only, which suites were in use. "We have a total of ten guests. There are two vacant suites on level two, a vacancy on level one and one suite available on the penthouse floor."

Noelle nodded. Satisfied. She allowed herself a brief moment of relief. "Let me take a look at the private register."

Gina retrieved the leather-bound journal from the safe and handed it to Noelle.

Noelle scanned the names, nodding at each familiar one, until she reached the name Cole Richards. She frowned. "Who is this?" She pointed to the last entry.

Gina peered across the desk to the line that Noelle indicated with a French manicured finger.

"I'm sure I saw him last night, Mrs. Maxwell," she assured with confidence. "He checked in about an hour ago. He's on level three. He gave me this." She showed Noelle the check.

Noelle's brown eyes briefly widened in surprise. "$75,000.00?" She did a quick mental calculation. "He intends to stay for an entire month?"

"That's what he said."

"Did he provide the required references?"

"Yes. I filed them away. Would you like to see them?"

"Please."

Gina exited through the door directly behind her desk into the back office. Momentarily she returned with a sealed folder. She handed it to Noelle.

"I'll just take this to my office. I'll be sure to return it before the end of the day."

"Of course." Gina started to feel uneasy. A tiny spot just beneath her left eye began to twitch—a sure sign. Her father always said that she was psychic, and her feelings were generally on target. She only hoped that this time her intuition was off.

Noelle turned to leave.

"Mrs. Maxwell?"

Noelle came around looking at Gina quizzically.

"Didn't everyone who was here last night receive a personal invitation?"

"Yes. Unless they were the guest of someone who did. Why do you ask?"

"Then Mr. Richards must be a friend or the guest of someone that you know."

"That remains to be seen." She smiled briefly and headed in the direction of her office.

Gina swallowed back her trepidations. As she marked Noelle's departure, she had the unsettling sensation that trouble was on the horizon. But she had her own secret to concern herself with, and it would take all of her diplomatic skills to keep it under wraps. If Noelle were ever to find out, she would surely lose this fabulous job.

Noelle took the short ride on the glass elevator to the lower level where her office was housed.

Within moments she'd broken open the plastic seal and had methodically run over the details that it contained.

There was a personal letter from her friend Senator Richard Thomas of California. He described Cole Richards in glowing terms, saying that they had been associates for several years and he was very familiar with Mr. Richards' entrepreneurial skills in the aeronautical industry.

Planes. The thought evoked painful memories. She shoved them to the back of her mind. She set the letter aside and looked over the brief personal profile.

He was 35 years old, preferred privacy, home state New York. He would be staying for one month in suite number 9. He listed his occupation as an Aeronautical Consultant. No guests were expected.

Pensively she looked across the room and focused on the Picasso abstract, absently replacing the pages and closing the folder.

Suite number 9. That was on the east wing, set off by itself, she recalled. Braxton had designed it specifically for those that wanted the utmost privacy.

For some reason, Cole Richards had sparked her curiosity. She leaned back in her leather seat and Jordan's words of wisdom echoed in her mind. *Never leave anything to chance. You always stay ahead of your opponent by already knowing what they're trying to find out.*

Slowly she pushed herself away from her desk. Perhaps she'd pay a personal visit to her special guest. Just to satisfy her curiosity, of course.

Hesitantly, Noelle stood in front of suite number 9. Maybe this wasn't such a good idea. After all, the profile did indicate that Mr. Richards wanted his privacy. Then again, she reasoned, as owner of Liaisons it was her responsibility to be assured that her guests' anonymity was not compromised by any unscrupulous individual, which this Cole Richards very well could be. She felt mildly justified.

Inhaling deeply she knocked on the door, then waited for what seemed like an eternity. She was beginning to truly feel ridiculous. She turned to leave just as the door was snatched open.

"Yes?"

The familiar voice vibrated down her spine and momentarily held her in place. As she turned around to face him, her eyes locked on the bare, wet chest then drifted down to the white towel that scarcely covered his middle. Her mouth went dry and her face felt flushed, and for the life of her she couldn't think of anything logical to explain her appearance. Standing before him she, once again, felt like the young inexperienced waitress instead of the twenty-eight-year-old businesswoman.

He merely stared at her, seeming totally nonplussed by his half-naked appearance. His cavalier attitude snapped her to her senses.

She cleared her throat. "I'm sorry, Monsieur Richards. It seems that I've come at a bad time."

He gave her a crooked smile. "Now why would you say that, Mrs. Maxwell?"

She quickly realized from his tone that he was teasing her, apparently taking great pleasure from their encounter.

"Would you like to come in while I—uh—put something on? I was expecting room service."

Noelle straightened her shoulders and forced her gaze up from below his waist to focus on his eyes. She quickly discovered that wasn't much better.

"I want to make a practice of visiting all of my guests," she replied. "Especially those that intend to stay with us for a while."

The smooth cadence of her voice reminded him of hot nights on sandy beaches with a full moon glowing above. *Sensual.*

"But I think I should come at another time. I'm sorry to have disturbed you." She made a move to leave.

He reached out and touched her shoulder and she swore that must be what an electric shock felt like.

His voice was low, throbbing. “I hope it’s not a problem that I’ll be staying for a while.” His fingers began to burn with the contact. Reluctantly he removed his hand. “I need the rest.” His smile held an invitation.

“I didn’t mean to give the impression that your stay was a problem.” She touched her hand to her chest. “I apologize.”

“None needed.” His eyes held hers.

Noelle was the first to look away.

“I, I must be going. If there’s anything you need . . .”

“I’ll be sure to let you know.”

Noelle gave him one last fleeting look, turned on her heel and walked quickly down the carpeted corridor.

Trent leaned casually against the door frame watching her hasty departure. The cool mint green linen dress just barely skimmed her knees. Last night he thought he’d had the perfect view of those luscious legs. Now he knew what had been left to the imagination.

He surprised himself with the control he exerted while she stood in front of him. It had taken every ounce of self-restraint to still the urges that pulsed through his loins, while she stood there looking so flustered, assured and delectable all at once.

Now that she knew he was there, the next phase of his plan had to be executed.

He shut the door. In a little more than ninety days, the notes would be called in. Everything that Jordan worked for would come tumbling down. The only person who could salvage his empire was Noelle. And the one she needed to learn the ropes from was him. The last man on earth she’d have anything to do with. He had to get her to trust him. Or at least trust Cole Richards.

CHAPTER 4

En route to her office, Noelle made good on her statement to Cole Richards. She took a short stroll through the gardens, the three dining rooms, the pool and the exercise room. She made a point to speak to each guest personally. Everyone that she met confirmed that the service and accommodations surpassed all expectations.

She should be elated, but instead she felt more under the microscope than ever. All eyes would be on Liaisons and her for the next few months. Everything had to be better than perfect.

The fact that Cole Richards was to be a long-term guest, mildly complicated matters. He made her feel things, think things, want things. She couldn't allow herself to be distracted by him or anyone. Not now.

Arriving in her office, Noelle sorted through the mail and reviewed the bills that required her signature for payment. She casually flicked through the stack until she came across a plain white envelope addressed to her from Jordan's attorney in Los Angeles.

Curious, she tore it open. As she read the unbelievable contents the words began to blur and her hands trembled.

Screaming denial rang in her brain. This must be some macabre joke. But as she continued to read the familiar scrawl she knew that it was true.

The light knocking on the door, nearly caused her to cry out. She cleared her throat and swallowed back the tears. The knock came again. She pushed control into her voice.

"Yes? Come in."

The door swung open. "Well. Good afternoon." Tempest whisked in closing the door behind her. She took a seat on the low sleek, leather couch. "Whew. I'm exhausted. What a night."

"I know. It was better than I expected," Noelle answered absently.

Tempest frowned. "You don't sound like you're too pleased."

Noelle briefly shook her head. "Of course I'm pleased. Why shouldn't I be? Liaisons's opening surpassed everything that I ever dreamed," she concluded, pointedly avoiding Tempest's steady gaze.

Tempest pursed her full red lips and crossed her legs.

"How long have we been friends, Noelle?"

The question caught Noelle off guard. She forced a laugh. "For more than eight years. Why?"

"We've always been honest with each other, right?"

"Of course. What are you getting at?"

"Something's bothering you. And I want to know what it is. Maybe I can help."

Slowly Noelle rose from her seat and turned away to face the window that covered the expanse of the wall. Her view took in the outdoor pool and rested on Cole Richards as he emerged from the water. His muscles rippled with every move. Her pulse picked up its pace while she watched him stride across the pavement into the villa.

She turned away from the window and forced a smile as she faced her friend. "I only wish there were something you could do."

Tempest rose. "Is there a problem with Liaisons? Are you ill? Talk to me," she pleaded softly.

Noelle's lids fluttered as she tried to hold back her tears. She crossed her arms, embracing herself as if the act could contain the torrent of emotions that threatened to overflow.

Alarmed, Tempest hurried to her side, bracing Noelle's shoulders. "Noelle, what is it?" She guided Noelle to the couch. "Whatever it is, it can be worked out," Tempest assured, her soothing voice washing over Noelle.

Noelle solemnly shook her head and wiped the tears away from her cheeks.

"It's just so bizarre."

Tempest heard the strain in her voice. "What is?" she coaxed.

Noelle angled her chin toward the desk. "Over there. On the desk there's a letter. From Jordan."

Trent returned to his suite. His body felt rejuvenated after the vigorous swim. His mind was clearer. Physical exercise always had a positive impact on him. Whenever he felt stressed or worried he found a way to expel it in some form of activity.

Swimming was just one outlet, but flying was his passion. He'd been flying since he was eighteen. He'd gotten his pilot's license at twenty and was a certified instructor by twenty-two.

His skills as a pilot became public knowledge after a stint with the air-force. His unit, led by him, had successfully pulled off a rescue mission of an American diplomat held in the Middle East.

From there he wrote his own ticket. He became a pilot for hire, flying anywhere, anytime. Which was how he met Jordan Maxwell and became his personal pilot and business partner.

Without warning, images of Noelle pushed thoughts of Jordan out of his mind. He clenched his teeth. He had to stay focused.

He stepped out of his wet trunks and strode naked across the room. It was now or never, he thought as he dialed the villa operator.

"Yes, Mr. Richards?"

"I need to rent a car within the hour.

"That's no problem. Just follow the instructions on the voice-activated system when I switch you to the rental department."

"Thank you."

Exactly as he'd dictated, a midnight blue Lexus LS was waiting for him when he exited the facility. He slipped behind the wheel and headed to-ward Los Angeles.

Tempest read the letter with a mixture of disbelief and alarm. It was obvious, after the first few lines, that Jordan had written this letter well before the accident. She could easily understand and sympathize with Noelle's shock. What was curious, however, was her nagging sensation that Jordan seemed to have known well in advance that he wouldn't be returning home. She wondered if Noelle had the same feeling.

Gently she placed the letter on the desk and returned to Noelle's side. "Are you all right?"

Noelle nodded.

"Noelle, was there something going on in Jordan's life that could have prompted him to write this letter?"

She shook her head slowly. "No. Nothing that I know of."

Tempest took a thoughtful breath before speaking. "It's just that . . . well, it sounds as if he knew something. Or had planned something."

Noelle sprung up from the couch. Her brown eyes blazed. "Are you trying to imply that Jordan planned his own death?" Her voice rose to a tremulous pitch. "Are you?" she demanded.

"Noelle. Calm down. The letter just doesn't sound right. He says that you would know what to do. That your life together was what made him go on for as long as he did. That he'd trust you to be able to run his busi-ness and everything would fall into place. Noelle, whether you want to accept it or not, this is a farewell letter."

All of the restraint that Noelle had maintained crumpled at those telling words. She seemed to deflate like a pierced balloon. The tears that she'd held at bay ran freely down her chiseled cheeks. But her voice was surprisingly strong when she spoke.

"I didn't want to believe it," she said slowly, "I didn't want to think that he would intentionally abandon me. Then to ask me to trust Trent Dixon is more than I can bear."

Tempest stretched her arm across Noelle's shoulders. "I know that you hold this Dixon guy responsible for the plane crash. I know that it's hard for you to accept that he survived and Jordan didn't. But if Jordan trusted him, why can't you?"

Noelle tossed her head in dismissal. Her eyes pierced Tempest's. "Yes, Jordan trusted him. He trusted him with his life and Trent Dixon destroyed that trust!"

"It was an accident Noelle. The inquiry cleared Dixon of any wrongdoing. It was a malfunction."

"But Trent was responsible for the maintenance of the plane," she countered. "He was responsible."

Tempest began to feel that she was fighting a losing battle. She tried one last time.

"You don't even know Trent Dixon. Did it ever occur to you that he's going through his own hell? Jordan left the reins of his enterprise in Dixon's hands. Whether you like it or not, you're going to have to deal with him. At least until the terms of the will are fulfilled. As this letter says, after the year is up, Dixon is to turn the company over to you."

Noelle's lids briefly lowered in reluctant acceptance. "I've never been interested in running Jordan's business. He knew that. He *knew* that. We were always completely at odds over his business practices and his vision for the company. For all I care, Trent Dixon can have it."

But with those words an eerie thought rushed to the surface.

She turned to Tempest, her eyes wide with awakening. "Suppose this letter is just a ploy by Dixon to lure me into a sense of security so that he could take the company from me without a fight?"

Tempest wrestled with the idea for a moment. "But how would he have gotten Jordan to write this letter? This is Jordan's handwriting isn't it?"

Noelle stood up and began to pace, biting on her thumbnail as she thought.

"It looks like Jordan's writing. But Trent was the closest person to him. He could easily have studied his handwriting over the years."

Tempest slowly shook her head and sighed. "Where did the letter come from?"

"It was hand delivered this morning from our attorney's office in L.A."

"Have you called your attorney?"

"That would be pointless. Joseph Malone was more Jordan's attorney than mine. He's one of those types that sticks to the letter of confidentiality. I'm sure he's under some strict instructions."

"Then who else may know something?"

Noelle turned back toward the window. Snatches of her conversation the night before rang in her head.

"The man I met last night," she said slowly. "He said he was with Jordan when he bought the villa." She turned toward Tempest. "He's here. Now. Cole Richards knew Jordan."

CHAPTER 5

Trent spent the better part of the day in his other hotel suite in Los Angeles. He had an arm's length of calls to make to the Maxwell headquarters in Sudan and Hong Kong. He couldn't risk them being billed to him at Liaisons.

According to the reports that he'd received, everything was in order. Or at least as well as could be expected with the revolution in full swing. Import and export of anything other than food and medicine was out of the question. The United Nations was taking steps to intervene, but there was no telling how long that would take.

Finally, wrapping up his business late in the day he headed back to Liaisons.

As he sped across the winding highways in the rented Lexus, he questioned his tactics. Maybe he should have been honest with Noelle and absorbed her eminent outrage. But it was too late now. He had no other choice than to follow through. Noelle Maxwell believed that he was Cole Richards and it would remain so until the time was right to tell her the truth.

He made the last curve into the long drive of Liaisons and turned into the underground garage.

Tonight, he thought.

Noelle took special care to prepare herself for the evening ahead. After the shocking ordeal of the morning she needed the time to relax before mingling with the guests.

Her attempts to subtly locate Cole Richards had proven to be fruitless. He'd apparently left the villa earlier in the day and had yet to return.

She sighed as she sat before her mirror applying her makeup to the flawless copper skin. She felt certain that Cole Richards held the key to some information about Jordan and the fatal plane crash. What it was she couldn't be certain, but she would have to find a way to gain his help.

Satisfied with her polished look, she crossed the room and selected a fitted gown of black lycra. The off-the-shoulder neckline was dotted with tiny rhinestones. She slipped the gown over her nude body. The simple act wrought steamy visions of how Cole Richards looked at her the previous night and how sensual he'd made her feel.

Unconsciously, standing before the full-length mirror, her hands involuntarily stroked her heated body. Briefly she shut her eyes as powerful flashes of long unfulfilled desire ripped through her.

What would his hands feel like, his mouth, his . . . Her eyes flew open. Her breath came in short, choppy waves. She stared unbelievably at herself in the mirror, her hands still cupping her full breasts.

She flung her hands to her sides. With a shuddering breath she spun away from the telltale image.

Forcing herself to concentrate, she stepped into her strapless black heels, picked up her rhinestone purse and walked purposefully from her room.

The glass enclosed dining room, situated on the rooftop of the villa, had already begun to fill with eager diners. Part of the policy of Liaisons was to cater to the guests' every dietary whim. Upon arrival, every guest filled out a complete guide to their special requirements and the Liaisons' chef met their requests with verve. The immense kitchen was stocked with everything from Nathan's hot dogs to exotic Far East cuisine.

Momentarily, Noelle stood at the threshold of the dining room quietly observing the guests, and hoping to catch a glimpse of Tempest and Braxton, to no avail. However, she was totally satisfied that her fantasy hideaway had become her reality. Maybe now the gossipmongers would begin to take her seriously. There was no way that anyone could doubt that Liaisons was a huge success. And she'd only just begun.

"Checking on your guests again?"

The decidedly intimate voice came from behind her.

Noelle stole a glance over her shoulder to see Cole Richards standing a mere breath away. Her pulse shuddered as her brief glance told her that he was even more handsome than when she'd last seen him. If that were possible.

He stepped around to stand at her side.

"It's my responsibility to make sure that everyone at Liaisons is well taken care of, *Monsieur* Richards."

His slow smile taunted her. "I'm sure that everyone appreciates your conscientiousness." He paused, noting the seriousness of her expression. "Please call me Cole. I'm sure we'll be seeing enough of each other to be able to drop formalities."

Her expression slowly relaxed. "I suppose you're right. You must excuse me if I seem . . ."

"Anxious?" he said completing her sentence.

Her smile was tremulous as she nodded.

"It's just that I've worked so hard for so long to," she spread her hand in explanation, "make this all happen. I just want everything to be perfect."

He saw the shadow of doubt flicker in those beautiful brown eyes and he had to reassure her.

"Believe me, I can't imagine anyone thinking otherwise." He lowered his gaze and then looked directly at her and added gently, "I'm sure Jordan would be very proud of what you've accomplished."

"You knew my husband well?" she asked, smoothly sidestepping the compliment.

"Yes. Very well."

Noelle recognized her opportunity. She straightened her shoulders and tilted her head.

"Would you care to join me for dinner—Cole?"

He took her elbow and grinned. "I thought you'd never ask. I'm starved."

Dinner conversation was easy, unstrained and at times filled with laughter. They talked about old movies, the economy, hobbies, places that they had been and found that they had a lot in common. The unspoken realization was tantalizing.

"Your chef is magnificent," Trent complimented, pushing slightly away from the table. "I can't remember ever having poached salmon that could compare to this."

Noelle smiled appreciatively.

"Jordan and I met Paul, the chef, when we were in Paris," Noelle explained. "I decided then and there that if I were to ever have this dream of mine come true, I would make sure that Paul was my chef."

Trent brushed his lips with the linen napkin then tucked it beneath his empty plate. "So you thought about Liaisons for a while?"

Noelle nodded. "All of the years that I worked at my aunt's cafe in New Orleans, I envisioned a place of my own. Something unlike any other," she added wistfully,

"You've outdone yourself." He looked around the elegant dining hall, then back at Noelle. When his dark eyes settled on her, she felt her insides flutter. "I can't imagine all the time and work it took to put this all together."

She sighed. "I had a good teacher."

For several moments they sat in companionable silence, sipping the last of their wine, each caught in momentary memories of Jordan Maxwell.

"Would you like to take a walk with me around the grounds?" Trent asked. "I haven't had a chance to see very much."

Noelle smiled. "I'd like that very much."

They talked softly as they strolled across the grass covered slopes, with Noelle pointing out her favorite spots and explaining where some of her ideas had arisen.

"I wanted to try to recreate some of the wonderful things that I'd seen in my travels and bring them all together in one place.

"Like the fountains over there." She pointed in the direction of the enormous marble fountains. "I'd seen those in Greece. The ideas for the pillars came from seeing the ruins in Rome. The hieroglyphics on the stone wall in the steam rooms came from my visits to the tombs in Egypt."

Trent was visibly impressed, Noelle noticed with a touch of pride.

"You've obviously traveled a great deal. Not many people are that lucky."

"Jordan tried to make sure that the whole world would be an education for me."

Noelle slowed down and stopped walking. Trent halted his step and turned toward her. His expression registered concern.

"Is something wrong?"

She stood still for several moments framing the questions in her mind. "How well did you know Jordan? When did you see him last?"

He knew the questions were inevitable, and had dreaded this very moment from the time he mentioned that he'd been with Jordan at the purchase of Liaisons. Careless. He hated having to lie to her. She was so beautiful, so sincere, nothing like the person that he'd envisioned. But he felt he had no other choice.

He stepped cautiously closer. She looked so fragile and vulnerable. Her luminous brown eyes were wide with expectation.

"We worked—together," he began, "on several projects."

Noelle's brow creased. "I don't remember Jordan ever mentioning you."

He thought quickly. "I was more of a consultant. He called me in from time to time."

She lowered her gaze to the ground. Her voice was barely above a whisper. Trent strained to catch each word.

"I hadn't seen Jordan for three months before the—accident. He'd spent his time traveling and then when the revolt started, he told me he couldn't get away, there were too many things to take care of."

Slowly she looked up, her eyes glistening with memories. "I'm sorry," she said, swallowing back a sob. "I didn't mean to drag you into my problems." She sniffed and smiled weakly.

His gut twisted with guilt. "It's all right," he assured her softly. He pulled a monogrammed handkerchief from the breast pocket of his midnight blue dinner jacket and handed it to her. Instantly he realized his error.

The initials TMD hypnotized him. He held his breath while Noelle dabbed at her eyes.

"Thank you Cole." She handed him the handkerchief. His relief was almost palpable. Noelle read it as discomfort. "I didn't mean to embarrass you. I don't usually do this kind of thing. Especially around strangers."

His eyes roved over her face. "I was hoping that we were more than strangers." He grinned mischievously. "Especially after this morning, Mrs. Maxwell," he teased, his look bringing back swift memories of their earlier encounter at his suite. His crooked smile made Noelle laugh in spite of herself.

"I guess you're right." She eyed him coyly surprising herself with her directness. "So what does that make us—exactly?"

He stepped closer, until he was near enough to feel the heat from her body, and was sure that she could hear his racing heart.

She felt the intimate caress of his eyes when he looked at her and held her breath as he spoke.

"I'd say that makes us two people who are on their way to something very," he touched her chin with the tip of his finger, "very special."

When she looked up into his eyes, he saw a mixture of longing and doubt. "What do you say to that?" he asked softly.

She hesitated, reluctant to say what she was truly feeling. Things were moving too fast.

"I'd say it's time that we changed the subject."

Trent smoothly recovered without missing a step, much to Noelle's relief. The feelings she had about Cole Richards were coming too hot, too fast. She had to put on the brakes.

He grinned and shoved his hands in his pants pockets, reminding her of a little boy caught with his fingers in the cookie jar.

"And to what would you like to change the subject?"

Noelle breathed deeply. "What exactly did you do for Maxwell Enterprises?" She looked directly into his eyes.

Trent casually averted his gaze. "I was responsible for recommending particular aircrafts to suit the need." He spread his hand in explanation as he continued. "I compared capabilities, costs, shopped around, kept up on the latest models, made necessary negotiations." He shrugged, offhandedly. "Things like that."

Slowly Noelle nodded while she absorbed the information. Then her head snapped up.

"Would that cover personal aircrafts as well?" Her pulse raced and so did Trent's. He thought he knew where this was headed and he didn't like the direction. But he couldn't divert the inevitable collision.

"In some cases," he replied with caution.

"Cole." She stretched out her hand and clasped his arm. "I want you to find out what happened to my husband's plane."

"What?" That request he didn't expect. "I—I, didn't the FAA rule it as an accident?"

"I don't care what the FAA said!" Her slender hands clenched into fists. "I have a feeling that something happened. Something that the FAA and my own investigator were unable to find. Jordan was too careful, too conscientious about everything. He never would have flown in a plane that had even the remotest problem."

Her dark brown eyes locked with his. "And neither would Trent Dixon. Unless he knew . . ." Her voice trailed off with her thoughts.

"Knew what?"

She shook her head in uncertainty. "I'm not sure," she said finally. "All I know is that I'll never be able to go on with my life until I do know—for sure. And I believe that you're the one who can help me."

He read the silent plea in her eyes and he almost weakened.

"But you even said that you'd hired an investigator and he couldn't come up with anything. The FAA couldn't come up with anything. Why are you so sure that I can?"

Her features softened when she spoke. "You don't have to answer me now. Just promise me that you'll think about it."

Trent briefly shut his eyes, realizing that at that moment, with her looking at him as if he was the only man on earth; if Noelle Maxwell had asked him to jump off of the Golden Gate bridge in his birthday suit he would have agreed. He nodded.

"Thank you," she whispered.

With that aside Noelle took up their stroll again, heading back in the direction of the main house. She spoke softly as they walked.

"Sometimes," she began, "I feel as though I'm trapped in some sort of limbo. Unable to go forward, unable to go back. My unresolved feelings have me locked into a fortress without windows or doors."

"But you are moving on with your life. You've opened Liaisons. It's obviously a success."

She laughed a self-deprecating laugh. "This is all part of the fortress."

His dark eyes squinted in confusion. "I don't understand."

She touched his arm lightly and instantly felt the heat spread through her fingers. "It's a longer story than I care to tell." She turned away.

For several moments he stood behind her, entranced by her solitary beauty. The iridescent glow from the half moon seemed to cast a halo around her black clad body, every detail of her form defined under the moonlight. He was spellbound by the sensuous voice, moved to undeniable arousal by her very existence in his life and pained by the fear and loneliness that was her life. *Damn it Jordan! What have you done to her—to me?*

He eased closer and turned her around into the circle of his arms.

"Maybe one day you'll tell me," he said gently. His eyes trailed languidly over her face and he felt her heart slam against his chest.

She stared at him, transfixed by an overwhelming anticipation that was almost unbearable. She struggled to control the spiraling emotions and failed as his head lowered. His mouth met her parted lips.

The contact was as fiery as an arson's blaze. She felt her entire body ignite, yet she shivered in his arms. He pulled her closer, molding her body to his.

His own mind and body convulsed in a barrage of explosive emotion. His thoughts ran in circles as he tried to control the instantaneous passion that welled within him.

He felt as if he'd known her forever and then not at all. He wanted to taste every inch of her, make her his own. His eager tongue explored her mouth and when she willing responded he knew that he was lost.

Noelle searched his mouth. Her slender arms clung to him, her only means of knowing that she was still on earth finding herself within the warm cavern.

How long had she waited to feel this way? A day? A week—forever? Somehow she believed her search was over. Cole would show her what it was like to be a real woman.

Then reality stung her with vehemence. She couldn't. Not with this man. Not with someone who knew Jordan. Then their long-kept secret would be discovered. She couldn't do that to Jordan's memory.

Without warning, she tore herself from Trent's embrace. She shook her head warning off his spontaneous approach.

"No. Please. I shouldn't have done that." She turned away and started up the small incline toward the entrance.

Trent took off after her, reaching her just before she came to the door. He grabbed her arm. "I wanted to," he said in a raspy voice.

Noelle remained with her back to him afraid to see the truth that she sensed would be in his eyes.

"I've wanted to from the moment I saw you, Noelle. So don't blame yourself."

Slowly she turned to face him. He saw the doubt in her eyes. He reached out and cupped her cheek in his hand.

"What are you so afraid of?" he asked gently.

She tilted up her chin, exhibiting a confident air. "You've got it all wrong. I just don't want you to think that I was trying to . . ." She searched for the word.

"Romance me into helping you," he said finishing her sentence once again. The beginnings of a smile tilted his full lips. "Like I said, Mrs. Maxwell, I wanted that kiss."

The light in his eyes ignited. "And I think you wanted it, too."

He moved his hand down to stroke her arm.

She stared at him for a brief moment. "Good night, Mr. Richards." Her tone was suddenly formal. "Please let me know if you'll accept my request."

Without another word she turned away, hurrying into the safety of the villa.

For several moments Trent leaned against the ornate pillar, silently fuming. He could have kicked himself. He'd obviously misread her. He shook his head at his own macho stupidity. Just because he let his hormones lead the way didn't mean that she was on the same wave length.

He slammed his fist against the pillar. Damn it! This was going to be even more difficult than he thought. Not only did he have to hide his identity, and keep his feelings for Noelle in check, he also had to get her to realize that he wasn't some oversexed, oversized teenager on the make.

Noelle lay in her bed staring sightlessly up at the sheer netting that draped her bed. For years she'd kept a lid on her desires. She'd willingly substituted gratitude and loyalty for physical pleasure. And now, in one fell swoop, Cole Richards walks into her life and opens up the trap door to her heart.

She squeezed her eyes shut. She couldn't let herself be swept away by a torrid desire for a man she hardly knew. And even if she did, which was highly unlikely, she'd had no experience with casual affairs and wouldn't know how to conduct one. For all the years of her marriage she'd stuck to the letter of her vows. *Forsaking all others.* She'd never allowed temptation, unhappiness, or physical incompleteness to lead her into infidelity. Although she wasn't particularly religious as an adult, her childhood years of churchgoing had left its indelible mark.

In any event, Cole Richards appeared to be the type of man who would never settle down and she knew she could never tolerate that.

Could she even trust a man, any man with her feelings, with them knowing who she was and the millions that she represented? Why would Cole Richards be any different from the others who had been attracted by the wealth and power? This time couldn't be any different. Could it?

She turned on her left side, trying to still the racing beat of her heart. Even as she did visions of Cole, the scent of him, the feel and taste of him filled her.

She flipped onto her right side, pushing her face into the pillow. She'd just have to find some way of dealing with the irresponsible way he made her feel. She'd disguised her true feelings for years. This time wouldn't be any different. Because Cole Richards was going to help her prove that Trent Dixon caused Jordan's death whether he wanted to or not.

Nothing could interfere with that.

CHAPTER 6

Tempest spotted Noelle across the courtyard and waved to her. Even before Tempest reached where she stood, Noelle saw the lines of strain beneath the striking hazel eyes.

"Are you all right, *chère?*" Noelle asked when Tempest approached.

"Just a little tired," Tempest answered lamely.

Noelle looked hard at her friend. "Now how long have we been friends?" Noelle taunted, tossing Tempest's own question back at her.

Tempest sighed heavily and sat down on the bench beneath a huge transplanted palm tree. Noelle sat beside her and waited.

"Braxton left last night," she blurted out.

Noelle frowned. "Just like that?" She snapped her fingers for emphasis.

"Yes. Just like that." Tempest repeated the gesture.

"I don't understand."

"He claims he has another job in Brazil that needs his immediate attention."

"But isn't your daughter, Kai, coming in today?"

Tempest nodded. "I'm on my way to the airport now to meet her and Mrs. Harding."

"I thought Braxton was going to use this time to spend with you and Kai?"

"That's what I thought," Tempest complained. "We spent the entire night arguing about it. He still insisted that he had to go."

That would explain why she didn't see them at dinner last night,

Noelle guessed. She searched for something comforting to say. "Perhaps it is important. I can't imagine that he would leave without seeing his daughter if it wasn't urgent."

Tempest stood up, smoothing the aqua-colored suit jacket. She looked off toward the horizon.

"Things have been very strained between Braxton and me for a while," she admitted softly. She turned toward Noelle. "Our schedules are so hectic we hardly see each other. Then when we do—" her voice trembled, "it's almost like we're two strangers. It was never like that between us, even after being separated for those six years after I left Virginia and went to New York. When we found each other again it was like those lost years had never happened."

Noelle was shocked. She'd always imagined that Tempest and Braxton were the perfect couple. If you had wanted to write a book about a happy marriage, they would be the ones to write about. They had been through so much to be together. It was hard for her to believe that their marriage could be in trouble. But then Noelle examined her own marriage. Everyone believed that it was *My Fair Lady* come true. But at what cost?

Noelle stood up and put her arm around Tempest's shoulder. "I didn't know," she said gently. "I only wish that I had the answers to make things better. All I can say is that as long as you and Braxton continue to love each other, everything will work out. You'll see."

"I hope you're right. And I do know that I love him, more than anything in the world." She forced a smile, still unable to put into words what was truly troubling her. She pushed aside her troubles. "How about you? Are you feeling better today?"

Noelle wanted to tell her about her evening with Cole, about the way she felt when she was with him. She decided that it wasn't the best time to discuss her budding feelings for Cole in light of Tempest's problems.

"Actually, yes. As a matter of fact, I thought about what you said about the attorney. Maybe I will call him."

"I think that's the right decision. The worst that could happen is that he won't tell you anything."

Tempest checked her watch. "I've got to go. The flight is arriving in L.A. Mrs. Harding got my instructions wrong and booked the flight into LAX airport."

An idea came to Noelle. "Would you mind some company?"

"Of course not. It's not the shortest drive in the world."

"Maybe I'll just pay my attorney Monsieur Malone a surprise visit."

Tempest brightened. "Perfect. I love surprises. If you catch him off guard he won't have time to prepare a story."

"Exactly!" Noelle grinned. She linked her arm through Tempest's. "Let's go."

* * *

Trent meticulously reviewed the data that had been faxed to him on Liaisons. He'd set up a small office in his hotel suite in L.A. It was fully equipped with a computer, printer, a copy and a fax machine. He'd already had his computer linked via modem to the main headquarters in Sudan and in Hong Kong.

The financial stability of Liaisons was excellent. He'd verified the credibility of the accountants, attorneys and had conducted a background check on all of Liaisons's staff.

As he leaned back in his chair he breathed a sigh of relief. Noelle Maxwell was unquestionably an astonishing businesswoman, not merely a woman in business. There were no outstanding debts. All of the structures exceeded building codes and revenue was pouring in.

If he had any doubts about her capabilities they had certainly been laid to rest.

He closed the thick manila folder and stood up, shoving his hands in his jeans pockets as he did. To look at her one would easily assume that she was merely a pampered heiress with delusions of grandeur, he mused. To the contrary, Noelle was a woman of substance, with talents yet untapped. But did she have what it took to manage an empire as complex as Jordan's? More importantly would she be able to handle the truth once it was revealed to her and possibly give up her one dream to save Jordan's? Of that he was still unsure.

His own personal feelings about her seemed to be clouding his judgment. He wanted her. He wanted her like he hadn't wanted any other woman. And the intensity of his emotions made him feel vulnerable. A feeling that was totally foreign to him.

He'd already revealed too much to her last night. It had probably cost him his credibility in her eyes. He couldn't let that happen again. He owed it to Jordan to see that the instructions of his will were carried out. Emotional entanglement with his widow was not part of the package.

"I'll see you later this evening," Noelle called out as Tempest waved and drove away.

For several moments Noelle stood in front of the building that housed Joseph Malone's suite of offices. He was obnoxious as far as she was concerned and she knew that he didn't hold her in very high regard. Whatever civility he showed her was purely due to the very large retainer that Jordan had paid him.

She pushed through the glass door and boarded the elevator to the third floor, wondering all the while what made her think that he would tell her anything.

The reception area was paneled with dark maplewood. Any semblance of sound was easily absorbed into the thick grey carpet. It reminded her of a scene from some old black-and-white "B" mystery movie. *Yuk.*

She walked directly to the secretary's desk, with her three-inch, sling-back heels sinking into the carpet with each step. She had the hilarious notion of being swallowed by grey quicksand.

Alice Bernstein, the middle-aged secretary, looked up at her over her wire-rimmed glasses.

Her face flushed when she recognized Noelle. "Mrs. Maxwell, what brings you here?"

Force of habit compelled her to quickly check the appointment calendar on her desk. "I don't see your name in *the book.*" She said the last word with an almost holy deference. "Was someone expecting you?" She removed her glasses and looked every bit like the affronted secretary.

"No Alice, I don't have an appointment. But I would like to see Monsieur Malone. Is he free?"

Alice Bernstein's silver curls seemed to spring to life.

"Oh—Mrs. Maxwell, you know that it is quite impossible to see Mr. Malone without an appointment." She reshuffled the small, neat stack of files on her desk. Alice took pride in the one fact that her life was dictated by order. Any interference threw her completely off balance and the sudden appearance of Noelle Maxwell had done just that. She didn't like it one bit. She reached for her always handy cup of water and took a sip. She immediately felt more composed and in control. She squared her chin.

"If you'd like to give me a date and time when you're free, I'd be happy to . . ."

"I'm free right now, Alice. And I'd like it very much if you'd tell Monsieur Malone that I'm here," she stated firmly.

Noelle stood her ground tossing back the icy stare with one of her own. Generally, Alice Bernstein had the ability to unnerve Noelle. Even as she stood before her, she had the inclination to make a bee line for the elevator. But she wouldn't let the old general intimidate her today. She wasn't leaving until she had accomplished what she'd come for.

Alice was completely astonished. She wasn't used to anyone not following her instructions. Especially Noelle Maxwell. All one usually had to do was raise an eyebrow and she'd back down. When did she finally get some backbone? Alice had to admit, although never to Noelle, that she admired her nerve.

Alice loudly cleared her throat.

"If you'll just have a seat over there." With her pen she indicated a row of grey chairs. "I'll see if Mr. Malone can spare you a few moments." She picked up the phone.

Noelle released the long-held breath. "Thank you."

Moments later, Joseph Malone flung open his door. "Noelle," he boomed in a deep basso voice. "Please come in."

It always amazed her that this reed of a man could have such a powerful voice. She supposed that's what made him such a master in the courtroom. He was just as rangy and taut as ever, she noted. He'd always reminded her of a predator ready to swoop down on an unsuspecting victim.

As Noelle approached, he placed his bony arm protectively around her shoulder, ushering her into his office. Noelle cringed.

"Now, what can I do for you?"

Noelle took a seat opposite the maplewood desk and crossed her legs. She reached into her pocketbook and produced the letter from Jordan.

"I'd like you to explain this to me."

Briefly he scanned the letter and returned it to her.

"I really can't see how I can explain the contents, Noelle. I wasn't privy to the . . ."

"Please don't patronize me, Joseph. You know perfectly well what I mean. Where was this letter? And why am I just receiving it from your office?"

Joseph pursed his thin, pale lips, placing his index finger thoughtfully across them.

"I had instructions," he said simply. "I was to have this envelope delivered to you, one day after the official opening of Liaisons."

"What? Jordan didn't even know that I would go through with it."

"Perhaps. But, if and when you did, you were to receive this letter."

Noelle exhaled heavily. "Is there anything else I should know, Joseph?"

The pain in her voice almost touched him, but he pushed it away. He was no longer obligated to her. The last retainer check had been cashed upon delivery of the letter. But why did she have to look at him with those eyes so full of anguish? Something inside of his chest twisted.

He cleared his throat. "There is a codicil to your late husband's will."

"What are you talking about? I was there when it was read."

Joseph nodded indulgently. "Yes and according to my instructions, the codicil was only to be read by Trent Dixon."

Her head began to pound.

"I see." She stood up. "And I suppose I'm not to be privy to that either?"

"I'm afraid not. My instructions were quite clear."

"Thank you for your time, Joseph," she tossed at him, more annoyed at herself for having thought that their encounter could have been any different.

He rounded the desk, reaching the door a step before her.

"I wish there was something else I could tell you, Noelle," he said with as much sincerity as he could summon.

Noelle only nodded as she crossed the threshold.

Joseph had a rare attack of conscience as he watched her leave.

"Maybe Mr. Dixon would be willing to tell you. I understand he's here in Los Angeles."

Noelle halted her step and turned around. "How do you know?" Her heart thundered.

"I called the headquarters in Sudan yesterday. I was told he'd come to California two days ago."

Trent finished the last of his paperwork. Languidly he stretched his tight muscles. He had to get out of this room. Hours on the phone and behind the computer had left him numb. A long flight around the countryside would be ideal about now. But what he really wanted to do was return to Liaisons and see Noelle. He hadn't been able to stop thinking about her. She seemed to creep into his thoughts at the most inopportune times. Like now.

The throbbing between his thighs was almost unbearable. Maybe what he really needed was a cold shower.

He switched off the humming machines, grabbed his denim jacket and headed out of the door.

Noelle exited the building and proceeded to walk, oblivious to the rows of boutiques and the flow of human traffic.

Trent Dixon was somewhere in Los Angeles. He was the only one who had the answers to her questions. The thought of his proximity unnerved her. Why was he here? Had he come to spy on her? He could be anywhere, walking right beside her and she wouldn't know it. That fact raised her blood pressure. She didn't have the faintest notion of what he looked like. He'd never accompanied Jordan on his trips to the U.S., since he was responsible for operations in Jordan's absence. Trent Dixon could run her over with a Mack truck, right this minute, and she wouldn't know it was him. Her temper rose as her thoughts ran in circles.

The head-on collision knocked her purse from her hand.

"Noelle?" Trent instinctively grabbed her shoulders to steady her, then reached down to retrieve her purse. "Are you okay?"

"Y-es," she stammered, surprised and embarrassed to see Cole Richards in the middle of Los Angeles. "I'm fine. Sorry. I guess I wasn't watching where I was going."

"You must be deep in thought."

She gave him a weak smile. "Something like that." She took a quick look around, observing her surroundings for the first time. The large marquee of the hotel loomed above her head and her thoughts scurried off in a dangerous direction.

He was probably there to meet someone, she thought. Did he spend the night here after he'd left her weak from his kisses?

An unfamiliar wave of jealousy swept through her. Her body tensed.

"Did you think about my request?" she asked in a tight voice.

Confusion registered on Trent's face with the swift change in Noelle's mood.

"Is something bothering you, Noelle?"

"What else could be bothering me?" she almost snapped. She looked away unable to meet the questioning gaze.

Trent avoided answering the question, by posing one of his own. "I was going to get something to eat. I'd like it very much if you'd join me. Then we can talk. Would you?"

When she dared to look back at him, she was, once again, consumed by those onyx eyes that had haunted her nights, by the lips that she longed to taste again and by the captivating scent that heated her blood.

He'd begun to think that she hadn't heard him or had chosen not to respond—when she finally answered.

"Do you know your way around?" she asked in that sexy faint accent that drove him crazy.

"Maybe you can give me the tour again," he replied, his tone intentionally intimate.

Noelle cleared her throat. "There's a great outdoor cafe about a block down. I'm sure you'd like it."

"With you, I'm sure I would."

For a brief moment they both stared at each other, the busy world around them going totally unnoticed.

"We're going to cause a scene in a minute," Trent said, his smile teasing. "People are beginning to stare."

Self-consciously Noelle looked around, feeling that everyone could see what was going on inside of her.

Her voice was slightly tremulous. "Then I guess we should be going."

Trent slipped her arm through the curve of his. "Lead the way."

Lunch was brief, almost strained. Both of them were harboring their own thoughts and skirting the real issues that bubbled like molten lava beneath their composed surfaces.

"You were right about this place," Trent offered, breaking the rather long train of silence. "The food here is great." He smiled. "But they can't touch Liaisons's with a stick."

"I hope that everyone who comes will feel the same way." She fiddled with her napkin to avoid looking at him.

Trent reached across the table to still her fingers. He covered her hand with his. The immediate warmth spread through her.

"I thought about your request to . . . find out what happened."

She looked directly at him and his stomach lurched with longing.

"And?"

"And I've decided to help you."

The brilliant smile that he received was worth all the deceit.

"Thank you. I'll make it worth your while. Whatever the price."

His brows creased both in disbelief and guilt. "I couldn't possibly take any money from you." His voice rose in agitation. "I'm not doing this for the money."

"I didn't mean to offend you, but I think it would only be fair. In fact, I insist."

Trent's jaw clenched. He looked away. How could he possibly accept money from her knowing that the person she was looking for was sitting right in front of her and that he would have to do whatever was necessary to keep that information from her until the time was right.

His gaze returned to her. "I won't accept anything from you until after the job is done. That's the only way," he added firmly.

Noelle considered for a moment. "If that's the only way you'll agree, then I guess I don't have a choice."

"Then it's settled."

She nodded.

Trent leaned back in his seat and exhaled deeply. What in the hell had he gotten himself into?

"Do you have plans for the rest of the day?" he asked.

"No, I don't, actually. I was supposed to call the villa and send for a car and driver, but after my visit with Joseph Malone . . ."

The mention of Malone's name caused Trent's pulse to gallop. He'd completely forgotten about the carnivorous attorney. He was the one person who could identify him on sight.

". . . so your job may not be so difficult after all."

Trent slowly returned to the conversation. "What? I'm sorry."

"I said, Joseph Malone told me that Trent Dixon was here in Los Angeles."

Just great. "That will make things easier," he said lamely.

A thought occurred to Noelle. "You spent time in Sudan with Jordan," she stated more than asked. "Did you ever meet Trent Dixon? What does he look like?"

Oh, God. Trent cleared his throat. "I never had the chance to meet him. I guess our paths just didn't cross. Why don't we get out of here?" Trent suggested, before Noelle had a chance to respond. He swiftly wiped his mouth and pushed away from the table.

Before Noelle knew what was happening he was standing behind her chair to help her up.

Her eyebrows arched. "Why are you in such a rush all of a sudden? Is something wrong?" she asked in bewilderment.

"Of course not. But there's no point in sitting here when we can be exploring. You did promise to show me around." He forced a smile as they walked toward the door.

Noelle shrugged to camouflage her confusion. "I guess we could drive out to the movie studios, or into Beverly Hills." She looked at him skeptically. "What do you want to do?"

He wanted to say, get as much distance between me and Malone as possible, but instead, "How about a drive out to the beach? Next to flying, the waves always help me to think. The sun will be setting in a few hours. It's been a long time since I saw the sun set over the water."

His full lips curved into that sensuous smile that made her feel weak. "It sounds wonderful."

Her voice felt like the brush of silk against his ears. "My car is in the hotel garage."

The mention of the hotel caused Noelle's initial misgivings and jealousies to resurface. It was ridiculous to feel this way, she knew, but for whatever reason, she couldn't seem to help it.

Trent watched the warm brown eyes turn suddenly cold and distant. "Noelle, for the last time, what is it?"

"If we're going to the beach, we should get started," she answered in a cool tone.

Trent fell in step next to Noelle. He kept his confusion to himself in the hope that she would eventually reveal what was bothering her.

She couldn't keep doing this, she thought. It was unfair to Cole to suspect him of anything. And what if he was in the hotel with another woman. There were no strings tying them together. But still, she didn't like how the thoughts made her feel. If nothing else, they had to work together to find Trent and the truth.

If there was any possibility that what she was beginning to feel for Cole could ever be reciprocated, she needed to know what else or who else was in his life. She needed to put her concerns to rest.

As casually as she could, she asked the question that had been burning her tongue.

"So . . . what brought you into L.A.? I thought Liaisons had everything that a person could want. Please don't say that we're lacking something." She kept her eyes straight ahead as they continued toward the hotel.

Trent struggled to keep from smiling. So that was it! She saw me coming out of the hotel and thought I was with someone. *A woman.*

"Well, I came in town earlier this morning. I had a business appointment with a potential client." She could feel his eyes looking down at her with that smile that made her believe he could read her mind.

Noelle felt her whole body heat with embarrassment. Now she felt totally ridiculous again. Cole Richards had an uncanny knack for having that effect on her.

She swallowed the lump in her throat. "Oh," was all she could say.

They turned into the garage entrance. Trent handed the attendant his ticket stub and they waited for his car to be brought out.

Trent turned toward Noelle and tilted her chin up with his fingertip. The intensity of his expression caused Noelle to tremble beneath his gaze. She held her breath and when he looked into that face, all the promises that he'd made to himself vanished.

His voice was low, penetrating. "I want to kiss you again, Noelle." His eyes swept searchingly over her face. "What do you say to that?"

For a moment she couldn't think, couldn't breathe, as his head slowly lowered. His muscular arms encircled her.

His lips gently touched down on hers, once, then twice ending with his tongue awakening every nerve in her body.

Involuntarily, she grasped his forearms, mostly to keep her balance, but also to assure herself that this was no dream.

But the intimate moment was cut short when the roar of the Lexus engine filled the torrid air.

Reluctantly, Trent eased away, planting one last kiss on Noelle's parted lips. "There's more," he groaned in a thick voice. "Believe that."

CHAPTER 7

"But why did Daddy have to leave so soon? Why didn't he wait for me?" Kai demanded, her wide dark eyes piercing her mother's.

Tempest absorbed the pain of her daughter's disappointment so potently, it felt like a steel weight that had leveled her heart. *Damn you Braxton! How could you do this?*

Tempest sat down on the couch and pulled Kai down next to her. She put her arm around her daughter's slumped shoulders and eased her closer.

"Listen to me baby," Tempest said softly. "It was very, very important work that your daddy had to do. You know how much he loves you." She kissed the top of Kai's head. "He would never miss a chance to spend time with you if it weren't very important." *How many more lies will I have to tell my child?*

Kai forcibly tugged herself away and sprung up from the couch.

"It's always something," Kai said, her ten-year-old voice rising in anger. "He's never around anymore." She spun around to face her mother. Those large black eyes, identical to her father's, were glistening with unspent tears.

"I'm tired of traveling all over the world. I want to live like the rest of my friends. I want to have a regular life and a regular family."

Tempest rose and took Kai into her embrace, fighting desperately to hide her own tears.

"It'll be all right, baby. I promise," she cooed. "We're going to be a regular family. I promise you."

Tempest peered over Kai's head at Mrs. Harding. Clara Harding had been a part of Tempest's life since she was six years old. Clara was more of a second mother than a housekeeper and she treated Tempest and Kai like they were her very own children.

"Clara would you run a bath for Kai, please? Then afterwards I'll take both of you on a tour of Liaisons. We're going to make the most of this visit."

She forced herself to smile when she looked down at Kai's upturned face.

"And I think my beautiful daughter hasn't seen anything until she's seen Liaisons."

She turned Kai toward Mrs. Harding. "So get moving. There's plenty to do. And I know your godmother is waiting to see you."

Kai smiled slightly at the mention of her godmother, Noelle. Reluctantly she did as she was told and followed Mrs. Harding out of the room.

Tempest smothered a sob with her hand. "I'm not going to let you keep doing this Braxton. You're not going to keep hurting us like this. No more!"

She stormed off into her bedroom and placed an overseas call to Brazil.

"I'm glad I keep a blanket in my trunk." Trent stretched his long muscular limbs. "Old habit." He turned his head to see Noelle perched gingerly on the edge of the blanket.

"Relax, Noelle," he urged, raising up on one elbow.

She laughed nervously. "This outfit isn't exactly beachwear."

He took a quick glance at the lemon yellow, sleeveless linen dress and matching strapless shoes. He wanted to tell her that he could fix all that by simply helping her out of it. But he knew that wouldn't go over too well.

"What was it like living in New Orleans?" he asked instead. "It's one place I've always wanted to visit."

Noelle visibly relaxed. She sighed with a wistful smile. "It was all I knew for most of my life. Mardi Gras, hundreds of tiny cafes, seafood, crowds. I thought every place in the world had all-night jazz clubs, and hordes of people roaming the street in bizarre costumes on holidays." She laughed at the recollection, then sobered. "We were poor, and I thought I was happy." She peeked at him over her shoulder. "I guess that's how it is when you have nothing to compare it to."

"And now?"

"Hmmm. Well, I suppose most people would think I have the perfect life. Clothes. Money. The ability to travel whenever and wherever I want. I've seen my life displayed in so many magazines and newspapers I almost started to believe the stories myself . . ." Her voice trailed off. "But I think deep inside I'm still that simple girl, working in my aunt's cafe. I still have dreams and hopes."

Trent traced circles in the sand with his finger as he listened. Hesitantly, without looking up he said, "I would think that with Jordan all of your dreams would have come true." He instantly saw her withdraw at the mention of Jordan and regretted uttering his name.

"Things aren't always as they seem," she said.

He inched closer, needing to know. "This may be none of my business," he ventured, "but—were you really happy in your marriage?"

Noelle lowered her head and hugged her knees to her chest. Trent strained to hear her.

"At times. I think Jordan truly believed that showering a person with gifts and buying them anything that they could ever dream of would make them happy. But that kind of happiness is only temporary." She looked off toward the horizon. "That's not to say that we never shared joyful times together, because we did. Then at others I felt like I was trapped in some sort of nightmare." She shook her head as visions of ugly fights sprung before her eyes.

"If you were a real woman you'd find a way to satisfy me." Jordan had yelled. "Go on, find yourself another man! I'll even pay for it. Like I've paid for everything else in your life." With those painful words he'd stormed out and locked himself in the guest room leaving her alone in their enormous bedroom. Yet she'd stayed because she saw beneath the outward rage. It was never her that he was truly angry with. She was simply his available target.

She'd always felt that if she could somehow destroy the barrier that Jordan had constructed around himself, he would release all his insecurity.

She shook off the vision with a toss of her head.

"What about you?" she asked, needing to change the subject.

Trent chuckled softly. "I definitely didn't have the fantasy storybook life. I was adopted when I was about two. I never knew my natural parents. But I was always happy. I had two of the greatest people as parents anyone could want. They made sure I had the best they could afford, which included four years at Columbia University.

This revelation deeply touched Noelle. She could sense by his tone the depth of his feelings for his parents. And she envied him. Then something he said struck her. "You said you had two of the greatest parents." She hesitated a moment. "Did something happen?"

Trent inhaled deeply remembering all too vividly the day of James Dixon's heart attack.

"My father died when I was in my sophomore year of college. Heart attack."

Instinctively Noelle touched his arm in a comforting gesture. "I'm sorry," she said softly, knowing all too well the feelings of loss.

Trent nodded. After several moments he went on to tell her about his two adopted sisters who he obviously adored, and his twin niece and nephew who both swore that they were going to be great pilots just like their uncle.

"They all live in Philadelphia," he concluded. "We don't see each other much," he chuckled in that deep baritone, "but we do have a helluva phone bill!"

Noelle laughed with him as she realized how their lives were parallel in some respects. She felt that invisible bond, that had been present since their first meeting, intensify. Her one regret was that she didn't have the loving family that she so much wanted.

"Do you plan on having a family someday?" she asked tentatively.

"Most definitely! I want a house full of kids, so I can give them all the things that I had. And more." His eyes roamed slowly over her face. "Most of all—I want a wonderful woman to share my life with."

She felt breathless and hot as he stared at her as if she were the only person in the world. "That . . . sounds . . . wonderful." Her eyes held his as he leaned, slowly closer.

The warmth of his lips brushed her shoulder like the whisper of a breeze. A tremor rushed through her and her eyes slid closed.

Trent slipped his arms around her, sliding his hands down her thighs. He eased closer, pressing his chest against her back.

Her hands grasped his roving fingers, locking them above her knees.

"Cole," she whispered in a strangled voice.

"Sssh. No . . . time for . . . talking."

The setting sun cast a brilliant orange glow across the horizon, bathing them in its iridescent light. Giving this intimate moment an almost surreal aura.

He planted a row of kisses along her neck, her shoulders. "You're beautiful," he whispered in her ear.

Instinctively she arched her back when his hands trailed teasingly up her waistline. She'd fantasized about this moment from the very first night that they'd met. She imagined his strong hands roving freely across her body, tasted his lips against her own, inhaled his scent until it became a part of the very air she breathed. Now it was real. She'd never felt such a powerful attraction towards anyone. Not even when she first met Jordan. This was different. And for her this wasn't something totally physical. She trusted Cole. She trusted him with her heart.

Trent smoothly leaned Noelle back into the cradle of his arm until his face was only inches above her own. He felt his heart hammer mercilessly and he was sure that Noelle must think he was some oversexed gigolo on the prowl. But he couldn't stop himself as he moaned against her neck. He couldn't stop the waves of excitement that shook his body.

Yet, even as he kissed and caressed her, seeping between the vapors of his longing were faint strains of doubt. Noelle had been married to and loved by one of the most powerful black men in the world. A man who had made one of the greatest impacts on his life. His friend. His mentor. A surrogate father in his young adult years. Yes, he'd had his share of romances, crisscrossing all the barriers. But Noelle. Noelle, she was different. Whatever happened between them, he knew, would change them both forever.

He wanted everything to be perfect. He wanted to be sure that with every move he made, her moments with Jordan would dissolve from her mind like sugar in hot water.

As he held her like she was the most precious and delicate of jewels, she felt herself come alive for the first time in her life. She wanted him. Desperately. She wanted to know and feel, fully, what it was like to be totally loved—like a woman. She wanted what she had been denied for all the years that she'd been with Jordan.

She felt herself being swept away by the hunger of desire that seemed more powerful than the force of the crashing waves.

But she couldn't do it. She couldn't allow this man, her husband's friend, to discover what had been kept secret for the duration of her marriage. She couldn't dismantle Jordan's image in Cole's eyes.

Trent lowered his head to, once again, kiss her the way he'd dreamed.

Noelle suddenly turned away, and with surprising strength, pushed him off of her, forcing him onto the sand.

"What, the . . ."

"No . . . Cole . . . I'm sorry . . . I can't." Her heart thundered. Her skin was aflame. She couldn't face the accusing look, the disbelief and hurt that she knew hung in his eyes.

With as much grace as she could summon, she rose from the blanket, purposely keeping her back to him, wrapping her arms protectively around her body.

Trent pulled himself onto his hands and knees until he was in a crouched position. He dropped his head onto his knees. He felt like a first-class fool.

He was so sure that this was what Noelle wanted too. This time. The atmosphere, the fire between them. All perfect. He'd gone against his better judgment. He knew he shouldn't get involved with her. It was too complicated. But he couldn't seem to help himself. He was falling for her. Hard. And that fact made what he was doing to her that much more despicable.

"I'm sorry." His voice barely reached her.

"No. I'm the one that's sorry," she said solemnly. "It's not your fault."

She turned around to face him and he looked up. Her brown eyes glistened with tears and it pierced his heart. Trent believed them to be tears of sadness, but they were tears of longing. She wanted him so desperately it was an almost physical pain and to see the look of anguish on his face only added to her own misery. She trusted him. But could she trust him enough to tell him the truth?

Slowly she knelt down in front of him. "Cole," she began softly but then couldn't go on.

He looked at her with an intensity that set her soul on fire. She gently stroked his bearded jaw and he clasped her hand against his lips, kissing her palm.

"Whatever it is, Noelle, you can tell me. I'll understand. If you're not ready, if I'm not what you want, you can tell me." He kissed her palm again. "You can," he whispered urgently.

Sadly she shook her head. "It's all so complicated." She tugged on her bottom lip with her teeth. "And sordid, and I . . . don't want to talk about it. Not now. I can't." She looked away.

"Noelle," he turned her face toward him. He kept his hand on her cheek and she cradled it against her shoulder. "Whatever you want, I want for you. Whenever you're ready, I'm here."

She smiled weakly. "Thank you, Cole."

Each time that she said the name Cole, his gut twisted with guilt. How much longer could he keep deceiving her? How much longer before she discovered the truth on her own? Then what?

"I'll tell you what," he offered, forcing cheer into his voice, "why don't we head on back and have one of Paul's fabulous meals and relax?"

Noelle nodded with relief. But the mention of Liaisons brought back her conversation with Joseph Malone.

Frowning she looked at Trent. "If Trent is in L.A. why hasn't he contacted me? He wasn't scheduled for another two weeks. What do you think he's up to?"

Trent looked away toward the darkened horizon, forcing his thoughts to catch up with the change in topics. He stood up and brushed off his jeans, but kept his eyes focused on his shoes as he continued to brush off his clothes.

"Maybe your attorney got his information wrong."

Noelle shook her head emphatically. "Joseph Malone never has the wrong information."

Don't I know it. He began to move restlessly, eager to change the topic.

"Then maybe Dixon decided to visit friends," he shrugged dismissively, "or relax for a while before he came to see you." *Please change the subject.*

"Maybe," she sighed, not totally convinced.

"Just wait until he turns up," he advised, finally daring to look at her. "There's no point in stirring things up. And I'll find out what I can until then. I've already sent for the FAA report."

She slipped the dark glasses in her purse. "I guess you're right," she admitted half-heartedly. Trent relaxed a little. "I just wish I knew why he was here two weeks early."

He put his arm around her waist, and snatched up the blanket with his other hand. Noelle tucked her purse under her arm.

"I'm sure we'll find out soon enough. In the meantime, let's get back. Your guests await!"

Noelle grinned up at him. "Thank you," she said softly, but her eyes said so much more, and Trent wondered again what secret bound her heart.

After Trent dropped Noelle off at Liaisons, she headed straight to Gina's office to get a rundown on the day's activities.

"I know there's nothing we can do right now," Gina said softly into the phone. "But we have to be patient. You know that. Everyone will just have to understand. When the time is right."

The sharp knock on Gina's office door made her jump.

"I have to go. Someone's here. Yes. As soon as I can. Bye." She quickly hung up the phone.

"Yes. Come in," she said in her cheeriest voice.

Noelle stepped into the small, neat office and closed the door behind her.

"Sorry to disturb you, Gina."

"No. No problem, Mrs. Maxwell." Gina cleared her throat as she stood up. "Please sit down. I guess you want the report."

Noelle looked at her quizzically. "Is something wrong? You seem . . . edgy."

"Oh. It's nothing. Just a slight headache. Nothing that two aspirin won't cure." Noelle noticed that Gina's smile didn't quite reach her eyes.

"Well be sure to take care of yourself. I know how hard you push yourself. Tomorrow is your day off isn't it?"

Noelle tucked away every bit of information about her staff in her head. It was a gift that constantly amazed Gina. And she was sure it was one of the reasons why Noelle had such a good rapport with her employees. That's why it made her so damned angry when she'd hear some of those wealthy bitches talk about Noelle as if she were some incompetent child who'd gotten lucky. Noelle had more class and intelligence than all of them rolled up together.

"Yes it is," Gina answered. "I think I'll just stay home and relax."

"You be sure you do that," she admonished, pointing a flawlessly manicured finger at Gina.

"I promise," Gina grinned. "Here's the report." She picked up the two-page report from her desk and handed it to Noelle.

"Thanks." Noelle rose from her seat. "Don't forget what I said," she warned.

"I won't Mrs. Maxwell."

"See you when you get back. And how is your father by the way?"

"Oh," she smiled, "he's doing very well. As a matter of fact he may be going over to the Sudan on behalf of the United Nations, depending on what happens over there in the next few weeks."

"If anyone can have an impact on the rebel forces, Kenyatta Nkiru can," Noelle offered, remembering quite clearly the dynamic impression that he'd left on her when he'd come to see this "magical place" that his headstrong daughter had opted for instead of a career in politics. He was certainly a man to be reckoned with.

Noelle was updated periodically on the impact that the revolution was having on Jordan's business, but had steered clear of interfering. She had some very definite opinions on what should be done. However, she'd never give Trent Dixon the satisfaction of shooting them down. Let him handle it. She intended to stay as far away from Maxwell Enterprises as possible.

"Anyway, enjoy your day off and give my regards to your father."

"I will."

Noelle left the office with the vague sensation that Gina had something else on her mind beside a headache. But, then again, everyone was entitled to their secrets. She had enough of her own to attest to that.

Tossing aside thoughts of Gina, they scurried off in the direction of Cole. She'd had a wonderful afternoon with him. He was everything that she could hope for in a man.

She frowned. And yet she still wasn't sure about giving herself to him completely. She knew he wanted her as much as she wanted him. But would he wait around long enough for her to come to grips with the ghosts of the past? As she headed for her office a cynical inner voice penetrated her conscious thoughts. It was curious that both he and Dixon were pilots and both of them had worked for Jordan. But the similarity ended there, she decided. There was no way that . . .

"Auntie!"

The all-too-familiar childlike voice snapped Noelle out of her reverie. Her face lit up when she saw her goddaughter run toward her, the unsettling comparison immediately forgotten.

"Kai!" She swept her up in her arms and squeezed her hard before putting her down. "How are you sweetheart? You've grown up so much since I last saw you."

Kai beamed. "I'm in the fifth grade now," she said proudly.

"And I'm sure you're the smartest and the prettiest girl in your class."

Kai's cheery expression changed.

Noelle kneeled down. "What's wrong, *chère?*"

Kai pouted. "I never stay in one school long enough to find out," she spat out with a vehemence that shook Noelle.

She looked over Kai's head to see Tempest standing behind her daughter. The expression on her face said that there was much more to be told.

"But you're such a lucky girl, Kai. There are so many children who would love to travel around the world," she said gently.

"Not me!"

Noelle looked up at Tempest who only shook her head sadly.

"Well, since you're here, why don't we make a deal?"

Kai looked up with a bit of interest.

"What kind of deal?"

"I'm going to make sure that you have the best time possible. And you're going to put all those . . . thoughts out of your head and enjoy yourself. How's that?"

"Can I have room service?"

Noelle grinned and kissed her cheek. "Of course."

"Okay. It's a deal."

Noelle stood up and took Kai's hand. Her smile was full of compassion when she looked at Tempest. "So," she breathed, "what have you both been up to?"

"Just trying to get Kai and Mrs. Harding settled in," Tempest offered. She placed her arm around her daughter.

Noelle looked down at Kai. "I bet your mother hasn't shown you the stables. I know how much you like to ride. Would you like to ride before dinner?"

Kai jumped up and down. "Yeah!"

"Great. Wait right here and I'll have someone take you over. I'll be right back," she said to Tempest.

Moments later she returned with Gina.

"This is Gina Nkiru, Kai. She runs things around here and she loves horses, too."

"Hi," Kai said shyly.

"Hello, Kai. Mrs. Maxwell told me how much you love to ride, and I know just the horse for you," she smiled. "Are you ready?"

Kai nodded happily.

"Then let's go. I'll have her back to her room before the dinner hour," Gina assured both women.

"Thank you," Tempest said.

When Kai and Gina were out of earshot, Noelle turned to Tempest. "Let's take a stroll over to the atrium. You look like you need to talk."

Tempest nodded, thankful, once again, for Noelle's perceptiveness.

They settled comfortably on the cushioned bench. The airy space offered a sense of peace and tranquility. Enclosed in glass with a beveled skylight, the large space was amass with tropical plants and trees from around the world. It was like bringing the very essence of nature right to your feet.

Tempest slowly began to relax, allowing the serenity to replace the hurt and turmoil that raged within her.

"Talk to me," Noelle coaxed.

Tempest shook her head. "I wish I knew where to begin."

"Start anywhere."

Tempest took a long deep breath, then blurted out the words that had tormented her. "I think Braxton is having an affair." She covered her mouth with her hand as if the very act could take back the damnation.

"No. Not Braxton," Noelle sputtered in disbelief. "Why, why would you think something like that?"

"What else could it be, Noelle? He's changed. He's always busy, always away. Hushed conversations, special meetings." She turned toward Noelle, her hazel eyes flashing. "What does that say to you?"

For a moment Noelle couldn't find the words to dispel Tempest's accusation. No one knew Braxton better than Tempest. If she believed that Braxton was having an affair, she had good reason. The thought that he could hurt Tempest in such a way enraged Noelle. But in the midst of Tempest's hurt it would do no good to display her true feelings. That's not what she needed now.

She spoke calmly. "Have you spoken to Braxton?"

"No. I called the construction site in Brazil and was told that he was unavailable. Humph. *Very* unlikely. Braxton can always be reached."

"Before he left, did he say when he would be back in the States?"

"He said he wasn't sure. If he couldn't get back before we leave in two weeks, he'd meet us in New York."

Noelle took both of Tempest's hands in her own. "Listen to me. There's no point in building a case against him until you've talked. You and Braxton have a second chance at a life together. Not many people do. Don't throw that away with unfounded suspicions.

"Be patient. I know it's hard. But if your marriage is as important to you as I know it is, just be patient."

Noelle's smile was gentle. "When you talk with him, be honest about how you feel. Take the chance. Tell him your fears, and what you want. It's the only way he'll know."

Tempest succumbed to a weak smile and sniffed. "When did you get so wise?" she asked softly.

Noelle's eyes drifted around her garden of Eden, then back to Tempest. "Right this minute," she answered in a voice filled with revelation. Maybe what she longed for was right at her fingertips, she thought. And maybe she should take the chance.

"And what brought it about?" Tempest wanted to know.

"Cole Richards," she answered simply.

CHAPTER 8

Trent immediately returned to his room. He had work to do in order to pull this whole bizarre plan off. Under the pulsing surge of the steamy shower, he tried to keep his mind focused on his objectives. But no matter how hard he tried to concentrate on contracts, bank loans and Maxwell Enterprises, his thoughts shifted to Noelle.

With each passing day, he mused, lathering his hard body with Aramis soap, he became more drawn to her. She was everything he could ever wish for in a woman. Having gotten to know her, she had unconsciously changed his whole perception of her. Not only was she beautiful, but she was sensitive and had more business sense than many seasoned veterans.

The streaming water rushed over his face. He braced his hands against the black tiled walls, letting the water pound against him in the futile hope that it could somehow wash away the unending desire that coursed through him.

He stood to lose it all. The woman. The job. Everything. All because of a promise to a dead man.

He shut off the water and wrapped a towel around his waist. He had no choice. He'd never go back on his word. Maybe by some miracle, when this was all over, she'd find a way to forgive him.

He checked the clock. He had about two hours to return to L.A. in time to meet his friend Nick Hunter. Nick was due in town to check into some potential real estate for his new club. It had been a while since they'd seen each other, but they made a habit of keeping in touch. He'd contacted Nick before he left Sudan to let him know where he'd be staying. He was glad that he did. It would do him good to talk with someone he trusted. When Trent had offered to put him up during his stay, Nick was more than happy with the idea of utilizing Trent's hotel room.

He grinned sardonically as he towel-dried, imagining what his caustic buddy would say about his latest liaison.

Noelle sat in front of her dressing room mirror, absently brushing her hair while she recalled her confession to Tempest. She had to admit that she felt better having finally gotten her feelings for Cole off her chest. Tempest had been elated for her and urged her to pursue the budding relationship. She had every intention of taking her advice.

She smiled. Even in the middle of everything that was going on in Tempest's life, Tempest still was happy for her and supportive of her. That was a true friend.

Dressed for dinner, in an emerald green, crepe cocktail dress, Noelle entered the rooftop dining hall, hoping to see Cole. Not spotting him, she wandered over to the bar where two women were engaged in animated conversation. She heard her name mentioned and stopped in her tracks.

". . . the place looks good," one woman said to the other, whom Noelle recognized as Suzanne Donaldson, editor for one of Los Angeles's leading women's magazine. "But," she continued, "we all know that beauty has nothing to do with brains. She'll probably run the place into the ground in a matter of months. She may have the Maxwell name, but she'll always be just another waitress!"

The two women nodded in agreement, with Noelle still going unnoticed.

"I still cannot imagine how Jordan Maxwell, of all people, would have reduced himself to marrying such backwater trash."

"You know what they say: you can take the girl out of the swamp," Suzanne continued, "but you can't take the swamp out of the girl!" They both fell into affected laughter.

"What always amazed me," Noelle said in a silky voice, taking pleasure in the horror registered on their faces when they saw her, "was that backwater trash isn't strictly reserved for New Orleans. Have a lovely evening, *ladies*. And I use the term *ladies* very loosely."

They both tried to sputter explanations and apologies which fell on deaf ears.

Noelle's flesh burned, her ears rang, her pulse raced. She wouldn't scream. She wouldn't go running to her room like a wounded puppy. Not anymore. She'd do like she'd always done, store the humiliating comments in that secret compartment that no one could reach.

She should be used to it by now, she thought, swallowing back the lump of anger that welled in her throat. But how did you get used to the pain?

She put on her best smile and stopped at each table to ask a question here, make a comment there or offer a dinner suggestion. Then she was gone.

She desperately wanted to escape to the sanctity of her room, she thought, taking the outdoor elevator to the lower salon. But that would be the equivalent of running away. She wouldn't give them the satisfaction.

She emerged on the first level and ran into Tempest and Kai who were on their way to dinner.

"Have you eaten already?" Tempest asked, surprised at Noelle's unusually early departure.

"No. I'm not really hungry." She looked down at Kai, purposely avoiding Tempest's searching gaze. "And how was your ride, sweetheart?"

"It was great, auntie. I'm going to ride Blaize again tomorrow."

"Wonderful. I knew there'd be something here that you'd enjoy." She turned toward Tempest. "You two have a good evening. I'm going to check on a few things, then go over to my office. I have some paperwork to clear up." Her smile was empty as she absently patted Kai on the head.

Tempest wasn't convinced, but decided against pursuing the issue until a later date.

"If you're sure."

Noelle nodded. "They're running a Denzel Washington marathon in the theater downstairs, if you want to go."

Tempest looked down at Kai, who grinned broadly. "Maybe we will. I'll talk with you later." Their eyes held for a moment and they parted.

Noelle strolled to the garden in the hopes of finding Cole, to no avail. She thought about going to his suite, but changed her mind. Just thinking about being alone with him again, in close quarters, made her anxious.

Tomorrow was another day. She headed for her office, before turning in for the night.

"How in the hell did you get yourself into this mess?" Nick asked, shaking his dark head in amazement. He lifted his glass and took a sip of cognac, eyeing Trent over the rim. "And Jordan's widow on top of that." He took a long swallow and closed his eyes as the fiery liquid slid down his throat. "Man you have truly gone over the edge."

"Listen man," Trent interrupted, knowing that at any moment, Nick would be on a monologue roll. "I've said the same things and asked the same questions myself." He dropped down on the sofa, stretching his long legs out in front of him. He leaned back, bracing his head with laced fingers. "I'm in it and I can't get out of it. And quite frankly," he gave Nick a pointed look, "I don't want to."

"She really means that much to you? So quickly?" Nick asked in a combination of amazement and acceptance. He and Trent had been friends since the air force. He'd roamed the country with Trent. They traded clothes, secrets and sometimes women. He'd seen women come into and go out of Trent's life and never had he seen Trent care one way or the other. Until now.

"Yeah," Trent nodded solemnly. "She does." He leaned forward resting his arms on his thighs. "But once she finds out who I am, and why I'm here, it'll be all over. I don't want to lose her."

"So what are you gonna do?"

"I've been asking myself that very same question."

Joseph Malone rolled over and snuggled closer to the warm body next to him. When he first met her, nearly two years prior, she had made an immediate impact on him.

Her vibrancy, candor, razor-sharp intelligence, not to mention natural beauty, had been just the medicine he needed after a very ugly divorce. She made him feel human again.

It was his inside connections that had placed her in the front running for her very lucrative position. He had fallen in love and at times he believed that he was actually mellowing. The positive effect that she had in his life had slowly begun to radiate outward. He was beginning to feel compassion for other people. The incredulity of that notion still amazed him.

Gina sighed softly as her eyes slowly opened to see Joseph smiling down at her.

"You look like you're thinking pleasant thoughts," she whispered, while her warm brown eyes went sweeping over him.

A broader smile tugged at his mouth, softening the often hard look that was his trademark.

She stroked his chiseled chin as if seeing him for the first time. When she'd truly come to know Joseph, she saw in him what many others couldn't.

His tough-guy exterior was all a facade. He'd grown so accustomed to dealing with irascible clients, cutthroat attorneys, huge fortunes, and corporate treachery, that he'd surreptitiously assumed the mantle in order to survive. Beneath it all was a lonely man who needed someone to look after his needs for a change. And that's what Gina intended to do.

Although there was nearly fifteen years difference in their ages, they were compatible on every level—Cut from the same cloth, as her father would say.

"I was thinking about you," he responded in that basso voice that made many quiver in their footsteps. "I'm tired of hiding us from the world, Gina. I want to marry you, and having a secret wife will be a bit difficult."

Gina came fully awake and shifted in the bed. They'd had this conversation a half dozen times over the past year and her answer had always been the same: "We have to wait." But just how long would he wait for her to tell her boss that she was marrying a man who had always been less than decent to Noelle—tell her father, who would be outraged at a mixed union? What would Noelle think of her and her choice? Would she assume that Gina was there to spy on her and take information back to Joseph? And ultimately to Trent Dixon? Gina admired Noelle for her courage, her strength and her achievements. What Noelle and her father thought of her mattered a great deal. But was it more important than salvaging the best relationship she'd ever had? These were the questions that rattled her, and Gina knew she'd have to make a decision soon.

She sat up and tossed the dark paisley sheet off her nude body, simultaneously swinging her long legs over the side of the bed to stand up.

"We decided to wait, Joe," she said without much conviction, keeping her back to him and giving him an ample view of her shapely bottom.

"*You* decided we should wait," he countered, running his fingers through his tousled salt-and-pepper hair. He got out of bed and crossed the room to stand behind her, his suntanned body in sharp contrast to her ebony tones.

His voice dropped to a lower octave. "I don't want to wait any longer," he said, brushing his lips across her shoulders. He slipped his arms around her narrow waist. "And I want you to make a decision one way or the other."

Gina spun around inches from his face. Her eyes narrowed. "Is that an ultimatum, Joseph?"

His jaw clenched. "Yes."

"You should know me well enough to know that I don't take ultimatums very kindly. Even from you, Joseph."

She tugged away, snatched up her discarded clothing from the floor and stormed off into the bathroom, slamming the door behind her.

Trent returned to Liaisons shortly after midnight. He'd explained his plan to Nick, who after several hours of debate had reluctantly accepted defeat. In days gone by Nick wouldn't have batted an eye at such an outrageous plot. But since he'd settled down with his wife, Parris, and opened his own nightclub in New York, Nick Hunter was a changed man. Trent shook his head in amazement. What love could do to a person . . .

He opened the door to his suite and switched on the recessed lights. Was he doing the right thing? he wondered for the umpteenth time, discarding his jacket on a nearby chair. Or was he only complicating matters further?

He couldn't be sure. But the one thing that he was certain of was that he had fallen in love with Noelle and he'd do whatever it took to share that love with her. If only for the moment.

First thing in the morning he would reserve a plane.

* * *

Bright and early the following morning, Noelle sat at her desk reviewing the total revenue against the accounts payables. She couldn't believe her eyes.

Liaisons had been open for less than a month and already they were three million dollars in the black. Her check from Maxwell Enterprises had arrived in the mail, adding to the growing revenue. But she had made plans for that money, just as she had done for the past four years. She tucked it away, and smiled, knowing exactly how she would put it to use.

She scanned the guest list. Reservations were booked through the entire year, with a waiting list for the following. To say that this venture was a success was a complete understatement. Potential patrons were so eager to secure a suite that deposits were still pouring in months in advance.

"I wonder what those two wenches would have to say to that?" she asked out loud, the astonishing success temporarily offsetting the hurting comments.

Satisfied, she closed the large green ledger and pushed away from her desk, thankful, once again, that Jordan had insisted that she take business management and accounting courses.

Jordan. She still felt slight pangs of melancholy when she thought of him. Although their marriage had been far from ideal, they had found a way to be good for each other. Somehow they filled a need in each other's lives. He was the strong older man who had never been present in her life, and she was his greatest accomplishment.

She turned toward her panoramic window which looked out across the entire lower level of the west wing and the indoor, Olympic-sized pool. From the other side, the imported, tinted glass looked like a mirror—it allowed her to look out while maintaining her privacy.

Watching the early morning swimmers brought back vivid images of Cole when he'd emerged from the pool. Instantly her body became infused with a pulsing heat. She wanted him. There was no longer any doubt in her mind. And at the very next opportunity she would show him just how much.

A knock on her office door intruded on her steamy thoughts. She took a settling breath and smoothed the raw silk shirtdress of red and gold. Jordan had had it specially made for her on one of his numerous trips to Hong Kong.

"Come in."

The door came slowly open and Trent stepped in.

At once she was taken aback by this blatantly gorgeous man. His white cotton shirt was open down the front, almost to his navel and the black baggy pants brushed teasingly against the muscular thighs when he moved. He carried a black leather jacket over his arm and an inviting smile was on the bearded face.

She stood completely still behind her desk certain that her knees, which had suddenly turned to Jell-O, wouldn't carry her one step.

Her smile matched his.

"Good morning." He stepped fully into the room. "I'm sorry about not seeing you last night." His mouth tipped in a half smile. "I guess I was more exhausted than I thought."

"No problem. I had plenty to keep me busy."

Their eyes held and neither spoke, as though afraid that any movement, any spoken word might disturb the hypnotic pull that transfixed them at that moment.

Trent slowly walked forward, stopping on the opposite side of Noelle's desk. He leaned across, bracing one hand on the desk, the other cupped Noelle's face. He drew her closer until their lips met.

"It was a problem for me," he whispered against her mouth. "I dreamed of you all night." He pulled slightly back so that he could look into her eyes. "I don't want to just dream about you at night, Noelle. I want you to be there with me. Especially when I wake up in the morning."

Her pulse pounded so loudly in her ears, she couldn't be sure that she'd heard him.

He straightened. His dark eyes were holding her in place. "I want you to come away with me for the weekend. I want us to have the time to get to know each other. Better. I know," he continued, suddenly feeling that he was treading on shaky ground, "that I may be presuming too much. I've made some mistakes where you and I are concerned. But I just feel that we have something special going on here, Noelle. And I think you feel it, too.

"The hell with waiting for the right time. Time doesn't wait for anyone. Come away with me. Let me show you just . . ."

"Yes," she whispered, feeling the flooding of uncontrollable joy whip through her. "Yes," she repeated, "I'll go away with you."

Without another word, Trent rounded the desk and pulled her hungrily into his arms, molding her against him. His mouth swept down over hers, his tongue urgent and demanding.

And she responded. The velvet warmth of his kiss was sending spirals of passion racing through her. She allowed herself to succumb totally to the full domination of his lips, and knew that this was only the beginning.

CHAPTER 9

Trent eased back. "You won't regret this. I promise you," he said against her mouth. "I can arrange it for us to leave tonight. If you're ready."

Noelle's heart sank. "I can't. Not tonight. Gina is off today. She won't be back until tomorrow." She sighed. "That's the earliest I can get away."

Trent straightened, looking at her with warm eyes. "I can wait." He checked his watch. "I have some errands to run. I'll see you at dinner?"

"Sounds wonderful," she responded in that voice that thrilled him.

He gave her a long breathless kiss that left her longing for more.

"See you later." He made a move to leave.

"Oh, Cole, before you go—have you gotten any information yet?"

He fought to keep from averting his gaze as the lies formed on his tongue.

"As a matter of fact, I'm going to pick up the report this afternoon. I have someone who'll be working on it while we're away."

"Really. Who?"

"You'll meet him soon enough. I've got to go," he added hurriedly.

Before she had a chance to respond, he was out of the door.

Briefly she wondered who this *someone* was, but decided that she'd put her faith in Cole so she would just let him handle it. She felt confident that whoever he had selected to help uncover the truth about the crash, he was someone competent.

In the meantime, she thought, with her excitement building, she had plans to make, and a million details to attend to before she left.

Momentarily, she closed her eyes, and tried to imagine what an entire, uninterrupted weekend with Cole Richards would be like.

Just as Noelle had promised Kai, room service had delivered breakfast to their suite. She ate the full-course breakfast with relish, completely amazing her mother and Mrs. Harding with her enormous appetite.

Tempest shook her head and smiled as she watched her daughter consume everything on her plate.

"Where do you put it all, Kai?" Tempest teased.

"Hmmm, all over" she answered with a mouth full of syrup-drenched pancakes. "I have to keep my strength up," she added. "I have a big day today."

Tempest's hazel eyes widened in curiosity. "Is that right? And would you mind sharing what this big day is?"

Kai downed her glass of milk and wiped her mouth with a linen napkin. "Well, the man that works in the stable said he would have Blaize ready for me this morning. And I met a girl yesterday on the track. She's here with her parents. We're going to the dance class in the gym. Then we're going to play with her dolls." Kai's eyes lit up. "She has dolls from all over the world! And she said I could play with them. Then we're going to get our hair done at the hair salon downstairs."

"Get your hair done?" Tempest asked incredulously.

Kai's head bobbed up and down. "Yeah, I talked to the lady in the salon yesterday. I told her that my mother designed this w-h-o-l-e place and that Noelle was my godmother." Kai grinned. "She said we could have the full treatment," she concluded triumphantly.

Tempest was momentarily speechless. Was this the same girl who only yesterday was on the border of misery?

"Well I see you have your day all mapped out. I would like to meet this new friend of yours and her parents."

"Okay."

The phone rang in the background and was quickly picked up by Mrs. Harding.

"Tempest," Clara called from the next room, "the phone is for you."

Tempest pushed away from the table and entered the small sitting room. "Who is it?" she asked as Clara stood with the phone in her hand.

"It's your husband." She handed Tempest the phone, looking at her with eyes full of compassion. Gently she patted her shoulder as she left.

Tempest had been the daughter she'd never had. She'd helped Tempest's grandmother, Ella, raise her. When Tempest had returned home from college, pregnant and afraid, Clara had rallied to her side. Everyone, except her, thought that Tempest's marriage to David Lang was the answer to their prayers. That turned out to be disastrous. Not only because David proved himself to be nothing more than a greed-driven politician, but because Tempest had never stopped loving Braxton, the father of her child.

Clara would move hell and earth to see to it that Tempest and Kai were happy and protected. She knew how much Tempest adored her husband and she knew all that they had been through to be together.

She could only pray that whatever the trouble was between them that they would work it out. She had never seen two people who loved each other more. It would just about kill her to see them apart.

Clara returned to the small dining room to check on her often-mischievous charge.

For several moments, Tempest held the phone against her chest searching her mind for the right words. Slowly she put the phone to her ear.

"Hello, Braxton."

"How are you? How's Kai?"

"We're both fine." She paused. "You really disappointed her, Braxton. You know that don't you?" She felt her adrenaline begin to pump. She fought to control the rising anger that was becoming evident in her voice.

"It couldn't be helped. I thought I explained that to you."

"You explained it. But that's not good enough and you know it." She took a calming breath. "You're going to have to decide what it is you want, Braxton."

On the other end of the world, Braxton felt the weight of Tempest's hurt and confusion. If only he could tell her. But the time wasn't right. Not just yet. He could only hope that what he was doing could make up for all of the disappointments that he had caused.

"Listen to me, baby, everything is going to be fine. I'll be back by next week. There are just a few things I have to take care of first and then I'll be on the first plane out of here."

Tempest was not satisfied and couldn't resist twisting the knife of guilt just a bit deeper. "Then when's the next plane? Will it be on Kai's birthday this time or the day before our anniversary? Christmas? New Year's? When?"

"This isn't getting us anywhere, Tempest," he tossed back. His voice rose. "I didn't call to get into an overseas argument with you." Braxton struggled to control his own erupting temper, knowing that the reason why they were arguing at all was because of him. He tried to believe that the way he was handling things would be best for everyone. But at what cost?

"Listen, T, I'm sorry. I know you're upset. I know Kai was disappointed. I didn't set out to hurt you or her."

Tempest struggled with her swirling emotions. Listening to him, in that voice that she loved, she could almost believe anything he said.

Times like this reminded her of how they used to be. How they could be if he'd just let them.

"Can I speak to Kai?" he asked, the hesitation apparent even over the distance.

She cleared the knot in her throat. "I'll get her."

"Wait. Before you go, I just want to say that we do have some things to talk about. Our future." She felt her stomach twist. "It's just that now isn't the time. I promise, I'll be there as soon as I can. We'll straighten everything out then. And in the meantime, just remember that no matter what—I love you."

Without responding, she placed the receiver on the table and went to find Kai. *No matter what.*

Trent arrived at his suite in L.A. to find Nick comfortably playing his saxophone.

"Hey man," Nick greeted, looking up as Trent breezed through the door. "I didn't expect you until later."

Trent pulled off his leather jacket as he crossed the room and tossed it in a vacant chair. "Yeah, I know, but I talked to Noelle this morning."

"And?"

"And she agreed to go away with me for the weekend." He flopped down on the couch.

"Great! Then why do you look so gloomy?" Nick gently placed the sax on the floor.

Trent blew out a frustrated breath, and shook his head. "I know I should be thrilled. It's what I wanted since the first time I met her. But . . ."

"But what?"

"It's all gotten so complicated. Maybe if I'd told her the truth in the beginning, we still could have worked things out." But even as he said the words, he knew that was an impossibility.

"But you didn't."

"I know that!" He jumped up from his seat and jammed his hands in his pockets, pacing. "And I'm going to complicate things further by sleeping with her. Then what?"

"Then you'll just have to deal with it." Nick leaned back and looked at Trent hard. "Or you could tell her the truth, now, before this scheme of yours really blows up in your face and everybody else's."

Trent ceased his pacing and turned on Nick. "And what about the company? What about the thousands of people who will be out of jobs? What about my promise to Jordan? Not to mention the loans from the bank that are gonna come barreling down any minute." He tossed his hands up in the air and looked toward the ceiling as if searching for the answers. His voice lowered. "She hates Trent Dixon, Nick. She blames him for causing Jordan's death. Even though the reports say something different. Do you honestly think that she's going to shower me with love and affection when she finds out the truth? When she finds out that she's slept with the man she thinks killed her husband? There's not enough explaining in the world to pull that one off."

He turned away, disgusted with himself and what he'd done.

"You can fix all of that by telling her now. You know it and I know it. Let the decision be hers."

Trent was audibly silent.

"You can't. Can you?"

Trent's jaw clenched. "No. I can't. I want her too much. If I can only have this one time with her, then so be it. Because I know, as sure as hell, that once she finds out she'll never come near me again. All I have, Nick," he continued, hoping that his friend would understand, "is now."

Noelle completed a series of phone calls to tie up some loose ends with the villa. Then she stopped by Tempest's suite and shared her good news, and was enthusiastically ordered to have a great time. Then she went to check on Carol, the young trainee who filled in for Gina.

Upon arriving at the reception lounge, she was surprised to find Gina in her usual spot behind the long counter.

"Gina. What on earth are you doing here? You're supposed to be off today."

Gina tried to smile. "I know. I had a change in plans and decided to come to work instead."

"A change in getting some rest?" Noelle asked, perplexed, quickly reflecting on the conversation of the previous day.

"I guess I didn't need as much rest as I thought," she responded, trying to keep the edge out of her voice.

Noelle hid her surprise at Gina's obviously annoyed reply. "Well, you know what you need," she said, trying to sound pleasant and take the tension out of the air. "How's that headache?"

"Much better thanks." Gina kept her eyes focused on the ledger. "Is there something I can do for you?"

"Actually, I just came up to check on Carol. I thought I would have to wait until tomorrow to go out of town, but since you're here, I can leave sooner than I anticipated. That is, of course, if you feel up to managing things yourself. You will have to spend the weekend here." Foresight had prompted Noelle to include several small suites for staff members who might have to stay over for an unexpected reason. In a state plagued by earthquakes, floods, fires and mudslides, one just never knew.

She angled her head to the side and peered at Gina quizzically.

Gina finally raised her eyes up from the book in front of her. "I don't see a problem." She forced a smile. "If there's anything special I should be alerted to, just let me know. I'm sure everything will be fine."

"Wonderful. You have all the schedules and the reservations are in place. So . . ." she grinned, raising then lowering her shoulders, "I guess Liaisons will function fine without me for a few days."

"Don't worry about a thing, Mrs. Maxwell. Your villa is in good hands."

Noelle stretched her hand across the counter that divided them, and she placed her hand over Gina's. "I know you'll do a wonderful job, Gina. I have all the trust in the world in you and your capabilities." She smiled again. "I'll stop by before I go."

"I'll be here."

Noelle turned to leave, confident that with Gina at the helm she had nothing to concern herself with. Nothing at all.

CHAPTER 10

A misty rain had begun to fall as Trent pulled the Lexus into the underground garage of Liaisons. He hurried across the manicured grounds. He swore under his breath. The last thing he now needed was to catch a cold. His decision to have a secluded suite precluded him from using the elevator that only went to the main wings. This was one time he really could have used that convenience.

By the time he reached the entrance, the rain was falling in buckets. Maybe it was best that he and Noelle weren't able to get away tonight.

Ever since the crash, he had steered away from flying in anything but clear weather. Flashes of that last flight with Jordan still plagued him. Many nights, he'd wake up in cold sweats, screaming and trembling like a frightened child, his body racked with pain from the many breaks that his body had suffered when they plunged into the sea. Especially nights like this.

He pushed through the glass doors and entered the main lobby, just as a flash of lightning illuminated the heavens. Shaking off the dripping water and ominous thoughts, he crossed the marble floors and headed for the elevator, anxious to get out of his drenched clothing.

He hadn't been in his room for more than a few minutes, having only taken off his shirt when there was a hesitant knock at his door.

"Who is it?" He ripped out the words impatiently, while running a towel across his wet hair. A blast of thunder muffled the response.

He snatched the door open and his whole demeanor quickly changed.

"Monsieur Richards, I seem to always catch you at a bad time," she grinned mischievously.

He reached across the threshold and grabbed her arms, pulling her into his. "There is no bad time when it comes to you," he whispered against her mouth. His tongue traced the soft fullness of her lips, sending tremors shimmying through her body.

Reluctantly he eased away without completely letting her go. His eyes swept hungrily over her. "To what do I owe this very pleasant surprise?"

"I have news."

"Come into my parlor," he teased, bowing low as she passed him.

". . . so we can leave tonight," she concluded, quite pleased with the way things had turned out and anxious to leave before she had any pangs of doubt.

Trent was decidedly quiet.

"Is something wrong? I thought you would be happy."

"No. It's not that, of course I'm happy. It's just that . . ." he could never tell her the real reason, the root of his fears.

"Just what? You've changed your mind, is that it?" She was beginning to feel utterly foolish for having rushed over to him ready to throw herself in his arms like some, some . . .

"Tonight would be fine, Noelle. I'll just have to make a few calls to confirm the changes. That's all." He kissed her lightly. "What time will you be ready?"

"How's six?" she answered, relieved.

"No problem."

"There is one thing, though, Cole."

"What's that?"

"I'd rather meet you somewhere." she looked at the floor. "I mean, I don't . . ."

He cupped her chin, forcing her to look at him. "Believe me, you don't have to explain. I understand perfectly. Meet me at Cochran Airways, it's about . . ."

"I know . . . exactly . . . where it is." She swallowed. "Jordan used to fly from there quite often when he flew in his . . . private plane."

How could he have been so stupid? Of course Jordan used that private airstrip. Hadn't he made enough reservations on Jordan's behalf?

His smile was both apologetic and teasing at the same time. "I hope you won't hold it against me," the words rekindling for her the night that they'd first met.

"There's no way you could have known," she said softly. She breathed deeply. "And just where are you taking me, Cole Richards, that we need a plane?"

"Now if I told you that, you'd know as much as I did. And there'd be no point in all this being a surprise. So get going and I'll meet you at six."

Noelle pretended to pout as she was escorted to the door.

Trent kissed her tenderly. "Until later."

"Bye," she whispered.

He closed the door behind her and shut his eyes. Please don't let the nightmares come. Not tonight. Please, he silently prayed.

Noelle tossed her overnight bag in the trunk of her Mercedes, and hurried around to the driver's seat. Normally, it would take about forty-five minutes to arrive at the airstrip, but in this weather she had allowed herself an extra half hour. The last thing she wanted was to get stuck.

The windshield wipers worked wildly to keep the driving rain off of the windows. It was a losing battle. She slowed the car to fifteen miles per hour as visibility was almost impossible.

How in the world would they be able to fly anywhere in this weather? she worried. It was a night very much like this one that . . .

This was different, she assured herself. She wasn't flying on the open seas. She wasn't traveling in a faulty aircraft. She wasn't flying with someone who didn't check every detail. Cole Richards wasn't Trent Dixon. Cole was someone who could be trusted.

The lights from the airstrip loomed ahead. Another ten minutes and she'd be there. Her heart picked up its pace as she contemplated the trip.

This was a big step she was taking. This was the first man she'd been with since Jordan's death. The first man period. The thought began to frighten her.

What if she couldn't measure up to Cole's expectations? What if he were turned off by the fact that she was . . . No, he wouldn't do that. He would be gentle. He would be loving. He would fulfill her as she'd been longing to be fulfilled. He would teach her and she would be a willing student.

Still, she was afraid. Afraid of what Cole's discovery would do to his image of Jordan. The persona that Jordan presented to the world was infinitely important to him. He reveled in his power and masculinity. But before the next few days were over, that image would come crumbling down. Was she ready to do that to him? Even after all of this time?

She pulled onto the dirt road that led to the hanger. She saw the Lexus parked up ahead. For several paralyzing moments she sat in her car, unable to get out.

It isn't too late to turn around, an inner voice warned. She took a deep breath and opened the door, retrieved her bag from the trunk and entered the hanger.

Her legs felt weak as she walked the few yards to where Trent was animatedly engaged in conversation with the owner's son. Trent turned when he heard footsteps approach. The panicked look on Noelle's face stopped him in midsentence.

"Noelle, what's wrong? Is everything alright at Liaisons?" He crossed the floor in quick strides to where she stood.

"Y-yes," she muttered. "It was just a bumpy ride. The weather is terrible. Are we going to be able to fly?"

Trent put his arm around her waist. "Mr. Cochran assures me that our flight path is relatively clear. The storm is moving away. We'll just have a tail wind to contend with."

"You don't have a thing to worry about," Bill Cochran assured. If you'll both follow me, I'll take you to the plane." As the three crossed the large open space, Bill Cochran wondered why this man had insisted that he not mention his real name. He'd dealt with Trent over the phone on numerous occasions and always had Jordan's plane in tip-top shape. Trent Dixon's credentials as a pilot were above reproach. Now Trent was with Maxwell's widow, pretending to be someone else. Why? Then again it was none of his business, the huge fee that he'd been paid was enough to dismiss any questions.

"Please excuse my manners, Bill," Noelle apologized as they neared the plane. "How is your father?"

"Arthritis has him pretty bad. Days like this keep him indoors. But other than that, he's as grumpy as ever," he chuckled.

Noelle easily recalled the burly older man whose every word sounded like an order. It must be a result of his years in the army she'd always concluded.

Bill Cochran briefly ran a perfunctory check of the instruments, made mention of where everything was located, and handed Trent the flight plan.

He patted Trent on the back as Trent took his seat in the cockpit.

"Y'all have a safe flight, now," Bill Cochran ordered. He tipped his hat toward Noelle. "You take care Mrs. Maxwell. It was good seeing you again."

"Thank you, Bill. You, too. And please give my regards to your father." Noelle eased down into the passenger seat, directly behind Trent. She strapped herself in, as Bill exited the plane.

"All set?" Trent said over his shoulder.

"As ready as I'll ever be."

The engine rumbled beneath them and within minutes they were in the air.

Gina tried to be patient as she explained yet again to Suzanne Donaldson that she could not issue refunds in the form of cash.

"I'll be more than happy to write you a check. But that's the best I can offer on such short notice."

"Well if that's all you can do, I suppose I have no choice," she scoffed. "I'll stop down to pick it up on my way out. Do have it ready." She turned away in a huff and sauntered off toward the elevators.

"I'm more than happy to be rid of you," Gina said under her breath. Suzanne Donaldson was a royal pain. She carried herself around as if the whole world owed her something. Good riddance. She could easily have given her a refund from the vault, she smiled wickedly, but why make life easy for her? She didn't like her from the moment she set foot in the door. She'd overheard several of the nasty comments she'd made about Noelle to the other guests and that just added spice to her distaste.

The phone rang. "Liaisons. Gina Nkiru speaking. May I help you?"

"Yes, Ms. Nkiru," answered the masculine voice. "I certainly hope you can help me. This is Senator Thomas speaking."

Why was that name familiar?

"Yes, Senator Thomas. How may I help you?"

"I'll be in town for a few days, and I was hoping that there was a possibility that you may have a vacancy."

Now she remembered. He was the reference for Cole Richards.

"As a matter of fact, Senator, we do have a vacancy. We had an early checkout."

"Wonderful."

"When would you be arriving?"

"I'll be arriving by mid-week. I'll be staying for three days."

"I'll be sure to have your suite ready."

"By the way, is Mrs. Maxwell around?"

"No. I'm sorry she's out of town for the weekend. She'll be back on Sunday."

"Very good. I'm looking forward to seeing her again."

"I'm sure she'll be happy to see you, too. And Mr. Richards also."

"Excuse me?"

"Cole Richards, the gentleman that you referred."

Senator Thomas paused. "You must be mistaken. I don't know anyone by that name. And I certainly didn't recommend anyone."

A hot flush swept through her. "I probably am mistaken," she said, hoping that the panic wasn't evident in her voice. "There've been so many reservations lately, I must have gotten the name confused."

"Well, in any case, if you should hear from Mrs. Maxwell, do tell her about my arrival."

"I will."

Gina replaced the receiver with a shaky hand. Oh, God. Not only had she done the unspeakable by mentioning another guest by name, that guest's references were false. And if his references were false what else about him didn't ring true?

She hurried into her office and retrieved Cole's file. There it was, a glowing reference letter from Senator Thomas. Her heart thudded. It was her responsibility to verify all references. But Cole Richards just seemed so above board, and he'd left such a large deposit, she just didn't think . . .

She shoved the folder back in the file. She couldn't tell Noelle. She'd lose her job for sure.

What had she done? And who was Cole Richards?

CHAPTER 11

By the time Trent and Noelle landed in the Napa Valley, the rain had all but stopped, replaced by a growing chill in the air. A car was waiting to pick them up and twenty minutes later, they pulled up to a quaint little bed and breakfast inn, named Meagan's Place.

"I hope you like it," Trent said nervously, as he guided Noelle across the cobblestone path. He chuckled. "It doesn't compare to Liaisons, but I thought you might enjoy a slower pace for a few days."

Before they reached the door, Noelle tugged on Trent's hand, causing him to turn around.

Worry was reflected in his eyes.

"I'm sure I'll love it," she said softly, allaying his fears with a heavenly smile. "And I'll love it even more because you took the time to think about me."

"That I did," he responded. "This whole weekend is for you, Noelle. I want everything to be perfect for you."

"It already is."

Gently, he took her in his arms and kissed her tenderly, then eased away. "Come on," he said in a low, intimate voice, "I want to show you our room."

Noelle welcomed the fire that was already roaring in the fireplace, taking out the chill that had seeped through her bones.

Her eyes ran over their inviting quarters. The partially drawn drapes gave them a splendid view of the mountains with the sun hanging low over the peaks. The entire room was done in warm prints, the wallpaper matching the throw pillows and bedding.

But the focal point of the room was the enormous four-poster, mahogany bed that sat at an inviting angle near the bay window. Draperies in the same pattern, hung over the posters. Overstuffed pillows and thick down quilts begged the observer to sink onto them. Small, rectangular tables of the same mahogany were adorned with bowls of fresh flowers, giving the entire room an outdoor scent.

Everything about the room said, Welcome.

She spun around, her face beaming when she looked at Trent. "It's beautiful. I could stay here forever!"

He walked toward her, pulling her against him. "That's the whole idea," he growled into her neck. "But first," he moved away and took her hand, "I say we get something to eat before we barricade ourselves in here." His smile was teasing.

"I thought you'd never ask."

There were only two other couples present in the homey dining room. The menu was simple but appetizing.

Noelle ordered clam chowder for starters, a tossed salad, and fried catfish strips with yellow rice.

"This reminds me of New Orleans," she said biting into a tempting morsel of fish. "I haven't had catfish this good since my aunt made it."

Trent grinned. "I'm glad you like it." He cut into his two-inch porterhouse steak. "When was the last time you saw your aunt?"

Noelle leaned slightly back in her chair. "It's been quite some time," she admitted. "She hasn't been well over the years. She wasn't able to come to Jordan's funeral. We, Jordan and I, usually visited her once a year." She smiled at the memory. "She never changed over the years. Right up until the last time I saw her she was still giving orders and demanding sweat and blood from her staff."

"Seems like a very interesting lady. Maybe that's where you get your tenacity from."

Noelle's eyebrows arched in an unspoken question.

"You're a determined woman, Noelle," he said, by way of explanation. "There's no doubt about that. I believe that if you put your mind to it, you could do anything you set out to do." *Even run Maxwell Enterprises.*

She sighed heavily. "Perhaps. I really don't see myself as the extraordinary businesswoman that some have made me out to be. I'm just doing what I like. I've always enjoyed seeing people happy and well fed," she added with a grin. "I just feel fortunate to have the financial ability to do what I want. Not many people have that opportunity."

"You're a very lucky woman in many regards, Noelle."

"I feel especially lucky now," she said, looking into his eyes. "More so than in a very long time."

"I hope I'm the reason."

"Maybe," she teased. She focused on her plate. "This place is really lovely. You were right, I did need a change."

"I thought we could take a flight out to the wineries tomorrow."

Noelle nodded in agreement. "It's funny, but as long as I've lived in California, I've never been to a winery. It was something I always intended to do, but never got around to it."

"Then it'll be a new experience for both of us. Something I can go back and tell the folks at home about."

Noelle took a sip of spring water. "What do you plan to do when you . . . leave California?" she blurted out.

The question had been gnawing at her ever since she'd accepted his offer to go away for the weekend. *This was the nineties,* she tried to remind herself, but at heart, she was still old-fashioned. She wanted to at least pretend that there was some future for them on the horizon. Even if it was only for a little while.

The suddenness of the question caught Trent off guard. What could he possibly tell her that remotely resembled the truth?

"I hadn't really thought about it," he answered smoothly. Then shrugged, "I don't have any new contracts at the moment. So maybe I'll just hang out here for a while." His look held her. "How would you feel about that?"

"I think I'd like that very much," she answered without hesitation.

He reached across the table and took her hand in his.

"I'm not going to fill your head with promises, Noelle. I'm not going to tell you that there's a rosy future for us, although I'd like it to be. But the reality is, my job takes me all over the world. I haven't been in one spot for more than a couple of months at a time in years. Maybe one day . . ." He looked deep into her eyes. "With the right ingredients, I could plant some roots."

Noelle was the first to look away. "I understand. I don't want you to think that I was trying to . . ."

"Tie me down?"

She nodded.

"I couldn't possibly think that. Not about you. Actually," his tone turned teasing, "getting tied down doesn't sound like such a bad idea." His lips curled up into a grin.

It took several minutes for the comment to sink in. When it did, Noelle felt her face flush with heat. She couldn't meet his taunting eyes, but started to laugh in spite of herself.

"Monsieur Richards," she gasped, affecting offense, "I'm not that kind of girl."

His voice settled down to a low throb. "Then I can't wait to see what kind of *woman* you are."

She glanced away, hoping that he didn't see the inexperience written all over her face.

"In the meantime," he said quickly, wanting to alleviate her obvious discomfort, "why don't we take a stroll around the grounds?" He pushed away from the table and came around to help her out of her seat.

The sun was slowly setting over the hilltops. For miles the lush green valleys resembled giant waves, permanently etched onto canvas.

A cool, after-shower breeze blew caressingly around them. Noelle snuggled closer to Trent as they walked, welcoming his warmth.

"I didn't know what I'd been missing all of these years," she said softly. "It takes your breath away."

He stopped and turned her to face him. "It's almost as beautiful as you Noelle." When he stood there looking down at her, he wished that it could always be this way with them. Open. Carefree. Full of wonder and expectation. But he knew that this brief moment in time was only temporary. He had no right to hope for anything more. But whatever he could take from their time together he knew it would have to last him a lifetime. A lifetime without Noelle.

He leaned down and kissed her with such tenderness that her heart felt like it would split in two. At that moment she felt that she would do anything to be with this man. To make a life with him. To forge a future with him. Did she dare to hope? To dream? If only for the moment.

In silent understanding they turned back toward the inn.

The only light in the room emanated from the fireplace, sending light and shadow dancing across the walls. She was grateful for the semidarkness, hoping that it would camouflage the anxiety that hung in her eyes. Her fingers trembled as she made a task out of unpacking her bag, for some inexplicable reason wanting to delay the inevitable.

She did want this, didn't she? she questioned, gingerly laying her chiffon gown across the bed, that had been turned down in their absence. She'd come this far. There was no turning back. Her heart thundered.

Trent stepped up behind her, kissing the back of her neck and she nearly leaped out of her skin.

"I didn't mean to startle you," he apologized, reaching around and handing her a glass of champagne. "Here, take a sip."

Obediently, she did as she was instructed. She didn't taste a thing.

Trent pinched the glass from her fingers and placed it on the bedside table. He turned her around to face him.

"I won't do anything you don't want me to do, Noelle. I realize this is a big step for you. You're not the kind of woman who would take . . . something like this lightly. Believe this, if you believe nothing else. This time with you is special to me. More than I could ever explain. I've wanted you from the moment I saw you, maybe even before. In my dreams." He gently stroked her face and she felt as if all of the air had been absorbed from the room.

His hands trailed down her arms and he took her hands in his, leading her out of the bedroom.

Trent pushed open the connecting door which led to a spacious bath. Without a word, he turned on the shower and within moments the room was filled with steam.

"I won't do anything," he repeated, untying the knot on her wrap-around dress, "that you don't want me to." He kissed her neck, separating the folds of the dress as he did.

Noelle bit her lip to stifle a cry, when his mouth slid down to caress the exposed skin of her breasts.

The fine mist from the steam enveloped them, dampening her skin. The air seemed to sizzle as her dress slid off her to fall like a whisper around her feet. His hands lovingly explored the delicious curves of her body. His eyes, heavy with desire seared across her flesh. She trembled as the stroking of his fingers sent jolts rushing through her.

"You're beautiful," he groaned, slipping one strap off her shoulder and then the other. He cupped her full breasts in his hand, grazing her erect nipples with tantalizing flicks of his tongue.

Noelle felt lightheaded as wave upon wave of unsatisfied hunger engulfed her. She clasped his head with her hand as he took one succulent tip into his mouth and then the other.

From somewhere far off she heard ragged moans, almost a plea, and realized that it had come from deep within her. She tried to speak to tell him how wonderful he made her feel but she couldn't find her voice, as his hands trailed downward, pushing her black lace panties over her hips.

Hesitantly, he took a step back. His eyes refused to believe the magnificence of the person who stood in front of him. She was a pure work of art, a sculptor's dream. Her tall, voluptuous frame belied her outward slenderness. Full, erect breasts cried out to be touched. Her delicately narrow waist, flared out to rounded hips. Hips made for loving, was his one rational thought, as his eyes trailed downward to the long, shapely legs that he couldn't wait to be imprisoned by.

Standing before him, Noelle felt truly beautiful for the first time in her life. The look of pure adoration, that emanated from his eyes, not simply wanton lust, warmed her to her soul.

Tentatively she reached out a shaky hand and slowly unbuttoned his shirt. With more calm than she thought she was capable of managing, she pushed his shirt over his broad shoulders.

She wanted to discover him, to understand and commit to memory every inch of that glorious body. Boldly, she first unbuckled his pants then loosened the zipper.

Instinctively, his hand grabbed hers pressing it solidly against his throbbing member. She shuddered as the thudding pulse of his desire welled within her grasp.

His intoxicating groan urged her on as she stroked him, learning the curves, the sleekness, the power of him.

He struggled for control, but knew that he could no longer withstand the seduction of her caress.

His mouth covered hers hungrily, drinking in the sweetness, exploring and discovering new depths, new heights. He pulled her to him, pressing her soft flesh against the hard lines of his.

Unable to be denied a moment longer, he guided her into the shower.

The surging water cascaded over their bodies, drenching them, cooling them, heating them, binding them.

He drew her nearer, sliding the jasmine-scented soap over her form. The sensuous feel ignited unimaginable longing.

Her eyes slid shut as the foamy lather liquified and dripped languidly down the crevices of her body. She braced herself against the tile wall as Trent neared.

He pressed himself against her. The frothy suds were joining them erotically together.

Noelle stroked the hard contours of his broad back, sending shivers of incendiary delight down his spine.

"I want you, Noelle," he moaned against her neck. His lips ran a path across her shoulders. "I want to make love to you. Now."

CHAPTER 12

Lovingly and with tender care he placed her on the bed. The flames from the fireplace kept dancing off of her still damp body, giving her an almost surreal aura.

For several moments he stood above her, hesitant to touch her. Afraid that just the slightest contact would send him over the edge.

And then, as if in a dream, she reached out for him, beckoning him with her eyes. She whispered his name.

"Cole."

Slowly, hypnotically he lowered himself onto her waiting body. Only a breath separated them.

He touched her cheek then covered it with a kiss. His mouth closed over hers swallowing her quiet moan.

Expertly, his hard thighs separated her pliant ones. His wide hands caressed her thighs, her hips, raising them to meet him.

His mouth drifted down to take a taut nipple fully into his mouth. She cried out his name as he pushed against her and met resistance. Startled, he searched her face with his eyes. The unasked question hanging in the air between them.

She clung to him, arching her body to join with his. Urging him on. No longer caring what he discovered, only knowing that at this moment she must have him within her. His mouth came down on hers, his tongue dancing against the walls, stifling her cries. Her eyes squeezed shut as he pushed past the thin barrier that separated them.

The briefest moment of piercing pain was immediately replaced with an overwhelming sensation of sublime joy.

Slowly, tenderly he moved within her, bracing her hips to meet his rhythm, sending sensation after sensation of pleasure whipping through her.

She never imagined it could be like this. All of her unfulfilled days, and countless lonely nights had not prepared her for this ecstasy.

She wanted to please him and instinctively her innate sexual nature took over. She stroked him, called out his name, slowed the tempo, moved her hips solidly against his thrusts.

Trent groaned out loud, clawing at the sheets as her undulations steered him toward the brink of total submission.

Faster they traveled, discovering in each other a world that neither knew existed. Until now. In each other's arms, bound by a calling older than time.

Tears of exquisite joy ran down her cheeks as the pulsing, throbbing beat of release wound its way through her body.

She wanted to scream, to laugh, to cry. She wanted this moment to last forever, but intuitively she knew that the climactic end was rapidly approaching.

Trent's heart raced. Every fiber of his being threatened to explode. This couldn't be real, he thought hazily, as Noelle's long legs tightened around his waist.

He sunk deeper within her, pulling her hips savagely against his final shuddering thrusts.

Through the cloud of dizzying fulfillment, he heard her cry out his name over and again as her spasmodic response drained the last of the fiery liquid.

Quietly they lay nestled in each other's arms. Trent cradled Noelle protectively against him, listening to her heart beat rhythmically against his chest. What had taken place between them still had him awestruck. How could it be possible that she was . . . ? His mind was still too cloudy to sift through the possibilities. He'd find a way to get her to talk about it. But all he wanted to do right now was hold her.

It was more than she could ever have hoped to expect. Cole was all that she'd imagined him to be and so much more, she thought. He'd awakened in her that strong passion that was always just beneath the surface. She felt complete, different somehow—as if some magical force had altered her life. That magic was Cole. She had no regrets.

Trent turned fully on his side. "Noelle," he said gently, "do you want to tell me what went on with you and Jordan?"

She tried to turn her face away, but he wouldn't allow it.

"Does it change anything?"

"Like what, Noelle?"

"Like what you think about Jordan?"

"Jordan? Is that what's been bothering you all along? You were worried that if we made love I'd find out that you were still a virgin?"

She barely nodded. "I was worried about how your opinion of Jordan would change."

"Whatever went on between the two of you could never change the kind of man Jordan was, Noelle."

"It's just that Jordan always prided himself on his masculinity. Maybe even more so because of his . . . problem. I'm sure that's the reason why he was so driven." She bit her lip. "I was in a four-year marriage that was never consummated. It's almost too bizarre to be real. But it is. I lived it."

"Did you . . . know before you married him?"

She shook her head. "I had no idea. I always believed that he was being an old-fashioned gentleman and wanted to wait." She expelled a shuddering breath. "On our wedding night," she began hesitantly, "he made me . . . do things, then he taunted me, insulted me, told me that I was the reason that he couldn't make love to me."

She held back a sob. "I tried. Night after night. I did everything he told me, but nothing ever happened. I felt so inadequate as a woman, as a wife.

"Then one night, after another of our terrible arguments about my incompetence, he finally just broke down. He told me how much he loved me, how he believed that he had finally found the one woman that could change him. But he said he realized that nothing could change the fact that he was no longer a "real man." And probably never would be again.

"He told me if I wanted to leave him he would understand. He even offered to let me have a lover on the side." She looked up into Trent's eyes. "But I couldn't do that. I wouldn't do that. My wedding vows still meant something to me. In sickness and in health," she said deliberately. "Jordan had been everything to me, mentor, friend, protector, provider. He opened up the world to me. I would never leave him because I'd come to realize that Jordan needed me, although he'd never openly admit such vulnerability. And I think he knew that I'd never leave. He appreciated me, and I guess he loved me in his own way. I guess Jordan hoped I would be the one to make a man out of him. And when I couldn't . . ." Her voice drifted away.

Trent was stunned by this intimate confession. He knew that it took a lot for her to reveal the most private details of her life with Jordan. But now, the pieces of the puzzle were beginning to slowly come together. He'd never understood why Jordan had requested such an enormous favor from him. It was becoming clearer. Now it all made sense, Trent realized. That would explain why he was never seen running around with various women and why he married an innocent like Noelle. Jordan's illness had rendered him impotent. A man like Jordan wouldn't risk that crushing secret getting out because of some casual fling. He had to get married to maintain his image.

"But what about you Noelle? What were you to have? Jordan spent the majority of the time out of the country."

"I kept myself busy with my studies, traveling, trying unsuccessfully, to fit into Jordan's world. But he more than compensated for his shortcomings in our love life." She laughed mirthlessly. "Jordan showered me with gifts, cars, jewelry. All of my clothes are handmade, my shoes are imported."

"But what about you, Noelle?" he asked again.

It was several moments before she spoke. "He made me feel special, for the first time in my life," she said plaintively. "Jordan took me from a life of poverty and little hope, and gave me salvation. I owed Jordan. I admired him, looked up to him, depended on him. I know that he was cruel at times with his words, but his anger was not at me." She looked away thoughtfully. "He was angry at himself," for not really being the man that he presented to the world." She paused, her next words seeping out through the crevices of her loss. "In one careless moment all that I knew was taken away from me. And I have no one to blame except Trent Dixon. I hate him for what he's done, to me and to Jordan."

She swallowed. "But to answer your question, my life, at least the one I'd come to know, was empty as far as real love was concerned. Even with all of the trinkets to fill it up." Her voice softened and she looked at him with the discovery of love in her eyes. "Until I met you."

The blade of guilt twisted deeper into his gut. Noelle had worshipped Jordan. There was no question about that. She worshipped him as a child worships a parent, he realized with sudden clarity. He was the father that she had missed. Just as Jordan had become for him. He could never make that up to her. But damn it, it wasn't his fault. Or was it? He could have said no. He should have just refused. But he knew how important it was to Jordan. After all that Jordan had meant to him, he couldn't deny him that final wish. If Jordan couldn't get him to do it, eventually he would have found someone else. Perhaps someone not as competent as himself and that could have proven to be even more disastrous. More importantly, Jordan was determined that Noelle be spared . . .

"Cole?" The gentle, cadence of her voice pulled him back. "I didn't mean to put you on the spot. I just want you to understand. Until now, I've never discussed the intimate details of my marriage with anyone before. It's always been too . . ."

He put a finger to her lips and focused on her, seeing her from yet another perspective. "Yes, I do understand, Noelle. I understand more than I ever thought I could. I'm just glad that you thought enough of me to confide in me. You're a remarkable woman and you deserve nothing but happiness."

He leaned down and kissed her tenderly, then slowly, patiently, he rekindled the flames that danced just below the surface, with the insistent circular motions of his hands.

This time, Noelle led the way, guiding him to all of the spots that she'd discovered aroused her. She felt a sense of wild abandon in his arms. Her own driving need shocked her. She wanted to learn everything, know everything at once. And she wanted Cole to teach her.

She was more than a dream come true, Trent gasped, as Noelle's velvet tongue trailed steadily down his chest. He visibly trembled when she took him in her hand, hesitating but a moment. Then all he felt was a searing white heat shooting through his body as she enveloped him.

CHAPTER 13

A light tapping on the window permeated Trent's dreams. It was raining. He was in the air, trying to fly above the storm. His palms were wet from perspiration.

"This is crazy, Jordan," he yelled over the roar of the Cessna's engine. "We should turn back. You don't have to do this. There has to be another way."

"We made a deal, Trent. There is no other way," Jordan answered back as another sharp pain ripped through his insides. He doubled over. "You . . . can't back out now."

Trent's heart raced. What was he doing? The slightest error and they would both be dead.

A bolt of lightning blazed through the heavens.

"Did you make the adjustments?" Jordan asked, sweat beading on his forehead.

"Yes," Trent answered succinctly.

"I want you to make sure that every detail of my will is carried out to the letter." He spoke through clenched teeth. "She can do it. I know she can. And she deserves the chance. She thinks she just wants to run some hotel, but I know better. She's better than that, because I made her what she is. Noelle has been groomed all of these years for just this moment. She just hasn't realized it yet. She'll see. You'll make her see, what power, real power, can do. She'll never have to feel inferior to anyone again."

The plane suddenly lurched to one side, being tossed around by the raging winds like sheets on a line. Jordan was seized with another attack of excruciating pain. An animal-like cry was torn from his throat.

Trent cringed at the sound. Jordan had gone on like this for months, Trent thought, as he fought to keep the plane in the air. He'd refused to see a doctor and wouldn't return home. "I can't let her see me like this," he'd said on more than one occasion. "And you'd better not breathe a word to her!"

They were several miles off shore, having flown out of Thailand on their way to Hong Kong. He and Jordan had been finalizing the reorganization operations with Mr. Takaka who was to take over the headquarters in Hong Kong. It was obvious to Trent and to Takaka that Maxwell Enterprises needed to rethink how it did business and find alternatives to expand. But Jordan had been adamant about not changing a thing about his corporation. He was positive that after the *minor* revolt in Sudan was settled, the exporting of goods would be resumed.

For all of Jordan's business sense he refused to see that his enterprise was in serious trouble. The fact that he had negotiated for close to fifty million dollars to refinance his shipping and airlines only compounded the problem. With trade being cut off at the knees because of the rebel forces, Maxwell Enterprises was losing thousands of dollars per day. They needed to diversify.

"How far are we from the shore?" Jordan asked, breaking into Trent's troubling thoughts.

"About fifteen miles."

"It's time."

Trent briefly looked over his shoulder and saw the look of absolute peace and resolution on Jordan's face.

They'd gone over the plan a hundred times over the past month. *It must be made to look like an accident,* Jordan had insisted. He didn't want Trent implicated in anyway. *If* Trent got out of the plane alive.

Trent adjusted the dials, set the controls on automatic. He reached for the headphone and called in the distress signal. When Hong Kong responded to the desperate call for help, he ignored it. Just as he had been instructed. He slipped on his life jacket and unfastened his seat belt.

His throat constricted when he rose from his seat. His eyes clouded with burning tears of regret, fear, and the imminent loss of someone who meant so much to him.

"No good-byes," Jordan said.

Trent dropped down on his knees and embraced him.

"Just go," Jordan croaked in a tight voice.

Then suddenly the plane shook like it had been hit with enemy fire, tossing Trent across the small seating space. Sparks shot up from the control panel. The small twin-engine Cessna began a stomach-pitching descent to the dark waters below.

Oh, my God, Trent thought desperately. It wasn't supposed to happen like this. It was too soon. They were going down. He wasn't going to make it.

The roar of Jordan's voice snapped him to his senses. "Get out, Trent! Now, before it's too late. Now!"

"Cole. Cole. Wake up!" Noelle gently, then with more urgency shook his shoulder. He was drenched in perspiration.

Trent's eyes flew open and he looked wildly around as if he didn't know where he was. His body was racked with unforgotten physical pain.

Noelle became frightened seeing the look of pure terror carved on his face. "Cole, please," she begged. "It's all right. You were having a dream." Cautiously, she reached out and touched his cheek. The contact seemed to draw him back.

Slowly his eyes began to focus. He breathed in short panting breaths. He struggled to sit up, and seeing the look of agonized concern on Noelle's face, he knew it had happened again.

"Are you all right?" she asked gently, as her fear for him was slowly ebbing.

He nodded. His voice was unsteady. "That must have been some dream."

Noelle eased off of the bed and got a towel from the dressing table.

"Do you want to talk about it?" she asked, carefully drawing the towel across his damp body. "They say it helps."

He rubbed his eyes with the tips of his fingers. "You know, I can't remember what it was about."

"You can't remember?" she asked in disbelief. "You practically leap out of your skin, groan like you're being tortured and wake up bathed in sweat, and you can't remember what it was about!"

Trent took a deep breath, and hung his head in resignation. He flung himself back down against the pillows, and stared up at the ceiling. "All right, all right I do remember. At least some of it," he admitted. "I was dreaming about . . . a flight that I was on."

"And?"

"And, it was pretty scary."

"What was so scary about it? Was it when you were in the air force?"

"Yes," he answered, almost too quickly, thankful for a way out.

"We were on a rescue mission, in the middle of a storm. One of the planes was lost and mine almost went down." At least that was true, he consoled himself.

"Oh, Cole," she reached out and stroked his cheek. "I'm so sorry."

"I'm sorry that you had to witness that. I haven't had an attack in a long time."

"Well, it's over now," she soothed, easing down next to him and cradling him against her breasts. "Try and get some sleep." She kissed the top of his head and held him, listening to his breathing return to normal.

Instinctively, she understood that when he crawled on top of her and entered her without so much as a word, it was solely an act to assure himself of his connection to life. He simply needed her at that moment, without question, without recriminations. She willingly gave herself to the driving thrusts that quenched her thirsty body, and she became one with the ragged moans of his release.

As Noelle finally drifted off to sleep, a nagging thought hovered just on the fringes of her consciousness. She could have sworn that Cole had called out Jordan's name in his sleep.

"How are you feeling this morning?" Noelle asked as she stood in front of the mirror brushing her hair.

"Pretty damned good," Trent grinned, sliding up behind her and nibbling her neck.

Joy bubbled in her laughter. "We'll never get out of here if you keep that up."

"Hmm," he slipped his arms around her bare waist, "that sounds like an excellent idea."

She swiveled around and leaned lightly into him, tilting her face upward to his. "Now, Monsieur Richards, I didn't come here with you to be ravished!" She giggled as she fought to maintain a sense of seriousness. "I came here to see the vineyards."

"Well, madame," he responded, pulling her solidly against him, "I think you've come to the wrong place." His mouth covered hers in a hungry kiss that left her weak with wanting.

"Last night was beautiful, Noelle," he whispered against her lips. His nimble fingers trailed up and down her back. "You were beautiful." His eyes washed over her. "I've never been with anyone who's made me feel the way you do."

"You made me happy Cole. More than you'll ever know. What happened between us was special." She looked away. "I know you've been with other women . . ."

"Don't."

"No. Please let me finish. And I could only hope that I made you happy. Because no matter what happens between us, I'll always remember this time together. Always." She looked up at him and everything that she felt was mirrored in her eyes.

Trent felt a surge of guilt sweep through him like a tidal wave. He'd taken away her most precious gift with lies, and deceit. Romanced her out of her virginity on the pretext of being someone she thought she could trust, could put her faith in.

What had he become? Had his own needs and desires superseded the feelings of others? Had he been under Jordan's tutelage for so long that he was becoming like him?

Then he was no better than Jordan Maxwell who made the stakes so high the other players could never stay in the game.

He cupped her face in his hands. His eyes grew serious. "This—this is no casual thing with me, Noelle. You're too important to me for that. Don't you ever forget that. Ever." He seared her lips with a kiss.

"Maybe you're right," he grinned, leaning back and catching his breath, "I think we should get out of here." And he would have to find a way out of this web that he'd woven.

Nick studied the fax that had come over the machine moments earlier. Several of the Maxwell sites had been completely shut down. One of the jets was confiscated and its contents looted. There was complete anarchy in the streets.

He placed the long sheet of paper on the table. How would this affect the loans that Trent spoke about? Nick worried. If no money was coming in from shipping and air transport, how were they going to pay off the bank and all the other expenses? The letter didn't state how much loss had been sustained, but he could only imagine that it was in the millions.

This is what Jordan had left for Noelle to walk into? It was incomprehensible that Jordan couldn't have foreseen what was happening. He was too astute a businessman not to plan ahead. He breathed deeply. Trent did mention that there were other circumstances that compelled Jordan to handle things the way that he did. Must have been some mighty powerful circumstances, he thought, picking up his jacket.

Things would be so much simpler, he thought, if Trent would tell her the real reasons behind what had taken place that night. But he knew Trent as a man who stood by his word. He would never tell her, no matter what the cost to himself.

Nick walked toward the door. He'd make the call to Liaisons when he returned.

"If you'll follow me," the sunshine-blond tour guide instructed, "I'll show you the pressing machines."

"You mean they don't stomp the grapes with their feet?" Trent spouted, appalled.

"Please don't pay him any attention," Noelle interjected. "It's the sun." She nudged him in the rib with her elbow. "Behave," she whispered under her breath.

"Yes, Mommy."

She nudged him again, only harder. And they both giggled as they followed the small group.

* * *

Once back outdoors, Noelle playfully chastised Trent.

"Cole, why can't you behave yourself? You tortured that poor girl to death with your twenty questions."

"Aw, she loved it," he chuckled. "I'm sure we made her day."

Noelle shook her head. "You're probably right," she admitted.

He suddenly swept her up in his arms and spun her around until she squealed. Dizzy with laughter, they both collapsed on the grassy knoll.

"What do you want to do now?" Trent grinned as he nibbled on her lip.

"I'm starved. What about you?"

"Let's eat."

The pungent aroma of wine floated through the air. Trent spread a patchwork quilt on the grass, while Noelle unpacked the contents of their picnic basket.

"The inn thought of everything," Noelle commented, looking at the assortment of cheeses, dips, cold cuts, salad, fresh fruit and breads. "Maybe this is a feature that I could add to Liaisons," she mused out loud.

"You mean Liaisons doesn't prepare picnic baskets?" he asked, feigning horror. "Who would have thought such a thing!"

Noelle gave him a good shove. "Don't be obnoxious. It's just that I want to make sure that my guests have everything that they could want. I think picnic baskets would be a nice, homey touch."

"Believe me, baby, I'm pretty sure, none of your clients have ever sat their rear ends down on damp grass, fought off insects, or eaten food out of a basket." He took a hearty bite from his apple.

Noelle looked offended. "What is that supposed to mean?"

He sat up and looked at her. "You didn't create Liaisons for the non-wealthy, the underclass, and you know it. Liaisons is the hideaway for the rich, the elite. They don't come to Liaisons to be reminded of poverty. They want to be pampered, their every whim catered to with zest. They wouldn't know a picnic basket if it hit them in their Rolls Royces."

"That's a pretty narrow-minded conclusion," she tossed back. "Especially coming from someone whose had their share of the finer pleasures of life!"

He took the barb in stride. "I just think that when you dreamed of Liaisons, you wanted it to be as far away from all the poverty you've ever known. There's nothing wrong with that," he qualified. "But sometimes," he added thoughtfully, "we get so blinded by the beautiful life we forget where we've come from."

She turned away. He couldn't be any further from the truth at least where she was concerned. She wanted to laugh, but her anger and disappointment wouldn't let her. She'd expected that he would have thought more of her than that.

But she couldn't realistically expect him to be able to see beyond the obvious. Liaisons was a diversion. It was created for the very reasons that he mentioned, but the ultimate goal lay beyond the naked eye. It was a part of her life that she'd shared with no one. It was her one joy.

And she wasn't ready to part with that secret. Not just yet.

She played along. "Perhaps you're right, Cole. I probably have gotten too far away from my roots. I guess I never thought of it that way before," she said easily.

"I didn't mean anything by all that, Noelle. It's just that I know you're such a caring person. I wouldn't ever want to see you get jaded by everything that's around you."

"If I have nothing else, I have integrity. I could never become *one of them.* But believe me, I know what I'm doing."

Trent spotted the glint of challenge in her eye. He believed her.

"I had a wonderful day," Noelle said to Trent as they lay stretched out on the blanket, looking up at the setting sun. "Thank you."

"I think," he replied, "it was something long overdue for you. I would guess that you've spent the past year doing nothing else but trying to get Liaisons off the ground."

"That's true. I haven't had much of a social life in so long, I'd almost forgotten how pleasant it could be."

"The other day," he started tentatively, "you asked me what were my plans for the future. But what about you?"

She sighed. "I haven't given it much thought, actually."

"Have you ever considered taking over Jordan's business?"

"Jordan and I had very different views when it came to Maxwell Enterprises."

"Such as?"

She tried to think of a response that wouldn't sound too condescending.

"To put it simply, in business and in some aspects of his personal life, Jordan was a man strictly after personal gain. He had no concerns where it . . . came to the greater good."

Trent looked confused. "His business employed hundreds of people. That had to mean something."

Noelle pursed her lips, then took a sip of water before she spoke. "This may sound callous," she offered, "but in my opinion, Jordan took whatever he wanted at whatever the cost and generally gave nothing back. At least not on a humanitarian level," she qualified. "Jordan was propelled by money and power and what that could afford him. If someone else happened to benefit as a result, it was purely accidental."

Trent thought about it for a moment and had to admit that it was true.

"Did you ever discuss it with him?"

"Of course I did. But he wouldn't hear of doing anything differently. He said his business flourished with a strong hand and he didn't get into business for humanitarian reasons.

"Even though I resented his tactics and some of his ethics, I could never deny that he was incomparable when it came to business. You couldn't help but admire his ability to turn nothing into something. The barren lands of Sudan are a perfect example." And so am I, she thought. "No one imagined that it could be possible to establish a thriving enterprise in that region of the world," she continued. "Jordan had a vision and he made it a reality, whatever were his methods."

Trent leaned closer. "What would you do if given the chance?" he asked.

Noelle's eyes brightened. "If given the chance I would change the total direction of the company. Or at least expand its objectives." Her voice blossomed with excitement. "I would develop housing, schools, and hospitals in the areas where Maxwell Enterprises has its largest holdings. I would enlist the services of the community in building these facilities so that they would have a sense of ownership.

"Not only would they have jobs, but places to live and hospitals to attend to their health needs. Instead of constantly bringing in outside sources, use the internal resources," she concluded.

Trent was astounded by her insight and the validity of her vision.

"It's hard to believe that Jordan wouldn't have jumped at something like that."

"Believe it," she said simply.

"Have you ever discussed your ideas with—Trent Dixon?"

Her face hardened. "I have absolutely nothing to say to that man. And certainly nothing that has to do with the business. He was a hired hand, paid to do Jordan's bidding. I'm quite sure that he wouldn't want to upset the status quo."

"Maybe if you . . ."

"Did you hear what I said?" she railed, her eyes flashing. "I have nothing to say to him. Nothing!"

She rolled her eyes in disgust and stared off into the distance. "My marriage may not have been made in heaven, but it was all I knew. All I had to rely on," she said in a choked voice. "Trent Dixon shattered my world. The only reason why Liaisons even exists is because of Jordan's death. It's a painful consolation. But it gives me the incentive to make it the best it can be. I'd like nothing better than to see Trent Dixon rot in jail for all eternity, and take Maxwell Enterprises with him. I have what I want," she added with finality.

Trent felt a chilling numbness slowly weave its way through his veins. Noelle's unyielding hatred for Trent left him without words.

It was painfully clear that Noelle would never forgive him, no matter what information he could come up with. And he could never tell her the truth.

The only way to convince her of his innocence would be to break his word to Jordan. That—he could never do.

He swallowed back the lump of acceptance. These next two days would be their last together. Of that he was certain.

CHAPTER 14

Gina returned to her station at the front desk. The dinner hour was over and she'd made her rounds. In a matter of days Senator Thomas would arrive. Her pulse raced. How would she ever explain this mix-up to Noelle? Maybe, she thought, if she could find out who Cole Richards really was before Noelle returned, she could head off what she knew would be a disaster.

The spot just beneath her left eye twitched. The same sensation she'd had several weeks ago filled her. There had to be something she could do. But what?

The phone rang.

"Liaisons. Gina Nkiru speaking."

"Hello, this is Trent Dixon. May I speak with Mrs. Maxwell?"

Trent Dixon! "Uh, I'm sorry Mr. Dixon, Mrs. Maxwell is unavailable. May I help you with something?"

"We were to meet this week. But unfortunately something has come up and I won't be able to see her. Would you tell her that I'll call and reschedule?"

"Of course."

"Thank you."

The connection was broken.

Gina replaced the receiver. Noelle would be relieved, Gina thought, as she wrote down the message. She knew Trent Dixon wasn't someone Noelle was looking forward to meeting. At least that was one less thing to worry about. But Cole Richards, or whoever he was, was still an issue.

She hadn't spoken to Joseph since the night she walked out on him. Several times she'd attempted to call him but changed her mind halfway through dialing. This time she would swallow her pride. He was the only person she could think of that could find the answers. She prayed that he would help her.

The evening was warm. A soft breeze blew in from the partially opened window. The lights were turned down low and the murmurs of the television hummed in the background.

"Tell me more about your family, Cole," Noelle coaxed as they lay in each other's arms.

"Hmm, let's see. My older sister, Diane, she's the one with the twins, she works at a small law firm in Eaton."

"She's an attorney?"

"She thinks she is," Trent chuckled. "She's a paralegal, but you could never tell her she's not an attorney. Every chance she gets she's spouting the law, no matter what the topic."

They both laughed.

"But she's a doll. Unfortunately she can be a little hard around the edges," he admitted. "The firm she works for handles a lot of suits against large corporations and wealthy individuals who have, in some way, stepped on the toes of the little people. She considers herself a champion of the underclass. That compounded with a nasty divorce a year ago makes her a little difficult. But she's attending law school now. She should be finished in about another year. My other sister is Stephanie. Steph has nothing else on her mind except having a good time. She has more boyfriends than she can keep up with. She has the biggest heart of anyone so tiny. Everyone's issue is her personal heartache."

Noelle smiled, envisioning his night and day sisters. "And where do you fit in?"

"I'm the baby," he said humbly.

"And I'm sure you were spoiled rotten with two older sisters doting on you."

"I must admit, I had it made. But my parents didn't let me get away with much. They made sure that I knew how to do everything, including cooking to sewing. My mother always said I had to know how to take care of myself because she couldn't see how any woman in her right mind would put up with me."

"Were you a troublesome little boy?" she grinned, snuggling closer.

He laughed. "I was always in one scrape or the other when I was growing up. Usually it was because I had gotten involved in some outrageous scheme with my buddies from school. I spent an unusual amount of time in the principal's office."

"You certainly haven't outgrown your mischievous streak," she said, smiling as she recalled his behavior at the vineyards.

"Well some things never change," he said, rolling on top of her. "As a matter of fact," he kissed her lips, "I feel some mischief coming on right about now."

His mouth covered hers, while his searching fingers found their way beneath her short gown. Gently he caressed the tender flesh.

"I don't think you'll be needing this," he said in a raspy voice, skillfully slipping the gown over her head. He held her hands above her, dipping his head to suckle a taut nipple.

He felt her body tremble as his tongue circled the delectable orb.

"Cole," she moaned, "I want to touch you."

"No. Not this time. This is for you."

With each stroke of his tongue, with each tender touch he made her body come alive in ways she never knew possible.

Her mind ran in circles as she felt the flames of passion ignite within her.

Languidly his mouth sought out her moist center and lights exploded before her eyes. She cried out as her body involuntarily arched. Her shuddering moans crescendoed to ragged gasps filling the night air with erotic music.

He played along her willing body like a concert pianist propelling his instrument to greater heights. Her own spontaneous reactions incited him, filling him to near bursting.

She wanted to be with him always, she realized through the haze of her swirling emotions. She wanted to wake with him, sleep with him, share his dreams.

And as he gently buried himself deep within the satiny sheath, he said in a ragged breath just before his mouth covered hers, "I love you, Noelle."

The words so simple, yet so powerful, filled her with a warmth that was beyond reply. Let them be real, she prayed, as she clung desperately to him.

Joseph hung up the phone, still trying to absorb what Gina had said to him. This man that Noelle was with apparently wasn't who he claimed to be.

He rose from his seat by the window and crossed the small sitting room to the bar. He poured a glass of scotch over ice. If he were to discover who Cole Richards was, would Gina be willing to reconsider his marriage proposal?

She was scared. There was no question about that. Her job meant everything to her. More than he did, he realized, sadly. But maybe if he found a way to help her, she'd finally see just how important she was to him.

He took a sip from the glass. The information that Gina had provided was sketchy. And he couldn't rely on the profile that had been submitted to Liaisons.

He shook his head. This man was obviously after something. But what?

First thing in the morning, he'd make some calls. Hopefully, he thought, turning off the lights and walking into his bedroom, he could give Gina what she was looking for and she'd give him what he wanted most. *Her.*

Deep in thought, Nick lay in bed. He had some serious doubts about what he had done. He truly couldn't see how a phone call could actually help Trent out of this hole that he'd dug for himself. He said it would buy him some time. But time for what?

He clicked off the light. He could only hope that after the dust settled, Noelle would be able to forgive what Trent had done. Although he couldn't agree with Trent's methods, he could sympathize with his dilemma. Trent deserved some happiness. But for the life of him, he couldn't see how this could turn out happy for anyone.

Braxton looked over the documents with a sense of loss and relief. Carefully, he signed the last page and handed the papers to his partner, Scott.

"Signed and sealed," Braxton said, forcing a smile.

"You're sure you want to do this?" Scott asked.

Braxton nodded. "I've thought about it long and hard. It'll be the best thing for everyone."

Scott slipped the documents into a manila folder. "I still think you should have discussed it with Tempest first. Secrets aren't what relationships thrive on."

"You know what she would have said. This way was best. Anyway, I'll still have my hand in things. My father built this architectural business from scratch. I don't intend to just turn my back on it completely. But my family needs me more than this firm does."

"You still have a ninety-day option, if you should change your mind."

Braxton heaved a sigh and nodded. "Listen, buddy, I have a plane to catch." He shook Scott's hand.

"Don't worry about anything," Scott offered.

"Why should I?" he joked, "I taught you everything you know."

Scott slapped him on the back, and grinned. "Yeah, right."

"I'll call you when I get to San Francisco."

* * *

Joseph was in his office earlier than usual. The staff had yet to arrive. He checked his fax machine. Waiting for him was the copy of the profile of Cole Richards that Gina had sent. He scanned the details.

Richards claimed to be a consultant for Jordan. That's odd, Joseph mused. He handled all of the contracts for every employee that Jordan hired. He'd never even heard of him.

He sat down at his desk and reviewed the other details. Everything looked perfect. No wonder Gina didn't question anything.

He reached for the phone and dialed the number to the private investigator that he used from time to time.

"Good morning, Mike, Joseph Malone. Listen I need a quick favor. I want you to look into the background of a Cole Richards. He claims to be an aeronautical consultant, with a home base in New York."

"No problem. How soon do you need the info?"

"Yesterday."

"I'll get right on it."

"Thanks, Mike. There's a big one in this for you."

"Isn't it always?" he chuckled.

Joseph hung up the phone. "I really hope you appreciate this, Gina," he said out loud. But he had to admit, his own curiosity was getting the best of him. Why would someone want to pretend to be someone they're not in order to get close to Noelle? What did they have to hide?

Noelle and Trent spent the next day touring the countryside, stopping in at the little shops, picking up gifts and simply enjoying each other's company.

Noelle had a shopping bag full of souvenirs and Trent had a bag to match.

"I'm about shopped out," Trent breathed as they emerged from the last antique store on the road.

"What do you want to do now?" she asked.

"I hear they have a boat ride, well more of a yacht ride, just outside of the valley. How about if we take these back to the inn, change for dinner and spend our evening under the stars?"

"That sounds wonderful."

He leaned down and kissed the tip of her nose. "I was hoping you'd say that."

Hand in hand they returned to the car and headed for the inn.

On the return ride, Noelle leaned back and closed her eyes, letting the warm breeze whip across her face. She was in heaven. These past days with Cole had been more glorious than her wildest dreams. She felt like an entirely new person. A person who meant something. A person worth caring about for the *right* reasons.

She angled her head to the side to subtly study his profile. She smiled. Last night, he'd said he loved her. Did he really mean it? she worried again. She had been reluctant to bring it up in the fear that he may deny it. Or maybe he only said it because he felt he should. At least for the moment she could live with the glorious possibility that his feelings for her were real.

A part of her was still afraid to reveal her true feelings for him. She didn't want him to feel obligated to return the sentiments. He'd made it pretty clear that he wasn't making any promises.

She was a big girl. She'd just have to accept the fact that after this magical weekend Cole Richards might very well walk out of her life.

"What are you thinking about, baby?" Trent asked, catching a glimpse of her out of the corner of his eye.

Noelle's smile was wistful. "Just that I wish that I had the power to freeze time."

He turned to look at her, brushing her chestnut hair away from her eyes. He eased the car onto the shoulder of the road. He turned toward her. "If we froze time," he said, loving her more with each passing minute, "then we'd never be able to reach our destiny."

"And where is that?" she asked hopefully.

He leaned across the stick shift and gently kissed her lips. His eyes caressed her face, so full of expectation he thought, his heart heavy with regret.

"Only time will tell," he answered finally.

She looked away, suddenly consumed by a sense of loss. She wanted him to want her as desperately as she wanted him. She wanted him to say more. To say that their destiny was one in the same. He wanted to go back in time and change everything—make it right.

"You're right," she said, forcing cheer into her voice. "And our immediate future is waiting for us at the pier."

They returned to the inn in silence, both trapped in their own tumultuous thoughts. Each wanting the same thing but unable to cross the barrier to claim it.

Beneath the star-encrusted sky, the *Alexis II* glided smoothly along the still waters.

Trent pulled Noelle closer, needing her nearness. He took a sip from his glass of champagne and looked toward the horizon.

"We'll be heading back to the pier soon," he said.

She didn't want to think about it. The closer they neared the pier, the sooner their night would end. And then tomorrow would come and they'd have to return to Liaisons.

She sighed. "As much as I love Liaisons," she looked up into his eyes, "I'll miss being here." She hesitated a moment. "I'll miss this time we've shared together."

He wished that he could offer her more than just the moment, but he couldn't. Instead he hugged her closer.

"Let's not think about tomorrow. Let's make the most of the time we have."

Noelle nodded, taking Trent's arm as they strolled along the deck.

"I've been thinking about your ideas for Maxwell Enterprises," Trent said, hesitantly. "I think you should do it. It would be just the thing to turn the company around. It's really suffering enormous losses because of the revolt. The people are revolting against the government because of all of the things that you mentioned."

"Is the company really in trouble?" she asked, hearing this news for the first time. The reports that she received on the company were generally glorious, with only hints of the real problems.

"From what I understand, things are getting pretty bad."

"Maybe that's why Trent wants to see me." She tossed the information around in her head. "If Jordan's company is in trouble, then Trent must want something from me that he can't handle himself. That would explain his sudden need to come to the States. But it still doesn't explain why he hasn't shown up yet, if the situation is urgent."

She looked to Trent for answers.

"Hopefully, when we return, we'll have some answers," he offered.

They disembarked from the yacht and walked toward the car.

"Think about it, Noelle," he continued. "Jordan groomed you for business and you've obviously proven that you have the capabilities to handle anything."

"You really think so?"

"I know so," he answered, helping her into her seat. He took his place behind the wheel.

"But Trent has complete control over the company. There's no way that he'd be willing to share in the power."

"Maybe you don't know him as well as you think you do."

She looked at him curiously. "You almost sound as if you do."

"No. Uh, of course not," he said quickly. "It's just that, well, maybe you should give him a chance. If Jordan trusted him, perhaps you can, too."

Hadn't Tempest said the same thing? Hadn't Jordan said as much in his letter? Now Cole. She thought about it for a minute. She trusted Cole and she trusted his instincts. Maybe he was right.

"Before I make any decision one way or the other, I want to hear what your investigator friend has to say. If he can show me, without a doubt, that Trent Dixon has absolutely nothing to do with the crash—then—I'll think about it."

He stared straight ahead, keeping his eyes on the road. Ironically, his plan seemed to be working. He could only hope now that Nick did his part.

CHAPTER 15

Tempest heard the sound of soft footsteps entering her bedroom. It must be Kai, she thought, pulling herself out of a light sleep. She glanced at the clock: 1:00 A.M. Kai couldn't possibly be hungry.

She sat up in bed just as the light came on.

"Braxton!" She came fully awake. "When . . . what?"

He crossed the room in long quick strides and sat down beside her.

"I've missed you like crazy," he said, covering her mouth with a warm kiss, stilling any further questions. He sat back and looked at her.

"I know it's early," he began, "but we need to talk."

Her heart raced. "All right."

"I know the past few months have been hell on you and Kai. I know I've been awful to live with, at least when I'm around," he added. "But things are going to change."

Tempest looked away, then back at him. "You've said that so many times, B.J., what makes now any different?

"I've sold the company."

Tempest paused before she spoke. "You did what?"

"I sold the company to Scott. He'll be running things from now on."

"You can't be serious. Why didn't you talk to me about it? That's a decision we should have made together Braxton. Didn't you trust me enough to discuss it with me?" She still couldn't believe that he'd made such a monumental decision without her. Maybe their marriage was in more trouble than she thought.

"I didn't tell you because I knew you'd say not to do it."

"But Braxton, that company means everything to you. It was your father's."

"I know. But it doesn't mean more than keeping you and our daughter happy. My months out of the country, and my hopping from one project to the next, have put a real strain on us. I haven't been there for you and Kai when I should have been. I'll do whatever it takes, T. I don't want to lose you, and I felt you drifting away. Or maybe it was me. I just couldn't stand it."

She was filled with mixed emotions. Everything she'd been thinking had been wrong. She'd been on the verge of accusing him of having an affair, and all the while he was . . . How could she have doubted him?

"So all those trips, all those hushed phone calls, they were about the company." Her tone was more of a statement than a question.

He nodded. "I had to make sure that everything was in place. I had some developments underway and I couldn't step aside until I was sure that they were completed." He lowered his gaze. "I realize now that I should have been honest with you. It would have avoided so much hurt and confusion. I prejudged you, and I guess I was too stubborn to see past doing it my way. I know how persuasive you can be." He grinned slightly. "I didn't want you to talk me out of it."

"Are you sure this is what you want?"

"I'm positive."

"But what are you going to do?"

"I've leased some space in New York, near your office at the World Trade Center. I plan to set up operations there. But only for local jobs." He smiled. "No more jet-setting for me."

"I can't believe you did this," she said, fighting back tears.

"It's done. Now we can be a family. The family that you and Kai deserve. Nothing is more important to me than that. If I have the two of you, everything else will fall in place."

He lowered his head. "I think I got too caught up in the glamour of it all. Traveling around the world, making ridiculous sums of money. I'd forgotten why I'd gotten into architecture—to build houses for people. Not monuments to the wealthy who'll never really live in them."

"Oh, Braxton." She hugged him fiercely. "If this is what you want, then I want it for you. We already have enough money to last us a lifetime. I was just so afraid," she choked back a sob.

He eased her away and looked into her eyes. "Afraid? Of what?"

"I was afraid that you were planning on leaving me," she cried.

"Oh, God." He crushed her against him. "I'd never leave you. Never," he whispered against her hair. "You're my world. I couldn't make it without you."

"I've waited so long to hear you say that again."

He eased her down on the bed, hovering over her. "You'll never have to wait again," he promised. "I'm gonna keep reminding you every chance I get."

"No more secrets," she whispered softly against his mouth.

"No more," he promised.

Trent tossed his jacket on the chintz ottoman when he walked through the door of their room. His conscience had been gnawing at him relentlessly all evening.

He'd been so close to telling her the truth but had taken the coward's way out by trying to convince himself that the hurt to Noelle would be too devastating. The reality was, he was more afraid of what the truth would do to him.

At least he had been able to get her to rethink her stance on Maxwell Enterprises. Her vision was brilliant. It was exactly what the corporation needed.

"What are you thinking about?" Noelle asked, sidling up behind him.

He turned and pulled her into his arms. "This may sound very unromantic, but I was thinking about your plan to expand Maxwell." He looked at her speculatively.

"Oh." She backed away.

"I really believe that you should push for it Noelle," he urged.

Her eyebrows arched in question. "You seem overly concerned about Maxwell Enterprises. Any reason?" She folded her arms in front of her.

He swallowed and glanced away, not daring to meet her penetrating gaze.

"It's just that Jordan was a friend and I'd hate to see everything he worked for go down the tubes." He shrugged dismissively. "That's all. And anyway I'm sure that whatever happens would have some impact on you. Aren't you concerned about that?"

She moved his jacket aside and sat down, crossing her long legs at the knee. Her voice was decidedly flat.

"Liaisons has afforded me the ability to be independently wealthy. I've made some wise investments over the years. I'm sure I won't suffer one way or the other—no matter what happens to Jordan's business."

She stared at him hard, vaguely gaining a sense that there was more to his interest than he was letting on.

After Jordan's death, my goal has been to finally make a life for myself separate and apart from him and his name. I don't intend to spend the rest of my life living off of what he accomplished."

She thought of the enormous holdings that she had established in the reconstruction efforts of South Central L.A. After the riots, she had systematically sponsored many of the store owners and local contractors to rebuild. If she lived to be a hundred she'd never be able to spend all of the money that she would receive in dividends over the coming years.

So instead, she funneled the money to help the poor communities of California. She was adamant, however, about staying in the background and keeping her name out of the papers. But she gained her satisfaction from seeing the many victims of poverty gain a leg up on life.

"I never wanted to be a part of the big picture," she continued, keeping her thoughts to herself. "You don't have to hear applause to be appreciated."

"You never cease to amaze me," he said, kneeling down beside her. "Every moment that I'm with you, you reveal another layer of that Noelle Maxwell mystique." He smiled and held her hands in his. "What else do you have in store?"

She searched his eyes for some clue of what she was feeling. "Only time will tell," she answered quietly. For the first time since they'd met she had the fleeting sensation that she didn't know who he was.

Gina parked her Volvo in front of Joseph's ocean-front cottage. She'd taken a chance in coming without calling, but her nerves wouldn't let her rest. Noelle would be back tomorrow. She had to know what she was facing.

It was nearly 1:00 A.M. She'd left Carol in charge of things while she made the hour drive.

She was banking on Joseph's feelings for her to somehow help her out of this fiasco. He had no real reason to want to do anything for her, not after she'd walked out on him. But he'd at least listened to her when she'd phoned, although reluctantly. He said he would call her, but she hadn't heard a word from him since she sent the fax.

She couldn't wait any longer. Hesitantly, then with more determination, she walked up the four steps to the front door. The bell chimed.

Gina waited nervously, switching her purse from one hand to the other. She began to lose her resolve. What was she really doing standing on Joseph's doorstep in the middle of the night? She took a step back and started to turn away, when the door was pulled open.

"Gina?"

She spun around.

"Joseph. I, I'm sorry to just come by like this but . . ."

His voice was surprisingly gentle. "Do you want to come in?" He reached out and took her hand before she could respond.

"Can I get you anything," he offered, once they were inside. He poured himself a drink of scotch over ice.

"No. Thank you, I'm fine." She sat on the edge of the low sofa, her hands folded in front of her.

He leaned casually against the oak-finished bar, gazing at her appreciatively.

"So, to what do I owe this late-night pleasure?"

Gina studied her hands, then looked up. "I had to know if you found out anything," she said weakly.

"A simple phone call could have done the trick." He slowly walked toward her. "Are you sure that's the only reason you drove all the way out here in the middle of the night?" His finger stroked her cheek.

When he looked at her like that, as if she were the most important woman in the world, she couldn't think straight. He was right, and she knew it. She could have phoned. But deep in her heart she'd wanted to see him. Ever since their last night together, she hadn't been herself. Her temper was short, she hadn't slept well, and she'd made an inexcusable mistake. Mistakes were something totally out of character for her.

"You always could see right through me," she finally admitted, a glimmer of her true feelings dancing in her eyes.

Joseph took her hands and pulled her up. "I've missed you, Gina. I don't want to lose you." He sighed heavily and held her tightly against him. "I'll do whatever it takes to keep you in my life. No more pressure." He kissed the top of her head. "I promise."

She held him to her, pressing her cheek against his chest. She listened to the rapid pounding of his heart and realized that it matched her own. She knew how much it took for him to say what he did. Joseph Malone was a proud man and he'd put his ego aside for her. He'd willingly stayed in the background like the unmentionable lover in an illicit affair. He deserved better than what she'd given him.

She tilted her head back and looked into his warm eyes. "No more hiding, Joe," she said, feeling a sense of relief wash over her. "So long as you're with me, I'll deal with my father's outrage, Noelle's disappointment and anything else that gets tossed our way."

"Are you sure?" he asked, daring to hope.

"Absolutely," she smiled.

"You won't regret this, Gina." He kissed her lightly then with more urgency, his need for her mounting with every beat of his heart. "Stay with me tonight," he groaned against her mouth.

"I wish I could," she whispered, breathless with emotion. "But I can't. I left my assistant, Carol, in charge of things. I told her I'd be back in a couple of hours."

"Tomorrow then?" He caressed her hips, urging her closer against him.

"I'll be here as soon as I get off."

Reluctantly, she backed out of his embrace. "I'd better be going."

She picked up her purse and Joseph walked her out. When they reached the door, she stopped and turned. "I'd almost forgotten my other reason for coming," she said sheepishly. Have you heard anything?"

"Not yet. It'll probably take a couple of days."

Disappointment registered on her face.

"You said that this Cole Richards, or whoever he is, is with Noelle?"

"I'm pretty sure that they're together. Both of them left on the same day and haven't been back. She just seems so happy, Joe. I mean really happy for the first time in months. If I'm the cause of this imposter creating any trouble or hurting Noelle, I don't know what I'll do."

"Don't worry." He braced her shoulders firmly. "We'll get to the bottom of it. What troubles me," he continued, "is, what reason would someone have to conceal their identity from her? Why is it so important that she not know who he really is?"

"Maybe he's just some money-hungry con man out to see what he can get." But even as she said the words, she didn't really believe it herself.

"Perhaps," Joseph responded, half-heartedly. "I just have a nagging feeling that it goes deeper than that."

As Gina drove along the darkened highway en route to Liaisons, she had that same nagging feeling.

CHAPTER 16

Trent and Noelle lay side by side, listening to the latest update on the revolt in Sudan. The United Nations was in the process of sending over an ambassador to see if he could initiate some sort of agreement between the rival forces.

The starving inhabitants were demanding a fair share in the running of their country. They wanted housing, jobs and doctors to care for the sick. Unfortunately, the newscaster continued, the government was unable to provide these things as the country was on the brink of financial collapse. Ambassador Kenyatta Nkiru was scheduled to arrive at the end of the week.

The wheels began to spin in Noelle's head. She sat up in bed.

"Cole, do you really believe that my plan could work?" she asked cautiously.

"Of course I do."

"But how could I ever hope to get it off the ground?"

He pulled himself into a sitting position. "I'm sure there's a way. You have plenty of contacts."

She thought about her options and then it dawned on her.

"Ambassador Nkiru is Gina's father."

Trent nodded. "Yes?"

"If I could meet with him before he left, maybe we could put together a proposal that everyone would be satisfied with."

"Are you sure you're in a position to pull something like that off?"

"I'd have to pull some money from the reconstruction in South Central," she blurted out, and wished she hadn't.

Trent's reaction was instantaneous. "You'd have to do what?"

She sighed in resignation, lying back on the down filled pillows. She stared up at the ceiling as she spoke.

"I've been contributing my dividends from Maxwell Enterprises and my investments into the rebuilding efforts of South Central. After the riots and I saw, first hand, the devastation, I had to do something. Even with government loans, it's not enough. Jordan never knew," she confessed. "He would have never understood."

Trent was momentarily speechless. To say that she was an enigma said little about Noelle. Before he'd met her, he believed her to be no more than a pampered princess. But day after day he witnessed the depth of her compassion, her intelligence, her acute business sense and her unbridled passion. Her own humility humbled him.

"Noelle, I don't know what to say."

"You don't have to say anything. And actually, I'd prefer that you didn't. I meant it when I said I didn't want to be in the limelight."

"But do you really believe that you can stay in the background if you present your case to Nkiru?"

"From the first time that I met him, I realized that he was a man of discretion. If I can be assured that my name won't be mentioned, I'll do whatever I can."

As casually as he could manage, he asked, "What about Trent Dixon?"

"I'll find a way to deal with him," she answered firmly. "If I have to buy him out, then I will. With any luck, he'll wind up in jail and he won't be my problem," she concluded with icy finality.

Trent felt the chill of her words as strongly as an arctic blast. He swallowed. "I know you're doing the right thing, Noelle."

"It's because of you," she said softly.

"Me?"

"Yes, you," she smiled, caressing his bearded cheek. "If you hadn't gotten me to really think about this, I don't believe it would have occurred to me to even try. You convinced me that it's possible."

"Noelle, you have talents that you haven't even touched yet. The future is yours for the taking."

"Is it?" she asked hopefully, searching his eyes with her own.

"Whatever you want."

"Anything?" She leaned toward him. Her heart pounded.

"Anything," he whispered as her lips met his.

Tentatively her tongue sought out his, inflaming her as they met. Her nimble fingers stroked his face, his bare chest. She began reacquainting herself with the rough and soft texture of his sienna skin.

He reached out to touch her and she held him back with a firm hand. "This is for you," she said in a throaty whisper.

Her eager lips trailed down the length of his body, nibbling, kissing, awakening every fiber of his being.

She raised herself up, straddling him while holding his hand solidly in place above his head. Her eyes hung heavy with desire when she looked down at him, enclosing him within the heated walls.

She took him to heaven and beyond with each gyration, every rise and fall of her hips.

Her eyes slammed shut as he rose to meet her. She cried out as the sun, the moon and the stars all collided into a brilliant white heat within her.

She lost herself, consumed by her own driving need and his pulsing desire to sweep her above the mountaintops, across the valleys, soaring over the oceans to meet in a world that they had created.

He pulled himself away from her grasping hold, reaching up to cup her tender breasts, kneading the taut nipples until she called out his name in a mixture of agony and ecstasy.

They traveled together in a race older than time, searching for that supreme release that can only be found in the joining of two perfect lovers.

In one swift motion, he turned her onto her back, hurtling them over the last soul-drenching mile of their sublime journey.

"I love you, too," she whispered in a ragged voice as the last shuddering spasm slammed deep within her.

And the pang of guilt twisted deeper into his heart.

Gina returned to the front desk, just as the phone rang. It was nearly 6:00 A.M. she realized.

"I'll take it," she quickly said to Carol.

"Liaisons, Gina Nkiru speaking."

"Gina, I'm glad I caught you. It's Noelle."

Gina held her breath. "Mrs. Maxwell, is everything all right? I didn't expect to hear from you."

"Everything is fine, Gina," she said wiggling away from Trent as he tried to nibble her ear. "I'm calling because I need to speak with your father. It's urgent. Do you think you can get in touch with him?"

It was 9:00 A.M. in New York, she quickly calculated. Her father was a notorious early riser. She was sure he had been up and around and in his office at the embassy for hours by now.

"Certainly. But I know he must be preparing for his trip. You did see the news?"

"That's exactly why I need to speak with him. *Before* he leaves," she emphasized. "Please try to reach him and you must impress upon him the importance of contacting me. Will you do that?"

"I'll—call—right away," she agreed, her exotic face creasing in wonder.

Noelle breathed a sigh of relief. "Thank you. I should be back no later than noon today. How is everything? Any important messages?"

Her heart skipped. "Everything is fine. There were a few messages," she added with hesitation. "But they can wait until you return."

"Good. Then I'll see you in a few hours. And Gina—"

She felt her stomach pitch. "Yes, Mrs. Maxwell?"

"Get some rest."

Gina smiled with relief as her stomach returned to its rightful place. "I was on my way."

"Good-bye."

Noelle hung up and Gina replaced the receiver with a shaky hand. Her conscience was troubling her so badly she'd begun to get paranoid, thinking that with every word Noelle already knew.

But she'd find out soon enough, she thought miserably.

She picked up the phone and dialed the embassy in New York.

Noelle and Trent sat side by side, each immersed in their own troubling thoughts. The short flight back to Cochran Airways was filled with unspoken questions.

She wanted to ask him; Where did they go from here? But she was afraid of the answer. She didn't think she could bear to actually know that their days together were coming to an end.

He wanted to ask her if she really meant what she'd said last night, or was it only said in the throes of passion. He didn't dare hope that what she felt for him was real. It would only make their inevitable parting that much more painful.

"I hope Gina was able to reach her father," Noelle said lamely, attempting to break the heavy silence that hung between them.

"I'm sure she did. The only thing to concern yourself with now, is convincing him to present your plan."

"I just hope he'll have time to see me before he leaves."

They lapsed into another poignant silence as the Cessna hovered over the landing strip.

The plane gently touched down, and Trent automatically shut off all of the controls.

He turned to Noelle. "Well, here we are, safe and sound." His forced smile wasn't missed by Noelle.

Noelle looked away, but she was unable to hold back the thoughts that tripped through her head.

"Cole, before we go back, I have something I want to say to you."

He looked at her expectantly, with a mixture of false hope and much trepidation.

"Last night, I—I told you that I loved you—and . . ."

"You don't have to explain anything, Noelle." He reached for and held her hand.

"But I do. I know you said the same thing to me." She looked into his eyes and was rewarded with a nod of confirmation. "I don't want to hold you to that, and—I don't want you to feel obligated to—continue this relationship because of what I said.

"I mean, I realize that you, we, made no promises to each other." She looked down at their entwined hands, then eased hers away. "And I don't expect any now."

She sat back, straightened her shoulders and expelled a long-held breath.

She was offering him a way out, and like a fool he knew he was going to take it. Awkwardly, he cleared his throat.

"I—wish I knew what to say."

Her voice was thick with disappointment. "You don't have to say anything." She reached inside of her purse and retrieved her long-discarded, dark sunglasses. "Everything has been said," she added softly, slipping the glasses in place.

She forced a smile. "We should be getting back. I'm anxious to talk with Gina." She turned away, not trusting the dark glasses to hide the tears that welled in her eyes. She unhooked the latch of the door and with her back to him she said softly, "Thank you for an unforgettable weekend."

She stepped out of the plane into the blazing California sunshine.

As she sped along the freeway, she promised herself that she would not cry. If nothing else came out of this weekend with Cole, she had been made to realize that she had the power to change the destiny of thousands less fortunate. She'd discovered what real love truly felt like. She had uncovered her womanhood. And for those things she would always have a place in her heart for him.

Gina saw Noelle the moment she stepped through the revolving doors. Her pulse raced. She still hadn't heard from Joseph. And Cole Richards, or whoever he was, was no where to be seen.

Maybe she'd been wrong when she told Joseph that Noelle and Cole were together. Noelle had never mentioned anything, but Gina had a strong sense that something was going on. She could tell by the way Noelle's eyes sparkled whenever she saw him, and from the intimate way they spoke to each other whenever she caught a glimpse of them together.

Those things, compounded by the fact that both of them left Liaisons on the same day, had heightened her suspicions. Could she have been wrong?

"Gina," Noelle greeted. "How's everything? Did you speak with your father?" she asked anxiously.

"Everything is just fine. Here are your messages." She handed Noelle the rectangular slips of paper. She took them but didn't look at them. "I spoke to my father this morning."

"And?"

"He said he couldn't promise you, but he'd try to make a detour before he left. In any case, he said he would call you this evening."

Noelle bit her bottom lip as she pondered her alternatives. "Would it be a problem if I contacted him myself?"

"I don't think so. I can give you the number." She quickly jotted down the number to the embassy on the memo pad affixed with the Liaisons letterhead.

"*Merci.* I'll let you know what happens." She turned without another word and headed to her suite, with her three-inch heels clicking purposefully against the marble floor.

When Noelle returned to her room she immediately went for the phone, her messages from Trent Dixon and Senator Thomas completely forgotten.

Trent sat in his car and watched Noelle's Mercedes until it disappeared along the stretch of highway. They had agreed that he would wait a reasonable amount of time before he returned. How long was reasonable? he asked himself. An hour? Two? Forever?

He wished that he could make things different. He wished that he could continue to be Cole Richards and never have to step into Trent Dixon's shoes again.

The irony was, for all of his deceit, everything was working out in spite of it. He hadn't given Noelle enough credit in the beginning. She was an intelligent, reasonable woman. He could have convinced her from the start that in order for Maxwell Enterprises to survive she would have to step in.

It was too late now. The damage had already been done. There was no going back.

He turned the key in the ignition and the Lexus engine roared to life.

Maybe the best thing to do would be to return to Sudan and try to put this behind him as quickly as possible—to forget Noelle.

He pulled off onto the highway and headed for Los Angeles. As the road unfolded before him, vivid images of Noelle sprung to life. Her smile. Her sparkling laughter. Her exquisite body wrapped in his arms.

At that moment, when he rounded the curve, he knew that he would never share a greater love, and what he was about to do would be the most difficult task of his life.

CHAPTER 17

Noelle had been unsuccessful in trying to reach Ambassador Nkiru, but she'd left a message. Now there was nothing else she could do except to wait.

In the meantime, since Gina seemed to have everything under control, she began to unpack.

The first item that she touched brought back a pang of remembrance. She lifted the filmy nightie and held it against her face, closing her eyes as she brushed it against her cheek.

His scent still lingered on it. She held it closer as visions of their nights together filled her with an incredible warmth.

She'd given him an easy way out, and he took it, she thought, the hurt blooming anew. Was it that simple for him to walk away from what they'd shared? She couldn't believe that he didn't feel something for her. She knew, deep in her soul, that when he'd said he loved her, he meant it. How could he turn his back on her—on them?

Her gown floated from her fingers onto the bed. Floated away like the dreams that she'd had for herself and Cole.

Slowly she walked across the room to stare sightlessly across the expansive grounds that held Liaisons.

She had everything that anyone could ever want. Wealth. Power. The ability to make a difference. Even now she was on the brink of challenging the stone walls of a government.

But in truth, she had nothing. She was still the poor, orphaned girl serving food to the masses. The only difference was that the patrons dressed up for dinner, and the ambiance was the epitome of elegance.

Suzanne Donaldson was right when she said you could take the girl out of the swamp . . .

Who was she really fooling? All of her philanthropic work would never change who she really was. She'd believed that Jordan was her knight in shining armor. For a time he was. But even him, with all of his money, his gifts, his tutoring—he'd done it all for personal reasons, she realized sadly. Jordan's need to create something from nothing was manifested in her. She was his greatest creation. And her need to have her dreamlike life had allowed it.

But Cole, what were his reasons for wanting her, even briefly? She might never know, she concluded.

She sighed heavily. There was no point in berating herself for what had taken place between them. She had wanted it to happen and part of her would always be glad because of it.

She would treasure the memories and just tuck them away for safe keeping.

Noelle turned from the window, just as there was a knock on her door. Her heart leaped as she quickly crossed the room and entered the small foyer. *Cole.*

She pulled open the door, her face flush with expectation.

"I'm happy to see you, too," Tempest greeted, crossing the threshold and kissing Noelle solidly on the cheek.

Noelle struggled to hide her disappointment. "Miss me?" she asked, closing the door.

"Of course, this place isn't the same without you. Oh, Noelle," she clasped her hands to her chest, unable to subdue her happiness a moment longer. "He's back! Braxton's back." She looked up to the ceiling, a brilliant smile illuminating her face.

Noelle instantly pushed aside her own worries and took Tempest's hand. She led her over to the small couch and they sat down.

"Tell me. What happened?"

Tempest spun out everything from Braxton's surprise arrival to the sale of his architectural business.

"We're going to stay in New York," she concluded. "We're finally going to be a family. Kai is ecstatic. She and Braxton are spending the day together celebrating. *We* celebrated last night," she added coyly.

Noelle grinned knowingly. "I'm so happy for you. You see, everything did work out. I told you if you really love him, give him a chance."

"I cringe every time I think I almost accused him of having an affair." She shook her head. "I still can't believe that I could have thought such a thing. Harboring secrets and doubts can be devastating," she said softly.

"If we had only talked with each other about how we really felt, so much pain could have been avoided."

She turned to look at Noelle and for the first time noticed the emptiness that was carefully hidden behind the practiced smile.

"What about you?" she probed gently. "I can tell something's wrong."

Noelle rose from her seat and turned away, crossing her arms protectively around her waist.

"Everything is fine."

"Look me in the eye and tell me that," Tempest insisted.

Noelle didn't move.

Tempest got up and came around in front of her.

Noelle angled her head to the side to avoid contact with Tempest's riveting gaze. She bit her lip to keep it from quivering.

Tempest held Noelle's arm. "What in the world happened? And don't tell me, nothing. I'm not leaving here until you tell me."

Noelle threw up her hands in defeat, then covered her mouth to stifle a sob. "Everything and nothing," she finally said in a weak voice.

"Very clever. Now what is that supposed to mean?"

Noelle sat back down, staring intently at the intricate pattern of the Oriental rug.

She started slowly, reliving each detail as she spoke, up to and including telling Cole that he didn't owe her anything.

When she finished, nearly a half hour later, Tempest was shocked.

Here was a woman who she truly believed she knew better than anyone, only to find out that she'd been living in an unconsummated marriage for four, lonely years. What type of character must it have taken to stand it for so long and never whisper a word? Noelle's obvious loyalty to Jordan overwhelmed her. Tempest's admiration for Noelle amplified ten times over.

And now when she finally believed that she'd found that special someone, he, too, had abandoned her. Only this time it was much worse. Noelle was not in awe of Cole, as she had been of Jordan. She didn't feel obligated to stay with him. She was unquestionably in love with him.

"Less than a week ago," Tempest began, "you and I sat on opposite sides of the fence. It was *you* who gave me encouragement. It was *you* who told me to stick it out, because you knew how I felt."

She touched Noelle's chin, turning her face toward her. She looked deep into the sad brown eyes. "Prejudging nearly destroyed my marriage. Don't assume anything. If you love him, Noelle, don't let him go," she implored. "Everyone doesn't get a second chance."

"Did you make the call?" Trent asked Nick.

"Yeah. Just like you said."

Trent nodded and took a sip from his drink. He sat down on the couch and intently read the printouts that had arrived in his absence. Things were worse than he thought. He would have to return sooner than he'd planned.

"Is that all you have to say?" Nick probed, taking a seat opposite Trent. He'd been in the suite for over an hour and had yet to mention a word about his weekend other than Noelle's idea for development in Sudan.

Trent's jaw clenched. "I have to get away," he said, his voice devoid of emotion.

"You're just gonna walk away from her? No explanation? Nothing? I can't believe you'd do something like that."

"I don't have any other choice."

Nick shook his head in disappointment. "I would have thought you were a bigger man than that, Trent. Even for you this is low."

Trent jumped up, tossing the last of his drink down his throat. His eyes narrowed. "What would you suggest, O wise one?" he asked sarcastically.

"You know what I'd suggest. So don't ask."

"Oh, of course," he spat, his voice escalating in misdirected anger, "I should just walk right up to her and say, Noelle, I just wanted you to know that you've slept with your husband's murderer. See you later. Does that about sum it up for you, buddy?"

"Listen," Nick countered, his voice rising to match Trent's, "don't get pissed with me just because you let your hormones take the place of your brain! You knew what you were doing and you did it anyway. And the only person who's going to suffer is Noelle."

Trent turned on him. "Really? Do you honestly think she's the only one who's going to suffer?" His face hardened into a mask of pain. "Don't you think I'm feeling it, too?"

Nick crossed the room and stood in front of Trent. "I know you're feeling it," he said quietly. "That's why you've finally got to do what's right."

Trent turned away. "It sounds so simple," he said in a detached voice. "I only wish that it was." He hesitated. "But I know you're right," he admitted reluctantly. "You've been right from the beginning." He paused for a long moment. "I'll tell her," he said finally. "Once she presents this proposal to the Sudanese government, I'll tell her. I know that if I say anything now, she'll back out. And for all of the wrong reasons."

"I don't think you give this woman enough credit, Trent. From everything that you've told me about her she doesn't seem like the kind of woman who would put her personal opinion above the good of so many."

Trent shook his head. "I can't take that chance. This is too important. If I say anything now, I know she'll think I was just using her."

"Well, weren't you?"

"Maybe at first. But then," he looked across the room at Nick, "but then I fell in love with her, Nick, and everything changed." He hung his head. "Everything."

"And how does she feel?"

Trent swallowed. "She feels the same way." He spun away and pounded his fist against the wall, rattling the abstract portrait. "Damn it Nick, all I can think about is Noelle. I sleep, eat and dream her. I wanted her so badly, I just completely lost all sense of reality. And I still want her." His voice strengthened with determination. "I want her up until the very last minute I can have her."

He crossed the room in long, determined strides, snatching up his discarded jacket. "I'll call you," he said, as he slammed the door behind him.

The soft sound of music could just be heard over the surging rush of water. Noelle closed her eyes, letting the beat of the music and the pulse of the steamy water relax her.

She'd thought long and hard about what Tempest had said. She couldn't deny the fact that there were still too many things left unfinished between her and Cole. She owed it to herself to lay her cards on the table. She would go to him, she decided, and tell him exactly how she felt. She certainly had nothing to lose.

Noelle heard the insistent knocking on her door just as she stepped out of the shower. She slipped on a white silk robe and went to answer. Something must be wrong, she worried, crossing the room in bare feet. No one would come to her room, without calling first, unless it was an emergency.

She pulled the door open. Her heart lurched madly. And before she had a chance to react, Trent stepped through and pushed the door shut. Noelle took a cautious step back.

"Cole, I . . ."

He gathered her in his arms smothering her mouth and any questions in a soul-searching kiss.

Instinctively she responded, succumbing to the persuasiveness of his kisses. Her own spontaneous reaction to him rendered her powerless against the magnitude of his hunger.

Her head spun as the delightful shiver of wanting whipped through her. He'd come to her, she thought, wildly. Everything was going to work out.

Before she knew what was happening, Trent's nimble fingers had found their way between the folds of her robe, igniting the bare skin beneath. She let out a soft gasp.

Urgently he lowered her down to the thick carpeted floor. She clung to him, too overwhelmed to speak.

"I know I shouldn't have come here. But I can't stop thinking about you," he groaned in a ragged whisper, his breath hot against her exposed neck. Like a man starved for physical contact, he kissed her ears, her cheeks, caressed her narrow waist, suckled her breasts. "I couldn't imagine the night without you."

He rose up on his knees and tore the shirt from his body. The tiny buttons scattered across the floor. He quickly unbuckled his pants and kicked them away, holding her in place with the heated intensity of his gaze.

Then, as if in slow motion, he lowered himself above her. "I love you Noelle," he whispered, "more than I've ever loved any other woman. Don't ever doubt that."

It's true, her heart sang madly. She cradled his face in her hands, her eyes glistening with pure joy.

"I love you, too, Cole," she cried. "And nothing else matters." Her eyes slid shut as his lips met hers, her willing body welcoming their union.

Joseph stared in disbelief at the handwritten report in front of him. How could this be possible?

He turned over his options in his head. If he told Gina, she would be forced to confess her screw-up to Noelle and undoubtedly lose her job. If he went to Noelle, she would certainly think that he'd concocted the entire story.

He leaned back in his leather chair, steepling his long fingers against his chin. There had to be another way, and there had to be some crucial bit of information that he was missing.

He reached across his desk and buzzed for his secretary.

"Yes, Mr. Malone," Alice answered promptly.

"Alice get me the entire file on Jordan Maxwell. And check with all of the hotels in Los Angeles. I want to find out if Trent Dixon is registered in any of them."

"Right away, Mr. Malone."

There had to be something in the file that he'd missed. Something that would explain everything.

His private line rang.

"Yes?"

"Joseph, it's me Gina."

"Gina." He thought quickly. "I'm sorry but I still don't have anything yet. It's taking longer than I thought."

Gina swallowed. "Joseph, I just got a call from Senator Thomas. He pushed up his arrival. He'll be here late this evening."

Somehow Noelle and Trent found their way to her bedroom. A soft breeze blew in from the terrace window. The afternoon sun blazed through the sheer curtains. Noelle curled closer to Trent, listening to the pulse beat in his neck.

"I'm glad you came, Cole," she said softly. "There're so many things I want to say to you."

Trent took a deep, guilty breath. He knew he couldn't let her go on believing that there was any hope for a future with them. It was an impossibility.

He kissed the top of her head. "I'm leaving in the morning, Noelle," he blurted out before he had a chance to change his mind.

Her head pounded. She couldn't be hearing right. A suffocating sensation tightened her throat. *He didn't say that he was leaving.* "But you'll be coming back." She struggled for control.

"I don't think so," he answered softly.

A new anguish lashed at her heart.

"I got an offer to do a major consulting job in Washington. It could take—a long time," he added weakly.

Her voice trembled. "How long?"

"Months."

"I see." But she didn't see. She couldn't and she didn't want to.

She got up from the bed and slipped back into her robe, for the first time feeling naked before his eyes.

She wouldn't cry, she vowed. She'd walked into this relationship with her eyes wide open. No promises had been made. So nothing had been broken. Except her heart, which was shattering into tiny bits.

Her throat constricted. She spun toward him, her eyes burning with restrained agony. "Will you write?"

She sounded like a wounded child, begging for release from the pain, he thought mournfully.

He got up and went to her and was met with stony resistance. She kept her arms wrapped stiffly around her body.

He held her shoulders instead. "Noelle, I—I wish things could be different." He struggled for words. "I wish that our lives were different. But they're not. I can't offer you the things that you need. The things that you deserve."

You can, she thought wildly, feeling her world slipping from beneath her feet. *You are what I need. All that I need.*

She remained silent.

He turned away, unable to look at the despair that darkened her eyes.

"I'd better go," he said softly.

"I think that's best."

She stood motionless, facing the window, listening intently to every move of his departure.

The sound of his voice rocked her.

"I got the report from my investigator," he said to her stiff back.

Her voice was empty of emotion. "Just leave it on the table—on your way out."

The next sound she heard was the door closing softly behind him.

Slowly she turned around, her glistening eyes searching the space that they had so recently shared. *Empty.*

Drawn like a magnet, she walked over to the bed, absently touching the sheets. His scent still lingered in the air. She breathed deeply, and turned away.

All of the hurt, the loneliness, the insults, the inability to fit in, could never compare to the devastation that consumed her heart at this moment.

But as with all of the other hurts, she would store it away where it couldn't touch her. She would go on with her life as she'd always done. She would continue to conquer the obstacles and she would do it alone. As she'd always done.

Purposefully, she walked into the small sitting room and saw the thin brown envelope on the table.

She picked up the envelope and stared at it for several long minutes. Then she ripped it to shreds. Letting the pieces fall to the floor. The only emotion she had left now was her hatred for Trent. It would be what propelled her. It would make her forget Cole. She couldn't risk the chance that the words contained on those pages would vindicate him. Then she would have nothing to hold on to.

It was over, he thought, tossing the last of his possessions in his bag. He looked around the room for the last time.

I thought you were a better man than that. Nick's accusing words echoed in his head.

He picked up his suitcase and garment bag and walked out of the door.

Maybe he'd make a stop in Philadelphia and see his family before he returned to Sudan. He would need the fortification of his family to face the turmoil that would confront him in the coming weeks.

The company could survive only if Noelle's proposal was accepted.

He stepped onto the elevator. He'd have to find another job, of course, but that could wait. He pressed the button for the lobby. But he did want to tie up all of the loose ends.

Maybe one day, Noelle would somehow find out the truth about Jordan and find her way back to him. *Right.*

He cursed the day he'd made that pact. But if he hadn't, he might have never experienced the love he shared with Noelle. That would have to be his consolation.

He walked up to the registration counter.

"Mr. Richards," Gina said, *or whoever you are,* "what can I do for you?"

"I'm checking out." He placed his key on the countertop.

"Is something wrong? Are the accommodations a problem? I'd be happy to . . ."

"No." He waved his hand in dismissal. "Believe me everything here is wonderful." He smiled and the room lit up. Gina could instantly see Noelle's attraction. "I have some urgent business to attend to and I have to leave earlier than I expected."

"Well if you'll just wait a moment, I'll calculate your bill and draw up a check for a refund. Unless you'd prefer it in cash."

He reached down and picked up his luggage. "No refund is necessary."

"But Mr. Richards, our policy is . . ."

"Believe me, my stay here was well worth every cent."

"At least let me call Mrs. Maxwell. I'm sure she'll want to know you're leaving."

"She knows," he said. And Gina could have sworn she heard a tinge of sadness in his deep voice.

She followed him with her eyes as he crossed the marble lobby. Just before he reached the door, Noelle emerged from the elevator. For a brief, painful moment their eyes held. In that instant, Gina witnessed the undeniable electricity that sparked like fireworks between them, and the sadness that lingered in their gazes.

And then he was gone.

She saw Noelle raise her chin in determination as she turned and walked away.

Noelle sat in her office, perilously close to tears. She stared at the mail, the invoices, the reports without seeing them.

How long would the pain last? she wondered. A week? A month? Eternity?

One thing she was certain of, she realized, she couldn't allow what had happened between her and Cole to overshadow her entire life. If she'd learned one thing from Jordan, it was that you could never allow your personal feelings to compromise your business objectives.

She spun her chair around to face the window. In retrospect it was the same movement Jordan had exhibited when he was in deep thought, she realized suddenly. What would he have done, she wondered?

Then, a long-forgotten memory struggled to the surface and took shape in her head.

Jordan was sitting at his desk, much as she was now, pensively staring out of the window. Less than an hour earlier, they'd had a heated argument about his exporting of goods out of Sudan. She had been vehement in her disapproval and had questioned his ethics. She could immediately see that her emotional outburst affected him, even though his face remained impassive. But his dark eyes held the sting of her words.

When she'd walked into his office, much later, and found him there, his voice was calm, his eyes direct and full of purpose. He turned from the window to face her.

"I understand your objections to what I do, Noelle," he'd said. "But I can never let personal feelings, even yours, compromise my business objectives. Maxwell Enterprises is in the business of making money. What I do makes money. Unfortunately, it may not be in the manner you see fit." He stood up, his broad shoulders filling his Italian suit jacket. "One day you'll understand that."

Maybe now she finally understood.

She stood up. And her objectives were to make Liaisons the most successful enterprise of its kind. She would reshape Maxwell Enterprises. She would throw all of her energies and her resources to reaching her goals. And in time, Cole Richards would be no more than a vague memory.

She could do that, she thought, with renewed determination. She could wish him away. She could do anything. Hadn't she been told that a million times? She—was Noelle St. James-Maxwell. And the process would begin *now.*

CHAPTER 18

Nick sat in open-mouthed disbelief. The magnitude of what Trent had revealed to him left him speechless.

Now everything made sense in a mad, almost insane kind of way. Jordan Maxwell had been a troubled man. A man consumed by his own power, and he had skillfully wielded that power around Trent.

"Who else knows about this?" Nick finally asked.

Trent heaved a sigh. "No one. The only person who could come close to putting the pieces together would be Joseph Malone, Jordan's attorney."

"You can't just leave it like this, Trent."

"I have no other choice. I swore I would never tell her."

"But what could it matter now? He's dead. And it wasn't your fault. She's got to find out eventually."

"Not from me. And now, in my stupidity, I've complicated matters so much that she'd probably believe that I'm making the whole thing up.

"You see, Jordan never wanted Noelle to run the corporation out of loyalty. That was the one thing he was adamant about. He understood that the main reason why she stayed in the marriage was out of loyalty. He didn't want her to spend the rest of her life feeling like she owed him something. If she ever found out what was really going on, that would be her reason. That's just the type of woman she is."

Nick ran his hand across his smooth face. "I wish there was something I could do, besides say that I'm sorry."

Trent chuckled mirthlessly. "*You're* sorry. No one could be sorrier than I am."

"Did you give her the report?"

Trent nodded.

"Well, it clearly says that you had nothing to do with the crash. Wasn't that the proof that she needed?"

"I wish it were that simple. The report doesn't explain why I've been lying to her all of this time." He paused then looked directly at Nick. "And the report will never explain what really happened."

Nick frowned. "What do you mean?"

"There are things that have been removed."

Gina sat in her office and dialed Joseph's private line. He answered on the first ring.

"It's me Joseph. There've been some changes."

"What kind of changes?" he asked scanning the hotel information that Alice had just brought in.

"Cole Richards checked out about a half hour ago."

His head snapped up. "Did he say why or where he was going?"

"He just said he had some important business come up."

Joseph's jaw clenched. *He didn't go very far.*

"How soon can you get away?" he asked.

"I'm off at seven."

"Can you meet me at my house?"

"What is it Joseph? Have you found out anything?"

"Let's just say that the pieces are beginning to fall in place. I'll know more later. I have to make a few calls and go out for a while. I'll see you tonight."

He hung up, and quickly dialed the Los Angeles Hilton.

"Hilton Hotel," the clipped voice answered.

"Yes, I'm trying to reach Mr. Trent Dixon."

"I'll put you through to the switchboard."

The phone rang three times before it was answered.

"Hilton Hotel."

"Trent Dixon please."

"One moment."

The phone rang at least a dozen times. Joseph was just about to hang up.

"Hello?"

"Trent! Joseph Malone. I heard you were in town. I'm glad I caught you." He paused. "We need to talk. I'm on my way to your hotel. I can be there in fifteen minutes." Joseph hung up before Trent had a chance to respond.

* * *

"Ambassador Nkiru, I'm so happy you called."

"My daughter said it was urgent," he responded, the soft lilt of his homeland of Ghana evident in his voice. "What can I do for you?"

For the next half hour, Noelle laid out the details of her plan to Nkiru. "I have the resources to do this Mr.—Ambassador Nkiru. I'm sure that if you intervene with this proposal the government would be responsive." She held her breath.

Kenyatta Nkiru could hardly believe what he had just heard. How long had the government of Sudan waited for some relief from their poverty? The nations of the world had all but ignored them until it began to hit them in their pockets. Was this Noelle's objective also? He thought not.

"Mrs. Maxwell, your offer, though generous, may be too late. There has been such widespread destruction, it would take years to rebuild. What the people need now is food, immediate shelter and medicine. And who would train these people to do all of the things that you suggested?"

"Maxwell Enterprises would provide the initial training until the people were self-sufficient."

"You realize of course, that this idea of yours would be counterproductive to your own government?"

"What do you mean? How could the U.S. not want the people to be self-sufficient?"

"If all the people of the third world could fend for themselves there would be no need for *divine* intervention. The military budget is extremely high. And there are many who want to make sure that it stays that way. Now if there was no need to ship armaments and send in troops . . ." His voice trailed off.

A cold chill ran through her. "What can we do?"

"If you are as committed to this as you say you are, we'll find a way. Together. I'll be in touch with you as soon as I can."

"Thank you, Ambassador."

"No. Thank *you.*"

Noelle sat back, taking in the frightening words that had been hinted at but not spoken.

She was more determined than ever to make this a reality. And as much as she hated to admit it, she was going to need Trent Dixon's help. Whether she wanted it or not.

CHAPTER 19

Noelle did a careful review of her financial assets. She would have to do some quick juggling.

She placed a call to her accountant, Sam Waters. Sam had been Noelle's personal accountant and financial advisor for the past five years. He knew her assets and liabilities like his own name. He was the type of man that she could call in the middle of the night and ask what her bank balances were, and he'd rattle them off without opening his eyes. Numbers were Sam Waters's life.

He'd given her sound financial advice over the years and he watched with pleasure as her fortune multiplied.

But Sam was annoyingly cautious, Noelle came to realize. He was never willing to take risks. He liked cold hard numbers, not big question marks.

That characteristic had them in their latest debate.

"I know what I'm doing Sam," Noelle said patiently for the third time. "I want my two largest personal accounts consolidated. I have to be able to show that I have the financial base to implement this plan successfully. I can't have my money spread all over."

"But Noelle," he cautioned, "do you realize the incredible amount of tax you'll have to pay on that money if you do that?" Automatically he punched numbers into his calculator.

"Of course I do. I worked out the figures. "$90,000.00."

She was right. As usual, he smiled. One thing he always admired about Noelle was her ability to manage numbers. She understood them and used them to her advantage. She would have made an excellent CPA, he always thought.

"All right. If you're sure," he finally agreed. "I'll get the ball rolling and contact the bank. They're going to have a fit when you pull out all of that money. It may effect your leverage with them if you ever want to borrow in the future."

Noelle thought about that for a moment. "You're right. Leave $100,000.00 in the account at Commerce and transfer the rest to First National. I'll send you my dividend check from Maxwell Enterprises, by messenger tomorrow. Deposit that with the $100,000.00. That should keep them happy."

Sam relaxed a little. "Wise decision. I'll call you tomorrow."

Next, she contacted her broker and advised her to liquidate $50,000.00 worth of her stock. Nina Armstrong was one of the top brokers in L.A. Her sixth sense when it came to picking the winners was almost eerie.

Fortunately, Nina took instruction extremely well and rarely did she question Noelle's judgment.

Noelle intended to use that cash to cover her monthly donation to the shop owner's fund in South Central. It would be a little short, this time, but she knew the anonymous donation would be well appreciated.

For the next two hours, Noelle sat in front of her computer, carefully detailing every phase of her proposal.

When she was done, the completed document was twenty pages long.

She leaned back in her seat and rotated her tight shoulders.

If only she could have the same control over her personal life, she thought miserably.

She pushed away from her desk and stood up. She'd promised herself that she would put Cole behind her and go on with her life. But it seemed as though whenever she took a breath she thought of him. *Maybe she should stop breathing*, she thought morosely.

She checked her gold, Cartier watch. The dinner hour was approaching. But she had enough time to change.

She switched off her computer and turned off the lights. Off in the distance she heard the low roar of a jet. Briefly she wondered if Cole was on that plane.

Joseph sat in the darkness of his den. The only light emanated from the last rays of sunshine.

His meeting with Trent had numbed him. He looked at the report that sat on his lap.

He had been so sure that he could nail Trent for somehow trying to manipulate Noelle. That theory went out of the window. Trent was as much a victim in this as Noelle.

He always knew that Jordan Maxwell was a force to be reckoned with. How many times had Jordan been able to convince wary stockholders that it was in their best interest to buy additional shares of stock, even when the stock market was falling? He was a great orator. He should have been in politics, Joseph mused. Jordan could make you believe that the moon rose at daybreak, if he chose. He was a shrewd businessman with the uncanny ability to zero in on a person's weakness and capitalize on it. What was more astounding was that it generally turned out to be in their best interest in the long run. Jordan ultimately achieved their lifelong loyalty as a result. Even from his grave, he was still the great manipulator. It was frightening.

After Joseph had departed from the suite, Trent and Nick sat quietly facing each other.

"What do you think Malone's going to do with what you told him?" Nick finally asked.

"I'm sure he'll go to Noelle with it. Why wouldn't he? I always knew he never gave her much credence. He'd probably get some kind of sadistic pleasure out of seeing the look on her face."

Nick hesitated a moment, reluctant to bring up the issue again, but knew that he must.

"Don't you think it would be better—a lot easier on Noelle—if it came from you? From what you're telling me about Malone, there's no telling what he might actually say."

Trent stared at his hands as if he hadn't heard anything Nick said.

Without a word he got up, shoving his hands in his pockets. His expression was impassive.

He gave Nick a sidelong glance. "You know I hate it when you're right. I'm going to take a shower and change. Then I'm going to drive out to see Noelle."

He started to move away, then stopped to toss a parting remark at the smug expression on Nick's face.

"I'm going, if for no other reason, just to shut you up. Finally."

"Whatever works," Nick grinned.

Noelle sat in front of her dressing-table mirror and applied a light stroke of coral lipstick to her mouth. With a thin black pencil, she lightly outlined the bottom rim of her eyes, making the chestnut brown orbs even more pronounced.

From her jewelry box, she selected a pair of diamond-and-gold teardrop earrings, the matching bracelet and choker.

She ran a wide-tooth comb through her chestnut hair, letting the satiny strands fall into place. Her hair had grown, she noticed, lifting the thick bang over her eyebrow. She decided not to cut it. *New life, new look,* she mused.

She had selected a sleeveless, calf-length Dior dress of off-white crepe.

The two rows of buttons were fourteen-carat gold. The scoop neck showed off the choker to perfection. And the hip-high slits on either side gave ample walking room for her long legs.

She stood up and assessed herself in the full-length mirror. Now, if she only had someone to share her evening with, everything *would* be perfect.

She pushed aside the thought. She had guests who were expecting to see their sparkling hostess attending to their every need. She wouldn't disappoint them.

Trent slipped on his midnight blue Armani dinner jacket, over a pale-blue silk shirt.

He noticed a slight tremor in his fingers as he knotted the geometric, navy blue and pink silk tie. *Nerves.*

He stepped out into the sitting room, hearing the baleful strains of Nick's saxophone.

Nick stopped playing and looked up when Trent entered the room.

"Wish me luck," Trent said.

"You got it."

"See you later. Hopefully in one piece."

Trent tried to focus on the endless stretch of highway, but his thoughts kept drifting to his impending confrontation with Noelle.

How would he ever fully explain what he had done and why?

He stepped on the gas, screeching around the narrow turn, barely missing an oncoming sedan. *Damn, that was close.* His pulse raced as he tried to concentrate.

Images of Noelle loomed before him. He visualized her as he'd last seen her. The pain in her eyes was almost accusing. She didn't deserve that.

He wanted to erase that haunted look and replace it with the look of love that had filled and revived him. A look that he knew was reserved only for him.

His thoughts veered off to Joseph Malone. He stepped on the gas. He had to get to Noelle and explain before Joseph did. If he hadn't gotten to her already. If he didn't get to her first, he knew he wouldn't stand a chance in hell of salvaging anything.

His mind raced. His thoughts were colliding with one another. He didn't even see the other car coming.

Senator Thomas had yet to arrive before Gina left for the evening. If there was any justice in the world, maybe he would get called to make some national decision and not show up. Miracles like that never happen, she thought, pulling up in front of Joseph's white stucco house.

The house was dark. *Odd.* He did say to meet him when she got off.

Since he was expecting her, she used the spare key that he'd given her and let herself in.

She walked inside and switched on the hall light. That's when she saw his silhouette in the semidarkness.

"Joseph?"

She walked briskly down the corridor to the den. She switched on the light.

Slowly he turned his head in her direction. His smile was vacant.

"Joseph, are you all right?" She hurried across the room.

"Sit down."

She took a seat next to him and her heart raced with dread.

"What is it Joe? You're scaring me."

"I'm sorry. I didn't mean to. We need to talk—about what I found out."

"What is it?"

"I located Trent Dixon. I spoke with him."

Her eyes widened. "And?"

"I can't use what I found out, Gina. I won't. Noelle will have to find out some other way. It won't be from me."

"But Joseph, I don't understand. What could Trent have possibly said to you?"

Trent sat in his car, looking at the flashing lights of the police van up ahead. His head ached. He was lucky that the accident hadn't been worse. While no one was seriously hurt, the driver of the other car had insisted to the police that Trent must be drunk to have come flying around that curve and into the wrong lane.

Quick reflexes had allowed both drivers to barely escape a head-on collision.

Trent massaged his head. Joseph was probably bending Noelle's ear by now, he thought miserably. He couldn't begin to imagine what Joseph's version would do to her.

". . . Sir. Sir."

Trent snapped out of his thoughts and found a bright flashlight beaming in his face.

"Here's your license and registration. Do you want to go to the hospital?"

"No officer. I'm fine. Is it all right if I leave now?"

The officer looked toward the other vehicle. "You can go. But I suggest that you pay attention. These roads can be tricky if you're not familiar with them."

"Thank you, officer."

"Damn out-of-state drivers," he mumbled.

Slowly Trent eased the car out of the ditch and back onto the highway. *I'm probably too late,* he thought.

Noelle's first stop for the evening was the kitchen. It was bustling with activity.

Paul was busy giving out instructions and personally taste-testing the array of food and pastry that encompassed the entire state-of-the-art kitchen.

A cacophony of aromas assaulted her senses. She thought of her late-night dinners with Cole.

She moved on.

From there she went to the rooftop dining room. Tables were already occupied. She spotted Tempest and Braxton, their heads bent in intimate conversation. *At least someone was happy.*

She put her smile in place and stepped into the dining room.

There was a live jazz band playing some Miles Davis favorites in the background.

Noelle crossed the room and stopped at the table occupied by Gladys and Dionne, who after a little persuading agreed to do a duet at the end of the band's set.

After seeing to the seated guests, she went to the arch of the entrance-way, to greet the incoming diners.

It seemed like an eternity since she stood in this very same spot and Cole walked through the door, she mused, smiling and shaking hands as the interesting assemblage of who's who entered the room.

Finally all but two tables were full. Satisfied, she turned away to make the rest of her rounds and walked smack into solid, hard muscle.

"This isn't the first time we've met like this," the voice that thrilled her said, bracing her shoulders to steady her.

Her eyes slowly trailed upward from the broad chest and locked onto the dark eyes that seemed to hold her in place.

Her voice sounded faint to her own ears. "Cole."

He felt her tremble through his fingertips.

"I had to come. I couldn't leave things the way they were between us."

She cleared her throat, and straightened her shoulders.

"I thought you'd made yourself pretty clear," she said stiffly. She eased out of his grasp, so he wouldn't feel the tremors that shook her body.

"Can we go somewhere and talk?"

"About what, Cole?" She wrapped her arms around her waist. Her eyes narrowed and her voice took on a steely edge. "Do you want to reaffirm your undying love for me and take me to bed—one more time, and then make your apologies?" she hissed. *She wouldn't cry.*

He lowered his gaze. "I deserved that." He looked up. "But it's not what it seems. It's much more complicated than that."

"Is it really?" she shot back.

"Please, Noelle."

For several interminable moments, they stood facing each other. A myriad of conflicting emotions assaulted her.

Her heart longed to be with him, to hear him out. Maybe there was some explanation that he could give her to take the emptiness away.

But her mind said—*no.* She couldn't subject herself to anymore hurt. It would be so much easier to just walk away. Yet she knew she would always have so many unanswered questions if she did.

"Please, Noelle," he repeated.

Her resolve weakened. She took a brief look over her shoulder. Everyone was absorbed in their conversation. The scene between her and Cole was going completely unnoticed.

"All right," she finally agreed. "Let's go out into the garden."

She brushed past him and walked out. Trent caught up with her as they reached the elevator.

Once inside they stood like two sentinels, stiff and silent. She wanted to ask him about the small gash over his eyebrow, but elected to feign indifference.

From the corner of his eye he watched her motionless form. She was so beautiful, and so hurt. His heart ached. It was his fault. She had every right to feel the way she did about him.

How could he make it all go away? He still struggled with the words he knew he would have to speak. What words could ever explain his role in this colossal game of deceit? She was right. All he really wanted to do was hold her—tell her how much he loved her and spend the rest of his life making her happy.

She couldn't look at him, because she knew if she did, she would run into his arms and tell him that nothing else mattered. Her heart pounded so forcefully it felt as if it would explode. Why had he come back? Why couldn't he just stay out of her life?

But deep inside of her soul, she knew that she would never stop wanting him even if he left this very minute and went to the end of the earth.

The doors slowly opened on the lobby level.

Noelle stepped out. Trent followed until they were side by side.

Trent saw him first, but it was too late.

Noelle kept her eyes straight ahead and didn't see Senator Thomas until she heard his voice.

"Noelle!" he called from across the wide corridor.

She stopped and turned, her eyes widening in surprise.

Trent tried to keep walking but Noelle stopped him with a touch.

Senator Thomas moved surprisingly quick for a man of his girth, Noelle thought absently.

The senator's smile was broad and encompassing, as he reached for Noelle and kissed her cheek. "Wonderful to see you."

Trent felt everything rapidly slipping away, when Thomas stuck out his hand.

"Trent Dixon. How long has it been?"

Trapped in a slow-motion nightmare, Noelle turned toward Trent and stared wordlessly at him as a wave of nausea threatened to overwhelm her.

CHAPTER 20

Her thoughts crashed against one another. Everything ceased to move. She couldn't think. She struggled to breathe.

This mustn't be true. But it was. Somewhere deep inside her soul, she knew.

The little slip-ups. His unusual knowledge about the business. The nightmare! It wasn't an air force accident. It was the crash with Jordan.

Lies! All lies!

She'd given herself to her husband's murderer. *Why was it so cold?* She began to tremble visibly.

"Noelle." The senator's voice drifted like a disembodied force to her brain. "Are you all right? You look ill."

Trent reached for her. "Noelle—please."

Her expression turned into a marble effigy of contempt. "Don't touch me," she whispered in a strangled voice.

Thomas scowled at Trent. "What's going on? Is he bothering you? I'll get . . ."

She held up her hand. "You're right, Richard," she said weakly. "I don't feel well." She didn't need a scene. Her smile was tremulous. "Working too hard. I just need some air."

She spun away, nearly running for the exit.

Trent started off after her, but Thomas grabbed his arm.

"I don't know what's going on here and maybe I don't need to know. But you and I have known each other for a while Trent, and your reputation with the ladies precedes you."

The senator remembered all too well their rivalry over the same woman. Trent had won, and the senator's pride was still bruised, years later. That score was never settled. But Noelle wasn't that kind of woman. He'd realized that, years ago, the moment Jordan had introduced his new wife.

"I'd hate to find out that you're the cause of her distress." His stony eyes locked with Trent's. "You do understand me?"

Trent snatched his arm away. "You're right, Richard, this doesn't concern you." He turned without another word and ran for the exit.

By the time he reached the garden, Noelle was in her car tearing out of the driveway.

Burning tears nearly blinded her as she sped down the open roadway. Her head was pounding. She had to get away, as far away from Trent Dixon as possible.

How could she have been so blind, so gullible? She'd been used, masterfully, by the one man she'd sworn to despise.

"Oh, Jordan, I'm so sorry," she cried out loud. "You wanted me to trust him and unknowingly I did. I trusted him with my heart, my body."

Every scene of their lovemaking burst before her eyes. An agonized scream tore from her throat.

The high beam of headlights reflected in her rear-view mirror. Another car was barreling down on her. *Cole—Trent.* She stepped on the accelerator.

The speeding Lexus raced to close the distance between them.

Noelle took a sharp turn onto the back road that she knew so well. Within moments, she was swallowed up in the darkness.

Trent lost sight of her as the taillights disappeared into tiny specks.

CHAPTER 21

Noelle continued to drive with no destination in mind. She kept driving aimlessly down the road until she reached the highway entrance. Somehow she found her way onto the exit to Los Angeles. All she knew was that she had to put as much distance as possible between her and Cole—Trent Dixon.

When she finally slowed down she was in the heart of Los Angeles. She looked around and saw the marquee of the Los Angeles Hilton Hotel. *This was where she'd seen him that day.*

What made her pull into the garage and walk to the reception desk, she didn't know. She seemed to be drawn by an invisible magnet, but hoping to find what?

"I'm looking for Cole, I mean, Trent Dixon's room," she said to the hotel clerk. How long would it take her to get the name Cole Richards out of her mind? she wondered absently.

"I'll ring the room," the clerk advised.

"I'd, uh, prefer if you didn't," Noelle said, putting on her best smile. "I want to surprise him."

"It's really against hotel policy," the clerk protested. "Mr. Dixon didn't advise us to allow . . ."

"Is there a problem?"

Noelle turned in the direction of the voice. A rather tall, unquestionably handsome man, dressed in faded jeans and a T-shirt approached. By his outfit, he couldn't be hotel staff, Noelle quickly surmised, unless he was security. She'd leave quietly, she thought.

Nick stood next to Noelle and immediately knew who she was. Everything that Trent had said about her was magnified a hundred times over.

"You must be Noelle," he said, his soothing voice putting her at ease. He looked across the desk at the clerk. "It's all right, miss," he smiled.

He took Noelle's arm and angled his chin in the direction of the lounge. "Let's go in here."

Obediently, Noelle allowed herself to be escorted into the dimly lit room.

He helped her into her chair and took a seat opposite her at the round table.

"Would you like something to drink? You look a bit shaken."

"No. No thank you." She fidgeted with the paper napkin and wondered, again, why she had come here.

Nick tried to figure out how to break the ice. She was obviously so distressed that she would walk away with a complete stranger.

"I guess you're wondering who I am," he said looking at her from beneath long, curling lashes.

She twisted her napkin between her fingers and didn't respond.

"I'm Nick Hunter, Trent's friend."

For the first time since they sat down, she actually looked at him.

Her eyes registered on his face. "You're a friend of Cole's?" She swallowed. "Trent's?"

Nick nodded. "He came to see you, didn't he?" he asked gently.

Her bottom lip quivered. "Yes."

"Then you know everything."

She stared directly at him, each word that she uttered a condemnation, cold and exacting.

"All I know, Nick Hunter, is that your friend lied to me for some sick reason. He used me for his own, personal satisfaction. And I fell for it—every sweet word." Her voice broke. "Every sweet touch."

She turned her head to hide the tears and abruptly rose from her seat. "I don't even know why I came here."

Nick got up and put a restraining hand on her arm. "Wait. Please. What did he tell you?"

"He didn't tell me anything. We ran into an old friend of his."

"Joseph Malone?"

"What?"

"Did Joseph Malone come to see you?"

She frowned in confusion. "Why would he?"

"He paid Trent a visit today."

"What? Why?"

"Please sit back down," he urged. He released her arm when she did.

"Listen, Trent got in this thing way over his head." Nick took a breath.

"The bottom line is, he made a promise, more of a pact with your husband. A pact that he swore to Jordan he'd never reveal to you."

"What kind of pact?" Noelle asked bewildered. "What are you talking about? And what does Joseph have to do with it?"

"Trent wouldn't tell me everything. And I left the room when Malone showed up. All I know is that it had to do with the accident. Trent didn't cause it. Jordan manipulated him, and ultimately you as well."

"You're lying for him. I don't believe you!" she said through clenched teeth, her eyes sparking with rage. "Trent did it. What other reason could he have for trying to pass himself off as someone else? He knew how I felt about him and about what he'd done. It was the only way he could—get to me. To score some points."

"You don't have to believe me, Noelle. But believe this. I've known Trent Dixon for more years than I care to count. And what I know about him is that he's a man of his word." His voice softened. "He'd risk losing you rather than break that promise he made to Jordan. That should say something about the kind of man he is."

He halted, waiting for his words to sink in. "Another thing I know—he loves you. And I don't think you'd be this upset if you didn't feel the same way."

He reached across the table and covered her hand with his. "You fell in love with the man, not the name. Doesn't that tell you something?"

Noelle looked at Nick, seeing the sincerity in his eyes. And suddenly she knew that what he'd said was true.

"So what do I do now? I've got to know. If Trent won't tell me, then I know who will." She abruptly rose to leave.

"Where are you going?"

"To see Joseph Malone."

Nick got up. "I'm going with you."

They walked toward the exit.

"Where's Trent?" Nick asked.

"I don't know. He tried to follow me, but I lost him on the back roads out of the villa."

"He'll eventually come back here. Do you want to wait it out?"

"No. I need to talk with Joseph, now. The next time I see Trent I want the slate to be clear between us. He'll never have to tell me anything he swore he wouldn't."

Maybe it was better this way, Trent thought as the lights from the airstrip winked, up ahead. Maybe he deserved this for using Thomas' name. Maybe it was fate.

Fate had taken it out of his hands.

He switched on the windshield wipers as a slow drizzle began to fall.

Everything was coming apart. In ten days the banks would demand their money and when they didn't get it, Noelle would lose Liaisons. And if she doesn't step in as CEO, as required by the agreement, Maxwell Enterprises will collapse. But Jordan, Trent mused, I believe Noelle may just outwit you this time. *The student teaching the teacher.* Noelle was resourceful. She had a brilliant mind and more business acumen that even Jordan had given her credit for. Knowing Noelle as he did, Noelle would find a way to run Maxwell and keep the villa. He felt certain that she would be able to put her plan in motion. Would it be in time?

He parked the car in front of the hangar and got out.

Bill Cochran trotted out to meet him.

"Mr. Dixon. What are you doing out here?"

"I need a plane," he stated in a flat voice.

"I'll juice one up for you. Going far?"

His laugh was hollow. "As far as I can."

Moments later he was in the air, soaring above the clouds, high up in the environment that he loved.

He let his mind wander, forgetting about the rain, his fears. He forced his body to relax as the comforting sensation of flight seeped through his veins.

Thunder rolled around him, but he ignored it. He should have followed Nick's advice a long time ago, he mused, as the tiny plane was buffeted around the heavens.

Visibility was getting poor, and the winds were picking up. He checked the dials. He was losing altitude.

He tried to pull the nose up but it wouldn't budge.

He tried again.

Nothing.

Bill Cochran cupped his hand over his eyes and looked up. He could have sworn that plane was at a funny angle. He shrugged. Dixon knew what he was doing. He turned to get in out of the rain when he caught a glimpse of thick, black smoke trailing through the air.

He trotted forward to get a better look, when flames leaped from the engine. He tore off toward the hangar to call for help, when the explosion threw him to the ground.

CHAPTER 22

By the time Noelle and Nick pulled up in front of Joseph's house, it was raining heavily.

"Maybe we should have called first," Nick said, quickly coming around to open the door for Noelle.

She stepped out. "No. That would have just given him time to think of a way out of it."

They darted toward the door together and stood under the shelter of the canopy. Noelle rang the bell.

"Are you expecting anyone?" Gina asked, slipping into a robe.

Joseph frowned. "No. I'll get rid of whoever it is." He opened the door. His face reddened.

"Noelle?" He tightened the belt on his robe and looked nervously at Noelle and Nick. "What are you doing here? Is something wrong?"

"Something is very wrong, Joe. And I think you know about it."

"If it's something to do with the will, I'd be happy to . . ."

"It's a lot deeper than that," she said, cutting him off. "May we come in? Or would you rather have this conversation on your porch?"

He quickly glanced over his shoulder, thinking of Gina.

"Come in," he said finally. He led them into the den.

"I understand you've already met Nick Hunter," she said following him down the hallway.

"Yes," he answered halfheartedly. "We've met."

After they were seated, Noelle wasted no time in getting to the point.

"I know that Cole Richards is really Trent Dixon. I want you to tell me the rest."

"How did you find out?" Joseph asked slowly.

"Senator Richard Thomas arrived at Liaisons this evening. He recognized Trent. It seems they're old friends."

Joe pursed his lips. "Then I don't see why you're here."

Noelle leaned forward. "I need your help Joseph. I know we haven't had the best of relationships over the years, but I hope that you will put your feelings for me aside and tell me what was in Jordan's codicil. Whatever it is, it's the reason why Trent felt compelled to masquerade as Cole Richards." She paused. "Trent won't tell me, because he made some sort of pact with Jordan. You were Jordan's attorney. You had to be a part of it."

Joe leaned back and rested his head against the cushion. He inhaled deeply, weighing his options. He could stick by lawyer-client privilege. But at this point, he knew that premise was absurd.

He looked across at Noelle for a short moment and in that instant he plainly saw the love she had for Trent. He'd seen the same look in Gina's eyes. It was undeniable. And for the first time in his life he understood it.

His conscience tore at him. From the day that he'd written the document, he knew it was a cruel epitaph. But who was he to argue? Jordan was one of his biggest clients.

"Tell her, Joseph."

All eyes turned toward the doorway where Gina stood.

Noelle's mouth opened, but no words came out.

Gina walked to Joseph's side and took his hand.

"Believe me, Joseph didn't know that Trent Dixon was masquerading as Cole Richards." She sat down on the arm of the chair. She looked at him, then back to Noelle who was still trying to digest what was unfolding in front of her.

"He only found out yesterday that Cole Richards never existed."

Noelle finally found her voice. "Did you know what was going on Gina?"

"No, Mrs. Maxwell. Believe me, I had no idea. I only found out he wasn't who he said, when the senator called."

Gina lowered her eyes. "I let it slip that his reference, Cole Richards was staying with us. The senator had never heard of him. I guess I panicked. I called Joseph. When you called, I was too afraid to tell you. I was hoping that Joe could help in some way. And he did."

Gina turned to Joe. She took his hands in hers, giving him the strength and comfort that he needed.

"Tell her the rest," she urged him gently.

Slowly he nodded. "It'll probably be easier if I just let you read the codicil."

He pushed himself up from his seat and left the room. In his small office he spun the dial on the wall safe.

"How long have—you been seeing each other?" Noelle asked Gina hesitantly.

"Almost two years. He's really a wonderful person, Mrs. Maxwell," she emphasized. "I know that may be hard for you, or anyone to believe, but he is."

Noelle looked at Gina and saw the strength of her love and conviction reflected in her eyes. "Gina, if you feel that strongly about him, then I know it must be true." She smiled gently. "I always told you I had the greatest confidence in the world in you. As long as you're happy, that's what's important."

Joseph stood in the doorway, catching the last strains of the conversation. He and Gina had greatly underestimated Noelle Maxwell. He'd been wrong about her from the beginning. He had been so blinded by the dollar signs and protecting Jordan's interests, when he really should have been protecting Noelle's.

Maybe now he could begin to make that up to her. This was the first step.

He walked into the room. Without a word, he handed her the copy of Jordan's codicil.

CHAPTER 23

The rescue squad combed the wooded area. Wreckage was everywhere. But no body had been found.

The news crew from KABC in Los Angeles were the first reporters on the scene.

"This is the kinda stuff that makes the eleven o'clock," Bill overheard one of the cameramen say.

He stayed as far away from them as possible. He didn't want to be interviewed.

The fire department worked feverishly to extinguish the many small blazes that had erupted from the sparks.

Bill nervously paced back and forth in front of the hangar. He knew there'd be an investigation. His father would be furious. It was his responsibility to make sure each aircraft was in perfect running condition.

But over the past few months, revenue had been low. Bills were piling up. So he'd used shortcuts to curtail some of the costs. Instead of bringing in the technicians to service the planes, he'd done much of the maintenance himself. He'd been lucky. Until now.

"Over here!" Bill heard one of the workers yell.

There was a flurry of activity as a half-dozen men from the rescue squad, followed by two cameramen and the anchor woman from KABC, ran toward the beckoning voice.

Moments later, the screeching wail of the ambulance's siren pierced the night air.

Bill watched in dread as the red and white vehicle raced down the roadway.

A short, rather heavyset man approached and identified himself as Detective Dumont.

"You run this operation?" he asked, gruffly.

Bill nodded, nervously. "Yeah, me and my pop."

Dumont pulled out his notebook and began to ask a series of questions.

"What was the time of departure? Did the victim seem sober at the time? Where was he going? Was his pilot's license checked?"

Dumont scribbled down all of the answers, then snapped his book shut.

"Oh, one more question, Mr. Cochran. Is there anyone that you know of that should be contacted?"

"He was here the other day with a lady," Bill offered.

"You have a name?"

"Noelle Maxwell."

Dumont's eyes widened. "*The* Noelle Maxwell that just opened that ritzy joint in the valley?"

"Yes sir."

He flipped his pad back open and made a note. "Thank you. I'll be sure she's notified."

He had always wanted to get a peek at Liaisons. Now he had a damned good reason.

Noelle was visibly shaken when she completed reading the contents of the will.

"I—just can't believe Jordan would do such a thing," she said in a strained monotone. She looked up at Joseph as if searching for some explanation.

"He was determined that you would take over the running of the company. At any cost," Joe said. "Trent was to see to it that you were capable of managing it. Jordan knew that you would never do it voluntarily because you'd always been very clear in your views of the corporation and its methods of operation. So Jordan made sure you had no alternative. He used Liaisons as collateral for the bank loans. And he knew you'd do whatever it took to save Liaisons. You would have to step in as CEO with all of your resources. Jordan viewed Liaisons as a lark, so to speak. If you found a way to keep it . . ." Joseph shrugged his shoulders.

"Trent was caught in the middle," Nick added. "Even though he had promised Jordan that he would carry out his wishes, he wanted to ensure that you didn't lose Liaisons in the process."

"That would explain his insistence on my pursuing the expansion of Maxwell Enterprises," Noelle said almost to herself. "But something else is missing," she continued. "Jordan was not the kind of man to just blindly pursue anything. I realize that his company meant everything to him. Something motivated him to go to such lengths, beside the fact that he wanted me to run it."

"The only person who would know that is Trent," Joseph said.

Noelle rose. "I can't thank you enough, Joseph," she said sincerely. "I know this was difficult for you to do."

Joseph heaved a sigh. "It's something I should have done a long time ago."

Noelle and Nick returned to the car.

"I've got to find him, Nick," she said, quickly turning on the ignition. "He's off somewhere believing the worst, thinking that I hate him for what he's done. I've got to find him before he leaves."

CHAPTER 24

It was well after 2:00 A.M. by the time Detective Dumont arrived at Liaisons.

As soon as he stepped through the door the atmosphere made him hold in his stomach, stand up straight, and wish that he had shined his shoes.

Self-consciously, he smoothed his wrinkled suit as he approached the reception desk. He tried not to act like a tourist as he took in the decor from the corner of his eye.

Carol was completely absorbed in her latest romance novel. She had just reached the part where the two lovers were on the brink of making love.

Dumont cleared his throat so loudly, she dropped her book with a thud.

"I'm so sorry," she apologized, her face crimson with embarrassment. "May I help you?"

He flashed his badge, and she nearly choked.

"I'm looking for Noelle Maxwell," he said sternly, enjoying the look of fear in her eyes. That was the one pleasure in being a cop, he'd always thought, you had the power to intimidate. And he enjoyed it to the fullest every chance he got.

Carol swallowed back the knot in her throat.

"Mrs. Maxwell is not in the building." She tried to remember what she was supposed to say next, but the big burly cop who looked like he wanted to grind her to pieces, made her forget everything.

He wanted to laugh, but instead he hardened his look even more. He leaned across the counter.

"Do you know how she can be reached?"

"I can call her on her car phone," she offered up as sacrifice.

"You do that."

With shaky fingers Carol punched the numbers into the mobile phone. It rang ten times before she hung up.

"No answer."

"Okay." His demeanor softened. He'd had enough fun for the evening. "When she returns, or as soon as you hear from her, tell her that a friend of hers, Trent Dixon, is in Memorial Hospital. She should try to get there as soon as possible."

Carol quickly jotted down the information. She looked up and smiled weakly. "I'll be sure to give her the message."

"Good girl." He started to leave, then stopped. "How much does it cost to spend a night in a place like this?"

"$2,500.00," she said, "all amenities included," she added gaining immense pleasure from the look of astonishment on his face.

He left without another word.

Carol looked down at the neatly written message and wondered who Trent Dixon was.

Noelle hadn't said a word all the way back to the Hilton.

Once they returned to the suite, and discovered that Trent had not come back, Noelle insisted, against Nick's protestations that she had to get back. The combination of the emotional shocks that she had endured—together with pure exhaustion—were taking their toll. She wanted to be alone. She needed to think.

"Are you sure you can make the drive back alone?" Nick worried.

"I'll be fine. I've done it dozens of times. And anyway I want to be there in case Trent decides to come back."

She reached through the open car window and clasped his hand. "Thank you for everything, Nick. Trent is really lucky to have a friend like you."

He gave her a half smile. "I tell him that all the time."

"Call me when he arrives. I'm beginning to worry."

He hadn't wanted to say anything, but he was starting to worry also.

Dr. Kevin Holloway was the Chief of Surgery at Memorial Hospital. He was on duty when Trent was rushed into the trauma room. He'd practiced internal medicine for nearly twenty years. Most people would be hardened by the pain and suffering they witnessed daily. But for Kevin Holloway, each case was special and each patient's life was just as precious as the next.

"Vitals are weak, doc," the EMS worker said. "We had to resuscitate on the way over."

Holloway quickly peered into Trent's dilated pupils with his pen light. His trained eyes did a rapid visual assessment of the external injuries, while his fingers gently probed the inert body.

He looked over at his nurse. "Get Carson in here, stat. I'm going to need him in the O.R. If he's not in the building, have him paged. And order a CAT scan."

"Yes, doctor." The nurse rushed from the room.

Moments later, the squalling sound of the intercom blared throughout the hospital.

"Dr. Matthew Carson. Dr. Carson, trauma room one, stat."

Within moments, Matthew Carson appeared at Trent's side. To look at him, one would never imagine that this painfully thin, rather meek-looking man, was one of the leading neurosurgeons in the state. Most people thought that he was no more than twenty-five years old. He was much closer to forty.

"What've we got?" Carson asked.

"Plane crash. He's pretty messed up inside," Holloway explained. "We're trying to stabilize him before going into the O.R. No known relatives. The police are trying to track them down."

Carson took a look into Trent's eyes. "Hmm, not good. Has a CAT scan been ordered?"

"Done."

"Has he been conscious at all?"

"Not a peep. That's why I want you in the O.R. to observe. Just in case."

"Let's go. I'll look at the pictures then."

Each step was a task. Every fiber of her being ached. Her eyes felt like they had been loaded with sand. Her brain seemed to have turned to sludge, from her having tried to absorb everything that had taken place over the past few hours.

She still found it hard to believe the things that she'd been told. She thought she knew her husband. In reality, she didn't know him at all.

Jordan had been driven by his own obsession for control.

From the moment that he'd walked through the doors of her aunt's cafe, he'd controlled her life. She had been so desperate for escape from the life she lived, that she had willingly succumbed.

Even now, when she had finally found her place in the world and a man to share it with, he was still in control.

Noelle pushed through the doorway of Liaisons. She wouldn't allow him to control her any longer. If she'd learned nothing else from Jordan, she learned what power can do. And she intended to use hers to the fullest.

She was so caught up in her own thoughts, she didn't stop by reception, but went straight to the elevator. She'd take a quick shower and then call Nick. Hopefully, Trent had returned by now.

She pressed the UP button, just as Carol ran up behind her.

"Mrs. Maxwell."

Noelle spun around, a smile of greeting on her face.

"Mrs. Maxwell," she began breathlessly, "the police were here."

The smile faded in degrees. "What?"

She nodded vigorously. "He left this message for you." She stuck out the slip of paper.

Noelle read the words and her hand began to tremble.

"How—long ago was he here?"

"About an hour." Carol looked at Noelle's stricken face. "Are you all right, Mrs. Maxwell?"

Noelle nodded, but knew she was far from all right.

She felt frozen. For several moments she just stared at the piece of paper. She couldn't think straight. She didn't know what to do first.

The elevator door opened and Noelle snapped to attention. She had to go to him.

"If anyone is looking for me, I'll be at Memorial Hospital."

She brushed past Carol, ran across the corridor and out the door.

CHAPTER 25

Memorial Hospital was more than a half hour away. Only critical cases were taken to Memorial. Her heart pounded. *Trent was critical.*

She floored the gas. She'd be there in fifteen minutes.

Nick couldn't sleep. The soundless television watched him. He glanced at the bedside clock. It was almost 4:00 A.M. Trent hadn't returned and he hadn't called.

Maybe he'd gone back to Liaisons. He reached for the phone. But something on the screen caught his attention. He pressed the volume button on the remote control.

". . . we're here at Cochran Airstrip where a little more than an hour ago, a small aircraft registered to Trent Dixon, an employee of Maxwell Enterprises, has gone down . . ."

Nick sat straight up in the bed.

". . . the victim has been rushed to Memorial Hospital in critical condition. We'll have . . ."

He didn't hear any more. He grabbed the phone and dialed Liaisons.

Mrs. Maxwell isn't available," Carol informed the caller. "She left about five minutes ago."

"Did she say where she was going? Nick pressed.

"Oh, yes. She's on her way to Memorial Hospital. She did say to . . ." The dial tone hummed in her ear.

Carol shook her head dismissively as she replaced the receiver. *This has been some night.*

Nurses and doctors alike turned and stared when Noelle ran down the hospital corridor to the information desk.

She looked like someone straight out of a Hollywood movie, from her obviously expensive clothing to the stylish hairdo, right to those brilliant brown eyes.

Breathless, Noelle stopped at information.

"There was a man brought in about an hour ago. Trent Dixon. Where is he?"

The overworked receptionist checked the computer.

"He's in surgery, ma'am."

She felt faint.

"Are you a relative?"

"Yes. No." Noelle wrung her hands. "I'm a close friend."

"You can go up to the third floor. Dr. Holloway is in charge of the case."

"Merci."

When Noelle arrived on the third floor, she was escorted to a small lounge area by a nurse.

"It may be a while," the nurse advised. "There's a coffee machine against the wall."

"Will someone let me know what's happening?" She knew she sounded like a frightened child but she couldn't help it.

The nurse patted Noelle's shoulder. "As soon as they come out of surgery, I'll let Dr. Holloway know you're here," she said soothingly, seeing the anguish in her eyes.

Noelle swallowed and struggled not to cry. "Thank you."

The nurse turned away and left Noelle alone in the room.

"I can't lose you. Not now," she cried in a strangled whisper.

"How are his vitals?" Holloway called out over his mask.

"Weak. His pressure is dropping. Fast."

The surgical nurse wiped Holloway's brow.

"I can't stop this bleeding."

"We're losing him, doc."

Suddenly, the ominous sound of the heart monitor blared in a piercing, steady drone.

"Paddles!" Holloway barked. *Don't let me lose this one,* he prayed.

Nick rushed through the lounge door, and found Noelle huddled in the corner of the tweed sofa.

She looked up and the agony he saw in her tear-filled eyes tore through his gut as sharp as a samurai sword.

He hurried to her side and put his arm around her trembling shoulders. The last of her strength crumbled. Hot tears ran down her cheeks as deep sobs racked her insides. He held her in silence until the tears slowly ebbed. His eyes asked the unspoken question.

"He's in surgery," Noelle was able to say.

Nick briefly shut his eyes in relief. "Have you heard anything?"

She shook her head. "How did you know?" She sniffed back the tears and wiped her eyes with the paper napkin that she'd balled in her fist.

"It was on the news."

"A car accident?" she asked, bewildered.

"That's what you think happened? Didn't anyone tell you?"

"No. Tell me what? Nick, what happened?"

He took a breath. "Trent was flying. He went back to Cochran and rented a plane. I don't know all of the details, but the plane went down. He was apparently thrown clear—before it exploded."

She felt as if she'd been slammed against a brick wall. She wanted to scream, but no sound would come from her mouth.

The nightmare came hurtling back. Only now she was fully awake. *Jordan. Trent.* It was happening all over again and she felt herself slipping into that dark abyss of unspeakable pain.

"There's nothing else we can do," Holloway said heavily. He left the operating room.

Exhausted, mentally and physically, he stripped off his hospital garb.

Carson joined him at the sink. "You think they found any family members?"

"Hopefully."

"You want to tell them, or should I?"

"I guess I should. I'm the doctor of record."

Carson patted him solidly on the back. "If it's any consolation buddy, you did a helluva job. No one else could have done more."

Holloway barely nodded his thanks.

CHAPTER 26

Noelle and Nick both jumped up when a grim-faced man in a white hospital jacket came to the door. He stepped inside and approached Noelle.

"Mrs. Maxwell?"

She nodded.

"I'm Dr. Holloway.

She shook his extended hand.

Noelle held her breath and prayed.

"Please tell me, Doctor."

He looked at Nick.

"It's all right," she assured, the panic rising. "He's a close friend."

When they were both seated, Dr. Holloway explained what had transpired.

"Mr. Dixon sustained internal as well as head injuries. He was in shock and unconscious when he was brought in. We repaired what we could, and set his leg. During the operation his heart stopped."

Noelle's breath caught and she covered her mouth to stifle a cry. Nick held her hand.

"Go on, Doctor," he said.

"We were able to revive him," he paused, "but he's in a coma."

Noelle's eyes squeezed shut.

"Now, I'm not promising anything. I want you both to understand that. However, the next seventy-two hours are critical. He lost a great deal of blood and we don't know the extent of the damage to the brain. He's going to receive the best medical care possible. But it's up to him. He has to want to pull through."

Dr. Holloway stood up. "If there's any way you can contact his family, I would suggest that you do."

"When can I see him?" Noelle asked in a tight voice.

"He'll be in recovery until tomorrow afternoon. Then we'll move him to intensive care. I would say tomorrow evening."

They both nodded.

"You both might as well go home and get some rest. There's nothing else to do right now." His voice softened. "Your friend looks like he's in good physical condition. That's a plus in his favor."

They both nodded, the first glimmer of hope shining faintly.

"Get some rest," Holloway said again. "And please leave a number where you can be reached. Just stop off at the nurses' station on your way out."

When they were alone, Noelle collapsed in Nick's arms. The tears that she had fought to hide while the doctor was with them, were released in low, tortured sobs.

"He'll be all right," he soothed, gently rubbing her back. "You heard the doctor. Trent is strong. He'll pull out of this."

"All I can think of," she choked, "is that I'm going to lose him. It's like Jordan all over again. And I don't think I can live through it. I want to have the chance to tell him that everything is going to work out. I want to tell him how much I love him," she cried.

"You will," Nick assured softly. "You will. Now, let's go home and get some rest."

When they'd reached her car, Nick put his arm around Noelle's shoulders. "Drive carefully," he advised.

"Why don't you stay at Liaisons," she suggested. "We have vacant rooms reserved for the staff in case of emergencies. No one is scheduled to spend the night," she said, easily recalling the staff log.

"Sounds great. It'll give me a chance to see what Trent has been raving about. He thinks the world of you," he said softly, a warm smile playing at the corners of his lips.

She looked up at him, her eyes softening, "I feel the same way about him."

By the time they arrived at the villa, the sun was high in the sky. Several of the early risers were already on the tennis court, and there was a lone rider taking a turn around the track.

To Nick it seemed that he'd stepped into his wildest fantasy. He was dumbfounded. He began to look at Noelle with a newfound respect. Trent was right, he mused. She is remarkable.

There was no doubt that Liaisons was her creation. Every sculpture, window dressing, piece of artwork all had her distinctive signature.

"It's a bit small, don't you think?" he teased.

Noelle laughed for the first time in what seemed like weeks and it felt good. She took his arm. "You haven't seen anything yet, Monsieur Hunter."

Once Noelle stopped by reception to let Carol know she had returned, she personally escorted Nick to his room.

Noelle looked hesitant as she opened the door a crack.

"I do want to apologize that there were no full suites available. I hope that you'll be comfortable here." She opened the door the rest of the way.

Nick stood in the doorway with his mouth open. "This is the staff quarters? How can I get hired?"

Noelle breathed a sigh of relief. She wanted him to be comfortable.

He stepped in and sunk into the two-inch thick, oriental carpet. The room was done in muted shades of grey and mauve.

The cozy living room was fully equipped with a high-tech stereo system, a fully loaded bar, and an efficiency kitchen.

The bedroom repeated the same shades with the addition of a soft green that ran throughout the printed draperies and matching bed ensemble.

"I'm sorry that there's no Jacuzzi, but you're welcome to use the one in the gym."

"I'll keep that in mind," he grinned.

"Well—I'll let you get settled. There are a million things I need to take care of."

Nick walked over to her and braced her shoulders. He looked into her questioning eyes. "Please try and get some rest. I'm sure your staff is capable of handling everything."

She looked away. The hard and painful realities came rushing back.

"I'll try. I'm going to call the hospital and see if there's been any change."

"You'll let me know if you hear anything?"

"Of course."

She turned to leave, then stopped at the door. She looked at Nick over her shoulder. "Thank you for everything, Nick. And most of all thank you for helping me to see beyond the surface."

"No thanks needed. Everything is going to be fine. Count on it."

She pressed her lips together and nodded.

Noelle returned to her room. Alone, again the tumultuous thoughts enveloped her.

Heavily she sat down on the couch.

Was it just yesterday that she and Trent had made love not two feet from where she sat?

Slowly she got up and walked to her bedroom door. For several long moments she stood there recalling awakening in Trent's arms.

Her eyes misted over when she remembered, all too painfully, the moment she heard the door close behind him.

She would give anything to have even those last moments together again. To be held in his arms—to be loved by him again.

Her throat tightened. She turned away from the telltale bed, knowing she would not be able to sleep.

Crossing the room, she went to the phone and dialed the hospital.

There'd been no change, she was informed, and he hadn't been moved out of recovery. His condition was still critical, but stable.

She thanked the nurse and hung up. Looking down at the telephone table, she caught a glimpse of the edge of a piece of paper sticking out from beneath her address book.

She picked up the slips of paper that had the telephone messages.

Senator Thomas will be arriving tomorrow.

Trent Dixon will not be meeting with you as planned.

Her heart skittered, when she saw the note with Trent's name on it. Even though Nick had confessed that he'd placed the call at Trent's request, hoping to buy more time, it was still disturbing to be plainly reminded of the reasons behind it.

She studied the neatly written notes in Gina's familiar handwriting. The last few hours of her life had almost been prophesied on two tiny pieces of paper.

Would anything have been different if she'd seen them sooner? Could this tragedy have been avoided if she'd mentioned to Trent that Senator Thomas was arriving?

There was no point in trying to go back, she realized with a pang. There was nothing she could change about the past. All she could do now was pray that Trent would be a part of her future.

She shuddered to think that the last time she saw him could be the final time.

CHAPTER 27

After a quick, refreshing shower and a change of clothes, Noelle went to the lower level to check on things before going to the hospital.

Gina was at the desk when she arrived. The look of sympathy in Gina's eyes told her that she already knew.

"I'm sorry, Mrs. Maxwell. I saw the news report. How is he?"

"He's critical. And he's in a coma." She swallowed. "They, the doctors, don't know when he'll come out of it."

"I don't know what to say."

"I'll be staying at the hospital. I want to be there when he wakes up."

"Of course. Do you want me to stay over?"

"If you don't mind. I'd feel much better knowing that you're here. Oh—one more thing. I put together a proposal that your father needs to review before he leaves. It's in my office. Would you be sure that he gets it in the overnight mail."

"I'll take care of it and call my father to let him know to expect a package."

"*Merci.*" She hesitated, while Gina watched expectantly. "Gina," she began slowly, "I just want to say that no matter what difficulties Joseph and I have had in the past, I'm truly happy for you both. I know you were reluctant to let me know about your relationship and I understand your reasons. But I hope we can put that all behind us."

Thoughts of Trent surrounded her as she spoke. "Life is too short," she said with quiet conviction, "to let past wrongs stand in the way of the future."

"Thank you, Mrs. Maxwell. You don't know what that means to me."

"I think I do," she smiled. "And I also think it's time that you started calling me Noelle."

As Gina watched Noelle depart, she once again had to marvel at the extraordinary woman that she was. Even in the midst of everything that she was enduring, she still had time for others.

She could only hope that, one day soon, Noelle would finally have the happiness that she deserved.

Before leaving for the hospital, she went to her office and called her accountant, Sam and her broker, Nina. Both of them confirmed that the transactions had taken place.

Noelle paid Tempest and Braxton an unannounced visit. For the next hour, she told them everything that had happened—at least all that she knew.

Tempest held her, letting her cry softly, while Braxton tried to reassure her that Trent would pull through.

By the time she left them, she felt physically spent yet emotionally lifted. True friends was something that she desperately needed, right then, and they had proven themselves once again. They had not judged, or condemned, but had been loving and supportive.

"Don't forget the words of wisdom you gave me," Tempest said, standing with Noelle at the door. "If you love each other, be patient." Tempest smiled and Noelle hugged her.

"I'm going to miss you terribly," Noelle whispered softly, hugging her tighter.

"I wish we didn't have to leave, but we have to get back to New York tomorrow. But you know I'm always just a phone call away," Tempest said softly. "I'll be here until tomorrow night if you need me."

"Thank you for everything. I'll call you. And give Kai a kiss for me."

"I will."

After Noelle left, Tempest stood for several moments facing her husband.

"She's been through so much, B.J., my heart aches for her."

He gathered his wife in his arms and kissed the top of her head.

"She's found her happiness, baby. I just hope that she'll stay as happy as we are."

Nick quietly hung up the phone. He covered his tired eyes with his hands. That had to be one of the most difficult calls he'd ever had to make.

The doorbell chimed. He pulled himself off the side of the bed and went to answer it.

"Noelle, come in." He could immediately tell that she'd been crying. Her eyes were slightly red and puffy. He began to think the worst.

"Has something happened? Did the hospital call?" They walked into the small living room and sat down.

"No. No." she quickly answered. "I called, but there've been no changes."

"I was able to reach his sister, Stephanie, in Philadelphia." He shook his head. "She was almost hysterical. But she calmed down long enough to say that she would inform the family."

Noelle took his hand. "I know that must have been difficult for you."

He heaved a sigh and nodded. "She said she'd call back once they made flight arrangements. So I need to stay here and wait for the call."

"Of course."

"Anyway," he tried to smile, "Trent doesn't need to see my ugly mug when he opens his eyes." He saw her lip tremble. "He will open his eyes," he repeated with certainty.

"And I want to be there when he does." She got up and walked to the door. "I'll call you as soon as there's any news. If you need anything at all, let Gina know. She'll take care of it. I'll also make arrangements for Trent's family to stay here at the villa. It'll be too much for them to try to arrange for a hotel on such short notice."

Nick shook his head in amazement. "I know they'll appreciate that."

"It's the least I can do." Her voice threatened to break. "I just feel that somehow this is all my fault."

"That's absurd. You couldn't have known."

She looked directly into his eyes. "If it hadn't been for me and my obsession with trying to prove that Trent was guilty of . . ." she looked away, "he wouldn't have felt forced into this twisted scheme." She spun away, suddenly ashamed.

Nick grabbed her shoulder, turning her around. His eyes zeroed in on her. "Don't do this to yourself. You're as much a victim in all this as Trent. What matters now is not who's wrong, but what you're going to do to make things right."

She bit down on her bottom lip. "I know you're right but I can't help how I feel. I've spent the past year fueling my hatred for a man I'd never met, blaming him for something he didn't do." She looked up at him, her eyes laden with guilt. She shook her head in despair. "I'll never forgive myself if I don't get the chance to make it up to him."

She wrapped her arms around her waist. "I can't imagine what he's been going through for the past year. I even went so far as to destroy the report he'd gotten because I didn't want to find out that I may have been wrong."

"That's all behind you now. Think positive."

"I'll try."

* * *

Noelle tossed a small overnight bag, filled with toiletries onto the passenger seat of her car, along with a light blanket and a pillow. She was determined that she was not moving until he awakened. If they threw her out into the hall, at least she would be prepared.

She'd dressed in a designer jogging suit of purple and white with matching Nike sneakers. The waiting may take some time, she'd reasoned, at the very least she wanted to be comfortable.

She'd taken care of all of the tiny details at the villa and was confident that Gina could handle any problems that might arise.

All she had to do now, was focus all of her energies on Trent.

CHAPTER 28

Noelle took a steadying breath as she stood outside of Trent's hospital room. She drew on the final reserves of her strength to help her face whatever lay on the other side.

Doctor Holloway had warned her that it could be an unnerving sight. He'd offered to accompany her, but she had adamantly declined.

She pushed open the heavy blue and white door. The stark white walls rushed toward her, while the mournful bleeps from the monitors seeped through her veins, becoming one with her own heartbeat.

She felt like she was suffocating. She took deep, gulping breaths. For a split second she shut her eyes, as she stepped across the doorway. She knew that just beyond the jutting wall was Trent.

Steeling herself, she slowly walked around the curve.

Her heart slammed against her chest. She covered her mouth to smother the gasp that rose from the pit of her stomach.

Her throat constricted as she cautiously stepped forward. He was so still, unmoving beneath the sterile white sheets. The only sign that he was even breathing was the steady beep of the monitor.

Carefully she drew closer until she was inches from his side. A hot tear rolled down her cheek when she looked down at the bruised face. There was a thick bandage over his right eye and another on his cheek. She swallowed back the knot of anguish that lodged in her throat.

Her fingers trembled as she reached out to touch him, needing desperately to confirm, for herself, what the machines already knew.

The instant that her fingertips touched his warm flesh, a sudden wave of euphoric relief swept through her.

Her eyes filled and ran over.

"Trent, you're going to be fine, *cher,*" she cried softly. Gently she stroked his arm. "I'm here. We have so much to talk about. So many things I need to say to you."

She lowered her head and lightly rested it on his chest. The steady beat of his heart filled her.

"I love you, Trent," she cooed. "Nothing else matters except how we feel about each other."

Blindly she sat down on one of the two, white plastic chairs. For the next few hours, she sat unmoved, talking softly to him, believing, without a doubt, that he heard every word she said.

Nick found her quietly talking to him, smiling intermittently as she revisited their brief, but passionate time together. He felt like the third wheel, rolling in on a very intimate moment. He turned to leave.

"Nick." The strangely ragged voice reached across the sterile room.

"Hi," he whispered almost as if the sound of his voice might awaken the sleeping patient.

Noelle motioned him over.

"Any change?" he asked, pulling up the matching white chair.

She shook her head. "He hasn't moved." She continued to stroke his arm. "But I know he hears me," she firmly stated, as if challenging Nick to disagree.

He chose to ignore the statement, rather than upset her. He'd never believed all that stuff about talking to people in comas. It might work on television, but this was real life.

Instead, he stated, "I heard from Trent's sister, Stephanie. They can't get a flight out until tomorrow. They'll arrive early in the morning. She said the family really appreciates your offer."

"So they'll be staying?"

"Yes."

"Good. I'll let Gina know to make arrangements." She turned her attention back to Trent.

"Have you seen the doctor?" Nick asked.

"He was here when I arrived. He said Trent is stable and we'll just have to wait."

"Why don't you go for a walk. Take a break and stretch. I'll stay here with him."

She shook her head emphatically. "He may wake up, and I wouldn't be here. I can't leave," she insisted.

"Okay. Have you eaten?"

The mention of food suddenly reminded her of how hungry she was. She hadn't eaten since early the day before.

"Food has been the last thing on my mind," she said with a fragile smile. "But I am hungry."

"I'll see what I can find in the hospital cafeteria."

"Something light for me," she said. "Fruit or a yogurt. I don't want to send my stomach into shock."

"No problem. I'll be back shortly."

She turned back to Trent's still body. Lovingly she caressed his cheek.

"I think I understand why you had to do what you did," she said softly. "I thought I knew my husband, but I didn't. What he did to you I can never forget. But we can't let that stand between us." She remembered Tempest's words, *harboring secrets and doubts can destroy a relationship.* "Trent," she pleaded, "come back to me so that I can make it all up to you."

A nurse entered soundlessly, did a brief check of the monitors and changed the I.V. just as Nick returned.

He placed the small tray on the bedside stand. It went unnoticed by Noelle who kept her eyes locked on Trent.

Without a word, Nick gently patted her shoulder. This was their time, he thought. He wasn't needed there. Quietly he closed the door behind him.

The sun was slowly setting over the mountaintops. Noelle switched on the small nightlight. Slowly, achingly, she rose from the chair.

Her body was painfully stiff from having sat in one place for so many hours. She arched her back and rotated her head.

On shaky legs she walked toward the window. She looked through the partially open blinds. She saw the weaving roads, the flow of human traffic, the flickering lights. Life moved on, she realized, even as one life hung by a precarious thread.

She twirled the wand on the venetian blinds, letting the last rays of sunlight filter through.

Suddenly, she spun around when a soft groan mixed with the tin-tin sound of the blinds.

With renewed agility, she ran across the room.

"Trent," she whispered. "Trent, it's me, Noelle." Her voice began to tremble. "I'm here, sweetheart."

She held his hand tighter, willing him up from the darkness that had captured him. "Come back to me. You can do it," she urged.

Ever so slowly his fingers wrapped around her hand. A ragged groan rose from deep within his throat. His eyes flickered open, then slid closed.

"I love you, *mon cher,*" she cried. "Please!"

Somewhere far off he heard that familiar voice, that he so loved, drift to him like a lazy tide. Every nerve-ending in his body screamed in pain.

But the voice soothed him, almost lulling him back into that peaceful sleep where there was no pain, no agony of loss.

He had nothing to come back to. There was no reason to fight against the darkness. The only thing he had ever really wanted was not to be had by him.

It was better this way, his mind said. It's easier to just let go and get swept away to eternal peace.

But that voice kept calling out to him, whispering, reaching out, not letting him escape. He couldn't fight the voice. It was more powerful than the desire to sleep.

"Noelle." The raw whisper was the sweetest symphony to her ears.

She held his hand to her face. "I'm here, I'm here." Her throat ached as she fought to control the scream of joy that struggled for release.

The agonizing effort to open his eyes, was almost more than he could stand. But he had to reach the voice.

Gradually his eyes opened.

She stroked his head and leaned over the guardrail, directly in his line of vision.

"You're back," she cried in a strangled voice. "You're back."

Hot, salty tears flowed unchecked down her cheeks and onto his.

She rested her head on his chest. "Everything is all right now," she said.

Weakly he squeezed her hand and somewhere deep inside his soul, he knew it was.

CHAPTER 29

"Well," Dr. Holloway said, giving Trent a brief exam, "you're a very lucky man. You have a difficult recovery ahead of you and you'll probably experience severe headaches for a few days. Maybe weeks. But," he turned to include Noelle in his smile, "I predict a full recovery. Don't stay too long," he added. "Our patient is going to need a lot of rest."

"When can I leave?" Trent croaked.

"That depends. I'll have Dr. Carson run another series of head x-rays. So long as there's no infection from the operation and the pictures are good, I'd say in about a week. Maybe less."

"Thank you, Doctor," Noelle grinned.

"You'll definitely need peace and quiet during your recovery. You won't be able to get around much on that leg for a while either."

"Don't worry, Dr. Holloway." She looked at Trent with adoring eyes. "I intend to take very good care of him."

Holloway winked at Trent. "You're luckier than I thought." He walked to the door. "I'll check on you in the morning."

Nick approached the bed with a big grin on his face. He said in a stage whisper, "If they're worried about head injuries, they can forget it. With that hard head of yours it would take an atom bomb to do any damage."

"Very funny," Trent tossed back in a hoarse voice. "Anyway, step aside, you're blocking my view."

"Hey," Nick held up his hands. "No problem. Consider me gone." He gave Noelle a kiss on the cheek. "I'll see you later." He turned back to

Trent. "Your whole family will be descending on you tomorrow. Don't let her wear you out!" he teased.

"Beat it," Trent warned with a crooked smile.

Nick waved good-bye and left.

Noelle took a deep breath and stepped closer. "How are you feeling?"

"Sort of like I've been in a plane crash." He tried to laugh but a sharp pain shot through his head.

Noelle clutched his hand. He closed his eyes and spoke through the pain. "Did you mean it—when you said you'd take care of me?"

She leaned down and kissed his forehead. "Of course I did."

"Good." He began to drift off to sleep. His voice was thick. "I—like the sound of that. We have—so—much to talk about. So much I need to tell you."

Noelle stroked his arm. "We have plenty of time for that," she whispered, but he was already sound asleep.

After speaking briefly with the doctor, he assured her that Trent would sleep through the night. Noelle took the opportunity to return to Liaisons. She wanted to personally see to the accommodations for Trent's family.

Suddenly, the thought of meeting them made her nervous, as she strutted through the two adjoining suites that were set aside for their use.

She spewed out rapid-fire instructions. "Please be sure to stock the refrigerator with soft drinks, juices, condiments and light snacks from the kitchen," she instructed Joann, her head of housekeeping. "We don't have information on their dietary requests. So we'll just have everything available."

Noelle's trained eyes rapidly assessed the rooms. "We just received a new shipment of floral bedding. Have these bedrooms changed. I want the rooms to have a cheery atmosphere. They'll need it."

"Yes, Mrs. Maxwell."

"Be sure that there are fresh flowers and baskets of fruit in both suites."

"Yes, Mrs. Maxwell."

Noelle looked around anxiously. She wanted everything to be perfect, and realized that she was transferring her anxiety to Joann. She turned and looked at Joann who stared back with something resembling awe.

"I'm sorry if I sound too demanding," Noelle apologized. "It's just that these visitors are very important to me."

"No apology necessary. I understand." She felt thrilled just to be in the same room with Noelle.

"*Merci.*" She smiled warmly at Joann and hurried from the room. She'd already arranged to have a car pick them up from the airport and bring them to Liaisons, then to the hospital.

She mentally ticked off the things yet to be done as she entered the elevator. *Call hospital, change clothes.* Her stomach growled. *Get something to eat!*

The elevator doors opened and she went directly to her room. She looked around as if seeing through new eyes. The last time she was in these very same rooms, she was filled with apprehension and cold fear. Now, she felt like she could finally smile again.

Trent was going to be well. They were going to work things out between them. True, there were still a lot of unanswered questions. But they would all be answered in time. Liaisons was flourishing and she had very positive vibrations about her proposal to Nkiru.

Everything was right with her world. She had someone to love and he loved her. She felt alive and vibrant again.

Nothing could change that.

Noelle prepared for her evening tour of the villa. Now that Trent was stable, and she had the assurance from Dr. Holloway that Trent would sleep through the night, she didn't feel guilty about meeting her routine obligations.

She selected a coral cocktail dress of satin with a chiffon overskirt in a pale orange. The combination gave the dress an iridescent shimmer.

The wide waistband gave unquestionable definition to her narrow waist. The bodice was framed by stand-away off-shoulder sleeves, giving the observer an ample view of the satiny copper skin.

She felt radiant and she looked it as heads turned when she entered the dining room.

Almost immediately, Senator Thomas saw her enter and motioned her to his table. He'd hoped to see her tonight. He'd desired Noelle from the moment Jordan had introduced them years ago. Seeing her again served to reinforce that desire. He'd never dared to cross that line while Jordan was alive, knowing that Jordan would have ruined him without batting an eye. Plus Noelle never seemed to be the kind of woman who would cheat on her husband.

But now. Now was a different story. Jordan was definitely out of the picture and her would-be suitor was incapacitated.

"Please join me for a few moments," he requested when she'd reached his table.

"Just a few." She sat down as he helped her into her seat. He stood behind her for several moments longer than necessary, deeply inhaling her intoxicating perfume.

"Noelle, you're looking—extraordinary," he breathed heavily. His eyes raked over her. "I hope you're feeling better. I was worried." His light brown eyes reflected concern.

She smiled confidently. "I am. Thank you, Richard."

At first glance, Richard Thomas gave the impression of being a rather average-looking man, Noelle always thought. But upon close observation he was decidedly handsome in a practiced sort of way.

His smooth ebony skin was flawless, his dress impeccable and the full head of salt-and-pepper hair capped off the look of distinction. Richard Thomas was a big man in stature and gave all who met him a sense of trust and security. He inspired confidence—an attribute that had made him adored by his constituency.

"I heard about Dixon. Sad." He shook his head slowly, the picture of concern. "Have you gotten any word on his condition?" He looked at her from beneath long lashes.

"As a matter of fact, I was at the hospital when he came out of the coma."

Her face visibly brightened, Richard noticed, annoyed. *Dixon wouldn't get this one.* Not if he had anything to do with it.

"The doctors say he'll be fine," Noelle added.

"I'm sure he will be. Trent and I go back quite a way. Actually I met him for the first time when Jordan purchased this villa. Dixon has a very unscrupulous reputation." He chuckled lightly. "I hope you weren't taken in by any of his, uh, schemes." He took a sip from his glass of wine.

Noelle frowned. "I'm sure that whatever Trent may or may not have done in the past has no bearing on who he is now."

Richard pursed his lips, covering them with his finger.

"Oh, Noelle," he said in a patronizing tone, "no wonder Jordan was so madly in love with you. You're still so innocent."

Noelle stiffened. "You don't know anything about me," she snapped.

"Please I didn't mean to offend you." He placed his hand on her bare arm and his fingers began to tingle. "It's just that," he looked around as though making sure they couldn't be overheard," I wouldn't want to see you hurt." He paused for effect.

"Trent Dixon has a long track record for romancing rich women and taking them for all they're worth. He has a very expensive lifestyle. Even Jordan couldn't afford his habits," he chuckled again.

A hundred troubling thoughts ran through her head at once. *The lies.* His interest in what she did with the business. *The lies.* If he married her, he'd be set for life. The community property laws in California were very liberal. Had she been blinded again?

"I don't see how all of this has anything to do with me," she said, cautiously.

"Of course it doesn't have anything to do with you. But you can never be too careful. I just feel it's my duty—as a friend of Jordan's to—warn you."

He smiled, watching her expression change from confidence to doubt as his words slowly penetrated.

"Please excuse me." She pushed away from the table.

He stood up. "I was hoping you would stay for dinner."

"I'm sorry, Richard." She felt confused and suddenly afraid. "I still have rounds to make."

"Maybe tomorrow then?"

"Maybe." She hurried from the room.

What Richard said couldn't be true. Trent wasn't after her for her money. He couldn't be. It was Jordan. Jordan convinced him to trick her into running Maxwell Enterprises.

Her mind spun. But what kind of man was Trent? She had no idea he lied before since the lies flowed so easily. Had he always lied—even to Jordan?

The pulse in her temple began to pound. She rushed for the elevator and ran into Tempest as she was coming out.

"Noelle, where are you . . ." She saw the stricken look on her face. "What's wrong? Has something more happened to Trent?"

Noelle shook her head. "I-I'm just tired. I was going to my room."

Tempest looked at her skeptically. "I know you, and I always know when something is wrong."

How could she tell her that she'd been a fool—that she'd been used?

"I'll be in my room, Noelle if you want to talk."

"I'll be fine," she said weakly. She stepped into the elevator, leaving Tempest with an unsettling feeling.

Alone in her room, she went over every detail from the moment she'd met Trent.

Every move that he'd made had been choreographed to seduce her. He clouded her head with words of love. He praised her business sense. He sympathized with her marital problems.

She had been so starved for love and affection, she played right into his hands.

Within hours his family would be arriving and she'd have to pretend to be cordial. She'd have to pretend that nothing was wrong.

A chill ran through her. She couldn't face him. She wouldn't look into his eyes and feel weak. She wouldn't listen to anymore lies.

Anguish gripped her. She fell onto her knees, huddling into a tight ball and cried. She cried for all of her losses—her parents, her youth, Jordan and Cole. Cole because that's who she fell in love with. But he was gone forever.

CHAPTER 30

At 10:00 A.M. the white, stretch limousine carrying Trent's family pulled in front of Liaisons.

Stephanie hopped out first. Her large brown eyes widened in astonishment. "Damn!"

"Watch your mouth!" her mother, Janice, warned as she stepped out of the car. But even she had to stop in wonder as the enormous villa spread out before her.

"Don't get all excited," her older sister Diane stated. "You know how these rich people are. She'll probably write this off as some tax deduction." She turned up her broad nose in distaste.

"Your antiestablishment rhetoric is rearing its ugly head again," her mother said.

"Diane," Steph cut in, "lighten up."

"I just want to get to the hospital," Janice said, "and get my son home."

Gina buzzed Noelle on her office intercom.

"Yes, Gina."

"The Dixons are here."

"Thank you."

Noelle had hardly more than an hour sleep all night. She kept seeing Trent lying so helpless in the hospital. Then she'd heard Richard's scathing denunciation.

Maybe Richard was wrong about Trent, she'd told herself at least a hundred times. But then reality would hit and all of the events that had led to this moment confirmed her fears.

Her head ached. She felt hollow, devoid of emotion.

Somehow she'd make her excuses. She wasn't going back to the hospital.

Her private line rang.

"Yes? Noelle Maxwell."

"Noelle. This is Ambassador Nkiru. I presented your proposal at an open session of the U.N. this morning."

This morning? she thought she was confused, then remembered that it was one o'clock in the afternoon in New York.

"I have good news. It was decided that I would present the offer to the Sudanese government."

He sounded so enthusiastic, she thought absently. Her voice was empty. "That's wonderful."

"However," he rushed on, "the cabinet members want to meet with you."

"That's fine," she continued in the same monotone.

"They want you here by tomorrow. Can you arrange for a flight?"

Her excuse dropped in her lap. She didn't have to pretend to have a headache, or sudden illness. Maybe when she arrived in New York, she'd just stay for a while.

"I'll be there."

"Excellent. I'll book a room for you at the Plaza. And Noelle, you're doing a wonderful thing."

She broke the connection without commenting further. Now to face the family.

"I hope you liked your rooms," Noelle was saying as she escorted them back to the limo.

"Everything is exquisite," Janice said enthusiastically.

Diane looked at Noelle from the corner of her eye and was painfully reminded of Roxanne, the woman who had lured her husband away from her and his family. She swallowed back the knot of remembrance. So what if the champagne gold pantsuit that Noelle wore so gracefully was a Halston original, or that the studs in her ears were real diamonds, she thought jealously. So what if she was gracious and thoughtful, she mused angrily, unable to find the flaws that she sought. She knew her type. And the quicker her brother was out of this fake world the better off he'd be.

Didn't the dark glasses clearly state that she was a product of her environment? What did she have to hide? Diane went on silently.

"Give my best to Trent," Noelle forced herself to say.

"Aren't you coming?" Janice asked.

Stephanie looked at Noelle quizzically and could have sworn she saw shadows of pain lurking in her brown eyes just before she slipped on her dark sunglasses.

"No. I can't. I have to go out of town—on business. I'm sure Trent will understand." She smiled. "Now that his family is here he doesn't need me hovering around."

Stephanie watched Noelle closely and listened to the very subtle tremor in her voice. She'd always been good at seeing beyond the surface and this woman was definitely hurting. She wondered why.

Noelle waved until the car was out of sight. Without looking back, she went directly to her office to make her flight arrangements to New York.

"You can't all go in at once," Dr. Holloway advised patiently. "Two visitors at a time and only for five minutes each."

There was a loud groan from the family and verbal protestations from Steph.

"We flew all night, have been terrified about my brother, and we only get five minutes! That's totally unfair."

Dr. Holloway gave her that doctorly look that he gave to all difficult family members. "We have to think about what's best for the patient. If he gets too tired, it will take longer for him to recover. You don't want that, do you?" His steady gaze included everyone.

"Hospitals have rules, Steph," Diane admonished in that know-it-all tone that Stephanie hated. "Just like there are laws that have to be followed. If not, there'd be total chaos." She gave her sister a self-satisfied look.

Stephanie cut Diane a sidelong glance and rolled her eyes. She was about two seconds from telling her ever-righteous sister just where to go. But refrained since they were in front of a stranger.

"I only want what's best for my brother," Stephanie assured the doctor.

"Very well. Two visitors. Five minutes."

They all nodded in agreement. Dr. Holloway continued down the hall.

"Steph you go first," Diane said. "I'll go with Mom." They both knew from experience that Diane was the only one who could control their mother's hysterics, especially when it came to Trent. The last thing that Trent needed now, was his mother falling apart.

"Come on Ma," Diane directed, taking her mother by the arm and moving her away from Trent's door. "Now you be strong," she cautioned in a no nonsense voice. "You don't want to upset Trent." She looked over her shoulder at her sister with an *I have everything under control look.*

Less than a minute after Stephanie had entered the room, Trent's struggling laughter could be heard. Steph always had that effect on him, Diane realized grudgingly.

* * *

"So that's *the* Mrs. Maxwell. Nice to have *friends* like that. She's pretty wonderful," Steph added with a conspiratorial wink. "A person could get used to living like that. She have any brothers?"

Trent winced when he chuckled. "Sorry Sis."

Stephanie pouted, then stepped closer. "You just get well, baby bro'. I'll find me a man on my own," she teased. She smiled down at Trent and her heart swelled. She loved her brother dearly and couldn't have loved him more if they had been joined by blood. It was like that with all three of them, even though Diane did get on her last nerve. Their adoptive parents had raised them to love each other unquestionably.

"Get some rest," she said kissing his cheek. "You're gonna need it," she added. "Ma and the wicked witch are next."

Trent tried not to laugh because it hurt too much.

"I'll be back tomorrow," Stephanie said. "I can't wait to get the full tour of Liaisons." Her face beamed. "No one back home is gonna believe me."

She bent down and kissed his cheek again. Her eyes softened. "I love you," she said in a near whisper.

"Same here."

"See you tomorrow."

Moments later Diane and his mother walked in. He could immediately see that his mother was struggling for control and that Diane had her under strict orders.

Janice hurried over to his bedside and gently embraced him. "Oh, my poor baby," she wailed. "What have you gone and done to yourself now?"

"I'll be okay, Ma," he said, trying to sound stronger than he felt.

Diane stepped closer. "I hope that you're planning on pursuing an investigation. I'm sure you can sue the company."

"I just want to get out of here, Di."

"Well you'll be coming home with us to recuperate."

"No. I'm staying at Liaisons."

"You need to be home with your family. This whole glitzy life out here is not you. And your friend Noelle is just like all the other rich and famous."

"You don't know her," Trent snapped back, feeling his temper rise. Diane could raise his blood pressure in a wink. "She's not like Roxanne." He mentioned her ex-husband's mistress.

Diane felt the implication of his words as if she'd been slapped with a cold towel. "Believe me, I know her type," she sniffed.

Trent didn't have the strength to argue.

"I want you to come home, too, sweetheart," his mother pleaded. "I'll be there to take care of you."

"Ma, I appreciate that, but Noelle has already made the same offer. It'll be easier on me if I don't have to travel for a while."

"She must be planning on getting you a nurse," Diane said, "because she's not going to be there."

Trent frowned. "What are you talking about?"

"When we were leaving today, she said to send her regards and that she was going out of town on business."

Trent felt a sinking sensation in the pit of his stomach. She wouldn't do that without calling. What could have happened?

"We'll see you tomorrow, Son." His mother kissed his forehead. Diane did the same.

Trent gave them a faltering smile as they left.

For several moments, Trent lay staring up at the ceiling. Diane must be wrong, he concluded. He knew how she felt about wealthy people. She was always barely able to hide her contempt for the work he did with Maxwell Enterprises.

Noelle wouldn't just leave without saying anything, he reaffirmed. Any minute now, she would walk through that door.

By late afternoon, she hadn't arrived. Nor had she called. The sinking sensation intensified.

He couldn't stand it any longer. Painfully, he inched his way toward the bedside phone. The normally simple task took agonizing minutes to accomplish. He was bathed in sweat.

Panting he dialed Liaisons.

Minutes later he was hanging up. Disbelief clouded his thinking. *Mrs. Maxwell is out of town for an indeterminate length of time,* he was informed. He'd tried to reach Gina, but she was unavailable.

She'd just left, without a word. He couldn't understand that.

He looked up and Nick walked through the door.

"Where's Noelle?" Trent demanded.

Nick stood next to the bed. He avoided looking into his eyes. Trent felt ice spread through his belly.

"She said to tell you that she's leaving on business." He halted. His gaze wavered.

"And?"

"And she hoped you'd be long gone when she returned."

CHAPTER 31

Noelle arrived in New York and checked into her hotel room at the Plaza.

She didn't notice the exquisite decor or the breathtaking New York skyline that was visible from her bedroom window. All she could think about was Richard's very candid characterization of Trent and what a fool she had been.

She sank down on the bed. Even after everything that had happened between her and Trent, she had allowed herself to be persuaded to believe that he had been sincere in his feelings for her. She had given him a second chance, despite her reservations. That was all part of the act, Richard had said.

She'd never admit to him that she too had been taken in by Trent's charm. It was too humiliating and too painful.

Mindlessly, she undressed and crawled beneath the covers, wishing that she could stay there, hidden away from the world forever.

Even in her dreams she found no refuge in sleep. With every toss, every turn, Trent was there, smiling, caressing, loving her, making her feel complete. Unwillingly she felt her body ignite with an undeniable longing.

And then the adoring eyes would change to jeering ones, taunting her, laughing at her. She struggled to get away, running down a dark road, but everywhere she turned, once-friendly faces changed to mocking ones—pointing laughing fingers at her.

At the end of the long road, Trent stood with open arms beckoning her to him. Weightlessly, she ran to him, with joy bubbling in her throat. He'd come to rescue her. Just as she reached him, the light of love in his eyes was extinguished, replaced with contempt.

Long fingers reached out for her. She screamed and came fully awake.

She sat up in bed, shivering, burning tears running down her cheeks. She hugged her knees to her chest, and let the pain-filled sobs envelop her.

Trent awakened the following morning with that same sinking feeling. Maybe it was all a dream, he thought, but he knew that it wasn't. He still could not imagine why Noelle would leave him.

Maybe her being at the hospital, sitting at his bedside had been an act. How many times had he heard how important it was for the coma victim to feel that there were people around who cared. It was crucial to their recovery.

He closed his eyes. Noelle was just that type of person. He could very well imagine that she would totally set aside her own feelings for someone else.

He'd been surprised even to find her at the hospital. The last time they'd seen each other he felt the power of her hatred.

Last night, before Nick left to return to New York, he'd said that he and Noelle had talked. He said he was sure she understood that he wasn't to blame. She seemed convinced. Even Nick couldn't understand the sudden change.

Maybe he'd just do like his folks had suggested and return with them to Philadelphia. It was becoming obvious, with each passing hour, that Noelle had closed the chapter on their lives. He would tell the doctor he wanted to leave immediately. The sooner he put some distance between himself and Noelle the better.

Miraculously, Noelle had been able to sound coherent as she stood before the cabinet of the United Nations.

Her confidence grew from her firm belief that she could make a difference. In clear, nonpolitical language, she reviewed the details of her reconstruction efforts in Sudan.

"You were magnificent," Ambassador Nkiru stated to Noelle over lunch. They were dining in one of the rooms reserved for cabinet members.

"I just wanted to emphasize how important this is." She took a forkful of her seafood platter. "You're sure they'll be able to keep my name out of it?"

"All that will be mentioned is that this is an endeavor by Maxwell Enterprises."

She looked down at her plate. Trent would get the credit and that was fine. Let him have it. She'd firmly outlined the reorganization process to the note holders and had guaranteed repayment of the loans. She was no longer in jeopardy of losing Liaisons. She no longer had the desire to care.

"How long will you be staying in New York?" Nkiru asked.

She smiled wanly. "I haven't been to New York in years. I think I'll just take my time and see the sights."

"I'm sure you'll find plenty to do." He pushed away from the table, wiping his mouth with the paper napkin. "I've got to be going. My plane leaves in an hour. Will you be able to get back to the hotel? I can get a car."

She held up her hand. "Please don't bother. I'll be fine. And I could use the exercise." She stood up and firmly shook his hand. "Have a safe trip."

"And you have a pleasant stay."

It was still early afternoon when Noelle stepped out of the United Nations. The warm spring air was filled with the sounds of birds, laughter and promise.

With no specific destination in mind, she strolled casually along the busy Manhattan streets—a sharp contrast to the lull of San Francisco.

She peeked into the elaborate store windows and pangs of melancholy rushed through her. She and Trent had done the very same thing in the Napa Valley. It seemed like a lifetime ago.

Everywhere that she looked, couples were holding hands, touching, hugging one another, whispering words of love. Spring was the time for love, she thought miserably.

She moved on and kept walking until she found herself at Twenty-eighth Street and Fourth Avenue.

The bold gold letters splashed across the crystal clear windowpane caught her attention. *Rhythms.* Curious, she came closer to read the posting in the window. It was a supper club with live jazz entertainment. It may be a bit early for dinner, she realized, but she could hear the soft beat of the music beckoning to her.

Her spirits lifted. When was the last time she was out alone, doing something spontaneous? She couldn't remember. She thought about it for a minute and decided to go in. The combination of aching feet and a budding appetite were the final motivators.

Once her eyes adjusted to the dimly lit interior she could see that the club was actually a converted brownstone.

The front of the club had a small dining room and bar as well as a working fireplace. The hard parquet floors were covered with bright African print area rugs. Large plants stood in the corners.

Since no one seemed to be rushing to seat her, she took a quick tour.

Upstairs were three large rooms, one for dancing and two for dining. Each of them had a small bandstand for entertainment. Several tables were occupied and the sound of Nancy Wilson's voice filtered through the hidden speakers.

Just as she was about to descend the stairs, she caught the sound of a very familiar voice in the midst of a conversation.

Nick turned almost at the same moment that she did.

Her brown eyes widened in shock. What was he doing here? The next to the last person she needed to see was a friend of Trent's—especially this friend.

She turned away and began to go downstairs, but not before Nick grabbed her arm.

"Wait a minute," he commanded.

She spun around, her eyes glaring in anger and humiliation.

"What are you doing here?" he demanded to know.

"I could ask you the same question," she snapped back through clenched teeth.

He walked down two steps and stood directly above her.

"This is my place," he said simply. "And quite frankly I don't know if I want you in here. Anyone who could do what you did to Trent isn't welcome here." His eyes hardened into narrow slits.

Noelle swallowed back her astonishment.

"Are you crazy?" Her voice rose and customers began to stare. "What *I've* done?" she asked incredulously. "He—he used me!" she cried. "He was going to do to me what he'd done to all the others. It all fits, and you were a part of it. You helped him with his lies."

"To all the others?" Nick's glare lost some of its steam. His utter disbelief momentarily derailed her anger. "Now you're talking crazy."

"Oh really." She tugged her arm away. "I had a chat with Senator Thomas. He told me everything."

Nick rolled his eyes up toward the ceiling. "Come on," he ordered. "I'm gonna talk and you're gonna listen." His unwavering tone didn't leave room for argument. He ushered her down the staircase.

He found an unoccupied table in the far corner on the ground floor. They had complete privacy.

Nick folded his large hands on the table. He lifted his eyes to look at Noelle.

"Let me get right to the point. Richard Thomas is a pig."

"Sure, tell me anything to cover for Trent." She turned her head away and folded her arms, stubbornly in front of her.

"I'm doing the talking, remember?" Nick said stonily.

She snapped her head around, her eyes challenging, but she did not speak.

Then in gentler tones, he continued. "A nasty rivalry has been going on between Trent and Richard for years. Richard was really head over heels in love with this woman in Texas when we were stationed there. But she only had eyes for Trent. Richard also wanted Jordan to put out large amounts of money to finance his reelection bid. Trent convinced Jordan that it wasn't a wise move because of Richard's negative third-world views. Jordan agreed. And . . ." Nick added, looking at Noelle hard, "rumor had it that Richard had his eyes on you, but was too afraid that Jordan would cut him off at the knees if he ever tried anything."

Noelle leaned forward in her seat and covered her face with her hand. "He told me all of that to get back at Trent," she said in a hollow voice.

Nick nodded. "Richard has a very long memory, but a very short attention span. His relationships never last."

"I just walked out on him," she said looking across the table at Nick. "I never gave Trent a chance. I was so anxious to believe the worst. How can I keep doing this to him?"

"You can't."

She caught his pointed look.

"I've got to get back and settle things once and for all." She stood up. "I wouldn't blame him if he wanted nothing to do with me."

"He's not that kind of guy." The warmth in his smile echoed in his voice. "If you give him half a chance, I bet he could prove it to you."

Noelle's eyes filled with gratitude. "How many times am I going to have to thank you?"

"As often as necessary," he grinned.

When they reached the exit, he pulled out a business card from the pocket of his jacket and handed it to her.

"The next time you're in New York, look me up. My home number is on the back."

She reached up on tiptoe and kissed his cheek. "I certainly will."

Noelle took a cab back to the Plaza. In no time at all, she'd packed her bags and had contacted the airport. There was one more flight out to LAX Airport. She would have to be on standby, but she didn't care.

She arrived in Los Angeles at 7:00 P.M and took a cab straight to Memorial Hospital, only to be informed that Trent had signed himself out less than eight hours earlier. She couldn't speak with Dr. Holloway, he was in surgery.

All she could do now was return to Liaisons and hope that he'd gone there.

An hour later she walked through the doorway of her villa. Gina was at the front desk.

"Mrs.—I mean, Noelle, we didn't expect you back so soon."

Noelle's heart raced. "Are the Dixons still here?" she asked in a rush.

"No. They checked out early this afternoon."

She dreaded the answer to her next question. "Did Trent go with them?"

"His mother said they were picking him up from the hospital on their way to the airport."

Noelle felt all of her hope slowly seep out of her like a leaky tire.

"Thank you, Gina." She turned away. There was nothing else she could do. At least for now. What she needed was some rest. The rapid change in time zones was catching up to her with a vengeance.

She blinked her eyes hard to clear them. Her legs began to feel like they were weighted down with cement. The short walk to the elevator was like traveling a desert mile.

She pressed the UP button, and then took a peek in the lounge. While she waited, Richard came out.

Rage bloomed with frightening potency within her. The strength of it gave her renewed vitality.

Richard caught sight of her and came in her direction, his smile broad and inviting.

Noelle stood motionless, her ability to camouflage her innermost feelings swung into full gear. She smiled sweetly.

"Noelle, I've been looking for you. I'd hoped that I could persuade you to join me for a—late dinner."

"Richard," she said calmly, the smile never leaving her face, "the sight of you turns my stomach." He blinked back his shock. "If you want a meal, or anything else for that matter, I suggest, strongly, that you get it somewhere else. The last place I ever want to set eyes on you again," she continued in that same sweet voice, "is in my villa! Save your maligning verbiage for the Senate floor."

His mouth dropped open and he took a faltering step back as though struck.

She turned triumphantly on her heels and stepped into the elevator feeling utterly wonderful.

When she reached her room she knew it was too late to call Nick in New York.

She dug in her purse and pulled out his business card and placed it on her nightstand. She'd call him first thing in the morning.

Diane had decided to take a week off and help her mother care for Trent. She couldn't be happier to have her brother home again. She just wished he would stop brooding. She knew it was about Noelle, but he was better off without her. He just didn't know it yet. She had the perfect woman for him, a friend of hers who worked at the law firm. As soon as he was better, she'd set something up.

* * *

Trent lay in his old room, listening to the familiar sounds of his childhood home.

He thought of Noelle. He had hoped that they would finally have a life together. But it was painfully obvious that she hadn't forgiven him.

He had no one to blame but himself. He'd lied to her, over and again. He deserved the sentence that had been meted out to him. But that would never stop him from loving her. With every breath he took, he thought of her. The pain was more powerful than the physical injuries he'd sustained. Those injuries would heal, but the loss of Noelle would always leave a dull ache in his spirit.

He looked toward the phone and thought of calling her. Maybe if he had the chance to explain, he could somehow make her understand that he never set out to hurt her.

He turned his head away. There was no point, he decided. She'd made her decision. He'd have to respect that.

He forced his eyes to close and instantly visions of Noelle blossomed with life.

Noelle awakened with the sun. It was nearly 9:00 A.M. in New York. She reached for the card on the table and dialed Nick's home number. A sleepy female voice answered, then gave the phone to Nick.

"I'm sorry to call so early, Nick, but Trent signed himself out of the hospital. I'm sure he's in Philadelphia."

Nick grunted. "Hold on."

Several moments later he was back on the line. "This is the number to his mother's house."

She quickly copied down the number. "Thanks again."

"You're batting a thousand," he teased. "Good luck," he added seriously.

She depressed the button and quickly dialed the number. Her pulse pounded in her ears. She felt warm. Please be there, she silently prayed.

The phone rang four times on the other end before it was answered.

"Hello?"

"Mrs. Dixon?"

"Yes."

"Good morning. This is Noelle Maxwell. I'm trying to reach Trent."

Janice Dixon flinched. She remembered all of the things that Diane had said to her about this woman. Maybe Diane was right. She'd already seen how hurt Trent was now. She wanted the best for her son. She cleared her throat.

"I'm sorry, Mrs. Maxwell he—doesn't want to speak with you. And I think it would be best if you didn't call back. But thank you again for your hospitality." She quickly hung up, and for an instant she wondered if she'd done the right thing.

Noelle swore that her heart stopped beating.

CHAPTER 32

For the next three weeks, Noelle functioned as if she were in a dream. She couldn't remember ever feeling so empty inside.

Even the news that her proposal had been accepted didn't revive her crushed spirits. She simply called Mr. Takaka in Hong Kong and explained that Trent was temporarily unable to run the operations and he would have to begin the reorganization of Maxwell Enterprises. She seemed to have lost interest in everything.

She continued to meet and greet the continual flow of guests. She attended all of the necessary meetings, and took a trip to Washington to meet with the Secretary of State to finalize the plans and keep a watchful eye on her business. But her heart was not in it.

Sitting alone in her room one evening, her phone rang. She had long since stopped hoping that the caller would be Trent.

She answered the call in the same monotone that had become a part of her.

"Hello?"

"Mrs. Maxwell?"

"Yes. Who is this?"

"Mrs. Maxwell, this is Stephanie Dixon, Trent's sister.

Her stomach lurched and she sat straight up.

"Yes, Stephanie, is something wrong? Has something happened to Trent?"

"Something's wrong all right, and that something is my big-mouth sister, and gullible mother."

Stephanie went on to explain that her mother had blurted out to her the conversation that she had with Noelle and how she wasn't sure that she'd done the right thing by not letting her speak with Trent. Stephanie was livid.

"Trent never knew that you called. And he's too stubborn to contact you. I don't know what went on between the two of you," she continued, "but I can't stand for my brother to be hurting like this. I know he loves you. He has that same look in his eyes that you did. And the only time he seems to brighten at all is when I mention your name."

Noelle choked back a sob of joy.

"He still can't get around very well. But he's using crutches. So do you think you can come out here?"

Ecstasy bubbled in her voice. "I can be there tomorrow," Noelle gushed.

"If you can tell me what time your flight is arriving, I'll meet you at the airport."

"That would be wonderful."

"Take my work number and call me as soon as you can."

"I will. Thank you, Stephanie. Thank you so much."

"Anything for my brother," she said. "You're just the medicine he needs."

Noelle could barely sleep. Her thoughts scrambled around in circles. Would her prayers finally be answered? It was almost more than she could stand.

She was so anxious to see him, she arrived at the airport more than an hour early. The added wait only heightened her anxiety.

Suppose Stephanie was wrong, she worried on the five-hour flight. Suppose Trent didn't want to see her after all this time. What would she do?

By the time the plane landed she was a nervous wreck. Luckily, as soon as she walked through the arrival gates, she spotted Stephanie waving at her.

"I didn't tell him you were coming," Stephanie said as she drove the red Acura Legend skillfully through the Philadelphia traffic. "The surprise will do him good."

"What if he refuses to see me?"

Stephanie turned briefly and looked at Noelle's troubled expression. "He wants to see you," she said with assurance. "Believe me. He's just too proud to admit it." She patted Noelle's hand. "Everything is going to be fine."

Soon they pulled up in front of a small frame house. The front lawn was neatly manicured and the house itself gave off a feeling of serenity.

So this is where Trent grew up, she thought, imagining him as a boy running through the yard.

"Here we are," Stephanie announced. She hopped out and opened the door for Noelle, who suddenly seemed frozen to her seat.

"Don't look so panicked," she said. "He won't bite your head off. Come on," she coaxed with a smile.

Noelle stood nervously at the front door, while Stephanie dug in her bag for her keys. "My mother is out," she informed Noelle. "And thank heavens, Diane is back at work. So you two will have the house to yourselves."

She opened the door and they stepped inside.

Noelle was pleasantly surprised at the size of the house. It was much larger than she'd envisioned.

The entry foyer led to the living room where Stephanie instructed her to wait.

"He's probably in the backyard," she said. "Wait here. I'll be right back."

Noelle paced like a caged tigress, barely taking in her surroundings. What did catch her eye was the row of photographs that graced the mantel.

There were several pictures of Steph and Diane at various stages in their lives. But the ones she really looked at were the pictures of Trent.

There was one of him in his Little League uniform—photos of his graduation from high school and college—and a picture of him in his air-force uniform, his chest full of medals.

She turned, suddenly, her heart thundering when she heard voices approaching.

"I told you I didn't want to see anyone, Steph," Trent growled.

"Well at least try to be nice."

"Who is it anyway?"

Stephanie didn't have to answer as she left him at the door and quietly slipped away.

His large, muscular body framed the doorway, and Noelle's heart stood still. He was more gorgeous than ever she realized with a pang. And the slight scar over his right eyebrow gave him an even more devastating look.

When he saw Noelle standing there in a sunshine yellow dress, he was certain that he was imagining things. His head pounded. He wanted to move toward the apparition but his feet seemed to be glued to the ground.

"Noelle?"

The sound of her name coming from his lips filled her with an exquisite joy.

She took one cautious step forward, another and then another, until she was only inches away.

His crutches clattered to the floor as he reached out and crushed her against his body. She was real!

"Noelle," he said over and again. His lips swept down on hers, burning against her, filling her with unimaginable sweetness.

She moaned helplessly against his mouth, touching him, stroking him, relishing in the feel of him against her.

His honey sweet tongue dove into her mouth, searching wildly for all that he'd thought he lost. His fingers raked through her hair, kneaded her spine, pulled her ever closer to his hardened body.

She arched her neck as his mouth trailed hungrily down the open collar of her dress. She cried out his name when his scalding lips touched the half moons of her breasts.

Languidly he raised his head and stared deeply into her tear-filled eyes. "I never thought I'd see you again," he said in a ragged whisper. He stroked her cheek as if still not believing that she was real.

"So many things have gone wrong between us, Trent," she said in a shaky voice. "I want to make it right."

"I've missed you so much Noelle," he said, taking a reluctant step back. "I thought I'd go out of my mind because I believed you'd walked out on me."

"I was a fool to let anything or anyone come between how I feel about you."

"And how *do* you feel about me?" he asked, a soft smile teasing the corners of his mouth.

"I love you madly."

He exhaled deeply. "Let's go outside and talk," he said. "There's so much I have to tell you. And if we stay in here," he added his eyes raking over her, "there's no telling what may happen. I'd hate for Mom to walk in on us in a compromising position." He grinned mischievously.

She tossed her head back and laughed out loud, a deep and soul-stirring laugh that lifted her spirits to the heavens.

Under the warm afternoon sunshine, Trent, in measured tones, explained to Noelle what had happened on the day that changed their lives.

"Jordan was very ill, Noelle," he began slowly. He turned his head and looked at her. "He was dying of cancer."

Noelle's eyes registered shock but she didn't speak.

"He didn't want you to know. He knew that if he told you, you would stick by him out of loyalty. He couldn't bear having you watch him deteriorate. He said it wasn't fair to you after everything that you'd been through with him.

"I never understood what he meant by that until you told me about your marriage." He took a deep breath. "He convinced me that the only way out was to orchestrate his death." He paused. "I did rig the plane."

Her heart jumped.

"But that's not what caused the crash. We were hit by lightning just like the reports said. That's what actually caused the malfunction."

Noelle covered her mouth with her hands.

"In his own way, Jordan was doing what he thought was best for you, Noelle. He never wanted me to run Maxwell Enterprises forever. It was for you. He wanted to show you and the world that you were capable of handling it. You'd never have to feel inferior to anyone again. He wanted you to have Maxwell Enterprises. But he knew you'd never take it willingly, so he fixed that too."

"The bank loans, using Liaisons as collateral," she said in a faraway voice.

Trent nodded.

"I was to give you one year to get the villa off the ground and out of your system. When everything fell apart you'd have no other choice but to take the reins if you wanted to save the villa. He knew that would be your motivation. The only thing he didn't bargain for was that Liaisons would be so successful in such a short period of time."

"You knew how important the villa was to me," she said softly. "You wanted to make sure that I didn't lose it."

He nodded.

"And you believed that if I knew who you were from the beginning I would have found another way out of Jordan's plans for me."

"That's part of it," he admitted. "But from the first time that I saw you, I wanted you." His eyes held hers. "I knew how much you hated me. If you realized who I was, I wouldn't have gotten within a mile of you.

"I made a promise to Jordan, and I'm a man of my word, Noelle. I idolized Jordan." His eyes drifted off toward the horizon as distant memories rushed past. "He was more than just my employer, he was my friend. He was like a father to me, and I think he knew that's what I needed. And like a dutiful son I pledged my allegiance to him.

"Even though I stood the risk of losing you, I couldn't tell you." He hung his head, then looked up. "And then I fell in love with you and I couldn't back out. I wanted you more than life itself and the thought that you would turn away from me because of who I was—it terrified me."

She reached out and touched his face. Tears of happiness and regret slid freely down her cheeks.

"You'll never have to worry about losing me. I almost let my misplaced hatred destroy me, destroy us. Nothing can ever come between us again." Thoughts of Tempest and Braxton swirled before her. They too had come perilously close to losing each other because of doubts and pride. But their love had bound them irrevocably together as Trent's love and hers would do.

He brushed the tears from her face. "Jordan truly loved you in his own way, Noelle."

"I see that now," she said sadly. "Maybe by some strange twist of fate, this was all meant to be." She smiled wistfully. "If I know Jordan, he probably had this whole thing planned." She could easily imagine that Jordan would have dropped Trent in her lap, somehow, mystically knowing the outcome.

She looked off toward the drifting clouds and remembered Jordan's words in his letter. *Put your trust in Trent.* And she knew that she would.

EPILOGUE

The wedding of Noelle St. James-Maxwell to Trenton Mark Dixon hit every reputable newspaper and tabloid in California.

Her gown was hand-sewn and imported from Paris and copied in every bridal shop across the state. All of the major networks carried coverage of the elaborate wedding held on the great lawn of Liaisons.

Tempest walked regally as her matron of honor and Nick stood proud as Trent's best man. Even Ambassador Nkiru attended and gave his blessing to Gina and Joseph.

All of Trent's family attended and even Diane had to admit that her brother was really happy.

Noelle's aunt Chantal sat in a place of honor and cried bittersweet tears at the extraordinary beauty of her niece.

Every celebrity from sports to the big screen was in attendance. It was truly a fairy-tale wedding come true.

Hundreds of miles away, Noelle and Trent spent their honeymoon night under a blanket of stars on a secluded strip of the Riviera. The warm breeze blowing off the ocean gently caressed their beach-clad bodies.

Noelle snuggled closer to her husband. "Can it always be this way?" she asked softly, stroking the warm skin of his bare chest.

Trent kissed the top of her head. "For as long as we make it," he answered.

Gently, he rolled on top of her. His dark eyes swept lovingly over her face. "I've searched for you all of my life, Noelle. And with every breath I take I promise to spend the rest of my days making your every wish come true."

His mouth slowly descended onto hers, sending spirals of desire shooting through her. She held onto her husband, wrapping him in the warmth of her love.π

They had traveled a long and painful road to find each other, but their triumph was well worth the struggle that they had endured. They no longer had to be satisfied with stolen moments of happiness. They had forever.

As Trent gently eased her suit from her body and joined her, forever, with him, she knew, unquestionably, that she had found the love that she had been seeking. The ghosts of her past were finally at rest. And silently she thanked Jordan for sending real love to her—at last.

Scandalous

To my mom and dad . . . without you where would I be?

To my three beautiful children, Nichole, Dawne and Matthew, who teach me every day what hard work and true love are all about.

CHAPTER 1

Tiny beads of moisture clung to Vaughn's nude body as though unwilling to relinquish the hold of her satiny ebony skin. She stepped out of the shower and padded into her bedroom, allowing the warm spring breeze to finish the work her towel had missed.

Sitting on the edge of her bed, she took an almost sensual pleasure in languidly smoothing scented body oil over her damp skin. It was one of the few luxuries she allowed herself. With her grueling schedule as assemblywoman for the State of Virginia, Vaughn Hamilton found that leisure time was a rare commodity.

Completing the ritual, she stood in front of the full-length mirror, critically assessing her reflection. As a young girl, she'd always been overly sensitive about her dark complexion. Her father, on the other hand, had always called her his "ebony princess." But back in the old days, ebony was not the thing to be. And the old chant "the blacker the berry, the sweeter the juice" didn't ease the pain from the taunts she'd received as a child. She'd grown up longing for the fair skin and long, silky hair preferred by society. As a result, she'd tried to overcompensate in every other area of her life by being the very best at everything she did, as though that would somehow make people overlook how dark she was. Fortunately, with maturity, she'd grown to be proud of her ebony coloring and had long ago dismissed the notion that to be light was right.

She angled her chin toward the mirror—her profile side—a flicker of a smile tugging at her full lips, revealing deep dimples. All in all, hers was a pleasing face, she mused, and her long, shapely body only added to the total picture. She strove hard to keep it in top shape, from the food she put in it, to the clothes she put on it, to the rigorous exercise regimen she adhered to devoutly. As a result, her small, rounded breasts were high and firm to the touch. Her narrow waist was the envy of her few close friends. Her rounded hips and tight thighs tapered down to striking "showgirl legs," as her mother would call them.

She took a long look at her body. But then a shadow passed across her deep brown eyes, darkening them to an almost inky black. Her long, slender fingers lovingly, almost reverently, stroked the blade-thin faint scar. She turned away from the reflection as the mists of her past swept over her. It was always there—mocking her, reminding her.

How often had her mother tried to persuade her to have it removed by plastic surgery? "No one need ever know, darling," her mother, Sheila, had said. Vaughn exhaled a deep breath. *She* needed to know. *She* needed to be reminded—every day of her life.

But for now she'd push those thoughts behind her, she decided with finality. She jutted her chin forward. Tonight she had to be focused, refreshed, and full of energy. Tonight was the beginning of a new direction in her political career. She couldn't let anything interfere with that, especially ghosts from the past. This was a night she'd dreamed of for years. A shimmer of doubt creased her brow. Hadn't she? Or was it her father's dream? Momentarily she squeezed her eyes shut. At some point her father's, Judge Elliott Hamilton, great aspirations for her had become her own, driving her relentlessly—to the exclusion of everything and everyone else. Regardless, she was a politician and she loved the job.

"It *is* my dream," she said aloud, "and I'm going to capture it." If there was ever any doubt, it was too late now. There would be over two hundred guests awaiting her arrival at her parents' estate in Norfolk. There was no turning back.

Meticulously, Vaughn continued preparing for the evening ahead. Every notable person in Virginia's political circles as well as many renowned business people would be in attendance. *Her father's friends.* Although she'd made a name for herself as Virginia's assemblywoman, she couldn't honestly say she'd made an array of friends in those circles. At least, not the kind who could push her over the election hurdle. That was her choice. She had very firm views that she refused to compromise. As a result, there were many of her male counterparts who'd be more than happy to see the "iron maiden" fall on her opinionated behind. Especially Paul Lawrence, her subconscious voice whispered. It's over, she reminded herself. He'd gotten what he'd wanted from her, and it was over. She inhaled a shuddering breath as visions of their brief but tumultuous relationship rushed through her.

But as her bid for Congress loomed large, her father had insisted she surround herself with these people of influence. He had arranged for this first of many fundraisers. As much as she disliked the elbow-rubbing and gratuitous smiles, she knew that it was just one of the steps necessary to achieve her goals.

Driving the two hours to her parents' home, she felt the beat of her heart quicken as the Jaguar brought her closer to her destination. Her hands unconsciously gripped the wheel. She could almost hear her mother's words of disappointment when she arrived, once again, without an escort. That, too, was her choice. The life she'd chosen did not allow room for a relationship. Not now. Or maybe she just hadn't met a man willing enough or strong enough to withstand the pressures of the life she led. At least, that's what she told others. But the reality was, a husband and a family were not in the cards for her. That choice had been snatched away from her long ago. And sometime during the countless lonely, sleepless nights, she'd resigned herself to that fact.

Putting her trepidations aside, Vaughn eased the Jaguar into the private garage behind her parents' hundred-plus acres of property.

Her father had purchased the palatial estate on the anniversary of his tenth year on the Superior Court bench. There, Vaughn had always felt like a fish out of water, alone and confused in the countless rooms and winding hallways. It was no wonder that when she was gratefully out on her own, she'd chosen a simple two-bedroom townhouse in the heart of Richmond, surrounded by houses and plenty of neighbors.

Even now, at thirty-six, she still had an overwhelming sense of being swallowed whole each time she walked through these ornate doors.

Fortifying herself with a deep breath, Vaughn walked determinedly toward the house. As she approached, she could hear the faint strains of a live band. Daddy had spared no expense, she thought, with a slow shake of her head. She bypassed the front entrance and went around to the back door, which opened onto an enormous kitchen.

The crowded room was bustling with activity and overflowing with mouthwatering aromas. At least a dozen waiters and waitresses, and the cooks and the chef, were jockeying for position.

In the midst of it all stood her mother, directing traffic and giving orders in her distinctive southern modulation. Sheila inspected a tray of hors d'oeuvre a tiny Asian waitress carried, then nodded her approval. Sheila looked up and her chestnut brown eyes rested lovingly on her daughter.

"Vaughn, sugar." She crossed the space with outstretched arms and enfolded Vaughn in a tight embrace. Sheila whispered in her ear, "It's not proper for a lady to make her entrance from the back door." Sheila felt Vaughn's body tighten as Vaughn tried to contain a chuckle. Sheila pulled her head back to look into Vaughn's gleaming eyes. She pursed her lips in displeasure at her daughter's faux pas. But Vaughn's humor was contagious, and Sheila's lips trembled at the edges as she struggled to keep from smiling. She kissed Vaughn's cheeks and slipped her arm around her daughter's tiny waist. "Listen baby," she added in a stage whisper, sounding more like the girl who'd grown up in rural Georgia than the woman who now played hostess to political dignitaries. "Our days of entering from the kitchen are long over, and don't you forget it. Anybody see you doin' some mess like that gonna set us back fifty years!"

Instantly, both women broke out into deep, soul-stirring laughter, the kind that reminded Vaughn of the way she and her mother had often laughed together before . . . everything had changed. Exiting the kitchen, Sheila peered over Vaughn's shoulder. "You came alone?" The question, which was more of a commentary, made Vaughn cringe. Her smile slowly dissolved.

"Yes, Mama. I came alone," Vaughn conceded on a sigh.

Sheila's perfectly made-up caramel-toned face twisted in a combination of annoyance and disappointment. "Truly, child, I just don't understand you. You're beautiful, important, intelligent . . ."

"M-other, please, not tonight," Vaughn snapped, in a low, sharp voice. Briefly she shut her eyes. Then, on a softer note, she added, "Please, Mama. I really have enough on my mind."

"Well, never mind," Sheila said, with a toss of her expertly coiffed auburn head, her diamond stud earrings twinkling in the light. "There'll be plenty of eligible men here tonight. You can believe that." Her brows lifted in emphasis. Sheila took her daughter's hand and guided her out of the kitchen. "Hopefully, one of them will meet the insurmountable standards you've set for yourself." And fill the emptiness that shadows that wonderful heart of yours, she added silently.

Vaughn dutifully followed her mother into the main area of the house. Momentarily, Vaughn's breath caught. The huge hall, which could easily hold a hundred people, had been transformed into a glittering ballroom.

The crystal chandelier glowed brilliantly with soft white light. The antique tables that braced the entry arch to the dining hall overflowed with fresh flowers. The black and white marble floors were polished to an "I-can-see-myself" gloss.

Beyond, in the dining hall, small, circular tables covered in pale rose linen cloths were topped with single tapers that lent the room an iridescent glow. On one side of the room, long tables were covered with exotic fruits, huge bowls of fresh salads, and cold seafood. On the other side a bar had been set up, complete with two *fine* bartenders. Maybe this single thing ain't all it's cracked up to be, Vaughn thought wickedly.

"Mama, everything is beautiful," Vaughn enthused.

Sheila beamed with pride. "I'm glad you like it. Nothing is too good for you, sweetheart." She gave her another quick peck on the cheek.

"Make yourself comfortable. I'm going to find your father. The guests have already begun to arrive. And do mingle," she ordered, over her shoulder.

Before Vaughn could respond, her mother was off in a whirl of sequins and diamonds. With no other choice, Vaughn wandered over to the bar and requested a glass of white wine, the only drink she could pretend to tolerate.

With her wineglass in hand, she strolled over to the terrace. The doors were wide open, allowing the fragrant scent of cherry blossoms to waft through the night air. She inhaled deeply as snatches of conversation drifted to her ears. Her pulse raced. She turned toward the voices and her heart slammed painfully against her chest. There, not ten feet away, involved in what appeared to be an intimate conversation, were Paul Lawrence and a woman who seemed to hang onto his every word. Vaughn's hand trembled and she nearly spilled her wine.

How long had it been since she'd seen him? Not long enough. She should have known he'd be here tonight. She couldn't let the sight of him rattle her. Just because their relationship was over didn't mean he'd drop off the face of the earth, as she'd prayed he would. There was no way Paul would miss the opportunity to rub elbows with the politicos who'd put him into the district attorney's office . . . even if it meant they'd have to face each other again. Vaughn stood as still as stone, the old fury rising in her like molten lava.

"I hope that's champagne you're drinking."

Vaughn's tense expression was transformed into one of serenity, her outrage slipping off like discarded clothing. Slowly she turned toward the sound of the familiar voice, an easy smile of welcome deepening the dimples in her cheeks.

"Daddy."

Elliott Hamilton embraced his daughter in a tight hug. But her attention was swiftly diverted to the figure that stood behind his broad frame. It took all the social training, she'd endured over the years for her to keep from staring.

Elliott released his daughter and stepped to her left, possessively slipping his arm around her waist. The movement steadied her and gave her a perfect full-figured view. Her mouth was suddenly dry, Paul all but forgotten.

"Justin, I'd like you to meet my daughter, the next congresswoman from Virginia. Vaughn, this is Justin Montgomery."

It seemed as though everything happened in slow motion. First, there was that smile of his, which made his dark eyes sparkle and crinkle at the edges. Then, the strong arm that reached out, his large hand open and welcoming, waiting to envelop hers.

When Vaughn mindlessly slipped her hand into his, her brain seemed to short-circuit. A rush of electric energy raced through her arm, exploding in a wave of heat that radiated throughout her body.

"It's a pleasure, Ms. Hamilton," he was saying, in a voice that vaguely reminded her of the ocean, deep and soothing.

The sudden explosion of heat that erupted in Justin's gut stunned him with its intensity. He felt himself being helplessly pulled into the depths of her brown eyes. He'd seen her before. Countless times—glimpses in restaurants and at public meetings, and in newspaper photos and television ads. But he'd never had the opportunity until now to meet her face to face. She had a natural charisma that was impossible to resist. Before tonight, she'd been but an image that he'd admired. The real thing was an entirely different story, one that left the usually unflappable Justin Montgomery totally off center.

Vaughn found her voice and quickly recovered her manners.

"Pleased to meet you, Mr. Montgomery." The name struck a familiar chord in her brain, but she couldn't seem to get her thoughts to focus with him staring at her as if he could peer beyond her facade of calm.

The corner of his full mouth, traced by a fine mustache, inched upward in a grin. "I've heard a lot of good things about you, Ms. Hamilton."

"I'm sure my father's been exaggerating again." She gave her father a feigned glance of reprimand.

Elliott Hamilton held up his palms in defense. "Honestly, sweetheart, I wish I could take the credit." He smiled benevolently. "But since Mr. Montgomery just arrived, I haven't had a chance to launch into my repertoire of accolades."

Vaughn's eyebrow arched in question. Her gaze swung back to Justin.

He shrugged nonchalantly, his dark eyes flickering over her. "Word gets around."

They both realized then that they still held hands and self-consciously released their hold.

Elliott gently patted Justin's back. "If you'll excuse us, Justin, Senator Willis and his wife have arrived. And my wife is waving to me frantically."

Vaughn peeked over the heads of the incoming guests and caught a glimpse of the stately Senator Willis. Her stomach clenched and a cold rush of unforgotten hurt suddenly overwhelmed her with poignant memories. A wistful smile of reminiscence lifted her mouth as she saw Brian's young face in his father's.

"Vaughn." The intonation of her name snapped her out of her reverie.

"Nice to meet you, Mr. Montgomery," she said with a brilliant smile. "I hope you enjoy the party. Excuse me . . ." She turned to leave, following closely behind her father's footsteps, when that voice reached out and caught her in mid-stride.

"Justin," he said, with that smile that could make a woman do the kinds of things she'd only fantasized about.

Glancing at him over her shoulder, she smiled in acknowledgment, then quickly turned away to begin the ritual of smiling, greeting, and playing the role to the line of guests waiting to meet her.

Justin kept a subtle eye on the guest of honor for the early part of the evening—over the rim of his champagne glass, throughout the six-course meal, from a corner shaded by a blooming potted tree, and from the center of the dance floor, where he glided effortlessly with an array of faceless beauties.

Her every movement was fluid and almost choreographed in its perfection, Justin thought. Her shimmering spaghetti-strap black gown dotted with countless black sequins and tiny rhinestones, fit that lithe body like a glove. Damn! Every time he looked at her, his thoughts ran off in dangerous directions and his body threatened to let everyone know exactly what was on his mind.

He continued to watch Vaughn closely, waiting for his opportunity to approach her, when he saw District Attorney Paul Lawrence go up to her, accompanied by a woman who hung onto his arm. Justin had paid such close attention to Vaughn for the better part of the evening that he instantly sensed her tension upon the arrival of Paul Lawrence. He waited for the flash of dimples, but the smile never came, and Justin cautiously waited with a mixture of curiosity and concern.

"Vaughn, it's good to see you again," Paul greeted her, showing her his famous campaign smile.

"Paul. It's been awhile," Vaughn replied in a monotone.

"This is Victoria Fleming. Vikki, Vaughn Hamilton, our guest of honor."

Victoria stuck out her pale porcelain hand and smiled effusively, her shimmering red hair glistening in the light. "This is a wonderful party," Vikki said, apparently oblivious to the tension that sparked like electricity between Paul and Vaughn. "I wish you the best of luck with your campaign."

"Thank you. I appreciate that."

Paul tightened his hold on Victoria's waist. "Vaughn doesn't need luck. She has a judge for a father," Paul taunted, the smile never leaving his face.

Vaughn felt as if she'd been slapped, but she didn't miss a beat. "You would know," she tossed back coolly.

Paul's hazel eyes darkened and his honey-toned skin flushed. "If there's anything my office can do," Paul said, "do give me a call. You know I'd be happy to help in any way that I can."

"I'm sure. Nice to meet you, Vikki." She inclined her head to Paul, turned, and walked away, her fury barely contained as she headed for the terrace, her heels beating a vicious rhythm against the marble floor.

She gripped the rail of the balcony with such force, her fingertips began to burn from the pressure.

"Can I refresh that drink, Ms. Hamilton?"

Vaughn turned with a start, but all traces of her distress were masked, by her public face. She stared into the searching brown eyes. Her stomach fluttered. "Mr. Hamilton."

"Justin," he corrected.

She cleared her throat and looked down at her half empty glass. "No, thank you . . . Justin. I'm not really a drinker."

"I know," he grinned. "You've been nursing that for hours."

Vaughn felt a rush of embarrassment sweep through her, but it was quickly replaced with a sense of warning. "You're very observant," she replied pointedly.

Justin stepped closer and leaned his hip against the rail. The soft, sensual scent of her floated to him, momentarily clouding his thoughts. His eyes settled on her upturned face and he realized that he'd never before seen a woman with such flawless ebony skin. It seemed to radiate with a vitality that was magnified by sculpted cheekbones and large, luminous brown eyes that must surely peer into one's soul. And that mouth! What would those luscious lips feel like, pressed against his?

"Is something wrong?" she asked, beginning to feel as if she were being disrobed.

"That was my next question to you," he said, recovering smoothly.

Vaughn tilted her head in question. "I beg your pardon?"

Justin angled his chin in the direction of Paul and his date. "Mr. Lawrence seemed to have rubbed you the wrong way," he stated casually.

Vaughn turned away to look out onto the expansive lawn below. "Have you spent your entire evening watching me?" she asked, both flattered and defensive.

"Pretty much," Justin said, a hint of amusement rippling through his deep voice.

Vaughn turned to look at him and saw the beginnings of a smile tug at the corners of his lips.

"It seems I'm learning an awful lot about you very quickly . . . Justin. You're observant and blunt. Is there anything else I should know?"

"There's plenty." He stepped a bit closer and her pulse raced. "Unfortunately, it would take a lot longer than one night to reveal it all."

Her heart beat so fast she was afraid she'd stop breathing altogether. Why did he have to look at her like that—as though he were truly interested in her. She had yet to meet a man who didn't want her because of her power and political influence. Paul was a perfect example of that. She was sure that this Justin Montgomery was no different. Her defenses kicked in. She was sure he had an agenda, and she wasn't going to be on his itinerary of things to do.

Vaughn took a deep, steadying breath and exhaled. "Well, Justin, that's a great line. However, I'm not interested."

"Hmmm, very defensive," he said, stifling a chuckle.

Her dark eyes flashed until she caught the gleam of amusement in his. She suddenly felt totally ridiculous for acting like a shrew.

"I'm sorry," she said finally. She looked around, her dark eyes sweeping across the throng of guests who had come to contribute to her nomination campaign. "I don't really like fundraisers," she admitted on a long sigh.

"Who would?" he agreed gently. "Who would *like* pretending to adore a bunch of stuffed shirts."

She smiled. "I'm glad you understand," she replied softly, surprising herself at her candor. He was a perfect stranger.

Justin turned and braced his hip against the balcony railing. Vaughn stood with her back to it. Inches separated them.

"Why are you involved, then," he asked, "in politics? If you don't like . . . all this?"

Vaughn sighed wistfully. "Maybe one day I'll tell you all about it." She took a sip of the warm wine.

Why did I say that? she wondered.

Justin turned sideways and looked down at her. "I hope that's a platform promise, Ms. Hamilton, because I intend to hold you to it."

She gazed up at him and saw the warm sincerity in his eyes and let the caress of his voice wash over her.

She swallowed hard, and their eyes held for what seemed an eternity. She didn't realize that he'd taken the glass from her hand, and she couldn't find her voice to either accept or decline when he swept her onto the dance floor.

The band was playing a slow, bluesy Nancy Wilson song, and Vaughn felt her tense body slowly begin to relax in the comforting embrace of Justin's arms. Their bodies seemed to fit together like puzzle pieces, Vaughn realized with alarm.

They danced in silence through three numbers before Justin spoke. "Actually," he said, speaking into the silky texture of her upswept hair, "you'd make an excellent politician."

Vaughn arched her neck to look quizzically up at him. Her dimples flashed for the first time in hours. "Why is that?"

"You have a knack for evading direct questions."

"I *am* a politician," Vaughn snapped. "What do you mean?" she said more softly.

"You very skillfully avoided answering me about Paul Lawrence. He seemed to have upset you earlier." Then he smiled sheepishly. "I couldn't help but notice."

"Some things are better left unsaid," she answered quietly.

The music ended and Vaughn stepped out of Justin's arms. "I have a question for you," she said.

"Shoot."

"Are you acquainted with Paul?"

"In a manner of speaking."

"Now, you're beginning to sound like a politician," she countered with a smile.

"Touché. Paul and I have crossed paths on several occasions."

"Personally or professionally?"

"Professionally."

Vaughn's brows rose in surprise. "He didn't try to convict you of anything?" she asked drolly.

Justin laughed heartily. The deep sound rumbled through his chest. It made her feel warm and tingly inside. "No. We stood on opposite sides of the table."

"You're an attorney?"

"Don't say it with such disdain," he said, pretending offense. "Politicians and lawyers don't make such strange bedfellows, you know."

Her dimples winked at him. "I deserved that one."

They fell in step next to each other and headed for the bar.

"So, who do you work for?" Vaughn asked.

"Scotch-and-soda, and a white wine for our hostess," he said to the bartender. He turned his lazy gaze on Vaughn. "I don't work for anyone," he said, evasively. "I have a small private practice."

Vaughn held her snappy retort in check. She was beginning to enjoy the verbal sparring. "Alone, or with partners?"

"I have two partners," he said matter-of-factly.

"Really?" Her interest peaked. "What's the name of your firm?"

He looked her full in the face, a bold grin lighting his eyes. "Montgomery, Phillips, and Michaels."

It took all she had for her mouth not to drop open in astonished embarrassment. "You're *that* Justin Montgomery?"

"I guess so," he chuckled. "Disappointed?"

"You don't have some 'little' practice! You have one of the busiest firms in D.C." His notoriety didn't end there, Vaughn thought. Justin Montgomery was also known for his eye for investments, which had afforded him a luxurious life-style.

Justin noted that she'd expertly sidestepped his question once again. He shrugged his broad shoulders. "We keep busy."

"I know your partners—Khendra Phillips and Sean Michaels. They were involved in a major case a couple of years back." How could anyone not notice Khendra Phillips, with her gleaming auburn tresses, wide eyes, and expressive mouth? Khendra always reminded Vaughn of the singer-turned-actress, Sheryl Lee Ralph, of *Dreamgirls* fame. And Khendra's husband, Sean Michaels, was to die for.

He nodded. "Those are the ones."

Her brow crinkled. "How come you and I have never crossed paths?"

"I try to keep a low profile. Actually," he took a sip of his drink, "I do more speaking engagements than litigation. I let those two hotshots handle that. They say it keeps the spark in their marriage going."

As she listened, glimmers of press clips flashed through her head. Her past was haunting her more than usual tonight. "I see," she said stiffly. "Listen, Justin . . . I really should mingle with the other guests. They are paying a lot of money to be here tonight." Her smile was devoid of emotion. "Please excuse me."

She made a move to leave. Justin touched her arm and a tremor raced through her. "Is it something I said?" he asked, perplexed by her sudden change in attitude.

"It was nice talking with you, Justin. Good luck with your practice."

He stared at her hard. "There you go again, avoiding my question."

She returned his look without flinching. "Thanks for the drink. And the dance," she said with finality. She eased away and was quickly swallowed up in the crowd.

Justin stayed long enough to listen to the round of toasts on behalf of Vaughn, who made a point of avoiding him for the rest of his stay. Shortly after, he said his goodbyes.

Just as he was heading for the door, Vaughn crossed his path. She stopped short.

"I hope you enjoyed yourself tonight. I appreciate your coming," she said formally.

"Listen," he began, his thick brows forming a thunderous line, "I don't know what happened between us back there. But if I've offended you in any way, I apologize. I know that sometimes I have a tendency to come on a little strong." He stepped closer, cutting off the space and the air between them. Her head swam and her pulse pounded in her ears as the heavenly scent of him rushed to her brain. "But I'm also known for going after what I want—in the courtroom and out." His dark eyes stared deeply into hers. "This isn't the end, Ms. Hamilton." He raised a finger and gently stroked her jaw. "Not by any means. You can either do this the easy way," he shrugged his shoulder, "or my way. It's your choice." His smile was devilishly wicked, but his eyes were deadly serious.

Vaughn's eyes widened in disbelief. Who the hell did he think he was, anyway? Vaughn thought in a rush, her thoughts finally focusing. She was an assemblywoman for the state of Virginia. She was the daughter of a Superior Court judge. How dared he talk to her as if she were just . . . just a woman? As she opened her mouth to tell him just where he could go, he leaned down and placed a silencing kiss on her pouting lips. "Think about it," he said, brushing past her. "*I* will."

Vaughn spun around in open-mouthed astonishment to watch his casual departure as though nothing more had transpired between them than an impersonal goodbye.

"Wasn't that Justin Montgomery I just saw kissing you?" came a friendly voice practically in her ear.

Vaughn turned quickly back around, her thoughts spinning. She forced her mind to clear as her eyes rested on her best friend and chief of staff, Crystal Porter.

"Crystal," she responded stupidly.

"Very good," she teased. "Now, back to my question."

"Oh, that," Vaughn answered casually, recovering her poise. She waved her hand in dismissal. "Just a friendly goodbye, that's all." Her dimples flashed.

Crystal's thick eyebrows arched in disbelief. "You can tell me anything, girlfriend. But you know that I know better." Her voice lowered to a sassy whisper. "You haven't let anyone, or should I say, any *man,* get close enough to you even to smell your perfume, let alone give you a kiss. And on the mouth, at that." She pursed her lips and peered at Vaughn from beneath thick black lashes.

"Don't be dramatic, Crystal. That's not true."

"Yeah, right. Anyway, it's time to make your goodbye and thank-you speech to the masses."

"Thanks." They began walking toward the dining room. "Actually, I'll be glad when this whole night is over," she said, trying unsuccessfully to shake off the lingering effects of Justin's kiss.

"You think you will. But you know you love the limelight. You were born for this sort of stuff. And Virginia would be a helluva better place if you had a seat in Congress."

Vaughn squeezed Crystal's arm. "I don't know what I'd do without you, Chris."

"Sure you do. You'd hire someone *almost* as qualified as I am. Because you know *I'm* the best."

"Yeah, you keep reminding me. Now, let's go and get these people out of here."

"Go for it. And lay it on thick," she added with a smile, as Vaughn made her way to the front of the hall.

Flashbulbs and applause competed feverishly as Vaughn spoke both passionately and humorously about her bid for Congress.

". . . your presence here tonight renews my determination to win this election. I stand by my conviction that government is ultimately responsible for its people." A roar of applause filled the room. "I intend to take the voices and needs of my constituency to Capitol Hill. I have no intention of becoming," she paused for effect, "one of the good ol' boys."

Laughter filled the air. "My stand on women's rights has caused storm clouds to gather, but that's what umbrellas are for."

"The crowd loves her and the press adores her," Sheila whispered to Crystal as she eased up beside her, both of them watching Vaughn enchant the ballroom crowd.

"She definitely has what it takes, Mrs. Hamilton. There's no question about that."

"But there's a long road ahead," Sheila continued. "There'll be those who'd rather she stayed at home, barefoot and pregnant, than run for higher office. You be there for her, Crystal," Sheila pressed, squeezing Crystal's arm for emphasis.

Crystal turned to look at Sheila, the faint hint of warning in her voice sending a shudder of alarm skimming up her spine. "I'm sure we can handle any mud that gets slung," Crystal assured. "Vaughn is tough."

"She'll have to be tougher," Elliott interjected, joining the two women. "There's no room in politics for the weak of heart." He put his hand around his wife's waist. "I've paved the way for that girl. I know she's not going to let me down."

Sheila straightened her shoulders and fixed a smile on her face. "Of course she won't, sugar," Sheila assured her husband, even as a sense of foreboding found a haven in her heart.

The room erupted into thunderous applause as Vaughn concluded her speech. She joined her parents on the sidelines.

"Whew. That's that," Vaughn breathed with relief.

"You did good, girl," Crystal said giving her a brief hug.

"Thanks." Vaughn grinned. Crystal Porter was the only person she knew who could turn *girl* into a three-syllable word.

"This is only the beginning, princess," Elliott said. "So you'd best be prepared." He clamped his lips around the unlit pipe that was his trademark.

"I will, Daddy. I will," she said wearily. "Mama, I'm going to be heading home. I'm beat."

"I know you are, sugar. You must have shaken a thousand hands tonight."

"Not to mention the countless wet kisses," Crystal chimed in.

Vaughn switched her gaze to Crystal, her eyes flashing in annoyance.

"What?" Crystal asked innocently.

Vaughn shook her head. "Never mind. I'm getting out of here. Mama, Daddy, I'll speak to you both tomorrow."

"If you're that tired, Vaughn," her father said, "I think it best you stay here tonight. You don't need to be driving home half asleep."

She heard the beginnings of an order in his voice but she wasn't having it. Not tonight. "I'll be fine." She kissed his cheek and then her mother's. "I promise. I'll call as soon as I get in."

Elliott frowned and gnawed on his pipe, not at all pleased. But there was no point in getting his shorts twisted in a knot on such an auspicious night. This one time he'd let her rebellious streak go. "You just make sure you do that."

"Goodnight, everyone," Vaughn said wearily. "Chris, do you need a ride?"

"No. I have my car. I'll see you on Monday. Be safe."

Vaughn waved and swept out the door, deeply relieved to be out from under the supervision of her father. She couldn't wait to get home and hop into bed.

As she slowly pulled out of the drive and onto the street, the sound of a honking horn caught her attention. She peered through the darkness and saw the headlights of a parked car at the edge of the six-foot iron gate. Cautiously, she eased the car down the lane. Quickly she checked that her windows were up and the doors were locked. Just because you paid a lot of money to live someplace didn't protect you from crime, she thought nervously. Norfolk's crime statistics could attest to that. She pressed her foot on the gas, intent on speeding past the waiting auto before the driver had a chance to know what was happening.

Her black Jaguar jetted forward, but not before the driver stepped in front of her car. "Holy. . . ." she screeched, as she slammed on the brakes. The momentum threw her against the steering wheel. For several long moments she sat shivering in her seat, her head pressed against hands that couldn't seem to release the wheel.

The sharp tapping on her window caused her to gasp in alarm. Her head snapped up. Her eyes, wide with fright, darkened into two dangerous slits. She bit down on her lip to keep from expelling a spew of expletives. Like a flash of lightning she unfastened her seatbelt, popped the locks on the door, and flung it open, nearly knocking down the unfortunate soul who was about to wish he hadn't gotten up that morning.

She jumped out of the car, hands on hips, eyes blazing. "Are you totally out of your mind? I could have killed you, you damned idiot!"

Justin leaned casually against the hood of the Jaguar. He folded his arms across his chest. "Now, it wouldn't have looked very good for your campaign image if you'd run me over."

"What?" she sputtered. "You are out of your mind!" Her chest heaved in and out, enticingly, Justin noted, as she tried to get her breathing under control.

Justin stepped around in front of her. "I just felt this was a good way to get your attention. And to let you know that I was very serious about what I said earlier."

Now, she really couldn't breathe. Not with him standing close enough for her to see the sparkle in his eyes. Oh, God. "What *is* it that you want,

Mr. Montgomery?" she asked, completely exasperated and totally at a loss as to how to deal with this unpredictable, gorgeous man.

"I thought I made myself clear earlier," he said in a rough whisper. "Obviously, I didn't do a very good job." He stepped even closer, allowing only a breath to separate them. "Maybe this will help."

Vaughn felt hypnotized, immobilized, as his steady gaze held her in place. By degrees he lowered his head until his lips gently touched down on hers. Ever so slowly, Justin's mouth grazed over her own, commanding her to yield to him.

She felt her head spin, her stomach flutter, her heart race with blinding speed. She felt as if a whirlpool had taken up residence within her. Unwillingly, her body began to unwind as Justin's hand cupped the back of her head, pulling her deeper into the kiss. Without thought, her fingers reached up and stroked his smooth cheeks. His arms wound down around her, welding them together.

She heard his low groan mix with her sigh as the tip of his tongue flicked across her lips. Then, without warning, the tantalizing sensations that ripped through her ceased. Justin eased back without totally releasing her, once again stunned by the sudden impact of the emotions that heated every fiber of his body.

"How about if I follow you home to make sure you get there safely?" he whispered, drawing in a deep breath to calm himself.

Wordlessly she nodded and stepped back out of his embrace. Like an automaton, she slipped into the driver's seat of her car, fastened her seatbelt, and put the car in gear. She shook her head to clear her thoughts, wondering if what had just transpired was real, or if she'd just imagined the whole erotic episode. But when she looked up and saw his headlights cut a path through the pitch black night, she knew it was all too real.

Slowly, she pulled out ahead, and as promised, Justin followed her for the full two-hour drive to her townhouse. It took all her concentration to get home in one piece. Her thoughts kept shifting between the road ahead and the man behind the wheel of the midnight blue BMW.

Mercifully, Vaughn parked the car in her driveway, fully expecting Justin to get out of his car. He didn't, and she found herself acutely disappointed. Instead, he waited for her to put her key in the door, turn on the hall light, and lock the door behind her. On shaky legs, Vaughn momentarily leaned against the locked door. When she heard the sound of his car pull out of the drive, she hurried to the window to see the taillights disappear.

Vaughn let out a shuddering breath, then wearily went upstairs to her bedroom. She walked across the pale peach carpet, mechanically dialed her parents' home, and told them she'd arrived safely. Numbly she listened to her mother tell her what a success the evening had been and that she was hoping she and Vaughn could get together for lunch during the week. Vaughn only half listened, agreeing to whatever was being said. Her thoughts wouldn't stay focused. Finally, her mother said goodnight.

Undressing, then cleansing the remnants of makeup from her face, she began to relive every single detail of her encounter with Justin Montgomery from the moment she'd met him. It all seemed like a dream, she thought with wonder. Even as she slipped under the satin sheets, she had the unsettling sensation that at any moment Justin was going to pop out from beneath her bed or step out of her closet. It took all she had not to peek under the floral quilt. As she drifted off to sleep, the beginnings of a smile tugged at her lips. "Looks like we're gonna do it your way, Mr. Montgomery," she said softly. "But I'm not going to be so easy next time."

CHAPTER 2

All night long, Vaughn tossed and turned, visions of Justin assaulting her from every angle. She relived his touch, savored his kiss, longed to inhale the scent of him once again. But with the start of a new day, her senses seemed to have returned. The previous evening took on a sense of unreality and became more distant as her days were filled with plans for her campaign. It was the nights that were difficult. In the still of the evening she recalled vividly the thrill of being in his arms. She'd dreamed of him again and awakened with a tingling sensation that had left her body feeling totally unsatisfied.

What in the devil did I let happen that night? she wondered, as the steamy shower cascaded over her. Have I been so starved for affection that I let the first aggressive man I meet dominate my thoughts, day and night? No way, she thought, shutting off the water and stepping out of the stall. No way.

He must want something, just like everyone else. She had to admit, though, he ran a good game. She chuckled at her own gullibility. However, determined to put thoughts of Justin Montgomery out of her head, she dressed in her sweatsuit and sneakers and took her morning run around the park. But if she thought she could run him out of her system, she was truly mistaken. With each step she took, she surreptitiously peeked over her shoulder, expecting, even hoping, that Justin would step from behind a tree to kiss her breathless once more. She swore she saw his face in every other man she passed. She imagined she caught a whiff of his cologne as a group of cyclists sped by. This is crazy, she mused, making the turn back onto her street. She wiped the perspiration from her forehead with her wristband and ran smack into Justin as he stepped out of her front gate.

"Well, good morning," he greeted, steadying her with a strong grip. "This is a great look for you," he teased, his eyes roving over her.

For the first time since she'd been a child, she was self-conscious about her looks. She knew that her dark skin must be about as shiny as a pair of polished shoes. Perspiration ran in rivulets down her face. This is just great, she thought. The very thought that he could have caught her in this very unflattering light suddenly ticked her off and all of her frustration and longing over the past two weeks overflowed.

She took a step back so that she could look him full in the face. Her eyes narrowed and her neck arched to an arrogant angle. She planted her hands firmly on her flaring hips.

"Let me tell you something . . . Jus-tin," she spat out his name with vehemence. "First you come on to me like gangbusters, then you plant yourself in front of my car and scare the hell out of me. Then you kiss me like you've known me all your life and follow me home." And then I don't hear from you, she wanted to say, but didn't. "Then you have the audacity to pop up on my doorstep unannounced, and all you have to say is, 'this is a great look for you'?" She leaned dangerously forward, rising on tiptoe to press home her point. "No, buddy, it doesn't work like that. Not with me. Maybe this sweet-talking routine of yours has worked in the past, but I'm not buying it," she concluded in a huff, pointing her finger at him like a dagger.

The corner of his lip inched up in a grin and she instantly felt her resolve begin to waver. "Well, I guess I deserved that," he said mildly, seemingly unruffled by her tirade. It took all his willpower to keep from staring at the rapid rise and fall of her breasts. "That's why I stopped by this morning. I wanted to take you to brunch to make up for being such a . . ." he peered quizzically at her. "What did you call me again?" He placed his forefinger on his lip in contemplation. "Ah, yes, a gangbuster. Yeah, to make up for coming on like a gangbuster." Mischief danced in his eyes. "I just don't know what came over me," he concluded, all innocence and light. "But most of all," he took a step closer, "I couldn't seem to get you out of my head."

Vaughn's shoulders slumped. She expelled a long-held breath and shook her head, but she refused to give in to the smile that threatened to ruin her tough stance. Vaughn cocked her head to the side. "Mr. Montgomery, I hope your pockets are deep, because I'm starved and you have a lot of making up to do." She spun away and headed for her door. "Wait in your car," she instructed over her shoulder. "I'll be out in twenty minutes."

"Ooh, I love it when you talk to me like that," he called out, amusement rippling through his voice.

This time Vaughn did give in to the joy that bubbled within her. She laughed all the way up the stairs to her room and didn't stop until she'd showered, finished dressing in a pair of designer jeans and matching shirt, put on a pair of Italian loafers, and grabbed a navy wool jacket from the hall closet. Just for today, she pledged, slipping into her jacket, I'll put my mistrust, my politics, and my old hurts aside and enjoy this time with a very sexy man who makes it so easy to forget. She stepped out the door, determined and confident, strutted around to the passenger side of his car, and slid in.

"Twenty-five minutes," Justin said, checking his watch before pulling the car onto the road. "You said twenty. I was beginning to get worried."

"Right." She rolled her eyes, intent on pretending annoyance. "Just drive, before I change my mind." But the confidence that she'd had only moments before seemed to dissolve by the second as the close proximity of Justin Montgomery took its full effect on her. What am I doing? she worried, the strong manly scent of him scrambling her thoughts.

For several minutes they drove in silence, the steady rhythm of the car stereo the only sound. Vaughn fiddled with the gold button on her jacket and had nearly pulled it off when Justin's voice broke the silence.

"I've never known a woman named Vaughn. It's quite unusual." He looked at her from the corner of his eye. "Is it a family name?"

She smiled briefly. How many times in school and in business had she been mistaken for a man when her name was read on the register or her résumé was reviewed by prospective employers? She secretly enjoyed the looks of surprise when she'd answered in attendance or appeared at an interview. She only wished that the reason for her unusual name was because someone cared that much about her to have her carry on the name.

"My father wanted a boy." Justin caught the hint of wistfulness in her voice. He looked at her curiously, but her face remained impassive. "I guess it was his way of saying to hell with fate," she concluded.

"He's definitely tempted fate on a lot of levels."

"He certainly has," she answered shortly.

"Have I hit a sore spot?"

Vaughn snapped her head in his direction. "Why would you ask something like that?" she countered defensively.

"I watched you with your father last night and the way that you responded to him. Now when his name comes up you get all tense."

Vaughn straightened up in her seat. "I didn't think it was that obvious," she replied quietly, disconcerted that the public mask she'd so expertly kept in place had slipped. Or was it simply that this man—this devastating man—had seemed to see through all the barricades she'd erected, apparently without effort? The thought stirred her uncomfortably.

"It is. But if you'd rather not talk about it, then we won't."

"Then I guess we won't."

"Fine. What *would* you like to talk about?"

She hesitated a beat. "I'd like to talk about why you're so intent on squeezing your way into my life, for starters."

"Good comeback," he said jovially. "How about if I give you a full confession over brunch? We're almost there."

For the first time since she'd stepped into the car, she took note of her surroundings. The smell of the James River filled the interior. Vaughn turned her head toward Justin and stared at him through narrowed eyes.

"I thought a nice midday riverboat cruise on the *Annabel Lee* would be nice," Justin offered, in response to Vaughn's questioning look. "I hear the food is excellent. There's a live band, and most important, you can't get away from me unless you decide to jump overboard." He squinted his beautiful brown eyes at her. "That was the deciding factor."

"Very funny," Vaughn said. "And very thoughtful," she added, with a dimpled smile that set Justin's pulse racing.

"I was hoping you'd say that." Unable to resist the temptation of tasting her again, he quickly leaned over and kissed her moist mouth. Relishing the sweetness anew, he sucked on her bottom lip and Vaughn felt the tremors of yearning explode within her. Reluctantly, Justin released her. "I'm just a thoughtful guy." His voice lowered to a thrilling throb and his eyes held her in an invisible embrace. "If you give me half a chance, Vaughn Hamilton, I can show you just how thoughtful I can be."

Her heart thumped, then settled down to its normal rhythm. "You're off to a flying start," she said softly.

Momentarily, with her looking at him with those glorious eyes and bewitching smile, he had the insane notion to pull off and take her as far away from civilization as possible, then ravish that luscious body until she begged him to stop. Fortunately, good judgment took over. He expelled a shaky breath. "Which is exactly what we're gonna have to do if we don't want to get left at the dock. That boat leaves in about five minutes."

Laughing, hand in hand, they ran across the dock and darted up the gangplank. Vaughn thought for a few moments about how sudden and wild her actions were with Mr. Montgomery. What was it about him? Why did he strike such a chord within her? Why did she allow him to get so close? She shook her head. She wasn't going to think about that now. Now, she was going to hold tightly to his hand and remember how good it feels to do something as simple as hold a man's hand. She felt carefree and young again, and she never wanted the feeling to end.

Once on board, Vaughn was treated to an afternoon of pure magic.

The exquisite seafood cuisine, the soothing sounds of the band, and most of all, the comfort of being in Justin's company. He was every bit the gentleman. He saw to her every need. He made her laugh with his sharp wit and exceptional talent for mimicking the other passengers on board. Above all, he made her feel special, truly important.

By degrees her guard came down and she found herself talking about things, personal things, that she had kept buried for years.

"I really don't know how I got involved in politics," she confessed, as they strolled arm in arm across the deck and out onto the boardwalk. "My father seemed to have my whole life mapped out even before I was born. For as long as I can remember I was surrounded by politicians and attending political events. I imagine the Kennedys know what my life was like. My father's idea of a family outing was to have my mother and me sit in the spectator box in court while he presided." She laughed.

Justin heard the false note of gaiety in her voice and slipped his arm around her waist, pulling her close. "Didn't you have any say so? I mean, wasn't your father interested in what you wanted to do?"

"You obviously don't know him very well. There *is* no way but his way. There's no argument, no debate." She sighed. "To tell you the truth, I never knew any other kind of life. It's kind of hard to debate when you have nothing to compare it with."

"What about your friends? Didn't they have interests?"

"Coincidentally," she grinned, "all my friends were children of my father's friends. Who, of course, were politicians."

Justin shook his head sadly. "Doesn't seem like you had much of a childhood."

"It wasn't that bad," she said unconvincingly. "After a point, I really got into it and found that I was good at what I did. I graduated at the top of my class and worked at one of the top law firms in D.C. When my father suggested that I run for the state assembly four years ago, I did, without question."

"And now you're ready to move on to bigger and better things," Justin added.

Vaughn nodded. "But this time I want to be sure that *when* I win, it's because of me, and not because of my father's influence."

"All anyone has to do is take a look at your record," Justin said, quickly coming to her defense. "*You* accomplished those things. *You* got the funding in place to open the youth and senior centers and got the bill passed to crack down on drugs in Richmond. Not your father."

His vehemence warmed her. "That may be true. But there are plenty of people who can't see past my name to who I really am. Too many opponents want to believe that the only reason I've gotten this far is because my father is a judge. I work hard at proving them wrong every day."

"That's where I come in," Justin said, turning her into his embrace. He gazed down into her upturned face. "From the moment I met you," he whispered gently, "I knew I wanted you in my life. I can't remember ever feeling this strongly about anyone or anything." He slowly caressed her cheek with the tip of his finger. "You're an incredible woman, Vaughn, and I want to be the one to make you realize just how incredible." His head lowered and her breath stopped somewhere in her chest. "Not as a politician, or as a judge's daughter." His lips were inches away from hers. "But as a woman."

Justin's mouth slowly, seductively covered hers. His arms tightened around her, pulling her solidly against the hard lines of his frame. She felt as if she'd dived under water—weightless, free, as her mouth opened, welcoming the texture of his exploring tongue.

Wave after wave of pleasure rushed through her being, awakening long-buried desires, forcing them to the surface with a power that was frightening. Yet a warning voice nipped at the shreds of her consciousness. *Too soon . . . too fast.* She sank deeper into the kiss. *After something . . . what?* Her fingers clutched him for support. *The headlines . . . his life, mine . . .*

Suddenly Vaughn tore herself from Justin's embrace. Breathless and shaky, she turned away, commanding composure. Justin clasped her shoulders in a firm grip. Her felt her tense beneath his fingertips. Slowly he turned her around to face him, his own heart ready to burst with the unnatural rapid beating.

When she turned, Justin fully expected to see doubt, longing, confusion, happiness—even desire, spilling across her exquisite face. Any of those emotions he could easily have dealt with. But not the look of pure dismissal that hardened her features like granite.

CHAPTER 3

"Vaughn," Justin said in a hushed voice. "What is it? What have I done?" He held her shoulders, feeling the subtle shudders ripple through her. "Damn it, Vaughn, don't look at me as if I'm beneath contempt. Talk to me!"

Vaughn swallowed deeply and took a gulping breath. She turned her gaze away and looked out toward the rolling waters. Her jaw clenched. "I can't," she finally said in a broken whisper. She shook her head and eased away from Justin's hold. "I wish I could. But it's impossible." She spun around and looked up at him, her warm brown eyes filled with a pain so palpable it reached out and squeezed his heart. "Maybe it would be best if we just cut this afternoon short." Her voice strengthened as it picked up volume. Justin saw the mask subtly slip into place. "The reality is, I'm not in a position to get involved in a relationship right now. I shouldn't have led you to believe otherwise. There's too much at stake," she added self-righteously.

She began to sound more and more like a politician as she rambled on, Justin noted with wry amusement. Well, he'd just let her finish and get it off her chest, and then he had a thing or two to tell her, once and for all.

"The fact is, I must concentrate on my campaign. Too many people are relying on me. My energies have to be focused at this point." And I certainly can't focus on anything with *you* in my life, she thought longingly. She took a breath and lifted her chin. "Believe me," she said, a bit more gently, "you're a . . . desirable man." Justin almost lost his composure and laughed out loud as he watched her try to keep a rein on her emotions. "Under other circumstances . . ." She didn't complete her sentence, because what could she honestly say? Could she tell him that if things were different, she wouldn't hesitate to give in to all the feelings that were wreaking havoc with her heart? Could she tell him that if a part of her hadn't been obliterated, she would feel differently about the future? Could she tell him that her lessons in love had nearly destroyed her? No. She couldn't.

Justin had watched her every move since she'd begun her litany of dismissal. She wanted him, and he knew it. She wanted him so badly that it scared the hell out of her. But there was also something else, something hidden so deep it leaped beyond just a fear of a relationship. He was never a man who gave up on anything he wanted. And he wanted Vaughn Hamilton more than anything he'd ever wanted before. She could throw up all the roadblocks she wanted, but he'd knock down every one of them until she finally and unequivocally removed that mask for him and him alone. And he would be there to help her unleash the passion that he knew smoldered beneath that polished surface.

"Are you about finished?" he asked pointedly.

Vaughn nodded.

"Then I think you ought to know that I don't give two damns about your campaign, your constituents, or your blasted busy schedule that's supposed to keep you so occupied that you won't have a life! Will all of that keep you warm in bed at night?" He answered his own question. "No. I think not. Not like I can . . . and will."

The heat of his erotic threat whipped through her and pounded in her veins. Vaughn's mouth opened, then closed instantly.

He took a breath and his voice softened. His gaze implored her to listen with her heart. "What I do care about is you, Vaughn. For some godforsaken reason, I care about you. Don't ask me why or how. I don't know. Everything is happening too fast for me. But I don't want to stop it. I couldn't if I tried."

He reached out and stroked her cheek with the tip of his finger. A shiver ran through her body at the feather-light touch. Her eyes briefly fluttered closed.

"What's happening between us . . ." He shook his head, searching for the words. His hands opened to her and tightened into fists. "It only happens once in a lifetime, Vaughn. The passion, the connection, the vibrations that run like live wires between us . . . can you say that you're sure you'll find this again? Are you sure you've ever had it before?" He bent slightly down to meet her at eye level. He held her shoulders, willing his fingers to transfer his emotions to her.

"I don't want to know about your past. Let's begin from here, now, today, as if all the yesterdays never happened. We can start slowly." He grinned encouragingly. "Or at whatever pace you choose." The flicker of a smile sparkled in Vaughn's eyes. "But whatever you do, give this a chance." He paused a moment, then began again, his voice dropping an octave. "I know you want this." He stepped closer. "You know how I can tell?" he asked arrogantly, the light of mischief dancing in his eyes.

"No. How can you tell?" Vaughn whispered, softening at his touch.

"Because every time I hold you in my arms, like this . . ." He enfolded her in a gentle embrace. His mouth lowered to whisper above hers. "And kiss you, as I'm going to do . . ."

"Yes," she breathed.

"I can feel every fiber in your body dissolve into hot liquid and burn through my veins like a white heat. You're in my blood, Vaughn. Just as I'm in yours."

His mouth tentatively touched down and covered hers. He felt her tremble and pulled her securely against him, clamping his palm behind her head, urging her deeper into the kiss.

Her mouth willingly opened, drawing in the tangy taste of his exploring tongue. Their tongues, their lips, their hearts danced exotically with each other, heightening, then lessening the explosive intensity that poured through them.

The sensation of her hardened nipples brushing against the fabric of her shirt nearly caused her to cry out. Vaughn pressed herself closer to Justin to relieve the maddening pressure in her breasts.

Their muted sounds of desire filtered through the early evening air as their bodies welded together in tantalizing contact. Justin's own shaft of desire bloomed painfully hot and hard, pulsing against the stirring gyrations of Vaughn's hips.

This time it was Justin who broke contact. He pulled her solidly against him, burying his face in her hair. A low groan rose from deep in his stomach. With great effort, he brought his breathing under control.

"That's how I know," he said raggedly, willing his body to contain the shudders that whipped through him.

Vaughn eased back and looked up into his eyes. A slow, seductive smile curved her lips. Her dimples deepened. Her eyes trailed languidly over his face. "I think you're right, Mr. Montgomery," she conceded in a whisper. "But we're going to take it very slowly," she added softly, "very slowly. I don't want to make any more mistakes in my life, Justin." Vaughn reached up and cupped his cheek. He turned his face into her palm and kissed her open hand. "You've got to be patient with me, Justin."

"I'll be whatever I have to be, Vaughn. If it's what you want."

She let out a deep sigh. "Then I guess this is the start," she said, hope, fear, and joy filling her voice at once.

"You won't regret it," he assured her solemnly.

"If I do, you'll be sorry I did," she warned, poking him playfully in the chest, needing this moment of frivolity to regain her equilibrium.

"You're on!" He smacked her solidly on the lips with a kiss to seal the pact.

"Well," she breathed, "I hope you still have plenty of money left in your pockets, because I seem to have worked up an appetite."

Justin let out a hearty laugh, wrapped his arm around her, and ushered her to his car. "Your appetite will be the one thing to topple this relationship, lady." They both laughed, the sound bright and promising as the budding blooms of spring.

Over the next few weeks, Vaughn and Justin spent all their free time together—discreetly. Their lives consisted of concerts, sharing late-night dinners, and home-cooked meals as Vaughn attempted to keep her private life out of the public eye. They talked of world affairs and of her campaign plans, took long drives in the midnight hours of spring. From that first night forward, their destinies were irrevocably sealed.

CHAPTER 4

Simone Rivers sat in the small living area of her Spelman College dorm. Like a sponge she absorbed yet another news article in the *Atlanta Journal,* detailing the fundraising event of the season for Vaughn Hamilton. She had avidly followed the rise of the many African-American female politicians for years. The few details she'd gleaned about Vaughn Hamilton only confirmed her conviction to become just like the woman.

Simone folded the paper and placed it on the dinette table. Unfortunately, Simone didn't have the political connections Vaughn had. She didn't have a judge for a father or a political socialite for a mother. Her foster parents were simple people. Her foster father worked for the Atlanta post office, and her foster mother was a part-time librarian. What Simone did have were determination and an unquenchable thirst for knowledge. And this summer she was determined to do her undergraduate internship in a political environment outside Atlanta. And she hoped to get to meet Vaughn Hamilton in the process.

She sighed heavily, drawing the attention of her roommate, Jean.

"Sounds deep," Jean commented, peeking over the edge of her textbook.

Simone shrugged. "I was just reading this article on Vaughn Hamilton's big shindig last week."

"And?"

"I really admire women like her—women who are willing to go against the odds and take what they want. Women who aren't intimidated by outside forces, but who are secure in who they are." Her light brown eyes glowed with admiration.

"Sounds like you'd make a great walking advertisement for her campaign," Jean teased.

"Very funny." Simone rolled her eyes in annoyance. She hated it when Jean teased her about her political zeal.

"Don't get all bent, Simone. You know I was just kidding," Jean said, half apologetically. Jean was a biology major, and politics was the furthest thing from Jean's mind. She tried valiantly to keep up with Simone's rhetoric and name dropping, but the whole abstract concept of politics crashed against her logical, analytical brain like a mack truck. However, it was Jean's unshakeable reason that Simone sometimes relied on to keep her focused on her goals. Jean returned her attention to her textbook when her eyes brightened with what she thought was a brilliant idea.

"Hey, if Hamilton is running, she has to have a campaign staff. Why don't you try to get an internship with her this summer?"

Simone gave a weak smile. "I'm way ahead of you on that one." She plopped down on the plaid couch and stretched out her long legs. "I called about two weeks ago. One of her aides told me that they had just filled their quota for summer interns."

"Hmmm. Bad break. That would have been perfect."

The two friends sat in silence, both caught up in trying to arrive at an alternative solution.

Simone folded her arms beneath her small breasts and twisted her lips in consternation. She knew she'd waited too long to make her contacts. But until two weeks ago, she wasn't sure how she'd have managed living expenses outside of her dorm. She knew that her parents had spent most of their savings to send her to college. Or at least, that's what she'd thought; until they'd revealed to her that upon her nineteenth birthday, which was in three weeks, she'd have access to an account in the amount of $250,000. They'd refused to say how they'd amassed that much money, only that it was now hers. She was still reeling from the shock.

"Hey," Jean said suddenly, making Simone jump in surprise. "Remember about three months ago when that f-i-n-e brother, um, um, whatshisname?" She popped her fingers trying to make the name materialize. "Montgomery!" she cried triumphantly.

Simone sat up in her seat, her thoughts racing. "Right. When he came here to speak, he said he'd be happy to help out with internship and job referrals," she shouted. "And I was really impressed with his stance on children's rights and advocacy." How could she have forgotten? She'd been so preoccupied with working with Vaughn Hamilton that she'd completely overlooked Justin Montgomery's generous offer.

Briefly she thought of her own situation and what an impact his presentation had had on her at the time. It had really made her think it was possible to find the truth, that the law was there to be used, if you knew how. That was what she'd wanted more than anything, to learn how to use the law to find the truth. And now she had the means to do it.

"Do you still have his card?" Jean asked.

"I hope so." Simone popped up and trotted off to her room with Jean close on her heels. Simone reached up to the top shelf of the closet and took down a well-worn shoebox.

Sitting on the edge of her bed, Simone and Jean sifted through the myriad papers, old love letters, and news clippings.

"Here it is," Simone said jubilantly, holding up the cream-colored card.

"Great. Give him a call," Jean urged, nudging Simone.

"Today's Saturday, silly."

"Oh, yeah, right." Her bright idea momentarily dimmed. "Well," Jean said, "that gives you two days to prepare a knock-'em-dead internship-of-the-year presentation speech."

Simone grinned. "That's just what I'm gonna do. By the time I finish my pitch to Mr. Montgomery, he'll be begging me to join his staff!" She turned toward her friend, her black eyes sparking with fire and her soft but firm voice growing serious. "I have a real strong feeling about this, Jean." She clutched the card in her hand. "I really believe that this internship is going to be the turning point in my life."

Lucus Stone tossed his copy of the *Washington Post* across the glass table in disgust. The grainy black-and-white photo of Vaughn Hamilton stared back at him, beautiful, smiling, and confident, a combination that would not be ignored by the voters.

So, the daughter of Elliott Hamilton was truly running against him. The whole notion was almost funny, that this *woman* thought she had what it took to run against him and win. His deep blue eyes darkened. He'd held his congressional seat for over a decade, virtually unopposed, and he had no intention of losing. Especially to a woman. Especially *this* woman. He didn't give a damn who her father was. Vaughn Hamilton was no match for him.

He stood up and ran his hand across his smooth chin, then through the shock of glistening gray hair that gave him an air of confidence and maturity that his constituency loved. However, he mused, there was no point in taking chances. The political tides changed rapidly, and Lucus Stone was never one to be caught adrift. And he was never one to leave anything to chance. He crossed the room in smooth strides and reached for the phone. Punching in the numbers, he waited.

"Hello?" answered a sleepy male voice.

"David, it's me."

David Cain slowly sat up in bed, forcing himself awake. Lucus Stone never called him at home unless it was urgent. His thoughts scrambled for organization. "Good morning, Mr. Stone. What can I do for you?"

"It's afternoon," Lucus corrected tersely. "Did you see today's paper?" he asked, demanding to know but also realizing that this miscreant hadn't even gotten out of bed for the day.

"Uh, no." David rubbed the last of the sleep out of his light brown eyes.

"Well, get it and read it. Meet me at my office in an hour. I have a job for you." Lucus broke the connection.

David stared at the receiver. What could be so important that Stone would want to see him at his office on a Saturday? He tossed the twisted sheets off his muscular body and got out of bed. Knowing Stone, he'd better have every line of the newspaper committed to memory by the time they met. He stalked across the lush bedroom and into the adjacent bath.

David turned on the faucets full blast. He'd worked for Stone before on a variety of projects over the years. Everything ranging from local deliveries to intimate investigations of very influential people. Lucus Stone had over the years compiled a dossier on anyone of importance in government office. He was the modern-day J. Edgar Hoover. He was feared but respected. However, Stone's methods for combating his opponents remained questionable in Cain's mind. Little did Stone know that Cain, too, had been compiling a dossier—just for insurance, of course. That secret knowledge caused a slow smile to lift the corner of Cain's wide mouth.

The steaming water rushed over the mass of rippling bronze muscles as Cain flexed and contemplated what his latest project would be.

Sheila Hamilton sat opposite her husband at the white wicker table that had been placed on the balcony. A lush spring breeze blew caressingly over her supple caramel skin, rustled the blooming greenery, and gently stirred the grass. The air was filled with anticipation as the new season primed itself to burst forth. But instead of the sense of expectation that Sheila normally felt at this time of year, she was filled with a sense of foreboding.

"Elliott," she said softly, distracting him from a case review that lay open in front of him.

Determined not to show his annoyance at the interruption, he slowly removed his glasses from the bridge of his nose and counted, silently, to ten, placing the bifocals on the table. "Yes, dear?" he said evenly, pleased with himself for maintaining control. Control was important, he reminded himself daily. Control dictated every facet of his life—or else there would be chaos, he reasoned. He looked across at his wife.

She hated it when he stared at her like that. It made her feel as if she were under a microscope, a curiosity to be examined. Sheila adjusted herself in her seat and took a deep breath. "Elliott," she began again, "I have a very bad feeling about this entire . . . campaign thing," she expelled, shaking her head with concern. Her smooth brow creased as she continued. She leaned forward. "We've been lucky these past years, Elliott," she said in a hushed but steady voice. "You know that. There's no way that someone, somewhere, isn't going to dig up the dirt. This isn't some local assembly position, Elliott. This is a congressional seat. She'll be up against an incumbent who hasn't been defeated in nearly a dozen years! Lucus Stone is ruthless when it comes to opposition. And now, Vaughn will be that opposition." Her anxiety over her daughter's future filtered through her voice and registered in a web of tension on her face.

Elliott stood up. His wide jaw clenched. His ebony skin seemed to darken further with unspent outrage. He squinted his eyes into two warning slits.

"I will discuss this one last time, Sheila. I have paved the way for Vaughn all her life," he said, with a shake of his balding head for emphasis. "Everything has been taken care of for years. There's nothing anyone can do to her or to us. I won't allow it. Do you think for one minute that I haven't foreseen this day and planned for it? Nothing will stop Vaughn from reaching my goals. Nothing!" he said with finality. He straightened and adjusted his pants over the slightly protruding paunch. Then, in a soothing voice, "Everything will be fine, dear. There's no point in you worrying. Haven't I always taken care of everything?" He gave her a benevolent smile, patted her hand absently, and got up and strolled into the house.

Sheila Hamilton watched her husband leave, and her heart sank. When had things changed? It seemed only moments ago the young Elliott Hamilton, full of dreams, ambition, and himself, had burst into her life. From the first moment they'd met, Sheila had known that Elliott was destined for great things. He'd caught her up in his dreams. He'd made her a part of his plans. He'd promised her a life of influence, happiness, and luxury. He'd delivered all that he'd promised, and more. And she believed he could do anything he set his mind to do.

Sheila always knew that Elliott was a man driven, and with good reason. He came from a family that had virtually nothing. He was the first member of his family to have an education beyond the ninth grade. But Elliott had changed. He'd become consumed by his own dreams, to be fulfilled and exceeded by Vaughn. At any cost.

She shut her eyes and the old pain resurfaced and twisted her heart. She pressed her fist to her chest. She was afraid. This was the first time in her forty years of marriage that she didn't believe her dynamic husband had the power to make the impossible a reality. What was more frightening was that she could not intervene. To do so would destroy her marriage and possibly ruin Elliott's career, and she knew she would lose the greatest love of all . . . Vaughn's.

Simone hadn't told anyone about the money, not even Jean. She just had the irrational feeling that if she spoke about it, it would all somehow disappear. She knew that the notion was ridiculous, but that still didn't stop her from checking the account every other day—just to be sure.

She sat down on her bed, staring blankly at the array of posters, class schedules, and activity notices tacked to her bulletin board. Somehow she believed that the money was either a clue to her past or a doorway to her future. It was up to her to decide which path to choose.

Her gaze drifted, then rested on a picture of her foster parents that sat on her dresser. She smiled wistfully. She picked up the picture and looked at it lovingly. She loved her foster parents. There was no doubt in her mind about that. Linda and Philip Clark were everything a child could want. They cared for her and loved her unquestionably, regardless of the origins of her birth. Yet deep in her soul remained the silent yearning to know from where she'd come. And why—why had she been abandoned? Why was she so unworthy of her natural parents' love? That question had gnawed at her all of her nineteen years. At times it made her feel worthless, unlovable, and insecure. She hadn't been wanted from birth. That was a heavy burden. Then there were those times she'd even had doubts about her foster parents' love. Why had they never adopted her and given her their name? They had an explanation, a flimsy one, but an explanation nonetheless. One which worked well during her adolescence, but failed to hold up to teenage scrutiny. Eventually she'd stopped asking, but the underlying pain had always remained with her.

Over the years, Simone had valiantly shielded herself from her insecurities, forcing herself to excel. By eighteen, she'd amassed trophies in track and field, tennis and swimming. She'd skipped grades on three separate occasions, had always remained at the top of her classes, and now had the opportunity to graduate a semester early if she could secure an internship to satisfy the requirements for a political science major. Simone was an achiever, a planner and a stickler for being prepared. Which was what she had to be when she made her call.

Simone pushed herself up off the bed, deciding to take a jog around the track and try to organize her thoughts in preparation for her phone call to Justin Montgomery. When she returned from her run she would finish putting together her package containing her cover letter, résumé, and letters of recommendation from her professors. She knew her head would be clearer when she returned. Physical activity had a way of smoothing out the rough edges for Simone. Whenever she had a difficult test or a presentation to make or was struggling through a personal dilemma, she would run or swim. The ultimate result was that her head was always clearer and she had more perspective. For the moment she would put her myriad thoughts and emotions on hold and wait to unleash them on the track.

Her tight thighs and calves expanded and contracted as her sneakered feet pounded against the gravel track. Her arms pumped. Her thick ponytail swung defiantly against the wind. Her slender frame cut an alluring silhouette against the lush green background.

As Simone jogged, the rush of adrenaline pumped through her veins and the clean spring air filled her lungs, clearing her head and crystallizing her thoughts. It was at the moment she rounded the track for the third time that she realized just how she would use her inheritance.

David nearly busted a gut trying to contain himself when Lucus Stone dropped Vaughn Hamilton's name as his next assignment. To say he'd take great pleasure in getting the goods on that bitch was an understatement. He never thought he'd have the opportunity to make her pay for what she'd done to him. Now he had his chance.

He slammed the door of his red Mustang convertible and started whistling a tuneless song. The engine roared to life and David started to laugh, a deep, dark, dangerous laugh that built to a crescendo as he pulled into D.C. traffic and headed for his office in Georgetown. Shortly after, he pulled into the small parking lot and headed for the building that was sandwiched between a real estate office and a women's boutique.

He trotted up the three flights of stairs to his office. Tossing his suit jacket onto the wooden chair, he crossed the small room to the locked file cabinet. Selecting the key from his ring, he opened the grey metal file drawer and quickly found the file he needed.

David smiled as he flipped the Lucas Stone file open and made several notations on the back sheets. He closed the folder and leaned back in his chair, staring at the letters emblazoned on his open door. *David Cain, Political Consultant.* A man for hire, he thought.

He put his feet up on his wooden desk, ruminating about the road he'd traveled to get to where he was. He'd been detoured; there was no question about it. David had been groomed for a life of law and politics. He'd focused all his ambitions on achieving the life of power and prestige that he craved.

Graduating at the top of his law class at George Washington University, he'd easily landed a cushy job with McPhearson, Ekhardt, one of the leading law firms in the District of Columbia. He was headed for great things, until his focus became misdirected when he set his sights on the young attorney Vaughn Hamilton. She was magnificent, everything that he had ever desired in a woman. She was ambitious and intelligent, she was competitive, and most of all, she had the right connections.

He looked at the black-and-white photo of her smiling face in the newspaper. She'd remained virtually the same. The years had been good to her. There was only the subtle change around her eyes. More mature? More worldly? He couldn't be sure. David, however, *had* changed, at least physically. His body had filled out, and he'd maintained it vigorously. The result was broad, muscular shoulders and biceps. His thighs were thick and they rippled with power. He was no longer the smooth-faced young attorney-on-the-rise. His square chin was covered in a smooth, finely tapered beard that lent maturity and a sense of mystery to his face. Gone was the full-blown natural hair and in its place was a very short, tapered cut. Yes, on sight, David Cain was a different man. But inside, the burning desire to have what he knew he deserved remained the same.

A picture of Vaughn as she'd looked on that last day flashed before him. Even now, after so many years, his groin still grew rigid at the very thought of her. That weakness infuriated him. It had cost him his career. He spun around in his chair to face the soft rays of sunshine coming through the tinted windowpane. The movement only served to aggravate the tension between his legs.

If it wasn't for her and her stuck-up, virtuous, holier-than-thou attitude, he could have *been* a Lucus Stone instead of a hired hand. She thought she was better than him, above his advances. What she really was was a frigid bitch who needed a man to teach her a good lesson.

Now he had the opportunity to pay her back in spades. It was one job he would truly enjoy. He closed his eyes and laced his fingers behind his head. Visions of the voluptuous Vaughn Hamilton flashed before him. He twisted uncomfortably in his seat. Now for a plan, he thought.

CHAPTER 5

It was almost business as usual when Vaughn floated into her office on Monday morning. Almost, because there was a definite feeling of electric energy in the air that hadn't been present when she'd left on Friday. She'd spent yet another glorious weekend with Justin, and until this very moment, work was the farthest thing from her mind.

The phones were ringing off the hook, staff members were racing around, and when she reached her office, she saw through her open doorway that there were enough phone messages and faxes to start a small avalanche.

"Ugh," she said out loud, and stepped into the artsy office.

"You ain't seen nothing yet," Crystal said from her favorite overstuffed chair behind the door.

Vaughn jumped in surprise. "Darn it, Crystal, if you don't stop doing that, you're going to give me a heart attack!"

"Puh-leese," Crystal tossed off, rising from her throne. "I've been sitting in this same damn spot every morning for the past four years. You need to stop." Crystal sucked her teeth in dismissal of Vaughn's complaint.

"Yeah," Vaughn huffed, hanging up her teal Burberry trenchcoat on the cherrywood coat rack. "And every morning for the past four years you've been scaring me out of my pantyhose!" She rolled her eyes hard at Crystal and tried not to laugh.

Crystal boldly ignored her. "Girl, get over it. We have work to do." She strutted over to the desk and deposited a stack of letters and folders.

"Every newspaper in the tri-state area wants an interview. We gotta get busy."

Vaughn smiled as she watched Crystal flip through her notepad. Underneath that down-home-girl facade lay the mind of a brilliant strategic planner and a heart of gold. Vaughn wouldn't trade Crystal in for a whole staff full of Yale grads. The girl was awesome. But between friends, Crystal was just plain ole' Chris from the projects. Vaughn and Crystal were physically opposite in every respect. Where Vaughn was dark, slender, and tall, Crystal was fair, with skin the color of sautéed butter and eyes that shimmered like the blue-green Caribbean. She had wide hips and the kind of high, firm behind women paid money to possess. Her hair, when she decided to wear it out, nearly reached her waist and was blacker than pitch, a result of her distant Trinidad heritage.

When Vaughn and Crystal had first met on their college campus, Vaughn had silently envied Crystal's light tones and Barbie doll hair. It wasn't until years later that Vaughn had discovered that Crystal had her own insecurities about her looks. Crystal, too, had never felt accepted by her peers. She was taunted for "thinking" she was white—boys wanted her only for her looks, and most girls hated her on sight. In retaliation, Crystal had adopted that wise-talking street-girl persona—to be one of the crowd. It was only with Vaughn that she allowed her depth to shine through. The friendship of Vaughn and Crystal was like a catharsis for both of them, and it had blossomed into more than just friendship over the years.

"So," Crystal began, once Vaughn was seated. "I've scheduled three news conferences for you. One today, and two on Wednesday, and an interview with Channel 6 . . ." she checked her watch, "in about two hours." She paced the room as she spoke, only briefly checking the notes she'd committed to memory. "I contacted Lucus Stone's office this morning to see if I could arrange an informal debate. They weren't having me today," she stated cynically. "But I'll be back at them in a couple of weeks, after we get some heavy press coverage. They'll be ready to talk then."

Vaughn took it all in as Crystal continued with her agenda, which included luncheons, meetings, and follow-up appointments. But even as she listened, a part of her was totally detached from the conversation. That part was focused on Justin and the glorious two days they'd spent together.

She felt as if she'd been transformed into someone else, and she was scared. There was no doubt about that. Her track record as far as love and romance were concerned was dismal at best. The few serious relationships she'd been involved with had ended disastrously. The traumatic ending of her young love affair with Brian Willis had irrevocably changed her life and made her cautious of relationships. Her liaisons in between had been meaningless until she'd met Paul. She thought he'd be the one, but her brief relationship with Paul Lawrence had been the ultimate in betrayal. Though their relationship had been over for nearly two years, she'd remained wary of would-be suitors. Every man who'd come into her life had ultimately wanted something other than her; from a political favor, to money, to casual sex, to an appointment on her staff.

She knew that she was taking a big risk with Justin. But for the first time, she was with a man who had his own and didn't need her or her influence to further his own goals. Justin clearly had no political aspirations. He had his own money and a flourishing career. Most of all, he made her feel—God, he made her feel—way deep down in her soul, a place that she didn't know was still living and breathing within her. Just the thought of him made her toes tingle and her pulse pound.

She realized they'd barely known each other a month. Twenty-seven fabulous days, to be exact. She was still overwhelmed. She knew that her emotions were doing an Indy 500, but she couldn't help it and she no longer wanted to. She deserved to be held, to be kissed senseless, to be loved. She needed to start living again. It was long overdue.

"I've never known a nonstop, 'til you drop schedule could put a smile on your face," Crystal said, effectively cutting into Vaughn's steamy thoughts. Vaughn's face burned with embarrassment.

"Sorry. I was just thinking. But," she qualified, raising her index finger, "I heard every word you said."

"Hmmm. That remains to be seen," Crystal breathed, unconvinced and very curious. She took a seat opposite Vaughn, crossed her legs, put down her pad, and stared wide-eyed at her boss.

"What?" Vaughn questioned innocently, knowing full well that Crystal was waiting for a scoop.

"Don't what me," Crystal admonished. "What, or better yet, *who* put that starry look in your eyes and the glow on your face? If I didn't know better, I'd swear you looked happy."

Vaughn laughed out loud, albeit a bit nervously, at Crystal's blunt observation. Generally, Vaughn was able to camouflage her true feelings expertly. It was a bit unsettling to discover that where Justin Montgomery was concerned, that practiced skill was disintegrating rapidly.

Vaughn sat back and began shuffling the papers and folders on her desk in an attempt to recover her composure and avoid Crystal's pointed gaze. She cleared her throat.

"Can't I look happy?" she asked lamely, stalling for time.

"Of course you can," Chris replied gently. "It's just that it's so rare." She paused. "And it's been so long," she added softly, her eyes filled with warmth for her friend. Crystal, more than anyone, was aware of the tight reins that Vaughn kept around her heart. Hers was the shoulder Vaughn had cried on after that fiasco with Paul. But Crystal also knew that there was something deep in Vaughn's past, a wound that would not heal, and one that Vaughn had refused to disclose. There was a part of Vaughn's past that she kept entirely out of reach. Crystal stood up and patted Vaughn's busy hands, stilling them. "Listen, I'm not prying. I never have. If you're happy—whatever the reason—I'm happy. If you feel like talking, you know I'm always here."

Vaughn smiled up at her friend of over fifteen years. "Thanks," she said softly. "I know."

"Good." Then Crystal did a quick switchback to her role as chief of staff. "Once you've gotten that smile off your face, go over your agenda and let me know if there need to be any changes. Not that anything *can* be changed." She smiled mischievously. "But you know how I like your input."

Vaughn flashed what could only be termed a sneer. Crystal stuck out her tongue in response.

"I'll be back in an hour." Crystal headed for the door.

"Could you send Tess in? I need to respond to these letters."

"I'll send her right in." Crystal closed the door softly behind her.

As soon as Vaughn was alone, her thoughts drifted back to Justin. She wondered what he was doing right now. Was he thinking of her? Her heart beat a little faster. What was he wearing today? Did he splash on that cologne that made her brain turn to mush?

She shook her head to clear her thoughts. What was happening to her? This daydreaming and fantasizing was so unlike her. She seemed to have become engulfed in a whirlwind, a storm of unimaginable power. She was spinning helplessly. It was a heady, frightening sensation. For the first time in her life, at least since her teens, her emotions seemed to be totally out of her control. She couldn't seem to rein them in and put on the brakes. Although there had been other men in her life, she had always felt some sense of control over her feelings, some sense of reality. Not now. And Justin Montgomery was the eye of her storm.

The light tapping on her door and the ringing of the phone competed for her attention.

"Come in," she called out, while reaching for her private line.

"Yes. Vaughn Hamilton."

"Good morning, Vaughn."

Her stomach did a quick lurch. "Hi, Dad." She waved Tess inside and motioned for her to sit. "How are you?"

"I'm fine. I thought we could meet for lunch and discuss a few things."

Vaughn frowned slightly. She didn't like the sound of "discuss a few things." "Has something come up, Daddy? Because if it's not urgent, I really have a full schedule today."

"I believe it would be in your best interest to fit me into your schedule. There are matters that must be dealt with immediately. What time is good for you?" he continued.

Vaughn sighed heavily and clenched her jaw. She knew she'd give in even as she told her father about her agenda. But she at least wanted to make him feel a twinge of guilt for disrupting her day, though she knew he wouldn't.

"How about 2:30?" she said flatly. "I'd really appreciate it if you could come here. It's going to be difficult for me to get away."

"I'll be there at two," he replied. "Court reconvenes at three. See you then." Elliott Hamilton hung up the receiver and looked, once again, at the pages in front of him. He pressed his lips together and slid his glasses from his nose. With his free hand, he rubbed it roughly across his face. He didn't like it; he didn't like it one bit. Vaughn had to be brought under control. Everything rested on appearances. He'd worked too hard to get her to where she was today. He wasn't going to let her ruin it; that's all there was to it. He slapped his hand against his mahogany desk with finality. That's all there was to it.

The Chaney Building, which housed Justin's suite of offices, loomed ahead. Moments later, Justin eased his BMW into the underground parking garage and swung into his spot. He looked across the lanes and saw that Sean and Khendra's Lexus LS was also parked in their usual spot. Good, he needed to talk to Sean.

Retrieving his briefcase and his black leather trenchcoat from the backseat, he automatically activated the alarm system and locked the doors. In long, brisk strides, he crossed the gray and white concrete and entered the elevator that would take him to his offices on the sixteenth floor.

Justin pushed through the heavy, ornately carved wood doors that led to the immense reception area. Although he'd been coming through those same doors for nearly three years, he still had sudden flashes that it was all fantasy. Yet, this was his. He'd worked for it and everything, including every detail in the wood, had his markings. It was all a tribute to his enormous success, both in the courtroom and out. It was as a result of his success that he now had the time and opportunity to pursue other avenues, such as public speaking, advocacy, and writing that book that had been gnawing at him for years. And now, he finally had time for a woman in his life. He smiled unconsciously as visions of Vaughn bloomed ripe. He had the time to devote himself to making this relationship work and not have his work destroy the relationship—as it had between him and Janice.

Years later, it still hurt. Janice had been his first love, and his young heart had been fired with romance and ambition. He'd wanted Janice along for the ride. They'd married, had a child almost immediately, and before Justin had realized what had happened, they were divorced and Janice was gone, along with their infant daughter.

He'd expended his savings, his skills, and all the resources available to him trying to locate his ex-wife and child. They'd virtually disappeared off the face of the earth. Finally, after years of frustration, he'd given up and dove into his work with an incomparable intensity.

For that reason he'd become a devout advocate of children's rights. He truly believed that he could somehow make an impact on legislatures to repeal the laws governing the sealing of adoption and foster care placement records and allow those children to lawfully find their natural parents. He had been a catalyst in helping to establish several organizations across the country who assisted parents and children in finding each other. It was his hope that although Janice saw no need to have him involved in their daughter's life, his child would somehow find him through the channels now available. That hope was like an eternal flame that burned in his heart. If and when his dream of reuniting with his daughter was realized, he wanted Vaughn to be a part of that ultimate joy.

"Good morning, Mr. Montgomery," Barbara Crenshaw, his executive assistant, greeted him cheerily. Her soft gray-green eyes warmed at the sight of him.

"Morning, Barb. Any messages?"

"They're on your desk. Do you want coffee or should I send out for breakfast?"

"Coffee will be fine. I want to get my notes together for the staff meeting."

"I'll be right in."

Justin waved and nodded acknowledgment to the bevy of staff members that made up his team as he wound his way through the maze of offices that led to his own. Once inside the soundproof room, he hung up his coat, rounded his desk, and punched in the extension for Sean's line.

"Good morning, Phillips here," came the distinctly feminine voice.

Justin smiled broadly. "How can that man of yours ever get any work done if you're in his office doing who knows what when I'm not looking?"

Khendra's husky laughter filtered through the phone. "Who says we're here to work? We just come in to get a change of atmosphere," she teased, enjoying the bantering that went on between them. "I presume you want to speak to my handsome, brilliant husband," she added, giving her husband a quick wink.

"Well, only if you're not keeping him too preoccupied to talk to me, of course," Justin joked.

"Let me just check and see if he wants to be distracted, by business, that is, this early in the morning." Khendra chuckled. "Listen," she said, switching gears, "I was just going over the reports on the Harrison murder case. I think we should take it, Justin. I know I can pull this off."

"Great. Bring your notes. We'll discuss it at the meeting."

"Here's Sean."

"Hey, Justin. What's up?" Sean's voice came over the wire.

"I was hoping you, uh, had some free time this morning, before the meeting."

Sean immediately caught the hitch of hesitation in Justin's voice. His thick eyebrows arched. Justin was never hesitant about anything.

"Sure. You want me to stop in now?"

"Yeah. Barb is bringing in coffee. Have you had breakfast?"

"We just finished. I just need to make two short calls and I'll be right down."

"Thanks."

"Justin?"

"Yeah, Sean."

"Is everything all right? You don't sound like yourself."

Justin thought for a moment and almost laughed out loud. He wasn't himself. "Everything's fine. Better than fine. That's what I want to talk with you about. See you in a few."

Justin reached again for the phone. His smile was broad. This time he dialed an outside number to the local florist.

Shortly there was a light knock on Justin's office door.

"Come in."

Sean strutted in, the picture of polish, power, and control. Sean was a connoisseur of fine clothing. His instincts and tenacity when it came to criminal law could be paralleled only by his wife, Khendra. But Sean knew when to relax and enjoy the good life he'd built for himself. He spent hours in the gym and on the racquetball court, which was where he and Justin had met nearly eight years before. They'd become fast friends, sharing a variety of similar interests. Justin had come to rely not only on Sean's legal judgment, but on his personal judgment as well.

"What's up, partner?" Sean asked, breezing in and taking a seat opposite Justin.

Justin stood up, slinging his hands into his pockets. He turned dark eyes on Sean. "I'm thinking about making some . . . changes."

Sean's eyebrows rose in question. He remained silent and listened as Justin revealed a side of himself that Sean hadn't known existed.

The morning flew by with blinding speed. Before Vaughn had completed half of her tasks for the day, it was time to meet her father for lunch. She'd had Tess order two jumbo salad specials, knowing that they would be both filling and in keeping with her father's diet, which he readily ignored.

Her midday interview with Channel 6 had gone off smoothly; the statements she'd made to the reporter from the *Herald* would be in the next day's paper. She'd gone through half her mail, returned nearly a dozen phone calls, and remained sane through it all. To cap off a morning of success, she'd just received a huge bouquet of two dozen red roses from Justin. The whole office was buzzing. And she knew that as soon as Crystal was finished with her meeting, she'd be beating down her door for some answers. She'd tried to call Justin to thank him for his thoughtful gift, but he was tied up in a staff meeting.

In the meantime, she had her father to deal with. She checked her watch. Ten to two. He'd be arriving in minutes. Vaughn straightened her desk and crossed the parquet floor to the small conference table that held their lunch. She looked over the array of salads, breads, and low-calorie dressings. Everything was in place.

The brief knock on the door signaled her father's arrival.

"A little noisy around here today, I see," Elliott commented, hanging up his coat on the rack. He took out his pipe and slipped it between his teeth.

Vaughn crossed the room and gave her father a quick kiss. "I took the liberty of ordering lunch," she said, crossing to the table. "I thought we could eat and talk."

Elliott took a seat without comment. He looked across at his daughter and waited for her to be seated.

"Would you like some spring water, or tea?" she asked nervously, the ominous look of her father rattling her. He waved the offer away. She sat down like an errant schoolgirl waiting to be reprimanded. She became angry at herself. She influenced all sorts of men and women and changed government policy. So, why did her father still have the ability to rattle her nerves?

"I want to get straight to the point of this meeting," Elliott began without preamble. "I just received a report today on your activities over the weekend."

For an instant she was sure she couldn't have heard correctly. "You what?"

"You were seen at the docks on Saturday, with that Montgomery fellow in a very compromising position to say the least."

Vaughn felt the heat of embarrassment and anger burn her face. She shot up from her seat. "Are you saying that you had me followed?" she asked, her voice rising in indignation and disbelief.

Elliott cleared his throat and shot her a thunderous look. "Let's just say that your activities have been brought to my attention."

Vaughn spun away, barely able to contain the fury and humiliation that welled inside her.

"Sit down!" Elliott ordered.

"I will not," she tossed back, spinning around to confront him, her face a blanket of outrage. "How dare you? How dare you have me followed? What right do you have to interfere in my private life?"

"I have every right," he countered. "Wasn't your experience with Paul enough to teach you a lesson? And Brian," he added. The impact of his last comment had the desired effect, he noted, as he saw her resistance crumble.

The cold, on-target remark was like a splash of ice water. Vaughn felt her eyes sting with tears that threatened to overflow. Her throat tightened. She would not allow him to see her cry. Never again, she vowed. She remained standing, stiff and defiant, meeting her father's eyes head on.

"Vaughn," he said, almost gently, "I have only your best interests at heart. I want to protect you. Now is not the time for you to get . . . involved." He cleared his throat. "The last thing you need is for the tabloids to pick up on any relationships you may be having. They'll eat you alive. You'll have enough to contend with without the added burden of a relationship that couldn't possibly go anywhere. For heaven's sake, child, you only just met the man. I gave you more credit than that."

"Did you really?" she asked hollowly. "I didn't think you gave me much credit for anything, Daddy."

"Don't be ridiculous. Of course I do. If I didn't believe in your abilities, do you think I'd have guided your career for so many years? I want the best for you, sweetheart. But I want you to realize your ambitions *before* you make any commitments. You need to be sure of who you're dealing with and ultimately of what they want from you. Everyone wants something, Vaughn; you know that as well as I do. It's the nature of our lives. A mistake now could be disastrous for your career."

Is that all she would ever have? she wondered numbly. A career? What about love, a family, a man in her life who loved her for who she was? Was Justin the right man? Maybe her father was correct. Hadn't he always been right? Hadn't he always *made* everything right?

He reached across the table and patted her cold hands. "I know you'll realize the truth in what I'm telling you. Put an end to this, *before* it gets out of hand. I know you may not agree with me now. But if you think with your head and not with your heart, you'll see that I'm right."

Vaughn's eyes trailed across the room to her desk and settled on the brilliant bouquet of flowers. Inhaling deeply, she nodded.

Elliott rose. "Then it's settled." He rounded the table and briefly touched his lips to her cheek. "You won't regret this, sweetheart."

Vaughn pressed her lips together to keep them from trembling. Elliott collected his coat. His goodbye went unanswered.

Mechanically, Vaughn rose, crossed the room, and locked her office door. She turned and pressed her back against it. She squeezed her eyes shut and fought down the tremors that raced up and down her spine.

What was she going to do? Her political career was already a daunting struggle, but now she would have to put her energies into fighting her father as well?

Slowly she recrossed the room and sank down onto the low couch that braced the far wall of the airy office. A part of her knew that her father was right. She *didn't* know Justin Montgomery. Her past experiences had demonstrated time and time again that the men in her life had proved disastrous, on many levels. Was Justin any different?

Her father was one of those men as well. For reasons she couldn't fathom, she at times found it almost impossible to get from under his spell. Her father had dictated every aspect of her life for so long, that she felt incapable of making an independent decision.

Vaughn sucked on her bottom lip. She'd always succumbed to her father's demands and expectations. She stood up and took a deep breath, her face resolute, her eyes glowing with rebellion. Until now. This time she would prove her father wrong. Justin would prove him wrong.

CHAPTER 6

Over lunch in a small café on Pennsylvania Avenue, Sean and Khendra talked animatedly about the pending Harrison murder case. It was one of the most noteworthy cases to have arisen in decades. All of the players were very public people, and the prime suspect was one of the most prominent athletes in America.

"I'm sure that the family will be agreeable to retaining us," Khendra stated, taking a sip of Perrier. "We have the manpower and the experience. And the D.A. has so much circumstantial evidence, it's almost funny."

Sean nodded in agreement. "Unfortunately," he said, "circumstantial evidence has convicted a lot of people."

"True. But I don't think there's a jury in this country that will convict Harrison based on the evidence collected to date."

Momentarily they lapsed into silence. The waiter appeared with their order.

"There's something else that I wanted to talk with you about, Khen," Sean said, changing topics. He hesitated.

"Well?"

"I had the strangest conversation today with Justin."

Khendra looked at him curiously. She pushed a wayward strand of hair away from her face. "Justin, strange? What a contradiction in terms." She slipped a forkful of pasta salad into her mouth.

"Believe me." He paused briefly. "Justin is contemplating giving up his practice and devoting all his energies to advocacy and public speaking."

Khendra's eyes widened, the fork that she held suspended between the plate and her mouth. "What? I don't believe it."

Sean shook his head. "It's the same thing I said. But he was very adamant."

"What is he going to do with the firm? I mean, what about the cases, the staff . . . ?"

Sean held up his hand. "This is the clincher. He wants us to buy him out and take over."

Khendra sat in open-mouthed astonishment. Her fork clinked against the china plate. She tried to absorb what she'd been told. How many years had she and Sean talked about starting their own practice? But they'd been too loyal to Justin to pull up stakes? And now he was handing them their dream on a silver platter. It was almost too good to be true.

Khendra straightened in her seat. "How long have we known Justin?"

"About eight years."

"Right. And knowing Justin, he never does anything on the spur of the moment and without a real strong reason." She took a deep breath. "There's more to this than he's telling."

"I didn't want to say anything, but that's what I was thinking."

"What do you think it is?" she asked.

"I wish I knew."

Khendra smiled coyly, her eyebrow arched. "Don't you think it's up to us to find out?"

Sean saw the spark in her eyes and knew that those wheels were turning a mile a minute. "What are you thinking, Khen? I know that look." He peered at her from beneath heavy black lashes.

"I say we need to do some investigating on our own. As much as I would love for us to have our own practice, I want to be sure it's for all the right reasons."

"Agreed. What do you want to do?"

Khendra reached across the table and took her husband's hand in hers, running her fingertip languidly along his palm. Sean felt himself instantly harden at her touch. She leaned enticingly forward, giving him the barest glimpse of the swell of her breasts. Her normally husky voice lowered another octave. "Why don't we take a long lunch and discuss this further . . . at home?"

Sean grinned devilishly, his eyes darkening to a smoky sable. He leaned across the table to place a titillating kiss on Khendra's moist lips. "That's the best offer I've had all day."

Justin finally had a free minute to return Vaughn's phone call. Just anticipating hearing her voice brought a warm smile to his lips. These past few weeks had changed him deeply. Vaughn was like some wild dream come true. He knew he'd have to take his time to convince her to cross those walls she'd erected. Instinctively he knew she'd been burned before, and she was right to be cautious. What woman wouldn't be, given the circumstances of their meeting?

He smiled. Everything was going to work out; he could feel it. He reached across his desk and pulled the phone closer. He dialed her number. Waiting, he leaned back and put his feet up on the desk. He patted the breast pocket of his jacket. The tickets were in place. He'd had to twist a few arms and call in a few favors to get his hands on them. But he knew it would be worth it. The concert and then a late dinner tonight, he mused, listening to the ringing on the other end.

Vaughn stared at the phone. It was her private line. It was probably her father again, wanting to add more fuel to the fire. She sighed heavily.

Justin frowned. Maybe she'd stepped out, he concluded. He leaned over to return the receiver to the cradle when he heard Vaughn's voice. He snatched the phone back.

"Vaughn. Hello. It's Justin."

Vaughn squeezed her eyes shut. Maybe it would have been better if it had been her father on the other end. She wasn't ready to talk with Justin. She was still too torn.

"Justin . . . hello. I really can't talk right now. I was on my way out to a press conference." She swallowed and ordered her heart to slow down. *Oh, Justin.* She gripped the phone. Since her conversation with her father and her momentary flash of rebellion, she'd had some time to think things through. She'd come to a decision.

"No problem. I won't keep you. I wanted to entice you to a night of music and great food. I have two tickets to the Carpenter Center for the Performing Arts. There's a jazz concert there tonight with all of the favorites. The list is incredible. Then I thought we'd have a late dinner at the Strawberry Café. How does that sound? I can't wait to see you again," he ended on a husky note.

"It, it sounds wonderful, Justin. But I really can't . . . not tonight." She straightened her shoulders and forced a tone of airiness into her voice. "You wouldn't believe the kind of day I've been having. I won't be any good to anyone, including myself, by the end of this day. I'd probably fall asleep."

"What's wrong, Vaughn?" he asked bluntly. "And don't tell me it's the job. You've been doing this for years. It's second nature. What's the real reason you don't want to see me tonight? More second thoughts?"

He was too good at seeing through her, she thought miserably, even over the phone. "Justin, listen," she began. "Believe me, I'd love to spend the evening with you." *You don't know how much.* "But circumstances . . . won't permit it."

Justin's jaw clenched so hard his head began to hurt. What was he going to have to do to get her to trust him, to let go? What had happened to her to make her so wary? He knew that he wanted Vaughn in his life, especially with the turn that it was about to take. But he wasn't sure he had the patience or the endurance to give what it was going to take to get through to her. Maybe it wasn't worth the effort.

Justin let out a long-held breath. "Fine," he expelled. "If that's what you want. Call me . . . when you have some time. Goodbye, Vaughn."

Vaughn heard the dial tone hum in her ear. She looked up to the ceiling, clutching the phone to her breasts. Her eyes stung. "It's best this way, Justin," she said, her voice trembling with emotion.

Justin slammed his fist against his desk and sprang from his seat, spinning it in a circle in the process. Recklessly, he raked his fingers through his close-cropped hair. Never had any woman made him so crazy! He spun away from the window, his face a mask of confused anger. Something had happened. Something or someone had gotten to her to make her do a 360 in less than twenty-four hours. He pressed his lips together. He was never one to just give up, not when it came to something he wanted. Vaughn was that something. She was the key, and he had no intention of letting her slip through his fingers. No matter what she said.

Simone had just returned to her dorm room after her last class for the day. It was nearly three o'clock. She wanted to place her call to Mr. Montgomery's office before it got too late. She tossed her knapsack onto her bed and snatched up the business card from her nightstand.

Quickly she said a silent prayer and then dialed.

"Montgomery, Phillips and Michaels," answered the polished voice.

Simone took a deep breath. "Yes, good afternoon. My name is Simone Rivers. I'm a student at Spelman."

"Yes?" Barbara inquired tersely. She had a desk full of work to complete before the end of the day and she wanted to get home at a reasonable hour.

"Mr. Montgomery had a speaking engagement here at the college several months ago," she stated quickly, sensing the woman's impatience. "He said he'd be looking for interns this summer. I'd like to apply for an internship with the firm."

Barbara frowned. "Why would you want to come all the way from Atlanta to D.C. for an internship?" she asked skeptically.

"I was very impressed with Mr. Montgomery's presentation, and I have similar advocacy interests. I feel this internship would be an excellent opportunity."

Barbara smiled indulgently. "I see. Well, Mr. Mont-gomery has to clear all internships. You'll have to mail in your qualifications and he'll be in touch with you."

Simone's faced beamed with delight. "Yes!" she mouthed silently, shooting a fist through the air. "May I fax my information to you? That would be a lot quicker."

Barbara's smile broadened. She liked the girl's tenacity. "That'd be fine. Take down this number."

Simone quickly jotted it down and repeated it back. "I'll send it right over," Simone said eagerly.

"Be sure to include a contact number. Either I or one of the paralegals will call you when we receive your information."

"Thank you. Oh, I'm sorry, who am I speaking with?"

"Barbara Crenshaw."

"Thank you for your time, Ms. Crenshaw. I look forward to hearing from you."

"You're welcome," Barbara said, returning the receiver to its cradle. She wondered what this young lady had to offer. Heaven knew they could use an extra hand around the office, especially if Khendra and Sean were going to be wrapped up in that Harrison mess. Most of the para-legals were still in school and only worked part-time. And the only one who showed any real promise was Chad Rushmore. The corner of her wide mouth lifted in a grin. Now, that was a young man who was going places, she thought. When the fax came in, she'd pass it on to him and let him give his impressions. There was no point in troubling Justin if there was no reason to show interest in Simone. She did seem quite determined, Barbara thought, returning her attention to her work. They'd just have to see.

Chad breezed into the office after picking up a set of transcripts just as the fax machine was spitting out the last page of Simone's internship package.

"Chad," Barbara greeted, "I'm glad you're back. I have something I want you to look over before I pass it along to Mr. Montgomery."

"Sure. What is it?" Chad stepped up to Barbara's desk, deposited his package, and took the curled pages. "A résumé?"

"Actually, it's an internship request. I got a call this afternoon from this young lady. She sounds promising. And her qualifications are outstanding."

Chad nodded as he skimmed the pages. She was impressive. Top of her class, outstanding recommendations from her professors, previous experience in a law firm. "I say, forget the internship, let's hire her!" he grinned, flashing even white teeth. At twenty-two, Chad had really come into his own. Gone was the lanky, uncoordinated boy of his youth. In his place was a six-foot-two, smooth-as-silk young man who knew where he was going.

Barbara watched him as he ran over the details of Simone's application. He'd come far in the three years he'd been with the firm. She remembered the day he'd arrived as an intern: uncertain, introverted, and a lousy dresser, she remembered with wry amusement. Now, looking at Chad, she wished she was fifteen years younger. Any young lady lucky enough to land Chad Rushmore would be one happy woman. The man was gorgeous.

"You have my vote, Barb," Chad said, looking up from the papers. He handed them back and leaned his thigh against her desk. "Are you going to pass it on to the big boss?"

"She certainly looks like she has potential. I'll add your recommendation to mine and see what he says."

"Good. Listen, I have some briefs to review. I'll be buried in my office for the next couple of hours. Then I'm cutting out. Anything you need from me?"

"As a matter of fact, yes. I'd really appreciate it if you could call this young lady back and let her know we received her information. She may have some questions about the internship program that you could answer, *firsthand,*" she qualified with a knowing smile.

"No problem," he grinned, remembering his own early days as an intern.

Barbara jotted down the number and handed it to Chad. "Thanks. I'll take care of it right away." He waved and strutted off to his office.

Barbara jotted down some notes about Simone, added Chad's comments, and headed for Justin's office.

Barbara arrived at Justin's door just as he was preparing to leave. "Oh, Mr. Montgomery, I didn't realize you'd be leaving so early. I'll just leave this on your desk."

"What is it?" Justin asked distractedly, slipping his arms into his coat.

"An application for an internship for the summer. The young woman seems extremely well qualified," she added.

"Fine. Just leave it. I'll take a look at it tomorrow."

Barbara noted the hard lines around Justin's mouth and the firm set of his jaw. "Is everything okay, Mr. Mont-gomery?"

Justin shot her a quick glance, grabbed his briefcase, and walked toward the door. "It will be," he said, snatching open the door. "It will be," he repeated under his breath.

"How long has she been in there?" Crystal asked Tess.

Tess sighed. "For the past couple of hours. She told me to hold all calls and she hasn't opened her door when I knocked."

Crystal frowned. She'd gotten wind of the fact that Vaughn's father had been on the premises earlier and she knew how Elliott Hamilton had the ability to unravel Vaughn with just a look. She wondered what bombshell he'd dropped today.

"You continue to hold her calls, Tess. I'm sure she's just swamped with work and doesn't want to be disturbed. You know how single-minded Vaughn can be when she gets her teeth into something." Crystal smiled. "I'll check on her."

Vaughn heard a light knock on her door. She couldn't continue to avoid her staff for the rest of the day. Slowly she got up and opened the door.

"Come on in," Vaughn said, straining to sound cheerful.

Crystal stepped in and spun around to face Vaughn. "You want to tell me why you've been locked up in your office for the entire afternoon?" Her eyes swept across the office. "And . . . who are those flowers from?"

A quick call to Vaughn's office prior to Justin's departure had confirmed that she was still there. He raced through the streets of D.C. and took I-95 to Richmond. If he didn't catch her at the office, he'd wait for her at her townhouse. One way or the other, he and Vaughn were going to talk. Today.

CHAPTER 7

Vaughn crossed the office, mindful of keeping her back to Crystal. How could she face her closest friend and tell her how weak, how spineless, she really was? How could she tell her that the woman who thousands admired for her strength and determination was no more than an overgrown daddy's girl? Slowly Vaughn turned around, her face a portrait of despair.

"Vaughn!" Crystal cried in alarm. "What is it?" She quickly crossed the room and stood in front of her friend. "Tell me. It can't be *that* bad."

Vaughn expelled a shaky laugh. "Oh, believe me, it's worse." Vaughn sat down behind her desk and took a deep breath. Crystal remained standing until the full impact of what Vaughn had revealed forced her to sit down.

"You and Justin Montgomery?" Crystal asked incredulously. She shook her head in bewilderment. "This is so unlike you, Vaughn, to just . . . leap into something."

Vaughn shot her a derisive look. Crystal held up her hands in defense. "Listen, I'm not saying there's anything wrong. Believe me. The Lord only knows I wish I could meet someone who could rock my world." She smiled warmly. "He must be one helluva man to win you over." Vividly Crystal recalled the anguish Vaughn had suffered through after the ending of her affair with Paul Lawrence. Paul had repeatedly professed his love for her, but Vaughn had opened her heart only to find out that he'd used her feelings for him to gain entrée into all the right circles, to attain favors and win supporters. Once he'd been elected to office, he'd dropped Vaughn like the plague. Crystal didn't think Vaughn would ever recover from that humiliation and hurt. Maybe this Justin Montgomery was just the medicine she needed. He was damn sure fine enough, Crystal thought, with a pang of remembrance from the night of the fund-raiser.

Vaughn felt her cheeks flame. "Yeah," she admitted softly. "He certainly is."

"But the thing that really has my head swimming is that Elliott had you followed. I mean, I know he has his ways, but this is going over the limit, even for him. You can't just sit back and let him do this to you . . . father or not," she added adamantly.

"That's what I've been wrestling with all afternoon, Crystal." She sighed heavily. "I've allowed my father to manipulate me for so long it's become second nature." She stood up, folding her arms tightly in front of her. "Except for buying the townhouse, I can't remember the last time I made an independent decision which didn't cause such a furor I didn't hear the end of it for months."

"But this is different, Vaughn . . . you *know* it is. This isn't about some purchase, or deciding what campaign strategy to use. This is about your life and what you want to do with it."

Vaughn's dark, troubled eyes met Crystal's. Crystal stood up and rounded the desk to stand next to Vaughn. "You know you have the strength. You know you have the determination. You've proved it time and time again in your career. Now, use those same qualities for your personal salvation. Vaughn," she pleaded, "if you allow your father to do this to you, to take away your happiness, you'll never know if you and Justin were meant to be. Don't you think you deserve to find out?"

By degrees the shroud that had covered her spirit was lifted. Vaughn felt a sweet release in the realization that for once in her life, she truly did have the power to make changes. If she backed down now, she knew she'd regret it for the rest of her life. And she'd never earn her father's respect, or her own.

"You're right, Crystal. I want this chance more than anything," she said, her voice lifting in strength. "There may never be another time. My father has controlled me for far too long. If this relationship between Justin and me falls apart tomorrow, I need to know that at least I tried."

Crystal squeezed Vaughn's shoulder. "And believe me, girl, if it doesn't work out, send him *this* way!"

Vaughn and Crystal burst into laughter, the doubt and tension vanishing into the air.

"Forget it, Crystal," Vaughn sputtered, catching her breath. "If it doesn't work, this sister is going to try again until she gets it right!"

A flurry of activity outside Vaughn's office effectively shortcircuited the momentary frivolity. The sound of raised voices penetrated the closed door. A worried look flashed between them as they hurried toward it. Vaughn reached it first, but she took a retreating step back as the door swung inward.

Justin stalked in, his full-length coat billowing around him with the force of his entry. Momentarily Vaughn had the notion of imagining Justin as the avenging superhero ready to pummel the enemy. *Her.*

"Justin," Vaughn said on a long breath, halting her retreat so that Justin was only a heartbeat away. Their eyes locked and held, communicating more than any words could convey.

Crystal looked from one to the other and visualized them as the perfect models for the cover of one of those steamy romance novels she loved. The electricity that snapped and sparked between them was enough to light up all of Richmond. If Vaughn let this hunk of a man go, she was definitely going to have to seek professional help for her friend.

Two steps behind Justin was Tess. "Ms. Hamilton, I'm so sorry," she apologized. "He just pushed his way past me. I tried to . . ."

"Don't worry about it, Tess," Vaughn responded absently, her eyes never leaving Justin's. The flicker of a smile teased her lips. "Mr. Montgomery has a tendency to come on like gangbusters every now and then."

When Vaughn's gaze slid past Justin's face, she saw Crystal nudging Tess out the door. The soft click let them know that they were totally alone.

"I'm glad you came, Justin," Vaughn began, quickly cutting him off before he could get started. "If you hadn't shown up here, I was coming to you."

Justin had been all geared up for a battle of wills. This spontaneous shift momentarily caught him off guard. His eyes narrowed suspiciously.

Vaughn turned away from him and walked toward the couch, where she sat down. She crossed her long legs, giving him a teasing view of her firm thighs. She stretched her arm across the back of the couch. Her eyes invited him to join her. Justin suddenly felt as if he'd been tossed into a seductive scene in a movie. Well, if this was to be his debut appearance, he was going to give an Academy Award performance.

With long, purposeful strides he came close, looking down at her intensely. Vaughn extended her hand and he took it, pulling her from her seated position right up against the hard lines of his body. Without words, without preamble, his mouth covered hers. As he crushed her in his embrace, his tongue forced her lips apart and plunged into the recesses of her warmth. A shudder rippled through her, sending sweet spirals of ecstasy singing through her veins. This was so right, she realized, sinking helplessly into the rapture of his kiss, giving back as much as she was getting. This was what she'd been searching for. At last she'd found it. She'd never let anything come between them again.

"Vaughn," he moaned against her mouth. He buried his face in her hair, inhaling the natural sweetness. "I thought . . ."

"Sssh," she whispered. "There's so much I need to tell you. So much I need to explain."

Reluctantly, Justin angled his head back slightly, looking questioningly down into her smoky eyes. His arm held her firmly around the waist. His finger traced the soft line of her jaw. Her eyes briefly fluttered closed as she fought down the tremor of his touch.

"Why don't we get out of here?" she asked huskily. "I don't want to be interrupted . . . by business."

"Get your things," he said in a rugged whisper.

"Hello, Ms. Rivers?"

"Yes," Simone answered, the smooth voice causing a flutter in her stomach.

"This is Chad Rushmore, of Montgomery, Phillips and Michaels."

Simone sat up straighter in bed, tossing her textbooks aside. "Hello, Mr. Rushmore."

"Ms. Crenshaw suggested that I call and advise you that we received your information. It's being passed along to Mr. Montgomery."

"Thank you."

"I must say, after looking over your credentials, I think you'd make an excellent intern."

Simone grinned with pleasure. "I'm glad you think so. I hope Mr. Montgomery feels the same way."

"Well, if my recommendation means anything, I'm sure you won't have a problem. If you do get the internship, we'll be working closely together."

Simone's heart thudded. "I hope everything will work out."

"So do I," Chad said sincerely. "I'm looking forward to meeting you." Chad took a deep breath then continued, "I'm sure someone will contact you shortly, Ms. Rivers," he added, regaining his composure.

"Thank you for calling," Simone said softly, wishing she could keep this silky-voiced man on the phone a little while longer.

"If you have any questions in the meantime," he added, wanting to delay their parting, "feel free to give me a call. I started out as an intern three years ago, and I'd be happy to fill you in on any of the details." He chuckled heartily. "From the ground floor up!"

"Really?" His laugh was deep and inviting, she thought wistfully. "How is it working for Mr. Montgomery?" Simone settled back against her stack of pillows.

"He's an okay guy. He expects your absolute best and he gives it back. If you prove yourself, there's nothing he wouldn't do to help further your career. He's the reason I was able to continue law school."

"Then he really is the way he comes across? It's not just a front?"

"Absolutely not. They don't come any better than Justin Montgomery."

"That's good to know. Now I'm sure I made the right choice in selecting his firm."

Simone heard a faint ringing in the background.

"That's my other line, Ms. Rivers; I've got to go. But good luck, and if you have any questions, just call me."

"Thank you, again, Mr. Rushmore."

"Sure. Goodbye."

"Goodbye," she replied softly. She placed the receiver on the cradle and briefly wondered if Chad Rushmore looked as delectable as he sounded.

While Chad jotted down the details of the phone call that had pulled him away from Simone, he wondered if the young Ms. Rivers looked as wonderful as she sounded. It'd be great to have someone to work with who was not only good to look at, but who understood the intensity of the legal profession. It had been a long time between relationships for him. He either didn't have the time, or the few women he met were only interested in how fat his wallet was. For some reason, he felt Simone would be different. What was he doing, fabricating a relationship with someone he'd never met? Now he was really losing it. It was definitely time to go home.

He concluded his conversation, made some final notations on the court transcripts, and checked his calendar for the following day. He really needed to get home and do some studying. The bar exam was in three months and he wanted to pass the first time out. But for reasons that he couldn't explain, he couldn't make out one word in his textbook that night. All he could see were different versions of Simone Rivers: tall, medium height; light, dark; short hair, long . . .

Finally he just gave up, fixed a sandwich, and overdosed on television.

"Why don't we leave your car in the garage and take mine?" Justin suggested. "We can come back and get your car later."

She slipped her hand into his. "That sounds fine," she nodded.

"Those reservations for the Strawberry Café are still good. It's an excellent place to talk," Justin suggested, as they approached his car.

Vaughn looked up into his questioning eyes. "To tell you the truth, Justin, as good as the café sounds, I really don't want to be around other people tonight."

His voice lowered. "You have a better suggestion?"

She smiled at him. "If you like crabmeat and shrimp casserole, tossed salad, and wild rice, I know just the place."

He squeezed her hand. "Would that happen to be on Lakewood Avenue, in a two-story townhouse owned by the renowned public servant Vaughn Hamilton?" he queried playfully.

"Good work, Sherlock," she teased. "I like a man with razor-sharp intelligence." She nudged him in the ribs.

"I hope you'll like more than my intelligence," he mimicked in a Dracula voice.

"Hmmm, and talented, too," she laughed.

Justin turned her into his embrace. His eyes swept over her upturned face. His fingers gently caressed her cheek. "There's so much more that I want to offer you, Vaughn," he said passionately. "I want you to believe that—always."

"I do, Justin," Vaughn whispered urgently. She placed a feather-light kiss on his palm. "I do."

The cozy townhouse was filled with the tangy aroma of simmering seafood. The sensuous sounds of Sarah Vaughn mingled with the tantalizing scent.

"If this tastes half as good as it smells," Justin said, adding a cup of diced mushrooms to the wild rice, "you'll have my vote for life."

"Well, if that's all it takes to get elected, I'd better get busy whipping up a batch for the voters."

Justin stroked her back as she sliced the tomatoes, and cucumbers, then sprinkled chopped sweet peppers as garnish. "We can eat in about ten minutes."

"Great. I don't think I can take the anticipation a moment longer. My stomach is calling out to me," he chuckled. "Loudly."

Vaughn smiled sympathetically. "Why don't you go in the living room and relax a minute? I have everything under control in here."

"Are you sure? I don't mind."

"Take advantage of being a guest. This is your last time. From here on out, it's equal work for equal food," she teased. Vaughn smiled, her eyes reflecting her hopes for their future.

"I like the sound of that." Justin pecked her playfully behind her ear and headed for the living room.

From his position on the couch, Justin could see Vaughn's movements in the kitchen. It gave him a warm feeling of security inside. It had been so long since he'd had a real home-cooked meal, and even longer since he'd shared it with someone who mattered to him. He'd enjoyed being married, although it had been short-lived. He liked the whole notion of having someone to share your life, your dreams, your emotions with. He wanted it again. He wanted the chance to start over, to make a new life and have a family. He wanted that chance with Vaughn. And if by some miracle he ever found his daughter, he couldn't think of any other woman he'd want to share that joy with.

"Dinner is served," Vaughn announced in an exaggerated accent.

"Hey, that's a pretty good imitation of the staid English butler," Justin chuckled, pushing himself up off the couch.

"I try. But I think you have me beaten with Dracula."

Justin smiled and took his place at the table. Vaughn had, at some point, lit a scented centerpiece which gave the room the soft scent of jasmine.

"Let's forget formalities," Vaughn said suddenly, the shimmer of mischief dancing around her lips. "Just dig in. Last one to empty his plate gets to do the dishes!"

"You're on," Justin challenged, and commenced to filling his plate with wild rice and topping it with a huge portion of the delectable casserole, drowning it in sauce. He added a heaping bowl of garden salad and snatched three slices of bread before Vaughn could wink.

She laughed out loud and shook her head in amazement as she watched Justin plow through his plate of food.

He looked up innocently, the fork suspended between his mouth and the plate. "I never back down from a challenge," he stated simply, and proceeded to finish off his plate of food.

The scrumptious meal was interrupted periodically only by brief comments on the state of the world, the weather, the concert they were missing, and their mutual interest in sports. Justin was careful to steer clear of anything too personal, or the reason why she'd wanted to speak with him. He felt confident that she would reveal what was troubling her as soon as she was ready. If there was one thing he'd learned about her, it was that Vaughn couldn't be pushed into anything.

Finally, Justin took a defeated breath and pushed back from the table. "I give up," he said. "I can't eat another thing. You win."

Vaughn leaned back, smugly satisfied. "The trick," she advised, "is to take small bites. It digests quicker—hence, more room for more food!" She smiled triumphantly.

"I'll try to remember that," he replied drolly. He stood up and stretched. "Well, point me in the direction of the dishwasher."

Vaughn tossed her head back and laughed. "No such luck, buddy. My mama didn't raise me to wash dishes in the dishwasher. Try good ole' Playtex gloves, hot water, and dishwashing liquid." Vaughn covered her mouth with her hand to stifle a giggle when she saw the look of total distress on Justin's face.

"You're kidding, of course."

Vaughn pressed her lips together and slowly shook her head.

"You're a wicked, wicked woman, Vaughn Hamilton," Justin said with mock solemnity.

"I work at it," she teased. She took his hand in hers. "The dishes can wait. We need to talk," she said seriously. Justin nodded and followed her to the loveseat.

"What would you like to talk about?"

Vaughn took a deep breath. "This seems silly considering my profession and all it entails," she said, as if speaking to herself, "but I really enjoy your company and I want to continue our relationship." She took Justin's hand in hers. "I'm in this relationship against my father's wishes."

"What do you mean? You're not a teenager," Justin commented.

"I know. I'm a woman who will soon wield incredible political power. Unfortunately, my power isn't effective over my father."

Slowly, painfully, Vaughn spoke of her life, her childhood, the invisible hold that her father had had over her, her insecurities, and finally, her father's recent ultimatum. She left nothing out except the painful year . . . after Brian.

Justin was stunned. For several long moments he said absolutely nothing, trying to absorb all he'd been told.

Suddenly, Vaughn felt as if she'd made the biggest mistake in her life by revealing such intimate details and most of all, her fears. She was certain that now that Justin saw how weak she was, he wouldn't want to have anything to do with her.

Justin's shock quickly turned to anger. To think that a father who supposedly loved his child unconditionally would use the love he received as a weapon! What kind of man was Elliott Hamilton? If he had the chance, he knew he would do everything in his power to show *his* daughter how much she was loved. He also knew there was more to this revelation than Vaughn was telling. For whatever her reasons, she still didn't trust him quite enough to confide in him. But that was all right. In time he knew she would. He turned to Vaughn, his eyes blazing. Vaughn held her breath, certain that Justin was a hot minute away from walking out the door.

"Vaughn, sweetheart." Relief washed over her in waves at the sound of the endearment. "I'm so sorry—for everything—everything you've been through. But most of all I feel outrage at your father for twisting your life into knots." He reached out and stroked her face. His jaw clenched. "I won't let him do that to you again, Vaughn. I swear to you I won't," he added fervently. "Your father is so sure that this relationship is destined for failure. He has you convinced that I'd be no different than any of the other career-grabbing, money-hungry predators who have crossed your path." His full lips lifted in a grin. "I told you," he said deeply, "I never back down from a challenge."

His fingers gripped her shoulders. "We can work through this, Vaughn. But only if you're willing to try. Are you?" he asked softly.

Vaughn swallowed back the knot of doubt and blinked away the water that floated in her eyes. Slowly, she nodded in agreement. "Yes. Yes, Justin, I am."

His eyes burned across her face. Gently, he pulled her into his arms.

"That's all I need to know," he breathed against her neck. "We'll take it slowly. Get to know each other." He leaned back and looked into her glistening eyes. "There's so much that I dream for us, Vaughn." He kissed the tip of her nose. He desperately wanted to tell her of his plans, of his search. But it could wait. "I've never felt this way about anyone before in my life. And I believe, deep down in my soul, that we can make this thing, this magic, between us work."

"Can we, Justin? Can we really?" she asked urgently, needing more than ever to know. "Politics can be an all-consuming way of life. Are you sure that's what you want?"

Justin breathed deeply. "I have to be honest with you, Vaughn. I'm not happy with the possibility that you'll have to devote so much of your time and energy to so many other people. I worry that there won't be any time left for us." He glanced away, then looked back into her questioning eyes. "But I'm willing to work through it."

Vaughn reached up and stroked his cheek, wishing she could wipe away the lines of worry. "If there was any way I could promise you it would be otherwise, I would. But you know I can't." She lowered her gaze. "All I can do is try." She smiled. "But we may be discussing something that's not even going to happen. I haven't won yet, you know."

Justin kissed her gently on the lips. "You will. I don't doubt that for a minute. Richmond has had its fill of Lucus Stone."

Vaughn snuggled closer to Justin. "I hope you're right."

"You have plenty of strong support, Vaughn." He tilted up her chin so that she had no other choice than to stare into his eyes. The connection made her stomach flutter. "And your strongest supporter is right here," he said. His gaze drifted down to the open neckline of her blouse.

"Justin . . ." she breathed.

"Sssh, don't say anything." He caressed her face. His finger trailed down her cheek to her neck. Vaughn struggled to push down the tremor that rippled through her. Justin's fingers explored the expanse of her neck. Feeling her pulse pound against the pads of his fingertips, he replaced his touch with his lips. The fire from his mouth burned across her collarbone and downward to the swell of her breasts. His tongue traced tiny, titillating circles on the exposed silken flesh. He pulled her tighter against his throbbing body, wishing he could magically soak her up into his very being.

Vaughn's lids fluttered closed as she absorbed the heat of Justin's touch. Her heart raced. Her breathing escalated. To feel like this again, she thought in wonder, so exquisite, so alive, was something she had not envisioned as part of her future. For so long she had shielded herself from romantic entanglements. Her past relationships had carved out a part of her heart and left her hollow and indifferent to men. Yet she dreamed of being reawakened, to know once again what it was like to savor the intimacy of being with a man she truly cared about. Justin was that man. She knew she wanted him. She didn't care that they'd only known each other for such a short period of time. She knew she'd said she wanted to take it slow, to be sure. But now, under the assault of his touch, all her resolve seemed to melt away. She wanted to prove to herself that through all the heartache she'd endured, she wasn't frigid, she wasn't the unfeeling "iron maiden" that she'd been dubbed.

Vaughn gripped Justin's arms, feeling the muscles tighten beneath her touch. Her hands spread across his chest, kneading the rock-hard body that pressed steadily against her own. Was it the real reason that she believed she wanted him so desperately, she thought suddenly—to prove something to herself—to reassure herself that she was still capable of making love to a man? Her body seemed to freeze as the thought took shape in her head. Slowly the fire that raged within her was extinguished.

Justin instantly felt the tension take hold of her body, even as his fingers deftly unfastened the top two buttons of her silk blouse. Her hands, which had only moments ago been as hot as a fire against his skin, were now as cold as ice as they grasped his hand, halting him.

"I . . . I can't," she said in a strangled voice. She tried to turn her face away from his look of concern, but Justin wouldn't allow it.

"Listen to me," he began, gaining some control over his ragged breathing. He held her chin between his fingers. "I told you once before, we won't do anything you don't want or aren't ready to do." His thumb gently brushed her bottom lip.

Her eyes filled and she swallowed back a sob. She lowered her gaze. "Justin, it's not you . . ."

"I don't need or want an explanation, Vaughn," he said gently. His lips tilted into a tremulous grin. "I haven't always been known as a patient man. But if patience is what you need . . . then it's a trait that I'd be more than happy to perfect." He inhaled, then breathed out heavily. "You're a special woman—woman," he teased, coaxing a shy smile from her. "And you're definitely worth waiting for. I'll just have to spend a lot of my free time taking cold showers."

Vaughn buried her head against his chest and they both released the tension that they had withheld in a bout of cleansing laughter. Their laughter, one a hearty bass, the other a throaty contralto, mingled in perfect harmony.

With her ear pressed against his chest, she heard and felt the contentment that rippled through him. And because of that she felt safe, secure. Somehow, she felt assured that Justin would wait, that he wasn't just saying what he thought she wanted to hear. When the time came for them to be together, it would be the right time for both of them, and it'd be for the right reasons.

"Well," Justin breathed, setting Vaughn gently away from him. "I'd better get to those dishes."

"I have a better idea," Vaughn said brightly, "let's do them together."

Justin looked deep into her eyes. "I like the sound of the word 'together' . . . especially when you say it," he said, tweaking her nose.

Vaughn grinned. "Me, too."

CHAPTER 8

"How could you, Elliott?" Sheila cried in anger. Her cinnamon eyes blazed. "You have no right to interfere in Vaughn's personal life—or to have her followed! She's not some adversary that you need to gather dirty secrets on. She's your daughter, for God's sake!"

Elliott got up from the bed and spun toward his wife, his eyes blazing with irrational fury. "I will not allow Vaughn to jeopardize her future ever again," he boomed. "She nearly ruined her life once with Brian Willis, then again with Paul. I will not sit by and watch her make a fool of herself in front of the entire state of Virginia!" He pointed an accusing finger at his wife. "You were the one who said that this was no ordinary campaign, that Stone was no ordinary opponent, that the risks were higher this time." He waved his arms in the air and pounded his fist against his palm as he continued his tirade. "I'm trying to protect her and us. If that girl messes up now, it's not something that can get swept under the rug. She's in the public eye. I won't be able to fix it again. I won't risk a scandal because of that impetuous girl!"

"First of all Elliott, that *girl* is a grown woman with a mind of her own. Maybe for once in her life she doesn't *want* you to fix it!" Sheila snatched up her robe, put on her slippers, and stormed toward the bedroom door.

"Where are you going?" Elliott demanded.

Sheila spun around, her eyes blazing. "Someplace you're not!" The door slammed so forcefully behind her exit that the gilded frame that held their family portrait nearly fell off the wall.

"I'll do whatever I have to do," Elliott vowed to the reverberating room. "Anything."

On the ride back to his apartment, Justin thought about his evening with Vaughn. His insides still throbbed with desire. He had to admit that his ability to restrain himself had surprised him. But without a doubt, he was willing to wait. That alone was a milestone of accomplishment for him. For whatever the reason, he was sure Vaughn Hamilton was a woman worth the wait, even as his body told him otherwise.

Hours later, sleep seemed an impossibility. By three A.M. Justin had done no more than toss and turn as erotic visions of Vaughn engulfed him. Moaning heavily, he flicked on the bedside lamp, then looked down at the tent in his sheet. Without humor he wondered if that old wives' tale of a cold shower had any validity.

On the other side of town, Vaughn wasn't faring much better. The constant heat and pulsing sensations that pumped through her center gave her no peace. She squeezed her eyes shut and pressed her hands against her stomach. How long had it been since she'd felt this driving need to be filled by a man? Had she ever truly felt this way before? Deep inside she knew she hadn't. Her youthful encounters had proved unfulfilling and traumatic. As an adult, she longed for something from a man that always seemed to be out of her reach. As a result, sex was an area of her life that had been tainted with failure and frustration. Consequently, she poured herself into her work to the exclusion of everything else. Until now. Just the thought of Justin's kisses, his skilled fingers exploring her body, caused her to tremble with need. Unbidden, her hands skimmed the contours of her body. Slowly she drew up her knees. She smiled, knowing that one day soon, she would finally experience, with Justin, what had eluded her.

Khendra eased closer to her husband, savoring the warmth of his body. Knowing his weak spot, she traced the hollow of his ear with her tongue. Sean moaned in his sleep and instinctively turned toward his wife. "I can't sleep," she whispered in his ear.

"Neither can I—*now,*" he whispered back. He slipped his hands beneath her back, pulling her close.

Khendra wiggled. "I want to talk."

Sean groaned. "Now?"

"Yes, now," she replied with a grin.

Sean flipped onto his back. "Go ahead, talk."

Khendra sat up in bed. "We still haven't decided how we're going to find out why Justin is really going to give up the practice. But a few things have been running through my head."

"I bet they have," Sean said drolly. Khendra rolled her eyes at her husband. He rubbed a hand across his face. "Sorry," he said halfheartedly. "Go ahead, I'm listening."

"Remember that night about two years ago when we had Justin over for dinner and he talked to us about his marriage and his daughter?"

"Yeah. And?"

"I think he plans to start searching for her again."

"But that's not enough of a reason to give up his practice! I can't see why he couldn't do both."

"Well, according to what he'd told us, his previous search had been all-consuming. I just have the feeling that this practice was something that he could throw himself into—to forget." She turned toward her husband. "I think he's accomplished everything he's wanted in life except finding his daughter."

Sean slowly shook his head. "I don't know, Khen. Personally, I think it's more than that. That's not to say that finding his daughter isn't part of the reason. I just don't think it's the whole reason." He sighed heavily. "Justin seemed almost . . . I can't find the words. Like, he's already found something. There was a spark in his eyes that I've never seen before. There was a lightness in his voice. He didn't look or sound like a man on a quest. More like someone who'd already conquered something and was savoring victory."

Khendra frowned, then turned questioning eyes on her husband. "Do you think it's a woman?" she asked, excitement rippling through her voice.

Sean chuckled. "Women have been known to have pretty strange effects on men. Kings have given up their thrones for a woman. Men have lost sleep because of a woman." Gently he eased on top of her. "Like now," he said deeply.

Khendra giggled and snuggled closer. "Is this your way of saying to stay out of Justin's business?"

"That's why I love you," Sean said, kissing her lightly on the lips. "You're so quick."

Yet even as Sean masterfully lit the flames of desire deep within her, she briefly wondered who the mystery woman in Justin's life was.

Justin was the first to arrive at his office the following morning. He had a full schedule and wanted to get an early start. Based on the staff meeting of the previous morning, it appeared that his firm would be handling the Harrison murder case. He knew that it would absorb all of Sean's and Khendra's time for months. Which would mean that he would have to put his plans on temporary hold.

Justin took a seat behind his desk. He'd wanted to tell Vaughn about

Janice and his daughter as well as his plans to find her. But Vaughn had enough to deal with at the moment. There would be plenty of time for him to discuss his painful marriage and his loss.

Flipping through the files on his desk, he saw the documents Barbara had given him the day before. He picked up the papers and read the résumé and recommendations for Simone Rivers. He was impressed. Nodding in approval of what he read, he scanned the last sheet, which was a preliminary recommendation from Chad and Barbara. This young woman was obviously worth seeing, he thought.

Justin reviewed her background once again, this time with a more critical eye. Simone would be about the same age as his daughter, he realized with a pang. Eighteen. Simone, he thought wistfully. Even the name was similar. He looked at the pages again. His heart beat a little faster. Simone Rivers had grown up in Atlanta. He'd met and married Janice in Atlanta. Janice had disappeared with his daughter in Atlanta.

He shook his head in denial. It couldn't be. Not after all this time. He couldn't believe Janice and Sam had been in Atlanta all along. It was impossible.

"Hey, boss."

Justin looked up to see Chad Rushmore standing in his open doorway. He forced his thoughts to clear.

"Rush." Chad grinned at the nickname. Justin cleared his throat. "You're here early." He placed the papers on his desk. Chad strolled into the office.

"I needed to get a jump start today. Looks like you had the same idea." Chad smiled broadly. He angled his chin toward the papers on Justin's desk. "I see you have the application for Simone Rivers."

"I was just going over it. Looks like a good candidate," he said, trying to sound casual.

"I think the same thing. I spoke with her last night."

Justin's eyes widened slightly. "You did?" There were a million questions he wanted to ask, but he valiantly controlled the urge.

"Barbara asked me to call and let her know that we'd received her info."

"What were your impressions?"

"She sounds just as good as she appears on paper. I think we should have her come down for an interview."

Justin's pulse escalated another notch. "Why don't you make the arrangements? Find out if she can come down at the end of the week. Offer to put her up in a hotel for the weekend. We'll take care of the flight arrangements."

"Great. I'll take care of it right away." He turned to leave.

"And Rush . . ."

Chad turned "Yes?"

Justin breathed deeply. "Uh, let me know what happens."

Chad looked at Justin curiously. "No problem. As soon as I know—you'll know."

Once Chad was gone, Justin looked again at the papers in front of him. Would Janice have changed Samantha's name to Simone? It seemed like a reasonable assumption. She'd probably changed her name as well. Which would explain why his searching had been fruitless. Could it be possible that the miracle he'd prayed for was actually within reach? He took a calming breath and pressed his palms against the desktop to stop the trembling. He wouldn't let his imagination run wild. It was a one-in-a-million chance that Simone was his daughter. But what if she was?

Vaughn was going over her morning schedule when Crystal breezed into her office, slapping the *Washington Post* onto her desk. "Take a look," Chris insisted.

Vaughn held her breath and picked up the paper, expecting bad news. Instead she read the glowing tribute that was written about her and her work over the past four years. She had the backing of the *Post!* Her eyes glowed with excitement. "I don't believe it," she said in awe. "Stone didn't even get backing from the *Post* on his last bid."

"Well, girlfriend, be prepared for a down-and-dirty fight. Stone isn't going to take too kindly to this. I'm sure we'll be hearing from his office real soon."

Vaughn sat back in her seat. "I can't wait," she said, rising to the challenge. "This is just the ammunition we need."

Crystal took a seat. "We need to plan our strategy. You know he's going to come at you full steam ahead. We need to be prepared for anything."

"I'll be ready," Vaughn said, full of confidence.

Crystal grew suddenly serious. "Vaughn," she began slowly. "The night of the fundraiser, your mom said something real strange to me."

Vaughn looked at her friend quizzically. "What did she say?"

"She said that I should be there for you. She sounded worried, Vaughn. Worried for reasons beyond just the stress of the campaign." She looked pointedly at Vaughn. "Do you know why?"

Vaughn's heart thudded once, then settled as she thought of the one thing that plagued her mother's thoughts. "I can't imagine what my mother could be so worried about. Maybe you were reading more into what she said."

"I don't think so, Vaughn. And I don't think that you do, either."

Vaughn looked away. "I don't know what you mean. You know how my mother can be sometimes."

"Yeah," Crystal nodded in agreement. "I know how she is. She's one of the most level headed people I know. Nothing much rattles your mom. But she was rattled. And please don't insult my intelligence by telling me that I'm imagining things, okay?"

"All right, maybe you weren't imagining things, but that doesn't mean I know what she was talking about," Vaughn countered defensively.

Crystal's eyes narrowed. She flipped her hair behind her ear. "Listen," she said calmly. "I'm your chief of staff, your campaign manager. But first and foremost, I'm your friend. If there's anything I need to know to help you or protect you, then I think you ought to tell me. We don't need any surprises, Vaughn." She looked solemnly at Vaughn, a faint smile shadowed her lips. "I only want to help."

"I know," Vaughn said heavily. "And I appreciate it. But there's nothing to worry about." Yet even as she said the words, she could only pray that they were true. "If there's anything I can think of, you'll be the first to know. I promise."

Crystal sighed and rose from her seat. "Fine." She flipped open her notebook. "You have a ten o'clock meeting with the community school board. Then you and I have to meet with Councilman Henderson at noon. Then there's the dinner tonight with One Hundred Black Women at seven."

"Are you planning to come to the dinner?"

"I'm thinking about it. You know I have that trip to New York in the morning. But if you think you'll need me, I'll go."

"Don't worry about it. I know you have plenty to do."

"Why don't you give Justin my ticket?" Crystal hedged.

Vaughn felt the flush heat her face. She smiled shyly. "Maybe I will."

"Did the two of you iron things out? He seemed mighty angry yesterday."

"We did," she said simply.

"I'm really glad to hear that. I hope everything works out with the two of you."

"So do I, Crystal. So do I."

Vaughn's private line rang. She hesitated before answering. Crystal took the hint.

"I'll see you later," she said softly as Vaughn picked up the phone.

Vaughn nodded and picked up the receiver. "Vaughn Hamilton," she said.

"Vaughn, I was hoping to catch you."

Vaughn's breath caught somewhere in her throat. "Paul."

"I just called to congratulate you. I saw the article in the *Post.* It looks like you're on your way."

"Thank you," she replied in a monotone. "I'm really swamped, Paul . . ."

"I know how busy you must be," he said. "I was hoping we could meet for lunch later on today."

"Excuse me?" She couldn't believe his audacity.

"Lunch. You know . . . eating . . . midday. People do that, you know."

"Yes. But you and I don't."

Paul laughed heartily. "You still haven't lost your charm, I see."

"Paul, I can't begin to imagine what you and I could possibly have to say to each other. Everything was all said and done two years ago. Remember?"

"Can't we put the past behind us?"

"And let history repeat itself? I don't think so. If there's nothing else, Paul, I really have to go."

"I think it would be in your best interests to meet me, Vaughn," he stated, his tone shifting from cajoling to blatantly serious.

The alarms went off in Vaughn's head "Why? What could I possibly do for your career now? Are you angling for a seat on the Supreme Court? How can I be of assistance this time?" she lashed out.

Paul exhaled heavily. "This has nothing to do with me, Vaughn, and everything to do with you."

"Then maybe you should just spit it out, because I have no intention of meeting you—now or any other time."

Paul quickly explored his options. "Have it your way. Watch yourself, Vaughn. There are big rumors running through town that Lucus Stone will do whatever is necessary to defeat you, even if it takes fabricating information. He's ruthless, and this endorsement from the *Post* will only fuel his fire."

Vaughn swallowed. "What brought on this wave of concern?"

"I owe you. I know I was a real bastard. I know I used you and your connections. I know I hurt you." He took a deep breath. "You didn't deserve it."

Vaughn was stunned into silence.

"Maybe this is my way of saying how sorry I am. I meant it that night when I said if there was anything I could do, I would."

"I . . . I don't know what to say."

"You don't have to say anything. Just take heed. Stone has some pretty unscrupulous people working for him. They'll do anything he says. Anything. Stone has no intention of losing to you."

"I'm prepared for whatever he throws at me."

"You'd better be. He plays for keeps."

She chose her words carefully. "I appreciate this, Paul. Really."

"Like I said, anything that I can do. Goodbye, and don't forget what I said. Watch your back."

Slowly Vaughn hung up the phone. Worry and an unnamed fear wiggled its way beneath her skin. Was Lucus Stone that desperate to retain his seat? Or was Paul trying to frighten her? She spun in her chair to face the window. The city of Richmond fanned out before her. Her heart pumped. Would Stone somehow uncover the truth to the past? But her father had promised that it was hidden forever. He swore that he took care of it. There was no way anyone would know. Even she never knew the whole truth. She squeezed her eyes shut and visions of the most painful day in her life bloomed before her . . .

Her father stood before her as she lay in bed. She had the covers pulled up to her chin, wishing that she could bury herself forever beneath the heavy quilts and never have to face the accusing, disappointed look in her father's eyes again. And then he told her. He gave her the news unemotionally. Then he simply turned and walked away. Her mother squeezed her hand and Vaughn broke out into wrenching sobs. She buried her face against her mother's breasts and cried for all she was worth. Her mother's only words to her were: "It's for the best, sweetheart. You may not believe that now, but it is. In time, you'll forget."

They never spoke of it again. But Vaughn never forgot, not for a minute.

The ringing of her intercom made her jump, effectively snapping her out of her disturbing thoughts.

"Ms. Hamilton, your ten o'clock meeting is in fifteen minutes. Should I call a car service?" Tess asked.

"Thanks, Tess—I brought my car. I'll be leaving in a moment," she added, collecting her thoughts. At the same time she hung up, Crystal knocked on the door and came in.

"Ready?" she asked.

"Just about." Vaughn quickly scanned her desk and snatched up the folder with her notes.

"I'll meet you out front," Crystal said.

"Be there in a minute."

David Cain sat quietly in his car in front of Vaughn's office building. He spotted Crystal the moment she stepped out the door. A slow smile eased across his handsome face. He'd seen her before in the newspaper photographs with Vaughn. He knew she was Vaughn's right hand. She was his opening. Now he just had to wait for the right opportunity.

Vaughn grabbed her jacket and was on her way out the door when her private line rang again. Hesitating, she debated whether or not to answer the phone. She wasn't sure if she could handle any more unwelcome news today. Finally, she decided to answer.

"Vaughn Hamilton."

"Hi, sweetheart."

"Justin," she sighed in audible relief. "I was going to call you."

"Well, as usual, we're on the same wave length. Any plans for tonight? I'd love to see you." Maybe tonight he could tell her about his suspicions.

Vaughn grinned like a schoolgirl. "As a matter of fact, I was hoping you would do me the honor of being my escort tonight."

"Where to, my fair lady?"

She briefly told him of the dinner being held in her honor.

"No problem. I'll pick you up at six-thirty."

"Perfect. I'll see you then. Listen, I'd love to stay and chat, but I have a meeting in about ten minutes."

"Go, go," he urged. "I'll see you tonight."

"I can't wait," she said softly.

"Neither can I."

Justin hung up the phone, a smile of anticipation lifting his full lips. Everything was going to work out, he reasoned. He was falling hard for Vaughn. He knew it. It was like falling off a building. It was mind numbing and exhilarating all at once, and most of all, it was unstoppable.

There was a light knock at his door.

"Come in."

"I got in contact with Simone Rivers," Chad said, as he stepped into the office.

Justin sat up straighter in his seat. "And?" he asked, trying to sound casual.

"Unfortunately, she said she can't get away for at least another week. She has finals."

Justin nodded, swallowing hard. "Just let her know to give us a call when she's ready," he said casually, fighting down his disappointment.

"Will do." Chad turned to leave, closing the door behind him. As he made his way back to his office, he considered the strange look on Justin's face. It was almost a look of expectation. But expectation of what? Justin didn't even know Simone Rivers. Or did he? It did seem as though Justin was going all out for the woman just for a simple interview. After all, she was just an internship candidate, not a potential partner.

He shrugged as he walked through the doors of his office. Simone Rivers certainly had a powerful effect on people, he mused, smiling at his own mixed feelings of curiosity and subtle yearnings. She certainly did. It would be interesting to see how this all turned out.

CHAPTER 9

"I'm going to cut out early," Crystal said to Vaughn. "I still have to pack and I want to unwind a bit."

"Sounds like a plan," Vaughn smiled. "I followed your advice," she added.

"Really? That's a first," she teased.

"I asked Justin to go with me to the dinner tonight."

"Great. I knew you had some sense."

"Very funny." Vaughn leaned back in her seat. "I have a real good feeling about Justin and me, Crystal. I really do." She sighed as she tried to formulate her thoughts into words. "It's like . . . he's like a breath of fresh air. He makes me feel alive again."

"I'm happy for you, Vaughn. I can't think of anyone who deserves happiness more than you do. I mean that."

"Thanks. I know you do."

Crystal hesitated a moment before posing her next question. "Have you spoken to your father again?"

Tension quickly coursed through her body at the mention of her father. "No."

Crystal nodded. "You know, you'll have to at some point."

"I know. But I'd like the opportunity to enjoy myself for a change before letting my father burst my bubble again. That confrontation can definitely wait."

"Hmmm. Well, anyway, I'm out of here. I'll give you a call tomorrow night when I get back in. That is, of course, if you're not otherwise engaged," she taunted playfully, with a rise and fall of her eyebrows.

"With any luck, maybe I will be," Vaughn tossed back good-naturedly.

"If there's any justice in this world," Crystal said, feigning a dramatic air, "maybe I'll luck out and find myself a handsome devil deserving of my love and adoration." She tossed her head back, pressed her hand to her chest, and let her eyes flutter closed.

Vaughn giggled. "You'll find someone. When the time is right," she assured her.

"So you say. Just because you've landed the greatest catch this side of the Chesapeake Bay doesn't mean I'll be so lucky." She pointed an authoritative finger at Vaughn. "You just have a great time tonight."

"I intend to. And tell your mom I said hello."

"Will do," Crystal said with a wave. "And remember," she tossed over her shoulder, "I want details, girl, details!" She breezed out the door leaving Vaughn with a broad smile on her face.

Crystal stepped out into the balmy spring air. Momentarily she stood on the steps of the building. David Cain watched patiently. Crystal thought about her options. She could go home and get an early start on her packing, or she could go over to Jade and relax for a good hour. She suddenly realized that the last thing she wanted to do right then was go home to an empty apartment. She opted for Jade. The local bar and restaurant was a favorite after-work spot for the Virginian politicos. Since it was still two hours before quitting time, she could have a relaxing meal without being sucked into any political forays. She headed for Jade, three blocks away.

Unnoticed, David made a U-turn and followed Crystal.

Justin, Sean, Khendra, and Chad sat around the conference table, painstakingly going over the documents they'd collected on the Harrison murder case.

"I can't believe that this is actually going to trial," Khendra moaned. "The evidence is ludicrous."

"He had motive. He had opportunity. And the whole world has heard about him beating the hell out of her two weeks before the murder," Justin stated. He looked up from the sheaf of papers in front of him, his eyes boring through those at the table. "Don't think for one minute that just because the evidence is flimsy the prosecution can't win this thing. All the world looks for a scapegoat. And Harrison can make the perfect example."

Khendra nodded, albeit reluctantly. "I know I sometimes let my arrogance get the better of me. But I know in my gut that we can beat this."

Justin smiled. "That's why you and that hotshot husband of yours are on this case. To win."

Sean leaned back, his dark eyes sliding toward his wife. They both grinned.

"I'm feeling left out," Chad complained good-naturedly. "Where do I fit into all this?"

"You, along with your hand-picked assistant, will be fully responsible for investigating every angle and following every lead on this case," Justin said.

"That's more like it."

"You'll have plenty to do, Rush," Sean added. "So forget about a social life for a while."

Chad thought momentarily about the possibility of working with Simone and the long days and nights ahead that might well be something to look forward to.

"That's about it, folks," Justin said, standing up. "I'll be expecting a weekly briefing on your progress before we go to trial."

The trio stood in unison and began to file out.

Sean stopped at the door and turned toward Justin. "How 'bout grabbing a beer, buddy? My treat."

Justin grinned "I wish I could." He shoved his papers into his briefcase. "But, my good friend, I have a date tonight."

Sean's eyebrows widened in speculation. "Anyone we know?"

Justin's grin expanded into a full-blown smile. "Actually, she is. But for now, I'd rather keep her under wraps." He threw his arm around Sean's shoulder as they walked out. "But I would like us all to get together soon—for dinner. Maybe my place."

"Sounds good," Sean said, as his late night conversation with Khendra replayed in his head. She was right again.

The dinner sponsored by One Hundred Black Women was an extraordinary affair. Every notable African-American female from across the country was in attendance and Vaughn was the honoree. Yet all she could think about for the entire evening was being alone with Justin. Every time she stole a glance in his gorgeous direction, her insides did a somersault. The evening seemed to drag on forever, until finally the last thank-you and goodnight had been said.

Justin had taken the liberty of hiring a chauffeur for the evening. As the black Lincoln Town Car cruised through the streets of downtown Richmond, Vaughn and Justin had the luxury of relaxing in each other's arms.

Vaughn leaned her head against Justin's shoulder. "I'm glad you came with me tonight. I don't know how I would have gotten through the evening without you there."

"And why is that?" he asked, placing a soft kiss on her forehead.

She angled her head and looked up into his eyes. "Because all I would have been able to think about was seeing and being with you," she said softly.

He cupped her chin in his palm. "Is that right?" he asked in a rough voice. "Funny how we seem to be thinking more and more alike." His eyes glided over her face and she felt her body ignite.

"Your place or mine?" she asked in a throaty whisper.

"Mine."

CHAPTER 10

Crystal was still humming as she tossed the last of her clothes into her suitcase. She still couldn't believe the evening she'd spent with David. David Hall was like a dream come true. He was handsome beyond description, funny, intelligent, gainfully employed, and on his way to New York in the morning!

The two hours that they'd spent together at Jade's had her feeling as if they'd known each other for a long time. When he'd approached her table just to say hello, she'd been momentarily reluctant to take him up on his request to join him at the bar for a drink. Eventually, she had, and so far, she hadn't regretted one minute. He was every bit the gentleman and had even waited until she'd gotten a cab. They'd made plans to meet at Union Station in the morning and share the ride to New York.

Her heart beat a bit faster. She looked at her reflection in the mirror and the glow that haloed her face was unmistakable. She'd finally found someone who sparked her interest. Hot damn! She'd give anything to have a crystal ball to see what the future held for her and David Hall.

It took all her willpower not to pick up the phone and call Vaughn. She was itching to tell her about David. But if Vaughn had the sense she was born with, she should be busy creating some unforgettable moments with Justin.

Vaughn and Justin spent most evenings together either out on the town or at her home. This would be her first look at how the man in her life lived. But she truly was not prepared for what awaited her.

Vaughn was moved to momentary speechlessness by the classy decor of Justin's home. If she'd expected either all-out opulence or downright bachelor bizarre, she found neither. Instead, Justin's modest but infinitely tasteful abode was furnished with a balanced mixture of the Afrocentric and the contemporary.

The color scheme was an intricate blend of olive walls contrasting ingeniously with soft golds and burnished orange and bronze. The effect was breathtaking. The dimmed recessed lighting gave an overall effect of tranquility and, yes, intimacy. Corner spaces were filled with either standing handcarved African sculptures or wrought-iron vases filled to overflowing with silk flowers and dried stems. The walls were adorned with artwork of various sizes and apparently, various stages of completion.

"Who's the artist?" Vaughn asked in admiration and a good deal of curiosity, walking closer to a particularly exquisite piece for a better inspection.

"I dabble here and there," he said quietly.

Vaughn spun around to face him, her eyes wide with shock. She turned back toward the painting and pointed. "You call that dabbling?" she cried, staring at a life-sized replica of a beautiful young woman sitting at a piano. "Your work . . . is fabulous." She turned back around to look at him and suddenly saw him through new eyes. This was a side of Justin Montgomery she would have never imagined. Everything that hung on his walls showed an intense depth, an understanding, a passion. "I would never have guessed," she said in wonder.

"Most people don't," he shrugged nonchalantly. "It's just a hobby."

"A hobby? Humph. If this is a hobby, you can definitely give up your day job." Justin chuckled modestly. "You're just full of surprises," she continued. "Your apartment is a showstopper. Did you do it all yourself?"

"As a matter of fact, I did." The last place he'd called home he'd shared with Janice and Samantha. Janice had been the one who'd decided what their home would look like. He didn't have the time, he thought, with a twinge of the old guilt. When she'd abandoned him he'd left everything behind. Here, he felt he could start over, erasing the memories by creating new ones. "It took a long time for me to get it the way I wanted it." He paused for effect. "But I'm a patient man," he concluded, looking deep into Vaughn's eyes. His meaning was unmistakable.

A flicker of a smile lifted her mouth as she crossed the room to stand directly in front of him. She looked up into his eyes and the heat of his gaze ignited a blaze at her core.

Tentatively, she raised her hand and stroked his rugged jaw as if committing the strong outline to memory. "I'm grateful for that, Justin," she said softly. "More than you'll ever know."

Justin clasped her outstretched hand into his, molding her palm against his cheek. "Some things are worth waiting for," he crooned gently. "And you're more than worth the wait."

Vaughn tilted her head to look him full in the eye. Her voice was a throaty whisper when she spoke. "I don't want to wait any longer."

His eyes suddenly sparkled. His heart thumped, then took up a racing rhythm. Justin took the hand that he held and maneuvered it behind her back, holding it there, causing her body to arch firmly against the hard lines of his.

"Vaughn," he groaned from deep in his throat. His head lowered. Vaughn's pulse beat erratically. His fingers felt like feathers as they brushed across her face, trailed along the tendons of her neck, then threaded through her hair to cup her head into his palm, pulling her deeper into the kiss.

Vaughn felt all her resistance, all her fears and doubts, melt away from the warmth of his embrace. Justin's exploring tongue taunted her lips, daring her to join him in the mating dance. And she did.

Her mouth sought his, savoring the texture, the fullness of his lips. The titillating contact of his tongue against hers sent sparks snapping through her veins. It felt as though their spirits had unified into one extraordinary fireball.

This wasn't simple sexual gratification she was satisfying, she realized, as desire raged like a desert storm within her. This was more than a joining of bodies; this was the uniting of souls. She knew that once she leaped across the precipice, there was no turning back. The thought that she was giving herself up totally for the first time in her life was at once frightening and all too tempting.

Never before had she felt the need to go beyond the mechanics, to reach deep inside herself and relinquish her control to someone else. Momentarily she stiffened as the thought of total submission took hold. Her thoughts twisted in confusion. To relinquish control of her body, her soul, to this man—any man—was no different than allowing her father to manipulate her, bend her to his will. Her father controlled her through the weakness of her guilt. If she fully succumbed to the allure of Justin's seduction, she would be at his mercy as well. Her body would betray her once again. She couldn't think, not with Justin's fingers magically unzipping her dress. She couldn't breathe. Flashing sparks of yearning whipped through her. Her dress slid off her shoulders and down to her waist, baring her uncovered breasts to his ardent gaze.

A rush of apprehension swept through her. The ghosts of her past leaped through her brain. The lights were dim, she reasoned, sinking deeper into the abyss of desire. He wouldn't know she prayed silently. But as Justin's mouth sought out and captured a hardened nipple between his teeth, all caution dissolved into a pool of liquid fire.

He wanted to scream out his pleasure when the velvety softness of her breasts brushed against his waiting lips. The texture of her taut nipples against his tongue nearly sent him over the edge.

He wanted to take her—here, now—on the hardwood floor of his living room, burying himself deep within the succulent walls that he knew awaited his entry. If he didn't, he knew that he would explode with longing.

But he knew that wasn't the way it would be between them. He wanted to savor every minute. He wanted to bring her to the utmost peak and hold her there until he knew she wanted him as desperately as he wanted her. If he had to bring her to the brink of completion—all night long—he would until she begged him to join her.

Vaughn felt the last of her resolve become consumed by the fire of her passion. In the instant that her soft cry mixed in harmony with Justin's deep groan, she fully understood that there had never been any other course to take but the road they had embarked upon.

Vaughn lifted herself up on her toes, pressing her bare upper body against the hard lines of his chest. Instantly she felt the powerful thumping of his heart and then the epicenter of his passion as Justin surged against her, cupping her firm derrière in the palms of his hands.

"Vaughn," he whispered over and over again in ragged breaths. She let her dress slip completely to the floor. All she wore beneath was a lacy black garter belt and sheer black hose.

The moment that Justin made the realization, he was sure that his heart would give out. To think that he'd sat next to her for hours and she was virtually naked beneath that dress was almost more than he could stand.

Cautiously, he stepped back to gain the full impact of what had only been in his imagination.

"You're . . . beautiful," he expelled in wonder. His dark eyes raked savagely across her body, scorching her with their intensity. Her breasts were high and round, like ripe fruits waiting to be tasted. Her small waist and taut stomach flared to provocative hips, and downward to long, shapely legs.

The vision of her standing there in nothing more than a garter belt and stockings blew him away. She was a sculptor's dream overlaid with silken ebony flesh that he knew he'd never get enough of.

Slowly, Justin eased to his knees. He slid his arm around her waist and pulled her to him. The heady scent of her incensed him beyond reason as he sought its source. The tip of his tongue boldly stroked her and Vaughn felt her knees give way. Her body involuntarily arched. A strangled cry rose from deep in her throat as she clung to him, her nails clawing his shoulders. Justin slipped his other arm around her thighs, bracing her solidly against his exploring mouth.

Tremors of unbelievable power shot through her as Justin delved deeper into her center. All sense of reality, time, and space eclipsed into a blinding white light. Vaughn threw her head back in delirious rapture.

Her eyes slammed shut as the steady pulse of fulfillment built to a crescendo within her. Just when she knew that her body had endured all it could stand, without sweet release, Justin slowed the tempo, steadily bringing her back down to earth.

At once she was both disappointed and still desperate for more of the sublime torture. Her deep moan floated through the torrid air, while Justin meticulously worked his way back up her body.

He covered every inch of her with tantalizing flicks of his tongue, nipping flesh with his teeth. Her body was one mass of electrified desire. She was sure that if she didn't have him buried deep within her—now—she would cease to exist.

Finally he reached the hollow of her neck and placed tiny, hot kisses along its base. He cupped his palms over each breast, massaging, caressing, kneading them until she cried out.

"Justin . . . please . . ."

"No," he groaned deep in his throat. "I've waited too long . . ." he breathed heavily. His lips burned across her neck, then behind her ears, as he ground out his erotic challenge. "I'm going to take you back and forth through the doorway of the promised land," he whispered hotly in her ear. Gently his fingers slipped between the slickened folds of her womanhood. Her knees gave way, but Justin held her fast. "But we won't go through together, until I know that you want me," his fingers intensified their probe, "as desperately as I want you." His mouth covered hers, stifling her cries when his fingers slid up into her center.

Her body shuddered. A plaintive cry tore from her throat. She felt weak and light-headed, as the very tip of his finger teased the one place that she wanted him to fill.

"Justin . . ." she moaned weakly.

"Tell me," he whispered deep in her ear. "Tell me."

"I want you," she answered back. She pressed herself against him and felt the hard shaft of his desire pulse against her inner thighs. She brushed her lips across the shell of his ear. "I want you . . . now." Her mouth covered his, demanding, controlling, beckoning. Her eager tongue deftly explored the tangy sweetness of his mouth. She drank of him, wanting to absorb him into her being. Her hands slid down from his face to his sides and firmly grabbed his arms and locked them behind his back in a steely grip.

"Now," she breathed huskily, "I'll show you the way to heaven." The butter softness of her hand encased him, steadily stroking him as her lips dropped hot, wet kisses across his burning flesh. Justin sucked in ragged breaths through his teeth. His deep groans filled the room when the pad of her thumb brushed teasingly across his tip.

Vaughn felt a sudden rush of inexplicable power, realizing that she could evoke such longing in her man. And he was *her man,* she thought giddily. The acceptance of that seemed to escalate her need for him. She wanted him—all of him—and she proved as much when her lips replaced her tender fingers.

"Yes!" Justin hissed. He groaned with undeniable pleasure as she played teasing games with her tongue. He clasped her head firmly in his hand and reluctantly eased her away. Through passion-drunk eyes he looked down into her face. "No more," he breathed, as a shudder raced up his spine.

He pulled her gently to her feet. "I believe I've run out of patience," he said on a jagged whisper. His mouth crashed down on hers, his tongue diving into her open mouth, a warning of what was to come.

Then, as easily as if she'd been no more than a baby, he lifted her nude body into his arms, cradling her gently against him, and strode into his bedroom.

Like a fragile treasure he lay her atop the down-filled comforter. For several unbearable moments he stood above her, momentarily overcome by the exquisiteness of her and the knowledge that soon she would be his completely.

His heart raced with anticipation and anxiety. A woman like Vaughn was sure to have been with other men. Men who, Justin was certain, did everything in their power to please her. He wanted to surpass every sexual experience she'd ever had. He wanted to be the one who'd be branded on her soul for all time. Because somewhere deep inside he understood that no one had ever reached that part of her.

"Justin?" she murmured, suddenly afraid that he no longer took pleasure in what he saw. Could he tell? she worried. Did he see the sins of her past? She felt truly naked and totally vulnerable under his unreadable gaze. But just as quickly her fears were extinguished when he smiled, his eyes still filled with longing, and yes, something deeper, she realized. The silent understanding that flashed between them deepened the yearning that had built near to bursting between her legs.

Vaughn raised her arms, silently asking him to join her. And he did. Straddling her supple form, he braced his weight on his arms. Tenderly, he brushed her face with countless tiny kisses, then down her neck, teasing the pulse that beat erratically in her throat. His wet lips seemed to sizzle across her heated flesh, causing her to cry out his name when his mouth reached her breasts and captured the hardened bud between his teeth. His tongue stroked first one, then the other, in maddeningly slow circles. In response, Vaughn arched her back, pushing the engorged mounds deeper into the recesses of his mouth.

"Mmmm," he moaned, spreading her thighs with a sweep of his knee. Gingerly he rested his full weight upon her, thrusting up her knees with the forward motion of his broad shoulders.

Lured to her, without guidance, he reached the passageway of fulfillment. Hesitating an instant, he looked one last time into her eyes. Then, simultaneously, his mouth covered hers while his hips plunged downward, engulfing his phallus in a hot tight cocoon of euphoria.

"The promised land," he groaned.

Vaughn snuggled closer to the warm, hard body next to her. A dreamy smile of contentment eased across her ebony face. God, she was happy—and satisfied! She couldn't begin to describe just how satisfied. Her toes curled at the memory of what had taken place between them. Justin was an exquisite, experienced lover. Powerful and gentle. Just thinking about how his rhythmic thrusts had pushed her to heaven and back caused an instantaneous throb to pulse between her thighs. How many times had they made love during the night? Somewhere along the line, she'd lost count but her body still seemed to vibrate with need.

What had he done to her? Her physical experiences with men were limited. Was this the way you were supposed to feel the morning after? If so, she knew what she'd been missing all those years, and she had no intention of traveling back down that road again. This was just too good! Her decadent thoughts made her giggle, the vibration stirring Justin in his sleep.

His arm, firmly locked around her waist, slid upward until his palm cupped one tender breast.

She moaned softly, thinking him to be reacting in his sleep. She pressed her back closer to his front to discover that Justin Montgomery was anything but asleep.

She tried to angle her head to look at him over her shoulder, but before she could, Justin had turned her fully on her stomach and rested his full weight upon her. He slipped his arm beneath her waist and raised her hips to meet him.

"Good morning," he groaned hot in her ear, finding his way into the fiery cavern that welcomed him. All Vaughn could do was sigh in pleasure as Justin took them on another ride of ecstasy.

The sun was high in the cloudless sky by the time Vaughn and Justin found their way out of bed.

She felt like a young girl in love for the first time. He was sure that ten years had been shaved off of his life. Vaughn was like a fountain of youth, pumping rejuvenating life into what had been an empty heart.

His smile was full of warmth as he watched the woman who seemed perfectly at home in his kitchen.

In the pit of his stomach was a strange stirring. It rose to his chest and seemed to make his heart pump faster. He felt warm all over and undeniably happy. Yet he was still reluctant to put a name to this sensation that ran rampant through him each time he looked at Vaughn. What could he expect from this relationship. She'd clearly stated that her time would be limited, that her priority was her faithful followers. So where did that leave him, exactly?

Before last night, he'd been sure that he was ready to just dive into this relationship—headfirst—and screw the consequences. Now, after being with her—within her, letting their souls touch—something had changed for him. He realized that with Vaughn he would totally lose himself. He would be consumed by the fire that she'd ignited within him. Before last night, the power that she'd had over him was purely imaginary.

Had he matured enough over the years to be ready to submit himself totally to a woman? Even now, with all the confusing thoughts tumbling through his head, he felt himself harden just by looking at her. He'd completely lost interest in what she was preparing for breakfast, but was more interested in how he could wrestle her out of his oxford-cloth shirt without ripping off all those damned buttons.

To hell with consequences, he thought vehemently. He hopped down from the stool and strode up behind her, pressing himself against her supple form.

Vaughn expelled a gasp of surprise, then giggled merrily while Justin teased her neck with nibbling kisses. Then suddenly he turned her around to face him. His dark eyes stared intently into her upturned face. She held her breath, mesmerized by the power of his gaze.

He blurted out huskily, "I think I've fallen in love with you."

The declaration was so impulsive, so unexpected, that it seemed to take both of them by surprise. Vaughn blinked away her disbelief.

For several breathless moments they both stared at each other with such startled expressions that they simultaneously erupted into fits of joyous laughter.

Justin pulled Vaughn snugly into his embrace, absorbing the feel of her, the scent of her, as their laughter slowly settled and the enormity of what he'd said fully took hold.

Did he say he loved her because they had great sex? she worried, listening to Justin's pounding heart. Was it what he thought she expected to hear the morning after? Did he expect some sort of favor now? When was the last time a man had said he'd loved her without some ulterior motive? She couldn't recall. Yet with Justin . . . did she dare hope?

Justin's words reverberated throughout his head. Why had he told her he loved her? It wasn't possible to fall in love with someone this quickly, was it? Yet nothing went by the book when it came to him and Vaughn. He knew the sex was damned great. There was no question about that. But he'd had great sex before and it had never made him say the "L" word. That was just it, he realized. It wasn't the sex. He and Vaughn had *made love,* in every sense of the words. For the very first time in his life he had truly, unquestionably, made love with a woman. That physical connection with her seemed to somehow transcend every aspect of his life. Their union had created love. Now he fully understood what making love was all about.

He might never be able to define it in words, but he knew in his heart that he had reached an apex in his life and it was due to one woman. This woman.

Justin leaned slightly back, placed the tip of his finger beneath Vaughn's chin, and tilted her head. Her dark eyes swam with questions, doubts, excitement, and reciprocation.

"I meant what I said," he told her softly. "I know it may seem impossible to believe that in a matter of weeks a person could fall in love." He took a deep breath and briefly shut his eyes. When he opened them again, he saw acceptance in hers. "But I have, and it's scaring the hell outta me." He grinned sheepishly.

Vaughn's mouth curved into a warm smile. Her eyes sparkled. She gently brushed his lips with her fingertips, which he lightly kissed.

"I've been so afraid of falling in love, Justin," she said with deliberate intensity. "Afraid of rejection, loss, hurt. All the love in my life has only caused me pain." Her eyes skimmed his face. "I don't feel afraid anymore," she whispered softly. Her delicate hands stroked his cheek. "Not anymore. I guess what I'm saying . . . is that I love you, too, Justin Montgomery."

His stomach tightened. His heart knocked hard against his chest. A welcome rush of relieved exhilaration spread through his veins. He heaved a sigh of relief. He lowered his head and touched it gently to hers. "I'll never hurt you, Vaughn," he vowed. "Never." He brushed her hair away from her face. "I promise you that." Ever so sweetly, he sealed his vow with a kiss.

Slowly, he eased away and took her hand, leading her back into the living room. He pulled her down beside him on the couch.

Her heart skittered when she saw the look of uncertainty on his face. "What?" she asked, a sudden fear knocking at the door of her happiness.

Justin breathed heavily. "There's something I need to talk with you about," he began slowly.

Oh, God, she thought. He's going to tell me he has a wife somewhere. But the painful story that Justin revealed was the last thing she expected to hear.

"I've decided to start looking for my daughter again," he concluded, after divulging the details of his tumultuous marriage.

For several long moments, Vaughn sat in silence, trying to put this revelation in perspective. He wanted her to be a part of his daughter's life. He wanted to give up his practice and devote his energies to finding Samantha. He thought that he might have a lead in Simone Rivers.

Rivers, she mused curiously, that was her mother's maiden name. It was almost too much to comprehend.

Her emotions ran the gamut. He'd cared enough about her to confide his deepest emotions, his greatest goals, his darkest fears. Was she willing to do the same? Not yet. Even now, years later, it was still too painful and now potentially too disastrous to discuss. The past was dead and buried. The vivid thought seemed to take on life within her, causing her to flinch. Justin saw her reaction as accusing.

Suddenly he sprang from his seat, jamming his hands into his robe pockets. He walked away from her and turned on the stereo, keeping his back stiffly toward her. His heart sank to a new low. Her physical response was not what he expected. He thought Vaughn to be the most compassionate woman he'd ever met. But maybe her compassion didn't extend beyond her public image. He was so engrossed in his dark thought that he didn't hear Vaughn come up behind him until she spoke.

"Whatever, you need, darling, I'll be there for you," she said, her voice full of the empathy he believed her to have.

Slowly he turned around and looked down into her face. Her eyes shimmered with unshed tears. "I can only imagine how difficult it's been for you all these years." With trembling fingers she caressed his stubble-roughened chin. She smiled gently. "You'll find her," she assured. "I know you will. And when you do, I'd like to be there."

With all the love that flowed through him, he wrapped her in his arms, burying his face in her hair. "Thank you for coming into my life," he whispered hoarsely. "Thank you."

CHAPTER 11

"So how long have you been working for the assemblywoman?" David asked Crystal as he handed her a cup of coffee.

Crystal smiled and shook her head. "Vaughn and I go so far back, I can't say where friendship ends and work begins. A lot of years, in other words," she said, taking a sip of the steamy brew.

The Amtrak train rumbled comfortably along the track. The scenery of downtown D.C. was soon out of view.

"So I guess you know her pretty well," he commented, settling comfortably in his seat.

"Yeah," Crystal grinned. "I'll introduce you once we get back." She paused. "Maybe we could all get together for dinner one night," she suggested hesitantly. "She's seeing Justin Montgomery these days. We could do a foursome."

Justin Montgomery. That information could prove useful. He cleared his throat and turned in his seat to look at her.

"To be honest, Crystal, I'm a very private person. I'm not really into group activities. I guess it comes from always having to deal with conference-goers and boards of directors," he lied smoothly. "And personal time," he added in an intimate tone, "is a special treat for me. I'd like to use it getting to know you better. My job requires a lot of travel. I don't want the little bit of time I have with you to be shared with anyone else." His eyes skimmed her face warmly and Crystal felt a definite tingle work its way through her body.

"Then we'll just have to make those times extra special."

He gave her hand a little squeeze. "I'd say we were well on our way." He grinned, giving her his best smile.

"Tell me more about what you do," Crystal said in an attempt to recover her equilibrium. David truly had her senses whirling.

He leaned back and sighed heavily. "It's really pretty boring stuff. I mean, compared to working for a politician."

"I want to hear all the boring details anyway," Crystal insisted, smiling brightly.

David shrugged. "Basically, I travel across the country and help businesses to get on a stronger footing. In other words, I analyze their finances, programs, goals, and things, and help them to do it better." He'd rehearsed this speech so many times in his head over the past few days he'd begun to believe it himself.

"That sounds great, David. You get to meet folks, travel, and have an impact on a lot of people. What could be boring about that?"

His full lips tilted into a half smile. "I guess it's what you make it," he said nonchalantly. "I've been doing this for so long it's just second nature. I don't even think about what I do beyond getting the job done as quickly and effectively as possible."

Crystal nodded. "It's inevitable to slip into complacency if you don't look beyond the small picture."

"That's true," David said absently, not really paying attention to her assessment. His mind was already on other things. "But enough about me, tell me about you." He gave her a meaningful look. "I want to know it all."

Crystal beamed. David was the first man she'd met in so long who didn't want to have a running monologue about himself, his accomplishments, his ex-wives or girlfriends, or his sexual prowess. David was definitely a welcome relief.

"What would you like to hear?"

David shrugged lightly. "Start with the present and work your way back," he suggested with an encouraging smile. "What does a chief of staff do, for starters?"

Crystal laughed. "All right."

This time he was paying attention. He absorbed every word. There was certainly some information he could use. As he watched her, smiling as she talked, he had a pang of guilt. The sudden sensation unnerved him. He shifted slightly in his seat. Crystal was actually a wonderful woman. She was bright, great looking, fun to be around. Sexy as hell. If things were different . . . but things weren't different, he admitted, adjusting his thoughts to the task at hand. Somewhere, buried inside, he wished it were. But, he reminded himself, he had a job to do. He wouldn't allow a mere attraction stand in the way of his goals. He settled deeper into his seat, put on his most ingratiating smile, and listened. Too bad, though, he mused. He could really have a thing for Crystal.

"What have you found out?" Elliott gruffly asked the caller.

"She didn't come home last night," was the wooden response.

Elliott's jaw clenched into a knot. He felt a burn in the pit of his stomach. "Where is she?" he spat.

"At 5836 Larchmont Road. Justin Montgomery's place."

The burning intensified. "Thank you." Slowly Elliott replaced the receiver. His large, dark hand curled into a fist and slammed down onto the desk. The coffee cup rattled, losing some of its contents on the maple desk.

A deep frown carved itself into his brow. His eyes darkened to a dangerous hue as he pondered his next move.

Downstairs, Sheila pushed the lightly buttered biscuit around on her plate. She was worried about Vaughn. She needed to talk to her about her father and this obsession he had about her. It was getting out of hand.

Sheila checked the wall clock. It was nearly eleven. Elliott had yet to come downstairs today. He was probably still brooding. That was just fine with her. He needed to think about what he'd done. She got up from the table, dumped the contents of her plate into the garbage, and proceeded out to the front hallway. Cautiously she looked, once, up the winding staircase—saw no one and heard nothing. Good, she thought, taking her purse and jacket from the hall closet. She had to get to the bank before noon.

"What do you want to do today?" Vaughn asked in a drowsy voice. After another session of toe-curling lovin', all *she* wanted to do was purr. She snuggled under Justin's arm and pressed her face against his smooth chest.

"Don't ask," he mumbled, pinching her bare behind.

"Ouch!" She slapped his arm. "Now I know the real reason why you want me," she pouted.

"If you say for your body," he grumbled deep in his chest, "you'd be damned right." He tenderly massaged her breasts to emphasize his point.

"How very chauvinistic," she cooed in a throaty whisper as sparks of yearning lit brightly within her.

"That's me," he chuckled, increasing the pressure.

"If I really thought that," Vaughn said on a long sigh, "we wouldn't stand a chance."

"Mmmm. I don't know about that," he countered, pulling her astride his throbbing body. "I think I'd just have to convince you I was the best thing that could happen to you."

Her voice shuddered as she felt the length and breath of him fill her. "I think you . . . may . . . be . . . right." Her eyes slid closed as Justin's hips rose and fell in a driving, demanding rhythm. Vaughn gripped the headboard to brace herself against Justin's powerful thrusts as he took them on a journey of unspeakable pleasure.

Hours later, fully clothed and playfully trying to keep their distance, Vaughn and Justin mapped out their day. Vaughn sat Indian-style on the loveseat, while Justin partially reclined on the sofa.

"At some point, I want to stop by my office. I'd like to show you the profile on Simone Rivers." He breathed heavily. "I know I shouldn't get my hopes up." He angled his head to look at her and met compassionate eyes. "But it's just this feeling I have. It may be farfetched, Vaughn, but anything is possible."

Vaughn unwrapped her long denim-clad legs, walked around the birchwood coffee table, and sat beside him.

Lovingly, she stroked his forehead, easing away the lines of tension that etched his brow. As she watched the strain slip from his face, she was once again engulfed in her own fears. The same sensation of wariness that had touched her when they'd first met needled her again. Suppose somehow, in some way, inadvertently, in his crusade he uncovered . . . She couldn't bear that. She wouldn't think about it. That would never happen.

"There's nothing wrong with hoping," she said softly. "I just don't want you to get hurt."

He nodded and took her hand. "I know, and I appreciate your concern." He pecked the back of her hand with a quick kiss and rose from the couch. "But I'm a big boy now." He smiled. "I can handle it."

Vaughn stood and slipped her arms around his waist. "In that case . . . big boy," she crooned in a good imitation of Mae West, "let's get ta' steppin'."

Simone had debated for the past few days whether or not she was doing the right thing. On one level, she believed she had the right to the truth. On another, she felt as if she was betraying her foster parents.

Simone sat down heavily on her bed and stared at the business card in her hand. *Child-Link, Inc.* She'd gotten the card ages ago at that same seminar Justin Mont-gomery had conducted on child advocacy. She knew the services were essentially free, but if they could find her real parents, she'd made up her mind she would donate half of her windfall to the organization.

She took a deep breath. She needed to put the wheels in motion before she went away. She reached for the phone and dialed. All her muscles tensed. She felt her pulse begin a steady upward spiral as she listened to the line connect and the phone ring.

"Good morning, Child-Link. Melissa Overton speaking. How may I help you?"

Simone swallowed hard. She gripped the receiver so tightly that her palm began to sweat. "Hello, um, my name is Simone and, uh, I'm wondering . . . hoping that you can help me find my parents . . ."

A warm breeze wrapped around them as they ate brunch at an outdoor café in Georgetown. The day was perfect, the air clean, the sky clear. Trees were blooming all around them. The scent of flowers and fresh-turned soil filled the air. Couples, singles, and families were out in force, taking full advantage of the glorious day.

"It's not necessary for us to take a trip to my office today," Justin said, taking a sip of iced herbal tea. "The day is too beautiful to waste a minute behind office doors."

"It's your call," Vaughn offered. She stabbed the last chunk of chicken salad with her fork and lifted it to her mouth. "What do you want to do instead?"

"Do you play tennis?" he questioned.There was a definite hint of challenge in his voice, Vaughn noted.

Her lip curved upward. "I have a nasty backhand," she taunted.

"I'll bet you dinner that I can beat you three sets out of five."

Vaughn tossed her head back, emitting a deep, husky laugh. Should she tell him that she'd been one tennis ball away from the Olympic team in her senior year of high school? Briefly she thought about those carefree days. She could have been a champion. But all her father saw in her future was law. And then there was Brian. But before those two events, she was good. She still taught at the inner city youth program. Well, Mr. Montgomery never backed down from a challenge, and neither would she. Anyway, she'd confess later—after the game. "You . . . are . . . on . . . buddy." She lowered her head. Her eyes squinted as she stared pointedly at him. "You truly don't have a clue as to what you're in for. As a matter of fact, hotshot, let's sweeten the pot."

Justin leaned forward meeting her gaze. "Let's."

"Not just dinner for one night, but for the whole week—home-cooked—winner's choice. You can cook—cain't cha?" She grinned devilishly.

"Ooh, aren't you the crafty one? I know my way around the kitchen." He chuckled deeply. "But that won't be *my* problem."

"Let's cut the rhetoric, buddy, and head to the courts. I want to see what you've got." Vaughn stood up.

Justin snatched her around the waist, pulling her fully against the hard lines of his body. His voice dropped to a pumping whisper. "I thought you already knew what I had."

"Call me curious," she breathed against his parted lips.

"Curious," he crooned softly, letting his lips brush lingeringly over hers. Reluctantly, he eased back. "Let's go before I change my mind and take you back home."

"I guess this is where we part ways," Crystal said, as she and David exited the train and emerged in bustling Pennsylvania Station.

"Only temporarily," he replied close to her ear. He checked his watch. "How long do you think your business with your mom will take?"

"The better part of the day. We have to meet with the attorneys and settle my dad's estate. It's not much," she added with a false grin of gaiety, "but my mother wants me there for moral support."

"How long has it been?" asked David, as they wound their way through the throng.

"Just about a year," she answered quietly. "The insurance company has been dragging their feet and they finally ran out of excuses."

"That's how they make their money," David said cynically, "by keeping yours."

Crystal nodded in agreement.

They exited the terminal and were instantly engulfed in the surge of travelers rushing for the honking cabs.

"Where can we meet?" David asked, as he hailed the next cab in line. "I'd like to see you this evening." He turned toward her. "And spend the day with you tomorrow, if that's possible."

Crystal was oblivious to the rush of sight and sound that swarmed around her. All she could hear was David's low, mesmerizing voice. All she could see were his caramel face and soulful brown eyes. Damn! she thought, I think I've hit the jackpot. She felt like clicking her heels.

"I'm sure we can work something out," she said lightly. She reached in her purse and took a scrap of paper and pen and jotted down her mother's phone number. "Here." She handed it to him. "I should be in after six tonight."

David tucked the paper into the pocket of his leather jacket. "I'll call you." He lowered his head and touched her lips with his. "Good luck today." He held open the cab door for her and she slid inside.

"Thanks," she said looking up. "I'll talk to you later."

David stood at the curb and watched the cab pull away. He checked his watch. He had six hours to kill. Since he'd told Crystal that he had business to take care of, he'd have to find something to do for the rest of the day.

He started walking up Seventh Avenue toward midtown. Well, this was

New York, he mused. There had to be something. But first he had a call to make. He found a phone booth and used his calling card to make the call.

"Stone residence," answered the slightly accented voice.

David recognized the lilting voice of the Bajan housekeeper immediately. A flash of her smooth copper body writhing beneath him magnified before his eyes.

"Trini, how are you?" he asked, his voice vibrating across the wires.

Trini's voice lowered to a sultry whisper. "David," she purred, letting the second syllable of his name ring lower than the first. Quickly, she scanned her surroundings and found herself alone. "When will I see you again, dah-lin'? It's been so—oo long."

"Soon, babe. I promise," he answered shortly. "But in the meantime, I need to speak to Lucus. Is he in?"

Trini tried to hide her disappointment behind a tone of impassivity. But underneath, she was hurt. She'd come to care a great deal about David Cain. So much so that she fed him private information about Congressman Stone. She would do just about anything for David. He was the first man she'd ever been with. She's grown accustomed to making wild love to him when the house was empty. It gave the whole act a sense of danger, which only heightened her desire for him. But if he wanted to play this silly waiting game, she could play, too.

"Hold the line," she said in a stiff voice. Without giving him a chance to respond, she went in search of her employer. He'd be sorry, she thought again, as her hips swayed in tune to an inner rhythm.

Moments later Lucus's deep voice filled the line.

Quickly, David sketched out the details of his new association with Vaughn's chief of staff, leaving out names.

"Excellent," Lucus said at David's conclusion. "Keep a close eye on things and keep me informed as details develop," he said, as though discussing a business transaction. That was a cardinal rule with Lucus. No names were ever to be mentioned over the phone, and anything that could be construed as "shady" was to be discussed in abstract terms—as a precaution.

"Get back to me on Monday," Lucus added. "We can discuss the particulars then."

"Sure thing."

Lucus broke the connection without saying another word. For several moments he stood with his hand resting on the phone. A slow smile crept across his lips, lifting them a fraction at the corners. Maybe David Cain really was worth all the money he paid him.

Melissa Overton stepped into her boss's office. "Excuse me, Elaine."

Elaine Carlyle looked up. Her sky blue eyes sparkled with warmth against her deep tan.

"Yes, Melissa, come in."

Melissa stepped into the small but functional office and took a seat opposite her.

"What's up? You have that look."

"We just got another one," Melissa said on a heavy sigh.

Elaine smiled benevolently at her newest recruit. "That's what we're here for, Mel."

"I know, I know. It's just that it's so painful to hear the desperation and hurt in their voices."

"You get used to it after a while."

Melissa sat further back in her chair and flipped her long, pale blond hair behind her ear. "It's just that I feel like I want to help everyone."

"Of course you do," assured Elaine. "We all feel that way. But it's not possible. All we can do is our best."

Melissa nodded in agreement. But somewhere deep inside she had sensed that with Simone Rivers it would be different. Very different.

Vaughn swiped the perspiration from her forehead with the back of her wristband. Like a Wimbledon champion, Vaughn leaned back in a perfect arc, tossed the white ball up into the air with her left hand, and sent it spinning at lightning speed with a fierce serve across the net.

Justin thought he was prepared. He'd braced himself He was poised on the balls of his sneakered feet, ready to dart in any direction. But nothing could have prepared him for the spinning tornado that whizzed past him as he leaped to his left, nearly hurling himself into the fence in the process.

Justin braced the mesh fence with both hands, bowing his head. He pushed his body out from the fence while still holding on, stretching his overworked muscles. He shook his head in disbelief. He would laugh, but hell, it wasn't funny. Vaughn Hamilton had whipped his tail. He still couldn't believe it.

He angled his head to the right in time to see her coming around the net, towel draped around her neck, long legs flexing and unflexing with each step. He felt himself harden just by looking at her. She may have won on this battlefield, he thought wryly. She drew closer. But he intended to the win tonight. She wasn't even breathing hard, he noticed with annoyance. But at least she wasn't gloating.

"Great game," she said with just the right amount of enthusiasm. She pecked him lightly on the lips.

Justin cut his eyes at her but remained ominously silent. It took all her willpower not to burst out laughing. But that would be mean, she thought merrily. Yet having him think that he'd been beaten by your garden-variety tennis player was meaner.

She slid her arm around his waist and eased up close. "I have a confession to make," she said innocently.

He looked down at her, suspicion simmering in his eyes. "What might that be? You're really Wilma Rudolph in disguise?"

"Not quite," she hedged. "Actually, I was an alternate for the Olympic team my senior year in high school. I'm also a part-time tennis instructor at the Racquet Club in Richmond." Her face crinkled into a sheepish, half-apologetic smile.

Justin's eyes were reduced to two dark slits of incredulity. Then suddenly he threw his head back and laughed so hard he almost choked.

"Now I feel better," he sputtered. "I was truly beginning to think that I'd lost it. I haven't played that bad since—since before I started playing."

Slowly he sobered and took a deep breath. He frowned. "Hey, wait a minute." He took her chin between his fingers and peered down into her eyes. "You agreed to this deal of ours under false pretenses."

"Oh, don't even feel it, Counselor," she tossed back. Mischief danced like a chorus line in her eyes. "There was nothing in the deal that said we had to say anything about our . . . skills. Anyway," she added smugly, "You were actin' so full of yourself that . . ."

"You felt it was your civic duty to bring me down a notch," he said, cutting her off.

"Exactly," she nodded. "After all, I *am* a public servant."

"What else is there about you that I should know?" he asked, pulling her fully against his burning muscles.

For just an instant, her heart stuttered at the question. Then, quickly realizing the innocence of it, she shook off the unsettling feeling.

"Now, that's up to you to discover, Counselor," she said coyly. Yet even as she said the words, a sense of dread spread through her.

CHAPTER 12

"You know what I think?" Justin asked, as they pulled into Vaughn's driveway.

"That I'm wonderful, irresistible, delightful to be with, and you can't stay away from me?" Vaughn quizzed demurely.

Justin looked at her from the corner of his eye and put the car in park. "Very amusing," he replied drolly. "But true. Unfortunately, that's not what I was thinking."

Vaughn pouted.

"I was thinking we'd make a good con team."

She frowned in confusion.

"You know, like the pool sharks," he explained. "We could pretend not to be able to play tennis. Lose a couple of sets and then, *bam!*" He slammed his fist into his palm for emphasis, turned to her, and smiled brightly. "Brilliant, right?"

"Yeah. About as bright as a five-watt bulb!" She playfully punched him in the arm.

"Just a thought," he chuckled, rubbing his arm. "You pack a pretty good wallop. Maybe we could get into the boxing game."

Vaughn cocked her head to the side and pursed her lips. "One more bright idea from you, and I'll be forced to knock your lights out. If you get my drift."

"Oh, better yet," he continued unperturbed. "The Enforcers. We could hire ourselves out . . ."

"Justin!"

"All right. All right," he said, laughing heartily. By degrees he sobered and grew serious. His dark eyes lovingly caressed her face. He leaned across the seat and gathered her close. He nuzzled her neck. "How 'bout if we just play house instead?" he breathed in her ear. "I come home to you," he whispered. "You come home to me—every night—and we see what happens."

Vaughn's heart was beating so fast, she could barely hear over the noise. *House? Us?* Did she hear correctly? She couldn't speak. She was too afraid.

He felt her hesitation in the tenseness that seeped through her body. He understood it. He knew he was pushing this relationship in a new direction. Was he even ready for the challenge? His own heart was racing at breakneck speed. Yet holding her, hearing her laughter, seeing her smile, made him know that this was what he wanted. He held his breath.

Myriad thoughts raced through her head. She was elated, frightened, confused, eager. She was a breath away from saying yes—when her defenses kicked in. Didn't he realize that anything she did could easily become public knowledge? The fact that she was "living" with someone would definitely work against her, even if this was the nineties. Stone would have a field day decrying her morals. She was certain Justin was aware of this. The more she thought about it, the more she convinced herself. Yet he'd asked her anyway. Why? Did he hope that in the heat of afterglow she would forget her dream? Her father's words filtered through her head. *"Everyone wants something. That's our lot."* But what did Justin really want?

Slowly, she eased out of his arms. She kept her eyes focused on her lap. She couldn't see the anxiety hovering in his gaze.

"I don't understand how you could ask me something like that," she stated, in a tone that concealed her inner turmoil. Her voice rose to a harsh note. "You know the kind of pressure I'm up against." She raised her eyes, but her vision was clouded by her own oratory, letting her swirling emotions give way to an irrational anger. "Yet you ask me to live with you and possibly ruin my chances at the election! That doesn't sound like someone who professes to love me, who—who has my best interests at heart." She clenched her hands into tight fists.

Justin felt as if he'd been slapped. He physically recoiled from the sting of her accusation. His nostrils flared with brewing anger. But his voice was tinged with the hurt that twisted his heart. "Do you think so little of me, Vaughn? What I asked came from my heart. Not from some ulterior motive to ruin your campaign," he ground out. He turned away from her and stared out the window. He gripped the steering wheel to keep himself from pulling her into his arms to make her understand the depth of his feelings. He wouldn't do that. Not anymore. "I guess you'd better be going. I'm sure you have some campaign strategy to map out." He pressed the button on the driver's side panel and released the lock.

Vaughn bit her bottom lip to keep it from trembling. Maybe she was wrong. Could she have been? She turned to him, afraid to touch him, afraid to cross the invisible line she had drawn. Words escaped her as she witnessed his hurt. He held himself as still as if he'd been cast in cement. Yet she didn't reach out across that barrier. She couldn't. Instead, she opened the door and closed it gently behind her.

Before she reached the steps of her townhouse, she heard the squeal of tires as the BMW sped out of the driveway and onto the street. Suddenly, she felt the enormous well of emptiness fill her until the tears were forced from her eyes.

The next few days were like walking down a dark tunnel—endless, with no light at the end. Vaughn was on auto-pilot, going through the functions of her office and her daily routine from pure memory. She seemed to have lost her enthusiasm, her sparkle. She hardly raised an eyebrow when Crystal bubbled over with details about the new man in her life. She went through the ritual of having lunch with her mother and listened, with one ear, to her concerns about her father. She hadn't heard a word from Justin, although she didn't expect to. More times than she cared to count she'd reached for the phone to call him. Each time she'd backed out. She still couldn't come to grips with her fears.

The entire office noticed the dramatic change in their boss, but Crystal was hell-bent on ousting this impostor who claimed to be Vaughn Hamilton.

It was about a week after her blow-up with Justin that Crystal had had just about enough of one-word conversations, with the high point being a nod of Vaughn's head.

"Tess," Crystal said, stepping up to the secretary's desk. "I'll be in Ms. Hamilton's office for a while. Hold all her calls."

Tess gave her a look that said, "Good luck." She'd long since given up on getting Vaughn back to normal.

Crystal knocked once on the door but didn't wait for an answer. She closed it solidly behind her and stepped in to find Vaughn staring pensively out the window, apparently unaware that Crystal had come in.

Crystal crossed the room and stood on the opposite side of the desk. She was startled when Vaughn spoke first.

"So you've come to talk," she stated matter-of-factly. Slowly she turned around. Her eyes seemed empty, her famous smile was gone. Whatever had turned her inside out was evident from the strain on her face.

Crystal stepped closer and took a deep breath. "What's going on with you, Vaughn? Everyone is worried about you. I've waited about as long as I intend to. You're gonna tell me something."

"I've just been taking a hard look at my life lately," she said in a flat voice. "I don't like what I see."

Crystal sat down and crossed her legs. "It wouldn't be the first time, Vaughn. It must be more than that. What is it? Is it Justin? Did something happen?"

Vaughn actually laughed, a hollow, empty laugh that chilled Crystal. "You could say that." She looked into Crystal's eyes. "I fell in love with a wonderful man. He asked me to move in with him and I pretty much told him to go to hell."

Crystal opened her mouth, then shut it. Her eyes widened. "What?" she finally sputtered.

"Justin asked me to move in with him. I accused him of trying to sabotage my campaign."

Crystal slowly shook her head in disbelief. "And of course, you've since realized that it's not true, but you haven't got the guts to call and tell him what a fool you really are?"

Vaughn pursed her lips and looked sheepish. "That about sums it up," she responded.

"You just don't know a good thing when it runs you over, do you? Damn girl, what's wrong with you? The man actually told you he loves you, wants to live with you, and you tell him to take a walk in traffic! You are a real piece of work. I . . ."

Vaughn held up one hand, the other on her hip. "Look, girl, I don't need this from you, okay? I already know that I have idiot written all over my face. I can't even remember the last time I felt this lousy." Suddenly her voice broke. She lowered her head to hide the tears. "I miss him, Crystal. I can barely breathe just thinking about him. But I'm so scared." She wrapped her arms around her waist to still the trembling.

Crystal came around the desk and put her arm around Vaughn's shoulders. "You've got to learn to trust again, Vaughn. Every man isn't like Paul. Go with your heart." She paused, then began again. "If you're not ready for a live-in thing, then just tell him. Don't cut him off at the knees."

"I know. That's what I've decided. Finally. I just don't think it's the right thing to do. At least, not now."

Crystal nodded in agreement. "So when are you going to stop torturing yourself and tell him how you really feel?"

Vaughn looked up. "Today. If he'll listen."

"That's more like it. Maybe now things can get back to normal."

Vaughn grinned. "I know I've been a real bitch lately. I'm sorry."

"Apology accepted."

Vaughn sat down with a sigh, then smiled up at her. She cocked her head to the side. "Now, what was this you were telling me about some guy you met?" she grinned.

* * *

The car was waiting at the airport, just as promised. Simone was whisked from the airport and into Richmond in no time. Her pulse quickened as they approached their destination. She desperately wanted to make a good impression. She'd had her nails done, purchased a new suit, and had her shoulder-length hair professionally styled for the first time in years.

"Here we are," the driver said, pulling up in front of the Chaney Building. He came around and opened the door.

Simone stepped out into the warm afternoon breeze and took a deep, calming breath. She took her briefcase and purse from the car and smoothed her pale peach linen suit. "Thank you. Will you wait, or should I take up my bags?"

"My instructions were for me to wait until your interview was concluded and then to take you to your hotel."

Simone swallowed. This was the life, she thought wistfully. "Well, I guess we'll see each other shortly," she smiled. She walked through the revolving doors.

Simone stepped off the elevator and walked toward the office. Barbara looked up and was pleased by the young woman who stood before her.

"Good afternoon. I'm Simone Rivers. I have an appointment with Mr. Montgomery."

Barbara stood up and extended her hand. "Ms. Rivers. It's a pleasure to finally meet you. I'm Barbara Crenshaw. We spoke on the phone."

"Oh, yes." Simone beamed, shaking Barbara's hand. "It's good to finally meet you."

Both Simone and Barbara turned in the direction of the opening hallway door. Instantly Simone knew that the lean, unquestionably handsome man was the image behind the voice.

Chad nearly halted in mid-step when his eyes locked with her shimmering brown ones. If this was Simone, then truly there was a heaven. He strode purposefully across the room, taking rapid-fire pictures of Simone in his mind's eye. She was taller than he'd envisioned. Her hair was longer. Her complexion richer, her figure curvier. She exceeded each and every one of his expectations. Jackpot!

"Good afternoon, ladies." His greeting included both women, but his gaze was on Simone. "You must be Ms. Rivers." He extended his hand and she slipped hers into his firm grasp.

"And you're Chad Rushmore," she said softly in return. "I'd know that voice anywhere." Her smile radiated the warmth she felt inside as she appraised him openly, gently unnerving him.

"I'm glad to see that you arrived safely."

"Thank you, Mr. Rushmore. Mr. Montgomery seemed to have taken care of everything."

"Call me Rush. All my friends do."

"I'd like that . . . Rush."

Barbara watched the exchange with wry amusement. She loudly cleared her throat, successfully disconnecting the electric charge in the air. "Chad, why don't you show Ms. Rivers around? Mr. Montgomery isn't expected for about an hour."

Chad tore his gaze away from Simone's face and slowly digested what was being said.

"No problem." He turned back toward Simone. "Are you ready?"

"Sure. Lead the way." She smiled and Chad could have sworn that his heart stopped.

"Maybe after the tour we could have lunch. If you're hungry, that is." Chad suggested.

"That sounds wonderful. The food on the plane left a lot to be desired."

Barbara watched them walk away and shook her head. It was about time Chad ran into someone who could cool his jets . . . or maybe turn up the heat, she chuckled to herself.

Justin had been like a caged bear since the fiasco with Vaughn. He hadn't had a decent night's sleep in days, which accounted for his unusual late-afternoon arrival. He'd needed the few extra hours to get himself together before going in today. The last thing he wanted to do was lose it when he met Simone. He'd been short tempered with his staff, his friends, strangers on the street, and every time he'd thought about Vaughn, which seemed to be continuously, his stomach twisted into knots.

As he stood in front of his full-length mirror and adjusted his maroon tie, his countenance grew solemn. This wasn't how he'd expected to feel today, of all days. He'd expected to feel exhilaration, anticipation, maybe even fear. But this indescribable desolation was unbearable. The only things that had kept him sane had been the single-mindedness with which he'd driven himself at work and in his business dealings, and his unwavering hope that Simone would be the daughter he'd lost. Yet even that excitement had been tainted by Vaughn's callousness.

His throat constricted. He'd opened his heart and soul to Vaughn. He'd exposed a part of himself that he'd never done for any woman, not even Janice. He'd trusted Vaughn to take his feelings and nurture them. Instead, she took, into her hand, what he'd offered of himself and she crushed it like something to be discarded. The pain of her rejection had ripped out a piece of him he wasn't sure could ever be repaired.

He inhaled deeply, ran a soft brush across his hair, and splashed on a dab of cologne. He'd find a way to rid his heart and his spirit of Vaughn. He knew that he couldn't spend the rest of his life feeling like he didn't want to face another day. Maybe, just maybe, he did have something to look forward to. Being a father again. Did he dare to hope?

CHAPTER 13

Four men sat solemnly around the hardwood table. Conversation was barely audible, the thick Persian carpets and paneled walls absorbing all sound. Waiters served drinks and brunch unobtrusively, seeming to blend into the "old-boy" decor.

The exclusive club on Sixteenth Street N.W. was a haven for the ultra-confidential conversation. It was rumored that the real decisions of the nation were made in these rooms. They were frequented by statesmen and businesspeople of every caliber, as well as those whose names remained unknown.

"I want you to meet with Montgomery within the next two weeks," the man at the head of the table advised. "Those are my instructions."

"From whom?" asked Stan Waters, the heaviest of the four. Stan Waters had been a considerable financial contributor to election campaigns over the years. Having his financial backing was like having your own godfather. His construction firm did big business with the government, and even though nothing was written down, decisions were never made without informing Stan Waters.

"There's no reason to concern yourself with that. Let it be my problem." His smile was practiced. "You get him to agree. I know you can. Any questions?" His dark gaze bore through each face intently.

There was a simultaneous nodding of heads.

"Good." He slapped his palms on the table. "Gentlemen, this meeting is adjourned. And," he cautioned as he motioned for the waiter, "this is not to be discussed with anyone. Understood?" Another round of nods. "Now, let's have lunch."

On the drive to his office, Justin felt his uneasiness over how he would react to meeting Simone mount. Would he recognize her on sight? Would she still resemble the pudgy little baby that he remembered? Of course she wouldn't, he rationalized. The last time he'd seen his daughter had been nearly nineteen years ago.

How would he know, he wondered, as he pulled his car into his parking space. What would he say? His pulse beat a rapid rhythm. He walked toward the elevator. Soon, he breathed heavily. Soon.

Simone and Chad had just returned from lunch and were waiting in the reception area when Justin entered. For several unbelievable moments, when Justin's gaze lighted on Simone, he was transported back through time to the moment he'd first seen his infant daughter.

His heart was swollen with pride and a fierce sense of determination that he would do everything in his power to protect this angel that had been sent to him from heaven. When he'd held his daughter for the first time, he'd been overcome with a love so powerful it had brought tears to his eyes. But somehow, over the ensuing months, his quest to carve out the best life possible for his wife and daughter had overshadowed everything else. And then they were gone. That void had never been filled—until now.

"Justin." Chad rose from his seat on the long sofa, as did Simone.

Slowly, Justin walked over to them and extended his hand to Simone. "I take it you're the Ms. Rivers I've heard so much about. Rush," he added, nodding to him in acknowledgment.

Simone smiled and Justin's heart constricted from the sweetness of it. "Yes, I am, Mr. Montgomery. It's a pleasure to meet you at last."

Justin cleared his throat. "Well . . . if you'll give me a few minutes to get settled, I'll be right with you and we can talk."

"Thank you," she said.

Justin crossed the room, fighting to keep his emotions shrouded under the guise of normalcy. "Any messages, Barbara?"

"There were two. One from Assemblywoman Hamilton, and another from a Mr. Waters." Barbara handed him the message slips.

It took all he had to keep his hand from trembling when he reached for the white slips of paper. *Vaughn.* He swallowed. "Thanks." He looked down at the number for Stan Waters as he headed for his office. He never did care for Waters and couldn't imagine what they would have to say to each other. He slipped the message into his jacket pocket and opened his office door.

Immediately he reached for the phone, then stopped. It had taken her a week to call him. The waiting had seemed like an eternity. Now, he wasn't sure if he wanted to hear what she had to say. He moved behind his desk and sat heavily down in his seat.

Suddenly, he wanted her to hurt just as badly as he'd been hurting. He wanted her to know the depths of his disillusionment. He wanted her to feel what it was like to have the love you offered tossed in your face.

He leaned across the desk and reached for the phone. He pressed the intercom.

"Yes, Mr. Montgomery," Barbara answered.

"Barb, send in Ms. Rivers, please."

"Right away."

Justin leaned back in his seat and waited. What would he say—what could he say that would explain the loss of nineteen years?

"It's quittin' time, girlfriend," Crystal said, stepping into Vaughn's office.

"Hmm-umm," Vaughn responded absently. She hadn't heard from Justin even after leaving two messages. It was becoming painfully obvious that he no longer wanted to have anything to do with her. "Uh, I'll be leaving soon. You go on ahead." She forced a smile.

"Trouble?" Crystal questioned.

Vaughn straightened her shoulders and inhaled deeply. "Nothing I can't handle."

Crystal gave her a long look, then shrugged. "If you say so. I'll see you in the morning. Don't forget to work on your notes for your meeting with the city council in the morning."

Vaughn waved away the suggestion. "Taken care of," she said. Work was the only activity that had kept her sound throughout the day as she'd waited in vain for the phone to ring.

"Then I'll see you in the morning. I'm meeting David in an hour. Got to rush home and change," Crystal added, trying to get a rise out of Vaughn.

Vaughn looked up from the papers on her desk. "Have fun."

Crystal shook her head once in defeat and closed the door silently behind her.

Vaughn sighed in audible relief when Crystal finally left. She didn't know how much longer she'd have been able to stand there and pretend everything was wonderful. When what she really wanted to do was crawl under the covers and cry.

She stuffed her notes in her briefcase, took a last look around the office and a fleeting look at the phone, and left.

For several moments she stood on the steps of the office building, her lightweight trenchcoat billowing around her. The evening sky was just beginning to darken. The heavens glowed a brilliant orange. The breeze was warm, the streets covered with after-work strollers and couples on their way to intimate dinners. There were all the elements she'd shared with Justin on so many nights just like this one. She had never felt so alone as she did at that moment.

Drawing on some inner strength, she walked to the corner and hailed a cab. She had no one to blame, she realized, as she sat back on the leather seat, no one but herself. She'd been a fool to think Justin could have been anything other than sincere. She'd taken what he'd offered her and she'd mangled it. And now he didn't want to have anything to do with her.

For so long she'd been brainwashed into believing that whatever her father had said was true, almost without question. She'd allowed his views to become her own. And now she had allowed them to destroy the one bit of happiness that she'd found in this lifetime.

"Driver." She tapped on the Plexiglas partition. "I've changed my mind. Please take me to 5836 Larchmont." She sat back and swallowed the trepidation that welled up in her throat. What if he wouldn't see her? What if . . . what if he was with someone else? She knew she wouldn't be able to stand that. Her mind raced through every uncomfortable scenario imaginable.

"Ms. . . . Ms." The driver craned his neck to look behind him. "Ain't this where you wanted to get out?"

Vaughn shook her head, snapping back to reality. "Oh. I'm sorry. How much is that?"

"Eight-fifty."

Vaughn dug in her purse and retrieved a ten-dollar bill. "Keep the change." She gathered her belongings, got out, and then stood like a statue in front of Justin's darkened house. There was no sign of anyone, no lights, no nothing.

In vain, she looked up and down the quiet, tree-lined street. What would she do now? The cab was long gone and this wasn't the type of neighborhood where you could flag one down. And the last thing she needed was to be caught standing outside his door like some lovesick puppy. She looked toward the corner in the hopes of spotting a phone. Nothing. Tears of disappointment, humiliation, and frustration slipped unnoticed down her cheeks.

After spending the better part of the afternoon with Simone, Justin was more convinced than ever that she was, in fact, his daughter, Samantha. There was no hard proof. He was now convinced that Janice had given up their daughter, which would fully explain why he could never find her.

She was the same age as Sam, even though their birthdays were months apart. It was probably all part of Janice's plan, he reasoned. Simone had Sam's coloring and she was everything that he would want his daughter to be. Yet there was still a part of him, a nagging part of him, that said he wanted Simone to be his daughter so desperately that he had created the scenario that would make it real.

As he drove through the darkened Richmond streets, he felt more than ever the overpowering need to be loved again. He needed to be held at this moment. He needed to be told that everything was going to work out. He needed to be vulnerable, for just a moment, and to shed his armor of impenetrability. He needed to be with Vaughn and the realization twisted the knife deeper into his heart. She didn't want him, at least, not in the way he wanted her. But he felt he had reached a point in his life where he had to have more than she was able or willing to give.

He turned onto his street. Maybe he had pushed too hard, too fast. He knew Vaughn was still on the wire about their relationship. He knew she had been terribly hurt in the past. He also understood that in her very public position she would be held up to the closest scrutiny. He breathed heavily. He'd been a first-class idiot. He'd let his ego dictate his behavior over the past week. Instead of getting to the root of what was really eating at her, he'd collected his marbles and quit the game. With that kind of attitude, he and Vaughn would never get anywhere. They were both too damned stubborn. Someone had to be willing to make the first move. To some men, the thought of making concessions when it came to a woman made them feel less than a man. But Justin didn't need the backing or approval of the brotherhood to validate himself. He always believed that it took a real man to realize what a woman needed to make her happy. Even if that meant making those concessions.

He stepped on the accelerator. As soon as he got home, he was going to call her. He was going to make her listen. Just as he'd done all the other times. He wasn't going to let her fears and the paranoia that her father had heaped on her destroy them. She was much too important. With that decided, he suddenly felt better than he had in days. He was in such a hurry to reach his door that he nearly missed the woman walking briskly down the street.

He slowed the car. It was beyond unusual, in this highly secluded neighborhood, to see a single woman walking the street at night. He frowned and then peered closer as the woman drew near. It couldn't be.

He pulled the car to a sudden stop alongside her. Vaughn snapped her head in his direction and her heart leaped to her throat.

"Damn," she swore under her breath. "Just what I need. How in the devil am I going to explain being here?" How about the truth, her conscience quizzed. She lifted her chin, adjusted her shoulder bag, and slung her hands in her trenchcoat pockets. Purposefully, she turned to face the now parked car and took a defiant step closer.

Justin stepped out and looked at her over the hood of the BMW. He swore he'd never seen anything so beautiful. His stomach knotted. Why had she come?

They both began to talk at once. "Vaughn, I . . . want . . ."

"I came to see you."

"I was going to call . . ." Justin rounded the car and stood in front of her.

Vaughn felt her heart slam mercilessly against her chest. The scent of him swam to her brain. Oh, God, how she'd missed him.

They seemed to reach for each other simultaneously. Her hand stroked his cheek, his cupped her delicate chin, tilting her face up to his. His eyes seemed to burn through her, she thought dizzily, heating all the places that had been so cold since she'd last been with him. How could she have ever thought for a minute that this man she loved beyond reason would do anything to intentionally hurt her?

Justin's eyes grazed lovingly across her face. There were so many things he wanted to say, but only one thing seemed to encapsule all that raged within his heart. "I love you, Vaughn," he whispered raggedly. "I know I'll always love you. And whatever it is . . ." He lowered his head until his lips were only a breath away from hers, "we'll work through it. We will if you'll just trust me. Please, baby, just trust me."

Vaughn had no words as Justin's luscious lips touched down on hers, then drew her into a soul-stirring kiss that was one step below heaven. How she longed to be held by him again, to be loved by him, to give herself to him as she had with no other man! She had been such a fool. Time and life were too short to allow anything to interfere with happiness. She would trust him this time. Completely. She would give one hundred percent of herself from this day forward. Never again did she want to feel the hollow pain that had filled her days without him.

Justin crushed her lush body fully against him, needing desperately to feel the heat of her flesh. He felt like a man who'd been deprived of water and then was finally led to the river to take his fill. He feasted on her lips, his tongue dancing with and enticing hers. His powerful fingers raked through her hair, commanding that she succumb to him. But this would never be enough, he realized, as the beat of passion pounded through his veins.

Gently, he broke the kiss. His eyes sparkled with a desire only to be surpassed by hers.

"Your place . . . or mine . . . ?" he groaned.

Vaughn smiled seductively at him. Her finger reached out and traced his full lips. "Since I'm in the neighborhood," she said in a throaty whisper, "let's try your place on for size."

CHAPTER 14

"I've been wrong about so many things," Vaughn confessed, as she lay on her side next to Justin. Gingerly, she traced the outline of his jaw. "It's just hard for me sometimes to say how I really feel." She hesitated. Justin caressed her back, encouraging her to continue. In a halting voice, she began again. "I've been conditioned to believe that every man is out to use me. My negative reflexes just kick in whenever someone tries to get close to me." Her eyes gazed lovingly into his. "What I should have really said is . . . I'm just not ready to live with you. But," she qualified with a tremulous smile, "that doesn't mean I'll feel that way forever. I just don't think that now is the right time."

Justin sighed heavily. "It was hard for me to accept what you said. But hindsight is always twenty-twenty. I know you're right, Vaughn, but I just couldn't handle the idea that you didn't want to be with me—and to hell with your real reasons. But guess what?"

"What?" she grinned.

"I'd rather have you with me on whatever terms than not at all."

"Oh, Justin." With a hunger that roared through her with unbelievable force, she pressed her starving body against his. In unison, their lips met, parted, and then enveloped each other.

Spirals of sweet pleasure swirled within her as she allowed Justin's every touch, every moan, every movement, to ignite the passion that she'd held in limbo.

With the gentleness of the most ardent lover, Justin sought out and found each and every needy corner of her body. Vaughn felt her bones liquefy as her body surrendered to the heat. Justin looked deep into her eyes, seeming to peer into the hidden corners of her soul. Her heart quickened. He cupped her face in his hands.

"There's more to your reasons than what you're telling me, isn't there?" he gently probed.

Vaughn swallowed. Could it really be that this man was truly capable of seeing into the dark spaces of her heart? Maybe now was the time to get everything out in the open—cleanse her heart and soul—time to voice her hurt and loss.

To do that would open wounds that should remain sealed. To do that would only resurface a flood of pain that she was sure she couldn't handle. It was a part of her life that she could not share with anyone, not even Justin.

"Whatever it is that you think you see," she whispered huskily, "we're here—now." She moistened her lips with the tip of her tongue, a gesture that sent Justin's blood pressure to the roof. "Make me forget it." Her eyes raked over his face. Her fingers dug into his back, pulling him to her. Her voice was the fire that raced through him.

"Whatever you want," he groaned deep in her ear, his tongue flicking across the delicate shell, while Vaughn's nimble fingers played a concerto down his broad chest, reaching the center of his lust.

She enveloped the power of him, feeling him pulse and throb at her touch. The contact served to heighten her own burning need while she stroked him in a slow, steady rhythm.

Justin's long moan filled the torrid air. His mouth covered hers, his tongue delving into the soft sweetness of her mouth, muffling his groans of pleasure.

To her amazement, the yearning that tore through her surpassed everything they'd experienced before. Her need for him was painful in its intensity. She felt herself float away, transported to a plateau of euphoria when Justin instinctively kneaded her throbbing breasts that cried out for his touch.

The pads of his thumbs grazed hungrily across the hardened tips of her breasts, sending lightning bolts of desire shooting to the core of her womanhood—flooding her, preparing her for him.

His strong hands slid down the curves of her body—lower—down her spine—lower across her hips, finding their way into the dark valley between her thighs. Lightly his fingers skimmed the thin ridge of skin that ran across the length of her pelvis. Vaughn's whole body tensed and Justin suspected that it was something she wouldn't want to discuss—a woman thing, he surmised. Instead of the questions that she held her breath against, Justin continued his exploration. The tip of his finger teased the tight bud of her dewy center, sending tremors hurtling through her.

A strangled cry welled up in her throat, her fears momentarily extinguished when Justin placed his weight lightly above her. His eyes bore into hers while his hands skimmed down her sides, bracing her thighs and raising them to lock around his back.

"I've missed you," he urgently whispered above her parted lips. "I didn't want to, but I did," he confessed. His fingers pressed deeper into her thighs. "This," he lowered his hips, pushing against her pulsing entryway, "is the new beginning for us." He pushed down further, crossing the rim of her opening.

Her body tightened from the pressure, then relaxed as the full force of him slowly filled her. His eyes squeezed shut as he allowed the first wave of rapture to engulf him. Involuntarily, her muscles contracted and Justin cried out her name, no longer able to hold back. He pulled up, then thrust downward, burying himself to the hilt within her.

Vaughn's body trembled as the total power of their union overtook her. It was sweet bliss, a symphony perfectly orchestrated as two vibrant instruments unified into one exquisite being.

The tempo was slow and pulsing, building to a shuddering crescendo. They played off each other, giving as much as taking equally, enjoying to the utmost the rise and fall of their bodies.

Never before had Justin known such joy as he allowed his body and soul to succumb to Vaughn's magical manipulations of his mind and heart.

Vaughn in hushed whispers told him how magnificent he made her feel, punctuating her words with driving thrusts of her hips—commanding him to take her—all of her—over the plateau and into the valley of release. And he did, masterfully propelling them over the last hurdle into a world of explosive ecstasy.

Smoldering in the afterglow, Justin's body still pulsed with need. He couldn't explain it—couldn't understand what was happening to him. Vaughn was like a sorceress who'd cast a powerful spell over him. He couldn't get through a minute of his day without thinking about her. He couldn't breathe without imagining her erotic scent. He hugged her tighter. She murmured softly in her sleep. Gently he brushed a lock of hair from her face and placed a soft kiss on her forehead. "I love you," he whispered with all the intensity that burned within him.

Vaughn stirred. Her eyes fluttered open. Her smile was as soft as a halo, illuminating all in its path, Justin thought.

"I know," she whispered. Her fingertip traced his luscious lips. "As much as I love you."

It was after midnight by the time Justin pulled up in front of Vaughn's townhouse. They were still talking about Justin's meeting with Simone when he parked the car. He walked with her to her door.

"Are you sure you don't want me to stay?" he asked, longing and mischief dancing in his eyes.

She bracketed his jaws in the palms of her hands. "If you stayed here tonight, I wouldn't get a moment's sleep. I have a big day tomorrow."

"Even if I promised to be good?" he crooned, hugging her snugly around the waist and rocking his hips sensuously against her.

"We both know you're good," she said, drawing out the last word erotically. She ran her tongue across her lips. "That's not the problem." She felt his hardness rub enticingly against her inner thighs. For a moment, she reconsidered. The last thing she wanted to do tonight was sleep alone. "Goodnight, Justin," she breathed raggedly, good judgment overriding the need that was steadily building up within her.

"You're gonna think about me," he warned, taking a slow step back without releasing her. His eyes crinkled at the corners. "You're gonna wish you'd said yes when you roll over in that big bed of yours and find yourself alone." He touched his fingertip to her nose. "You'll be sorry."

"I'm sure I will." She wondered where she found the strength to resist him.

"Tell you what," he said, "let's get away for a few days. Away from business, campaigns, and news polls."

Vaughn's smile widened. "Sounds heavenly."

"Let me make the arrangements. I want it to be a surprise." He took two more retreating steps.

"Yes, surprise me."

"Oh," he added, "I want you to meet Simone. Tomorrow. For dinner. We can show her the town before she goes back to school."

"I'd love to. If you let *me* pick the spot." She heard the eagerness in his voice and silently prayed that he wouldn't be hurt.

He stopped in mid-step and looked at her, his eyes beseeching her to understand. "She's everything I'd expected," he said wistfully. "I can't explain it, baby," he said, stepping back up to her, "but she's everything I'd ever dreamed of. I know it sounds crazy, but I just believe she is Samantha."

"Oh, Justin, sweetheart," she said gently. "For your sake, I hope that she is. But there's no way you can know for sure."

"There are ways," he said firmly. "And I'm going to prove it."

Her brow knitted. "How?"

"About two years ago, I started an organization called Child-Link . . ."

Flashes of news clippings dashed through Vaughn's mind, and the familiar feeling of misgiving that she'd experienced when they first met sprouted anew.

"The organization reunites families, searches out and uncovers sealed records." He swallowed. "It's about time I used it for my own benefit."

For some inexplicable reason, her heart was racing. Her stomach twisted. "Well," she breathed, steadying herself, "I'm sure that if they have you pushing them, they're bound to turn up something."

"And no matter what happens," he took her hands in his, "I want you with me."

She pressed her lips together and nodded. "I will be."

"I'll call you in the morning," he said, still reluctant to leave her. "Sleep well, baby. I'll see you in my dreams."

"I'll be waiting." She touched her fingers to her lips and then to his.

Lucus Stone sat at the head of the conference table at his congressional office in Richmond. His advisers sat on either side. All of them wore somber expressions.

Lucus stared long and hard at each face before he spoke. "What is going wrong?" he thundered suddenly, his deep voice reverberating through the room and sending a note of warning down their spines. He slammed his fist down onto the table, his blue eyes snapping like electric sparks. "I want answers."

Lucus's chief of public relations, Winston McGee, spoke first. "You've been in this business long enough to know that polls mean nothing this early on," he cajoled. "We just need to get you out there more, remind the voters about what you've done over the years. Do some more PSAs . . ."

"Shut up, Winston. If you'd been doing *half* of your job, Vaughn Hamilton would have never received this much press." He tossed the stack of newspapers down the length of the table. "Look at them, you idiots. She's in the papers every day! Every day! That's where I should be," he roared, stabbing his finger at his chest to punctuate his point. Lucus took several deep breaths, ran his hand through his shock of silver hair, and twisted his neck inside his shirt collar as if it had suddenly gotten too tight.

Julius Simpson, Lucus's political strategist, spoke up next. "We're into phase two," he said cryptically. "I'm confident that everything will be rectified shortly. We'll know more in about a week."

David Cain sat, as an observer, at the far end of the table in his role as consultant. He knew from the conversation that the issue being discussed was not completely above board and only those included in the execution of the plan were privy to Simpson's ambiguous remarks.

"What about that reporter at the *Weekly Globe?*" Lucus asked Winston.

"Just waiting for the go-ahead from me," Winston confirmed.

David's eyebrows rose a fraction of an inch in surprise. Lucus was going to use the rags to run Vaughn through the mill. He almost laughed at the irony of it all. The weekly tabloid was probably read and believed by more people than the *Post* and the *Times* combined. If Vaughn Hamilton wanted press coverage, she'd have more than she could handle.

"You're going to have to do better, David," Lucus stated, snapping

David out of his scandalous thoughts. "Time is running out. I need all the ammunition I can get, and quickly."

David nodded. There was no point trying to defend himself. Lucus wasn't the type of man who listened to excuses, even valid ones. He had to admit, though, as he continued to listen to the voices drone on around him, that he thought his job was going to be some pain-in-the-butt assignment. But the truth of it was that he was really getting to like Crystal. Unfortunately, that was the last thing he needed. Women who were able to get under your skin were nothing but trouble. Anyway, he concluded, heaving a sigh, after this was over, *they* were over.

But last night, when he was rocking Trini's world, he'd imagined she was Crystal. That spelled trouble. He'd had a devil of a time convincing Trini to see him, and when she did, all he could think about was Crystal. Trini had been madder than a cat in heat that he'd stayed away for so long. But he'd more than made up for his absence and Trini was more than happy to fill him in on Lucus Stone's extracurricular activities, most of which the good congressman would never want anyone to know, especially his wife.

His thoughts easily drifted back to Crystal. If only there were some way he could avoid hurting her, he mused, a slow frown lining his brow. But it was a dirty $50,000 job, and somebody had to do it. He was sure his payment would sufficiently compensate him for any emotional loss.

"I expect progress, gentlemen," Lucus concluded, as he stood. "We'll meet again next week." He pushed his chair back and strode out.

Elliott Hamilton returned to his chambers after the morning recess. He sat down heavily in an overstuffed leather chair. His clerk had placed a copy of the *Richmond Herald* on his desk and circled the glowing article about Vaughn.

Elliott glanced at the article and then out the window. At the moment, Vaughn was rallying well. But for how long? If she continued to act like some silly schoolgirl in love, there was bound to be some nosy news hound who'd pick up the scent and begin digging—maybe too deeply into her personal life. Although he'd taken every precaution over the years, there was always the possibility that some shred of damaging information could be unearthed.

A thin line of perspiration spread across his upper lip. If anyone ever found out what he'd done, he'd be ruined, his family name would be ridiculed, Vaughn's career would come to a halt. The only one who knew the truth was Sheila. He should never have confessed to her. But he'd needed her help. He'd convinced her that what he'd done was for the best. That was years ago when he was certain of his wife's love for him. Now . . . well, now he was no longer sure.

He had to be certain that the past was never resurrected. The best of men and women had been destroyed, their lives and careers ruined, when one dark element was brought to light. He could not allow that to happen. Justin Montgomery was the one who could ensure that.

Everything would be fine. He sighed heavily. The wheels were in motion. All he could do now was wait. And he'd be there for his daughter—as he'd always been—when she came running to him, crying, telling him that he'd been right. As always.

CHAPTER 15

Simone was in seventh heaven. The hotel Justin had selected for her was exquisite. Her room overlooked the river and she had a view of Richmond that spanned miles.

She lay across the queen-sized bed and mentally mapped out her day. She'd received an early morning call from Mr. Montgomery, inviting her to dinner before she returned to school the following afternoon. She'd have to go out and find something appropriate to wear. Her one hope was that he'd also invited Chad to come along.

Oooh, just thinking about him made her stomach knot up. He was absolutely wonderful. And it was pretty obvious that Mr. Montgomery was going to let her do her internship with his firm. She supposed this was a dinner to finalize the details. If so, then she could see Chad every day and maybe, just maybe, something could happen between them.

She slid her hands beneath her head and closed her eyes. She broke into a smile. Immediately she thought of the wonderful afternoon and early evening she'd spent with Chad. They'd gotten along so well, one would have thought they'd known each other all their lives. He was funny, charming, intelligent, and sexy. She giggled and wondered what he thought of her. She knew that he was in his twenties. She hoped he didn't think that she was some silly kid. After all, she would be nineteen soon.

Mr. Montgomery was pretty cool, too. He really seemed interested in her and in her life, not just about what she wanted to be when she grew up. He really made her feel as though he was listening to what she had to say. She'd found herself telling him about her life, about the emptiness of being a foster child, the insecurity of not knowing who her real parents were. While she talked, she knew that somehow he truly understood. She'd almost told him about Child-Link. She knew he was one of the founders, but she didn't want him to think she'd be so involved in finding her parents that she wouldn't be able to do her job.

Simone knew she would like working for him. There was something about him that touched her, almost a sense of the familiar. He was the type of man she'd want her real father to be.

She forced her eyes open and peered at the bedside clock. It was one in the afternoon. She'd better get a move on. But first she'd call Jean and tell her about all the wonderful things that were happening to her. She had a sense that they were going to get even better.

"Are you ready?" Crystal asked, breezing into Vaughn's office, looking radiant, Vaughn noted.

"Just stuffing the last piece of paper into my briefcase." She looked speculatively at Crystal. "And what—or should I say who—has you looking so bubbly? As if I didn't know."

Crystal grinned shyly. "David. Vaughn," she breathed airily, "he's the best thing to happen to me in so long. I've never been so happy."

"Well, there seems to be a lot of that going around lately," Vaughn teased, thinking immediately of Justin. "So when am I going to meet Mr. Wonderful?" she asked, slipping into her suit jacket. She looked across at Crystal and saw the momentary hesitation. Vaughn frowned. "Is something wrong?"

"No," Crystal replied a bit too quickly, Vaughn thought. "It's just that we have so little time to spend together, well . . ." she grinned and shrugged. "David doesn't want to share our time together until we get to know each other better. He travels a lot," she added hastily, realizing for the first time how odd that explanation sounded.

Vaughn's senses went on immediate alert. She didn't like the sound of this. It just didn't seem right that someone who was this important in a person's life wouldn't want to meet their friends. He sounded like someone who had something to hide. Although she realized the parallels in her own life with Justin, their initial reasons for discretion were entirely different.

Vaughn didn't bother to disguise her concern. "Are you sure everything is up front with this guy? I mean, I can understand comfy-cozy and all that, but don't you think this is taking it a bit too far?"

Crystal knew that Vaughn was right, but she would never admit it. Though in the still hours of the night, she wondered why David wanted to be so secretive. Most nights, when they did see each other, it was at her apartment. They generally went to out-of-the-way restaurants—when they did go out—David said it was so they wouldn't be disturbed by the tons of friends and politicians she was sure to run into.

"Why can't you just be happy for me?" Crystal snapped. "When you get all gooey over Justin, do I tell *you* that something funny must be going on?" She knew she was screeching, but she couldn't seem to stop. "No. I tell you to go for it. Be happy. But no, not you. Not cynical, suspicious-about-every-man Vaughn Hamilton," she railed. "Every guy is guilty until proved innocent in your book." Crystal's nostrils flared and she knew that she'd gone over the limits.

Vaughn swallowed hard. Her eyes burned. Her face remained unreadable. "I think we'd better be going," Vaughn said in a tight voice, barely under control. She snatched up her briefcase and tossed her trenchcoat over her arm. "Please shut the door on your way out," she said over her shoulder. "I'll be taking my own car. You can meet me there in yours."

Crystal squeezed her eyes shut as Vaughn stepped out of her office. She expelled a tremulous breath. What had she done? She'd hurt her friend for the sake of a man. She'd said horrible things, things Vaughn did not deserve.

She walked out of the office. This whole relationship thing was making her crazy. But she couldn't jeopardize her job and her best friend because of it. She'd apologize as soon as she and Vaughn had a moment together.

That moment never came. Vaughn kept an icy distance from Crystal for the balance of the day. She steered clear of her during the meeting with the city council, addressing her only when necessary. She pointedly told Crystal that she didn't have time to talk when they returned to the office. "Quite frankly, I don't give a damn what you have to say," she'd said, as calmly as if she were ordering lunch.

The only relief from the tension that coiled between them was that Vaughn left two hours early. She barely looked in Crystal's direction as she waved her goodbyes to her staff. The slight, noticed only by Crystal, set her teeth on edge. If that's the way she wanted it, then that's the way it would be, Crystal concluded, as she packed up for the day. If Vaughn didn't want to hear it, then she had nothing else to say.

Vaughn finally released the breath that she seemed to have held the entire day. She was still reeling from Crystal's stinging comments. How could Crystal say those things about her? she fretted, as she drove toward Justin's office. Didn't she realize that she had her best interests at heart? She and Crystal had been friends for so long, more like sisters. Nothing could have hurt her more.

She sighed heavily as she made her turn onto the highway. What she needed to concentrate on now was her evening with Justin and meeting Simone. Maybe when she calmed down and put things into perspective she'd be willing to listen to Crystal's explanation. Whatever that might be, she thought angrily. In the meantime, she needed to get home and change before meeting her dinner date.

"The forensic evidence is beginning to come in," Khendra said to the group sitting at the table. "I'm going to need your help here, Rush," she continued. "I'll sound like a babbling idiot if you can't turn this medicalese into layman's language."

Chad laughed heartily. "No problem, Khen, all that scientific stuff is right up my alley. Makes me feel like Quincy." He turned toward Simone and grinned. He spoke low enough so that only she could hear. "This is the kind of stuff you'll be working on while you're interning. I hope you have the stomach for it. It can get kind of grisly. But it's really fascinating."

Simone swallowed and gave a good imitation of a smile. "I'm sure it is."

"What have you turned up, Sean?" Justin asked his partner.

Sean leaned back in his seat and visualized the volumes of notes that he'd compiled over the past few weeks. "You know my specialty is appeals." He looked around the table and his eyes settled on his wife. "And although I have the greatest confidence in Khen's abilities, we have to be prepared for the possibility of a conviction."

Justin nodded in agreement and the trial team concurred.

"So what I've done is made a thorough search of every trial that was even remotely similar to the Harrison case." He passed out folders containing the information. "Just to summarize," he continued, "there have been thirty-six capital murders tried in Virginia. Only two have won on appeal."

Groans filled the room. "But, we could very well be number three."

"If we work it right, we won't have to worry about an appeal," Khendra cut in confidently.

Sean grinned. "Touché."

"Well, troops, we still have a lot of work to do," Justin concluded. "So dig in. We'll meet again next week, and I'll expect updates from everyone." He rose and everyone at the table began collecting his notes.

Sean eased up beside Justin. "So we finally get to meet your mystery woman, eh?" He nudged Justin in the ribs.

Justin chuckled. "Yeah, finally. Are you happy now? And I know your wife is about ready to burst." He winked in Khendra's direction.

"We've just been kind of worried about you lately. Especially after you said you wanted to sell the practice."

"I know. I know," Justin conceded, as they walked toward the door. "But I really want to devote more of my time to my own life now. I want to have time to pursue my investments and put more of a personal touch into the foundations that I've set up." They strolled down the hallway in the direction of Sean's office.

"And how does the mystery lady fit into all this?"

Justin slanted him a look. "Right next to me . . . all the way."

"This is getting better by the minute. You're really that serious?"

Justin nodded. "I can't believe it myself. I thought after Janice, it was over for me in that department. I mean, there have been women in my life, but no one important enough for me to look past tomorrow with."

"She must be some kind of lady," Sean hedged.

"And more." He checked his watch. It was twenty to six. Vaughn would be arriving shortly. He wanted to change his shirt and tie before they left for dinner. "Hey, why don't you and Khendra join us? It was just supposed to be my lady, myself, and Simone, but I've already invited Rush so that Simone wouldn't get bored. Two more at the table shouldn't be a problem."

"Sounds good to me. Let me check with Khen, and see if she feels like going. But I'm sure, knowing my wife, she wouldn't miss a chance to get your lady up close and personal, for a little interrogation in the powder room."

Both men laughed heartily, knowing that the ever-vigilant Khendra would never let anything get past her. She'd been just short of ruthless when it had come to the women that flitted in and out of Justin's life. No area of their lives was sacred to Khendra. But Justin's humor ran deeper. Just wait until Khen sees who the mystery lady is, he thought. He wondered how many test questions Khendra would be willing to spring on Vaughn.

"So . . . what do you think so far?" Chad asked Simone, as he opened the door to the lounge.

"I think I'm going to love working here. Except maybe for the forensic part."

Chad smiled. "Believe me, that's a small part of it. There's just so much more that goes into putting a case together."

Simone took a deep breath. "It's definitely not like television," she remarked.

They stepped into the lounge and sat on a long sofa. "I wonder where Mr. Montgomery is taking us to dinner tonight," Simone asked.

"Your guess is as good as mine. He said it was a surprise. I'm just glad he asked me to tag along."

Simone looked at him for a long moment. "So am I," she said softly.

Chad felt his chest tighten. "I was glad because . . . I could spend more time with you," he replied, not knowing where the words had come from.

Simone's eyes widened. But before she could respond, Barbara poked her head in.

"There you are. Justin was looking for you both."

Vaughn felt like a celebrity as she was introduced to Justin's staff. They rounded a corner.

"Here are Sean and Khendra's offices."

Justin knocked once on the door and stepped in. Sean and Khendra were huddled over a stack of briefs. They both looked up simultaneously when Justin and Vaughn entered. Vaughn was momentarily stunned by the intense power that was projected from their gaze. They would definitely make a formidable team.

Justin stretched out his hand toward Sean and Khendra as he made introductions. "Khendra, Sean, I'd like you to meet the Honorable Assemblywoman Vaughn Hamilton, the next congresswoman from the state of Virginia," he said in grandiose tones. He gave a sweeping bow to Vaughn and she felt as if she should be hearing trumpets.

Vaughn rolled her eyes to the ceiling and playfully pushed Justin to the side so she could walk around him. "Ignore him," she said, stepping into the room. "Sometimes he just has no control over his behavior." She gave him a conspiratorial wink.

Sean and Khendra gave each other a quick look. His was one of surprise; hers said, "I told you there was a woman behind his behavior."

Vaughn extended her hand to Khendra and then to Sean. "Please call me Vaughn," she said. "I get enough of 'Ms. this' and 'Honorable that' to send me into sugar shock." She smiled warmly.

"Now, that's more like it," Khendra stated, hopping down off the edge of the desk.

"Whatever the lady says," Sean added.

All three turned toward Justin, who stood innocently by the door.

"Hey, listen." He held his hands up. "Don't look at me. I was trying to be politically correct," he grinned.

Groans filled the room.

"Good to finally meet you. Justin's been so secretive lately." Khendra cut Justin a nasty look.

"Maybe everybody doesn't always want to tell you everything all the time," Sean teased, emphasizing every word.

Khendra laughed. "That's where my extraordinary powers of drawing conclusions come into full swing," she pointed out.

"Don't get them started," Justin warned Vaughn. "I've taken the liberty of inviting these two charming individuals to join us for dinner. Hopefully, they'll be able to behave themselves."

"The more the merrier," Vaughn grinned, truly pleased. This would finally give her a chance to get to know the people Justin thought so highly of.

Justin checked his watch. "So, we'll meet out front in about twenty minutes?"

"That should give us enough time to finish up," Sean said.

"I've been following your career for a few years now," Khendra was saying. "You've been doing extraordinary work in your district. It's just a damn shame that all our elected officials don't have the same agenda," she said vehemently.

"I know what you mean," Vaughn stated solemnly. "Politics has a way of turning you away from your objectives. There are so many special interest groups, it's a miracle anything ever gets accomplished in government."

"Enough talk about business," Justin cut in, taking Vaughn's hand. "See you both in a bit," he added, ushering Vaughn out of the office.

"Right this way, Assemblywoman Hamilton," he breathed in her ear. The sensation sent up a flurry of tingles that thrilled her down to her toes.

"Very funny, Counselor," she said in a husky whisper.

"If it were up to me," he continued, as they made their way down the hall, "everyone I introduced you to would be required to bow."

She angled her head to look quizzically up at him.

His look grew warm and serious. "Because you are without a doubt a queen. More specifically, *my* queen."

Vaughn's heart did a hard knock against her chest. Warmth spread through her as if heated water had been injected into her veins.

"You make me feel like a queen," she said softly.

"And I intend to keep doing just that—for as long as you let me." He took a deep breath. "Now, before I just pull you into one of these empty offices and ravish that luscious body, let's go find Rush and Simone."

Justin pushed open the swinging door that led to the reception area. "Did you find Rush and Simone, Barbara?"

"Yes," she smiled. "They should be in Chad's office."

Vaughn looked inquiringly from one to the other. "How come you call Chad 'Rush'?"

Justin chuckled. "I started calling him Rush when he first arrived about—hmmm—four years ago. His last name is Rushmore and he always reminded me of someone who was in a hurry to get ahead." Justin grinned wistfully as the early memories of Chad rumbled through his head.

"Well, that explains it," Vaughn grinned "I was beginning to get confused."

They turned to leave the way they'd come in.

"Oh, Mr. Montgomery," Barbara called. "You have messages."

"Thanks, Barb. If it's not urgent, just leave them on my desk. I'll have to return the calls on Monday."

"Sure thing, Mr. M." Barbara skimmed the notes again. Both of them were from Stan Waters. It was his third call in a little over a week, Barbara noted. According to Mr. Waters, Mr. Montgomery had not returned his call and had insinuated that he hadn't received his messages. Maybe he had no intention of returning the calls, Barbara had wanted to say. If there was one thing she was confident of, it was her ability as a top-rate legal secretary. Not giving messages was something that wasn't in the realm of possibility for Barbara Crenshaw. She got up from her seat, took the messages to Justin's office, and she left them dutifully on his desk.

Justin and Vaughn turned down the corridor toward Chad's office. Justin lowered his head to speak to Vaughn in an intimate whisper. "Did I tell you that you look delicious in that outfit?" He ran his hand lightly up her back.

Vaughn's eyes sparkled when she looked up at him. "As a matter of fact, you didn't," she answered coyly.

"Well, you do. You should wear red more often. It brings out the richness of that beautiful skin of yours."

From his reaction, Vaughn was glad she'd taken the time to change out of her business suit and into the red cotton jersey. The dress was totally simple. It had a short mock turtleneck and long sleeves and was cut in such a way that it defined every curve without being obvious. She added a wide gold bracelet, strappy red leather pumps, and sheer hose, held up by a fire-engine red garter belt.

"Keep up the sweet talk, Counselor, and we really may not make it to dinner." She gave him a quick wink just as they arrived at Chad's office.

The office door was open and Vaughn assumed that the young man behind the desk was Chad. A young woman with shoulder-length black hair had her back to them as they approached.

Justin stood in the open doorway partially blocking Simone's view. Justin stepped in as Chad got up from his seat. At the very moment Vaughn crossed the threshold, Simone turned around in her seat. Their eyes met and for a never-ending moment, Vaughn felt as if all the air had been sucked from her lungs. Her head began to spin when Simone got up and smiled an unforgettable smile.

Vaughn was certain that she must be trapped in some sort of bizarre episode of *Twilight Zone.* Her body became infused with heat. A thin line of perspiration trickled down her back. Voices were humming around her. She was sure it must be introductions taking place, but she couldn't hear anything over the buzzing in her ears.

"Vaughn . . . Vaughn," Justin was saying. "Are you all right?" He put his arm around her waist.

She took several gulps of air and laughed nervously. "I'm . . . so sorry. I felt so lightheaded all of a sudden." She forced a wavering smile. "I guess it's because I didn't eat today," she offered weakly.

"That's understandable," Simone answered in response.

Vaughn laughed in embarrassment. "What a way to make an entrance, huh?" she smiled.

"It could never be said that you don't know how to get an audiences' attention," Justin joked. But his eyes darkened with concern as he looked down at her.

Vaughn cleared her throat. She extended her hand to Simone and then to Chad. "I've heard so much about the two of you. It's a pleasure to finally meet you both. I'm looking forward to dinner so I can hear the uncut version," she teased with a genuine smile.

Chad and Simone grinned at the implication.

Slowly Vaughn was beginning to regain her composure, but the lingering effects of seeing Simone still had her nerves on edge.

"Are you two about ready?" Justin asked.

"My stomach says I'm on overtime," Chad grumbled good-naturedly.

The group chuckled as they filed out of the office. "My stomach is agreeing one hundred percent," Simone chimed in, "and I didn't even work today."

"A girl after my own heart," Vaughn said, smiling, looking at Simone over her shoulder.

"This meal isn't going to tap into my retirement account, is it?" Justin asked in mock concern.

"It just might," Vaughn said, only loudly enough for him to hear. "You know how hungry I can get." Slowly she moistened her lips with a flick of her tongue and Justin instantly felt his groin tighten. He was definitely going to have to tell her she was going to have to cut that out when they were in public. It could prove very embarrassing for him.

The two-hour dinner was a success. The soul food restaurant had some of the best fare in Richmond. The conversation was both stimulating and humorous.

Vaughn had the opportunity to see Justin through different eyes—how he interacted with his staff and his friends. She could see why he was so well liked. He treated everyone with the same degree of interest and respect. He was a born leader. It was apparent in the way he could subtly steer a conversation or make a suggestion that easily became accepted by all, and by the way his opinion was sought on any topic. Most of all, he didn't have to flaunt it, which was the quality that separated the real thing from the wannabes. But that didn't stop him from running his fingers across her thighs whenever he thought no one was watching. The sensuous feel of his fingertips seemed magnified because of the secrecy.

She also got a kick out of Khendra's not so subtle questions about her life and her views on relationships. It was hilariously apparent that Khendra had taken on the task of being Justin's keeper. Khendra Phillips-Michaels was even more charming than Vaughn had previously witnessed, she thought, as Khen flashed her famous dimpled smile that made her feel instantly at home. What made Khendra so compelling was not just her stunning looks, but a powerful aura of self-possession that could not be ignored. Khendra was not the kind of woman to wait around to be asked. She took control. Vaughn couldn't help but admire her. And her husband—Sean—hot was the first word that popped into her head. It was no wonder that he won all his cases. The jury was probably mesmerized by his charisma and believed whatever that gospel-sounding voice said. She was sure that this fine brother even looked good first thing in the morning. He, too, was dynamic, exhibiting an inner strength that he wore with the utmost confidence.

After about the first hour of talking with Simone, her high level of anxiety was finally reduced. Her initial reaction at seeing the striking resemblance to Brian had truly shaken her. They said that everyone in the world had a twin. Today, she could confirm that the old saying was true. Simone was as intelligent, as sweet, and as pretty as Justin had described. She could see how he could easily identify with Simone. She was the kind of young woman anyone would be proud to have as a daughter. And the longer she was in Simone's company, the closer she felt to her. It was a strange sensation. But Vaughn attributed it to Simone's ability to charm everyone she came into contact with.

"So, Simone, how do you like Virginia so far?" Vaughn asked.

"Everything has been wonderful. I'm looking forward to being here. It'll be a great way to celebrate my birthday," she grinned.

"When is it?" Chad questioned. "If you're going to be in town by then, maybe we could plan something."

"It's in two weeks. May twentieth."

Vaughn felt as if the breath was being squeezed out of her. Her head began to pound. Casually she took several sips of water to compose herself before she spoke. Maybe she had heard wrong.

"Did you say May twentieth?" she asked smoothly, magnificently camouflaging the tremor that seized her vocal cords.

"Yep," Simone affirmed. "I'll finally be nineteen."

"Nineteen!" Khendra sputtered. "And you're a senior? That's incredible. Your parents must be so proud."

"They are . . ."

The conversation continued without Vaughn. Although she smiled and nodded in all the right places, she was on automatic pilot. Her years of training to be in the public eye had taken over. She masked her dismay behind a practiced smile.

It must be just some bizarre coincidence. It had to be, she concluded. If she could just have a moment to get herself together, she knew she would be fine. She pushed back in her seat and slowly stood up. "If you all will excuse me a minute, I'm going to find the ladies' room."

"Woman—ladies' room—minute. Tell me what's wrong with that statement," Sean chuckled, and the whole table joined in.

"Very funny," all three women said at once, in varying tones of apathy, then turned to each other in amusement at the spontaneous response.

"I'll go with you," offered Simone.

Justin watched the two walk off and the conversation resumed. But he knew that something was wrong. He could tell by the almost imperceptible tremor in Vaughn's voice and the way that her eyes seemed to take on a glinty edge. Her smile was tight around the edges. Her note of laughter didn't ring true. Anyone who didn't know her, hadn't observed her as he had, would never be the wiser. He was beginning to worry.

At the start of dinner she'd seemed off center, but as the evening had progressed, she'd appeared to be her old self. Then suddenly she'd gotten this strange look in her eyes—just for an instant. The kind of expression a person has when they hear news that is too farfetched to believe.

"I'm really happy to finally meet you, Ms. Hamilton," Simone was saying, as they stood facing the mirror.

The sincerity in Simone's voice touched her. "I feel the same way." She smiled and applied a light stroke of lipstick.

"I've been following your career for years," she confessed. She turned so that she faced Vaughn's profile. "I know that this may sound corny, but I really admire you. You've been an inspiration for me over the years."

Slowly, Vaughn turned to face her. The shock hit her again, but not with as much force.

"I really appreciate that, Simone. It's important for me to know that I can make a difference." Something made her want to reach out and touch her. She placed her hand on Simone's shoulder. Her smile was filled with warmth. "Even if it's just one difference at a time."

Simone looked down at her shoes and then across at Vaughn. "When I come back next week, would it be all right if I came by your office? I'd really like to see how things operate."

Vaughn chuckled. "Believe me, sweetheart, it's not as glamorous as you think. But you're more than welcome to drop by."

They both began walking toward the door and for the first time that evening, Vaughn felt as if the weight had been lifted off her chest. The flutters that had gone berserk for the last few hours had finally ceased. In the place of all that undefined tension was an overwhelming sense of peace. She couldn't explain it. She just knew that it was so.

"Thanks, Ms. Hamilton," Simone beamed. "I really appreciate it."

"Your visit won't conflict with your work with Mr. Montgomery?"

Simone grinned confidently. "I think I can work something out."

Vaughn's eyes widened in amusement. "I'm sure you can, young lady. I'm sure you can."

Justin had dropped off Chad and then Simone. Vaughn had followed his lead in her car. He stepped up to her window after seeing Simone safely inside. Vaughn grinned up at him. "Where to?" she asked.

"How do you feel about an overnight guest?"

Vaughn smiled that slow, sexy smile that made Justin's stomach muscles tighten. "I'm sure I don't have anything for you to sleep in," she teased suggestively.

"I'm sure we can find something for me to sleep in, and I can guarantee that it will fit like a glove," he tossed back in a low, silky voice.

The slow heat of anticipation wound its way through her veins. "I feel a long night coming on." She winked and rolled up her window, then waited for Justin to return to his car, and they took off toward her townhouse.

In the kitchen, Vaughn prepared a pitcher of strawberry daiquiris while Justin selected some music for the CD player. She entered the dimly lit living room and placed the hand-carved tray with their refreshments on the coffee table.

Luther Vandross's "A House Is Not a Home" played soothingly in the background. Vaughn picked up their drinks and handed Justin his.

He reached for the glass, took a sip, then placed it on the mantel behind him. He turned toward her, giving her a smoldering look. "Did I tell you that you look incredible tonight?"

From the hunger in his gaze, Vaughn was glad that she'd decided to change into the gray satin lounging outfit. She took a slow sip from her glass, then placed hers next to his on the mantel. "As a matter of fact you did," she answered huskily.

Justin reached out and snaked his arm around her waist, pulling her close. Vaughn rested her head on his chest and let her eyes slide shut. Easily they glided together as one being to the sensuous sound of Luther.

"Feeling better?" Justin whispered into her hair. He felt the slightest hesitation in her step and knew that he'd been right. "You want to tell me about it?"

The firm but gentle cadence of his voice was almost enough to crumble any resistance that she had. She expelled a long, wistful sigh. "Simone seems like a wonderful girl," she said slowly, temporarily evading the question until she could put words to her emotions.

"Yes, she does. Did she measure up to my description?" He felt her nod her head in response. He waited, hoping she would say more, but she didn't.

The song ended and the CD player switched disks. The soul-stirring voice of Oleta Adams filled the room with "Get There."

"When are we going to get past the secrecy, Vaughn? When are you going to start trusting me?"

She heard the weariness in his voice, the hint of frustration. Guilt pricked her conscience.

"It's just that . . . well, nothing, really . . ."

Justin pulled slightly back to look down at her, but she wouldn't give him the satisfaction of returning his look. Instead, she pressed herself closer against him, as if she could burrow her way beneath his skin. They fell back into step.

"It's just what—what's been bothering you tonight?"

She wanted to just stay snuggled in his embrace, to listen to the steady beat of his heart, feel his warmth as the music washed over them. But instinctively she knew that Justin wasn't going to let her get away with it this time.

"I guess it's a combination of things," she finally admitted.

"I'm listening."

She took a deep breath and then told him about her argument with Crystal earlier in the day.

". . . It just really bothers me that after all these years of knowing each other she'd think so little of me. I can't understand why she can't see that I'm only looking out for her."

Justin slowly shook his head and chuckled softly, the closeness of their bodies causing vibrations to ripple through her in a delightfully sensual way.

"What's so funny?"

"Vaughn, no one likes to be told that the person they care about is no good for them. Of course she got defensive. Look at what happened between you and your father. Perfect example. I'm sure Crystal views you as someone she admires as both a friend and an employer. Someone she respects and quite possibly may be jealous of in some regard. So coming from you, it was probably a blow to her ego. By telling her that she should check this guy out, you were questioning her ability to make a good choice and she lashed out at you."

She angled her head back and looked up at him. His gaze widened in inquiry. Her bottom lip curled into what could only be described as a sneer.

"You just don't know how it ticks me off when you're right."

His eyes swept over her face and he gave her a wicked grin. "You must stay mighty ticked, seeing as I've been right about us since day one." He pulled her closer and nibbled on her ear. Her whole expression softened. She glided her hands up and down his back in time to Anita Baker's "Giving You the Best That I've Got. "Hmmm," was all she could say, as she let her body go with the music.

"How about if I go for the jackpot?" he hummed in her ear. He didn't wait for an answer. "You said it was a combination of things. So what else is bothering you? My senses tell me it has to do with Simone. Would you like to tell me why?"

CHAPTER 16

Crystal stared sightlessly up at the ceiling, unable to sleep. She looked across at David's peacefully sleeping form and all the things that Vaughn had said came crashing back.

As much as she hated to admit it, everything Vaughn implied was true. How much did she really know about David? Their whole world existed in her apartment. She'd never been to his. He claimed that he lived in a one-room apartment that was barely furnished and suitable only for someone who had no intention of being there for any length of time.

Yet even though her subconscious nagged her about the voids in their relationship, she'd been so bowled over by his attention that she didn't hesitate in sharing every aspect of her life with him. He seemed so interested—always wanting to know how her day went, what were they doing to ensure Vaughn's victory, and she'd always been candid, happy to share her triumphs, her strategies.

Now that she really thought about it, however, David's interest almost exclusively centered around her work and the campaign. A prickling of dread skittered up her spine. No. She was just being paranoid. Vaughn's innuendos that David had ulterior motives had gotten to her. After all, didn't he bring her flowers every time he came to see her? Didn't he buy her lovely gifts every time he went on a business trip? She was wearing one of the three satin teddies that he'd purchased. Didn't he tell her how much he cared about her when they made love?

Of course, all those things were true. She was being silly. But as much as she tried to convince herself, that uncomfortable feeling in the pit of her stomach would not go away.

Elliott hung up the phone in his study. His thick fingers braced the edge of his desk. Slowly, he surveyed the paneled room. One full wall, from floor to ceiling, was lined with heavy bound books covering everything of significance that had been written about the law. He'd never had time for recreational reading. His reading time was reserved for scholarly pursuits that would keep him abreast of every statute, appeal, and case across the globe.

His record on the bench was exemplary as a result of his seemingly limitless knowledge of the law. He ran his courtroom much like he ran his life, with iron-clad control. Ultimately it had afforded him an abundance of success and a coveted position on the Superior Court bench. His dream was to attain a place in history as a Supreme Court justice, following in the footsteps of Thurgood Marshall. It could happen. It would happen as long as his plan did not become unraveled by the potentially scandalous behavior of his daughter. However, even that was no longer a problem. He'd seen to that as well. Now, it was only a matter of time.

Vaughn just didn't understand. Their course was set years ago when he and Senator Willis were first launching their careers. They were in this together. He was so engrossed in his reflections that he didn't hear Sheila enter the thickly carpeted room until she spoke.

"It's two A.M., Elliott. When are you coming to bed?"

He blinked several times, shoving back the memories. He puffed out his chest and gently massaged the bridge of his nose. He looked up at his wife for a long moment. She was still so beautiful, he realized. Feelings of warmth quietly filled him. The sudden sensation shocked him. It had been so long since he'd felt anything other than the need to control. An overwhelming sense of loss swept through him, stinging his eyes and clenching his throat. For a brief moment he wanted to take his wife in his arms and turn back the clock. He sighed. Of course, that was impossible.

"Elliott?" She stepped closer. "Are you all right?" For a fleeting instant she swore she saw his expression soften when he looked at her. But then it was gone and she wasn't sure if she'd seen it at all or only wished it. He had on his public face, the one she'd come to live with. He and Vaughn were so much alike in that way, she mused, though not unkindly. They had the ability to shield their innermost emotions behind a mask. She, however, was not so talented. Even now she felt the lines of worry stretch across her forehead and the hollowness fill her eyes.

Elliott cleared his throat, pushed himself away from the desk, and stood up. "I was just on my way up." His voice was laden with a weight that Sheila knew he would never share. That part of their life was over. His voice was so low when he next spoke that it barely reached her. "Will we be sharing the same room tonight?"

Did she hear a hint of hopefulness in the question, or was it only her deepest desires ringing through her ears again? She smiled tightly. "I think that would be best." She started to walk toward the door. "There's no need to give the housekeeper something to gossip about," she added quietly. She reached for the doorknob and stopped. She turned expectantly toward her husband.

He came up behind her and gently put his hand on her shoulder. There was so much that he wanted to say—to tell her how sorry he was that she didn't love him anymore—how sorry he was about the way their lives had detoured. But he couldn't do that. It was eighteen years too late for regret.

"You're right," he answered pompously.

Tension ran through Vaughn's body and tightened it like a coil. How did she think she could hide her feelings from him? She'd been unsuccessful at that since the day they met.

Justin ran his hand slowly up and down her thigh. He knew he'd hit pay dirt when he felt her muscles tense beneath his fingers. He might have fallen into the habit of letting her sidestep his questions before, but not tonight. He had an undeniable sense that whatever was troubling her went very deep and maybe—just maybe—it was the root of her resistance. He wanted to know what Simone Rivers had to do with it.

The music ended and Vaughn eased out of Justin's arms. She moved toward the couch and sat down heavily. She looked up at him. His eyes grazed over her, taking in every nuance. Slowly he crossed the room and sat opposite her in the loveseat. He leaned slightly forward, his arms braced on his thighs. All his attention was riveted on her face.

Vaughn looked away—out toward the terrace—and down at her hands, which lay perfectly still in her lap. Where could she begin?

As if he'd read her thoughts, Justin said, "Why don't you start at the beginning." His voice was warm and comforting. Vaughn felt as if she could just wrap herself in it like a favorite comforter. His voice did that to her.

She smiled shyly. Then, methodically, she took him back with her eighteen years, to when she was a young, impressionable girl hungry for love and affection. She'd found it in Brian Willis's arms. "He was my first love." She took a deep breath and her gaze drifted off as she was swept away with her memories. "Brian was killed in a car accident a month before graduation." Her eyes filled, and a single tear slid down her prominent cheek. "He was Senator Willis's son, you see," her voice catching in her throat. "And it wouldn't have been . . . right." She hesitated for so long that Justin thought she wouldn't continue.

The memories overwhelmed her, choked her like noxious fumes. She felt the endless sense of loss carve a hole in her stomach.

Justin wanted to reach out and take her in his arms and make her hurt go away. At the same time, he wanted to ask her what was the significance of Brian being the senator's son. What wouldn't have been right? he wanted to know. But witnessing this metamorphosis of buried pain transform her, he realized that she'd been right all along. Some things were better left unsaid. Guilt pounded at him. "Vaughn, baby, you don't have to say more."

"Simone looks so much like him," she blurted out suddenly. Justin's eyes widened in astonishment. She covered her mouth to stifle the sob that bubbled up from her throat.

The corners of her mouth trembled when she tried to smile. She wiped the tears away with the back of her hand and sniffed. "You couldn't have known. It was just—such a shock when I first saw her." She swallowed hard. "All the memories just came rushing back when I saw her tonight." She sniffed again. Her eyes shimmered with tears. She wouldn't meet his gaze. "I guess it will just take some getting used to. They say we all have a twin somewhere."

Justin studied her and knew instantly that there was more to this than she was telling. He inhaled deeply and let out a long breath. This was not the end of it he determined. No more questions, no more prying, at least for now. He'd told her once at the start of their relationship that their pasts were behind them, and he wanted them to start new lives, with new memories. And still he tried to get her to talk about things from her past that she couldn't handle. Whatever it was obviously was too painful for her to deal with. The entire evening, from Vaughn's uncharacteristic behavior to her last revelation, left him with some disturbing questions. The pieces all had jagged edges, but somehow they fit together.

"They also say we all look alike," he chuckled lightly, pushing away his unsettling thoughts. Justin pushed up from his spot on the loveseat, rounded the table, and sat next to her on the couch. Without words they were in each other's arms. Justin lightly caressed her hair and placed tiny kisses on her cheeks. "I'm sorry," he murmured. "I shouldn't have pushed the issue. We're all entitled to a degree of privacy about our lives. I guess I was in my gangbuster mode." He felt her laughter ripple against his chest.

She tapped him playfully on the nose with the tip of her finger. "You definitely haven't lost your touch." She pressed her head against his chest and threaded her fingers through his. The steady beat of his heart against her ear was like a soothing balm to her spirit.

"Let's see what else I haven't lost," he uttered in a low rumble.

* * *

The sun was barely up in the sky when Justin eased from beneath Vaughn's heavenly scented quilt. They'd made plans to spend the rest of the weekend at Virginia Beach, and he wanted to get an early start. He still had to return to his house and toss a few things in a bag. He'd let Vaughn sleep until he returned.

Lovingly, he studied her sleeping form. This was what he wanted, he knew, watching the steady rise and fall of her breathing. He wanted to be able to come home to her every night and wake up with her every morning. He wanted her at his side.

Silently he eased down and placed a kiss on her smooth ebony forehead. She stirred in her sleep and he swore she whispered his name. Justin smiled at the possible reasons as he vividly recalled the torrid night of passion they'd shared. His groin throbbed just thinking of it. Who would ever believe this woman, who came across to the public as a levelheaded, conservative, hard-nosed politician, was actually the most erotic, insatiable woman he'd ever met? He shook his head in amazement and padded off to the bathroom.

Vaughn slowly pushed herself up through the final veils of sleep. Her heart thumped suddenly as the misty notion of something unsettling enveloped her. The first thought that materialized was Simone. Images of the young woman stood before her unfocused eyes. Her stomach dipped as if she were racing downward on a rollercoaster ride. The sound of running water invaded her senses. Slowly a feeling of security replaced the uneasiness as it retreated to the recesses of her mind and was soon forgotten. "Justin." She sighed contentedly and stretched, then slid out from beneath the cover. A trail of goosebumps broke out over her nude flesh. She gasped as the cool morning air brushed against her skin as she ran toward what she knew would be the heat of the bathroom.

She giggled like a scheming teenager as she turned the knob on the door. Maybe, if she worked it right, which she was confident she could, she'd convince Justin to take a quick jog with her before they set off for the day. And perhaps she'd convince him of a few other things in the meantime.

By the time Vaughn returned to her office on Monday, her whole attitude regarding the blow-up with Crystal was behind her. After talking it out with Justin and turning it over in her own head, she knew what she had to do. She was in no position to cast aspersions. What Crystal did in her private life was her own affair. If Crystal wanted her advice, then that's when she would give it. She and Justin had spent a wonderful weekend at his cottage in Virginia Beach, and she had no intention of coming down from the cloud she was on.

Her happiness was like a beacon as she walked quickly down the hall-greeting the staff as she headed to her office. She felt like she could take on the world and silently giggled, wondering if that's what good lovin' did to you.

She pushed open her office door, swung it closed behind her, and nearly choked on her own smile when she spotted Crystal sitting in her favorite spot in the little alcove behind the door.

"Crystal," she sputtered. Her pulse raced off at a fast trot, then settled. "You scared me right outta my pantyhose," she said, reciting the chant that was a longstanding ritual between them.

She waited for Crystal's practiced response but it didn't come. Instead Vaughn's gaze was met with uncertainty. Hesitantly, she reached out and touched Crystal's shoulder in a gesture of peace. "I just hope that you keep right on sittin' there, giving me a reality check every morning." Her throat tightened and she swallowed back the lump. "I don't know what I'd do if you weren't."

Crystal blinked to keep the tears from spilling. Then suddenly they both spoke at once.

"Vaughn, I just . . ."

"No, I jumped . . ."

They both erupted into infectious cleansing laughter and found themselves hugging. "Listen to us," Vaughn said after several long breaths, gaining a semblance of composure. "Two perfectly intelligent women, babbling like idiots."

Crystal stood back and took Vaughn's hands in hers. "I know you just had my best interests at heart." She lowered her lids, then met Vaughn's steady gaze. "I can handle it," she said with quiet conviction.

Vaughn gently squeezed Crystal's hand and smiled reassuringly. "I know you can."

Crystal let out a breath and released Vaughn's hands. "Now that we have all the mushy stuff out of the way, I have some news, girl." She maneuvered around to the small work table and sat down. Vaughn took a seat opposite her. Crystal slapped her palms down on the table and broke out in a sunshine grin. "The Lucus Stone camp wants to go head-to-head on television!"

Vaughn's eyes widened. "Why all of a sudden? That seemed like the last thing Stone wanted to do."

"Apparently, he feels you're getting too much press. You know my opinion—I think he's starting to feel the pressure."

Vaughn slowly nodded in agreement. Her expression grew serious. "I don't think we should give in right away. We set the parameters for the debate, we set the when and where."

"Exactly."

The wheels began to turn in Vaughn's head. She felt energized, like she always did when confronted with a challenge. "I need a synopsis on every bill Stone has voted on or against, and a recap of all of the polls." Her eyes grew pensive as she planned her strategy. "We need to get Imani Angoza, the image consultant. I want to make sure that the camera picks up the differences between us—not just color—not just male-female." She pursed her lips as she continued to think. "I want to lose that hard-edged image that I've been known to have. But I don't want to come across as a fluffy female, either. Getting the assembly seat was a whole different ballgame. We're in the big time now."

Crystal jotted everything down and nodded in agreement as Vaughn continued to map out their plan. She looked up and saw the same fire in Vaughn's eyes that had won her the assembly seat four years earlier. Just being in her presence at times like this was awe-inspiring. You couldn't help but catch the energy, Crystal thought in admiration. Vaughn was like the sun, radiating strength, determination, and power to everyone who came under her influence. This was the winning team, and she was happy to be a part of it.

Vaughn paced rhythmically across the hardwood floor, the heels of her blue suede pumps clicking a steady beat. "We'll need at least a month to prepare."

"Do you want Imani to do the mock interviews on video?"

"Perfect," Vaughn concurred. "Oh, and another thing," her finger cut through the air as she spoke. "We need to pull out our best slogans and put together two thirty-second commercials."

"That's going to dig real deep into the campaign funds."

Vaughn shrugged. "That's what it's there for. So let's use it."

"It's your call. But you may want to think about replenishing the pot with another fundraiser." Vaughn nodded. "I'll start working on the details and put together a schedule of when we set each step into motion and I'll start contacting all the players. We're going to need a top-of-the-line film crew and a producer."

"Check in the *Big Black Book*. I'm sure we can find a black-owned film company that can do the work and would jump at the opportunity. I really don't want to use the crew that's attached to this office. After a while, all their stuff looks the same."

"I know what you mean. We need a fresh approach."

"Exactly." Vaughn took a long, deep breath and let it out with a smile. "Well, girlfriend," she said, easing out of overdrive, "looks like we're in there!"

Crystal smiled brightly and held her hand up for a high-five. "You damned right!" They slapped palms and laughed like the friends they were.

Lucus Stone glared at the man who stood on the safe side of his desk with his hands clasped behind his back. "What's Hamilton's answer about the television appearance?" He cracked the knuckles of his right hand while he tapped cigarette ashes with his left.

Winston McGee pressed his lips together before he spoke. "I've spoken with her chief of staff. She said she'd get back to me in a few days with an answer."

Lucus squinted in disbelief. He was sure they'd have jumped at the chance. "Stay on top of it. If we don't get a positive response by the end of the week, set up a meeting with *our* friends from the press. We'll peg her as afraid to meet me head-on—that she's worried that her record won't stand up to mine—that she has something to hide." He leaned back.

"I have a feeling we'll be hearing from her," Winston offered. "I can't see her backing down."

"You're probably right. But I want to keep all my bases covered. She has until noon on Friday."

Crystal returned to her desk after her meeting with Vaughn just as her phone began to ring. "Assemblywoman Hamilton's office. Crystal Porter speaking," she answered crisply. She deposited her notes on the desk and hugged the phone between her shoulder and her ear as she sat down.

"Hey, baby. I'm back in town."

"David." For an instant, the suspicions raised by Vaughn reared their ugly heads, but she quickly discarded them. She got comfortable in her seat. "How are you? When did you get in?" she asked in one rushed breath. They hadn't seen each other in two days. To Crystal, it felt like a week. He'd left late Friday night for business in D.C. They hadn't spoken since.

"In answer to your first question, I'll be doing better when I see you. And to your second question, about ten minutes ago."

Crystal grinned. "When can we get together?"

"I was hoping tonight." He thought about the phone call he'd just received from Lucus and knew that he'd better get some new information, and quick.

Crystal's heart sank. She had so much work to do. She couldn't see getting out of the office before midnight. "Oh, David, I wish I could, but I'm swamped. We're right in the thick of things for the campaign."

David thought quickly. He needed to know what she knew. "Tell you what—why don't you bring your excess work home and leave at a reasonable hour, and I'll help you out at your place. You have a computer, that's half the battle."

She mulled it over for a minute. It could probably work, she thought, growing excited over the prospect of seeing him. She could make all her business calls from the office, set up the agenda on her office computer, and put the information on a disk. Then she'd just pop the disk into her

PC at home and finish up her paperwork there. If she mapped it out right, she'd have plenty of time to spend an intimate evening with David. The reality was, there were so many distractions and interruptions at the office that it would take until midnight to get finished.

"Sounds like a plan," she said finally. "But I'm holding you to your offer to help."

David let out a long held breath. "I'll even pick up dinner and bring it over," he added solicitously.

"Great. So I'll see you about eight?"

"I'll be there. 'Bye, babe."

David hung up the phone and laughed out loud. This was going to be easier than he'd thought. All he had to do was put his own disk in Crystal's computer and copy her information.

CHAPTER 17

"It was just great," Simone said to Jean over the phone. "Everyone was wonderful, and Ms. Hamilton was as nice as I thought she would be."

Jean stretched out on Simone's bed. "Looks like you really lucked out," she said. "But what I want to hear about is this Chad Rushmore."

"Mmmm," Simone sighed dreamily. "He's fine, intelligent, fun to be with . . ."

"Sounds almost too good to be true."

"Don't I know it. But we got along so great together. I can't wait to get back. He promised to take me around to see some of the sights in Richmond."

"Well, find out if he has a brother, or at least a friend. My love life could sure use a boost."

"Girl, if you'd get your nose out of those science books for a minute, you might be able to find somebody."

"Some of us have to study," she said wearily.

"Anyway," Simone continued, taking the barb in good humor. "I have to get my final approval from my professor and take the letter back with me next Monday."

"When are you heading out?"

"Late Friday afternoon. I need to call my folks and let them know, and I need to make travel arrangements. Mr. Montgomery said he'd arrange for me to stay at the Ramada Inn. It's not too far from the office, and I can take the train to work."

"How are you going to pay for all of this?"

Simone hesitated, deciding whether or not she should tell Jean about her involvement with Child-Link and the money that would be hers in a little over a week. Instead she said, "I think he and Ms. Hamilton have something going on," she said, sidestepping Jean's question.

"Get outta here!"

"That's what I think. But they're real cool with it."

"I wouldn't go spreading that around if I were you."

"Don't be silly. Of course I wouldn't. But suppose they are. Wouldn't that be something? I think they'd make such a fabulous couple." Simone slid her hands in her jean pockets, shuffled her feet for a second, then looked at Jean. "Listen," she said finally. "There's something I need to talk with you about. But you have to swear that you won't tell *anyone.*"

Vaughn lay stretched out on Justin's couch with her feet propped up on his lap. "Oooh, that feels good," she sighed heavily as Justin expertly massaged her stockinged feet. "I feel like I walked a million miles today."

"How is everything going?"

"Well, Crystal is working out the details. Things are really beginning to heat up with Stone. This television debate is going to be crucial."

"What's your plan of attack?" He moved his hands up from her feet to massage her calves. Vaughn closed her eyes and let herself float with the soothing sensations.

"Lucus is weak in the areas of housing revitalization and making a difference with the small-business owners and minorities. He may have a track record on some of the bigger issues, like foreign affairs, but I have him beaten hands down when it comes to direct contact with my constituents."

Justin nodded in agreement. "So that's going to be your platform," he stated more than asked.

"Umm-mmm, 'Vaughn Hamilton, a woman of the people, by the people, and for the people.' "

"I like it. It sounds hokey enough to be believable," he chortled.

Vaughn sat up and popped him on the top of his head. "Not funny. This is serious, Counselor."

Justin rubbed the spot on his head and grimaced. "I know, I know. Can't you take a joke?" he chuckled. He adjusted his position and slid up on the couch until he was lying next to her, then took one of his legs and locked it across her body to get comfortable. "If there's anything that I can do, let me know," he said earnestly. "I'm willing to help."

"Thanks." She kissed his forehead. "But what about your plans? What are you going to do about Simone—your practice?"

"First, I want to get to know Simone better—discreetly get some background information and then feed it to Child-Link and see what they come up with."

"Do you really think that Janice would have given your daughter up for foster care?"

"Anything's possible. I just want to be sure. At the very least, maybe we can find Simone's natural family. I got the feeling from her that it's something she really wants. It seems she has never accepted the fact that her parents gave her up."

Vaughn digested the information without further comment.

"As for the firm, I'm letting Sean and Khendra take on more responsibility. I'll oversee the Harrison trial, which will probably start shortly. But I want to spend more time on speaking engagements and working more closely with the organizations I've set up. I can't do that trapped in a courtroom." He turned his gaze on her, cupped her face in his hand, and spoke in a rough whisper. "Most of all, I'm going to work on us. I'm going to work on this relationship. I intend to get it right this time."

"I'd say you already had it right," she answered in a silken breath.

Justin's dark brown eyes warmed over her face. His lips met hers in a feather-light kiss, one so tender that it made her ache with longing. He threaded his fingers through her hair, pulling her deeper into the kiss, sending sparks of yearning through every nerve of her body. The honey-sweet heat of her mouth enveloped him as his tongue sought out and met hers in a sensual dance.

There was no denying it. She was in love with this man. Deeply, irrevocably in love. She hugged him fiercely to her, relishing the sensations his mouth created. The tip of his tongue danced across her lips, then plunged deeply inside her mouth. When this campaign was over, she thought dizzily, she would tell him everything. All of it, from the beginning. But for now . . .

Their low moans of desire blended together in harmony, heightening their need. Vaughn's fingers splayed across the expanse of Justin's chest, making enticing circles that spread shock waves through him. He reached behind her and unzipped her red dress, easing the soft fabric over her shoulders and down to her waist. His heart thudded wildly when his palms cupped her breasts and found them scantily clad in a red demi-cup bra that barely contained her fullness. His breathing stuttered. Just the thought of what she wore beneath her clothes drove him wild with desire. She was the most sensual woman he'd ever known and he couldn't get enough of her.

He adjusted his position, pinning her beneath him. He pressed his hips firmly down against her, desperately trying to relieve the hardened pressure. Vaughn arched her body, offering up her breasts as sweet sacrifice to Justin's caress. Her body shuddered as the excitement of his touch built a maddening sense of urgency in her body. Hungrily, her mouth covered his, cajoling, controlling the titillating kiss. Her tongue danced across his teeth and darted in and out of his hot mouth in deep thrusting motions, an invitation of what was to come.

She pressed her body closer. She wanted, needed more—to find a way to get closer to him—all of him—have him with her, beside her, inside her, filling her.

"Vaughn . . ." he groaned against her mouth. "I want you up here." His eyes burned savagely into hers. Their gazes locked and held.

She smiled a slow, sexy smile. Easing from beneath him, she stood up. In a slow, methodical dance of foreplay, they tantalized each other with the simple act of disrobing. Justin stretched out fully on the couch and unbuckled his belt. Vaughn unfastened the front clasp of her bra and let it fall away. He pulled down the zipper of his slacks and pushed them and his briefs down over his hips and off. She stepped out of her dress and half slip and stood nude except for a tiny red garter belt, sheer hose, and three-inch heels. Her lids lowered in sexy invitation.

"Oh, God," he moaned raggedly. "You don't know what you're doing to me."

She stepped provocatively toward him. "I think I do," she breathed. She leaned over his reclining form and touched her lips to his. The tips of her breasts grazed his smooth chest. The contact sent thrilling shocks through her body and she moaned audibly as she straddled him.

For several breathless moments she braced herself, motionless above him. She took the tiny packet from his fist and tore it open with her teeth. Slowly she placed the condom on his tip and rolled it slowly downward. Justin tugged on his bottom lip to keep from shouting out as her hot hands stroked him up and down. He grabbed her round derrière and pressed his fingers into the supple flesh.

"You're not going to make me wait—not a minute longer," he hissed through clenched teeth. In one upward thrust he pushed the length and breadth of him deep within her.

Vaughn arched her neck and cried out in unintelligible pleasure as the impact of his entry burst through her. Justin raised his head so that it rested on the arm of the couch, giving him easy access to her tempting breasts raised enticingly above him. His tongue laved one firm nipple and then the other, drawing the tip into his mouth. He suckled hard and long while running his tongue in maddening circles over his treasure.

Shudders ripped through her and radiated out. She dug her fingers into his shoulders to keep from collapsing above him. She rocked fiercely against him, driving forward to the rapturous release that they both craved.

She felt weightless and wanton, totally free, and thoroughly loved. There was no hiding from her emotions. She loved him more than she'd thought possible. And every act of loving they committed only solidified her feelings. The steady warmth of fulfillment began to pulse through her belly. The first contraction slammed so hard and sudden within her that the cry of his name hung in her throat until the next onslaught of his thrusts pushed her mercifully over the precipice of sweet release.

Justin held his breath when the first grip of her climax captured him. He wanted to go with her, but more—he wanted her to experience completion with the full power of him buried within her. When he felt the final shudders trigger through her, without breaking the connection between them, he lifted her and lowered them both to the carpeted floor.

For a little longer than a heartbeat, he looked into her sleepy gaze, slid his hands down the length of her thighs, and raised them high onto his back. "Look at me," he growled. Vaughn's eyes flickered across his face and she held her breath as he plunged again and again. The powerful eruption of his release pulsed convulsively within her.

"Yes!" she cried as ecstasy swept through her in an unending symphony.

CHAPTER 18

In the weeks since Simone had contacted her, Melissa Overton had been working diligently on her case. She'd checked every record, every detail. She'd taken a trip to Atlanta to visit the small town that Simone had grown up in. She'd asked questions. She'd gone to the foster care agency that had placed her. She'd reviewed newspaper clips and collected them all. The most curious of her discoveries was that the woman she'd met at the foster care agency had remembered distinctly a strange request that had been made. Whoever took in Simone was never to adopt her and she was to retain the last name of Rivers. Someone had done an incredible job of covering his tracks. Melissa knew from experience that people with money and power were capable of hiding anything. Whoever had given up Simone had money and power. That obviously limited the possibilities. How many black women living in the south had enough money and clout to cover their tracks for nearly nineteen years? Or had family money or influential friends done it?

A stack of reports and notes sat on her desk. She had a strong sensation that everything was finally coming together. This was going to be one of those cases that could be solved. With the information she'd been given by Simone about the mysterious bank account, she'd put a trace on the origins. It kept coming back to Virginia. In fact, all the information she'd been able to piece together pointed to Virginia. That's where the answers lay. She fed all the information into the computer. She did a search of all the black families in politics or business living in the Virginia area at the time of Simone's birth and fed that into the computer as well.

"Melissa," Elaine said, stepping into her office. Melissa looked up from her work and smiled inquiringly. "Yes?"

Elaine pulled up a chair. "I'm sorry to interrupt, but I just received a call from Mr. Montgomery." She cleared her throat. "He wants us to do some investigation into Simone Rivers's background."

Melissa's eyes widened.

"He seems to feel that she may be his daughter."

This time Melissa's mouth dropped open. "You're kidding? You're not kidding."

"I didn't tell him that Simone has already requested that we try to locate her natural parents, since each case is confidential." Melissa nodded. "I want to impress upon you the importance of handling his request with the utmost efficiency. I realize that you feel some affinity to Simone. But we have to remember that Mr. Montgomery is our benefactor. Without him we wouldn't be here."

Melissa straightened. "Mr. Montgomery never came across as someone who throws his weight around."

Elaine stood up. "Nevertheless. His request takes priority, and I want an update on your progress." She turned and left without another word.

Melissa slumped down in her chair. She wasn't going to back off Simone's case, no matter what Elaine said. If there was one thing she was certain of, Justin Montgomery was not Simone's father. The pieces didn't fit. She was sure it was someone else.

Vaughn and Crystal sat in her office going over the plans for the day. "I contacted Stone's office and told them we want the twenty-fifth for the air date. You start with Imani at the end of the week."

"Good. I'm going to be going away for a few days next week. I have to go to Georgia."

"This isn't a good time, Vaughn. There's too much happening."

"I have to," she said definitively.

Crystal took a deep breath. "Are you going to Atlanta?" she questioned softly. For as long as Vaughn and Crystal had been friends, Vaughn had disappeared to Atlanta without explanation. She would never tell her why, or how she could be reached; she'd just gone. It had always bothered Crystal, but she'd never really pressed the issue.

Vaughn nodded.

"What is it in Atlanta that compels you to make this pilgrimage every year?"

"It's not something I want to discuss, Chris, you know that."

"How long will you be gone?" she asked in frustration.

"At least two days. You can handle things until then."

Crystal got up. "I still don't think it's a good idea," she added, gathering up her notes.

Vaughn didn't respond.

"I'll talk with you later. Don't forget your appointment at city hall."

"I won't," Vaughn answered quietly.

Crystal slipped out, leaving Vaughn to her musings. The old feelings of melancholy crept through her. She knew what she was doing was masochistic, but it was her only way of making atonement. It was what would get her through the next 365 days. It was her secret promise to Brian.

Her phone rang, startling her out of her ruminating.

"Vaughn Hamilton," she answered succinctly.

"Vaughn, it's Paul."

Her eyebrows rose. "More cloak-and-dagger news?" she said, trying to still the sudden anxiety that settled over her.

"Call it what you want. But there are rumors flying that there's some potentially scandalous information that someone is planning to use against you."

Her pulse quickened "Do you know someone named David Cain?" Paul asked.

A stab of familiarity poked at her subconscience. "I knew someone named David Cain when I had my first law job," she answered hesitantly. "Why?"

"It seems he knows you very well, and he's working for Stone. And," he added, "he's been seen with your chief of staff, Crystal Porter."

A hot flush spread through her. It couldn't be, she thought, as her head spun. She'd had David dismissed for sexual harassment. She hadn't seen him in years. If it was the same David, maybe that was the reason why Crystal wouldn't introduce them. No. Crystal wouldn't do that. *She* was being duped as well. She swallowed hard.

"Thank you, Paul. But I'm really not concerned," she lied smoothly. "I'm sure Lucus has spies under every rock."

"Like I said before, Vaughn, be careful. You don't always know who your friends are, and that includes Justin Montgomery."

"What?" she sputtered.

"Listen, I have to go, I'm due in court. Take care, Vaughn."

When Vaughn hung up, her heart was pounding so hard she could hardly breathe. Her eyes swept the room unseeing as she tried to figure out what to do. Crystal wouldn't betray her; she just wouldn't. But damn it, pillow talk had destroyed too many people. And what did Paul mean about Justin? She thought about it for a minute and tossed it off as Paul's jealousy. Then again, how did he know? She had to talk with Justin.

Paul turned and faced the man in the chair. "All right, Elliott, I made your call. My debt to you is paid," he said angrily. "No more. I don't know what you're up to, but I don't want any part of it." He turned and stormed out of Elliott's chambers.

* * *

"I'm sorry, Ms. Hamilton, Mr. Montgomery is in court. The Harrison jury selection started today."

"Oh. How could I have forgotten? Would you just tell him that I called, and that it's important that he reach me as soon as he can?"

"Of course. I'm certain when they break for lunch he'll check in for his messages. I have a stack of them building up already," she added good-naturedly.

"I'm sure," she said absently, as Tess placed a stack of newspapers on her desk and tiptoed out. "Thank you, Barbara."

Barbara hung up and added Vaughn's message to the two from Stan Waters and took them to Justin's office. She ran into Simone in the corridor.

"How are you making out today, dear?" Barbara asked.

"So far, so good. I'm making copies of these briefs for Rush."

"Don't let him work you too hard," she teased.

"I won't." Simone smiled and went on her way. She was already looking forward to the end of the day. Rush had promised to take her to dinner.

Vaughn meticulously scanned every newspaper on her desk. Generally, this was Crystal's task, but she knew Crystal would be out of the office for the rest of the day. She reviewed all the articles Tess had circled. Then her eyes settled on one in the *Herald* and her heart skipped a beat.

There in black and white was a story of her impending makeover. The article alluded to the notion that she was attempting to soften her image, that she didn't want to come across as hard and distant.

Vaughn suddenly felt sick. She couldn't read any more. Her phone rang.

She snatched it up. "Yes?" she answered sharply.

"Have you seen today's papers?" her father boomed without any attempt at a greeting.

"Yes, I have," she said, as calmly as she could.

"How could anyone be privy to this information? It's obvious that you have leaks in your office. Or that Montgomery is telling tales out of school."

"Daddy, I really don't care to discuss this with you. Now, or at any other time. And as far as your innuendos about my staff and Justin—well—you're wrong. Whatever is going on in my office or behind my bedroom doors," she added for emphasis, "I will take care of."

"You think you can take care of this? You should have listened to me in the beginning. Get your professional life and your personal life together before it's too late! Too much work has gone into getting you to where you are. I won't stand by and see it all go up in smoke!" He slammed down the phone before she could respond.

By the time Justin had returned her call several hours later, her nerves were raw.

"I need to see you," she was saying, fighting to control the tremors in her voice.

"What is it, baby? What's happened?" Justin turned his back on the throng of people that walked the corridors of the courtroom. It was a madhouse. The press was everywhere, and the noise was deafening. He cupped his hand over the ear without the phone. "I can hardly hear you. It's crazy down here."

"Things are crazy here, too. We need to talk."

"We will. Can you meet me at my house tonight? Or do you want me to come to you when we finish up?"

"Come to my house. I'll fix a good home-cooked dinner and we'll talk." She swallowed. "I really need you, Justin."

"That's good to hear," he said softly. "I just hope I can help."

She bit her lip and nodded. "See you later."

Justin tried to keep his attention focused on the jury selection, but his mind kept skipping back to Vaughn and the note of urgency in her voice. That wasn't like her. She was always too cool and controlled. Something was definitely wrong.

Crystal left her meeting with the camera crew and headed home. She needed to check something. She, too, had seen the papers, and she was scared. There was only one way the press could have gotten that information. It was given to them. She was the only one who had it. The twisting and turning in her stomach intensified. Her head pounded. She made her exit onto the expressway and drove out of Richmond. She'd be home in another ten minutes.

Slamming the door to her car, she ran up the steps to her townhouse. Once inside, she went straight to her computer and clicked it on. She scanned the data stored in the system. Everything seemed to be in place. She checked her latest entry, which included Vaughn's agenda and the strategic plans. The date was right, but the time of the last adjustment was wrong. She knew she'd worked on the computer until nine. The file information said 11:30 P.M.

A sinking sensation overtook her. She felt dizzy. David had accessed her files; there was no other explanation. Suddenly, everything Vaughn had said came rushing back in nauseating waves. What had she done? Who was David Hart?

On shaky legs she stood up, crossed the room, and reached for the phone. She dialed the number David had given her. The phone rang twice and then the recorded message came on to inform her that the number had been disconnected. No further information was available.

CHAPTER 19

Justin, Sean, and Khendra returned to the office after the late-afternoon session. Everyone was exhausted.

"You were brilliant today, Justin, with the questioning of the potential jurors," Khendra congratulated him.

"Getting the right combination for the jury is crucial," he stated casually. His mind was really on Vaughn. "We still have plenty of work ahead of us," he added automatically.

"Speaking of which," Sean said, "I have a stack of work to plow through before I get out of here tonight."

Khendra put her arm around his shoulder "We'll go through it together. Two heads are faster than one." Sean grinned and pecked her on her cheek.

Khendra slanted a look at Justin and asked coyly, "So how's Vaughn doing these days?"

He wished he knew. "Doing well, so far as I know."

Khendra grinned. "Tell her I said hello, next time you see her."

"I'll do that," he replied, and veered off down the corridor to his office.

He gave a cursory glance to the pile of reports on his desk. The stack of yellow squares were a quick reminder that he had dozens of calls to return. He looked up. Four o'clock. He could still catch a few people at the office.

He sat down behind his desk and skimmed through the messages. *Stan Waters.* He'd avoided returning the man's calls long enough. Now it was bordering on rude. That was not how he was accustomed to doing business and he didn't want to be characterized as one who didn't return calls. But this Stan Waters just rubbed him the wrong way, and he couldn't begin to imagine what they could possibly have to say to each other.

He stared at the paper, then dialed the D.C. exchange. The phone was picked up on the second ring.

"Mr. Waters' line. May I help you?"

"This is Justin Montgomery. I'm returning Mr. Waters' call. Is he available?"

"Yes, he is, Mr. Montgomery. He's been trying to reach you. Please hold."

Justin expelled a breath through his teeth as he waited. The wait wasn't long.

"Mr. Montgomery," Stan intoned. "You're a hard man to catch up with."

"I've been busy," Justin said shortly. "I apologize for not getting back to you sooner. Now, what can I do for you?"

"Actually, Mr. Montgomery—may I call you Justin?"

Justin sighed silently. "Feel free."

"It's more what I can do for you, Justin."

"Please do us both a favor—*Stan*—don't be cryptic."

"This really isn't something that can be discussed over the phone. It's of great importance and it has to do with Assemblywoman Hamilton and her bid for Congress."

"What are you talking about?" His guard went up. "And what could you possibly have to discuss with me about Hamilton that would be of any concern to me?"

"I think it would be best if we met. There's a proposition that we'd like to offer. It would be in Ms. Hamilton's best interest if you took it."

Justin fought to control his boiling anger and the feeling of unease that spread through him.

"Why should I be interested?" he asked cautiously.

"We think that you are. We'd like to set up a meeting as soon as possible."

"Who is 'we'?" Justin asked, growing annoyed.

"You'll meet everyone at the meeting."

"I didn't say I'd be there."

"Let's put it this way, Justin. We have it from very reliable sources that you and Ms. Hamilton are—how shall I say?—involved. We also have information that could ruin her, permanently, in politics. You're the only one who can stop that. Now, are you interested in meeting with us?"

"When and where?"

* * *

Vaughn kept her mind off her problems by immersing herself in preparing dinner. She'd decided on smothered chicken, baked macaroni and cheese, and string beans, and she'd purchased a pint of butter pecan ice cream on the way home. For tonight she'd put aside her diet concerns and just enjoy. She definitely needed it.

She still couldn't believe that Crystal would deliberately have given David any information. Somehow he must have found a way to get it.

A tremor ran through her. How many years had it been since she'd seen David? Was it possible for anyone to carry a grudge that long? Was that even his reason for skulking back into her life and trying to destroy it?

Images of David Cain as he sat in the hearing room that last day flashed through her head. The look he'd given her when he was found guilty of the charges and dismissed from the firm had chilled her. The memory chilled her now. Yes. He was capable of carrying a grudge.

She shook her head to dispel the thoughts. Looking up at the kitchen clock, she saw that it was nearly seven. Hopefully, Justin would arrive soon. In the meantime, dinner was simmering and she wanted to change.

She took a quick shower and changed into a short silk top in mint green with matching pants that floated over her skin. She'd just finished dressing when the bell rang.

Vaughn leaped into Justin's arms when she opened the door.

"What did I do to rate a greeting like that?" he asked roughly kissing her on the mouth. For several long moments they embraced each other.

"Just being you—being here when I need you." She snaked her arms around his waist as they walked into the living room.

Justin took off his trenchcoat and then his suit jacket. He loosened his tie and unbuttoned the top button of his shirt. With a heavy sigh he sat down on the couch, then smiled wearily up at Vaughn. He patted the empty spot next to him and she eagerly sat down. He put his arm around her shoulder and pulled her close.

"Do you want to talk first or eat?"

"I know you must be starved. I can't imagine the kind of day you had with the trial starting."

He let out a breath. "It was rough, but I'm more concerned with you at the moment."

She smiled. "Let's do both. I'll talk while we eat."

Justin would have lost his appetite if he hadn't already been finished by the time Vaughn concluded her story. Flashes of his conversation with Stan Waters echoed in his head. Now his subtle innuendos about Vaughn took on a dangerous note. Vaughn was in serious trouble. Someone had no intention of letting her win this election. The prime suspect, of course, was Lucus Stone. And it was obvious that David Cain was on his payroll. How far Crystal was involved remained to be seen. Justin's jaw clenched. He sensed that it went further; how much further, he didn't know. As much as he wanted to tell her about his conversation with Waters, he decided against it. At least for now. The last thing she needed at this point was something else to worry about.

"First you need to talk with Crystal. I'm sure she's seen the papers by now. She has to know. What about your father? Do you think he would be any help?"

Vaughn laughed derisively. "He's already in a rage about the article. The last person I'd go to is him. I'll find a way to work through it. I'll deal with Crystal. I'm sure there's an explanation."

"In the meantime, I think you need to clamp down on everything that goes in and out of your office," he advised. "We need to keep a low profile as well," he added reluctantly, recalling Waters' implications. "There's no reason to stir up any more trouble or any more rumors."

"I know you're right but I just hate the thought that I can't trust the people around me, and most of all," she looked deeply into his eyes, "that we have to sneak around like two teenagers who have been grounded."

Justin motioned to her. She got up and went to sit on his lap. She rested her head on his shoulder. "Then my plans will be right on time. We'll be away from everyone and everything for two glorious days."

She sat up straight. Her eyes sparkled "What? Tell me."

"I've made plans for us to go to Nassau next weekend."

"Next weekend?" she stuttered.

"Yes." He gathered her close and nuzzled her neck. "I'll have you all to myself."

"I . . . I can't go, Justin."

He leaned back. His eyes squinted. "Why? I know you can get away for a weekend, Vaughn. You can't work seven days a week."

She pushed herself up and walked across the room. "I can't go," she repeated. "Not next weekend."

He, too, got up and crossed the room until he stood behind her. He took her arm and turned her around. "Look at me and tell me why."

Vaughn took a fortifying breath. "I can't talk about it." She turned her head away, but Justin grabbed her chin and turned her to face him.

"More secrets? When do they ever end with you, Vaughn?"

Her nostrils flared. "This has nothing to do with you, Justin. It's something that I have to take care of. And I don't want to talk about it."

He let her go and turned away. "Would you mind telling me where you're going?" he asked in a low voice. "Or is that asking too much?"

"To Atlanta."

Justin nodded without commenting.

A tense silence filled the air. Vaughn busied herself with straightening the kitchen.

"I guess I'd better get going," he said finally. She turned and he was standing in the doorway of the kitchen. Her heart lurched.

"Don't . . . go," she said in a halting voice, afraid of his response.

"Why not?"

She swallowed, then dried her hands on the striped towel. Slowly she walked over to him. She gazed up into his eyes. "I want you to stay," she said softly.

"You want a lot of things, Vaughn," he said shortly. "You want me, but just so much. You want to tell me things, but not too much. You want me in your life, but not too close. You can't have everything both ways. It doesn't work like that."

"I know that," she retorted in a tight voice. "If I could tell you, I would. And I will, in good time. Now is not the time."

"And who decides when it's a good time?"

She spun away and crossed her arms beneath her breasts. "Maybe it is best if you leave. Especially if the rest of the evening is going to go like this."

"Maybe we just shouldn't see each other for a while, Vaughn, until you figure out what kind of relationship you want."

Vaughn was stunned into silence. Without another word, Justin collected his things and quietly closed the door behind him.

CHAPTER 20

Justin sat in his office the following morning preparing for court, but his mind wasn't on the events of the day. It was on the events of the previous night. He'd hardly slept. Disturbing images of shadows and nameless faces haunted his dreams. He woke up in a sweat, thinking of Vaughn and of the forces that were in play against her. He, at least, was willing to help, but she kept shutting him out. There was only so much of that a person could take. Secrets were not supposed to be part of a loving relationship. Vaughn had too many of them, and he was beginning to wonder where they would all lead. Maybe he'd gone too far by telling her they needed to stop seeing each other, but he didn't know what else to do.

The sharp ringing of the phone cut off his thoughts.

"Montgomery," he answered tersely.

"Mr. Montgomery, this is Elaine Carlyle."

Justin sat up straighter in his seat. "Yes, Ms. Carlyle. How are you?"

"Fine. I just wanted to let you know that we're working on your request. So far, we haven't come up with anything definite yet."

His spirits sank. "I see. Well, I know these things take time."

"We're doing everything we can. I'll be sure to keep you posted."

"Thank you for calling. If you find out anything, even if it seems insignificant, please let me know."

"I certainly will. Goodbye."

Justin hung up and sighed heavily. Maybe this was all just an exercise in futility. The chances that Simone was his daughter were a million to one. He shook his head. Nothing seemed to be working out. He wanted to talk with Vaughn to see if she'd spoken with Crystal. But he wasn't going to involve himself. Hadn't she told him she'd handle it?

He pushed himself up from his seat. He had to be in court in a half hour. Everyone else's problems, including his own, would have to wait.

Vaughn expected Crystal to be in her usual spot when she stepped into her office. She wasn't there. She hung up her jacket and walked back out into the reception area.

"Tess?"

"Yes, Ms. Hamilton?"

"Has Crystal come in yet?"

"She was here earlier, but she said she had to go out and that she'd be back in about an hour."

"How long ago was that?"

"About forty-five minutes ago."

"When she gets in, would you . . ." Before she could finish her sentence, Crystal walked in. Vaughn could see immediately that she'd been crying.

"Good morning," Crystal said weakly, barely able to meet Vaughn's eyes. She took a deep breath and approached Vaughn. "We need to talk."

Vaughn nodded and turned toward her office. Crystal followed and closed the door behind her.

Vaughn turned around, leaning her body against the edge of her desk. "What happened, Crystal?"

Tears slowly trickled down Crystal's cheeks. Her body shook with silent sobs. "I'm . . . so . . . sorry. I was . . . an idiot. Somehow . . . David got into my computer. You were right all along." She covered her face with her hands and wept.

"I didn't want to be right, Crystal," she said gently. Slowly she crossed the room and put her arm around Crystal. "David Hart is really David Cain. He's working for Stone. David and I go way back. That's why he didn't want us to meet."

"What? Are you saying that you know him? He . . . he lied to me from the very beginning," she cried, the pain evident in her voice. "He only pretended to care about me to get to you."

"I'm sorry Crystal. I filed charges against David for sexual harassment when we worked together at the same law firm. He was dismissed."

"Oh, great. This just gets better by the minute," she groaned. "What are we going to do now?" She wiped the tears away with the back of her hand.

Vaughn took a breath and crossed the room to stand by the window. "First, I need to know everything David could have gotten his hands on." She turned and faced her. Her expression was one of compassion when she spoke. "I also need you to be perfectly honest with me." She paused a moment. "I know that when things get hot and heavy we tend to spill our guts out to the person who's keeping us warm at night." Crystal felt a hot flush rise up her neck. "I need to know everything you told him about me and the campaign. That's the only way we can begin damage control."

Crystal found a seat and sat down. Slowly, she went over everything she could recall having told David. When she finished, even she was stunned at the incredible amount of information she'd divulged. "I'll prepare my resignation," she said, rising from her seat.

"Is that what you really want to do?" Vaughn asked gently.

Crystal looked across at her. "You know I don't. I want to make things right. I want to be there when you win."

"Well, you can't very well do that if you quit."

Crystal sniffed, then smiled crookedly. "Are you sure?"

"I can't handle it without you," she answered honestly.

"I'll make this right, Vaughn, I swear I will."

"Do you know how to reach him?"

She looked away, silently embarrassed. "His number is disconnected. I've never been to where he lives." She swallowed. "I don't even have an address."

"It's not your fault. He had intentions of you only knowing so much. With any luck, maybe he crawled back under that rock of his," she said with disgust. "We'll work it out. In the meantime, you need to start revising our plans. We'll also have to plan a small press conference. I see I already have a stack of messages."

"I'll get right on it." She started to leave then stopped "Thank you, Vaughn," she whispered.

"That's what friends are for, girlfriend."

CHAPTER 21

With Crystal back in her own office, Vaughn had the first opportunity of the morning to be alone with her thoughts. The night she'd spent after Justin left was nothing short of hell. She was sure she hadn't gotten a decent minute of sleep for the entire night.

She sat down behind her desk and stared at nothingness. What was her life coming to? She questioned whether all that she had endured to get to this point had been worth the hurt—the losses. What would the future hold if she won the election? Would life be more of the same, only intensified?

When she entered politics, she understood the levels of power and what that meant. She also knew the lengths that people in power would go to to retain that power. For the most part, she had remained above and immune to the treachery that seeped through the halls of justice like a morning mist. Her father had been her benefactor, her shield. It was only now when she attempted to butt heads with the powerful elite that she felt the depth of their deceit. She no longer even believed that Elliott Hamilton could forestall the avalanche that was sure to come.

She knew now that the rumors and leaks to the press were only the beginning. The battlelines had been drawn, and she'd thrown her gauntlet into the den. A question gnawed incessantly in the back of her head: Was she capable of withstanding the onslaught of pressure that was inevitable in the months ahead? Yet, interwoven like a silken thread through the rough-hewn fabric of her life was Justin. Her thoughts, her feelings always went back to him—her ray of hope.

What about Justin—her life—*their* life? She knew that before she could be right and righteous with him, she'd first have to be right with herself. Perhaps this trip to Atlanta would be the cleansing one, the one to finally break her ties to the past so that she could live in the present and move on to the future. A future with Justin—that is, if he still wanted her when all of this ugliness was over. She knew she couldn't offer him anything less than one hundred percent. It would be a difficult road ahead—a lonely road. It would take all of her courage to meet the challenges that faced her. There were changes occurring in every area of her life and, in order to break free of the mental shackles that had controlled her for so long, she was going to have to be strong enough to withstand the changes.

David sat at the dining table of his co-op apartment, reading the morning paper. He lit a cigarette and took a sip of his coffee. Scanning the headlines, he stopped at a bold headline on page three: "ASSEMBLYWOMAN HAMILTON—SOFTENING HER HARD IMAGE." The article elaborated on Hamilton's decision to hire an image consulting firm in an attempt to improve her image and strengthen her appeal among male voters. This latest article also alluded to the notion that she'd exhausted her father's influence and had branched out to hang on the coattails of businessman, philanthropist, and legal wizard Justin Montgomery. It related Montgomery's association with the Harrison murder case and even hinted that Montgomery's law firm was getting preferential treatment because of his alleged connection to Hamilton.

David took a long gulp of coffee and chuckled heartily. "Now that's what I call payback," he snickered. Leaning back in his chair, he visualized the look of self-righteous indignation that must have twisted that beautiful ebony face of hers into knots. He sighed, contented. His work was done. He'd held up his end of the arrangement, now it was time for Stone to pay up. He reached for the phone and dialed Stone's office.

Elliott paced the confines of his judicial chambers like a caged panther. Livid could not begin to describe the intensity of his outrage. He pounded his thick fist against the table, scattering the damning newspaper onto the floor. He knew this would happen, but Vaughn was too lovestruck to listen. The only thing he could be grateful for, at this moment, was that he had foreseen the future and had prepared accordingly. He picked up the phone and dialed the private number. Gruffly announcing himself to the secretary, he was immediately put through to Stan Waters.

"Elliott, good morning."

"There's not a goddamned thing good about this morning! I need results, Stan. I want them now."

"Just calm down, Elliott," Stan countered. "I'm doing everything I can. I can't make the mountain come to me."

"Then you better get to it, Muhammad."

"I'll call you when everything is settled. I'm sure we'll have an answer by the end of the week."

Elliott took a deep breath and was on the brink of apologizing when he thought better of it. Stan Waters owed him. It wasn't the other way around.

"You know how to reach me," Elliott said, and hung up. As soon as he did, his line rang and, he snatched the receiver from the cradle.

"Elliott, have you seen today's paper?" Sheila asked in a tight voice.

"Yes," he replied shortly, knowing that there was more to come.

"She needs to get out of this now, Elliott. I have a very bad feeling about it. There are leaks in her own office. Reporters are digging into her private life. They . . ."

"I know. I know," he thundered, cutting her off. "All of this goes back to that Montgomery. If she hadn't gotten so starry-eyed over him, she would've been more focused and in-tune to what was going on right under her nose," he shouted. "I told her, but she wouldn't listen," he ended pompously.

"She deserves a life too, Elliott. She can't live in a vacuum of politics forever," she cried, reflecting on her own life of predictable loneliness and superficial joys.

"There'll be plenty of time for that later," he huffed. "Now she needs to concern herself with keeping her name out of the scandal sheets, and curtailing her association with Montgomery."

"Elliott," she warned, "stay out of Vaughn's personal life. You've done enough," she added, the simple words laced with innuendo. "Let her handle it."

"I'm due in court," he replied, ending any further conversation. "I'll see you this evening."

"Justin," Khendra called out to him as he hurried down the corridor of the courthouse. She picked up her step and quickly caught up with him. Her long-legged, high-heeled stride smoothly matched his. "Did you read the morning papers?" she inquired, shifting her briefcase from one hand to the other.

"Yeah, I read it," he answered gruffly. He'd read the inflammatory copy shortly before he'd left for court. The entire piece had his teeth on edge. Momentarily he wished that he was meeting with Stan Waters then instead of at the end of the week. He was beginning to believe that Waters may have some of the answers he needed.

"What the hell is going on?" she asked in a low whisper. "We can't afford to be connected to a smear campaign. Not with this kind of high-profile case." Her heels clicked rapidly against the marble floor.

"I'm well aware of that Khen," he answered in a tone that cautioned, *leave it alone.*

"I'm sorry. I didn't mean to jump all over you. It's just that . . ."

"I know you and Sean have worked your tails off on this case. I'm not going to let anything jeopardize that. Beyond everything else, it's not fair to our client." He took a long breath. "In the meantime, let's just deal with this jury selection."

Khendra fought to contain her curiosity, but lost the battle. "How's Vaughn taking her new level of notoriety?"

Justin slanted her a glance as he pushed open the courtroom door. "I wouldn't know," he answered tersely, holding the door open for her, then leaving Khendra with more questions than she dared to ask.

When court recessed for the day, Justin returned alone to his office. Making a cursory acknowledgment to the remaining members he passed, he headed for his office. Once inside, he closed and locked his door, then headed for the wet-bar tucked behind the roll away bookcase.

He couldn't remember the last time he'd had a real drink. All he knew was that he needed one now. He reached for the unopened bottle of Black Label, opened it, and poured the amber liquid into a glass filled with ice. Glass in hand, he walked over to the small sofa in the corner of his office and lowered himself down.

Staring out of the window, he watched the last rays of sunshine tumble over one another, struggling for survival over the horizon. Funny, that's how his thoughts were at the moment—each one struggling for dominance. *Vaughn. Simone. His practice. The trial. Samantha.*

The leaks from Vaughn's office had gone beyond just idle gossip and rumor. It now involved her private life and him. And with that, the ambiguous comments made by Stan Waters sounded more ominous. He wished he'd been able to move up the meeting date, but Waters would be out of town until the end of the week. If he didn't know better, he'd swear that it was merely a ploy to pique his interest.

Maybe what had happened between he and Vaughn last night was for the best. It was becoming crystal-clear that they needed to stay away from each other for everyone's sake. He took a long sip from his drink and squeezed his eyes shut as the liquid burned its way down his throat.

"Aaugh," he sputtered. "No wonder I gave this up." He put the glass down on the table next to the couch and sank back against the cushions, letting his thoughts take over. He wondered what Vaughn was doing—what was she wearing . . . ?

The knock on his door caused him to jump. He blinked and checked his watch. It was nine P.M. He'd dozed off. He pushed himself up and walked to the door.

"Sean, what's up? You're here pretty late," he said for lack of something better.

Sean stepped through the partially opened door. "I figured you'd need someone to talk to." He crossed the room to the bar and fixed himself a quick drink. "I elected myself," he announced, turning toward Justin with an expression that seemed to say, "I'm listening."

"Then I guess you'd better cop a squat," Justin said. "This may take awhile."

He thought he'd feel better after talking things out with Sean. But his revelations and introspections only intensified his confusion. He'd briefly told Sean about his nebulous conversation with Stan Waters and of the impending meeting. He'd also voiced his concerns about Vaughn's refusal to tell him why she had to go to Atlanta.

Sean's take on the rash of news articles was that it was just politics as usual. But he did agree that Justin should keep a low profile, although he couldn't fully agree with Justin's decision to stay away from Vaughn.

"She needs you more than ever, man. You gotta know that," Sean said.

"I do know. That's not the issue. The issue is, Vaughn has to come to terms with me and the kind of relationship she wants. I'm ready for the whole nine. She's still on the fence."

"Hey, its something you'll have to deal with. When she's ready she'll come around." Sean pulled himself up from his partially reclining position on the couch. "My advice—don't issue ultimatums. They generally backfire. You don't have to take the advice, just borrow it." He grinned, and clamped Justin heartily on the shoulder. "I'm outta here man. Full day tomorrow."

"Yeah, me too." Justin rose. "Hang on a minute. I'll walk out with you. And Sean . . ." Sean turned, his thick eyebrows arching into question marks. "Thanks," Justin said simply.

"Remember, I've been there. There were times before me and Khen got married that I thought I'd lost her forever. But we got it together. And look at us now," he chuckled, grinning broadly.

"Yeah, look," Justin teased. He threw his arm around Sean's shoulder, and they walked down the corridor to the elevator.

"What are we going to do about this?" Crystal asked, just short of losing her last shred of calm.

Vaughn braced her hips with her fists as she paced the length of the office. It was nearly 10 P.M. and this never-ending day seemed to have gone from bad to worse. She'd thought that Justin's declaration of the previous night had been her lowest point. Today proved that she had yet to reach it. After dealing with Crystal, she had the false hope that things would get better. Then she'd read the papers.

"My plan is simple," she said finally. "We do nothing. We won't rise to the bait. Questions will be answered honestly, but no additional information will be given."

Crystal nodded. "This is all my fault," she stated morosely. "If I hadn't been such an idiot . . ."

"There's no point in shouldering blame. What's done is done." She sighed heavily. "Let's go home. I've had it for today."

Vaughn arrived at her townhouse and immediately felt the emptiness swallow her. Over the short months she'd come to know and fall in love with Justin, he'd become an integral part of her life. The sudden realization that that portion of her life was halted, left her adrift, like a boat without an anchor.

Mechanically, she prepared for bed. When she returned from Atlanta at the end of the week, she would set everything straight with Justin. She just needed this one last time to put the past to rest. For an instant, she thought of calling him, but hesitated, her hand above the phone, then pushed the thought away.

It was 3 A.M. Justin still lay wide awake in the king-sized bed. Sean was right. Vaughn should be here with him. They should be figuring out this thing together. He breathed heavily, punched his pillow, and turned over on his side. How long was he going to be able to stand behind his own dictum and stay away from her? he wondered. Five days and counting, he groaned. If and when Vaughn was ready for a real relationship, he'd be waiting. Hopefully, it wouldn't take her too long to come to her senses, he ruminated, feeling the telltale effects of his body's reaction whenever her thought about her. He didn't know if he could stand the wait.

However, between the trial, the daily pile-up of work on his desk, and his calendar filling up with upcoming speaking engagements, Justin remained too exhausted to focus heavily on his personal life. He poured his energy into his work. His tenuous relationship with Simone strengthened daily. He felt so much empathy for her situation and for the countless youths like her. She'd confided in him about her fears, her insecurities, and her deep desire to find her real parents. Although, rationally, she could understand why parents gave up their children, on an emotional level, she refused to accept it. She wanted to find them, not just to validate her existence, but to show them what a success she was without them.

Listening to her hurt tore at Justin's heart. Whether Simone was his daughter or not, he silently pledged that he would do whatever was in his power to find her true parents.

Miraculously, the week sped by and he'd only thought of Vaughn a mere million times at last count. The idea that she hadn't called pricked his ego and his emotions. But, thankfully, there were no more news articles to stir up his already raw nerves.

As he prepared for his meeting with Stan Waters, he tried to evaluate all of the possibilities that could have precipitated Waters contacting him. He concluded that Vaughn was at the root of it.

As Justin pulled into the valet parking area of Hogarth's restaurant, where the meeting was being held, his thoughts veered toward Vaughn, raising countless questions. Where was she now? Was she thinking about him? Did she have any idea about Stan Waters? And he wondered if she'd already left for her mysterious trip to Atlanta.

"Yes, Mother, I'm on my way to the airport. My plane leaves in an hour," Vaughn said in a rush.

"I don't understand why you have to go to Atlanta at a time like this. With so much going on . . ."

Vaughn cut her off. "You don't understand, Mother. This is something I have to do. It's important to me. Can't you understand that?"

"Vaughn, honey," her mother sighed, "I just want you to be happy. With all of these rumors and articles runnin' rampant . . . I just don't like the idea of you traveling alone."

"I'll be fine," she said. "Listen, Mama, I've got to run. I'll call you when I return on Sunday."

"I wish you wouldn't do this, Vaughn."

"I have to."

While Vaughn sped along the highway en route to the airport, Justin sat in the company of four of the most influential men in Washington politics. He was being offered the opportunity to salvage Vaughn's life as she knew it.

CHAPTER 22

"I can't believe you'd have the gall to ask me something like this," Justin growled between clenched teeth. He tossed his napkin across his plate and stood.

Stan Waters grabbed his wrist. "Mr. Montgomery, I wouldn't be so hasty if I were you. I think you should sit down and listen. The careers of two very important people are at stake." He gave Justin a steady look, until he finally sat down.

"I can't begin to imagine what you could possibly have to say that would convince me to run against Vaughn Hamilton."

"But I do," Stan said. The three other men, Carlton Fitzhugh, owner of the largest hotel chain in Washington, J.T. Johnson publishing mogul, and Morgan Livingston, head of one of the most powerful lobbies on the Hill, all nodded in silent agreement.

"Listen," Justin cut in, holding up his hand to forestall any further comment. "If you thugs, which is how this is all shaping up to me, have something concrete to say, then put it on the table. Or you can continue your discussion without me."

"Very well. Simply put, if you do not take up our offer to run against Ms. Hamilton, we will release information about her activities that will topple her career.

"Ms. Hamilton can handle any trash that's put in those rags. She's been in the business long enough to know that it's all part of the game."

"Perhaps. But are you willing to test the power of the press? Remember

Gary Hart, Reverend Baker, Dukakis? Those are just a few—even the president is not immune."

Justin's pulse picked up a beat. His eyes narrowed as he leaned forward. "Are you saying that you were responsible for their downfall?" Stan Waters sat back and a slow smile of triumph inched across his mouth.

Justin rubbed his hand across his face. He shook his head. "You wouldn't do that. She's a judge's daughter. She has a clean record in the assembly. What kind of evidence do you have?"

Stan Waters pulled a small Manila envelope out of his breast pocket and slid it across the table toward Justin. Justin quickly skimmed the faces of the men at the table. Their expressions remained closed. Stan was sure that his powers of persuasion, alone, would be enough to convince Justin to enter the race. It was Elliott who insisted that Stan take along the sealed envelope for added insurance. Even he didn't know what the folded documents contained. But by the stony expression on Justin's face, the tension in his jaw, and the slight flaring of his nostrils, the papers had the desired effect.

Justin felt reality slide out from under him. Emotions raced so fast through his system, he couldn't latch on to them long enough to digest them. Anger, betrayal, a sense of disbelief, and ultimately resignation to the truth took hold. Yes, Vaughn did have plenty to hide, plenty to worry about. And she'd been hiding it from him along with everyone else. Slowly he refolded the papers and inserted them into the envelope. He slipped the envelope into the pocket of his jacket. "What makes you think I'd want to help her?" he asked cautiously.

"We know for a fact that you've been involved with Ms. Hamilton for some time. We're certain that you're not the kind of man who would sit back idly and watch her world crumble down around her. That's what makes you such a credible candidate. We want her out. Just think about what the positive publicity will do for the Harrison case. Then just imagine how negative publicity could destroy it."

"Are you threatening me?"

"Of course not. Just advising you of the facts."

"I have no desire to enter politics. I don't have the background or . . ."

"If you're concerned about your capabilities, believe me, you're quite capable. Anyone who has the wherewithal to operate a law firm, lobby for policy change, and start a string of foundations has more than enough qualifications to get the job done."

"I won't do this."

"Oh, I think you will. You see, Mr. Montgomery, you have the power to salvage or destroy a career. One phone call from me and Ms. Hamilton is finished."

He had to think. He needed time. He needed his own plan. "I'll have to think about this," he said finally.

Stan shook his head. "I'm sorry, but we're quite out of time. Your name must be put on the ballot immediately to be eligible for the general election."

"How do you expect me to make this kind of decision, just like that?" he spat.

"Decisions like this and more are made in a split second every day, Mr. Montgomery," Livingston said in a low lazy drawl. Justin slanted him a look but ignored the comment.

"What if I say yes? There's no guarantee that Ms. Hamilton would drop out of the race."

"That's not really your worry, Mr. Montgomery. We'll take care of everything."

Justin felt his chest heave with frustration. As much as he abhorred what she'd done, he knew he could not take part in her destruction. His dark eyes narrowed to slits. "What assurances do I have that this information won't be used?"

Stan Waters wiped his mouth with the linen napkin. "There would be no point in that, Mr. Montgomery," he said calmly, and signaled the waiter for a round of drinks. "We'll take that as a yes."

Before Justin had a chance to react, a series of light bulbs flashed in his face. Three reporters, two of whom he knew, began barreling him with questions about his sudden leap into the political pool. Somehow Justin had the presence of mind to repeat the standard "No comment at this time." And even as he tried to figure out how the press knew, he needed only to look at Stan Waters to find the answer to his question. For the first time since they all sat down, Stan Waters had little to say. He sat back in his seat and smiled.

Vaughn's plane landed in Atlanta shortly before 5 P.M.. If the cab kept up the steady speed in and out of rush hour traffic, she could reach the cemetery before it closed for the day.

She'd completed this ritual for the past fifteen years, she thought, leaning back against the worn leather of the cab. Today, May 20, would be the last. She'd never shared this secret part of her life with anyone. It had always been too sacred to her. Not even her mother knew the truth. Sheila believed that she made her yearly trip to Atlanta to visit Brian's grave, not the tiny headstone of her daughter.

"Keep the meter running," she instructed the driver as she alighted from the cab. Slowly, she entered the small, precisely cared for grounds with the two bouquets she'd purchased at the airport.

The short walk up the slight incline and across the stretch of emerald-green lawn gave Vaughn the opportunity to think. The old, dark, tumbling thoughts scrambled noisely around in her head, fighting to take shape as she neared the familiar marking.

Brian Everett Willis, Jr., beloved son of Claire and Brian Willis, Sr. Too young to know, was his epitaph. Gently she placed the bouquet across the headstone and touched the smooth, cool surface. She straightened up and moved away.

She rounded a short turn, and there, set on a hill beneath a weeping willow, was the headstone of her daughter.

As she neared, poignant memories of what caused her to be there rushed to the surface. This time, she allowed the memories to wash over her. She'd always shoved them aside and gone through the motions of her daily ritual. But today was different. Today was a day of cleansing.

It was three months before graduation. She and Brian had been seeing each other for the entire senior year. He'd been pressuring her to "give it up," as he put it. She'd refused, until finally, one night after coming home from a school dance, Brian used all of his youthful skills and she finally gave in—in the back of his car.

Her first experience was awkward, painful, and embarrassing. Brian swore that it would get better. It didn't. Their clumsy effort at lovemaking took place every Friday night, until Vaughn found out that she was pregnant.

At first she was terrified of her parents' reaction, and frightened for her own future. But everything would be fine, she convinced herself, as she waited for Brian on the porch of her home.

When his car pulled up, she tried to smile, but her lips were trembling so badly it was impossible. She hopped down the stairs and hurried around to the passenger side of the car and got in.

"Hey babe," Brian greeted. "Lookin' good tonight. I figured we'd go see a movie, grab something to eat and then . . ." He turned and winked at her.

Brian was probably the best looking guy in the elite private academy they attended. At eighteen he was already over six-feet tall, with smooth caramel-colored skin, silky dark brown hair, and the most exotic eyes she'd ever seen. He had thick silky eyebrows and long curling lashes that seemed to outline those remarkable eyes, dark and tipped up at the corners. Girls tripped over themselves trying to get Brian's attention. She told herself that she should feel lucky. The girls she knew would die to be in her shoes. But at that moment, she didn't feel so lucky.

"Brian, we need to talk."

He frowned and blew out a breath. "What about?"

"I . . . I went to the doctor today." She saw his eyes snap. She spilled out the rest before she lost her nerve. "I'm pregnant."

"Yeah. Who's is it?"

She felt as if she'd been drop-kicked. All of the air in her lungs rushed out in a gush. "What? You know you're the only one I've been with." Her voice rose in agitation along with her nerves. "How could you ask me something like that?"

"Easy. I ain't about having no babies. I have plans for my life and that's not one of them. If you went and got yourself pregnant, it's your problem."

Vaughn's heart was pounding so hard and so fast she couldn't think. Her hands started to shake. "It's your baby," she said firmly. "It may not fit in your plans, but it's in them." She folded her arms beneath her growing, tender breasts.

Brian made a noise of disgust. "I'm not really in the mood for hanging out tonight," he said, as though he hadn't heard a word she'd said. "Know what I mean?" He leaned across her stiff form and released the lock on the passenger door. She didn't have to be told. She took the hint.

"I'll call you," he said, as he put the car in gear. He turned and looked at her gently. "We'll talk. I promise," he said. As she watched him drive down the road, she knew he wouldn't call, and she felt very alone.

The next morning, news of the accident was in every paper and on every television station. Brian had been speeding around a sharp turn, lost control of his car, and slammed into a dividing wall. Vaughn was numb.

Elliott, who was a close friend of Brian's father, spoke at the eulogy at Brian Sr.'s request. Even back then they were enmeshed in politics. Brian Sr. was the district attorney and her father was a circuit court judge.

Vaughn's grief and guilt overwhelmed her. She believed it was her fault that Brian—upset by the news of her pregnancy—had driven so recklessly. All she had left of their youthful romance was the tiny baby growing inside of her.

It wasn't until two months later that she finally told her parents. Her mother wept, her father swore that he would kill the son of a bitch that took advantage of his daughter.

"Who's the father?" he demanded.

"Brian," she whispered.

Her father sank heavily into the chair. His face was a mask of horror. For several long moments the only sound in the spotless kitchen was the sound of her mother's muffled sobs.

When her father finally spoke again, his ominous voice was directed toward her mother. He refused to look at Vaughn. "Get her to a doctor in Atlanta. Find out how many months. Pack her bags. After graduation she's leaving. When she has the . . . child, she can come home and resume her life. No one is ever to speak of this again. No one is ever to know. No one."

Less than five hours after she received her high school diploma, Vaughn and her mother were on a plane bound for Atlanta. She arrived at the home of a mid-wife and was introduced as Valerie Mason.

Vaughn believed that the most tragic day of her life was the day she delivered by Cesarean section a healthy baby girl, who was taken from her only moments after the birth and was never to be seen by her again. That day dimmed in comparison to the morning about six weeks after her return home. Her father very calmly entered her room and told her that the baby's adoptive family had been abusive and that the baby was dead. That morning a part of her died as well. Lost was any hope of ever reuniting with her baby, and the pain lingered on every day of her life.

Now that she'd finally allowed the hurt to take shape, she was able to revisit a point in time that had irrevocably changed her life, and slowly she let go of the guilt. She recognized that it was not her fault. Brian drove his car into the wall. Her father selected the family that took her daughter. What she had been guilty of was not taking charge of her life sooner.

The images in front of her became cloudy. Her eyes wouldn't focus and she realized that she was crying. Standing in front of the marble headstone, she cried bitter tears.

The marble marker was more symbolic than anything else. She'd never been allowed to go to the funeral and she had no idea where her baby was buried. She'd selected the spot because she felt that her baby should be close to her father and near the family plot.

The engraving was simple. *Valerie Mason, You Were Loved.*

Vaughn straightened up and wiped her eyes. She'd given the baby the name she'd used at the hospice. Now it was time to let it go. Let go of the guilt, the remorse, the anger, and begin to heal. She placed the bouquet against the headstone. "Goodbye," she whispered, turned, and walked back to the waiting cab.

Justin paced his living room. He knew that what he'd agreed to was a mistake. But at the time, he didn't see any way around it. His motivation had been to protect Vaughn. They knew it and they used it.

He was nearly beside himself with frustration. His head pounded, his stomach was twisted into a knot, and he couldn't get his thoughts to focus. But he had to. He had to figure things out. He had to get to Vaughn and explain the situation to her before the entire bizarre episode exploded in her face. No matter what she'd done, she didn't deserve to find out on the eleven o'clock news. If he only knew where she went in Atlanta and when she'd be back . . . he could at least warn her. He'd already tried her office, but everyone had left for the weekend. Crystal Porter was his next hope but her number was unlisted. He'd already left three urgent messages on Vaughn's answering machine. There was nothing else he could do.

Finally, mentally and physically washed out, he collapsed in the loveseat. He rested his head against the back cushion and closed his eyes. Instantly, bursts of light reminiscent of the camera flashes popped before his eyes. Adrenaline charged through his veins and he pushed himself up out of his seat. Just as he began pacing again the phone rang.

He snatched up the cordless phone. "Yes," he barked.

"Listen, man, I don't know what the hell is going on," Sean stated, "but you'd better turn on the T.V. Now!"

In quick strides Justin crossed the room, grabbed the remote, and pushed the "on" button.

". . . In a surprise announcement today, businessman and criminal attorney Justin Montgomery threw his hat into the ring for the Democratic nomination for the congressional seat, just making the deadline . . ."

He didn't need to hear any more. All he could imagine was Vaughn's horror at finding out this way.

"Sean . . . are you still there?"

"Yeah. What's going on?"

"We need to talk."

"No kiddin'."

"Can you come here?"

"See you in twenty minutes."

Elliott watched the broadcast in the privacy of his study. Maybe now Vaughn would trust his judgment and listen to his plans for her success. It was obvious that Justin Montgomery meant her no good. Wasn't it? He'd be there waiting to comfort her when she came to him and admitted that he'd been right all along.

In the upstairs bedroom, Sheila's heart was breaking for her child. When would she ever find happiness? Could it be possible that Justin Montgomery had been using Vaughn all along? Was it he who'd leaked the information about Vaughn's plans to the press? As much as the evidence pointed an accusing finger at Justin Montgomery, a dark corner of her heart believed that he was just as much a victim as Vaughn. But to give voice to her suspicions would crumble the world as she knew it.

Instead of going to her hotel as she'd originally planned, Vaughn instructed the driver to take her back to the airport. There was no reason for her to remain in Atlanta. She'd done what she came to do. Now it was time to go back and begin to make things right between her and Justin. Her love for him could be all encompassing now, free from the ghosts of her past. She could love him as thoroughly as her heart allowed—as he allowed.

When she reached the airport she made a quick call to Crystal, but got her machine instead. She left her flight number and a message that she was on her way back. On the flight home she felt as if a weight had been lifted from her soul. Now she could tell Justin everything—about her pregnancy, her baby's untimely death, and her years of bending to her father's wishes. Each individual was in control of their own destiny, she reasoned. And now she would finally take control of hers.

She exited the plane. Her heart beat with anticipation. She couldn't wait to get home and call Justin. Maybe she'd just call him from inside of the terminal. The thought of hearing his voice made her smile. As she hurried across the runway and into the terminal, she saw Crystal running in her direction.

Something was wrong. Her pulse began to quicken as Crystal's anxiety-strained face came closer into view.

"Vaughn," Crystal said breathlessly, "I'm so glad you were on this flight. I got your message."

"Crystal, you're scaring me. What is it?"

"Let's get out of here." She looked quickly over her shoulder as she ushered Vaughn toward the baggage claim area.

"I don't even know how to tell you this, but I didn't want you to see it on T.V. or hear it on the radio."

"Hear what? See what?" she demanded.

"There she is!" The shout rang out through the terminal. Almost instantly, Vaughn and Crystal were surrounded by a small group of men and women.

Vaughn threw Crystal a look just as a flashbulb went off in her face. "It's Justin," Crystal tried to say, but was drowned out by the reporters' questions.

"Ms. Hamilton. Ms. Hamilton," shouted a woman from the *Herald*. "What are your feelings about Justin Montgomery entering the congressional election?"

Whatever she thought the question was going to be, nothing could have prepared her for this.

"Ms. Hamilton, is it true that you and Mr. Montgomery had a relationship and he used that relationship to further his political objectives?"

Vaughn felt as if the floor were giving way beneath her feet. Crystal was grabbing her arm and trying to steer her past the growing crowd.

There must be some sort of mistake, she kept thinking as she tried to form the words to answer the barrage of questions. But turning and seeing the look of regret on Crystal's face told her it was no mistake. Yes, she could easily walk away with the standard "No comment," but when she'd left her daughter's grave site, less than four hours earlier, she vowed to take charge of her destiny. It would have to start somewhere.

Vaughn halted her forward stride so suddenly that Crystal nearly fell over her own feet. Vaughn turned and faced the pursuing crowd. She took a steadying breath and assumed her public face. She smiled. "I look forward to a run-off with Mr. Montgomery. I'm sure he has his reasons for coming into the race so late. I can't imagine what those reasons are," she said cynically. "My office will be scheduling a press conference to respond to the questions." She started to walk off.

"Wait, Ms. Hamilton. What about the rumors of a relationship with Mr. Montgomery? What's the story?"

Her stomach dipped as she turned to face her inquisitors.

"That is absurd. I know Mr. Montgomery professionally and that's all. There's never been anything between us," she stated firmly. As she said the words, she knew that they were painfully true.

CHAPTER 23

Crystal was trying to tell her on the ride home about the news release earlier in the day, but Vaughn couldn't hear her. Her sense of betrayal ran so deep it had carved out a canyon in her soul. She was totally devoid of feelings. Her brain was no longer able to process the information that Crystal kept pouring into it.

The cab pulled up in front of Vaughn's townhouse. "Are you all right, Vaughn?" Crystal clasped her shoulder. "Do you want me to come up for a while?"

Vaughn looked at her, but didn't really see her. "No thanks." Her smile was in place. "You go on home. I'll see you Monday." Vaughn pushed the lock and started to open the door.

"Vaughn, you don't have to act like everything is alright. We both know that it isn't. Remember, I've been there too." For the first time since Vaughn had heard the news, Crystal thought she saw a flicker in her dark eyes. But just as quickly, her look became veiled and unreadable. *The Iron Maiden,* Crystal thought, suddenly overcome with sadness. "I'll be home if you need to talk," she said, as Vaughn stepped out of the cab.

"Thanks." She walked down the path to her door. She felt as if her feet had been weighted down in cement. If she could just make it to the other side of her door, she silently prayed. Once inside, she closed the door quietly behind her. And in that instant, all of the agony she'd withheld since her return washed over her in a nauseating wave. All of her anguish and loss over the years seemed to magnify one-hundredfold. "This couldn't be happening again. Not again," she cried. Instinctively she wrapped her arms around her body in a futile attempt to shield herself from the onslaught of pain that pummeled her mercilessly. Slowly, she slid down the surface of the door. Resting her head on her knees, she finally gave in to the wracking sobs that fought for release.

"What could they possibly have on her?" Sean asked.

"Trust me, if released her chances for this election or any other are zero."

Justin stretched out his legs and let his eyes slide shut. "I just need to talk to her. She's got to know from me what this is all about, and then I want her to explain."

Sean used the remote control to turn on the television.

". . . This just in," the newscaster was saying. "Congressional candidate Vaughn Hamilton was met at Dulles Airport this evening and questioned . . ."

Justin sprang up in his seat. His eyes were riveted to Vaughn's face on the screen, and what he saw made his gut twist. "Oh, no," he breathed. He got up and grabbed his coat. "I've got to go to her."

Sean was instantly on his feet. "Bad move, buddy. The press will probably be all over you. We don't need any more publicity. I'm telling you, stay put and hope that she calls you."

Justin heaved a sigh. "I know Vaughn. She won't call." He began to pace as the interview continued.

"There was never anything between us," he heard her say. And the moment he heard her utter the words, he knew that she meant it.

Vaughn spent her weekend expending her pent-up energy and frustration. She jogged, and played tennis until she fell into bed at night exhausted. Too tired to dream. Too tired to think about Justin. In one fell swoop he'd erased all of the joy of their relationship. He'd made her doubt herself and her ability to judge character. He'd made her feel unworthy, undeserving of true love. All of the insecurities she'd harbored about her womanhood he rekindled as expertly as he'd stoked the fires of her heart.

She'd refused to answer her phone or respond to the countless messages that flashed on her answering machine. Her father had called, feigning indignation. But the tone of his voice seemed to say, "I told you so." Her mother was beside herself with worry. But Vaughn called neither of them.

More times than she'd dared to count, she was tempted to answer Justin's phone calls. But what could he possibly say to explain his treachery?

Her father had been right all along and that reality made her ill. Even

Paul had tried to warn her. But more than anything, once the shock had worn off, she became angry. She wanted to hurt him, to humiliate him as he'd hurt and humiliated her. His betrayal fueled her desire to win—at any cost—and she would. She would control her destiny.

When she arrived at her office on Monday morning, the office was a flurry of activity. Phones were ringing incessantly. Staff members were racing up and down the hallway and, as usual, Crystal was in her spot in the alcove behind Vaughn's door. As soon as Vaughn walked in, Crystal jumped up.

"Where the devil have you been? I've been worried sick. Every newspaper in the state has been calling."

Vaughn gave her a cool smile. "That's exactly what we need," she said calmly. "Did you set up the press conference?"

"Tomorrow at 3 P.M.," Crystal said haltingly, completely taken aback by Vaughn's icy demeanor.

"If Justin Montgomery wants a fight, then he's got one on his hands. I'm in this thing to win," she said, a hard edge to her voice.

"He's called from the courthouse several times already this morning."

"Good. Let him keep calling. You talk to him the next time he calls and tell him we'll see him at the run-off election and not a minute before."

"Vaughn." Crystal stepped closer. "What's happening to you? This isn't like you. Why won't you at least listen to what he has to say? Maybe there's an explanation."

Vaughn rounded on Crystal so quickly, Crystal's next comment stuck in her throat. "Listen, let's clear this up now. He called this war and I'm not in it just for the skirmish." Her voice rose. "He used me, damn it! Just like Paul, just like . . . Brian. I'm not interested in his reasons why," she spat.

Crystal blinked back her shock, then nodded. "You're right. I just thought . . ."

"Let's get prepared for this press conference. I have my text prepared." She unsnapped the lock on her briefcase and pulled out several sheets of typed paper. She handed them to Crystal. "I need you to take a look at this and see if it needs revising."

Crystal took the papers and stared at Vaughn's rigid form, at the hard eyes and the mouth tight around the edges. She took a cautious step forward. "I'm sorry, Vaughn, about everything," she said quietly.

"Don't be. This is just what I needed. I'd begun to take this whole campaign thing too lightly. This is for real. It's like my father said, I'm going to have to be tougher. And I will be, Crystal." She looked at her with determination burning in her eyes. "Justin Montgomery taught me some valuable lessons. Trust is something that doesn't exist. Love is for fools. And no one is above deceit." She swallowed. "Even those who profess to love you." She turned away and blinked back the tears that scorched her eyes. "I need that speech back as soon as possible," she said softly.

"What does all of this mean for the law firm?" Simone asked Chad over her cup of tea.

Chad shook his head slowly. "I don't really know. I'm still in shock. Justin said he was having a staff meeting this afternoon." He shook his head again. "I mean, I know Justin has all of the qualifications to run for office, and he'd make a damned good candidate. I just never knew he was interested in politics—at least not to this extent." He took a swallow of his Pepsi.

Simone leaned slightly forward across the table and spoke in a hushed voice. "Actually, I kind of got the impression that Mr. Montgomery and Ms. Hamilton . . ." She let her thought hang in the air.

Chad smiled crookedly. "I had the same impression. I guess we were both wrong."

Melissa Overton had worked throughout the weekend on Simone's case. She knew she was close. In her work she'd discovered the name of the woman who had placed children in and around Atlanta during the time that Simone was born. She hoped that the woman would be willing to talk with her. What Melissa didn't know was that her boss, Elaine, was also working on the case on Justin's behalf.

Elaine's heart thundered in her chest as she read the report she'd accessed from Melissa's computer. Although the circumstances allowed for the remote possibility that Justin was Simone's father, the facts before her showed otherwise.

Elaine sighed. The information was rather curious. Everything pointed to Atlanta and a midwife. She put more names into the computer, using Simone's last name in the hope that Simone's mother had used that name at some point. The computer hummed and buzzed. Moments later, it produced a massive list of women whose last name was Rivers.

Meanwhile, Melissa had the same idea. She scanned her list, compared all the other variables: race, age, place of birth, proximity to Atlanta. She narrowed down the list to forty names. She knew she was on the threshold of discovery. Her palms began to sweat. Her fingers flew over the keys as she entered the commands: profession, married or single, deceased. She was certain that whoever Simone's mother was, she had had money and connections even nineteen years ago.

"The press is arriving," Crystal said as she stepped into Vaughn's office and closed the door.

"Did you set them up in the formal conference room?" Crystal nodded. "Let them simmer for a few minutes and I'll be in. I want them eager and hungry. Any word from David?" she asked, not looking at Crystal as she gathered her notes.

"No," Crystal mumbled, the word sticking in her throat. "I don't expect to hear from him again. I'm sure he knows that we realize what he's done," she said quietly, her humiliation renewed.

"You're probably right," she laughed mirthlessly, "but bad pennies always seem to keep turning up in one form or another." She took a breath and looked up, the emptiness that swam in her eyes jolted Crystal. A chill raced through her body. "Well, lets go," Vaughn said, "I have plenty to say."

David Cain stood over Lucus Stone like a brewing volcano ready to erupt. David's large, muscular body shook with rage.

"Take it or leave it," Lucus said, unmoved by David's display of temper.

"The deal was fifty grand." He slammed the envelope on the table. "Not fifteen!" He pressed his palms on the desk and leaned dangerously forward, so close he could smell the coffee on Lucus's breath. "I want the rest of my money, you slimy scum."

Lucus leaned back and chuckled. "Or what?" he asked calmly. "Your information was mediocre at best. I wanted more and you didn't deliver." He pushed the envelope toward David. "All your information is worth is in that envelope."

David straightened. "If you think you're gonna screw me outta what's mine," he smiled menacingly, "then you've finally tangled with the wrong guy."

Lucus leaned forward. His blue eyes darkened. "Don't ever threaten me, Cain. You don't have what it takes. Now, if you'd been able to pull off a coup like Justin Montgomery, you might be worth the other thirty-five thousand." He chuckled and shook his head. "This is rich. I wish I could've thought of it. Now things are really going to get interesting. I'm anxious to see what she has to say at her press conference today." He chuckled again.

David's anger slowly dissipated and was replace by incredulity. He was sure that Lucus was in some way responsible for Montgomery entering the race. If he wasn't, then who was?

"Take the money," Lucus said in his most patronizing tone. "We used your information and now our association is over. I'm sure that there's plenty you can do with fifteen thousand dollars."

David mindlessly retrieved the envelope. His thoughts tumbled over one another.

"Now, if you'll excuse me," Lucus said, interrupting David's thoughts, "its almost time for the press conference."

Court was recessed for the day at the noon break. Justin, Sean, and Khendra stepped out into the corridor and were immediately set upon by the press.

"Mr. Montgomery, what do you think Assemblywoman Hamilton will say at her conference today? Do you intend to face her in a formal debate? Why enter now? Are the rumors true about you and Assemblywoman Hamilton? What about the Harrison case?"

Sean and Khendra cut each other a glance. Justin held up his hands to stave off any further questions. "First, I'm in this race . . . because it was the right thing for me to do. As for Assemblywoman Hamilton's press conference, I have no idea what she'll be talking about. My entering the race has no bearing on this trial. Mr. Michaels and Ms. Phillips are more than competent. My participation at this point is strictly as an observer and advisor. Now, if you'll excuse us." He smiled magnanimously. "We'd like to catch the press conference also."

The trio shouldered their way through the reporters and camera crews and sprinted toward their waiting car.

"I sure as hell hope you know what you're doing," Sean said, taking his seat.

Justin stared out of the window as the car sped away. All he could hope for was that it would all be worth it. He loved her enough to sacrifice himself for her. If his actions could protect her from ruin, then he'd deal with the consequences. She had to know deep in her heart that he would never betray her. Everything would work out in the end.

". . . Are you saying that Mr. Montgomery is responsible for the leaks to the press about your campaign?"

"I would never say that," she replied calmly, her meaning clear. "But nothing is beyond speculation at this point."

Justin watched the cold, calculated way she answered the questions, and he was chilled. "How could she? She knows perfectly well that I had nothing to do with those leaks."

"The race is on, as they say. I stand behind my record. It's rather obvious that Mr. Montgomery sought me out in order to glean information for his own benefit . . ."

Justin sat alone in his office, watching the broadcast in silent disbelief. His hurt and shock slowly transformed into anger. He'd put himself on the line for her. He'd been patient. He'd loved her. And now, without ever giving him the benefit of the doubt—the chance to explain—she discarded him like an old pair of shoes.

He switched off the set. He couldn't stand to hear any more. He walked across the room and fixed himself a drink. In one gulp he downed it. If that's the way it was going to go down, then so be it. If she wanted the race "to be on," as she put it, then it was on. Slowly the long-reaching effects of his success in winning this election began to take shape. He'd be in a position to make changes, the kind of changes he'd been struggling to obtain from the sidelines. It wasn't the role he'd envisioned for himself, but it had been thrust upon him. This was the greatest challenge of his life, both personally and professionally. And he was never one to back down from a challenge.

Elliott, too, watched the broadcast from the television built into the wall of his chambers. This was the Vaughn Hamilton he'd raised to be a winner—decisive, strong, eloquent, and determined. This was the fire she needed. It would push her over the top. He smiled. All of his hard work, his dreams, even the years of deceit, would pay off. One day she'd understand that he'd only done it for her. All for her. And she'd thank him. When she stood on the House floor among the great leaders of the country, she'd thank him. And Justin Montgomery would be a forgotten memory.

CHAPTER 24

Chad stuck his head around the corner of the cubicle where Simone was typing some reports.

"Hi."

She swiveled her chair around and smiled. "Hi, yourself."

"How long are you planning on staying tonight?"

Simone glanced at her watch. It was after four. "I should be finished in about an hour." Her response held a note of expectation.

Chad stepped in and pushed his hands into his pockets. His subtle scent floated to her, making her feel warm and anxious inside. "I was thinking maybe we could get something to eat . . . later . . . after work."

Simone grinned. "Sounds good. Should I meet you out front?"

"Yeah. I'll be downstairs, say . . . five-thirty." He turned to leave.

"Rush?"

"Hmmm?"

"Did you see the press conference today?"

"Yes," he answered heavily. "I can't believe she said those things about Justin."

Simone folded her hands in front of her. "Neither can I. But then again, who knew that Mr. Montgomery was going to run for election?" she asked, still mystified by the strange twist of events.

"You have a point there. But I'm sure he has his reasons. He'll probably be talking to you soon anyway."

"About what?"

He leaned against the frame of the partition. "He's pulling together a small campaign staff. I just came from his office. With me involved with the trial, I suggested that you could probably help out until he pulls some people together."

Her eyes widened. "Really?"

He grinned that lopsided grin that made her stomach flutter. "Yes, really. So try to act surprised. See you in a while," he said with a wave.

No sooner had Chad left than her intercom was buzzed by Barbara.

"Yes, Barbara," she answered.

"Mr. Montgomery would like to see you before you leave, Simone."

"Thank you."

Simone took a quick look in the mirror of her compact. Satisfied, she got up and headed toward Justin's office.

Simone knocked lightly on Justin's office door.

"Come in," he said.

Simone stepped in. "Mr. Montgomery, you wanted to see me?"

Justin looked up and for the first time he made the connection that had been hovering on the fringes of his subconscience, struggling for clarity. All along he'd known there was something deep in Vaughn's past she wanted to hide. Her reaction to meeting Simone, her confession about Brian Willis, her father's hold over her. All of these thoughts raced through his head at once.

Now he understood why she was so reluctant to get involved with him—a man who publically advocated children's rights. She'd gotten pregnant by a powerful man's son, and she and her family hid it for nineteen years. Disbelief gave way to quiet fury. This young, beautiful woman who longed for her identity was the victim of years of deceit. And the woman he loved was a part of it from the beginning.

"Mr. Montgomery?" Simone said softly. "Are you all right?"

Justin blinked, then focused on Simone, and his heart ached for her. He cleared his throat and smiled half-heartedly, "Yes, I'm fine. Lot of things on my mind these days. Come in," he urged. "Sit down. I wanted to talk with you about working on my campaign."

Vaughn sat on the edge of her bed and rubbed her temples. Her entire day, the last few days, seemed like a dream. Less than seventy-two hours ago she'd been on the verge of laying her heart and soul at Justin's feet. She laughed mirthlessly and closed her eyes. Visions of Justin and their lovemaking loomed behind her closed lids. A tremor rippled through her.

What's done is done, she thought decisively. Never again would she give anyone the opportunity to touch her heart. It was her lot, as her father would say. She had a career to think about.

Her bedside phone rang, shattering the stillness of her room. Slowly she reached for the intrusive instrument. "Hello?"

"You were brilliant today, sweetheart," her father said.

"Thank you," she replied, without conviction.

"You showed everyone what you're truly made of. I'm very proud of you. Why don't you come out to the house this weekend? I know your mother would love to see you."

"I don't think so. I have too much to do."

"You're not brooding over Montgomery, are you? Because I tried to warn you. I . . ."

"I know, Daddy. And . . . you were right. But that's behind me now," she added, her voice growing in strength. "I have a campaign to concentrate on."

"Now that's what I wanted to hear. We need to plan another event. Soon."

She didn't want to contemplate another major function. Just the thought of it made her spirits sink. It would only remind her of when she and Justin first met. But she realized that she could no longer let the past paralyze her. "We will," she said finally. "You and Crystal work out the details."

"Good. I'll give her a call next week. Think about coming out for the weekend. You sound like you could use a change of pace."

"I'll think about it. But no promises."

They said their good-byes and Vaughn went to take a shower.

As the water rushed over her, she replayed the conversation with her father over in her head. Thinking back, she noted that he was uncharacteristically benevolent. She'd expected his cynicism, a string of "I told you so's." Her heart began to race. Why was he acting so differently now?

She turned off the shower and stepped out. As she padded back into her bedroom, her thoughts continued to turn to her father's odd behavior. Was it possible that he'd already known what was going to happen? A wave of nausea hit her. She shook her head, trying to push back the dark thoughts that were taking shape in her mind.

CHAPTER 25

Everyone had left the offices of Child-Link hours ago. Melissa was alone. She stared at her computer screen. She didn't know what she'd expected, but it wasn't this. The name flashed incessantly in front of her. *Sheila Rivers-Hamilton.* Simone Rivers was her granddaughter and Vaughn Hamilton was her mother.

It all made sense. Vaughn must have been eighteen or nineteen at the time. She'd been sent to the midwife to have her baby. The only name the infant had been left with was Rivers. Sheila's maiden name.

Melissa sat back and took a deep, shaky breath. What should she do? Simone had every right to know who her natural parents were. But how would the information effect the mother who'd apparently gone on with her life without looking back? Something like this could ruin Vaughn Hamilton professionally.

Melissa pressed the print key and waited until all of the information that she'd gathered printed. She tore off the sheets and stuck them in her purse. For several long moment she stared at the screen. She pressed the escape key and the computer asked if she wanted to save the information. She took a deep breath and pressed *no.*

David flipped through the files in his office and pulled out the folder on Lucus Stone. He tapped it thoughtfully against his palm. He'd been doing a lot of thinking since he'd left Stone's office. It seemed pretty clear that Stone had nothing to do with Montgomery entering the race. Which only left the people in her own party. He wasn't sure who and he really didn't want to know. The whole business was getting ugly, even for him.

He sat down on the edge of his desk and thought back to the days when he'd first met Vaughn. She was fabulous even then. They'd both come a long way since, albeit pursuing different avenues. He'd let his resentment eat away at him like a cancer over the years, never realizing that these feelings stemmed not from his loss of his law pursuits, but from Vaughn seeing him through tainted eyes. That he'd done himself. He was the only one to blame. And his twisted thinking had poisoned every facet of his life, until he was reduced to this—accepting payment for ruining another human being.

Maybe it was finally time that he take stock of himself and try to rectify some of his wrongs.

Vaughn searched through her phone book and found Paul Lawrence's home phone number. She knew that Paul and her father were still close. It never seemed to matter to her father that Paul had used her to reach his position as D.A. All her father saw was a competent, charismatic man that he'd help get into office. The rest be damned.

Paul had said he would help her. She just wondered how far he was willing to go. With her heart in her throat, she dialed his number.

The phone rang four times and she was certain that his machine was coming on. She had no intention of leaving a message and was just about to hang up when he answered.

"Hello?"

"Paul. This is Vaughn."

Paul sat up in bed and rubbed his eyes. A slow sense of dread creeped through his veins as he came fully awake.

"Vaughn you're the last person I expected to hear from."

"Paul I need your help," she stated quickly, sidestepping the small talk. "We need to talk and I need you to be honest with me."

"What is it?" he asked cautiously.

"I need to know if my father is involved with Justin Montgomery entering the race."

Paul shut his eyes and fell back against the pillows. What could he possibly tell her? How could he tell her? He hadn't felt good about this whole mess from the beginning. He wanted no part of it, but Elliott had played his trump card. He knew he owed Elliott a big favor for getting him elected, and he'd repaid him by making that call to Vaughn. He had pretty much known what Elliott was up to all along and he had sat back and done nothing.

"Paul? Did you hear me?"

Paul sighed heavily. "This isn't something to discuss over the phone," he said.

Vaughn's heart began to thunder. "Then where?" she asked as calmly as she could.

"I'll call your office in the morning. We'll arrange a meeting place."

"I'll be in by nine."

As soon as she hung up the phone, it rang. It was Crystal.

"Vaughn, it's me. David was just here."

"What?"

"He left me a folder full of incriminating information about Lucus Stone."

"How . . . I don't understand. When did he get an attack of conscience? And where did he get the information?"

"Apparently he's been getting inside information from Stone's housekeeper, along with sitting in on some under-the-table negotiations. From the little that I've read, Stone is up to his eyeballs in dirt."

Vaughn shook her head. "This certainly puts a new spin on things," she said, still trying to switch her focus from her conversation with Paul to the one at hand.

"What do you want to do?" Crystal asked.

"I'm not sure yet. I don't want to reduce myself to the same level as Stone by throwing more mud in the water." She thought for a minute. "Bring the file to the office tomorrow. I'm meeting with Paul. I'll let him handle it."

"Did you say Paul? You're kidding. Why?"

"I'd rather not talk about it right now."

Crystal pursed her lips and frowned. "Are you sure."

"Positive. I'll see you in the morning. Good night."

Justin had tried to reach Elaine Carlyle for the better part of the morning. He'd been unsuccessful. After talking with Simone the previous evening, he was more determined than ever to help her establish her parentage. His beliefs were strong, but he needed irrefutable proof. Elaine could help him.

The more he thought about the situation, the more enraged he became. His whole perception of Vaughn was distorted. He, of all people, knew the pain of not having one's child, and how important it was for children to know their parents. Vaughn and her family had gone against every principal that he held sacred.

Maybe Vaughn had been young at the time. Maybe her parents did force her to give her child away. But what had she ever done to try to find Simone—to make sure that her child was well taken care of, that Simone was loved? She'd done nothing. She'd hidden behind her father's judicial robes and her guilt for 19 years and never said a word. Her damned career was more important.

The knock on his door roused him out of his dark thoughts.

"Yes. Come in."

"Mr. Montgomery," Simone peeked her head around the door.

"Come in Simone."

"I was just getting ready to leave. Rush—Chad said he'd take me to the Amtrak station."

Justin got up and came around the desk. "When you get to Virginia, take a cab to the county clerk's office. They'll give you a file number for the case and . . ."

"I know," she grinned. "I have everything written down."

He smiled in return at the hint of dimples so reflective of her mother. He cleared his throat. "I'm sorry there's no one around to drive you, but we're swamped."

"I understand. This will be an adventure anyway." She paused. "About the campaign. Will I be working for you here or are you going to set up your headquarters someplace else?"

"Well," he said slowly, "for the time being it'll be easier for me to coordinate everything from here until I can settle a few of these outstanding cases."

She nodded, silently relieved that she would still be able to see Rush every day. "Well, I'd better get going. I still have a few things to take care of before I leave."

"You can just go on home when you're finished. There's no reason to come all the way back to the office."

"Thank you. I'll see you on Monday."

Simone returned to her desk just in time to snatch up her ringing phone.

"Montgomery, Phillips and Michaels," she said cheerfully. "Simone speaking."

"Ms. Rivers? Simone Rivers?"

"Yes," she answered hesitantly.

Melissa breathed in relief "This is Melissa Overton, from Child-Link."

Simone sat down. Her pulse pounded in her ears. "Yes. Have you found out anything?"

"I'm sorry to call you at work, but the only number I had was for your dorm in Atlanta. Your roommate gave me this number."

"That's fine, Melissa. What is it?" she asked in a rush.

"This is going against all of our policies, Simone. I shouldn't be handling it this way. But it's a lot bigger than I anticipated."

"You're scaring me," Simone said in a strained voice.

"I'm sorry. Listen, I've taken the day off. Is there any way that we could meet?"

"What? Why can't you tell me over the phone?"

"It really would be better if we met so that we could talk."

Simone tried to think. "I have to go into Virginia today. I'm getting ready to leave now."

"I can be there in three hours."

"Where should I meet you?"

CHAPTER 26

Vaughn scanned the typed pages of the file that Crystal had given her. Lucus Stone was involved in everything from ballot-tampering to extortion.

She closed the folder and slowly shook her head. It was still hard to believe. Well, she sighed, now she'd see how seriously Paul took his job as District Attorney.

She tucked the folder in her briefcase and prepared to leave. Her stomach seemed to tumble in slow motion every time she thought about her impending meeting with Paul. As much as she wanted him to confirm her suspicions about her father, a part of her didn't want to know that Lucus was capable of going to such lengths. Yet confirmation of her suspicions would vindicate Justin, something she desperately wanted. These past days of living with the thought of his betrayal, being alienated from him and pretending to be strong and indifferent to it all had been an endless trip to hell.

Now, what Paul would say would change the future course of her relationships with the two most important men in her life.

Paul was already seated at the restaurant when she arrived. He stood when he saw her enter, and waved her to his table. As she zig-zagged around the circular tables, she felt her heart thud and her pulse escalate. For an instant she had the juvenile notion to turn around and run. But her legs kept going until she was at the table and Paul was standing behind her, helping her to her seat.

"Do you want to order anything? I just ordered a salad," he said casually, in what Vaughn knew was his attempt to ease the tension.

"Umm, I guess I'll just have iced tea," she said evenly.

Paul signaled the waiter and gave him Vaughn's order. Once the waiter was gone, Paul looked down once at his folded hands and then across at Vaughn. Immediately, the look of regret in his eyes slammed into her. She felt her throat tighten.

She took a breath and tried to smile. "Why don't you just tell me, Paul—everything. I have to know."

He nodded. Then, in a steady, even voice, Paul outlined how her father had coerced Justin into running against her, and how Elliott made Justin believe that if he didn't, damaging information about Vaughn would be released.

"Why? Why?" Her face was tight with incredulity. "What purpose would it serve for Justin to run against me? My father wanted *me* to win the election."

Paul breathed heavily. He stretched his hand across the table and placed it atop both of hers. Her hands felt like blocks of ice and he tightened his hold. He looked steadily into her eyes and knew that Vaughn could handle anything he told her.

"Vaughn, your father is a man whose power and influence has—has twisted him. Your father intended to control you, always. He wanted you to be so hurt and enraged by Justin's defection that you would throw yourself entirely into the campaign." And that's exactly what she had done, she thought morosely. Paul continued, "He believed that Justin was a distraction to his plans for you."

Her eyes were on fire, but she wouldn't cry. "Is that the same thing that happened to us?" she asked quietly. Paul nodded.

She chuckled—a hollow, tortured sound. "What if Justin won the runoff? What would dear daddy have done then?"

"Justin would have been forced to pull out," Paul said slowly. "He never would have been allowed to get that far. And by that time your relationship would have been destroyed."

"Allowed? Destroyed? Dear God what kind of monster is my father?" She pressed her fist to her mouth to keep from screaming.

"Vaughn, I . . ."

"No." She shook her head vehemently. "I'm fine." She leaned over and took the folder from her briefcase. "Here." She slapped it on the tabletop. "I'm sure there's something in there of interest," she said woodenly. She stood and straightened her shoulders. "Thank you, Paul, for being honest with me. And as D.A. for the state, I believe that you should begin a thorough investigation into the activities of Judge Elliott Hamilton." She picked up her briefcase and purse, gave Paul a parting look, and walked out of the restaurant.

* * *

If she didn't have a late afternoon meeting she would just keep driving. Her chest heaved in and out as she fought to control the wrenching sobs that shook her body. Her eyes blurred with tears and she swiped them away with the back of her hand.

Justin. Oh, God, Justin. What he'd done for her was something that only a person who truly loved another would do. She had to talk with him. She had to tell him how they'd both been used. She had to tell him how much she loved him and how wrong she was, and beg him to forgive her.

There was a gas station up ahead and she pulled in to use the phone. She dialed Justin's office.

"Montgomery, Phillips and Michaels," Barbara answered crisply.

"Good afternoon. This is Vaughn Hamilton. Is Mr. Montgomery available?"

"No, he isn't," Barbara replied tersely. "He's in court."

"Oh, I see." She took a breath. "Is he expected back at the office?" she plowed on, ignoring the chill that seeped through the phone lines.

"That's hard to say."

Vaughn contained her annoyance. She understood that, under the circumstances, Barbara's distance was deserved. "Thank you," she said finally and hung up the phone. She returned to her car and headed back to her office. She'd see Justin and they'd talk; she was determined.

Elaine had debated long and hard about what she should do. She'd given Melissa specific instructions; all of the information on the Simone Rivers' case was to be channeled to her. This was a situation that she should handle. She'd gathered all of the data that she needed and her suspicions had been confirmed. Vaughn Hamilton was Simone's mother.

She'd wanted to discuss with Melissa a plan of action on how they would proceed, but Melissa had called in sick.

Elaine reached for her phone and dialed Richmond information.

Vaughn returned to work, hoping that she could catch Crystal before she left for the weekend.

"Has Crystal left yet?" Vaughn asked Tess, as she briskly walked down the hall to her office.

"About ten minutes ago. She had that meeting at City Hall."

"Right, I'd completely forgotten." Vaughn opened the door to her office and stepped inside. Moments later her intercom buzzed.

"Yes, Tess," she responded, leaning over the phone.

"There's an Elaine Carlyle on line two."

Vaughn frowned. "Who is she? If it's some committee meeting, tell her she needs to be put on the schedule."

"She says she's from Child-Link and that it's important."

Vaughn's frown deepened and her heart started to race. "Put her through."

Vaughn pressed down the flashing light. "Yes. This is Vaughn Hamilton. May I help you?" she asked, using her professional front, trying to ward off the terror that raced through her.

"I don't know quite how to put this, and I realize the high profile position you're in and what the news of something like this could do . . ."

"Please, Ms. Carlyle," Vaughn interrupted, barely able to contain her growing alarm, "just say whatever it is that's on your mind."

"Very well. Several months ago, a young woman called us requesting that we help her locate her natural parents."

Vaughn could hardly breath. "Yes . . ."

"Well, Ms. Hamilton, we've traced her parentage to you."

A swift heat whipped through Vaughn, making her feel suddenly lightheaded. "You must be mistaken. That's impossible," she whispered, gripping the phone to keep her hand from shaking.

"Ms. Hamilton, believe me, if I weren't 100 percent certain I never would have made this call," Elaine said with assurance. "Under normal circumstances we contact the client first and advise them of our findings." She cleared her throat. "However, in this case, with you being a public figure and running for office, I felt that it was best to notify you." She waited for a response but only heard Vaughn's heavy breathing. "Ms. Hamilton, this is highly irregular but if you wish, I can tell my client that you do not wish to be contacted by her. I know this comes as a shock and you probably need time to digest it all and think it over. Let me give you my number and you can call me with your decision on Monday."

Vaughn mechanically wrote down the number.

"Ms. Hamilton . . . ?"

"Yes," Vaughn said blankly, "I understand." In a daze she hung up the phone. But once she did, she realized that she'd hadn't asked the woman for the name of the girl who might be her daughter. But deep inside she knew that there was no need. She already knew. And with that came the knowledge of years of deception. Deception so deep and pervasive that acknowledging it crumbled the last remnants of the foundation upon which she'd built her life.

Justin exited the courtroom during the brief recess and went directly to the bank of pay phones down the corridor. Pulling the business card for Child-Link out of his breast pocket he dialed the number. After being kept on hold for several minutes, he heard Elaine Carlyle come on the line.

"Yes, Mr. Montgomery, this is Elaine."

"I want to know what you've found out," he replied without preamble.

Elaine hesitated.

"Well?"

"Mr. Montgomery, all I'm free to say about this case is that you are not Simone Rivers's father."

"That much I've figured out myself," he admitted with regret. He took a deep breath. "Did you find her parents?"

"Yes, we did, but I really . . ."

"Is Vaughn Hamilton Simone's mother?" he demanded. Elaine hesitated a moment too long. "Thank you Elaine, you've just answered my question."

CHAPTER 27

Vaughn went through the mechanics of her meeting. She smiled, nodded, and made all of the appropriate noises in all of the appropriate places. But her mind was racing to the confrontation that was ahead.

The implications of what had been done was enough to swallow her whole. She felt herself sinking into the quicksand of her father's malicious manipulations. But it was over now. It was over.

Mercifully, the meeting concluded, and Vaughn graciously begged off an invitation to accompany the group to dinner. She had to get to Norfolk.

It was already nightfall when Simone walked aimlessly through the streets, clutching the computer pages that spelled out her life.

At first Simone felt a surge of elation when she was told that Vaughn—the woman who she'd admired from afar for years—was her mother. But then the cold reality of her situation loomed before her. Vaughn Hamilton and her family were wealthy and powerful. Vaughn had grown up with the best of everything. Getting pregnant and keeping a baby was an inconvenience, an embarrassment. So the child had been disposed of. Vaughn went on with her life of luxury and privilege, while Simone's foster parents struggled to keep a roof over their heads. But what about the $250,000 in her account? Her foster parents had been vague in their explanation. Was it Vaughn's way of making restitution for the abandonment? Was she only worth $250,000?

The tears started again, flowing heavily down her cheeks. She swore that her heart was breaking. Somehow she found her way back to the station, but she knew she didn't want to be alone. Not tonight. She found a phone and dialed Chad's home number.

"Hello," came the deep voice.

"Rush," she cried. "It's me, Simone."

"Simone." Rush sat up in his chair at the kitchen table instantly alert. "What is it? You sound like you're crying. What happened?"

"Everything. They . . . they found my mother," she cried.

"What?"

"Y-es."

"Simone where are you?"

"I'm at the train station. Can you meet me? My train is boarding."

"Of course. I'll be there."

"Thank you," she sniffed.

"And Simone—everything is gonna be all right. Just keep it together, OK?"

"OK."

The two hour drive seemed endless. As Vaughn drove through the darkened roads, she tried to formulate the words she would say when she confronted her father and mother. As much as she hated to believe it, she knew that her own mother was involved. That hurt most of all.

As she approached the turn onto the property, her heart sped off at an alarming rate. She willed herself to be calm and for several moments she sat motionless in the car, the magnitude of her disbelief rendering her incapable of movement.

Somehow, she called upon the remains of her strength and her determination. She knew that whatever lies were uncovered and laid to rest on the other side of that door, she could handle them.

Clinging to that realization, she got out of the car and rang the bell. Moments later her mother came to the door, exquisitely dressed as usual.

When Sheila saw Vaughn her face lit up, and she stepped across the threshold to embrace her daughter in a tight hug.

"Vaughn, sugah, why didn't you let us know you were coming?" Sheila quickly realized that Vaughn was stiff as a board. She took a step back and assessed her daughter. "What is it?" She put her arm around Vaughn's shoulder and ushered her inside.

"Where's my father?" Vaughn asked stiffly.

"He's in the den. Vaughn, what on earth is wrong?"

Vaughn walked down the hallway past her mother, and pushed open the door to the den, slamming it against the wall.

Elliott scrambled upright in his recliner. "What the . . . ? Vaughn," he sputtered, "have you lost your mind?"

"I thought I would when I received a phone call today," Vaughn said in a voice thick with emotion. She crossed the room in angry strides until she stood above him. "Why did you tell me my baby was dead?" she screamed.

"Oh, my God," Sheila wailed.

"Tell me, damn you! What sick plan could have made you," her voice broke, "tell a young girl, your own child, that her child was dead?" Tears streamed down her face and her body trembled with fury.

"Vaughn, please," he began, his palms turned up in supplication. "You've got to understand that I did what I thought was best. You had a brilliant future ahead of you. I didn't want you to spend the rest of your life wondering—"

"No! You'd rather have me spend the rest of my life suffering and feeling guilty so that I'd continue to do your bidding! Did you know that every year on the date of my daughter's birth I go to a gravesite that I erected in her memory? Did you? Did you? And you were so hell-bent on your plans for me that you used the man that I love against me! Yes," she said venomously, "I know about that too." Then she rounded on her mother, who stood off to the side with her hands covering her mouth.

"And you," she pointed an accusing finger. "You knew all along. My own mother," Vaughn added sadly. "How could you do that to me?"

Sheila took a hesitant step forward. "Vaughn please. I-I didn't know what else to do. He's my husband. I had to stand by him." Sheila's shoulders shook as she wept. "But I kept tabs on her for years. I've been sending money every month so that she would have something."

"Does that somehow excuse you?" Vaughn asked icily.

Sheila shut her eyes and slowly shook her head.

Vaughn turned away, unable to bear the sight of either of them.

"Vaughn," her father said quietly, "I was on the verge of a promising career. Word of your illegitimate pregnancy by the son of the former D.A. would have been disastrous for everyone."

"Are you saying that Senator Willis was a part of this as well?" Vaughn asked, her disbelief kindled anew.

"Yes," he muttered.

"Where does it end?" she screamed. "Where? How far are you willing to go with your twisted plans for me?" Vaughn took a deep, steadying breath. "I think you should know," she said with an eerie calm, "that I've suggested to Paul Lawrence to begin a full investigation of you and your activities. My advice, since you're so concerned with scandal, is to submit your resignation the first thing Monday morning. And if I ever lay eyes on either of you again in this lifetime, it will be too soon."

With that, she turned and ran from the room, ignoring her mother's frantic appeals.

* * *

Vaughn sat on the edge of her couch, staring sightlessly at the television, emotionally and physically spent. The scene with her parents played relentlessly in her mind. She wanted to talk to Justin. She needed to see Simone. But how could she ever find the words to explain the treachery that had colored their lives?

Somewhere on the fringes of her conscience, she heard a ringing. She tried to ignore it, but the insistent sound drew her to the door. She pulled the door open and Justin stood before her startled eyes.

CHAPTER 28

"Justin," she cried in astonished relief. Before he could react or respond, she flung herself into his arms, clinging. to him like a life preserver. "Oh, Justin, Justin," she moaned over and over again. "My child, my baby, she's alive! I'm so sorry . . . they . . . they . . . my father . . . he used you," she rambled on hysterically. "I should have told you everything, but . . . I was ashamed . . . afraid. . . . Oh Justin, please forgive me . . ."

All of the anger, hurt, and disappointment that he'd erected inside of himself slowly ebbed and flowed out of his body. She hadn't known, he realized, relief surging through him. She hadn't known.

Like a man who'd been lost at sea, he grabbed hungrily at the hand she offered and wrapped her fiercely in his arms.

He kissed her hair, her cheeks, her eyes, whispering soothing sounds in her ear. "It's all right now," he cooed. "It's all right." He pushed the door closed and, holding her snugly against him, they walked into the living room to the couch.

Holding her shaky body securely next to his, he gently stroked her hair as he listened in pained silence to her halting story of her father's cruelty.

"I thought the worst," he said. "I thought you knew all along that your child was alive somewhere, and that you'd erased her from your life. I didn't want to believe that the woman I loved could be so cold."

She looked up at him through glistening eyes. "Do you still love me?" she asked, hesitantly.

He cupped her face in his hands and looked deeply into her eyes. "I'll always love you, Vaughn. More and more with each passing day." His eyes flickered over her face and then, slowly, he lowered his head until his lips were a mere breath away from hers. "Always," he whispered.

His moist, full lips touched down on her, feather-light and sweet, and Vaughn's spirits soared to the heavens. Their mouths melted together. Their tongues taunted and danced with each other's.

Justin pulled her closer, his strong fingers kneading the last strains of doubt and tension out of her slender frame.

Vaughn's shaky fingers fumbled with the buttons of his shirt, popping some in the process. Her body was suddenly on fire and she knew that only he could put out the flames. She practically ripped his shirt from his broad shoulders, exposing the smooth dark flesh.

She pressed her lips to the warm skin and flicked her tongue across his nipples, hardening them. Justin moaned raggedly when his hands cupped her breasts and squeezed them until she cried out in delight.

Suddenly, she pulled away and stood up. Slowly, provocatively she stripped out of her clothing until she was bare and beautiful before him.

Justin reached out and ran his finger across the blade-thin scar that ran the width of her pelvis. Their eyes met, and in them was a silent understanding and an acceptance that this was not a mark of sin, but a badge of honor.

She took his hand and pulled him to his feet, unfastened his pants, and pulled them and his briefs over his slim hips. His arousal was boldly evident, his erection seemed to throb for her touch.

Vaughn took him in her hand and steadily stroked him until his knees became weak with wanting. He snatched her hand away and slid his fingers into the dark, wet triangle between her legs.

Air pushed from her lungs in a gasp and she clutched him for support. Slowly, he lowered her to the floor and braced his weight above her on his arms.

"I've missed you," he said softly. "We're never going to be apart again." He spread her thighs with a sweep of his knee and rested his weight atop her. He pushed her thighs upward until her knees rested against his shoulders, allowing him the deepest entry.

His eyes grazed over her face and his mouth came down on hers smothering her cries as he plunged deep within her honey-coated walls.

Vaughn's body instantly arched in response, wanting every inch of him to fill her. She rocked her hips, urging him on, calling his name, telling him how he made her feel.

He took his time. Slow, deep, and steady was each rapturous thrust. He wanted her to know without question the depth of his feelings for her.

This act, this thing that was called making love, would forever seal them as one. Together they renewed their ceaseless love for each other, created a new foundation upon which the rest of their lives would be built. They banished doubt, erased secrets, and opened their hearts to the beautiful power of their mutual love.

When Justin felt the impending surge of her climax building deep within her womb, he knew that their release would transcend the physical, and transport them to a plateau where only those who have tasted magic could go.

Hours later, nestled in each other's arms, Justin and Vaughn tried to figure out the best way to tell Simone.

"She may find out sooner than you plan to tell her," Justin said as he stroked her bare back.

"But I want to be the one to tell her, not someone from the foundation. The woman said that she'd give me until Monday."

Justin peered at the television humming in the background, and saw that the ten o'clock news was on. "She should be back by now. I sent her into Virginia today to file some papers. If Rush hasn't spirited her away somewhere, she should be home," he chuckled.

Vaughn was silent for a long moment. "Hey, are you all right?" he asked.

"It's just that I'm wondering what kind of mother I'll be. Will she even accept me now? I mean, she's had two people who have been parents to her for nineteen years, and now here I come."

Justin hugged her tighter and kissed the top of her head. "I think you'll make a wonderful mother," he said sincerely. "And once you explain to Simone what happened, I think she'll understand. After all, she's been looking for you, too. We'll just have to deal with it."

She smiled up at him and touched a finger to his lips. "I like the sound of 'we,'." she said softly.

He returned her smile. "So do I, baby. So do I."

Justin leaned back and stretched, then a flurry of activity on the screen caught his attention. He pushed himself up on his elbow and reached for the remote to increase the volume.

"What?" Vaughn asked dreamily.

Justin angled his chin toward the television as the newscaster's voice filled the room.

". . . . several hours ago, *The Independent,* an Amtrak train, derailed just outside of Richmond . . ."

Vaughn clutched Justin's arm. ". . . Investigators speculate that track trouble caused the derailment. Three passengers are dead, including the motorman, and hundreds more are injured."

"Oh my God," Vaughn cried from beneath her hand.

". . . among the injured were several notables, including Senator Markam's aide, who was on tour along with some members of his staff, and also Simone Rivers, the assistant of congressional candidate, Justin Montgomery. . . . The condition of the survivors is undetermined at this point. The injured have been taken to neighboring hospitals."

"No. No. This can't be happening," Vaughn screamed. She jumped up from the floor. "I won't lose her, not now. I've got to get to her. I've got to . . ."

Justin grabbed her shoulders and gently shook her. "Calm down," he ordered. "We don't know how bad it is. She's a survivor, remember?" He looked down into Vaughn's eyes, willing her to calm down. "First things first. Get dressed, and I'll start making some calls and try to find out where they've taken her."

Vaughn nodded numbly. "Go," he said.

Justin snatched up his discarded clothing and started to get dressed. He tried calling Chad but got no answer. More than likely Chad was to meet Simone at the station. Then an idea occurred to him. Maybe Chad had the presence of mind to leave a message for him at home or on his voice mail at the office. He tried his home first and hit paydirt.

Chad had left a rushed message saying that Simone had been hurt. She was unconscious and taken to Memorial Hospital. Apparently, Chad had been the one who'd identified her and that was how the media got her name. Thank heavens for that, Justin thought, as he sprinted to the bedroom.

"She's at Memorial," he said quickly, stuffing his shirt into his pants. "We can be there in a half hour."

Her eyes flashed with hundreds of unasked questions.

"We won't know until we get there," he said on a breath.

By the time Justin and Vaughn arrived at the hospital, the corridor was teeming with reporters. One eagle-eyed journalist recognized them and shouted out their names. In an instant they were surrounded by cameras and microphones.

"Mr. Montgomery has there been any news on your assistant?" Justin tried to push his way through. He put his arm around Vaughn's waist and urged her forward. "Why are the two of you here together? Ms. Hamilton, Ms. Hamilton, why are you here tonight?"

Vaughn stopped in mid-step and turned to face the news-hungry crowd. "I'm here to see my daughter," she answered simply.

Flashbulbs went off, nearly blinding them as a surge of garbled questions were hurled at Vaughn.

Vaughn turned into Justin's arms and hurried down the long corridor.

CHAPTER 29

Simone drifted, weightless in a dark corner of her mind where everything was peaceful. Sudden images of her meeting with Melissa intruded and her head began to pound. If she woke up she would have to face the reality of her situation. Sleep, deep and peaceful, was better.

But somewhere far off, someone kept calling her name. Why was anyone bothering her? She just wanted to sleep.

"Come on Simone. You can do it. It's time to wake up now," the gentle voice coaxed.

Slowly her eyes flickered open, then quickly closed against the light and the pounding in her head. She moaned softly.

"She's coming around," the doctor said.

Cautiously, Vaughn stepped up to the bedside. "Simone," she called gently. She took Simone's limp hand in hers, and her heart constricted in her chest. "Simone wake up sweetheart."

Simone had heard that voice before. Her head pounded fiercely. Slowly, she opened her eyes again and tried to focus against the pain.

Her dark, sable eyes settled on Vaughn's face. "Go away," she croaked. "You didn't . . . want me . . . before. There's no reason to be . . . concerned now. You won't use me . . . to make you look good for . . . your campaign." She shut her eyes and her chest heaved with the effort of her talking.

"It's not what you think, Simone," Vaughn said slowly, holding her hand tighter and mildly encouraged by the fact that Simone didn't pull away. Vaughn gently stroked Simone's bandaged head.

"You don't have to talk. But please listen. There's so much I want to tell you."

Justin came up and stood beside Vaughn as she methodically recanted all of the events that had led up to this reunion.

From beneath closed lids, tears squeezed from Simone's eyes.

The next morning, with the press assembled in the conference room of Vaughn's offices, she made the most memorable statement of her career.

"Ladies and gentlemen, many years ago," she began slowly, "I had a child, who I believed was put up for adoption and then subsequently died." She took a breath and cleared her throat, looking steadily at the cameras and intense faces.

"It was less than 48 hours ago that I found out that none of that was true. My daughter is very much alive. I've always been a staunch supporter of women's rights, and my change in stature from single woman to single mother does not take away from my convictions. I intend to join Mr. Montgomery in his fight to set up organizations where families *can* be reunited." She paused. "And now I'll take your questions . . ."

Simone remained in the hospital for a week, and Justin and Vaughn were there every day. At first, Simone's relationship with Vaughn was cautious, but a genuine warmth and sense of trust steadily built between them. Vaughn had an opportunity to meet the Clarkes, and she was relieved in the knowledge that her daughter had been cared for by such truly loving people.

Vaughn was at Simone's bedside on the day of her release.

"I'd like it very much if you'd stay with me for a while . . ." Vaughn hedged. "If you want to."

Simone turned to her and smiled. "I think I want to very much."

Vaughn grinned. "I hope you won't mind having to wear dark glasses and a floppy hat."

Simone looked at her quizzically. "Why?"

"It seems that I'm in every paper and tabloid across the state these days. I usually have to sneak out of my back door just to get to the store."

"Is it because of the election?"

"Partly. And also because I've admitted to the press that I was a teenage mother."

"What will that do to your chances to get elected?"

Vaughn placed the last of Simone's belongings into the suitcase and looked up. "Since Justin dropped out, and Lucus Stone is under investigation," she shrugged her shoulders, "who knows? All of the women's rights advocates are supporting me, and there's been talk that Stone will be replaced. Whatever happens, I'm going to be spending some time learning how to be a mother."

Simone's smile was full. "It's really not hard you know. All you have to do is say yes to everything I ask you!"

"Right. You must be feeling better. Let's go."

Vaughn snuggled closer to Justin in the quiet of her bedroom, while Simone slept down the hall.

"I think everything is going to work out," she said quietly.

"So do I," he whispered back. "I know it's not going to be easy, but we have each other."

She sighed. "Maybe in time I'll even find it in my heart to forgive my parents. My father is a broken man since his resignation, and I know my mother is suffering. She believed she was doing the right thing and she did try to do what she could for Simone. She even gave Simone her maiden name."

"Maybe we should pay them a visit," Justin said softly. "And give them the opportunity to meet their beautiful granddaughter. Her paternal grandfather should meet her also. It'll be good for their souls."

Vaughn looked up at him. "That's why I love you," she grinned. "Justin, what do you plan to do about finding Samantha?"

"I have no intention of giving up. I just believe deep in my heart that I'll find her one day."

"I was hoping that you'd say that. We'll work on it together. Now that Sean and Khendra are running the practice, more or less, you have some time and since I'll be having some time on my hands . . ."

He looked at her curiously. "Time? Woman, with all that you have to do with the election just weeks away, where are you going to find time?"

"Well," she grinned wickedly. "I was hoping that you'd make an honest woman out of me. I'd hate to be the first pregnant congresswoman without a husband. Now that would be a scandal."

Justin bolted up in the bed. "What?" His eyes raced up and down her body. She smiled and nodded her head. "That's what happens when you don't take precautions," she whispered.

Gently, he placed his hand on her flat belly. "Really?"

"Really."

His look softened and he felt his insides tighten with joy. "I love you, woman," he said in awe.

"Why don'tcha come a little closer and show me just how much, big boy," she crooned in her best Mae West voice.

And he did.

EPILOGUE

The week before Vaughn won her congressional bid in a landslide, she and Justin were married in a quiet, private ceremony with Simone and Chad, Khendra and Sean, Crystal and her new beau, and Vaughn's parents. Her relationship with her parents was still strained, but the healing had begun.

Several weeks later, Justin filed papers to formally adopt Simone and she happily changed her name to Montgomery.

Although the small ceremony didn't make the national news, it did appear in the society section of a local paper in Georgia.

Samantha read the article and then carefully tucked it away with the others that she'd stumbled upon in the attic. The articles that her mother had been keeping from her for years. She put the last of her clothes in her small suitcase, checked her purse for identification and her money, and went downstairs.

Janice stood when Samantha walked into the room. She bit down on her lip to keep it from trembling.

"I'm ready," Samantha said, not wanting to meet her mother's pain-filled eyes.

"Are you sure this is what you want to do?" her mother asked in a tremulous voice.

"I have to."

Janice nodded and walked her to the door.

"My cab is here," Samantha said slowly.

Janice grabbed her daughter in her arms and hugged tightly. "I'm so sorry. I should have told you about your father a long time ago. One day I hope you'll find it in your heart to forgive me. I was so young and foolish and . . ."

Samantha blinked back her tears and slipped out of her mother's arms. "I'll call you," she said, and turned away.

"Tell your father that I'm sorry," Janice whispered.

When Samantha reached the airport, she checked her luggage and crossed the terminal to the bank of phones. With shaky fingers, she dug into her purse and pulled out the crumpled piece of paper that had her father's office number scribbled on it. She dialed.

Samantha held her breath as she waited for the phone to be answered.

"Montgomery, Phillips and Michaels," came the crisp voice.

"Mr. Montgomery, please," Samantha responded quickly.

"Please hold."

Moments later, the voice that she'd imagined only in her dreams filled her ears.

"Justin Montgomery."

"Daddy . . . it's Samantha . . ."

Deception

This novel is dedicated in loving memory of my grandmothers:
Clotilda Braithwaite and Mary Hill.
You both are always with me.

ACKNOWLEDGMENTS

I would like to extend my heartfelt thanks to my loving family, my friends, and fans who have been so supportive of me over the years and continue to give me encouragement. To the love of my life, who is the inspiration for all of my heroes! To my aunt Marjorie, who instilled in me a love of books and reading. I would also like to thank Sandra Kitt, who convinced me that revisions weren't as bad as they seemed and always has words of wisdom to share with me. To my dear friend and mentor, Nathasha Brooks, who published my very first short story. And many thanks to my editor, Monica Harris, who continues to believe in me and all that I do.

PROLOGUE

"Oh what a tangled web we weave,
when first we practice to deceive."

—Sir Walter Scott, *Marmion* (1808) stanza 17

"Just stay calm. Getting all worked up isn't going to solve anything," Terri muttered to her reflection as she partially wrapped her shoulder-length dreadlocks atop her head. Cool brown eyes stared back at her, revealing none of the turmoil that had precipitated her three-month leave of absence from her self-named corporation.

To look at thirty-year-old Terri Powers, no one would imagine what the past two years had done to her. Her New York–based public relations and advertising company had skyrocketed since its inception five years ago. With a minimal staff she had almost carried the company single-handedly. Because of that, she would always blame herself for the miscarriage of her baby. That trauma was compounded by the disintegration of her four-year marriage to photographer, Alan Martin.

She took a breath and slipped long silver earrings into her lobes. The reality was, her marriage to the flamboyant Alan Martin was over long before the divorce. She'd just been unwilling to see it. She and Alan were a disaster waiting to happen. Even now she questioned her attraction to him. She'd been young, eager for love, and eager to have someone love her back. She had been captivated by his charm, his vision and exuberance. His looks and his blatant sexuality only added to the total facade. So much so that she overlooked and made excuses for his flaws—which, she finally had to admit, were too numerous to mention. Her collapsed marriage she'd begun to deal with. The loss of her baby was something else entirely. A topic which she did not discuss with anyone. Losing her baby had resurrected too many painful memories, and her hopes for a family of her own had died with her child. Although her losses were more than a year behind her, the aftereffects had finally taken their toll and drained her spirit over the months. Pretending that everything was wonderful and right with the world took all that she had left, she thought sardonically.

It was to that end that she'd hired her VP, Mark Andrews, at a time when her world seemed to be slipping from beneath her feet. His resume was outstanding. He was charming, had a razor-sharp mind, was exceedingly good looking, and had brilliant ideas for company growth. The fact that he vaguely struck some familiar chord within her only endeared him all the more to her.

Over time, she'd given Mark more and more responsibility as the events of her life and the pressures of the job slowly overwhelmed her. Terri finally realized that for her own good and the good of the company, she needed to take a break. Now it was time to go back and reclaim the reins.

Terri frowned as she lightly coated her bow-shaped lips with a soft orange lipstick. Mark had crossed the line and deliberately ignored her instructions. If it hadn't been for her director of promotions, Stacy Williams, informing her of Mark's activities, the whole deal would have gone down without her knowledge or consent.

As things stood now, her company was in the midst of negotiations with a man that she wouldn't give the time of day. *Clinton Steele.* Everything that she'd ever read about the man set her teeth on edge. He was in the business of buying small African-American companies on the verge of collapse and turning them around for his own profit. From everything that she'd read, he paid the owners nothing near what the companies were worth. He called himself a businessman. Humph! She considered him nothing more than a predator—one whom she would have nothing to do with. To think that he wanted her company to run an ad campaign for him had her head spinning.

Terri strutted down the short foyer and slipped into her heels. Wouldn't they be surprised to see her returning to work three weeks earlier than scheduled. She smiled. If Mark Andrews and Clinton Steele thought that they would be dealing with the Terri who was haunted by her past, they were wrong. This was Terri Powers—new and improved, rested and rejuvenated. And someone had a lot of answering to do.

CHAPTER 1

"Good afternoon, gentlemen."

Sultry was the only word that stroked all of Clint's senses when the distinctly feminine voice, coated with just a hint of a Caribbean accent, pervaded the low rumble of male conversation.

"Terri." Her vice president, Mark Andrews, looked up and rose in greeting as did his client, Clinton Steele. "We were just going over Mr. Steele's proposal," Mark added, slipping back into his discarded charcoal gray suit jacket, in an effort to camouflage his surprise at her unannounced return.

Momentarily, Terri stood in the doorway, taking the moment to assess the man who towered head and shoulders above the six-foot-tall Mark, and was in sharp contrast to Mark's light cocoa complexion.

Clinton Steele's reputation preceded him, and from all appearances he confirmed Terri's image—from the expensive tailor-made suit to the formidable persona. But maybe it was those eyes. They seemed to have a way of mesmerizing you, she thought, feeling herself pulled into the bottomless inky pools that seemed to dance with dangerous lights. But then a flicker of something deeper flashed through those coal black orbs. An involuntary shudder ran up her spine. Then just as quickly the look was gone and replaced with what Terri believed to be condescension.

She'd seen that look before. Most men were either intimidated or mystified by her ethnic appearance, as though she either withheld or could unlock some great ancestral secret. Her shoulders straightened as she walked into the room.

Clint was immediately taken aback by the quiet power Terri exuded. Her shoulder-length, glistening ebony dreadlocks were not what he perceived to be the coiffure of the çosmopolitan woman. Rather hers was the image of a woman awakened to their nubian ancestry and determined to flaunt it in the most exotic of displays. Her obvious sense of cultural pride intrigued, yet put him off, his own sense of roots having been buried beneath years of equal opportunity rhetoric, stirring only periodically into the light.

The instant observation, combined with her cool appraisal of him, rubbed him the wrong way and nudged him off balance. His thick lashes lowered to shield his eyes, and his jaw involuntarily tightened.

Mark moved from around the table and stood between Terri and Clint, breaking through the tension-filled silence.

"Terri Powers, this is Clinton Steele, CEO of Hightower Enterprises."

Clint stretched out his large hand and enveloped Terri's petite one.

"Mr. Steele," Terri responded with a slight incline of her head, observing his perfectly clipped nails.

For one crazy moment Clint wanted to say *"your majesty,"* and he knew that if he opened his mouth, he'd say something equally ridiculous.

As a result he held her hand a moment longer than necessary, and Terri felt the tingling warmth spread through her fingers and glide up her arm. The sensation nearly caused her to snatch her hand away, but her inherent good manners interceded. Slowly she removed her hand, letting it fall casually to her side.

Terri raised her eyes to meet Clint's, and he quickly discovered that they were a fascinating shade of brown that seemed to darken or brighten with the play of light from the window.

"I'll leave the two of you to get acquainted," Mark interjected into the torrid air. "I'll be back shortly, and we can go over the details." He quickly exited the office, leaving Terri and Clint to face each other.

"I understand that we have business to discuss," Terri said, her low melodic voice again caressing him.

He watched her graceful movements as she moved to a leather chair at the head of the long oak conference table. Her sheath of golden linen barely shadowed the curves beneath, Clint realized with a twinge in his loins. He took a seat to Terri's right.

"Mark has informed me that you're interested in using our advertising services to promote your . . . new cable stations, Mr. Steele." She folded her hands in front of her.

Did he detect a note of sarcasm in her voice or was it just his imagination? "That's right." He rubbed a hand across his bearded chin. "Your agency comes highly recommended from everyone here in New York. And from all that Mark has told me, so far, I believe Powers Incorporated will do an excellent job."

Clint leaned back in his seat and boldly surveyed her sculpted mahogany features, letting his eyes drift down her long neck to the tempting vee in the front of her dress.

Terri felt a hot flush spread throughout her body from the intensity of Clint's appraisal. But she would not let his daring looks distract her.

"I'm sure that Mark also told you that I've been out—" she swallowed back the memories "—away for the past three months?" She raised a naturally arched eyebrow in question.

Yes, and what happened to cause that haunted look in your eyes? "He mentioned it."

Why did his voice seem to pump through her like an overactive pulse? "I'm sure what he didn't tell you, Mr. Steele, is that I have very firm beliefs about who I do business with."

The hairs on the back of Clint's neck began to tingle. "Don't we all?"

"In other words, Mr. Steele, I would appreciate it if you took your business elsewhere."

Clint's eyes creased into two dark slits. He leaned dangerously forward and the scent of his cologne raced to Terri's brain, quickening her heartbeat.

His voice lowered to a deep rumble. "Let me get this straight. I've been working my butt off in negotiations with *your* partner—" he pointed an accusing finger at Terri "—and now you're gonna tell me you don't want my business?"

Pure unadulterated anger flared in his black eyes and hardened the velvet voice. "What in the hell is going on around here? Is this some kind of game?"

"Had I been here, Mr. Steele," Terri answered calmly, not intimidated by the vehemence in his voice, "these talks would not have gone beyond the first phone call. Mr. Andrews is well aware of my policies. I'm sure that his . . . oversight was not intentional. However, *my* decision stands."

Terri rose regally from her seat, and Clint had the overwhelming sensation of being dismissed like a common errand boy by this very self-centered, arrogant—

"I'm sorry," Terri said gently, the soft sincerity of those two simple words mysteriously calming his fury. "I'm sure that this inexcusable situation has cost you a great deal of time and energy. I only wish that I could offer more than an apology."

Why did even her refusal sound so pleasant to his ear? "Have you at least looked over the proposal?" Clint found himself inexplicably yearning for her approval. The revelation pissed him off, but he couldn't seem to stop himself. "I'm certain that it will be a great campaign."

"I have looked it over. However, there's—"

"Is it money? You don't think it's adequate?"

Now she *was* annoyed. Why did they all think that money was the answer to everything? What about integrity?

"This has nothing to do with money," Terri answered, forcing a steady calm into her voice. "It wouldn't matter if your offer were ten times the amount. It's you, Mr. Steele, that I have the problem with. You and your business practices. I cannot in good conscience allow this company to be associated with Hightower Enterprises."

Clint felt as if all of the wind had been kicked out of him. All of his work, his sacrifices, his dreams and accomplishments, came to a grinding halt with just those few callous words. Did she have any idea what he'd been through . . . did she . . . ? Slowly he shook his head. Of course she didn't. No one did. That was the way he'd wanted things. Now, for the first time, he was paying for that choice.

Clint rose from his seat, looking at her with a mixture of regret—that she'd fallen prey to the things that had been said about him—and disappointment. He'd begun to look forward to working with this tempting woman against all of his reservations.

Terri held her breath as Clint's powerful body rose and spread before her. His dark blue suit fit the massive shoulders and muscularly long legs to exquisite perfection. She dared to steal a glance at the short wavy black hair that capped his proud head. For one dizzying moment she wondered what it would feel like to run her hands across it.

Had this been any other time . . . other circumstances . . . maybe . . . But she still had wounds to heal, emotions to mend, and unfortunately the darkly handsome Clinton Steele represented everything that she had grown to resent.

Terri extended her hand and the warmth of his grip shot through her again. Steadily her eyes held his.

"Perhaps my director of promotions, Stacy Williams, can give you some referrals, Mr. Steele. I could—"

"Believe me, you've done enough already." He shook his head, looked at her from beneath silken lashes, a sheepish grin tipping his lips. "I mean, I'm sure that I can find another agency."

Terri nodded her head and made a move to turn away. Clint's intentionally intimate tone stopped her.

"Regardless of what you may think of me, Ms. Powers, I still feel that you're the . . . that your agency is the best one for the job. If we can't be business associates, at least let's be friends. You *can* call me Clint."

The radiance of his smile washed over her like morning sunshine. Her heart thumped.

"Thank you for the compliment. However, in reference to your last statement, I must apologize again. Our association ends here, Mr. Steele. Good day."

She turned and walked from the office, leaving a fuming Clint and the heady scent of her *kush* body oil lingering behind.

Stepping out into the corridor, she forced her breathing to slow down to normal. What had happened to her in there? Taking a deep breath, she continued down the hallway, just as Mark left his office, to the conference room. Terri stopped short.

A feeling of disaster spread through him. "How did it go? I think this is one great deal, Terri," he said a bit too enthusiastically.

Terri glared at him. "We'll talk later. Right now I think you'd better soothe Mr. Steele's ruffled feathers. There's no deal, Mark. Understood? When you're through, I'll see you in my office."

She turned on her heel, leaving Mark to throw daggers at her back. She'd screwed him. Damnit!

Quickly Mark made his way down the hallway and rushed into the room just as Clint was putting the last of his notes in his briefcase.

"Clint," Mark began apologetically, spreading his hands in a plea. "I had no idea that she was going to react this way. I can assure you that everything was set," he lied. Actually, he had no idea that she would return to work three weeks early. He'd planned to have this deal signed and sealed before she returned.

Clint threw him a glowering look over his shoulder.

"I just need some time to talk with her," Mark added. "I'm sure I can get her to—"

Clint turned to Mark. "I don't beg for anything, Andrews. Boss lady has her reasons—fine. The hell with her. You should have known better than to waste my time."

"Listen, Clint," Mark implored, grasping at straws, "Terri's just being difficult. She's probably on a hate-all-men campaign. She's recently divorced, and she lost her baby. Today's her first day . . . ?

Mark's voice droned on as Clint absorbed the implications of what was being said. My God, what she'd been through was enough to floor anyone. Yet she'd stood there resolute and determined, only once letting emotion seep through that picture-perfect demeanor. His defenses weakened. How could you not admire a woman like that? He felt that he understood her. He knew all too well about pain and loss. That part of him wanted to soothe away the hurt that still lingered behind those mysterious brown eyes.

The snap of Clint's voice cut off Mark's litany.

"Try to see if you can get Ms. Powers to change her mind, and keep me posted."

Mark hid his surprise behind a wall of conversation. "I won't disappoint you, Clint. This deal is important to me, too." *You just don't know how much.*

Mark's calculating mind went into overdrive. He'd have to pull this off and soon, or . . . No. He refused to think about the possibilities.

"Will you be attending the reception tonight at Tavern on the Green for the producers?" Mark asked.

Clint picked up his briefcase. "I hadn't planned to. Why?"

"Well, I'll talk to Terri again. I'll be escorting her tonight. Maybe she'll be in a more receptive frame of mind," he concluded, giving Clint a sly grin.

Clint pursed his lips, considering what Mark had said. He generally shied away from formal affairs, believing them to be frivolous. But if it gave him the chance to see Terri again, he'd make an exception.

"I never confirmed my invitation," Clint said slowly, "but I don't think it should be a problem."

"Great. So I'll see you tonight."

Clint reluctantly shook Mark's hand and strode purposefully from the conference room.

There was one thing that bugged Clint more than anything else—a *brownnose.* And Mark Andrews fit the bill, he thought, as he waited for the elevator. But there was something else about Mark that disturbed him. He just couldn't put his finger on it. At least not yet. But he would. Maybe he'd just let Steve check him out.

Terri plopped down onto the overstuffed, cream-colored couch that stood against the far wall of her office. Waves of apprehension swept through her. She wasn't sure if what she was feeling was the stress of first-day jitters or the eruption of buried feelings that Clinton Steele had inadvertently dug up.

Adrenaline pumped through her limbs, forcing her body into action. She sprang up from her seat and paced the floor, crossing and recrossing the earthtone print area rug covering the parquet floor. Absently she stroked the polished wooden artwork and the array of greenery that adorned strategic locations throughout the tropiclike office.

Clinton Steel disturbed her. There was no other word for it. Without effort, he'd made her think and feel things that she'd promised herself she'd never fall prey to again. Her husband, Alan, had been enough.

Terri shut her eyes and wrapped her slender arms around her waist as if to ward off some unseen attacker, momentarily reliving the months of agony. The knocking on her office door jarred her back to the present.

She spun toward the door, blinking back the visions to focus on Mark standing in the doorway.

She cleared her throat. "Mark. Come in." She took a seat behind her desk.

"I think you're making a big mistake here, Terri," Mark began as he crossed the room and sat down, handing her a stack of documents to be signed.

She gave them a cursory glance and turned her attention back to Mark. "You know perfectly well how I feel about Hightower Enterprises."

"Your opinion is archaic!" he snapped. "You left me in charge, and I've been doing a damn good job of running things around here. At least give me the courtesy of believing that I know what I'm doing. Do you honestly think that you can get anywhere in this world being a Goody Two-shoes? Be for real, Terri."

Slowly she rose from her seat, her anger shielded behind her veil of serenity.

"You seem to have forgotten that this company is where it is today because we have values—whether you believe them to be legitimate or not." Her eyes locked onto him.

Mark heaved a sigh and ran a finger around his shirt collar. Alienating her was not the answer. "Listen," he said, forcing calm into his voice, "at least think about it. Three million dollars is nothing to sneeze at. Maybe this one time we could make an exception."

"I doubt it. But I will give the proposal the benefit of another look."

Mark's hopes lifted. "That's all I ask." He headed for the door, then paused. "Do you still want me to pick you up this evening?"

"What? Oh, I'd almost forgotten. Yes, thanks. Is eight o'clock good?"

"I'll be there," he said, opening the door.

Watching his hasty departure, Terri realized that something was very wrong.

The swish of Terri's black satin and chiffon gown blended delicately with the soft music and laughter that wafted from the ballroom.

Mark, clad in an elegant-fitting tuxedo, dutifully took Terri's elbow and escorted her down the carpeted corridor of Tavern on the Green. Stopping briefly to check Terri's stole, there were many who gave them a second look as the two made their way down the hall.

Bowing his close-cropped curly head, Mark whispered in Terri's diamond-studded ear, "Are you ready for your grand entrance?"

"No way," she whispered back as they neared the open ballroom. "And don't you dare leave me, Mark Andrews," she threatened. "You know how self-conscious I get in crowds. You're going to take your share of wet kisses and damp handshakes like a man," she teased.

"Thanks, I can't wait," he answered drolly, rubbing his index finger across his mustache.

At the entrance Terri was awestruck and took a moment to absorb the magnificence of the glittering room. Crystal chandeliers, lit by hundreds of candles, gave the room a dramatic, effervescent shimmer. The round dinner tables were covered with gold linen tablecloths, and crystal goblets stood as the centerpieces. The enormous buffet table was laden with every delicacy imaginable, the aromas taunting the senses.

The main ballroom opened out onto two huge rooms that led to enclosed balconies, giving a sweeping view of New York City. Complementing it all was the array of designer gowns and tuxedos that moved with the wearers like a second skin.

Mark felt Terri momentarily stiffen as the patrons turned to look at them as they stood in the archway. He gave the hand that held his arm an encouraging pat.

"Are you ready?"

Terri gave a tiny nod. Taking deep breaths and putting on their best smiles, they made their entrance.

Within moments Terri was separated from Mark and swept up in a flurry of greetings. Between hugs, handshakes, and rapid-fire conversation, Terri tried to peer over the sea of heads to locate Mark.

Finally she spotted him on the far side of the crowded ballroom, apparently in deep conversation with a striking-looking woman.

With her hopes of imminent rescue dashed, she continued to make conversation and field questions about her next endeavor.

"So, what's next, Ms. Powers?" asked Gordon Burke of Columbia Studios.

"This current project with the McPhearson Group and the networks will take up a great deal of time and energy," Terri confessed. "But I do have some proposals that have been submitted for our consideration."

"Would you care to elaborate?" asked a reporter from the *Times.*

"I don't think that would be fair to my prospective clients," she said, flashing an indulgent smile. She knew when she was being put on the spot, and her standard response was always a sure out.

Then, out of the corner of her eye, she saw that Mark was finally standing alone. Seeing a way out from the probing questions, she made her excuses.

"If you all will excuse me—" she lifted her chin in the direction of Mark "—I see my partner over there." She made her getaway, breathing a sigh of relief.

Shaking a few hands and giving smiles of acknowledgment along the way, she eventually made it across the packed room, only to be greeted by a look of pure enjoyment from Mark.

"You think this is all very funny, don't you?" Terri asked, twisting her full lips.

Mark smiled broadly. "Why, of course. Where else could a single man have the opportunity to be entertained by so many fabulous single women?"

"You are behaving yourself, aren't you, Mark Andrews?" she warned with a sparkle in her nut-brown eyes.

"That all depends on what you mean by behaving." He grinned and took a sip from his wineglass and wondered where Clint was.

Terri tapped Mark playfully on the arm while walking around him to the buffet table.

* * *

On the far side of the room, Clint made his entrance, accompanied by his vice president, Melissa Taylor. His six-foot-plus height cut an exquisite figure, bedecked in a black *Armani* tuxedo.

His arrival instantly caught Terri's attention, and an inexplicable heat rushed through her body. Her eyes were drawn to him like a magnet, totally oblivious to the shimmering female form that stood at his side. Terri quickly looked away. When she furtively looked back in his direction, she was shocked, yet thrilled, to find that his eyes were locked on her, openly assessing her, even as his stunning companion clung possessively to his arm.

He gave an almost unnoticeable nod of acknowledgment in her direction.

Flustered by the intensity of his stare, she nodded back and silently prayed that she wouldn't humiliate herself by dropping her food all over the thick carpet.

Holding on tightly to her plate, and with as much grace as she could summon, she walked across the room to her table, not daring to look back. Yet somehow she felt those warm eyes burning through her exposed back.

Clint had zeroed in on Terri almost immediately, and he couldn't help but admire the way the black gown seemed to float over her slender body. Or how her deep brown skin glowed radiantly, tantalizing the viewer with teasing peeks of bare flesh as the dress flowed with her movements.

He had an almost uncontrollable desire to run his fingers through the locks of ebony hair which she'd wrapped magnificently on top of her head. Unconsciously he squeezed his companion's arm to stifle the urge to touch her. There was no way that he could deny the instantaneous attraction he felt toward Terri. The powerful sensation unnerved him. She wasn't like any woman he'd ever known. He'd always been attracted to women like his wife, Desiree. Women who were needy, women who . . . Desiree is dead, he reminded himself. And it was his fault.

"Is something wrong?" Melissa asked, sensing the change in Clint's mood.

"No. Nothing's wrong," he answered offhandedly as they moved into the center of the room.

Melissa cut her eyes across the room to where Clint's gaze rested, then back to him in time to catch the look of longing in his eyes. "Why don't we find a table and get something to eat? I'm starved," Melissa said, a bit put off.

"You go ahead. I'll catch up with you later. There are a few old friends that I want to speak with first."

He gently eased her arm from his and crossed the floor, quickly engaging himself in a group discussion before she had a chance to protest.

For several moments Melissa stood alone, disappointed. Her hope of spending an elegant evening with Clint dissolved. But it was rare that she allowed her true feeling to show. And right now she needed something to soothe her injured ego. Putting on a practiced smile, she straightened her bare shoulders and began to do what was second nature—making men's heads turn.

Terri made a valiant effort to focus on the food in front of her while keeping up with the conversations of the movie executives that flowed abundantly. But her mind kept wandering back to Clint. What was he doing here? She dared not ask her dining companions, knowing that her true interests would be obvious. Perhaps she would have a chance to find out before—

"Would you care to dance?"

The rich rumble of the voice seemed to shimmer down her spine and arrest her heart. Instinctively she knew it was him and was almost afraid to look up. But the large warm hand gently held her shoulder, and a surge of heat swam to her head, clouding her judgment.

She turned to look up at him and the most devastating smile assaulted her, causing her breath to catch in her throat.

Terri felt hypnotized by the intensity of his dark, heated gaze. She didn't know whether or not she had even answered him before she was gently eased onto the dance floor. In a matter of seconds her body was pressed next to his as he artfully moved with the slow, pulsing music of the band.

The scent of his cologne enveloped her senses, and she felt an overwhelming urge to snuggle closer to the hard lines of his broad frame. Their bodies seemed to fit perfectly together, like pieces of a puzzle, each dip and curve matching the other, she mused. How long had it been since she'd been held in a man's arms?

Why did she have to feel so good? Clint wondered, his mind running in circles as he held her slender waist in one hand. He wanted to pull her fully against him, but dared not. He was sure that his untimely arousal would be evident.

The music drew to a conclusion, but he continued to hold her, searching for something to say, not yet ready to let her go.

She looked inquisitively up at him, a tentative smile lighting her face.

Finally he found his voice. "Can I get you something from the bar?"

"A glass of tonic water with lime would be perfect."

The melodic cadence of her voice floated to his ears. It almost didn't matter what she said as long as she would continue talking.

He placed his hand on the small of her back and ushered her toward the bar. "Two tonic waters with lime," he instructed the bartender, his eyes never leaving Terri's face.

Clint handed her the glass. "So we meet again," he stated, his eyes boring into hers.

"I wasn't aware that you would be attending."

"It was a last-minute decision." He took a sip of his drink, and his voice dipped intimately. "You look fabulous."

Terri lowered her eyes at the unabashed compliment.

"I hope there won't be any acceptance speeches tonight," he added, rescuing her from her apparent uneasiness.

"No," she breathed, thankful for the change in topic, "not tonight. This is more of a who's who gathering than anything else, Mr. Steele."

He looked at her for a long moment. "My friends call me Clint. I wish you would."

"You seem to have a lot of those," she commented.

He grinned slyly, his eyebrow lifting. "I didn't think you noticed."

A hot flush of embarrassment seared her cheeks.

"Don't be uncomfortable," he said smoothly as though reading her mind. "I've been watching you, too." His eyes trailed over her curvaceous form, and she felt her heart begin to race.

"So where is your escort—boyfriend . . . husband?" he probed in the hope that she would reveal or confirm what Mark had said.

Terri smiled, melting Clint's heart. "Sorry, none of the above. I came with Mark, who seems to have vanished. What about you? I thought I saw you with someone earlier."

He knew good and well that she saw him, but he was more than happy to play along. At least there were no stray boyfriends or husbands to contend with. "That was *my* business associate, Melissa Taylor, who seems to have made quite an impression on Mark."

Terri followed Clint's gaze across the room to see Mark and Melissa laughing intimately.

"Mark does have a way with women," she stated, a wry smile tilting her lips.

"Let's dance," Clint suggested in a low, urgent voice, taking her hand before she could deny him.

"I catch a faint accent in your voice," Clint whispered in her ear as they moved easily across the dance floor. "It's absolutely delicious."

Terri's pulse fluttered. "Barbados," she answered softly.

"Hmmm," he hummed into her hair. "Don't ever lose it."

The hours seemed to float away as Terri and Clint became enamored of each other's company. They talked of the places that they had traveled, the current economy and its effects on business. But whenever Terri directed questions to Clint about his line of work, he was subtly evasive.

"Let's not talk about work." He looked deep into her eyes. "Not tonight. I'd rather hear about you."

"There's really not that much to tell," she breathed as they walked side by side out to the balcony. "I came to the States when I was eight. I went to New York University and studied advertising and public relations. My business has been in existence for five years. That's basically all there is."

"I find that hard to believe. There has to be some life behind all of those facts and figures." He smiled encouragingly at her.

Terri stiffened. "I suppose there is," she said softly, "but I don't care to discuss it." She turned her head toward the skyline, wishing that the pain would somehow go away.

He raised a hand to touch her, wanting her to know that he'd be willing to listen, but he knew that she wouldn't give in. At least not yet.

"I know we got off to a bad start this afternoon," he began, pacing his words and her reaction. "I'd like the opportunity to change that."

Terri turned to him, the haunted look in her eyes stunning him with its intensity. She absently ran her hands down the sides of her gown, and Clint's insides went haywire with the motion. He forced himself to look at her eyes instead of those delicious hips.

"I have no idea what you mean."

"I mean," he said, taking a step closer, "I want you to see the real me."

"Why would that be important?"

"Because it's important to me," he stated simply.

Terri swallowed and placed her hand on the balcony railing. She looked at him from the corner of her eye. "What is it that you think I need to know?"

"That I'm not such a bad guy—and that I'm sure you've heard and read a lot of things about me that aren't true." He leaned against the railing, inching closer to her. "I'd like to correct that."

"Is this account that important to you?"

"It has nothing to do with the account."

"Your ego, perhaps?"

The implication riled him, but he remained unruffled, realizing the truth of her words. He chuckled and ran a hand across his beard in a sensuous motion that rushed through Terri in waves.

"You do have a lovely way of stepping on a person's ego," he answered lightly.

Terri lowered her long, sooty lashes and gave in to a grin that Clint wanted to kiss away. "Believe me, it's not my intention."

"That's good to know." He leaned closer. "Can we just forget about business for a minute?"

Terri nodded.

"I'd like to get to know you—outside of the office." His steady gaze held her, and she felt her pulse begin to pick up its pace.

"I've always been a man who speaks his mind," he continued, his voice dropping to a soothing beat. "And you interest me."

"In other words, you want to satisfy some curiosity?" she tossed back.

"Maybe."

Terri jutted her chin forward. "I'm not a curiosity piece, Mr. Steele," she said, emphasizing the word "piece."

Clint took the barb in stride. "You also have a way of twisting my words around."

Terri sighed. "What's your point, Mr. Steele?"

"I'd like to take you to . . . lunch."

Her heart thumped. "I don't think . . . ?

"Dinner?" He flashed her a taunting grin. "I'd love to prove you wrong," he challenged.

Terri knew her fragile emotional state was not yet equipped to handle a relationship, especially not one with a man who effortlessly made her senses go crazy. Yet she couldn't deny that she was just as interested. Maybe a night out was the medicine she needed after so many months of loneliness. And she was never one to back down from a challenge.

She looked boldly up at him. "How about tomorrow? I finish about seven."

His voice stroked her. "I'll meet you out front."

"I'll see you then. Good night, Mr. Steele." She made a move to leave in search of Mark, when Clint's captivating voice stopped her.

"It's Clint," he said, throwing her a heated look that turned her center into liquid fire.

Her voice wrapped around him in invitation. "I'll try to remember that."

CHAPTER 2

The following morning was filled with chaos. There were press releases to go out, writers to interview, and an assortment of trivial things that taxed the brain.

Yet even in the midst of the confusion and harried schedule, Terri could not shake Clinton Steele from her thoughts.

How could a man whose unsavory reputation preceded him evoke in her such warm feelings of desire? Terri had found herself lying awake the previous night reliving his touch, the depth of his voice, the scent of him that had clung to her hours after she'd left the reception.

She just found it difficult to believe that a man who could be so warm, so charming, so sensual would have done the unethical things that had been associated with him. Could she have been wrong?

The ringing of the phone intruded on her thoughts. She snatched up the receiver from its cradle.

"Terri Powers," she said, her mind snapping back to business.

"I thought I'd wait at least twenty-four hours before I called."

She swore that her heart stopped beating. A rush of heat flooded her body.

"Who is this?" Her fingers gripped the receiver—knowing.

His tone was lightly teasing. "I guess I shouldn't have been so presumptuous to think that you'd remember me." He paused a heartbeat of a second. "It's Mr. Ego."

She leaned back in her seat, took a silent deep breath, and smiled. "Mr. Steele. What can I do for you?"

"Ah, so you do remember."

Terri laughed outright. "You're not an easy man to forget."

"Then I guess that means we're still on for dinner."

His voice gently caressed her, and she trembled as if she'd been stroked by fire and ice.

"Yes. Of course. Did you have anyplace special in mind?"

"Why don't I surprise you?"

"All right. Just as long as it's not a late night. I have a very heavy schedule on Saturday."

"What might that be? If you don't mind my asking."

"Well, if you must know—" She pretended to sound annoyed but she was proud of her work, and it came through in her voice. "—I teach African dance to a group of kids in my building on Saturday morning."

Clint was impressed. "You're full of surprises, aren't you? Are your students any good?"

Laughter bubbled in her voice. "Let's just say they have potential."

"In that case, I promise to get you home early."

"Then I'll see you at seven."

Terri gently hung up the phone and tried to suppress the exhilaration that had taken control of her body. Then reality struggled for the upper hand. What in the world was she doing? She'd been divorced for only a year, although her marriage had been over before then—and now she was considering another man. A man who she had serious concerns with regarding his principles. Was it too soon? Well, maybe tonight she could put her unsettling feelings to rest.

The cheerful greeting from her friend and employee wrestled her away from her musings.

"Girl, it's good to have you back," Stacy declared as she hurried over and gave Terri a warm hug. "You have definitely been missed," she added in her North Carolinian drawl.

"Thanks," Terri chuckled, returning the embrace. "I feel as though I've been away forever instead of three months."

"It felt like forever," Stacy groaned as she took a seat on the sofa and slid her shoulder-length blond hair behind her ear with the tip of her finger. "With mad Mark Andrews in charge, I thought I'd go stark ravin' outta my mind."

Terri smiled knowingly. "He can be a bit much at times, but he's one of the best advertising men in the business. Unfortunately we don't always see eye to eye." A slight frown creased her otherwise smooth mahogany brow.

"I can tell by that look that you're not too pleased with that deal he's been working on with Hightower Enterprises," Stacy said. "I just got wind of it myself when I got back from vacation. I knew you'd want to know, and I was pretty sure that Mark hadn't breathed a word to you about it."

Her green eyes, fringed with long black lashes, widened in question, "Am I right?"

Terri slowly crossed the airy office and took a seat behind her desk, twirling one of her ebony locks between her slender fingers.

"That's an understatement. Mark knew perfectly well how I felt about Hightower Enterprises and its head honcho, Clinton Steele, in particular."

"So what are you going to do?"

"We met yesterday, and I initially told Steele to find another agency. However, I'm considering taking another look at the proposal. But there's some investigating I want to do on my own about Mr. Steele before I make my final decision." She paused a moment. "We're having dinner tonight."

Stacy looked at her quizzically. "Really? That's not usually your style."

Her eyes held a faraway look as she spoke. "Mr. Steele is a very unusual man."

"Do you want me to tag along?"

"No. I'm sure I can handle it. I suppose I could use the stimulation of a good debate to get my thoughts back in focus."

Stacy heard the emptiness that filled the usually rich voice that she had come to know so well. She spoke softly. "Terri . . . I know that the divorce and then losing the baby right on top of it has been hell. But, well, if you want to talk, you know I'm always here."

Terri forced a weak smile. "I know. But it will be a while before I can talk about it." She lowered her thick lashes. "I really just want to put it out of my mind, Stacy. At least I won't have to run into my ex anytime soon," she added cynically.

"I heard through the grapevine that Alan is in L.A."

Terri nodded, the acute pain of betrayal seizing her. "I can only hope that he finds what he thinks I couldn't give him."

Her turbulent four-year marriage to Alan Martin ran through her brain in a kaleidoscope of images. Everyone said that they made such a beautiful-looking couple, but that opposites must certainly attract. Terri, with her exotic natural beauty, had a sense of purpose rooted in the age-old philosophy of family and work for the common good. While Alan, with his playboy good looks, lived for the fast life, the quick money, and personal gratification.

It was a marriage almost doomed to fail, but Terri had loved Alan unselfishly almost to the point of losing a part of herself in the process. But after the first blush of passion began to fizzle, Terri saw how unalike they truly were.

Involuntarily her hand stroked across her empty stomach—a place that not long ago had been filled with budding life. Terri blamed herself for the breakup with Alan, feeling that she could not be the kind of woman that he wanted. She'd *never* allow herself to be that vulnerable to anyone again.

"Terri," Stacy called softly.

Terri shook her head, dispelling the visions, and focused on Stacy.

"Are you all right?"

"Sure," Terri answered absently. "I'm fine." She took a shaky breath and put on her best smile. "Now, if I'm ever going to get back in gear, I'd better get busy with the contracts for McPhearson. We're scheduled to meet in a few days."

"I have the promotional campaign almost all mapped out. I'd like you to take a look at it before I put on the final touches," Stacy said.

"You've done a great job on it so far. I can't see how they won't love it. If you're not busy this evening, maybe you can drop it off at my apartment. I'll go over it during the weekend."

"I'll try. If not, it'll be ready for you on Monday. But do you think you'll be up to it after a night on the town with Mr. Steele?" she teased.

Terri shook her head in amusement. "Very funny." She pushed herself up from her seat and walked Stacy to the door.

"Thanks for caring, Stacy." She gave her a warm look. "It means a lot."

Stacy patted Terri's shoulder. "Don't worry about it. Anytime."

Terri flashed a fleeting smile as Stacy left the office.

"Mark," Terri called.

He stopped and waited for her near the elevator.

"I'm going out to lunch. I was expecting a call from McPhearson's secretary. She hasn't called yet. If she calls while I'm out, I've told Andrea to pass the call to you."

She slipped into her lightweight, copper-colored trench coat.

"Do you want me to set up the meeting time?"

"Yes. Just check my calendar. I think any day next week will be fine."

"No problem. I'll take care of it. Oh, by the way, these need your signature." He angled his head to the pile of folders under his arm. "I'll leave them in your office."

"Have you reviewed them?"

"With a fine-tooth comb."

"I'll take your word for it. I really don't have the time to go through all of them. I'm swamped."

"I figured as much."

"I don't know what I'd do without you, Mark." She started to walk away.

Mark gave a derisive laugh that stopped her. "You'd do just fine. You have so far, haven't you?" he challenged, his tone heavy with sarcasm.

Terri frowned. The cynicism of the remark grated on her. "What is that supposed to mean?"

"All it means is what I said. You'd . . . do . . . just . . . fine." His jaw clenched.

"Is everything all right, Mark? You seem . . ."

"Listen," he sighed, "I apologize." He fingered the collar of his shirt and looked away. "I'm just a little tired—the pressure. That's all."

Terri noticed his nervous gesture. "Pressure never seemed to bother you before."

"Well there's a first time for everything," he snapped, his expression growing hard. "Have you had a chance to go over the Hightower proposal again?" he asked, quickly shifting the direction of the conversation.

"I'll get to them sometime next week," Terri answered warily.

"Then I'll check back by the middle of next week." He turned to walk away.

"Mark."

He turned to face her, his eyes widening in question.

"We need to make some time to talk."

"Really? About what?"

"About us."

"Us?" He tossed his head back and laughed. "You flatter me. I didn't know there was an us."

Terri cocked her head to the side and placed her hand on her rounded hip. "You know perfectly well what I mean. You've been on edge ever since I've been back."

"I think you're overexaggerating, Terri." He laughed mirthlessly. "I have work to do, and you have to do lunch." He turned and strode down the corridor, leaving her completely bewildered by his behavior.

Mark returned to his office, his agitation barely held in check. He reached for the phone, tapping his fingers impatiently on the desktop as he waited. Finally the line was answered.

"Melissa Taylor," said the low, controlled voice.

"Hi. This is Mark. I promised to call."

"How are you, Mark?"

"Fine. But I'd be even better if you'd have dinner with me."

Exiting the building, Terri turned left onto Lexington Avenue, ignoring the rush of lunch-goers as she strolled aimlessly down the busy street. Thoughts of her conversation with Mark unbalanced her usually light nature.

Something wasn't right. If she didn't know better, she'd think that Mark was jealous. Immediately she discarded the notion. She and Mark had worked side by side for nearly a year. She trusted him. She just couldn't imagine—

"You look lost."

She stopped short, a breath away from running into hard, muscular chest. Her heart thumped when she looked up into those eyes and down to the smile that spilled sunshine across her face.

"Clint . . . I mean . . ."

"You got it right the first time." His eyes roamed slowly over her. "Now that wasn't so hard, was it?"

Her eyes briefly focused on her beige suede shoes, and her only wish at that moment was that the tiny crack in the sidewalk would open and swallow her.

"I was on my way to grab a bite and decided to take a stroll," he said. "Are you out to lunch or just doing the window-shopping thing?"

Her eyes flashed at the last comment until she saw the laughter in his eyes. She couldn't stop the smile that matched his.

"That's better," he said, his voice enveloping her like a cocoon. "I'm not into the shopping part, but could I interest you in something from—" he quickly scanned the busy avenue "—Original Ray's?"

Her eyes followed his to the famous pizzeria across the street and her stomach gave a hungry twist at the mention of her favorite treat.

"Now don't tell me you don't eat pizza. That's almost un–African American."

This time she laughed outright, and he memorized the way her eyes crinkled when she laughed and the high sculpted cheekbones that gave credence to her Caribbean heritage.

Hesitating a moment, she sucked in her bottom lip, looking at him then across at the pizzeria.

"Okay." She held up a slender manicured finger tipped with soft orange. "But just one slice. I have to get back to the office."

"And," he said intimately, "I wouldn't want you to ruin your appetite for dinner." Then, like a conjurer, he took her proffered hand and it magically disappeared in his. Before she had the presence of mind to react, he was walking her across the street. As much as she hated to admit it, her hand felt fantastic in his.

"I guess you've heard all of the ugly rumors about me?" he asked, tearing off a piece of the steamy pizza and looking at her questioningly.

Terri took a deep breath. "Maybe. The question is, are they true?"

He smiled without humor. "That all depends. If you've heard that I'm a tough businessman, then it's true. If you've heard that I make it my business to take what I want in life, then that's also true." He shot her a penetrating look that made her avert her gaze.

"Beyond that—" he shrugged his broad shoulders "—I'm just your regular guy." He took a napkin and wiped his full lips, waiting for her response.

"You make it sound so matter of fact."

"I have nothing to be ashamed of."

Terri noticed the momentary flash of pain that hovered behind those dark eyes. Then it was gone. Briefly she wondered who or what had pierced the impenetrable armor.

"You're a very complex man, Clint."

He laughed a deep soul-stirring rumble. "I've been called worse. Coming from you, however, I take it as a compliment."

She took a nibble of her pizza and returned it to the paper plate.

"So have you changed your mind about me? My offer still stands." Hope filled his dark eyes.

Instead of a direct answer, she toyed with him. "I very rarely change my mind once it's made up. But I'm always open for discussion. *If* I have reason to listen."

His voice lowered to a deep whisper, his response rattling her feigned poise. "Then we have a lot more than business to talk about."

For several breathtaking seconds, their eyes held. "I've got to be getting back to the office," she said, smoothly disguising her shredded composure. "I'll see you later."

Without another word, he rose from his seat, rounded the table, and helped her on with her coat. The nearness of him set her heart racing and she knew she had to get away—fast.

"Thank you." She looked up at him one last time. "I've got to go," she breathed.

With that she made a hasty exit, darting in and out of the flow of traffic, the sensation of Clint nipping at her heels as eagerly as the fall breeze.

Terri massaged her temples. The figures just didn't seem to make sense. She shook her head. Maybe she was just tired. It was past six-thirty and she had been going over the books and comparing dates for hours. *Clint would be downstairs waiting.* Her pulse quickened at the thought.

Closing the huge ledger, she reached into her desk drawer for her purse just as Andrea, her secretary, tapped on the door and entered.

"Present for the boss," Andrea said, her face hidden behind long-stemmed flowers.

Terri eyed her secretary with skepticism. Andrea's arm was laden with what looked to be more than two dozen Casablanca lilies. Quickly she got up from her desk to help with the burden.

"Where on earth did these come from?" Terri asked.

"They just arrived."

Terri gently searched through the huge bouquet.

"There's no card, if that's what you're looking for."

Terri frowned. "Are you sure? How did they get here?" She placed the flowers on the desk and selected a vase from the credenza large enough to accommodate them.

"A messenger just brought them up. All I did was sign for them. They were addressed to you."

Terri was puzzled. "I don't understand. These are my favorite flowers," she said in a wispy voice. She pressed her face against the bouquet and inhaled the heady aroma. "But who knows that?"

"Obviously someone does." Andrea smiled. "I'll put these in water and bring them right back." She picked up the lilies and the vase and left the office.

"Thanks," Terri answered absently.

For several moments she paced the room, trying to figure out who could have sent the flowers. The only people who knew of her passion for lilies were her adopted parents, and she was sure that they hadn't sent them. They were hundreds of miles away and weren't the type of people who sent gifts just to be thoughtful. If it wasn't an act that would get them a blurb in the society column, they didn't bother. She'd probably mentioned it to several people, but to no one who would have gone to this extravagance. *Clint?*

She shook her head and smiled. "Don't look a gift horse in the mouth," she whispered, remembering her Nana's favorite line. Then she chuckled to herself, wondering for the zillionth time, what in the world was a gift horse anyway?

Moments later, Andrea returned with the lilies safely deposited in the crystal vase.

"Where should I put these, Ms. Powers?"

"On the small table by the window. That should give them just enough light."

"I'm all finished out front. If you don't need anything else, I'm going to go home."

"Of course, Andrea. I didn't mean to keep you here so late. I'll see you on Monday."

"Good night, Ms. Powers."

"Good night."

Left alone in the room Terri took one last look at her beautiful bouquet. It had been a long time since someone had sent her flowers. And she was going to enjoy every minute of it. She closed the door gently behind her.

Terri exited the building and was greeted by a cold burst of wind. October was a mysterious month. There was no telling what Mother Nature would send. The temperature had all ready dropped considerably since the afternoon, and she was thankful that she had decided to wear her trench coat. Her only wish was that she'd put in the lining.

Pulling the trench tightly around her trim body, she took a quick look up at the cloud-filled sky and wondered how far off was the first snowfall.

She checked her watch, noting that it was seven on the dot, and approached the curb to wait for Clint. Just as she neared the curb, a black Mercedes-Benz pulled up in front of her. Annoyed that the car had stopped and blocked her view of traffic, she started to walk to the corner just as the driver got out.

Leaning over the hood of the car, a look of pure mischief on his face, Clint held out one Casablanca lily between his fingers. "Can I take a few dozen lilies off your hands in exchange for dinner?"

CHAPTER 3

Terri tried to keep the conversation light and impersonal throughout dinner, but the mellow atmosphere and soft music at B. Smith's Restaurant lent itself to intimacy. Within a short space of time she found herself laughing at Clint's wry sense of humor and actually forgetting all of the things she'd heard and read about him.

He was animatedly recounting an incident that had occurred in the health club. "My friend, Steve, really had me just where he wanted me," he laughed. "There I was, spread-eagled on the bench with a hundred-pound weight hanging over my head."

"What did you do?"

"Cried uncle, what else?"

Terri shook her head in laughter, visualizing Clint's precarious plight.

"What do you do in your spare time?" he asked, loving the way her crimson dress hugged her curves.

"Read mostly. I play tennis in the summer, dance all year long, and I love riding through the park. But it's gotten so dangerous lately, I've cut back."

His voice lowered and raked over her. "I'd be more than happy to be your protector."

She looked at him coyly. "Maybe." *Now why did I say that?*

"That's the best answer you've given me to date. My faith in humanity is restored."

She lowered her thick lashes, her heart beating wildly. Then she looked up. "How did you know about the lilies?" she asked softly.

"I always make it my business to find out all I can about anything or anyone that interests me. In other words, I ask questions. I had my secretary dig up an article that was written about you in *Black Enterprise*. You mentioned your passion for the lilies in the article."

Her stomach lurched at the pointed look that he threw her way, but she kept her expression unreadable, which enticed Clint all the more.

"I believe I'll have to follow that philosophy," she replied.

"So, you've found something that has piqued your curiosity," he tossed back, enjoying the game.

"Perhaps. If there's anything of interest, I'll be sure to let you know." Her smile was a taunt, and Clint's insides tightened.

"Would you like anything else?" His voice was thick with the emotions that he struggled to control. Terri unwittingly brought out the passion in him that he hadn't felt for anyone in years. Every time he heard her voice or saw her face, he thought of what it would be like to unleash that cool control that she displayed so well.

"No. I'm stuffed. The red snapper was delicious." She finished the last of her spring water, secretly enjoying the heat that blazed in Clint's eyes and shook his voice.

"I'm glad you liked it. I haven't been here in a while, but the food is still the way I remember it."

"Do you come here often?"

"From time to time. Usually on business meetings."

The mention of business brought her back to reality.

"From the look on your face, you'd think I said a bad word." He stared at her.

"It just makes me wonder what you want with me. After all, you're in a very nasty business."

"Let me set the record straight." He took a deep breath. "I involve myself in businesses that are on the brink of folding, or businesses that I feel can be better managed by me. Where is the crime in that?"

"That's putting it delicately." She crumpled the linen napkin into a ball, her temper flaring.

"Delicate but true."

"You make what you do sound like a humanitarian gesture. How can you sleep at night knowing what you've done to so many people?"

He clenched his jaw. "I don't do anything that I'm not allowed to do within the law." Exasperation filled his voice. "If I make an offer to a company and they accept, what's the harm?"

"The harm is that they give you everything they've worked for, and you reap the benefits. You've built your fortune on the backs of other people. Our people!" Her voice rose in anger. "What gives you that right?"

Their eyes locked in a battle of wills.

Clint glared at her. How dare she make him feel guilty? He was never one to blow his own horn, and he'd be damned if he'd start now. If she really wanted to know about him, let her do her own homework.

Clint was the first to break the icy contact. "If you're ready, I'll drive you home," he said in a tight voice.

"I can catch a cab, thank you," she answered, annoyed with herself for letting her emotions get out of control.

Clint signaled for the waiter and paid the check. Terri rose to slip on her coat, but not before Clint rounded the table and took it from her.

Slowly, deliberately, he helped her into her coat, the nearness of him sending her pulse on a wild gallop. He pressed his lips close to her ear, inhaling her scent, his warm breath tingling her neck.

"I don't want the evening to end like this, Terri. I'm not interested in the campaign with your company. I can get another agency to do it. I want you and I to be friends—more than friends."

The suggestiveness of his words forced her to look up at him.

Was it sincerity that she saw brimming in those pools of midnight or was it something else?

"I—I don't know how that could be possible. We come from two different worlds."

"Not two different worlds, Terri. Two different points of view. But that's what makes a relationship interesting."

She stepped out of his grasp, her body on fire. She reached for her purse. Her voice shuddered. "I've got to be going."

"I'll get you a cab."

A cold wind blew viciously around them, and a shiver ran up Terri's spine. Clint instinctively put his arm around her shoulder, easing her next to his body.

Before she could protest, a yellow cab pulled up to the corner and she thankfully stepped out of his embrace.

Clint reached around her and opened the car door. With her nerves strung to near popping, she threw out her address in a gush.

"Get the lady home safely," Clint instructed the driver. He looked down at Terri's upturned face. "Until we meet again," he said softly, "and we will." He smiled and closed the car door.

It seemed an eternity before she finally reached her apartment on Twenty-eighth Street. Her head was pounding, and she massaged her temples hoping to relieve the nervous pressure.

Taking the short elevator ride up to the third floor, she put her key in the door and stepped into the cozy comfort of her apartment.

Mechanically she hung her coat on the brass coat rack and deposited her shoes in the foyer. Then she headed straight for the fireplace, and within moments the finely decorated rooms were filled with the warmth from the crackling flames.

Crossing the gleaming wood floors, she sank down into the cottony soft comfort of her bronze-colored couch, closing her eyes against the events of the evening. Instantly a vision of Clint bloomed before her, and she involuntarily trembled, remembering all too well the feel of him, the richness of his scent, the timbre of his voice.

She jumped back up from the couch, afraid of where her feelings were taking her, and turned on the stereo, hoping to muffle the rapid beating of her heart, just as the doorbell rang.

She frowned, wondering who could be ringing her bell. Then she remembered that Stacy had said she might stop by.

Without thinking further, she padded across the room and flung open the door, a small smile of expectation lighting her face.

Clint's lips swept down on hers. His arms enfolded her in a powerful grip. Terri's heart slammed against her breasts as she was helplessly carried away by the sensation of his lips.

Her mind commanded her to pull away, but her body succumbed to the temptation of his tongue toying with her lips, separating them as he entered her mouth. He tasted of wine and a touch of mint. How good the two were together, she thought dizzily.

How long had it been since she'd been held, been kissed, been made to feel like a woman by just a look? Suddenly the emptiness began to slowly fill and like one ravished with thirst, she drank of the waters.

He never knew a simple kiss could be like this. He stroked her back, delving into her mouth, wanting to seek out all of the hidden places. She was soft and strong all at once, a candy sweetness that demanded that he take more and more. He moaned against her mouth as arousal overtook him, hardening him to near bursting. His body demanded release, but his mind took control.

He released her, and she was sure that if it wasn't for the hand that still gripped the doorknob, she would have crumpled.

"I knew I'd forgotten something," he stated in a ragged voice, his eyes stripping her bare. With that he turned and strode down the corridor, leaving her trembling.

As she drifted off to sleep that night, her last conscious thought was that she'd have to do some serious checking on the devastating Mr. Steele.

CHAPTER 4

Rising early Monday morning, Terri completed her half hour of meditation, prepared her usual glass of carrot juice, and took a quick shower.

Searching through her closet she selected a brilliant green silk dress with fiery splashes of red and bold gold throughout. As an added accessory, she chose an oblong gold silk scarf that draped dramatically across her right shoulder. A small gold pin in the shape of Queen Nefertiti held the scarf in place. To take away from her girlish looks, she twisted her shoulder-length locks into an intricate twist on the top of her head, accentuating her sculpted features.

Satisfied with her look, she completed her outfit by selecting a pair of soft green suede pumps. With shoes and purse in hand, she padded to the door in stocking feet before slipping into her shoes.

She checked her watch. It was almost ten o'clock. She wasn't due in the office until after twelve. That would give her at least an hour of research time in the business library. She was going to dig up every article, news item, and gossip clipping that she could find on Clinton Steele and Hightower Enterprises.

Nearly two hours later, armed with a dossier full of information, Terri left the library, hailed a cab, and headed for her office. She was stunned to discover the volumes of information that had been written about Clint over the past ten years. It would take days, maybe even weeks, to sort through it all. But she would—of that she was sure.

She leaned back in the cab and considered her next step. As soon as she arrived at work, she'd give her friend, Lisa Barrett, a call. Lisa had worked as the head of proposals for the Gateway Foundation for fifteen years. Gateway solicited help from all of the major corporations in the United States to support charitable causes and community services. Any company worth its salt had contributed at some point. Powers, Inc., had made sizeable contributions over the years, and Terri was sure that if anyone knew about the inner workings of the businesses in New York it would be Lisa.

Arriving at her office, Terri quickly placed a call to Lisa.

"Lis, hi, it's Terri."

"Hey, hon, how are you? I haven't heard from you in days. Are you back at work?"

"In answer to your first question, I'm okay. And yes, I'm back at work, but I need a favor."

"Doesn't everybody," Lisa commented drolly. "What might yours be?"

"I need you to check out Clinton Steele. He owns—"

"Believe me, I know what he owns." Her voice was filled with amazement. "You're really moving into the big time. What do you want to know?"

"Anything that you can find. He made a bid for us to do an ad campaign, but I don't like what I've heard about him. Still, I'd like to give the man the benefit of the doubt."

"I'd like to give the man a lot of things, but doubt isn't one of them," Lisa quipped wistfully.

"Lisa," Terri moaned, "come on, this is serious."

"All right—all right. I'll see what I can find out."

"Thanks, Lis. Call me when you do."

With that out of the way, Terri diligently tried to focus on the meeting with McPhearson ahead of her. She'd prepared her notes, gone over Stacy's campaign strategy, and had dressed the part of the executive to the hilt.

Yet even with all of her preparation, she could not shake thoughts of Clint from her mind. Every free second for the past two days, visions of him assaulted her. She couldn't count how many times she'd relived his kiss. Just the thought of it sent jolts of electricity whistling through her veins. *Damn you, Clinton Steele! Why now, when my whole life is in a tailspin? And why you?*

Sighing deeply, she got up from her desk and smoothed her dress. She hadn't heard from him since that night, and maybe it was just as well. Things were getting too complicated too fast.

She checked the antique grandfather clock that stood against the wall. The representatives from McPhearson were due in her office any minute.

Where was Mark? she wondered, her agitation building. He should have been here an hour ago. She crossed the room in long-legged strides and pressed the intercom.

"Andrea?"

"Yes, Ms. Powers?"

"Has Mark arrived yet?"

"He just walked in."

"As soon as he's ready, would the two of you come in? You'll need to bring your Dictaphone, Andrea. I want every word recorded. And buzz Stacy also."

"Yes, Ms. Powers."

Terri returned to her desk just as her private line rang. "Terri Powers," she answered.

"Ms. Powers, this is Mr. McPhearson's secretary."

"Oh, yes. I wasn't expecting a call. Is there a delay in the meeting time?" She immediately flipped open her plan book, hugging the phone between her shoulder and her ear, pen poised and waiting.

"Uh, Ms. Powers—Mr. McPhearson wants me to inform you that he's changed his mind about the campaign."

"What?" She dropped the pen between the ivory pages. "I don't understand. Everything was set."

"That's all the information I have, Ms. Powers."

"Let me speak with Mr. McPhearson." Her pulse pounded in her ears.

"He's in a meeting."

Terri would have laughed at the practiced line if she wasn't so furious. "Would you have him call me as soon as he's through?"

"He's leaving directly for the airport when the meeting concludes."

"I see." Terri swallowed, her back stiffening. "Thank you."

Blindly she hung up the phone, a sinking feeling taking over. This deal was critical. She couldn't believe that McPhearson would pull out, just like that. There had to be some explanation, and she was damn sure going to find out what it was.

She paced the floor, her teeth biting her bottom lip, trying to contemplate a course of action.

There was a light tap at the door.

"Come in," Terri said offhandedly.

Stacy stepped in.

"All ready for the big boys?" Stacy asked. She took a seat at the round conference table on the far side of the office.

Terri blew out an exasperated breath. "McPhearson's secretary called."

"About what?" Stacy took a sip of black coffee and tossed her blond hair behind her ears.

"It wasn't what I wanted to hear. They reneged."

"What?"

"You heard right. They pulled out," Terri said.

"But why? They couldn't have gotten a better deal if they'd whipped it up themselves."

"Apparently they did."

"I don't believe it." She ran a hand through her hair.

"Neither do I."

"So now what?"

Terri raised her eyebrows. "I'll have to think it through and explore some other options. We'll really have to push for a confirmation with Viatek Studios. I want you to work on that right away."

Stacy nodded and jotted down some hasty notes. "Does Mark know about McPhearson?"

"I haven't seen Mark yet."

"This was his advertising deal originally, wasn't it?"

"Yes." Then almost as an afterthought, she added, "And so was the account that fell through with Conners, the independent producer," she said in a voice filled with awakening.

She turned to Stacy, her eyes burned with purpose. "As soon as I inform Mark that the deal has been canceled, I want you and I to go over Mark's files with a fine-tooth comb, as he puts it. I went over the books last week, and there are things that don't make sense. I thought it was because I was tired but now I wonder . . . ?

Stacy nodded, her sea green eyes reflecting Terri's concern. "I'll see what else I can dig up from the logs," Stacy added just as Andrea peeked her head in the door.

"Mark is here, Ms. Powers."

"Tell him to come in, Andrea."

Mark strolled in moments later, his light brown eyes shifting from one woman to the other. "Why the long faces?" He walked over to the water cooler and filled a paper cup.

"McPhearson canceled the deal," Terri stated. She watched for his reaction.

"You're kidding. I worked weeks on that deal." He ran his index finger around the collar of his shirt.

She registered the move. "I'm sure you did."

"What the hell is that supposed to mean?"

"It means we'll have to do some rearranging of our finances."

"Well, if you'd accept Steele's proposal we'd—"

She cut him off. "What time is your flight to Detroit?"

"I have to be at the airport in an hour."

Terri turned away, unable to look at him another minute. "Tell your folks I said hello. We'll talk when you get back."

"Fine!" Mark snatched up his notes and his briefcase and slammed out of the office.

Terri turned to Stacy. "As soon as he's out of the building, I want you to pull his files. Everything."

Hours later, exhausted and wanting to disbelieve what was in front of her, Terri closed the folders that Stacy had given her. The evidence was clear, and she had no alternative.

Slowly she got up from her desk, her heart heavy with regret, wondering what she could have done differently. She didn't know. All she could do now was prepare for Mark's return.

Stretching, her body aching with fatigue, she envisioned sinking into a steamy bubble bath, when a picture of Clint intruded on her thoughts. Her pulse raced at an alarming speed as she remembered the feel of his lips against hers . . . The part of her that wanted more, wondered what it would be like to make love with him.

This was getting crazy, she thought, angry at herself for fantasizing about a man who definitely was not for her. She hadn't heard from him since their dinner date, and the thought that he was playing games with her renewed her frustration and misgivings.

Gathering her purse and briefcase, she took her coat from the rack and began to leave the office just as the phone rang.

She started to let the answering service pick up the call but decided against it, thinking that it might be important.

"Terri Powers," she answered by rote.

"Terri, it's Clint."

Her heart skipped a beat. *Does he read my mind, or what?* "Yes?"

"I haven't been able to get you off of my mind."

Me either. Silence.

"How are you?"

If you only knew. "I've been better."

"You don't sound like yourself. Is something wrong?"

"I couldn't begin to explain." But she desperately wanted to. She wanted to feel his arms around her again, to hear his laughter, to taste his lips. But she couldn't.

"Listen, uh, I'm really tired, Clint. You wouldn't believe the day I've had."

"Maybe you should talk about it. That helps, you know."

"Not this time."

He wouldn't be dismissed. "Why don't I meet you? We could go for dinner or something. Maybe a drive." He drummed his fingers on the desk, waiting for her response.

"Clint, I really . . . ?

"I'll be downstairs in ten minutes. Wait for me, Terri."

The next sound she heard was the dial tone.

* * *

Terri waited in quiet agitation for the elevator to reach her floor. Why was he doing this to her? A better question was: Why was she doing this to herself? She knew perfectly well that Clint was not the kind of man to be taken lightly. What was more disturbing, he was the kind of man that fascinated her against her better judgment. That reality frightened her.

Finally the elevator arrived, and her heart raced as the metal box made its painstakingly slow descent.

She pulled her white cashmere coat tightly around her as a shiver jetted up her spine at the thought of seeing him. Maybe he wouldn't be there, and she could just escape to the sanctuary of her apartment. Just like she'd been doing for months, hiding from the possibility of life as she once knew it—too frightened to take any more chances. But there was another part of her that longed to be fulfilled again, the part that hoped he'd be waiting.

The doors of the elevator opened on the lobby level. Terri stepped out, her head held high. Casually she looked toward the revolving doors. Her spirits sank when she realized that Clint was nowhere in sight. Fine!

She strode purposefully forward, anticipation replaced with annoyance. Why did it matter? she chastised herself, pushing through the revolving doors. This was probably just another game to Clint.

Her temper rolled to the surface as she stood on the windy corner to hail a taxi. She waved her hand at an oncoming cab. As it approached, the cab's dome light flashed the "off duty" sign.

Terri went livid, wanting to scream and cry all at the same time. That was the final insult of the day. She really didn't know how much more she could—

"You weren't going to wait?"

Clint's voice seemed to massage her spine and unlock the tension that had gripped her. She turned toward the sound of his voice and looked up at him, the anxiety and frustration of the day brimming in her brown eyes. How easy it would be to just walk into his arms and let him soothe the aches away.

She remained immobile.

Something in the way she looked at him touched a hidden corner of his heart. He reached out and placed his large hands on her shoulders. "Terri, what's wrong?" Concern softened his voice. "You look like you've been crying."

Terri blinked and swallowed back the lump in her throat. "It's just the wind," she answered with a calmness that surprised her.

"I got stuck in traffic," he said by way of apology.

"Oh."

Why did he suddenly feel like a little boy having to explain his misbehavior? The awkward feeling left him unnerved. He shoved his hands in his coat pockets. "Can I at least give you a lift?"

She gave him a half smile and shrugged her right shoulder. "You could drop me off at my apartment. If you don't mind."

"No problem. My car is over—" He looked across the busy intersection to see a traffic cop sticking a ticket on his windshield.

"Hey!" he yelled as he immediately darted through traffic to the other side of the street. He snatched the ticket from the window, intent on making the offender eat it.

Clint strode over to the "brownie," as they were dubbed by New Yorkers for their brown uniforms, and shook the ticket in his face.

"Listen, buddy," Clint hissed, interrupting the officer from writing another ticket. "I was there for only a minute. What's the deal with this ticket?" He checked his watch. "It's five after seven. I can legally park here."

"Not by my watch," the brownie said, dismissing Clint.

"Your watch is wrong!" Clint stalked the officer as he moved to the next car.

"If you think so, then take it to court."

The officer walked away, leaving Clint to throw daggers at his back.

Terri gingerly eased alongside of an irate Clint, fighting hard to stifle the giggles that bubbled in her throat. This was the first time that she had truly seen the cool, controlled Clint totally bent out of shape. Her only regret was that she didn't have a camera.

"How much is it?" she asked in a tiny voice.

"Fifty damn dollars!" he spat, slamming his palm against the hood of the Benz. He looked at the ticket in disbelief, then across at Terri, whose face was contorting in silent hilarity.

"Go ahead—laugh," he said, his own anger giving way to the ridiculousness of it all. A reluctant grin lifted one side of his mouth.

Finally, through tears and giggles, she pointed a finger at him, the laughter still bubbling over. "You should have seen the look on your face," she said.

"You think this is all very amusing, don't you?" he said trying to sound threatening.

Terri wiped her eyes and took several deeps breaths. "Actually I do. I mean, let's face it, you can afford it."

"Now that makes me feel a helluva lot better."

"Well," Terri offered, pulling herself together, "I guess the least I could do is treat you to dinner. After all, if you hadn't come to see me, none of this—" she covered her budding smile with a gloved hand "—would have happened."

"You know what?" He looked at her hard and braced her shoulders. "I'm gonna take you up on your offer."

After a delicious meal in Chinatown, punctuated by congenial conversation, Clint drove Terri to her apartment building. The plush luxury of the Benz was like a soothing balm to her tense body. Slowly she began to relax, her voice a mere whisper when she spoke.

"I've always wanted to learn to drive a stick shift," she said dreamily, "but it's such a hassle with the stop and go Manhattan traffic."

"I know what you mean." He switched into second gear. "But after living in England and driving on the open road, it became second nature to me. I love the feel of power," he added, tossing her a searing look as he held on to the stick.

"I didn't know you lived in England."

"Yeah, for a while," he said, wishing that he'd never mentioned that part of his life. Just the idea of her saying she wanted to learn to drive a standard drove the knife of guilt through his gut, painfully reminding him of his daughter, whom he'd left behind in the care of his sister-in-law, because he'd caused her mother's—his wife's—death.

"You'll have to tell me about it some time."

"Hmm."

Terri looked at him from the corner of her eye, in time to see the hard, dark expression that passed across his face. She decided not to probe and leaned back against the leather cushion of the headrest. Maybe some other time.

Where had all of the tension gone? As much as she was reluctant to admit it, she enjoyed being in Clint's company. He made her laugh, he lightened her spirit. He was intelligent and witty, and he was undeniably sexy. Clint made her feel things that she hadn't felt in so long. Only this time it was more powerful, more compelling. And she wanted it.

"What are you thinking about?" he asked, breaking into her thoughts as he made the turn onto her street.

If she could have turned red, she would have been crimson. She felt certain that he could read her thoughts, and she felt suddenly exposed.

"Oh, just about some things at the office."

"You never did tell me what was bothering you." He pulled up in front of her door.

She looked at him, her voice softening. "It doesn't really matter now."

"If it affects you, Terri, then it matters."

She fumbled with her purse. "It's getting late. I—"

He reached for her, turning her to face him. "You keep running from me."

His voice wrapped around her.

"Every time we get close, you run from me like a scared little girl."

He gently stroked her face.

She held her breath.

"You're a woman, Terri." His eyes roamed over her, igniting her. "A desirable, sensual woman who I want in my life. But you have to give me a chance."

Could he possibly mean what he was telling her? Or was this just a ploy? Maybe he was right. How would she ever know, if she never gave him the chance? Curiosity won out.

"Would you like to come up for a nightcap?" She smiled a tentative smile. "I think I have some fruit juice and chips."

"Sounds perfect."

Terri opened her apartment door and immediately stepped out of her shoes, instructing Clint to do the same. She grinned at his perplexed look.

"When you leave your shoes at the door," she explained, "you leave all of the bad vibes behind you and just bring peace into your home."

"Hmm," Clint nodded, handing her his shoes, "sounds good to me."

"Well, come on in and make yourself comfortable. You can hang your coat on the rack." She pointed to the brass coat rack and headed for the living room. She turned on the CD player, and seconds later the music of Miles Davis blew a soulful tune in the background. Terri left Clint and went to prepare a platter of chips with a cheese dip and a bowl of pretzels.

"You have a great place, Terri," Clint commented, admiring the ethnic artwork and handcrafted sculpture. Huge earthen urns sat majestically in corners, overflowing with fresh-cut flowers in some and arrangements of silk in others.

"Thanks," she called from the kitchen, quietly pleased that he liked her taste. "Would you light a fire, please?"

"Sure." He walked to the fireplace and got the fire going. Finished, he roamed over to her bookcase and saw that she had volumes of poetry as well as what appeared to be every espionage and crime story ever written. What a strange combination, he thought, more fascinated than ever.

Terri entered the living room and placed the tray of snacks on the smoked-glass table.

"I see you've found out my secret," she said, walking up behind him. "I'm a closet poet with a murderous streak."

"The poet part I don't mind," he answered jovially, "it's the other half that scares me. Actually, as quiet as it's kept, I read a lot of poetry. It relaxes me. Especially after a rough day."

Terri's eyes widened in disbelief. "Really?"

"Let that be our little secret." He lowered his voice to a pseudo-whisper, "I don't want to ruin my dubious reputation."

Terri replied in kind. "Your secret is safe with me. Just don't cross me," she teased. "Come on and sit down. After I've been slaving over a hot stove for hours, I want you to eat every drop."

Clint chuckled as he followed her to the couch.

* * *

". . . So when I discovered that the books didn't jibe, it made me do some additional checking. To make a long story short, I don't like what I found." She was still reluctant to tell him too much. The last thing she needed was his sympathy or for him to think that she was totally incompetent. "I've worked hard to get to where I am, Clint. This company means everything to me. I've sacrificed a lot and I've given a lot. All I expect in return is honesty and a good day's work."

Could he dare tell her that he'd embarked on his own investigation? Good sense told him to hold off revealing his suspicions. He had to be absolutely positive, first. His years in business had honed his instincts. He was certain that something was amiss at her agency. Tentatively he put his arm around her. "What are you going to do now?"

"I have a few things in mind," she said, enjoying the weight of his arm around her shoulder. But she wasn't sure she should divulge her plan.

Clint moved a stray lock from her face and tucked it behind her ear, pleased with the silky quality of her hair.

She looked at him and felt her heart lurch.

With painful slowness, he lowered his head, his eyes holding hers. The flames from the fireplace appeared to dance in her eyes.

She knew her heart was going to explode into a million little pieces as his mouth slowly descended to meet her own.

The contact was incendiary, and Terri was certain that she heard fireworks erupt in the background.

The velvet warmth of his lips gently brushed over hers, taunting, tempting her with what was to come.

And it came.

The fire of his tongue played across her mouth as he spread his fingers through her twisted mane, pulling her completely against his hungry mouth.

Instinctively her lips parted and the tip of his tongue played teasing games, exploring her mouth, sending jolts of current surging through her.

He moaned against her lips, a deep carnal sound that vibrated to her center. Terri felt the heat race through her limbs as his fingers traced the pulse that pounded in her throat.

She wanted to scream when he pulled his mouth away from her lips, only to plant wet, hot kisses across her face, down her neck. Then he let his tongue play havoc in her ear and every fiber of her body ignited.

"Clint . . . ? She trembled against him.

A tingle of excitement ran through her as his hand trailed down the curve of her back, pulling her closer, caressing her, causing her body to arch, her rounded breasts to press against his chest, and he knew he would go out of his mind.

"I want you, Terri," he groaned in her ear.

His mouth covered hers again, his tongue slashing against hers, demanding, urgent.

Her arms tightened around his hard muscular frame. She stroked the strong tendons of his neck, the outline of his chest. She felt like she was falling, spinning weightless through space, and she never wanted the feeling to end. But she knew it had to stop. The door to her past was still ajar, and until she could empty it fully, no one else could enter.

His mind spun in a maelstrom of confusion. What was he doing? This was not part of the plan for his life. He wasn't supposed to feel this way, to want her from the depth of his being. His body ached to be a part of hers. But he couldn't do this to her. She was sure to think that he was just trying to romance her in order to get her to agree to the deal. He wanted her to want him for the right reasons, or not at all.

As if reading each other's minds, slowly they pulled away—each trying to control the shudders that ripped through them.

"I . . . I'm sorry." He stroked her cheek. "I didn't—"

"It's okay, Clint," Terri stuttered, breathless and in awe of what had almost taken place.

He gently pulled her into his embrace, fighting back the desires that wrestled to engulf him.

"I won't rush you, Terri," he whispered in a ragged breath. "As much as I may want to," he added with a soft smile.

She touched his lips with her own. "Thank you," she whispered.

Reluctantly he rose from the couch, "I'd better go." He smiled mischievously down at her, mimicking an old western movie. "I cain't guarantee your honor, m'am, if'n I stay."

Terri released a shaky laugh and stood up in front of him. She slipped her arms around his waist, looking up into his eyes.

"Then I'd say you'd better mosey on outta here, mister," she teased, matching his parody.

He held her for a long moment, burying his face in her hair, his confusion complete. Then he released her.

"I'll get your coat," she offered.

At the doorway Terri felt ridiculously like a teenager on her first date. Her nerves rattled, and her heart was pounding so loud she just knew Clint could hear every beat.

"I'll call you tomorrow," he said.

"I'd like that."

Clint leaned down and brushed her lips. The contact was too brief and he wanted more. Pulling her into his arms he kissed her fully, her own desire matching his every rhythm.

He eased away. "I've got to go," he said, his voice thick with desire. He started to leave, then turned back. "You'll be happy to know that I've found another advertising agency to do the work. So now there's no more business to interfere." His dark eyes bored into hers. "This is purely personal. The rest is up to you." He turned away, never looking back to see the expression of astonished relief spread across her face.

As if on a cloud, Terri glided back into the living room, a smile of contentment lighting her face as she replayed his final words. *This was purely personal.*

She changed the CD, replacing Miles Davis with Kenny G. Crossing the living room, she walked down the narrow hallway to the bathroom. Mechanically she turned on the tub water, adding her favorite bubble bath. Soon the herbal aroma filled the room, and her weary body nearly screamed for relief. Piece by piece she stripped out of her clothes and stepped into the steamy water.

Terri sank into the tub, the bubbles coming up to her chin. She closed her eyes, letting the steam envelop her, and a picture of Clint sprang to life before her eyes—and she trembled.

His mouth seemed to caress every part of her body, kneading all of the aches away. A soft moan of remembrance filtered through her lips, and she silently wished that he was there with her.

She felt the slow, steady warming that spread through her body and knew that it had nothing to do with the steaming water. And she wondered what it would have been like making love with Clint. How soon, if ever, would she know?

After a fantasy-filled half hour, Terri finally curled up into bed, sinking into the comfort of the freshly washed sheets. She reached for the book of poetry she kept by her nightstand, determined to ease away the last vestiges of tension and images of Clint.

Just as she was about to drift off to sleep, the ringing of the phone jarred her back to consciousness.

Annoyance replaced curiosity as she drowsily reached for the intrusive instrument.

"Hello?" she mumbled.

"Terri, it's me, Lisa."

"Lisa," she groaned. "It's late."

"I know. But I got the info you wanted. I thought you'd be interested."

Terri sat straight up in her bed. *Please let it be good.*

"Your Mr. Steele is, anonymously, one of the biggest individual benefactors that the Gateway Foundation has."

CHAPTER 5

The morning sun was barely up in the sky when Clint rose from his bed. He'd spent a torturous night, reliving what almost was. More times than he cared to count he'd reached for the phone to dial Terri's number. Each time, halfway through dialing, he'd hung up. The next move was Terri's. He'd put his cards on the table.

Pulling on a terry cloth robe he padded across the bedroom and opened his dresser drawer. Rifling through his possessions, he pulled out a cutoff T-shirt and an old pair of shorts. Crossing to the closet, he selected a navy blue sweat suit and a pair of sneakers. Usually a brisk run around the park revitalized him and cleared his head.

An hour later he lay sprawled across his king-sized bed, drenched in perspiration from his morning jog. His frustration was still alive and well.

Staring up at the stucco ceiling, his hands clasped behind his head, a slow smile of acceptance spread across his face. Terri was under his skin to stay, and no amount of jogging was going to change it.

Terri strode down the office corridor, looking neither left nor right. How could she have been so narrow minded and gullible to be taken in by rumors and speculation? She should have gone along with her instincts in the first place. She smiled ruefully. There was no way that her senses could have been that far off base if they went into crisis every time she thought of Clint.

She closed her office door with a thud, tossing her briefcase on the desk, her coat shortly behind.

Her head ached from the hours of reading she had done after Lisa's call. She'd forced herself to go through as many of the reports that she'd gotten from the library as she could before she'd fallen asleep. That, compounded with the company ledgers, was enough to keep her head spinning for weeks. But she had work to do, and it would begin with a process of elimination.

She reached for the phone and dialed Stacy's extension.

Stacy picked up on the second ring.

"Stacy Williams, here."

"Stacy, I need you in my office in an hour. In the meantime I want you to pull the accounting records for the past six months and compare them to the figures we came up with last night."

"Sure. Anything else?"

"The sooner the better. I want to get that SOB out of here as soon as possible."

"I'll get right on it."

"Thanks."

Terri hung up the phone, then proceeded to unlock the file cabinet, retrieving the files that she had examined the previous night. The pages in front of her seemed to laugh at her naivete.

She shook her head in disbelief. Powers, Inc., was on the brink of deep financial trouble, and she had let it happen. Her trusting nature had overruled her business judgment, and it had cost her dearly. For the past year she'd felt like a failure as a wife and then as a mother. All she had left was her business, and now even that was threatened.

No more.

She quickly crossed the office and went out into the small reception area. Andrea was just taking her seat.

"Good morning, Ms. Powers," she greeted cheerfully, then changed her tone when she saw the thunderclouds raging in Terri's dark eyes. "Is something wrong?"

"Not for long," she responded. "I need you to get Al Pierce, the accountant, on the phone. Tell him to stop whatever he's doing. I want him here within the hour, along with all of the records that have anything to do with Powers, Inc. Make sure that he understands that this is not a request. This is a command performance. If he gives you the slightest bit of a problem, put me on the line and I'll handle him."

"Yes, Ms. Powers," she said meekly.

"Thank you. Oh, and as soon as Mr. Andrews arrives, send him into my office."

Terri turned back toward her office before Andrea had a chance to respond.

Andrea couldn't remember ever seeing Terri this angry before. This must be serious, she thought, thankful that the boss's rage was not directed at her. She flipped through her Rolodex and found the accountant's number.

Clint stared pensively at the folders in front of him. He'd wrestled with what he had to do for several days. His decision was made. His friend Steve's investigation of Mark had come up with some very damning information, and he felt compelled to tell Terri whether she accepted his help or not.

The tapping on his office door snapped him to attention. Melissa strolled in.

"You wanted to see me, Clint?" she asked, beaming a brilliant smile.

"Yes. Have a seat."

Melissa took a seat opposite Clint, seductively crossing her long legs. She regarded him thoughtfully, gaining a joyous satisfaction in studying his profile. Her strong admiration and loyalty for Clint bordered on the romantic, but she was always careful never to cross that line. She sighed silently, wishing that one day he'd see past her brains to the woman who could rock his world.

"You've been seeing Mark Andrews?" His question was more of a statement, and Melissa wasn't sure if she should be angry or flattered by his interest.

"I won't even begin to ask you how you know," she stated candidly, the years of working together being enough of an answer. "Is there a problem that I should know about?"

Clint slowly crossed the room, sliding his hands into his pants pockets. He turned to face her.

"There could be. I got some bad vibes from him when the deal with Powers, Inc., fell through. Some things didn't sit right with me. I've had someone do some investigating on our Mr. Andrews, and I don't like what I've found out."

Melissa's heart tripped. The only man that had truly interested her in years had been Clint. There'd been others to fill the gaps, even Clint's buddy, Steve. When she met Mark, she thought that she had finally found someone to take her mind off of Clint—permanently. Or at least until Clint woke up and truly saw her. Now she had a bad feeling that she wasn't going to like what she was going to hear.

Melissa returned to her office, slamming the door behind her, the vehemence of her tirade toward Clint reverberating in her head. Her hurt and anger were so intense that she shook with its force. She swung back toward the closed door, wanting desperately to throw something. Then feeling totally impotent, tears of frustration and defeat filled her hazel eyes.

* * *

Terri and Stacy sat in Terri's office awaiting Mark and the accountant's arrival.

Stacy took a sip of her coffee. "I just can't believe that all of this was going on right under our noses."

"Neither can I," Terri replied, the soft lilt of her voice laden with regret.

Stacy shook her head just as Andrea peeked in the door.

"Ms. Powers, Mr. Pierce is here, and Mark just arrived. Should I buzz him?"

"Yes. But tell him to wait about ten minutes. Send Al in now."

"Who gave you authorization to allocate all of this money, Al?" Terri demanded, tossing the stack of check releases across the conference table.

Al Pierce swallowed and adjusted his glasses. He made a small showing of reviewing the documents in front of him. "Why, you did," he replied after several moments.

"In all of the years that we've been dealing with each other, when have I ever given you verbal instructions? Every transaction has been clearly written by me. Is that correct?"

"Yes. However, Mr. Andrews said that they were your instructions." He fidgeted in his seat, uncomfortable under her steady gaze.

"How much was he paying you to maintain two sets of books, Mr. Pierce?" she quizzed, throwing him totally off guard.

"I . . . I don't know what you mean," he mumbled, raking a nervous hand through his thick gray hair. "Certainly you don't think that—"

"Think what—that you and Mark were behind the scenes, undermining me for personal gain?" Her voice rose. "Is that what you think is on my mind?"

"Ms. Powers," he stood abruptly. "I resent the implication."

"Resent whatever you want, Al. You're through! And if I have anything to do with it, the only things you're ever going to add up again are cash register receipts," she spat. "Now get out of my sight and out of my office."

Al Pierce gathered up his belongings. "If you think that I'm your only problem, then you have more of a problem than you can imagine." He threw a cursory glance in Stacy's direction and stalked out the door.

"What was that supposed to mean?" Stacy asked.

"I really don't know. More than likely it was an idle comment." But silently she wondered if it were that simple. She inhaled deeply. "Now for round two," she said, her tone morose. "I think it would be best if I handled this one alone." She crossed her arms with resolve.

"Are you sure?"

Terri nodded gloomily. "If I need you for anything, I'll send Andrea for you."

Stacy rose reluctantly and slowly approached Terri, who stood as if cast in stone. "Listen," she began softly, "it all looks real bleak right now. But everything is going to work out."

"Sure," she whispered. "On your way out tell Andrea she can buzz Mark now."

They stood facing each other like two gladiators waiting for the signal to attack.

"I've had the misfortune of going over your records," Terri began, pacing her words evenly. "It's amazing how yours are so different from mine," she added with sarcasm. "You've tried to destroy me," she said, her voice edged in granite. "No wonder you were so hell bent on sealing the contract with Hightower. You needed the money to cover up what you'd done before I found out."

"You brought it on yourself," he tossed back in a malevolent tone that chilled her.

"What? You—with the help of Al Pierce—systematically set out to ruin this company. A company that I put together." She counted off his misdeeds on her fingers. "You sabotaged contracts, made us lose potential deals, lined your own pockets, and God knows what else. Then you have the gall to stand there and tell me that I brought it on myself! Do you hate me so much that you'd risk ruining this company and me as well as your own name in this industry?"

"Yes!" he shouted. "You'll never know how much. You with your holier-than-thou attitude. The woman who could do no wrong. This is no more than what you deserve. I was the one left with the crumbs of your success."

"Crumbs!" Her indignation came full circle. "You've always been a part of the success, Mark."

He chuckled. "But it was always Terri this and Terri that," he mimicked in a singsong voice. His face twisted into an ugly mask. "Terri Powers received the accolades, her name in the papers—not me." He jabbed a finger at his chest, glowering at her.

"So that's what it all boils down to, does it? You can't stomach working with a woman who has made it."

He looked away, clenching his jaw. "You're not a woman. If you were, you could've kept your husband and your baby!"

His personal attack stabbed her. She fought for control as nausea threatened to overtake her. "Not the kind of woman you expected me to be," she said smoothly camouflaging her hurt. "I want you out of here within the hour. Security will oversee your departure." She turned her back to him, her spine rigid.

Mark tossed her a hate-filled stare. "You've had your time to shine. I'll guarantee you that I'll have mine as well." He turned toward the door then stopped. "I was willing to risk anything to make you know how it feels to be forgotten. Now that you know everything," he paused, "you won't ever forget me again." He stormed out of the office, leaving the door swinging on its hinges.

For several moments Terri stood in the tension-filled silence that permeated the air. Finally she let out a breath that she didn't realize she'd held, and a tremor raced through her. She lowered her head, feeling weak and beaten.

She'd always prided herself on being fair to everyone. Or at least she'd thought so. How could she have not seen what was happening to Mark? She'd been so wrapped up in her own personal problems over the past months that she'd been blind to what was going on, allowing Mark free rein with the company. He'd used that trust against her.

His painful words rushed back at her, and her resentment and hurt resurfaced. No one could ever begin to imagine the pain and worthlessness that she'd felt. She'd shared her private hell with no one, and she wasn't sure if she ever could.

But she could not let it immobilize her. She forced her body to move, her mind to work. She still had work to do. It was time that she reclaimed control of her life, for better or worse.

Snatching her coat from the rack and putting her purse under her arm, she walked purposefully out of the office, stopping briefly at Andrea's desk.

"I'll be away from the office for the balance of the day. Any problems, call Stacy. She'll know what to do. Oh, and security will be escorting Mr. Andrews out of the building."

"Yes, Ms. Powers."

Terri stood in front of the elevator, her face resolute, her spirit determined. Her next stop was the offices of Hightower Enterprises.

CHAPTER 6

Clint had just hung up the phone when his secretary buzzed him on the intercom.

"Yes, Pat?"

"Mr. Steele, there's a Ms. Powers here to see you."

Clint's heart stirred with excitement. "Send her right in."

Quickly he stood up and put on his navy blue blazer and straightened his blue paisley tie. He approached the door just as Terri entered.

His full lips curved into an unconscious smile and widened in silent approval as he took in her regal, dark beauty. Her hair was swept away from her face, held in place by a wide headband, highlighting those large earthy brown eyes. The winterwhite cashmere coat was flung open, revealing the flowing dress that gently brushed her curves.

He ached to take her in his arms, but his smile slowly dissolved when he saw the shadow of despair hovering in her eyes.

Immediately he crossed the room to where she stood, ready to do battle with whoever had crossed her.

"Terri, what is it?"

She took a deep breath. "May I sit down?"

"Sure." He pulled up a high-back chair for her, one for himself, and sat down in front of her, his arms braced on his muscled thighs as he leaned forward.

She looked across at him, hesitant at first, but then decided to plunge right in. "I fired Mark today, along with the accountant," she said in a monotone.

Briefly Clint lowered his head, nodding in a way that let her know he understood. He looked up, his gaze holding hers. "I've had to fire my share of employees over the years, and it's never easy, especially under these circumstances. You not only feel guilt, you feel betrayed," he added softly.

Terri felt the weight slowly ease from her chest. She didn't realize until that moment how much she needed him to understand and not see her as weak and ineffectual.

"I take it Mark was the man behind the scenes all along?"

Terri nodded, a feeling of humiliation whipping through her, but her face remained resolute.

Clint easily saw through the facade of control. Once again he felt the overpowering need to take her in his arms, to protect her. But he sensed that wasn't what she needed or would accept. At least not now. That was one thing he was gradually learning about her—she did things in her own way, in her own time—without fanfare.

"Is there anything that I can do?"

She looked across at him, a weak smile tugging at her polished lips. "You could accept my apology."

His thick brows knitted. "Apology? For what?"

"For misjudging you. For doubting your sincerity. It's not like me to doubt people."

"Don't lose that part of yourself, Terri," he said, his voice full of warmth. "That's what makes you the wonderful woman that you are."

She looked away as though searching for words, then chuckled mirthlessly. "*That's* part of my problem. Being too trusting at the wrong times." She sighed deeply and Clint waited, knowing that she needed this time to come to a decision. One that would change the direction of their relationship. Then, as if a dam had sprung a leak, she slowly began to reveal bits and pieces of her failed marriage, her retreat from relationships as a result of Alan's infidelities, and her recent revelations about Clint.

The one thing that she left out was the loss of her baby, Clint noticed, a subject that must still be too painful to discuss. In time, he thought. In time. For now, he would treasure this small gift of trust that she'd given him.

". . . I was so wrong about so many things, Clint. And I always believed myself to be a fair-minded person. I let my own personal prejudices overshadow practical good sense." Her eyes leveled with his. "That was unfair to you. And when I did trust someone, it was the wrong person."

Warily Clint reached over and placed his hand on top of hers, and Terri swore that if he said anything sweet she would burst into tears.

"Thank you for that," he said, his voice a silken caress. "Thanks for trusting me enough to tell me. Just don't blame yourself. You had every reason to believe the things you did about Mark and about me."

"That doesn't excuse my behavior." She looked away, then turned to face him. "Why didn't you tell me?"

"What?" He knew what she was fishing for but refused to rise to the bait.

"About what you really do? Why do you allow the papers to print such trash about you? They have you portrayed as this vulture, that would walk over anyone to get what he wants. They never print the positive results of your business endeavors and the good that you do for struggling black businesses. It's despicable."

Clint lowered his head, then looked across at her. He shrugged his shoulders. "I suppose I want to keep that part of my life private. My reputation as a hard-nosed businessman has allowed me the financial flexibility to make those contributions. Let the public think what they want about me. Inside—" he pointed a finger at his chest "—I know what I'm about. That's what's important."

Terri nodded in understanding, pressed her lips together, and slowly rose. She felt totally vulnerable now, having shared some of her darkest moments and being witness to a side of Clint that she'd believed could not exist. The combination of new emotions crumbled her fragile sensibilities. She began to question her sudden spontaneity with him, realizing that it was brought on in a moment of weakness. Instinctively her defenses locked in place and she turned the subject to neutral ground. "My main concern right now is getting the company back on solid financial footing. I owe that to my staff."

Clint stood in front of her, catching a delicious whiff of her scent. He looked down into her upturned face. "How bad are things?"

Her smile was empty. "Bad enough."

"Listen, I could loan the company enough funds to get you over the hump."

Terri vehemently shook her ebony head, her locks swinging behind her. "No way. I got myself into this mess. I'll get myself out." Her voice softened, and her fingers splayed and stroked his arm. "But thank you. I appreciate the gesture."

He nodded and his admiration for her grew.

Terri pulled her coat around her and picked up her purse. "We're pretty close to clinching a deal with Viatek Studios. I feel very confident about it."

"I'm sure it will work out." His smile embraced her as he took a cautious step closer. "With you behind it, Viatek should consider themselves lucky."

She didn't trust herself to speak, feeling the heat of his nearness engulfing her. Instead, she eased away and moved toward the door.

Clint checked his watch. "Can I take you to lunch?"

"I'm sorry. I've got some things to take care of and I'm meeting a friend in about an hour. Maybe another time?" Her question was hopeful.

"I'll call you—soon."

She smiled. "All right. Good-bye, Clint." She turned to leave.

Clint's voice held her in place. "Terri," she looked up at him, expectantly, "I'm glad that everything is out in the open. I hope that we can move on from here."

She nodded in silent agreement.

But even as he said the words, the ache of his own hidden pain and buried truths burned his guilty conscience. He needed so desperately to open the doors to the feelings that raged within him. It had been so long since he'd shared the deepest part of himself with anyone. He wasn't sure if he still knew how. For now, all he could do was watch her walk away.

Terri picked up her glass of sparkling cider and took a sip.

"So what are your plans for the company?" Lisa asked over lunch. In all of the ten years that she'd known Terri, she'd never seen her so distraught. Terri was one of the most decent people that Lisa knew and the best friend she'd ever had. Terri was the last person who deserved the things that happened to her.

Terri took a deep breath, twirling the delicate glass between her fingers. "Well, the first thing is a total review of all of the files and a revamping of the staff. Stacy will take over Mark's responsibilities as of tomorrow. I plan to make an announcement in the morning. And of course I'll have to hire a new accountant." She gave a halfhearted grin.

Lisa nodded as she took a forkful of sauteed shrimp. "About Mark," she began slowly, "do you plan to press charges?"

Terri tossed the salad in her plate. "I thought about it, Lisa." She sighed. "But what's the point? Mark has dug his own ditch. Word travels fast in our circles. He'll never be trusted again. He's finished. That's enough punishment."

Lisa was unconvinced. "If you want my opinion, I'd say to press charges against the crummy bastard. Cutting him out of the *club* isn't enough," she added vehemently.

"I'll keep that in mind."

Lisa doubted that Terri would have a change of heart. Terri may not have been good in displaying her feelings, but she never wanted to see anyone hurt, no matter what they may have done to her. Terri kept her feelings bottled up inside, and Lisa didn't know what, or who, would ever make her change.

"So what's the progress with the advertising campaign for Viatek Studios?—moving on to a more pleasant topic."

"I'm positive we'll pull this off. If we do get it, I'll have to go to L.A."

"You don't sound too enthusiastic about the possibility." Lisa took another mouthful of her shrimp, her gaze full of question.

Terri hesitated a moment. "I was informed that Alan is being considered as the photographer." She had painstakingly tried to keep Alan in the recesses of her mind. She and Lisa had agreed after the divorce that any mention of Alan was taboo, and she regretted that the door was pried open once again.

The fork stopped midway between Lisa's mouth and the plate. "You're kidding."

"I wish I were."

"Can't Stacy handle this one?"

Terri shook her head. "No. Not really. Something this big I'd be required to deal with. There are contracts involved, and Stacy is not experienced enough in that area yet."

"So how does Alan fit in? He's not part of your package. You have your own photographer."

"I know. But Viatek has him as a subcontractor. He's worked with them before. And it seems that he's made quite a name for himself in L.A."

When was this woman gonna get a break? Lisa swore under her breath but gauged her words carefully.

"I know this may not be much of a consolation, but you've moved on with your life, Tee, and I'm sure that Alan's moved on with his."

"I'm sure he has," Terri said, her voice dripping with sarcasm. "Alan was always good for taking a situation and working it to his advantage . . . with someone."

Lisa took a deep breath. "Terri, what happened between you and Alan is a part of the past. There's no point in beating yourself to death about it because it didn't work out." Lisa cringed, remembering the countless warnings she had given Terri before she married Alan. He was a womanizer and as selfish as they came. But Lisa would never add salt to Terri's still open wounds by saying "I told you so." She had enough heartache to deal with.

"It didn't work out because of me," Terri said sadly. "Maybe if I'd been able to see past my own life and open up to accepting Alan completely in it, we'd be together today. And he wouldn't have had to go searching for what I couldn't give him."

"Don't be absurd! Alan was the consummate playboy, before and after you married him."

Lisa's temper rose as she fought to control the irritation that lifted her voice. She'd never told Terri that Alan had tried to make a play for her, too. That would have been too devastating for Terri to handle. She'd dealt with Alan herself, in no uncertain terms. She had the connections to cut the cords of his success with just one phone call. And she made sure that he knew it. It was months before he would even stay in the same room with her for more than a minute.

"My God, Terri, he had a part in it, too. A big part."

Lisa saw the veil of hurt descend over Terri's eyes.

"Listen, I'm sorry if I sound callous, but you can't keep doing this to yourself. I'm your friend, and I'd do anything in the world for you. I can't sit quietly by and see you tear yourself apart—especially over an SOB like Alan Martin."

Lisa reached across the table and took Terri's hand. Her voice lowered to a soothing whisper. "You're a wonderful person and when the time is right, that special someone is going to see it. Believe me."

Terri tried to absorb the veracity of Lisa's words. She knew Lisa was right. Alan was a bastard. But she'd loved and trusted him. She'd almost had his child. That wasn't something that you could just forget because someone told you so. Over time it had gotten easier, she had to admit. And maybe a special someone would be there to help her forget completely. A secret place in her heart hoped that the someone would be Clint.

Moments of silence passed with both women absorbed in their own private thoughts. Lisa desperately wanted to share the news of her recently discovered pregnancy with Terri, but deep inside she felt that the news would only add to Terri's misery rather than make her happy for her friend. She'd discussed it with her husband, Brian, and he'd advised against telling Terri, at least right away. Reluctantly Lisa had agreed. This was the first time in the ten years that she and Terri had been friends that she kept something this special from her. The feeling left her empty and a little melancholy. She searched for something to say to ease the tension-filled silence.

"Were you able to use the information I gave you on Clinton Steele?" Lisa asked finally. She instantly noticed the faraway look that passed across Terri's face and the faint smile that tugged at her lips. *Interesting.*

"Yes. Thanks," Terri said softly.

Lisa's brown eyes creased into a taunt as she leaned forward and ran a hand through her mop of auburn curls. "Come on, tell . . . tell."

"There's nothing to tell."

"Don't give me that. I'd know that little smirk of yours any day. So?"

"All right, all right. Just don't beg," Terri teased, itching to tell her friend about Clint.

She paused for a moment to collect her thoughts. She began slowly. "Well, at first, I had real misgivings about him. Everything that I had ever heard or read was negative. Hightower Enterprises was notorious for buying up smaller companies, and that's how he built his fortune—along with very wise investments in the stock market and profits from the companies." She laughed a self-deprecating laugh. "Little did I know that Mr.

Steele never took control of the companies, but helped to rebuild them for the owners. And when they were back on solid ground, Clint turned the reins back to the original owners if they decided that they wanted them. A lot of them didn't, of course, preferring to put that part of their lives behind them—"

"It's a shame," Lisa interjected, "that the media never tells that part of the story. They only publicize the buyouts, but not the positive end results. If you hadn't asked me to investigate him, I wouldn't have known myself. He actually started out as a runner on Wall Street. He's a remarkable man, Terri. Huge amounts of his profits go to the black colleges, universities, and community organizations."

"I know. The worst part is that I fell right into step with the bad press, eating up every word. And he never said a thing to me. He just let me believe those things about him, too proud to tell me anything different. He said he preferred to keep that side of his life private." Terri sucked on her bottom lip, disappointed in herself.

"So—where do things stand between the two of you now?"

A slow smile lifted Terri's lips. "Well, I never thought I'd be interested in anyone again, Lisa." Her eyes roamed off into the distance. "But there's just something about Clint that reeks of stability, honesty, and a magnetism that I can't shake." She wrapped her arms around herself as if to gather the warm feelings closer to her body. "He's very intense and I know very protective of his private life. He presents this rough, macho exterior to the world, but I've seen the vulnerability in his eyes. I've heard the gentleness in his voice. I think he's just afraid to show anyone that he has any weaknesses as if it could be used against him somehow. In that way we're a lot alike." She turned to look Lisa fully in the face, a radiant glow illuminating her features.

"It sounds as if it may be a lot more than that," Lisa gently probed.

Terri's gaze drifted away. "There are still so many things I have to work out, Lis, before I could even consider a real relationship again." She took a breath. "In the meantime, I still have my company and my career. That's what's important now."

Lisa heard the hollow lack of conviction that permeated Terri's voice. Her painful marriage to Alan had changed her. And Lisa slowly realized that the company and a career were no longer enough to fill Terri's life.

The only sounds that could be heard were the grunts and groans of the two men and the crack of the ball as it hit the racquet.

Clint slammed the tiny black sphere against the wall with all of the force of a speeding train, whizzing it past Steve on its return. Steve lunged for the ball with his racquet and slapped it back with equal force.

The game had been going on for nearly an hour, and the two men were drenched in sweat. Clint's rock-hard thighs bulged and tensed as he jetted back and forth across the marble court, playing like a man possessed. With each swing he tried to annihilate his frustration and rid his mind and body of Terri.

Terri.

That's all he could think about nonstop since she'd left his office a week ago, he realized grimly as he darted after the spinning ball. She seemed to creep into his subconscious when he least expected it. Like now. And he couldn't stand it. He hadn't called her or tried seeing her to maybe give her some space, and she'd made no attempt to contact him. The stalemate bruised his male ego and frustrated the hell out of him.

The ball spun past him on a return volley from Steve, and the game ended.

"Whew! How did you let that one get away from you, man?" Steve gasped, trotting over to Clint and patting him on the shoulder.

"I don't know," Clint grumbled, snatching a towel from on top of his bag. He roughly wiped his face, his breathing barely noticeable.

Steve reached for his own towel and draped it around his neck. He faced Clint, puffing hard. "You want to tell me what's buggin' you?"

Clint grabbed his gym bag and strode across the court toward the exit, ignoring Steve's question. "I'm going to the steam room," he threw over his shoulder. He stomped away, pushing through the swinging doors.

The two friends sat shoulder to shoulder in the steam-filled room, watching the ghostly images of the health club's patrons sitting in various positions. Steve knew Clint well enough to know not to push him. He'd open up in his own time. He always did. And Steve would be ready to listen.

Clint lowered his head, trying to form the words that were causing chaos in his life. Steve was the one person that he had confided in about his growing feelings for Terri. Periodically he grudgingly had to admit that he respected Steve's opinion. It was several long moments before Clint began to talk.

"It's hard to let go again, Steve," Clint began, his voice heavy with old guilt. He lowered his head. "Ever since Desiree, I just—"

Steve cut him off. "There's no way that you could have prevented what happened to Desiree. It wasn't your fault."

"It was my fault." He shook his head, pressing his palms against his eyes as the old wounds seeped open. "It was because of me."

"You don't know that."

Clint shot up from his perch. "Of course I know. Desiree took those pills because of me." He slapped his hand against his bare chest. "She got behind the wheel because of me!"

Steve looked up at his friend and saw the marks of guilt sear a path across Clint's face. "So your answer is to block out everything and wallow in a life of martyrdom? Is that supposed to make it right?"

Clint sliced hardened eyes toward Steve. "It's the only way I know how to be."

"It's the way you want to be. Haven't you learned anything?"

The question tore at Clint's gut. He visibly flinched but said nothing.

Steve continued to speak, but with a patience and wisdom that astounded Clint. "You've lived with this self-imposed guilt for three years, and I've watched it turn you into someone I hardly know. You've let it affect your relationship with your own daughter, man!" Steve's usual mild manner shifted to anger.

"Ashley doesn't understand that it hurts you to be around because she reminds you of Desiree. She's just four years old. A baby. Your baby! And Jillianne is no substitute for you, even if she is Desi's sister."

Steve took a long calming breath, searching for the words to shake some sense into his lifelong friend.

"For the first time in those three years I've finally seen you really care about someone again." He let out a breath. "Not many of us get a second chance. Don't blow it. If Terri is the one you want, you have to let her know, and stop playing these macho power games with her. The only person you're fooling is yourself. And by the looks of you, you haven't done too good of a job at that either."

Slowly Steve rose from the bench and clasped Clint on the shoulder, leaving him in the steam-filled room to sort out his turbulent thoughts.

CHAPTER 7

Terri and Stacy sat huddled over the round work desk in Mark's vacated office, putting together the final touches on the Viatek deal.

"I think that we should push the youth angle on this one," Stacy advised. "Since the director is in his early twenties, I'm sure that would be a great selling point."

Terri nodded, nibbling on the tip of her pen as she spoke. "We'll outline a thorough media saturation pushing that idea."

"I'll place some feelers out to the wire services, magazines, and morning talk shows," Stacy added, "and see who bites."

"That will definitely be a factor for the Viatek Board to consider if we can drum up a large interest from the media beforehand. You get on it, and let me know something definite by the end of the week. I want to tie the knot with them as soon as possible."

Stacy rose, tossing her sheet of golden hair behind her shoulder. "I never got a chance to say thanks." She slipped off her designer glasses, her green eyes sparkling.

Terri looked up, perplexed. "Thanks?"

"For giving me the promotion and for having the confidence in me to handle the job."

"Stacy, there's no question in my mind that you're the best person for the job. You have both the talent and the experience. You deserve it."

Stacy lowered her eyes, the depth of sincerity in Terri's words filling her with pride. Terri had given her a break when she needed it. Stacy had pounded the pavement for months before she'd landed the job with

Powers, Inc. Every ad agency that she'd interviewed with, the first thing the male owners thought was that she'd be quick and easy—and some weren't very subtle in their comments. They never took into consideration that behind her cover girl looks there was a brain and talent.

Disgusted and disillusioned, she'd been ready to pack her bags and return to North Carolina when she spotted the help wanted notice placed by Powers, Inc. The ad said that they were looking for a public relations specialist—Stacy had leaped at the chance. But after talking with Terri, who was so impressed with her qualifications and educational background, Terri designed a position specifically for her: director of promotions. Now, less than three years later, she was vice president at one of the fastest-growing and most innovative advertising agencies in the city.

Stacy looked across at Terri, a mischievous light dancing in her green eyes. "In that case," Stacy smiled brightly, looking around her new office with a sense of really belonging, "can I do some redecorating?"

Both women tossed their heads back and laughed.

"Go for it," Terri answered, delighted. "Give Tempest Dailey a call. I'm sure she'd love to make your visions a reality."

Terri headed back to her own office, for the first time in quite a while feeling positive about the future. A confident smile lit her face as she passed Andrea's desk.

"Oh, Ms. Powers."

Terri halted. "Yes, Andrea?"

Andrea flipped through her message pad and tore off a message. "This call just came in for you." She handed Terri the green and white slip of paper.

Terri looked down at the neat scrawl, and Clint's name leaped out at her. She forced her hand not to shake.

"Thank you," she said, never revealing the exhilaration she was feeling.

Terri walked into her office, gently closing the door behind her. "Please call" was checked off. Her heart thudded as she stared at the phone.

She reached for the phone, then stopped midway. Did she really want to pursue a relationship with Clint? She'd forced herself not to call him, much as she'd wanted to. She knew that she needed time to sort out her feelings about him and where their relationship was going. And she hadn't heard a word from him since that day in his office, even though he'd promised that he'd call her. She'd felt inexplicably abandoned at first, but then decided it was just as well. But now—

Abruptly she paced the office. She tugged on her bottom lip with her teeth, her arms wrapped around her waist. What was the harm in a phone call? At least she wouldn't have to look into those eyes that seemed to read her very soul.

Briefly she shut her eyes, and she heard the low rumble of his voice vibrate through her, and the air seemed to fill with his manly scent.

This was ridiculous, she thought, opening her eyes and turning toward the phone. It was only a phone call, she concluded, listening to that part of her that eagerly wanted to hear his voice again.

She reached for the phone just as the intercom buzzed.

"Yes, Andrea?"

"Mr. Steele is on line two."

She swallowed. "Thank you."

Terri took a deep breath and pressed the flashing red light.

"Clint," she breathed, "I was just getting ready to return your call."

"I thought I'd save you the trouble. How are you, Terri?"

The question was so simple, his voice so gentle, yet it aroused the complexity of how she was truly feeling. She couldn't begin to explain.

"I'm just fine. And yourself?"

"I wanted to know if your offer was still open," he said, his voice gently teasing.

"My offer? What on earth are you talking about?"

His voice dropped to a low throb. "Showing your appreciation for my offer to bail you out."

Terri felt her body go rigid with indignation. Clint heard the quick intake of breath and the unsaid "how dare you" in the brief silence that followed. He chuckled.

Terri opened her mouth to lash out a retort, but Clint cut her off. "I only wanted to know if you'd care to accompany me to *City Center* tomorrow night."

Terri felt her body slowly relax, and she envisioned the smile that must surely be brimming on his devilishly handsome face.

"Very funny." She tried to sound admonishing but failed miserably.

Clint's burst of hearty laughter was infectious, and she found herself laughing in answer.

By degrees the merriment ceased, and Clint's pulsing voice filtered through the lines. "How about it? The Dance Theater of Harlem is appearing."

Terri's eyes lit up. "Really! Oh, I love them. I studied with Arthur Mitchell for a while. They're fabulous," she enthused.

Clint grinned, enjoying her elation. "So I can take that as a no?"

"Don't be a wise guy. I'd love to go," she agreed happily.

"Should I pick you up at home or at the office? The show starts at eight, but I thought we could go to dinner first."

"That sounds wonderful. Why don't you meet me at the office. It'll save time. Is six good?"

"Perfect. I'll see you then, Terri."

* * *

Terri spent a fitful night anticipating the next evening with Clint. Every time she thought of him, her heart raced at breakneck speed and her eyes flew back open.

Finally, unable to rest, she rose from her bed, sat in the center of her bedroom floor with her legs crossed.

She closed her eyes and inhaled deeply until her breathing became slow and regular. She forced her mind to cleanse itself of troubling thoughts and began to visualize the lapping waves of the ocean, which always had a soothing effect on her.

Inch by inch she tightened then relaxed each muscle of her body, beginning with her toes all the way up to her head, which she slowly rotated.

After twenty minutes of meditation, she crawled into bed and was asleep within moments, to awaken the following morning feeling refreshed and invigorated.

The day sped by and before she realized it, six o'clock was rapidly approaching.

Quickly she straightened up her desk and collected her belongings, wondering all the while if Clint would like the outfit she had selected.

Slipping into her cream-colored wool cape, she picked up her purse and headed for the elevator. With each footfall, she commanded her heart to be still.

She walked across the lobby toward the exit. Clint was there waiting, looking for all the world as if he'd just stepped off the cover of *Ebony Man Magazine.* All of her preparation to quiet her jangling nerves was a complete fiasco when his heart-stopping smile embraced her.

"You look fabulous," Clint crooned, planting a smoldering kiss on her cheek. His eyes swept admiringly over her magenta palazzo pants of wool crepe with a matching trapeze jacket. He took her arm and guided her toward the revolving doors.

"Your chariot awaits, madam." He gave a mock bow and Terri smiled up at him, fully realizing that she had never felt happier.

They spent a glorious evening together with Terri intermittently telling Clint tales of her dance school days and relaying hilarious stories of her budding dance students. Clint animatedly recounted the days of his youth as a stock clerk in the local supermarket and the eccentric customers that frequented the central Harlem store.

That evening signaled a major turning point in their relationship, and they both sensed a new level of awareness in each other. Even the simple things that they shared took on new meaning. A mere brush of fingers was electrifying. A look spoke volumes. From that night they tried to spend all of their free time together, from racquetball, which Clint taught Terri with relish, to bike riding.

"Race you around the park," Terri challenged as they walked their bikes up to the entrance to Central Park's bike trail the following morning.

"You're on," he retorted with a wicked grin and suddenly zoomed out ahead of her.

Terri threw her leg over the seat and took off after him, yelling, "Cheater! Cheater!"

Clint threw his head back and roared with laughter even as she gained on him with startling speed. He enjoyed her competitive nature and her willingness to try new things. He even sat in on some of her dance classes and was amazed at her talent and her gentleness with her young students. As he witnessed her patience with them and the love and admiration that each of them had for her, he longed for his own daughter, and realized that he wanted Terri as a permanent fixture in his life. He'd have to find a way to tell her about his past and about Ashley, soon.

The more time that Terri spent with Clint, the more she realized all that they had in common. And Clint understood day by day that the budding feelings he had for Terri were in full bloom and pulsing with life. Their relationship steadily tread on new tempting territory, and the thrill of the unknown lent an intensity to their being together that was almost too much to withstand. Even so, Terri was completely thrown off by Clint's pointed invitation.

"I have a small cabin in the Poconos," Clint stated one evening over dinner. His voice took on a smooth storytelling tone. "It's a great place—wood-burning fireplace, snowcapped mountains in the background, good food, dancing, and plenty of indoor activities for nonskiers."

"It sounds great," Terri said, leaning back in the kitchen chair and eyeing him speculatively.

"I was planning on spending Thanksgiving weekend up there."

Her spirits instantly sank. She had hoped that they would spend the holidays together. She'd become used to Clint being a euphoric fixture in her life. The prospect of spending the holiday alone wilted her spirit. But she kept her disappointment well hidden.

She slowly rose from her seat and took the dishes into the kitchen, carefully avoiding Clint's all-seeing eyes.

"You'll be joining me," he said, as though it were an already moot point.

Terri nearly dropped the dishes in the sink. She turned cool confident eyes on him, totally in contrast to the wave of apprehension that flooded her. "Go away with you?" she asked, with a calmness that stunned her. "For the weekend?"

"I know you heard me," Clint said, rising from his seat and closing the distance between them in three fluid strides. He stood a breath away, and Terri felt the blood rush to her head and cloud her vision when she looked up at him. He lifted her chin with his index finger and held her eyes with his own. "So stop trying to stall for time."

She eased back until she was pressed against the sink. Her thoughts raced. The implication of any answer from her, one way or the other, would assuredly change the direction of their relationship—permanently. Was she ready? Yes, an inner voice whispered. Yes.

She straightened her shoulders, tilting her head to the side, her eyes taking on a smoky hue. Her voice dropped to a titillating whisper. "What day did you want to leave?"

Clint lowered his head by inches, his ebony eyes boring into her own. His powerful arms slipped around her, pulling her slender body fully against the hard lines of his. Slowly his mouth opened to cover hers.

"How about right now?" he groaned into her mouth as her silken tongue stroked hungrily across his lips.

CHAPTER 8

In silent amusement, Lisa sat on the chaise lounge with her long legs crossed at the ankle, watching Terri scurry around her bedroom.

"What should I take?" Terri moaned, after having already deposited half of her wardrobe on her bed.

"Why don't you just take everything?" Lisa advised. "Then you'll be sure to have the right outfit."

Terri halted, swung around, and saw the taunting smile. She turned dark eyes on Lisa, her hands planted firmly on her hips. "I thought you were here to help me. Not torment me with lousy jokes."

Lisa cracked up laughing, seeing the pained expression on Terri's dark face.

"You look like you have it together to me, girlfriend. You just need a bigger suitcase."

Terri rolled her eyes and sucked her teeth, a trait she'd inherited from her grandmother and doled out to those who really rubbed her the wrong way.

"You really vex me, ya know," Terri said, easily slipping into dialect, something she hadn't forgotten even after more than twenty years in the States. "Ya good fer nuttin' except to give me a hard way to go." Terri spun around in a huff and collapsed faceup across her bed, her mound of clothes fanning out around her.

"What am I going to do, Lis?" Terri whined.

Lisa sighed and pulled herself up from her resting spot with some difficulty, intending to put some order to the mess that Terri had created.

Terri eyed her curiously. "Are you putting on weight, or is it my imagination?"

Lisa knew she couldn't duck the inevitable forever. She was already having trouble fitting into her clothes, and Terri would have to know sooner or later.

Lisa pressed her lips together before she spoke and ran her fingers through her hair.

"You're not imagining things," she said softly. "I'm pregnant."

Terri felt a tightness in her chest and a momentary flicker of jealousy. Her own loss rekindled with painful intensity. But just as quickly as it had taken hold, it was released. Terri popped up from the bed and ran over to where Lisa stood and heartily embraced her.

"Oh, Lis, I'm so happy for you." She pressed a kiss to her friend's cheek. "I know this is something that you and Brian have wanted for so long."

Terri took a step back and peered down at Lisa's rounding stomach. "How many weeks?"

Lisa swallowed. "Two and a half months."

Terri frowned in confusion. "Two and a half months? You just found out?"

Slowly Lisa shook her head. "I knew a few weeks ago."

Hurt and disappointment filled her voice. "Then—why didn't you tell me?"

Lisa reached for Terri and braced her arms. Her eyes pleaded with her to understand. "I didn't want to upset you. After everything that you'd been through with Alan and then the baby . . . I just thought . . . ?

Terri's voice shook. "Lis, I would never begrudge you your big moment." She shook her head in amazement. "Even at the happiest time in your life, you thought about my feelings." Tears filled her eyes, but Terri blinked them away and sniffed. "You're some friend."

"You're not mad at me?" Lisa asked with caution.

"Of course not, silly. So long as I can be godmother."

Lisa beamed with relief. "Absolutely! Who else?"

"When's the big day?"

"The fifteenth of June."

"Time will go by so fast, you won't even realize it." Even as she spoke, the loss of her own baby loomed before her, and the emptiness threatened to engulf her once again. Swallowing the knot of pain, she steered her thoughts onto a happier trail.

"Well, since you're not going to be much use to me, before you know it, I'd better get all I can out of you while the going is good. Help me sort through these clothes!"

On the surface everything appeared to be the same between them. They chatted merrily, and Lisa teased Terri mercilessly as they selected

Terri's wardrobe for her long weekend rendezvous. But deep inside they both realized that they had moved into different worlds. A place they could no longer share, and the silent understanding of that reality left a hollow emptiness that echoed soundlessly in the room.

After Lisa left Terri's apartment to return home, Terri prepared a basket of food for the two-hour drive.

She filled a thermos with herbal tea, arranged a platter of fruit, chips, whole wheat crackers and assorted dips and placed it all in a wicker basket.

She checked her watch. Clint wanted them to be on their way by three o'clock in order to arrive before the rush, and give themselves time to get settled. He would be arriving in moments. She smiled. Clint had become such a familiar face over the preceding weeks that he was like a member of the family in the small six-tenant building.

Her pulse raced as she imagined the next five days—alone—with Clint.

She inhaled deeply, willing herself to be calm. Since the evening he'd asked her to go away with him, she'd been in a constant state of flux—exhilarated one minute and terrified the next. She couldn't count how many times she'd almost called him to back out. But desire and a deep-seated yearning for fulfillment would take over.

As a result she had made an appointment with her doctor and had a thorough exam. Dr. Walters said that Terri was in excellent health and that the miscarriage had not caused any lasting effects. Although Dr. Walters had advised Terri to take it slow, she'd assured Terri that she was just fine.

They discussed birth control and Terri was given a prescription, but the doctor strongly cautioned Terri to use additional protection for at least the first two weeks.

Even as she thought about it, her stomach fluttered. Her life was rapidly changing, moving in a completely new and hopefully positive direction. She had to put her past behind her and start fresh, she resolved. She could only dare to hope that Clint would remain a part of that future.

Terri took a quick look around her bedroom and spotted the stacks of notes and articles she'd gotten from the library. She made a mental note to get rid of them when she returned. Satisfied that she hadn't forgotten anything, she picked up her suitcase, walked into the living room, and placed the bag in the foyer just as the doorbell rang.

For several unbelievably long seconds, she stood there staring at the door, wondering what in the world she was getting herself into. The second ring jolted her into action. She pulled open the door and when she looked up at his smiling face, all of the anxiety seemed to melt away, replaced by a burning longing that she knew would be totally satisfied.

"I know you like jazz," Clint commented, giving Terri a sidelong glance as he shifted into third gear, "but I guarantee you'll love this." He leaned over and popped a CD into the player.

Seconds later the symphonic rhythms of Harry Connick Jr. filled the Benz. Terri closed her eyes. The quality was so crystal clear she could imagine herself in the concert hall with the young impresario in command of the orchestra.

Clint took a quick glance in her direction, satisfied by the grin that had spread across her face.

"Like?"

"Like," she said happily. "I've heard some of his work, but I haven't had time to pick up the tape. It's fabulous."

Clint's low voice reached out and stroked her. "There's more fabulous things where that came from."

Terri instantly felt a rush of heat sweep through her as she thought wickedly to herself, *you don't know how right you are.*

Clint only hoped that he could keep the demons of his past safely locked away.

Terri was beyond impressed as Clint gallantly bowed when he opened the door to his hideaway. The cabin was more fantastic than Clint described.

The first thing that caught the eye was the breathtaking view of the mountains seen through the enormous window that swept across one entire side of the cabin. Adding to the ambiance were the redwood rafters that majestically complemented the natural atmosphere, while giving the inhabitants a sense of home and comfort.

The polished wood floors gleamed, covered in areas with fluffy throw rugs, huge floor pillows, and a large fur rug that sat directly in front of the fireplace.

Terri stepped into the front room and looked around in wonder, taking in the wood and Italian leather furniture. Slowly she strolled into the inviting space and felt instantly at home.

The entire layout was a combination of rustic and ultramodern. The kitchen, which was directly to the right of the living area, was something straight out of *Architectural Digest.* Every electronic gadget known to man must have been installed. And it was spacious enough to have a helping hand in there without regretting it.

"Let me show you the upstairs," Clint offered.

Terri followed Clint up the wooden spiral staircase. The entire second floor was embraced by a balcony. From any room you could step out and look down onto the ground floor. It was magnificent.

"The bathroom is down the hall." Clint walked in the direction of the guest bathroom, opened the door, and flicked on the light.

The perfect-looking room was done all in light green and white, with matching towels, rugs, and curtains and recessed lighting that gave the cool green tiles a warm glow.

"Very nice," Terri commented softly.

Clint turned to his left and opened the next door. "This is the guest bedroom."

The room was warm and cozy, seeming to beg the visitor to step inside and stay awhile. The huge four-poster bed was covered with a multicolored quilt that looked as if it were hand sewn with love, with overstuffed pillows that you could sink into. The hardwood floors were covered with a thick ecru colored carpet. Two large windows draped in sheer white chiffon, with an overlay of crushed velvet that matched the carpet, opened onto a small balcony overlooking the ski village. There was a dresser topped with all of the basic toiletries, a nightstand, a large television, and a small fireplace, which added the finishing touch.

"I love it. Who did the decorating?"

The question momentarily threw him off. He and Desiree had purchased the cabin the year before their marriage and had tirelessly decorated every inch of it themselves. After her death, Clint had slowly begun to replace items, change color schemes, and eventually gave the place a new look. He knew that he would not have been able to continue to come here if the memories remained.

"I did."

Terri's eyebrows rose in question and in appreciation. "And you say I'm talented." She pointed a playful finger at his chest. "I think you may be in the wrong profession. Well, now that I'm suitably shocked, show me the rest of this *cabin.*"

Clint chuckled at the barb. "Right this way." Several feet away was the master bedroom. Clint swung open the door and stepped to the side to give Terri a full view.

The master suite was sprawling. In this room the hardwood floors were covered in a plush midnight blue carpet. Sitting in the center of the room was a lavish, king-sized, four-poster bed made of solid oak. The coverings were in the same midnight blue with gold and white throw pillows. All of the furnishings appeared to be hand carved from the same polished oak. The large bay window was draped in a sheer blue chiffon, trimmed in a brilliant gold that was repeated throughout the room. One wall contained a built-in bookcase that overflowed with volumes of work, next to which sat an elaborate state-of-the-art computer system.

Stepping into the room, Terri saw that it had its own private bath, with a built-in Jacuzzi. Once again, Terri came face to face with Clint's unrestrained tastes. He demanded the best from himself and everyone that came in contact with him, and that ideology transferred itself into his living space. Everything was just perfect, almost larger, better, than real life. The realization suddenly frightened her, and she wondered if he would expect the extraordinary from her as well.

Clint eased up behind her and slid his arms around her waist, dispelling the disturbing thoughts. He lowered his head and planted tiny, tempting kisses along her neck. A shiver of delight raced up Terri's spine as she arched her neck, inviting the sensation of his taunting mouth.

"Which room would you prefer?" he asked in a throaty whisper.

Her heart raced. She wasn't going to make it that easy on him. She turned into his embrace and looked up into his ebony eyes. A slow, seductive smile curved her lips, her lids lowered.

Clint's pulse quickened.

"The guest room is just perfect," she said softly. She waited for his reaction and was mildly disappointed. If there was any degree of surprise by her response, Clint hid it well.

He smiled. "Of course." Slowly he released her and stepped back. "I thought we could drive into town about seven. There's a great club that serves excellent seafood." He turned to leave, then said over his shoulder, "Dress casual."

While Terri adjusted to her new surroundings, the soft trill of music seemed to mysteriously float into her room. She looked around to all of the obvious locations in search of speakers. Her eyes trailed across the room and then upward to discover four hidden speakers tucked neatly into the wall above the oak molding.

Slowly she shook her head in amusement. Clint certainly knew how to live, and she wondered what other secrets lay hidden within the enchanting hideaway.

Clint returned to the lower level of the rambling abode. He lit the fire in the hearth, adjusted the volume of the music that flowed throughout the house, then began going through the cabinets and refrigerator to see if they were stocked to his satisfaction. He had left specific instructions with the middle-aged woman who came in weekly to check on things and straighten up. He was pleased to see that his instructions had been followed to the letter.

Satisfied that everything was in order, he decided to fix himself a light drink before changing for dinner.

He crossed the spacious living area to stand in front of the window, leaning casually against the wide beam, sipping a glass of white wine.

He stared unseeing at the swell of the hills and mountains that jutted erotically upward toward the heavens as one eager for a loving caress. He watched the maneuvers of a lone car as it threaded its way around the winding turns, which had been known to be treacherous, and down into the village below. Without warning, images of Desiree loomed before him, as real as if she'd stood by his side.

Swiftly the visions took hold, and his mind sped on a whirlwind of events that he had tried so desperately to forget.

It was four months after Ashley was born, and he and Desiree had decided to get away for the weekend. Their marriage was in trouble. Clint knew it, and Desiree demanded that they do something about it.

They'd been at the cabin for less than an hour when Desiree started in on him. She'd been doing that a lot, and it was driving him crazy. The doctor had assured him that it was postpartum depression and she'd get over it. Clint was seriously beginning to doubt it. The more she complained about his not being home, the more he stayed away, which compounded their already growing problem.

It was his fault, she'd accused over and again, her silken mane of chestnut hair swinging around her shoulders as she paced restlessly across the floor. Her hazel eyes blazed. He didn't have time for her or their infant daughter, she'd cried. Things were just so consuming at work, he'd argued. Why couldn't she understand? He loved her. Didn't she realize that? He didn't know how to love anyone other than himself and his work, she'd railed. There wasn't room in his life for anything else.

She'd stormed off to their bedroom, locking the door, refusing to let him in. After an hour of banging and begging her to listen, he'd finally given up and gone downstairs.

He'd tossed his weary body on the leather couch. He was so tired. Tired of the arguments, tired of the ways things were between them. Maybe even tired of what he'd become.

He hadn't known how long he lay there, thinking of the things Desiree had said. He'd thrown his arm across his eyes and tried to convince himself that he was right. But even to him, his explanations began to sound weak. Suddenly nothing was clear. Where had he gone wrong? He'd worked hard to get to where he was, and he lavished his wealth on his beautiful wife and daughter. He'd married his college sweetheart, and he'd made a solemn vow that she'd never again have to suffer the ravages of poverty. Her mother had worked two jobs to raise Desiree and her older sister, Jillianne. She never knew her father. They grew up in the tenements of Harlem, but the hard life never toughened up Desiree. Instead it made her insecure, needy, always seeking assurances and comfort. Clint was her knight in shining armor. She needed him and Clint needed just that.

His goal—to make the best life possible for his beloved Desiree—was all consuming. As a result, she had everything anyone could ever ask for.

A beautiful home, clothes, cars, bank accounts, luxury trips. So why was she so unhappy? She had everything.

And just as exhaustion had threatened to consume him, he'd heard the soft whisper of reality struggle to the surface. *Everything except you.*

The next thing he'd remembered was waking up to absolute stillness. His head snapped up from the couch when he'd realized that he'd dozed off. He tried to collect his fuzzy thoughts, knowing that he had to talk with Desiree. She was right.

Slowly over the years he had built a world and a life that he no longer shared with her. That wasn't part of their plan, their dream. Desiree needed him, more than the furs, the jewelry, the money. How many times had she said that and he had not heard her? It was just so hard for him to express his feelings. He'd never been shown tenderness in his youth. His father had instilled in him that real men didn't show their feelings. Women needed men to be strong and take care of the family. Words and acts of affection were for women. He didn't want to lose his wife and he knew he would if he didn't change.

He pulled himself up, swinging his long legs onto the floor. A sense of peace had filled him, and he'd believed that everything was going to be different. He could make it different. Hadn't he always been the master of his fate and ultimately Desiree's as well?

Quickly he'd bounded up the spiral stairs, a sense of purpose putting a lightness in his step.

He'd halted abruptly at the top of the staircase, a haunting sensation of foreboding rooting him to the ground.

The bedroom door was open. The room was dark, and he knew deep in his gut that Desiree was gone.

His body had jerked with dread when the shrill ringing of the phone reverberated throughout the cabin, and his world as he knew it came to a complete end.

"Clint . . . ?

Clint spun around, dark raging clouds swimming in his eyes. Her breath caught and for the barest instant, Terri was frightened.

"Terri." His voice sounded strangled, almost as though he hadn't expected to see her standing there.

"Are you all right?" She took a cautious step closer.

Clint fought back the urge to sweep her into his arms and exorcise his pain. Instead, the facade that he'd mastered so well slipped easily back in place.

"Yeah, sure. I'm fine. Just thinking . . . about . . . work."

"Oh." She nodded, somewhat mollified but not totally convinced. She took a step closer and reached out to touch him. His insides twisted.

The gentleness of her touch almost did him in. He couldn't let her see him break down or be weak. He had to be strong—always. Wasn't that what his father had always said. "You'll never get anywhere in this world, boy, being no weaklin'." The words still haunted him. But Terri was changing him in subtle ways, day by day, and he was afraid of the weakness, the vulnerability, that was sure to follow.

He brushed a light kiss across her lips. "Your outfit is perfect," he complimented smoothly, skillfully camouflaging his confusion. "Can I fix you anything before I change?"

"No. Thanks. I'm saving my appetite." She flashed him a smile that made the rhythm of his heart pick up a beat.

"Is that a threat?" he teased.

Instantly he held up his hands to ward off the onslaught of miniature blows that Terri rained upon his muscled body. He collapsed on the couch in a hysterical heap, pulling Terri solidly down on top of him.

But the frivolity slowly dissolved, and the deep rumble of his laughter softened into a provocative smile. His eyes darkened with dangerous lights, racing across her exquisite face. "I'm falling in love with you, Terri," he whispered roughly. "It seems that I've waited all of my life for you—for this moment to show you how much."

Elation surged through her veins as she trembled from the awesomeness of his confession. "Clint, I—"

"Shh. No words. Not now. Not yet." Terri held her breath when his hand clasped her head, pulling her slowly toward his waiting mouth.

She'd come to know these lips, the velvet feel of his tongue as it traced the cavern of her mouth. She'd savored the taste of him, felt the sensation of his kisses that thrilled her to her toes. She'd felt it all before.

This was different. There was an urgency, a yearning, a fire between them that was burning out of control—something that neither of them had permitted before—until now. And she felt the power of it in every fiber of her being. She shivered when the balls of his fingers played a concerto up and down her spine, compelling her to press deeper against the hard contours of his body—only to feel his undeniable arousal pulse steadily against her thigh.

Clint moaned almost painfully against her mouth, his fingers pressing into her back as he seductively ground his hips against her.

Terri's thoughts ran in chaotic disarray when Clint's hand slipped beneath her blouse. Her body shuddered when he pulled his lips away from hers, only to trail heated kisses along her neck, causing her to gasp with pleasure.

Her spontaneous reaction stirred him further, and he intensified his ministrations, caressing her full breasts in his palms. Her heartrending moan filled the music-soaked air, then floated away in a sensual melody.

Terri closed her eyes against the tumult of powerful sensations that ripped through her at his touch. The tips of her breasts hardened above his fingertips, sending ripples of raw electricity shooting through him. He locked her snugly in his arms, rising with her, as he stood and carried her across the floor in front of the fireplace.

Gently he lowered them both to the thick fur rug, partially covering her body with his weight.

He unbuttoned her silk blouse one tiny button at a time, while he basked in the flame of desire that danced in her eyes. With each button that came open, Clint placed a searing kiss on the exposed skin that beckoned to him. The prolonged anticipation was almost unbearable, but Terri knew that Clint was determined to take his time. Even if it took all night.

And it seemed that's exactly what was happening as the tip of Clint's tongue mercilessly sought out the hollow of her ear, and he whispered erotic, soothing, unintelligible sounds that flooded through her in waves.

Practiced hands freed her of the silk top and expertly removed the matching shirt and all beneath. Within moments, she lay bare and breathtaking before him, and he realized with awe that he had never seen such exquisite beauty.

She was an artist's treasure, with full high breasts that reached toward him longingly. Her flat stomach tapered to an hourglass waist, flaring outward to rounded hips and down to endlessly long dancer's legs.

Clint groaned, an almost physical agony gripping him as he lowered his head to suckle the sugar-tipped breasts and temper his thirst for her.

Terri's breathing escalated into short, stilted breaths as Clint lovingly stroked every inch of her body with his hungry mouth.

She pulled him to her, teasing his back with long sensuous strokes from slender fingers. Terri whispered his name over and again as wave upon wave of pleasure shot through her.

Slowly Clint rose above her and piece by piece shed his clothing, to hover naked above her.

Her breath caught as the firelight danced off his well-honed physique. The raw power of his body was almost terrifying. Hard, rippling muscle defined every inch of his massive frame. Gingerly she caressed the bulging biceps of his arms, causing him to shudder with pleasure.

Deliberately her hands traveled downward over his taut belly, seeking out the core of his arousal.

Clint's eyes slammed shut as he reared back in ecstasy. "Oh, God," he groaned. The butter soft fingers boldly enveloped him, nearly throwing him over the edge.

Hungrily his mouth covered hers, cutting off her cry as he joined them as one.

Millions of tiny lights seemed to explode at once, igniting every nerve in her body, as Clint found refuge within the honey-soaked walls.

She clung to him, wrapping her long legs around his waist while reality collided with fantasy. How long had it been since she'd felt such intense wanting—such a need to be connected and thoroughly loved? She gave herself to him—totally, willingly, irrevocably—welcoming the multitude of sensations that rocked her. "Clint," she whispered over and again, dizzy from the power of his thrusts into her welcoming body. "Love me some more," she moaned.

Together they found their own perfect rhythm, beating, moving steadily toward the pinnacle of complete satisfaction.

The flames from the hearth danced and sparked in a frenzy as though enchanted by the vision of loving before them. The overburdened heavens filled with moisture while the clouds rolled in competing formation, spilling onto the waiting hills and valleys, saturating the starving earth with a blanket of pure milky white, only to be swallowed up by the heat of their passion.

Terri's climactic cries of release were met by Clint's carnal response, taking them soaring upward to the mountaintop and over into the valley of total, unsurpassed bliss.

They clung together as one, nestled in the cushiony warmth of spent lovers, dinner all but forgotten. Terri had never felt so complete, so secure as she felt Clint's heart beat steadily against hers. This was what it was all about, she thought, pure happiness filling her. "I love you, Clinton Steele," she whispered, seconds before she drifted off into a satisfied sleep.

CHAPTER 9

"I'm starved," Clint mumbled wickedly in Terri's ear, stirring her out of a magnificent sleep. He pulled her closer, nuzzling her neck. "And I know just what'll satisfy my craving."

Tiny giggles bubbled up from her throat, while Clint ran his hands down her bare hips and nipped at her flesh.

"Clint!" she squealed, trying unsuccessfully to wiggle away from temptation.

Too late.

His velvet tongue and probing mouth sought out and captured her downy center. The explosion of sensations that followed tore through her like a volcanic eruption. Her body trembled, writhing beneath him as he delved deeper, stroking, teasing, caressing.

Her nails dug into his shoulders as she felt the shock waves of release make its steady climb—pulsing—stronger than a heartbeat.

She opened her mouth to cry out, but all sound and air seemed to catch in her throat as she was hurtled across the threshold of simple pleasure to the surreal world of absolute ecstasy.

Clint stood over the kitchen sink wearing only a pair of silk boxer shorts, running cold water over the pounds of shrimp. He turned a lecherous eye in Terri's direction. "You look great in my shirt," he commented, taking a long, slow look at her bare legs. He reached up and began rifling through the cabinets, then the refrigerator, pulling out an assortment of spices, spinach, mushrooms, a box of wild rice, and other goodies.

Languidly she curled up in the kitchen chair, tucking her long legs neatly beneath her.

She smiled, the glow of satisfaction illuminating her face. "Since you seemed to have discarded my clothing, I didn't have much of a choice."

He turned to her, his dark eyes raking across her face. He reached out and touched the top button on her shirt with his index finger. "This little number will be even easier to get you out of."

Terri clasped his hand in a grip that surprised him. She glared at him hard, but he saw the flickers of laughter dancing in her eyes. "Don't even think about it," she warned.

"Whoa!" Clint threw up his hands in feigned surrender. "Okay—just remember you said that." He gave her a quick peck on the lips and rubbed his hands together as one who'd come up with a master plan.

Clint surveyed the spread that spanned the long countertop. "Well, let's get this show on the road."

Clint tossed out instructions like a commando, sending Terri scurrying in one direction and then the other—mix this, get that. If she weren't so hungry, she would have laughed.

Finally, all of the effort paid off. Together they placed a small table in front of the fireplace and sat down to an exquisite meal.

"So . . . you are good for something," Terri commented drolly, sending Clint an appreciative look across the table.

Clint wiped his mouth with a linen napkin and chuckled. "Don't you dare tell anyone, either. Between cooking and poetry, I'd be finished."

Terri nearly choked on her wine as ripples of laughter edged up her throat.

"Trust me," she said, taking in small gulps of air, "no one would believe me."

He gazed at her, deep sincerity replacing the laughter in his eyes. "It doesn't matter about anyone else, Terri." He leaned closer. "Not anymore." He stroked her cheek. She tipped her head to the side holding his hand in place with the gentle pressure of her shoulder. "Only you matter to me." Terri held her breath as their gazes locked in a heartrending embrace. "I want you to keep that with you. Always," he said, his voice a velvet whisper.

"I will," she whispered.

And he meant it, even as his other life tapped impatiently against the glass wall he'd constructed around himself.

Mark turned over on his side, noting the sleeping form with a mixture of pleasure and disdain. She was good. There was no doubt about that, he thought. He cupped his head in his palm and leaned on his elbow.

Good enough to make a man forget his troubles. He absently stroked her sheeted hip.

Yes, Melissa Taylor was a man's dream come true in more ways than one. And he was determined to use her to his benefit. She was the key that would unlock the doors to a very solid future for him. He'd become a very patient man over the years. He'd learned long ago what it meant to wait. Only now, his waiting would no longer be without its rewards.

The voluptuous figure turned over. Long silken lashes fluttered open, and a slow smile crossed the chiseled face.

It was true, she thought dreamily, happiness spilling through her as she looked up at Mark. One of the most incredible nights of her life was no fantasy.

She'd had so many doubts about getting involved with Mark after the things that Clint had said. She'd been furious with Clint for spoiling her happiness. How dare he try to steal it from her when he'd never offered any of his own? He couldn't tell her what to do, or who to see. The things he'd said about Mark couldn't be true. Mark was a loving, gentle person. Maybe a little ambitious. But she liked that in a man. The quest for power was intoxicating. That's what had drawn her to Clint.

Clint. Just thinking about him in those terms turned her insides to fire. Without thinking she reached for Mark, hoping to put out the flame.

"Hmm." Mark leaned down and kissed her full, parted lips. She snuggled closer, shutting her eyes. Imagining.

They were partners now, she thought, as Mark expertly caressed her warming body. They were joined, body and soul. Hadn't Clint—Mark—said that?

"What are you thinking about?" Mark asked.

"Just how happy I am," she sighed, shaking off her illusion. She adjusted the sheet over her body and sat up.

Mark kissed her neck. "Did you get the information I asked for?"

She swallowed as a pang of guilt struck her. She was getting confused as the two men momentarily merged into one, until Mark caressed the twin swells beneath the sheet.

"Yes," she sighed, breathless, her thoughts slowly beginning to clear.

"That's my girl." He lowered his head, kissing her full on the lips. He pulled away. "Get it for me."

Melissa slipped out of the bed and padded across the floor to her briefcase. She'd been so angry with Clint these past few weeks, she thought. Angry and hurt. She'd barely said two words to him since their blowup about Mark. That only made it easier for her to turn a blind eye and do what Mark asked her. She'd gathered the information almost with a sense of glee. As though this one act would compensate for Clint's betrayal. Then why was she having these twinges of doubt?

"Are you coming or what?" Mark snapped, shaking her out of her swirling thoughts.

She returned with a sealed manila folder. Hesitating, she held the folder against her breasts. The confusion hovered, then it fled.

"What's wrong?"

"Why—why do you need all of this information?" Her voice sounded childlike, perplexed.

Mark's face hardened. "I thought we had an understanding, Mel. You don't ask questions. I do all the work, and you and I live happily ever after."

He held out one hand for the folder and rubbed her bare leg with the other. "Right?"

Reluctantly she handed over the folder, her pulse beating wildly. Mark smiled as he ripped open the seal absorbing every written detail.

Patiently Steve sat in the dark automobile, far enough away from the lamplight to go unnoticed, but close enough to the entrance of Melissa's apartment building to monitor the comings and goings. He checked his watch and yawned. Mark had arrived nearly three hours earlier and had yet to emerge. Steve noted that fact on his pad, then leaned back against the leather headrest.

The life of a private investigator was often a lonely one, he mused, suppressing the urge to light a cigarette. His chosen field made it difficult to maintain relationships. The women who had filtered in and out of his life could not appreciate the type of work he did or deal with his often bizarre hours. More often than not, when he met women he told them he was an investor. That generally went over well and for the most part he kept his line of work a secret. There were very few people who would ever suspect that the dashing, sweet-talking Steve Coleman was a PI.

He chuckled without humor, wishing that Melissa had never found out. He truly believed that something hot could have happened between them. Something permanent. From the moment he'd laid eyes on her in Clint's office three years earlier, he'd known she was the one for him. She'd just started working for Clint, and it took Steve nearly six months to get up the nerve to ask her out. Melissa's interest peaked, simmered, then dried up when she found out what he did for a living. Steve had fallen hard for Melissa, and her rejection of him had thrown him for a loop for a while.

Now, as fate would have it, here he was sitting outside of the bedroom window that he had hoped to have continued access to. He shook his head. Life was a bitch. 'Cause if it wasn't, he wouldn't be sitting there.

He twisted the cover off of the red-checked thermos and filled a cup with black coffee. He certainly hoped that Clint appreciated the personal sacrifice he was making. He took a swallow of coffee and waited.

* * *

Terri and Clint spent a glorious four days together. Clint taught Terri how to ski and tried valiantly to teach her to drive a stick shift. She taught him how to dance the latest dance steps at the clubs that they frequented and to use meditation as a means of relaxation.

Terri had never felt so happy, so fulfilled. Her days sparkled with fun and laughter, and her nights were heady with unbridled passion. Clint was a master at all that he did. He had irrevocably won her heart, and she was falling deeper in love with him day by day.

The hurt and disappointment of her marriage to Alan steadily faded under Clint's loving attention. He made her feel secure, worthwhile, and thoroughly adored. But she knew that their idyllic interlude was rapidly drawing to a close. The prospect of being without him left her feeling empty. And her upcoming trip to L.A. had suddenly lost its luster.

"I'll have to go to California when we get back," Terri said as they watched the snow fall silently outside their bedroom window.

"Really? The deal came through with Viatek?"

"Um-hum."

Clint turned on the stereo, then sat next to Terri on the window seat beneath the bay window. He put an arm around her shoulder and kissed her heartily on the cheek.

"Congratulations, babe. I knew you would pull it off. How long will you be gone?"

"Probably about two weeks," she answered in a thin voice.

He nuzzled against her neck, and she closed her eyes enjoying the sensation.

"How about if I meet you out there? Where will you be staying?"

"I'll be at the Hilton in L.A. But I don't know how much free time I'll have." She sighed as he nibbled at her ear.

"Your day has to end at some point. Besides, I don't think I can stand being away from you for two whole weeks." His voice lowered. "Not after the last four days."

Terri felt a hot flush seep through her at the mention of their intimate times together. She had never been so free with anyone before. Not even her husband. And the things they did with and to each other still left her shaky with need. Then the thought of Alan and his unmistakable presence in L.A. flung her back to reality.

She'd have to tell Clint eventually, and she could certainly use his emotional support. Now was as good a time as any.

She took a fortifying breath. "My ex-husband, Alan, is working on the project also," she expelled in a rush. She looked at Clint, her heart racing, her eyes searching, waiting for his reaction.

"I see." Slowly he got up from the window seat, and crossed the floor to the other side of the room, keeping his back to her. "Would you prefer if I stayed in New York?"

"It's not that. It's just—" she fumbled through her thoughts for a reasonable response.

"Are you sure you're over him?" he tossed out, the look of brewing accusation simmering in his eyes. It infuriated him immeasurably to think that she had a life before him, as unrealistic as he knew that to be. His own sudden insecurity translated into irrational fear. What if Alan won her back?

"How can you ask me something like that?" she snapped. "After what I *thought* you and I meant to each other—after everything that I've told you about Alan and I—how could you? Do you think that I can just turn off and on at will? Be with you one minute and with my ex-husband the next?" She sucked her teeth in disgust.

Clint's eyes clouded over and he felt his heart constrict, seeing the pained look on Terri's face. His stubborn streak set in with a vengeance, and he held his ground. He'd come too far with her, letting his feelings become totally exposed. He couldn't risk being hurt—losing again. He just couldn't. She was going to have to prove herself to him before he crossed that final threshold. How could he even contemplate telling her about Ashley if he wasn't sure of the woman he loved?

He slung his hands in his pants pockets and looked away. He inhaled deeply.

"Let's be realistic, Terri," he blew out in frustration. "Regardless of anything else, you were married to him. That counts for something. A husband isn't someone you can just erase from your mind." Or a wife, he thought, guilt stabbing him in the gut.

Terri witnessed the confusion and insecurity whip across his face and wrestle for position. Her heart went out to him.

Slowly she crossed the room until she stood directly in front of him. He clenched his jaw, refusing to look at her. Terri almost grinned as the image of a stubborn little boy took hold of her thoughts.

She took a deep breath. "Clint, it's over between Alan and me," she said softly. Warily she stroked his arm as she continued to speak. "He decided a long time ago that I wasn't enough woman for him." A hollow sound came from her throat. "I just had to find out the hard way."

Terri bit back the knot of regret. "There's no way that there could ever be anything between Alan and me again." She desperately wanted to tell him how abandoned she'd felt, how empty after she lost the baby. But the words wouldn't come. It was still so painful. Maybe one day . . . ? Clint lowered his head, then looked at her. His eyes flickered, then settled. "I can't stand the thought of you and him, of you and anyone," he grumbled, pulling her into his arms. He buried his face in her hair, inhaling her scent.

She listened to his heart slam against her ear as she snuggled near. "There's nothing for you to worry about," she assured in a soft whisper. "Nothing."

CHAPTER 10

They stood facing each other in front of Terri's apartment door.

"I'll call you tomorrow," Clint said. His eyes softened as he held her waist in both hands. "I don't know how I'm gonna make it through the night without you." He lowered his head and kissed her gently on the lips, then with more urgency as desire sent up its warning cries.

Terri quickly felt the steady beat of yearning seep through her as she surrendered to the tempting kiss.

Reluctantly Clint eased away. "I'd better go," he said in a ragged breath.

Terri reached up and caressed his cheek. "I feel the same way." Her eyes glided lovingly over his face. "I had a beautiful time, Clint."

He pulled her closer while fighting the urge to pick her up and take her to bed. "I'd say beautiful was putting it mildly." Abruptly he stepped back, reclaiming his composure. "Get some rest." He gave her one last long look, then turned and walked away.

Terri floated into her apartment, the euphoric aftereffects of her long weekend hovering around her like a halo. A smile of complete contentment stayed on her face as she glided into her bedroom and plopped down on her bed.

She took a brief look at the stack of news clippings and photocopies of information piled at the foot of her bed.

With a sigh she pushed herself up, intent on discarding the remains of a less happy time once and for all. She gathered up the stack and headed for the kitchen, when the ringing of the phone stopped her midway. She turned toward the phone, momentarily undecided which way to go, until the phone rang again. She looked at the stack under her arm, then at the phone, and decided to answer it first.

"Hello?"

"Terri! Hi. It's Lisa."

"Hey, Lis. I just walked in the door a few minutes ago," she said, placing the stack precariously on the edge of the nightstand, and trying unsuccessfully to hold it in place. While Lisa chattered, Terri watched the papers flutter to the floor.

"I was just calling to be nosey, girl. So . . . how was it?"

"Which part?" Terri teased, fighting to stifle a giggle as she gathered up the fallen papers.

"The best parts of course, smarty."

"Well, my dear, to put it in two words, absolutely incredible!"

"Now didn't I tell you your day was coming?"

"Yeah, girlfriend, and it just came and came."

"Whew, child!"

Both women erupted into a fit of laughter at the play on words.

"Listen," Terri said, trying to catch her breath between giggles, "let me get myself settled and I'll call you later."

"No. That's okay. You go ahead and get yourself together. Brian and I were going to a movie. Why don't we try to get together tomorrow?"

"Sounds good. I'll give you a call. If I don't forget," she added, frowning.

"Oh yeah, this is the big week, right?"

"Uh-huh. I'll be leaving Wednesday morning."

"Don't you dare skip town and leave me in suspense!"

"I won't—I promise." Terri giggled. "Give my love to your handsome husband."

"I will. Talk to you tomorrow."

"Bye, Lis." Terri hung up the phone with the same whimsical smile still on her face. Taking a long breath, she marched to the kitchen and dumped the pile of papers into the trash.

That part of my life is behind me, she thought. No more looking to the past. She'd done enough of that for too long. She'd buried herself in her old misery and now that she finally saw daylight, there was no turning back. Especially with Clint waiting at the end of that tunnel.

Resolved to her newfound philosophy, Terri sauntered to the bathroom and ran a steamy tub of water.

A half hour later, relaxed, happy, and drowsy, Terri slid under the sheets determined to get a full night's sleep. She'd fought hard for the past several hours to keep thoughts of Clint at bay, knowing that if she didn't she'd reach for the phone and sleep would be a total impossibility. She smiled when she thought of him and how things had changed, and before she realized it her mind and body were buzzing with visions and needs.

She tried closing her eyes, but a steady shudder of wanting tripped through her, warming her body. This was crazy! She'd be one wreck if she couldn't learn to spend a night without him.

Restless, she turned on her side, easily falling prey to the recollections of the nights of passion that flared between her and Clint. He was everything that she could want in a man—handsome, loving, secure, successful—and the most incredible lover.

Her body heated at the thought as if an inner dial had been switched to slow cook. Yet there was still something nipping at her. Something vague and unsettling. There was still that fine line that neither of them had dared to cross. So often during their weekend together, she'd wanted to tell him about the baby she'd miscarried, how it had affected her life, and how it had made her feel so inadequate about herself.

In the night when they had lain together, whispering to each other, she'd wanted to share with him the lonely childhood she'd lived, always the outcast, and how important a family of her own was to her. But something always held her back. That disturbed her. If they were ever to have a meaningful and trusting relationship, they were going to have to be honest with each other.

She turned over on her back and stared up at the ceiling, folding her hands across her stomach.

Children were important to her. She wanted a child of her own more than anything. Alan could never understand that, so her loss never affected him in the least. He never understood her desire to want to shower her affections on anyone other than him. But it was a deep obsession with her, as though a child would somehow eradicate her parents' lack of love for her during her youth. Everyone would always tell her that she was "special" because her parents had "chosen" her, as if that would make up for the loss of her real family. Funny, she never felt special, just different and alone.

Terri let out a long troubling sigh and slowly pulled herself upright. She looked at the clock: 11:30 P.M. At this rate she'd never get any rest. Tossing off the sheet and quilt, she swung her long legs over the side of the bed and got up, crossing to the center of the bedroom.

Several moments later, inhaling deeply, she let her mind and body sink into the relaxing tranquility of meditation. When she finally felt her mind and body going limp and free of tension, she expertly uncrossed her legs and rose in one graceful motion.

Trancelike, she crossed the room to her bed, but stopped short of sinking in, when her bare foot was tickled by the sensation of paper.

She bent down and picked up what appeared to be one of the countless newspaper articles she'd acquired on Clint.

Without thinking further, she started to put the article on her nightstand when the small foreign date and headline caught her attention.

Her breathing quickened, and suddenly it felt as though all of the air had been sucked out of the room. *API London 20 February—Businessman Clinton Steele's Wife Killed in Car Accident.*

Her eyes raced across the tiny black print, trying to absorb the information before she read the words. *Desiree . . . his wife of three years . . . found dead . . . Porsche turned over . . . leaving behind an infant daughter, Ashley . . . drugs may have been involved . . . husband questioned . . . ?*

Ashley, Desiree, the names began to blur. Clint had a daughter. A daughter! The startling reality slowly seeped through the fog that had blanketed her brain, then plunged her repeatedly with the blade of irrational jealousy.

The small slip of paper floated from her nerveless fingers. She felt light-headed and strangely empty, the conflicting combination leaving her bereft of any tangible emotion. It took several more moments for her to completely absorb what she'd read, and she replayed it in her mind.

Why had Clint never mentioned his wife? She shook her head in confusion. Her brow creased. Perhaps she could accept his reluctance to speak of his wife's death, but never to mention the fact that he had a child?

"A child. Clint has a child." The softly whispered words floated through the silent room, then echoed in her head like a schoolyard taunt.

Images of her painful childhood, the loneliness, the revelation of her beginnings as an accidental birth, being told casually over dinner that her brother, her reason for going on, was dead, and that she would no longer be spending any more summers with her beloved grandmother in the Caribbean—who, too, had passed away. All of it swept through her in a wave of remorse.

Slowly she sat down on the edge of her bed. Clint never once said anything about his daughter. Why? Where was she? Who took care of her?

Her blood thickened, then turned to ice in her veins. Something deep inside switched off. The light of hope dimmed, and the door to her heart slammed shut.

"This changes everything, Clint," she whispered into the night. And the realization of her own hypocrisy left her trembling.

"I could handle anything, Clint—anything." She lowered her head, her heart constricting with the weight of her selfishness. "But not someone else's child. I know what it's like to always be someone else's child. But how will I ever be able to make you understand so that you won't hate me?"

A broken sob struggled upward from her throat as the tears slowly spilled over her closed lids.

CHAPTER 11

"Ms. Powers, good morning. How was your holiday?" Andrea asked, with more enthusiasm than Terri could handle.

"It was fine, Andrea. Thank you." Terri adjusted the dark glasses on the bridge of her nose in an attempt to shield her swollen eyes. "Is Stacy in yet?"

"No. Not yet. She called and said she should be in around ten-thirty."

Terri nodded absently. "I need you to reschedule my flight reservations. I want to leave this morning instead of Wednesday."

Andrea looked quizzically at her boss but didn't question her. "Will you still be staying at the Hilton?"

"Yes. As soon as you confirm my flight, give them a call as well. Then contact the studio and advise them that I'll be arriving today. Perhaps they would care to get the initial meeting over earlier than scheduled. Let me know."

"Certainly," Andrea answered. "Ms. Powers, is something wrong? You don't look well."

"Everything's fine, Andrea. I guess I just did too much this weekend." She gave Andrea a weak smile and walked toward her office. Just as she reached the door, she stopped and turned toward Andrea. "Hold all of my calls today, will you?"

"Of course."

"And I'm not accepting any calls from Mr. Steele. Understood?"

"Yes, Ms. Powers." *So that was it.*

Terri walked into her office and closed the door softly behind her.

* * *

"The developers want you to come to Nassau in two weeks to take a look at how the work is going," Melissa advised, taking a seat on the couch and purposely avoiding his gaze.

Clint nodded. "Have our lawyers finished going over the contracts?"

"I'm expecting a call from Elliot Landau this afternoon," she answered in her most practiced professional voice.

Clint recognized the tone and knew that it stemmed from their argument, weeks ago, over Mark Andrews. She was still upset. But that was her problem. As long as she did her job, that was all he could expect. Although he reluctantly had to admit that he missed the light-hearted camaraderie that had always been a part of their relationship.

"I'm considering giving the Nassau account to Powers, Inc. What do you think?"

Inwardly she cringed. "Haven't you had enough problems from that woman? After all the work that was put into the cable television proposal and she just—" Melissa caught herself when she saw the dark look pass across Clint's features. She briefly looked away. "I mean, they're not the only agency in town."

Clint's jaw clenched. "Maybe we should discuss this later."

Melissa stiffened, drawing herself up to her full height. "Will that be all?" she asked in a clipped voice.

Clint stood and walked toward the window. "Yeah." He turned and looked over his shoulder as Melissa sauntered toward the door. "There is one thing."

Melissa halted and turned toward him. "Yes?"

"If you hear from the *real* Melissa Taylor, tell her I'm looking for her." He turned back toward the window while Melissa strutted out, a half grin lifting her lips.

Clint slammed down the phone, total disgust creasing his face. There were few things that really got on his nerves, but one of them was a secretary that ran interference.

He pushed himself up from his chair with such force, he sent the wheeled leather armchair sailing across the room.

What in the hell could be wrong? When he dropped Terri off last night, everything was fine. He'd made three phone calls to her office, only to be told she was unavailable.

"Unavailable!" His voice boomed around the room. "Why are you so suddenly unavailable, Terri?"

He loosened his tie, clenching his jaw. He sure as hell wasn't going to give up that easily. That secretary was going to tell him where Terri was whether she realized it or not!

He smiled devilishly. Next time charm would be the key.

* * *

The six-hour flight to Los Angeles International Airport had been delayed for nearly an hour. Terri impatiently tapped her foot as the cab sat in the midmorning traffic.

Annoyed, she checked her watch. So much for stopping off at the hotel. She was scheduled to be at the studio in less than twenty minutes. After her request that the meeting time be moved up, it wouldn't sit very well for her to show up late.

Thank heavens she'd had the presence of mind to wear her pink cotton suit beneath her winter coat. It would just have to do, she thought, amazed at the 70-degree weather near the end of November.

"Driver, I've changed my mind about the hotel. I won't have time. I need to go straight to Viatek Studios on the Boulevard."

Resigned to the fact that there was nothing she could do about her present situation, she settled back in the cab and popped open her briefcase. Absently she stroked the smooth burgundy leather surface, remembering all too well where the case had come from. It had been a congratulatory gift from Alan for her first major contract.

As much as she'd tried to prepare herself, she just couldn't shake the butterflies that had claimed a stake in her stomach. She knew that Lisa was right. It was over. Or was it?

She forced herself to push aside the unsettling thoughts and sifted through the proposals that she and Stacy had worked out. Her full lips tugged with pride, feeling assured that the movie executives would be pleased with the promotional campaign.

Finally the cab halted in front of the imposing studio. Terri reached into her purse and quickly paid the driver. She had five minutes to spare.

Hours later, tired but satisfied, Terri crossed the threshold of her hotel room. Her one consolation was that Alan had not been present at the meeting. However, he was expected the following day. She would just have to deal with the situation when it arose.

"Thank you very much," she said to the young bellhop who carried her bags. She slipped out of her shoes, stepped into the suite, and paid him.

"Thank *you,* Ms. Powers!" The young man beamed, eyeing the ten dollar bill in his hand. He backed out toward the door, smiling all the way.

Terri grinned wistfully, recalling her own college days waiting tables, cleaning hotel rooms, whatever it took to pay her tuition. She knew how much those tips meant when you were earning only minimum wage.

As if pulled by an unseen magnet, she crossed the sun-bleached wooden floor to the terrace. Swinging open the French doors, she was greeted by a whiff of salty sea air. She inhaled deeply of the scent and closed her eyes as images of her childhood blossomed before her.

How often had she and her brother, Malcolm, raced across the white, sandy beaches of Barbados with Nana always yelling for them not to stray too far? Nana had raised them since Terri was a two-year-old toddler, and when Malcolm came along she raised him as well. After the death of their mother in a boating accident and the disappearance of their respective fathers, Nana was the only relative that she and Malcolm had.

Malcolm.

The old knot tightened in her belly. His face was vague now. She'd tried to always keep his image engraved in her memory, but the years had slowly worn it away like water beating relentlessly against a rock. All that remained was a hazy figure with laughing eyes and an easy smile, which at times were so similar to Mark's. The thought brought on a shudder.

A deep sigh lifted her breasts, then drifted across the pale blue sky. What she did remember, all too clearly, were her baby brother's anguished pleas when the social workers separated them. Nana had gotten too ill to care for them. They had no one else. The last time she'd seen Malcolm was a week before his fifth birthday. She was only seven years old, and she promised him that she'd return.

Terri shook her head vehemently, trying desperately to dispel the painful memory. Her guilt, at times, was almost more than she could bear. She'd been Malcolm's only hope, and she'd abandoned him. Then he was gone—forever.

Moments later she slowly looked away, knowing that the solace she sought would not be found in the ocean depths.

Turning, she reentered the main room, picked up her two suitcases, and walked into the bedroom—oblivious to the white wicker decor. She urged her body to go through the ritual of unpacking and sorting through the stack of notes and documents she'd brought along, afraid to be alone with her thoughts. "An idle mind is the devil's workplace," she could hear her Nana say.

She tossed her lingerie into the dresser drawer, and without warning, her thoughts shifted erotically to Clint. She hugged her negligee to her face. How long could she put off not thinking, not feeling, not wanting Clint?

The weakness that she felt for him left her vulnerable, a sensation she was unable to handle. Even Alan had never been able to evoke such profound feelings of longing in her. She'd kept the key to her heart safely tucked away, out of reach. Clint had been able to unlock it as smoothly as a cat burglar slid into the family safe. The only difference was that his tools were charm and an irresistible sexuality that left her reeling. But feelings had been her downfall from the beginning. She could no longer allow them to misguide her.

With that determination made, she reached for the phone and dialed her office in New York. She had yet to let them know that she'd arrived or to pick up any important messages. It was already six o'clock New York time, and she knew that jet lag was right behind her.

She listened patiently as the phone hummed to life.

"Powers, Incorporated," the familiar voice answered.

"Hi, Andrea. It's me."

"Ms. Powers! How was the trip?"

"Long. Is everything all right?"

"Fine. Stacy has everything under control."

"Do I have any messages?"

"You sure do." Andrea flipped through her message pad and reeled off the messages, but dared not tell her that she had revealed her whereabouts to Mr. Steele. If she ever found out . . . ?"

Terri took hasty notes and fired out instructions on who to call back.

Andrea swallowed hard. "The last three messages are from Mr. Steele."

Terri felt her stomach shoot up to her throat.

"Really?" Her calm voice surprised her. "What did he say?"

"He asked to speak with you. And he wanted to know where you were."

"And . . . ?" She eased her stomach back into place with a silent gulp.

"And—" Andrea hesitated "—I told him you were unavailable." She knew her boss was adamant about giving out personal information. But he was just so nice and seemed to really care about Terri. And somehow, Andrea believed that she'd done the right thing.

"Is there anything else?"

"No. Everything is fine."

"Good. Well, tell Stacy that I'll call her in the morning and bring her up to date. I won't have time this evening. I was invited to a studio party."

"Wow. A real Hollywood party!"

Terri chuckled. "I'll fill you in on all the juicy details when I get back."

Andrea's eyes lit up. "Just bring me back an autograph of someone famous and gorgeous. Of the male gender, preferably," she sighed.

Terri shook her head in amusement. "I'll try. Talk to you tomorrow."

Slowly Terri replaced the phone in its cradle. She picked it up again and punched in the numbers to Clint's office. Then halfway to completion, she hung up.

She closed her eyes and hugged the receiver to her breasts. She wasn't ready to confront him. Not yet.

"Like I said, man, this thing with Melissa and Andrews is hot and heavy. I sat outside her window for a full night, and believe me, he never left." Steve tossed his notes across the desk toward Clint.

Clint's eyes narrowed. "With everything that we know about Andrews, I have to have some serious concerns about my own vulnerability with Melissa being the one on the inside."

Steve nodded. "It's possible," he began reluctantly, "that she may be feeding him info, but I find it hard to believe that Mel would stab you in the back. Her loyalty runs pretty deep."

"I know." Clint sighed, rubbing his hand across his bearded chin. "I guess on top of everything else, I don't want her to get hurt, either. That Andrews is a slime." He rolled his eyes in disgust.

"Listen, Mel's a big girl. She can take care of herself. I really think that the last thing you have to worry about is Mel, or her giving away company secrets."

The corner of Clint's lip lifted slyly. "Are you sure that the ole' fires aren't still lit for Mel, and that's why you can't see the real deal?"

Steve cut his eyes in Clint's direction. "Very funny. You really know how to twist the knife."

Clint popped up from his reclining position. "Just kiddin', man. Just kiddin'." He thumped Steve on the back.

Steve looked at Clint through thick lashes. His smooth eyebrows raised in question. "Speaking of fires, what's the latest with you and Ms. T?"

"That's a damn good question. I *thought* everything was great. After this past weekend I didn't think anything in life could ever be wrong."

"But?"

"But now she's pulling some kind of game on me. I called her office, and her secretary gave me the runaround, only to find out, after numerous attempts and considerable charm, that Terri left for L.A. early—Without saying a word to me!"

"You're kidding."

Clint began to pace. "Do I sound like I'm kidding?"

"Maybe something came up . . . suddenly."

"Too suddenly for her to call me?" Clint shook his head. "I find that hard to believe."

Steve smiled. "That sounds like your ego talkin'."

Clint flashed him a dangerous look, which Steve openly ignored.

"Do you think you're so damn irresistible that a woman like Terri is just going to up and change her whole agenda because she spent the weekend with you?" Steve laughed outright when he saw Clint practically swell up and explode before his eyes. He fought back the laughter. "But seriously. You know women, they run on emotion. Maybe she's trying to sort things out."

"What things?"

"How should I know? Whatever things they always have to figure out. Why don't you call her and find out for yourself instead of being pissed off."

"She's the one who took off without a word."

"And you're just going to leave it like that, I suppose?"

"I *suppose* you're right," Clint snapped sarcastically.

"Yeah, and look what happened the last time you were playing Mr.

Toughguy. You nearly blew it. Maybe she needs you to call her. For whatever the reason. From everything that you've told me about her, she doesn't seem like the kind of woman who'd play games."

Clint blew out an exasperated breath. "Damn, I hate it when you're right!" He grinned reluctantly at Steve.

Steve patted Clint on the shoulder. "Don't take it too hard," he chuckled. He looked up at the clock. "Hey, I've got to go. I have to meet a client in fifteen minutes. I'll check with you later."

Clint walked Steve to the door. "Thanks. For the info and the advice."

"Anytime." He began to leave, then turned back. "Women love surprises," he said in a stage whisper. He gave Clint a conspiratorial wink and strolled down the corridor.

Clint chuckled silently. "Surprises, huh?" He walked around his desk, sat down, and ran his hand across his beard, the beginnings of a very tempting idea brightening his darkly handsome face.

He reached for the phone and dialed the international operator. If he was going to make changes in his life, it would have to be on all fronts, beginning with his daughter. And there was no time like the present.

Patiently he listened to the lines hum and click, then finally ring countless miles across the ocean.

"Hello?" answered the polished English voice.

"Hi, Jill, it's me, Clint."

Jillianne tried to control the excitement that flooded her at the sound of her brother-in-law's voice.

"Clint, I was wondering when you were going to call." Her soft English accent drifted across the lines. "It's been weeks. When are you coming home?"

Her favorite question. "Soon." *My standard response.* "I'll definitely be home for the Christmas holidays."

Her spirits sank. "That long?"

"I know. I'm sorry. But I don't think I can get away any sooner. How's my girl?"

"Ashley's just fine and as busy as ever. She misses you."

Clint heard the silent reproach. "Is she awake? I'd like to talk with her."

"I just put her down for a nap."

"Oh." Disappointment filled him. He rubbed his hand across the beard that braced his jaws. "Please tell her that I called, Jill."

"Of course I will."

Seconds of silence ticked away. Jillianne gripped the phone until her knuckles locked, hoping that she could hold on to his voice just a little longer.

"How have you been, Jillianne?" Clint finally asked. "Have you been getting out?"

"I've been doing well. But you know I don't go out much."

The soft tinkle of her laughter filled his ears. So much like Desiree, he thought.

"Ashley keeps me suitably busy," she added.

He smiled as an image of his precocious daugher sprang to life. "You need more in your life than Ashley. What about a man? You're a beautiful woman, Jill. There must be countless available men waiting in the wings." He worried about his sister-in-law's solitary life. Ever since Desiree's death, Jillianne had devoted her entire life to him and Ashley. She deserved more than that.

"There are a few men, but none who really interest me."

If only she could tell him that the only man she'd ever wanted was him. Every time she thought about her love for Clint, guilt pummeled her. He had been married to her sister, and it didn't seem right that she should feel the way she did about him. Yet she couldn't help it. She'd been in love with Clint almost from the moment she saw him. She'd envied Clint's love for her sister. And God help her, she'd almost been relieved when her sister died, even as much as she'd loved Desiree.

"I'm sure that the right man is out there waiting for you, sweetheart. You deserve it."

Sweetheart. She hugged the endearment to her breasts. "But what would become of you and Ashley?"

"You let me worry about that," he said, his thoughts immediately turning to Terri. She'd make a wonderful wife and mother. He just knew it, although he had yet to tell Terri about Ashley. But he was certain that she would love Ashley just as much as he did.

A light tapping at his office door drew his attention.

"Hold on a moment, Jill."

He looked up and saw Melissa standing in the threshold. Clint crooked his finger, signaling Melissa to come in. He covered the mouthpiece. "I'll be right with you. I'm talking long distance."

He turned his attention back to his phone call. "Listen, hon, I've got to go. I'll call you in a few days. All right? And give Ashley a hug and kiss from me."

Jillianne shut her eyes. "Of course. We'll be waiting to hear from you."

"Take care of yourself."

"You, too, Clint," she said softly. Reluctantly Jill hung up the phone as she mentally ticked away the days until Clint would return. He had never so much as shown more than a brotherly interest in her. So she kept her secret, silently hoping that one day his eyes would open. To only her.

Clint replaced the receiver. "What are you doing here so late, Melissa? It's close to seven o'clock."

Melissa took a seat on the long leather couch that spanned one wall of the office. Her short black skirt crept seductively upward as she crossed her shapely legs.

Clint self-consciously tore his eyes away, but not before Melissa caught the look of appreciation that lit the ebony orbs.

"I had a few things I wanted to finish up," she said. She laced her long fingers together. "Was that our procurement office in Ghana?" She shrugged her shoulder. "I mean—you mentioned long distance."

Clint shook his head. "No, that was my sister-in-law in England. I was just checking in."

"Oh." The momentary grip of jealousy released her.

Clint looked at her for several long seconds. "Is something wrong?"

Melissa lowered her eyes, then looked up at him, framing the words in her mind. "Can we talk?"

Clint leaned forward, giving her his full attention. "Anytime."

Melissa swallowed. "I know I've been a real bitch lately."

Clint chuckled. "I wouldn't go that far." He smiled at her. "But pretty close."

"And—well—I thought I'd make it up to you."

"That's not necessary, Mel. I understand that you were upset, and sometimes we just say things."

"That's no excuse for the way I spoke to you. I realize that you were trying to look out for me." She ran an expertly manicured hand up and down her skirt. "I guess what I'm trying to say is that I'm sorry."

Clint rose from his seat and walked over to Melissa. He crouched down beside her, briefly catching the scent of her White Linen perfume. "No apology necessary," he said gently, his words tripping her heart.

She wanted to reach out and touch the slender silver threads that ran through his hair, but she knew better.

Her large hazel eyes held his, and what Clint saw in them took him aback. But just as quickly as that look had appeared, it vanished. Maybe he was just imagining the longing in her eyes. He really must be losing it, he thought. Melissa was the most controlled woman he had ever met—logical, dependable, sensible. That was Melissa.

Her voice drew him out of his reverie.

"I, uh, was wondering if I could take you to dinner?" She tilted her professionally coiffed head to the side and slightly lifted her shoulder. "Sort of a peace offering. My treat," she added in a hurry.

Maybe an evening with Melissa was just the distraction he needed to get his mind off Terri. Even if it was only temporary.

"Now that you mention it, I'm starved. And guess what? I think my calendar is free," he teased, chucking her playfully under the chin. He rose from his crouched position. "If you could wait about ten minutes, I'll be ready."

She nearly sighed aloud with relief. "I'll get my things and meet you in the lobby," she said, trying to control the breathless elation that gripped her voice.

Maybe tonight, she thought, as she hurried down the carpeted hallway to her office. Maybe tonight.

CHAPTER 12

The brilliant whitewashed walls of Alan Martin's beachfront duplex apartment were covered with the stark images of his profession.

Huge black and white photos of lush, naked models, the human eye magnified hundreds of times, breathtaking shots of storms at sea, not to mention the countless photos of the Hollywood elite, adorned every available wall space.

Alan took pride in his work and what his innate talent—to spot the perfect picture—had afforded him. He lived well as a result.

Prior to leaving New York, Alan had solidly established himself as one of the most sought after photographers in the business. His work was impeccable, appearing in ads and magazines across the country and in Europe. Arriving in Hollywood only enhanced his marketability. His morals, however, remained a hot topic of the social set. He wholeheartedly did everything he could to live up to his "bad boy" reputation.

Alan stepped out of the steamy bathroom, covered from the waist down in a printed towel.

Padding across the carpeted hallway, he entered his bedroom only to find his latest conquest sound asleep.

Indifferently he shook her until her bleary eyes opened and slowly focused.

"Hey, baby," she mumbled, flashing him a seductive smile.

"It's time to go, sweetheart. I have plans for the evening." He slid open his closet door and scanned his vast array of tailor-made suits.

"Can't I go with you?" she whined.

He threw her an exasperated look from soft brown eyes. "Listen, doll, I thought we understood each other. I don't mix business with pleasure."

The young woman pulled up the sheet to cover her exposed breasts. "But I thought I meant something to you, Al," she pouted, running a hand through her tousled hair.

"Of course you do, baby," he crooned by rote, not even remembering her name. A night of booze and drugs had dulled his memory. "But I have business to take care of, and it doesn't include you." He patted her hip. "So hurry it up."

He pulled out a lightweight, mustard-colored suit and collarless shirt. Secure in his prowess, he dropped the towel from his waist and meticulously began to dress.

Christy silently fumed. She'd been sure that her womanly charms would win her an invitation to the biggest bash this season. She'd expected Alan to take her along—in gratitude. This could have been her opportunity to be discovered. *Who could she connect with in a hurry to get herself invited?*

She stormed off to the bathroom, shutting the door solidly behind her.

Alan breathed a sigh of relief. He wasn't in the mood for a scene. He stepped into his pants and slipped into soft Gucci loafers. Crossing the room to his dresser, he selected his favorite cologne, dabbing it generously across his face. He picked up a diamond stud earring and inserted it into his left earlobe.

He turned toward the full-length mirror, admiring what he saw and wondered if Terri would feel the same way.

Clint leaned back against the red velvet chair. The intimate dining room was filled with late dinner patrons who frequented the Russian Tea Room after Broadway performances. The hushed voices, soft music, and tinkling of crystal and silver blended in perfect harmony.

"Dinner was delicious," he commented, briefly shutting his eyes in satisfaction. "I didn't realize how much I needed to get out."

He looked across the table at Melissa. "Thanks for asking me."

"It was my pleasure," she purred.

Clint rubbed his full belly. "It'll take hours of jogging to get this off," he joked.

Melissa's eyes sparkled. She leaned forward. "I didn't know you jogged. I love jogging." The lie dripped from her lips like honey.

"Really?" He was clearly surprised. Melissa didn't look like the kind of woman who ever broke a sweat. "Maybe we could get together sometime."

"Whenever you're ready." She quickly thought of all the gear she'd have to charge on her gold card.

Clint took a swallow from his fourth glass of wine. "I guess there are a lot of things we don't know about each other."

Melissa lowered her long lashes.

"I stay so busy with business, I've never taken the time to really get to know you," he added.

Her heart raced, searching for an opening. "That's to be expected. I mean—we haven't had time for more than a professional relationship." She looked at him suggestively.

He felt himself treading on dangerous ground, but the good food, easy music, and the wine, which he rarely drank, were all going to his head.

He smiled. "Perhaps that will change. Why don't you tell me about Melissa—the woman." His eyes held her captive as he languidly leaned back in his seat.

"Well," she began slowly, "I grew up in Chicago, attended Northwestern University, and graduated with honors."

He grinned indulgently. "Tell me something that I haven't read on your resume."

Melissa laughed softly. "What do you want to know?"

"What about your family? I'd love to know what kind of people raised such a remarkable woman."

She reached for a lie that would fulfill the image she thought he had of her. But before she spoke, she opted for the truth.

"I didn't really know my parents," she said in a near whisper, fiddling with her glass. "My mother was a nightclub singer. She traveled a lot. And my father—" she shrugged and her voice trailed off "—I spent most of my life living with my aunt and uncle. My mother visited occasionally, but she never stayed very long."

"Melissa—I'm sorry. I had no idea."

"It's all right." She gave him a pained smile. "I've learned to live with it."

"And very well I might add."

His warm words wrapped around her like a down quilt. She knew he'd understand, and her desire for him intensified like white heat.

Clint and Melissa pulled up in front of her apartment building on Ninety-sixth Street and Central Park West.

"I had a great time, Clint." She looked across at him. "And—I'm glad we had the time to talk."

She dug in her purse for her keys. "Uh, would you like to come in for a minute?"

The reality of his situation finally took root. What was he doing here—with Melissa—when it was Terri he wanted?

"No thanks, Mel. It's late, and we have a full day tomorrow." His skull was beginning to pound. He touched his head self-consciously. "And I think I need to sleep off all that wine." He offered her a crooked grin.

"Tomorrow then," she said softly.

She looked at him for a brief moment, imagining the feel of those luscious lips against hers. She knew she had to find out.

Without warning, she leaned toward him and pressed her moist lips against his, both startling and stimulating Clint with the fiery contact.

Instinctively he returned her kiss, until he felt Melissa's arms slip seductively around his neck, pulling him closer.

He eased away. "Mel—," he breathed, holding her at arm's length. He shook his head. "This isn't right. I'm sorry. I shouldn't have let it get this far."

She swallowed. "Clint, please. You don't have to apologize." She tore her gaze away from him. "It was my fault."

He took a deep breath. "Let's put it this way." He tilted up her chin with the tip of his index finger. "We got caught up in the moment." His smile was warm. "Still friends?"

She nodded.

"Good." He lightly kissed her forehead. "I'll see you in the office."

She turned and with as much dignity as she could summon, opened the car door and walked toward the building entrance.

Briefly Clint shut his eyes and took a breath of relief, thankful of what he'd gotten himself out of. What had he been thinking about? Without looking back, he sped off down the darkened street.

Melissa inserted her key in the lock, flicked on the hallway light, and tossed her purse and coat on the Queen Anne settee in the foyer.

Kicking off her shoes, she plopped down on the rich damask couch—a smile of total contentment outlining her full lips—committing to memory every detail of her evening with Clint.

The aroma of grilling steaks cooking on the huge open pit filled the late night air. Light-hearted laughter, pulsing music, and loud splashes in the Olympic-sized pool added to the opulence.

Everywhere that Terri turned, a familiar face was spotted. It was rumored that Spike Lee and John Singleton were expected. But in the meantime, she was tickled to see her favorite late-night talk show host being doused in the pool.

Slowly she threaded her way through the richly dressed crowd of revelers and headed toward the buffet table. Her mouth watered at the display of exotic delicacies. The studio obviously spared no expense, she observed.

Terri picked up a plate and made her selections. Taking her spoils, she strolled across the grounds and found an empty lounge chair near the pool, between two bikini-clad beauties.

Terri nibbled away while watching the comings and goings of the guests, when a waiter in formal attire stopped by her chair and offered a glass of champagne.

"No, thank you." She smiled, looking up at the waiter—then, over his shoulder, she caught sight of that familiar swagger coming in her direction.

Her whole being became infused with an unspeakable heat. She willed herself to get up and run, but her mind seemed to have lost all control of her limbs. Her body remained immobile, but her heart raced at breakneck speed.

Within moments he stood above her.

"Hi, Terri." His silky voice embraced her.

He was still so gorgeous. His café-au-lait complexion held a healthy glow and those eyes, the color of ginger, still held the old magnetism. She inclined her head in acknowledgment. "Alan."

Slowly she urged her breathing to return to normal and forced herself to smile. "You're looking well."

He crouched down next to her and stroked her bare arm. "You're as beautiful as ever," he said in a husky whisper.

He expertly scanned her flawless mahogany features, the layers of jet black locks that were wrapped stylishly atop a brilliant headdress of black and gold. His eyes quickly traveled downward. Momentarily he stared at the rise and fall of her full, round breasts, peeking teasingly out from her low-cut black and gold satin top. Then down to those legs that he remembered so well, covered in gold satin pants.

His hand trailed up her left arm.

With her right hand she lifted the wayward fingers and placed them solidly on the arm of the chair.

"Still have hand problems, I see," she stated in a flat voice.

He tossed back his head and let out a deep robust laugh, his diamond earring twinkling in the moonlight. Then he focused those cool browns on her.

"You haven't changed a bit either—*I* see."

The woman sitting next to Terri got up and strutted toward the pool. Alan's eyes followed the shapely form as she dove gracefully into the pool.

Terri's mind flashed backward to the countless stream of women who'd interrupted their life together. If she'd witnessed his behavior a year ago, her ego would have been crushed. But things were different now. She was different. Suddenly it didn't matter anymore. She finally realized, in that brief instant, that Alan was just Alan, and he'd be the same way if he was with her or any other woman. That long-awaited realization set her free.

She smiled an easy smile of acceptance and forgiveness, just as Alan returned his gaze to her, which he characteristically interpreted as being directed at him.

He grinned. "Why don't we get away from here—talk about—things? I could show you around. We could—"

Her voice was cool, controlled as she cut him off. "Forget it, Al. That was then, this is now. It's strictly business between us."

The smug smile slowly dissolved. "Business? Come on, baby, we had something." He eased closer, his warm breath fanning her face. "You know that as well as I do."

"Had, Al. Had." She made a move to get up. "And whatever it *was,* is a matter of perspective."

He put a restraining hand on her arm. "I was wrong. You have changed, Terri," he said, secretly pleased. He never could tolerate a woman who was too easy. That had been part of his and Terri's problem from the beginning. She gave too much, was always too willing to please, too trusting—just *too* everything. If you looked up the definition of a "good woman" in the dictionary, you'd see Terri's picture. She made it easy for him to live the kind of life he lived. It seemed as though the worse he behaved, the kinder and more giving she became. His stomach lurched with a mild pang of guilt.

She eased her arm away. "You're right about that, Alan. I have. In ways you'll never know." She rose from the chair. "If you'll excuse me, I think I'll find our host. See you later."

Alan pursed his lips in perturbance as he watched her move gracefully away and wondered why he had dumped "what's-her-name" for this. Well, what was life without a challenge? Terri would be in L.A. for two weeks. He was sure that he'd have her back in his bed long before then.

The evening wore on as the multitude of guests continued to ebb and flow throughout the magnificent expanse of property.

Although being in crowds usually unraveled her, Terri was thankful that she wasn't the focal point, and she was able to relax. She had to admit that she was truly enjoying herself as she raptly listened to tales of Hollywood scandals from a reporter from the *Globe.*

". . . They never knew that his wife had hired a photographer to sit outside of his window," chuckled the young reporter. "That is, until the photographer fell out of the tree and crashed into the bed of roses."

The small group laughed uproariously at the vision.

"How were they able to keep it out of the papers?" Terri wanted to know.

"Believe me, honey," commented Gail Holloway, the newest big-screen sex symbol, "when you have the kind of money and clout that Paul Arkin has, you can cover up anything."

Terri lifted her eyebrows. "I guess you're right."

Gail extended her hand. "I'm Gail."

"Terri."

"So what brings you out here? I can tell by your New York accent that you're not a native."

Terri grinned. "I'm working on the ad campaign for Jonathan Montgomery's newest film, *Outburst.*"

"You're kidding! I tested for the lead in that film. They said I was too—well, you know." She thought for a moment, putting a tapered finger to her famous lips. "So you must know Alan Martin? He's the public relations photographer."

"Oh, yes. I *know* Alan."

Gail caught the disapproving tone in Terri's voice. "Maybe more than just professionally?" she asked, her interest sparked.

"We worked together on a few projects in New York," she answered noncommittally.

"Hmm. Well, he's definitely an interesting specimen," Gail said, taking a sip from her glass of champagne.

She remembered all too well the long nights with Alan Martin when she'd first arrived in Hollywood. He might be a real dog, but his photos gave her that first big break. For that she would always be grateful.

The two striking women—one a rich mahogany, the other a golden saffron—caught the attention of every male eye as they passed. Neither of them took notice.

"When did you know you wanted to be an actress?" Terri asked, totally at ease in Gail's company.

"For as long as I can remember," she answered wistfully, flashing Terri the smile that made men want to reach out and touch her—among other things. "A lot of directors say that I have natural talent." Her voice lifted in pride. "I've never even been to acting school."

"That's fantastic. You must be very proud of your accomplishments."

"Oh, I am."

The two women stopped in front of the enormous buffet table and loaded their plates.

"Well, well, well. If it isn't the two most gorgeous women in this joint."

Terri and Gail turned simultaneously to find Alan standing behind them, a look of pure appreciation brewing in his eyes.

"Gail, sweetheart." He bowed his head and kissed her full lips. He slid a possessive hand around her tiny waist. "I didn't know you were acquainted with my ex-wife. She's pretty hot stuff back in New York."

Gail's picture-perfect face seemed to crumple, and Terri instantly knew that she, too, had been to bed with her roving ex-husband.

Gail swallowed. "Really?" She looked from one to the other, and it all sank in. This was *the* Terri Powers, of Powers, Inc. Damn! Al only briefly mentioned his marriage. He'd never gone into detail with her. Who would have thought that she would wind up chatting with his ex? To think that she'd been on the verge of telling Terri about some of the unforgettable nights she'd spent with Alan Martin. A brief chill scooted up her spine. But Gail quickly regained her composure. "How's everything with you, Al?"

"Couldn't be better." He grinned broadly. "I suppose Terri's already told you that she and I'll be working together." He gave Terri a pointed look. "Just like old times, eh, Terri?"

"Not quite." Her words were velvety smooth, but her meaning was coated in granite. She turned to Gail. "Listen, I'm going to leave. I have an early morning." She dipped into her purse, pulled out her business card, and handed it to Gail with a smile of understanding. "If you're ever in New York, look me up. And if you ever get tired of your PR people, give me a call. We're always looking for new clients."

Gail looked at the card and then at Terri, finding a new level of admiration for her.

Terri nodded curtly to Alan. "Good night."

"See you on the set," he replied smoothly.

"Whew, what's with you two?" Gail asked, shaking off the tension that had chilled the balmy air. "Nasty divorce?"

"Let's just say—unfinished business." He smiled that roguish smile. "But you and I don't have that problem." He leaned down and breathed in her ear. "We never leave things unfinished."

Out of the corner of his eye he caught a glance of "what's-her-name" on the arm of a studio executive. Alan smiled in her direction, silently admiring her for her ingenuity.

"Touché," he mouthed as she turned up her cosmetically corrected nose and sashayed away.

Clint lay sprawled across his king-sized bed, wearing nothing but a pair of silk boxer shorts. He stared up at the ceiling.

Thank heavens he hadn't let things get out of hand with Melissa, he thought. Never before had he allowed his professional relationships to cross the thin personal line. And certainly never within his own office. He wouldn't start now. What was worse, he'd never be able to explain that one to Terri.

Terri. How badly he wanted her. His loins ached with unfulfilled need.

She would be gone for two weeks. He wouldn't wait that long to see and talk with her again. That was too much time for things to go wrong between them. And she had some serious explaining to do.

He was going to do something about it—and soon. In the meantime, he got up from bed, determined to withstand a cold shower.

CHAPTER 13

Clint arrived at his office the following morning with a new sense of purpose. He stopped in front of his secretary's desk, his darkly handsome face beaming with excitement.

"Good morning, Mr. Steele. Don't you look happy this morning."

"I feel great, Pat." There was a slight tinge of wonder in his voice as though he, too, was realizing his joy for the first time. "I need you to do something for me right away."

"Of course." Pat automatically pulled out her notebook.

"Call the airline and book me on the next flight to L.A.—first class. Once you have confirmation, then reserve a suite for me at the Beverly Hilton. And pull together all of the data on the resort project in the Caribbean. I'll be taking it with me." He tapped the desk with his palm and jauntily strolled off to his office. "Oh, and Pat," he tossed over his shoulder, "don't forget to rent a car for me also."

Pat reached for her Rolodex just as Melissa approached.

Pat looked up. "Good morning, Ms. Taylor. I didn't know you were—"

"Did I hear Mr. Steele say that he was going to L.A.?"

"Yes. It was a surprise to me, too. I guess I'll have to cancel his appointment for—"

But before she could finish, Melissa turned on her heel and stormed off down the corridor.

Pat shrugged her narrow shoulders at everyone's peculiar behavior and proceeded to dial the airline.

* * *

Terri'd spent a night full of endless, erotic dreams of Clint. She awoke with every nerve ending on fire, her emotions strung to near breaking, but through sheer willpower she'd been able to push him to the back of her thoughts, if only temporarily, as she plowed through her day.

Her first day at the studio had been exhilarating. Even the time spent under Alan's watchful eye and provocative remarks hadn't been as painstaking as she'd anticipated.

Since she'd come to terms about Alan and concluded that the dissolution of their marriage was in no way her fault, she'd allowed herself to relax in his company—knowing that they could never be more than friends. So—she'd accepted his invitation to dinner. What could be the harm? She was confident that she could handle Alan Martin. She was no longer the young, love-struck girl who craved his love and attention. That hot little news flash would certainly raise Lisa's eyebrows a notch, she thought merrily.

He'd said he wanted to take her someplace elegant. She sucked on her bottom lip and searched her wardrobe for the appropriate ensemble.

Terri chose a sleeveless top in peach silk, with a white chiffon jacket and matching palazzo pants that had a peach satin lining.

She had to admit, however, as she lay the outfit on her bed, that it was because of Alan that she'd started her own business. His ambition and his vision were contagious. But while she was struggling to get her business off the ground, Alan was keeping himself busy by photographing and bedding every beautiful woman who crossed his path. She tossed the disturbing thoughts off and looked at her selection. Perfect, she decided and wondered what tricks good ole' Al had up his sleeve for tonight. Whatever it was, she decided with conviction, she was up to the challenge. But first a long, relaxing bath.

Alan slid behind the wheel of his red Audi convertible and pointed the nose in the direction of Terri's hotel.

His plan was simple. First dinner, dancing, a few drinks, a drive across the beach and then he'd invite her up to his apartment to see his etchings. *His etchings.* He cracked up, laughing at his own cleverness.

Thirty minutes later he pulled up in front of the Beverly Hilton Hotel. He tossed the valet his car keys and pushed through the revolving doors into the lobby.

He sauntered over to the front desk and asked for Terri.

"I'll ring her room. Just a moment, sir."

Alan turned sideways and leaned on the smooth oak desk, quietly observing the elegant women as they passed. He gave several a wink and was pleased to see that many winked back. *I haven't lost my touch.*

Several times he considered approaching a few and giving them his number but decided against it. It would be just his luck that Terri would come down and catch him in the act. That wouldn't do well for the night that he had planned.

Casually he turned his head toward the elevators just as Terri emerged.

His breath caught as he watched her seemingly float across the lobby floor. She had to be the most sensational-looking woman in the place. Now this—was a lady. *A lady.* Was this the first time he had attached that description to her?

His conscience nudged him in the ribs.

"Hi," she greeted. A radiant smile accompanied her salute. "I don't have to be led to the car blindfolded, do I?" she teased.

He looked at her as though seeing her for the very first time.

Her brow furrowed. "Is something wrong? Do I have lipstick on my teeth or something?"

Alan shoved his thoughts back into place. "No. Just a revelation."

"Well, I'm certainly not going to touch that one," she said, completely at a loss.

"Trust me." He took her arm and placed it in the crook of his. "If I told you, you wouldn't believe it."

She looked at him curiously. "I'm sure I wouldn't."

Dinner finished, Alan contemplated the veracity of his plan. Being in Terri's company had shaken him. She was nothing like the woman he once knew. And she never would be again. She was the kind of woman that you settled down with, not for one night, but forever. Without thinking further, he made the turn back onto the highway, away from the beach. So much for the best laid plans.

Terri never noticed the detour as she commented on the lush scenery and chatted about dinner.

"That restaurant was fabulous," she said emphatically.

"Angelo's is one of my favorites. I'm glad you liked it." He turned briefly and caught her profile.

"If I stay around here much longer, it'll be mine, too," she chuckled. Terri took a long searching look at Alan as he maneuvered around the turns, passing rows of swaying palm trees and picture-perfect homes. "Alan, you've really surprised me. You were actually a gentleman tonight."

Alan tossed his head back and laughed. "That's the first time anyone has ever used my name and gentleman all in the same sentence." He eased the car alongside the road and stopped.

He turned to face her, all humor absent from his demeanor. "That's because you bring out the best in me." He leaned toward her.

"Whoa! Now just hold on a minute. I thought we had an understanding." She subtly slid farther over in her seat.

"I really screwed things up between us, Terri. You deserved better than what I had to offer. I hurt you, and I know I can never make up to you for the loss of our baby, but . . . I want to try. I know I can." His voice was tender, almost a plea.

Terri sighed deeply before she spoke, measuring her words. "Alan, what's past is gone, buried. We can't go back. You don't want me, now, any more than you're going to want the next woman who catches your eye." She focused on her hands in her lap and continued without rancor. "I always thought it was me—something I was lacking." She looked across at him. "But it's just the way you are, Alan." She smiled and stroked his cheek. "I've tried to stop holding it against you and against me.

"The good thing is—" her voice held a gentle softness "—I don't have to deal with it. Let some other poor, unsuspecting soul fall for the 'Martin magic.' "

He was momentarily speechless, absorbing the simple truth of her words, and he didn't know whether to be relieved by her dismissal of him or pissed off. He generally didn't take too well to being turned down. No matter who it was.

"You're sure that's the way you want it?" he asked.

She nodded.

He lifted his eyebrows and exhaled. "Then I guess I'd better get you home." He turned the car in the direction of the hotel.

The balance of the ride was completed in silence, each having to come to grips with this newest crossroad of their turbulent relationship.

Terri leisurely stripped out of her clothing and put on a hand-printed, floor-length silk robe. She searched through her suitcase and pulled out a volume of poetry by Nikki Giovanni, one of her favorite poets.

Taking the book, she opened the French doors leading to the terrace and relaxed on the chaise lounge, intent on getting through several selections before turning in for the night.

But the warm sea breeze was like a balm to her bare skin. The air blew caressingly beneath her robe, teasing her, taunting her, stimulating her.

She leaned back and shut her eyes, absorbing this secret moment of inhibition. Languidly she ran her hand down her leg, then up across her smooth belly, heightening the electricity that charged unchecked through her veins.

Her imagination flew as she envisioned Clint's large strong hands caressing the places that she had touched. An unheeded sigh rose from deep within her as the liquid fire erupted, warming her center.

She wanted to shake off these tempting erotic feelings of longing, but she couldn't. Every fiber of her being screamed for Clint.

Shaken, she rose from her haven and walked aimlessly back into the suite, her thoughts a kaleidoscope of confusion.

She stopped at her bedroom door but was afraid to enter, sure that her unfulfilled desires would assault her once again. Maybe a cup of herbal tea would help to soothe her. She walked toward the phone, dialed room service, and placed her order.

She hung up and turned away just as the phone rang, startling her. Shaking her head to clear it, she took a calming breath and picked up the receiver.

"Hello?"

"Terri. It's me, Alan."

"Alan? Is something wrong?"

He hesitated a moment as a long-legged beauty, walking her dog, caught his eye.

"Alan?"

"Oh, sorry. Must be some interference. You know how these car phones are."

"No, I don't," she sighed, her sarcasm blatantly clear. "Is there a problem?"

"In a manner of speaking."

"Alan, don't be cryptic. I really don't have the energy."

He chuckled. "I need to see you."

"Excuse me?"

"You heard me. I need to see you. I'm five minutes away. I know I won't sleep tonight until I get this off my mind."

"Sorry to disappoint you, but forget it, with a capital 'F.' Now good—"

"Terri—wait."

She blew an exasperated breath into the mouthpiece. "You have five seconds."

"Terri, I still love you. I didn't realize it until tonight. If you'd let me come up, I'd show you just how much. Like old times, baby."

"Alan—the next sound you hear will be the dial tone."

She promptly dropped the phone onto the cradle and gave into the tremors that had taken hold of her.

Alan grinned as he heard the low hum buzz in his ear. He replaced the phone.

So his meek ex-wife had truly developed some backbone. But if she thought that was going to turn him off, she was sadly mistaken. If anything, it was a turn-on. No one turned him down. Not even ex-wives. His eyes narrowed. The hunt had only just begun. Automatically he shifted into gear and jetted down the freeway.

Stark, blinding outrage boiled and rose to the surface, exploding in a string of expletives.

How dare he? That self-centered SOB. Still in love with me! He wants to show me. He must think I'm crazy!

She paced the floor, her silk robe fanning outward and behind her. Rage flamed in her dark eyes. She balled her hands into small fists, wishing that she could land them where they would do some good. Right between Alan's big eyes.

After everything that he had done to her, put her through, and then left when she was at the lowest point in her life, he really thought that just seeing him again could erase her memory? He was an egomaniac.

She'd been a fool to be taken in by his charm once again. She'd let down her guard. No more. She was through. She'd have as little to do with Alan Martin as possible, and just try to get through the next week and a half the best she could. Without killing him!

She had to get her life on track. She wanted that life to be with Clint. But now . . . She shook her head in frustration and confusion, running her fingers through her locks. When would she ever have any happiness? Was it just not meant to be? When—

The knocking on the door halted her pacing in midstep.

Her heart raced as adrenaline pumped through her. Alan!

Well, they would have it out once and for all, she fumed. It was long overdue.

Terri stormed toward the door and nearly snatched it off its hinges. Her pulse was pounding so violently in her ears she wasn't sure what she said to the uniformed man who stood on the other side of the door.

CHAPTER 14

Melissa lay in bed, staring sightlessly up at the ceiling, unable to sleep. She felt Mark's muscular form adjust itself next to her.

He rolled over to face her. "Can't sleep?" he mumbled. He craned his neck to check the bedside clock. "It's nearly three A.M." He rolled on his back. "What's bugging you?"

"Clint is in L.A."

"And?"

"He's there with Terri. I just know it."

Mark sat straight up in the bed, sleep forgotten. "Why are you just telling me this? Your job is to tell me Clint's every move. Especially if Terri is anywhere in the vicinity. How in the hell do you expect our plans to materialize if you can't hold up your end?"

He threw off the blanket and sheet and stomped out of the bedroom into the kitchen. Melissa hurried behind him.

Gingerly she reached out and touched his back. He flinched as if touched by something unmentionable. "Mark, I—I'm sorry. I just had so many things on my mind. I—"

He spun to face her, his face a mask of anger. "Let this be the last time," he warned through clenched teeth. "We can't afford any slipups. How long will he be gone?"

"I think for the next week, at least."

Mark nodded. "That will give you plenty of time to get our plans in motion for that resort deal."

Melissa swallowed.

"It all hinges on you. Remember that. If you love me like you say you do, you'll do as I ask." His hand slowly rose and stroked her chin, then trailed down to the opening in her nightgown.

Then he abruptly turned away. "I need some time to think. Alone." He walked off into the living room, leaving Melissa to deal with her twisted thoughts and misplaced loyalties.

Mark opened a small desk drawer and pulled out the thin photo album that contained only one picture. He stared at the small, weather-beaten photograph, and his hatred was renewed.

The first thing Clint did when he arrived at the Hilton was place a call to the front desk to check and see if Terri was in her room.

"I'm sorry, sir. There doesn't seem to be any answer," the desk clerk had said.

"Thank you." He hung up the phone.

He'd tried several more times. All without success, until fatigue and jet lag won the battle.

When he next opened his eyes, it was the following morning, 10:30 Pacific time. Rubbing his eyes and stretching his stiff body, he made his way into the shower.

By the time he'd finished scrubbing the fatigue away and checking in with the front desk, he was informed that Terri had already left for the morning.

In that case, he decided, he'd pay her a surprise visit at the studio, take her to lunch, and find out what was going on between them. There was no way that he was going to let any more time slip away.

Once again he reached for the phone. This time he dialed the hotel florist and ordered a huge bouquet of Casablanca lilies.

Terri sat in the third row of the screening room, avidly watching the dailies from the previous day's shooting. She found that reviewing clips helped immensely in preparing a surefire ad campaign. Today, especially, they helped to take her mind off what a fool she'd made of herself when she'd flung open the door the previous night, only to find that room service had delivered her order. It was almost funny the way the young man looked at her, as though he expected her to leap at him with a knife—or something worse. He must have thought she had completely lost her mind.

She shook her head in silent amusement, clipped her notes together, and rubbed her eyes when the film came to an abrupt end. Checking her watch, she was surprised to see that it was nearly one o'clock. Stretching, then smoothing her salmon-colored skirt, she rose from her seat and inched her way out from the dark viewing room into the bright lights of the studio corridor. The drastic change in lighting made her want to slip on her sunglasses. But then she thought with wry amusement, she would truly look *Hollywoodish.* The image made her giggle out loud, causing several curious heads to turn in her direction. Flashing a "you know how it is" smile, she continued down the corridor.

Her stomach growled with hunger. But she wanted to make some last-minute recommendations to her original proposal based on the scenes that she'd just viewed. She smiled as the ideas began to formulate in her head. She was sure that the studio executives would love it.

Instead of running an ad campaign solely on clips from the movie, she wanted to do it more like a commercial. A take-off of the Calvin Klein commercials for Obsession and Eternity, with a variation of course to avoid any lawsuits. But it would be perfect. The male and female leads of *Outburst* oozed sexuality and would explode on the television screen with a clip like that. The audience wouldn't be able to get to the theaters fast enough.

Quickly she made her way down the busy corridor, sidestepping the multitude of studio employees, and turned left, heading for the small but efficient office that had been designated for her.

She stopped short when she opened the door and found Alan sitting behind the long wooden desk going over what appeared to be hundreds of photos. The conversation of the following evening came rushing back, infuriating her again.

His curly head snapped up when she entered. Automatically his smile slipped into place.

"Sorry to barge in on you like this, but they had some last-minute meeting or something and decided to utilize my space down the hall." His grin widened. "Hope you don't mind."

Terri inhaled, then blew out a deep breath. She spoke through her teeth. "And what if I do?"

Alan shrugged. "I guess we'll have to compromise. You get half of the room, and I'll get half. How's that?"

Terri's shoulders slumped. This was the last thing she needed today. And Alan didn't seem to have any memory of his last words to her. Just the thought that he could be so blasé fueled her temper to the boiling point.

Momentarily, she considered her other options in terms of work space. But before her thoughts had completely materialized, she knew that space at the studio was at a premium. She exhaled an annoyed breath and straightened her shoulders. She had work to do. There was no getting around it. She just would not let Alan interfere. Hopefully he'd have the good sense to act like the professional he claimed to be.

She stepped into the room, intentionally leaving the door cracked. Just in case.

She took a deep breath. "What are you working on?" she asked, more out of curiosity than civility. She stepped closer to the table.

Alan was in his element. His eyes lit up just like she remembered whenever Alan talked about his work. It was the only time that he seemed genuinely interested in anything.

He stood up and propped one hand on his hip, the other pointed out the various shots as he spoke.

"These were all done yesterday. I wanted to catch the lead characters unaware. I think the candid shots are going to go over well."

Terri nodded in agreement. "These are fabulous, Alan. I know the studio is going to love them." She picked several up for closer inspection.

Within moments they were engrossed in their individual projects—exchanging ideas, laughing, giving criticism as well as advice. For one frightening moment, it was almost like old times, Terri thought. Alan seemed to feel the same way when their eyes caught and held.

"Terri, I—"

"Alan, don't." She instinctively moved away, inching away from the table to the other side of the small room. Her heart raced.

"Just listen to me for a minute."

"There's nothing to say, Alan."

He quickly crossed the short distance between them and backed her against the wall. Her scent raced to his head, fanning his desire.

He reached out and grabbed her arms before she had the chance to move. Her eyes rounded with apprehension and a morbid sense of anticipation.

"Let go—"

But before she had a chance to finish, his mouth covered hers. He pushed his hard body solidly against hers, pinning her to the wall as he ground his hips against her unyielding body.

She tried to struggle, to break free, but that only aroused him all the more.

To Clint, who stood in disbelief in the open doorway, listening to Terri moan, it appeared that she was thoroughly enjoying every minute of her ex-husband's kisses.

CHAPTER 15

Anger, hurt, and humiliation fought for control of his emotions, blurring his vision. He didn't pay any attention to which direction he headed. All he knew was that he had to get out of there. Get some air. And he'd never give the two lovers the satisfaction of breaking up their little tryst by announcing his presence.

Terri reared back and slammed her knee deep in Alan's crotch. An agonizing cry erupted from his gut. Blinding pain shot through his body, so intense that his cry hung in his throat. He doubled over as nausea swept through him, and he began a descent to the floor. Terri gave him a little added incentive when her open palm connected with his face, sending him sprawling to the floor.

Somehow Clint found his way to the main entrance. He looked down at the bouquet of lilies in his hand and his stomach turned over with revulsion. Without thinking, he tossed them onto the receptionist's desk, pushed through the glass doors and out into the blazing California sunlight.

Terri's breathing filled the torrid office air in rapid, panting breaths. "If you ever—come near—me—or touch me—again, you'll wish you were dead."

She snatched her notes from the desk, causing the piles of photos to spiral to the floor as she swept past, leaving Alan in a heap on the floor, groaning for all he was worth. She threw him one last scathing look of disgust and slammed out of the door.

The first thing she did was rush to the ladies room, praying as she hurried down the hallway that she would have a moment of privacy.

It was no less a miracle that she found herself alone when she arrived. She went straight for the sink, immediately splashing cold water on her face. Her eyes stung with the tears that she refused to shed. And she swore that the water actually sizzled on her skin.

Bracing her hands on the sink, she lowered her head and tried to calm herself down long enough to think clearly. Her head pounded with the effort.

How could he? How could she have left herself so vulnerable to Alan? She'd given him credit where he didn't deserve any. A better question was, What was she going to do now? How in the world was she ever going to continue her work, knowing that he was always a heartbeat away? This was a nightmare, worse than any she could have imagined. And she had stepped right in it.

She shook her head. She needed time to think. She needed to get away from there as soon as possible.

She took one last look in the mirror, wiped off the last traces of her smudged lipstick, picked up her belongings, and headed for the exit.

"Oh, Ms. Powers!" The young receptionist popped up from her seat as Terri sped by her desk.

Terri kept heading for the door, totally oblivious to anyone or anything.

"Ms. Powers!" The young woman ran up behind her and stopped her just as she reached the door.

Terri turned around with a start—a look the receptionist would always remember, that reflected true terror.

The woman stammered. "I, uh, didn't mean—to startle you." She pushed the bouquet toward Terri. "Some man dropped these on my desk. When I checked the card, it had your name on it."

Terri's heart began to race mercilessly. Clint! Oh, God. With trembling fingers she took the bouquet of lilies.

"How long ago did he leave?"

"Not more than ten minutes. He tore out of here like there was a fire."

Terri swallowed back her greatest fear. "Did you know where he was coming from?"

"Of course. I'd directed him to your office when he came in. He asked me not to announce him. He said he—"

Terri didn't hear anything else but the buzzing noise that swept through her head. She spun away, clutching the bouquet to her breasts and raced through the door. She had to find him. To explain. But where?

She looked up and down the wide expanse of the studio lot. Clint was nowhere to be seen. She ran toward the parking lot.

When she finally found her car, her hands were shaking so badly she didn't think she would ever get the key in the ignition. She wanted to scream at this final act of frustration, until mercifully she was finally able to insert the key and start the car.

She tore off down the scenic freeway, the rented Mustang convertible leaving a halo of dust in her wake.

Terri arrived back at the Hilton in record time. She was heading directly for the elevator when the desk clerk called out to her.

"Ms. Powers." He came from behind the enormous oak desk. "Ms. Powers," he said as he approached, his sunburned face a mask of humility. "Please excuse our oversight. These messages came in for you last night." He handed the small slips of paper to Terri.

She barely looked at them—knowing.

"Please excuse the error. I suppose during the shift change last night—" he shrugged his shoulders "—there was some mix-up." He handed her one more message. "This was left for you this morning. But you had already departed."

Terri looked down at the neatly scrawled message. *I'm in suite 1701. Call me. Clint.*

She fought to keep the tremor out of her voice. "You mean, he's here in the hotel?"

The clerk looked exceedingly uncomfortable. "Well, uh, m'am, the gentleman checked out about fifteen minutes ago."

Terri felt weak, bordering on being ill. She struggled for calm. "Did he say where he was going by any chance?"

"I'm sorry. No m'am." He cleared his throat. "If this mix-up has caused you any inconvenience, I assure you I will bring it to the attention—"

But Terri didn't want to hear any more. Slowly she walked toward the elevator, still clutching the lilies. Whatever it was this ridiculous man was saying, it didn't matter. It was too late.

CHAPTER 16

Clint drove mindlessly, heedless of the picturesque homes and manicured lawns. *Faster.* The swaying palms blurred before his eyes as he whipped around the winding turns and mountainous roads.

He was a fool. He shifted into fifth gear, ignoring the roadway warning signs. *Faster.* The tires squealed, barely holding on to the tarred highway. He'd allowed himself to feel again and he'd been used, like a welcome mat in a snowstorm. He gripped the wheel. She was good. There was no denying that. He almost laughed, a malevolent smirk spreading across his lips. He'd begun to believe her whispered adorations, soft caresses, and moans of pleasure. *Idiot.* It was all a lie. But he loved her.

This time his heart constricted into a tight, twisted, anguished knot, then eased up to his throat in a ball of fire. An agonized groan of pain rose from his throat. Quickly, he swallowed it back as the entryway to Los Angeles International Airport loomed ahead.

Terri entered her suite just as the phone began to ring. She tossed the messages and bouquet of flowers on the foyer table and ran for the phone. Let it be Clint, she prayed.

"Hello." Her first word poured out in a gush.

"Terri, hi, it's Lisa."

Terri's high hopes fizzled away like a deflated balloon.

"Oh." She sat down on the wicker lounge chair, expelling a deep sigh.

"Well, if I'd known I was gonna get that kind of greeting, girlfriend, I would have saved my call. What's wrong?"

Terri shook her head. "You name it. Listen, I'm sorry to take it out on you," she added.

"I've got the time if you feel like talking. Is it Alan?"

Terri shut her eyes at the memory. "Among other things. And . . . oh, Lis," her voice broke. "Everything is wrong."

Through silent tears she explained, as best she could, what had transpired.

"Damn!" Lisa said, her own anger searing through the lines. "Talk about bad timing. I always knew that Alan was a real bastard. Now there's not even a name in the dictionary to describe him. So what are you going to do?"

"That's the fifty thousand dollar question." She blew out a shaky breath. "You know, Lis, I've really begun to second guess myself. I'm beginning to wonder if I'm too naive or just plain stupid."

"Terri, come on, you—"

"No. Seriously. It seems that every man that I trust kicks me right where it hurts. Look at what happened with Mark. I treated him like my own brother. And Alan . . . I was silly enough to give him the benefit of the doubt. Which he didn't deserve. Now Clint. I'm sure he believes everything he saw."

Terri massaged her eyes with her free hand. "Maybe it's just as well," she sighed. "Now I won't have to face him."

"Face him? About what?"

"I was going to break things off with him when I returned to New York."

"What? Why in the world would you do that? I thought you were in love with him."

Terri swallowed. "Just before I left for L.A., I came across a news clipping . . . ?

Lisa listened, her own heart breaking for her friend as Terri spilled out the long-buried memories and how they'd been forced to the surface with the information about Clint's daughter.

Lisa waited several long moments after Terri finished before she spoke. "Terri, hon, I know that someone else's child would be hard for you to deal with. Maybe you think you'd never be able to handle it. But I know you. I know the side of you that couldn't help but love a child. Any child. And if you love Clint, you'll love his daughter. In time. Don't let your fears destroy a chance at happiness."

Lisa waited, measuring the silence as her words sank in. "And what about Clint?" she asked gently. "If you're still intent on breaking off the relationship, don't you think he deserves to know the truth and not go on believing that you betrayed him with your ex-husband?"

Terri strolled off toward the terrace, hoping to find the strength and the words she would need to confront Clint. It would be another week before she would return to New York. A whole week to let the damage settle in.

She shut her eyes. Lisa was right. Clint did deserve to know the truth. Even if they didn't pursue their relationship, she couldn't let him continue to think so little of her.

CHAPTER 17

Everything was happening too fast. Melissa felt as if she were sinking into a pit of quicksand, and Mark was the anchor that weighted her body downward. He seemed to have cast some kind of bizarre spell over her, and she didn't have the willpower to break free. He'd convinced her, during their nights of unleashed passion, that what they were doing was justified—that Terri deserved to be brought down a notch for what she'd done to Mark over the past year. Most of all because she'd taken Clint away from her. And when Mark made her body sing with each stroke of his, she'd agreed over and again.

Melissa sprang up from her seat and began pacing her carpeted office, her svelte silhouette cutting a stunning figure against the plate-glass background.

Absently she chewed on a red-lacquered nail, contemplating what she should do, when the phone rang, halting her in midstep.

She took a long breath, then picked up the receiver.

"Melissa Taylor."

"Mel, it's me, Mark."

Automatically her pulse began to escalate, and she felt suddenly breathless. "Mark," she answered, forcing a lightness into her voice, "where are you?"

"At my apartment. Did you get a chance to check the files?"

She swallowed while her mind ran through a million reasons why she shouldn't give Mark the information.

"Yes, I did." She looked down at the stack of files on her desk. "I—I have them here."

"Great." He checked his watch. "I'll pick them up on my way out to the airport. See you in a few."

"Mark. Wait."

"What is it, Mel? I'm really pressed for time."

She ignored the annoyance in his voice and let the words pour out. "I don't know if I can go through with this."

"What do you mean, 'you don't know'? You'd better know! This is no time for you to start acting shaky. This is just the beginning." His voice grew hard. "I expect you to hold up your end. I don't like screwups." He slammed down the phone before she could respond.

Melissa shut her eyes as Mark's words tugged on the anchor.

Clint pushed open the glass doors of Avis Car Rental, his suitcase in one hand, his garment bag slung over his shoulder, and headed across the airport terminal. As he drew closer to the airline ticket agent, he knew he was making a decision that he would not allow himself to reverse once it was done.

Terri.

He hesitated as the huge flashing board announcing arrivals and departures seemed to beckon to him.

He moved forward.

"So far the project is developing smoothly. I even came up with some new ideas," Terri said into the phone, trying to sound enthusiastic.

"Then why don't you sound as excited as you should be?" Stacy probed, slipping her glasses off her nose.

Terri sighed. "I really don't feel up to talking about it, Stacy. But," she added quickly, "it has nothing to do with the job. Believe me, everything is fine."

"If you say so. Is there anything you need on this end?"

Terri frowned while she thought. "No. I don't think so. I'm sure you have everything under control."

"If you need me to come out there, just let me know. My new assistant is very capable of handling things in my absence. Just say the word."

"No. Honestly, everything is fine. It's just—never mind." She inhaled deeply. "Do I have any messages?" She continued to hold her breath while she waited for Stacy's response.

"Nothing urgent." Stacy flipped through her notes. "There's nothing here that can't wait until you get back. The one big bit of news is that we may have a new contract opportunity with Anita. Her agent called yesterday after he heard how well things were going with Viatek Studios. He suggested that we're being considered to handle the PR for her next album."

"Wow, that *is* big news." But not the news she really wanted to hear. "Listen, I've got to run. And you need to get home. It's nearly eight o'clock out there."

"I know. And I'm exhausted. I'll give you a call at the end of the week if there are any new developments."

"Good. Take care."

"You, too, and keep up the good work, boss!"

Terri chuckled. "Thanks."

Slowly she replaced the receiver. So Clint hadn't called. She didn't really expect that he would. Now she had no way of finding him. He wasn't in the hotel, and more than likely he was on his way back to New York.

Her already sunken spirits sank deeper. She hadn't remembered feeling quite this miserable for some time. She'd begun to believe that her days of heartache were behind her. Maybe she just wasn't meant to be happy.

At least her career was on stronger footing, she thought sardonically. At this pace she would be able to live very comfortably in a very short space of time. That would have to be her consolation.

Terri retraced her steps and picked up her briefcase from the table in the foyer, mentally convincing herself that she would push the myriad of unhappy thoughts to the back of her mind and try to concentrate on the final details of the ad campaign. Things were going too well for her to lose her edge now.

Curling up on the sofa, she pulled out her notes, painstakingly forcing herself to concentrate on the pages in front of her.

Just as she was finally beginning to absorb the words, the phone rang. This time annoyance replaced hope as she reached for the phone that sat on the white wicker end table.

"Hello?"

"Terri, don't hang up. Just listen to me. I know—"

Her hand began to shake, but her voice remained calm, controlled, steely. "If you ever come near me again, I'll have you arrested, Alan. Do you understand me? There is nothing—absolutely nothing—that you have to say to me."

"Terri, if you'd just let me come up and explain. Please, Terri, I'm sorry. I—"

Terri slammed the receiver into the cradle and tried to fight off the tremors that rocked her from head to foot. Her breathing rose into rapid, panting breaths as if she'd been chased by an assailant.

Dear Lord, this was a nightmare, she thought, a twinge of fear whipping through her, tempering her anger. Was Alan intent on stalking her during her entire stay, or was he trying to push her over the edge? Whatever his motivation, he seemed to be succeeding on the latter.

She buried her face in her hands, willing herself not to cry, when the doorbell rang, nearly jolting her out of her seat.

Terri sat wide eyed, staring blindly at the door. She couldn't—wouldn't—move.

It rang again, sending a chilling numbness up her spine. If she stayed quiet, she thought, Alan would just go away. Heaven only knew what would happen if she opened the door to him. Once he was inside, she was fair game. She shuddered. The worst part would be that no one would believe her story. She felt sure of that.

The bell rang again.

This time instead of fear she felt a sweeping sense of outrage. She could not allow him to reduce her to a quivering, non-functional mass of fear. She was better than that. If she submitted to this torment now, what else might he do to her?

Resistance welled up inside of her, renewing her. If she didn't face him down now, she'd never be able to live with herself.

Calling on all of her willpower, she urged her body to rise and compelled her feet to move, one foot after another.

She took a long calming breath, determination etched across her face. She reached the door, ready to face the inevitable, and snatched it open.

A sudden heat infused her. Her heart seemed to shimmy up to her throat and thump wildly as she watched the elevator doors slowly open to admit its lone passenger.

CHAPTER 18

"Clint." She only whispered his name when what she wanted to do was scream. Was it an apparition, or could the improbable be real? "Clint!"

This time sound found its way out of her throat, reaching him, wrapping around him, and he stopped, with one foot in the elevator and one foot out.

He turned toward the sound of the voice he'd come to know so well. Only moments ago he'd thought that he'd made a fool of himself for having come back. But just one look into her eyes and he knew that he hadn't made a mistake at all.

Terri was suddenly weak with joy as she watched that all too familiar stride move steadily toward her. A smile of total happiness lifted her full lips, making her face glow with radiance.

I love him, she thought with an intensity that shook her. And I'm going to make it right, she told herself as he drew nearer. I'm going to make it right.

Seconds later, without words, she was in his arms, burying herself in his embrace. She lifted her mouth to his, unable to still the desire to taste him once again.

She felt his heart slam against her breasts as his own longing for her mounted.

"I'm so sorry," she mumbled against his mouth. "It wasn't—"

"Shh," he crooned, welding her to the contours of his hardening frame. "I didn't give you a chance." His tongue lashed against hers. "I should've known better."

Unwillingly she eased back and looked into his eyes. "We have so much to talk about," she breathlessly whispered.

Her arms slid from around his neck, down his arms, and her hand found his.

"Come in. Let's talk."

Clint's coal black eyes flashed with rage as he listened to Terri recount the events that led up to the scene he'd witnessed at the studio.

Slowly he rose from his seat on the couch as Terri drew her story to conclusion.

He turned in her direction, and the look she saw blazing in his eyes sent shards of fear ripping through her. Immediately she stood up, placing her hands against his chest.

"Clint, don't. It's over."

"It's not over!" he bellowed. "He needs to be taught a lesson. I'm just the one to teach it to him."

"Clint, I'm asking you to leave it alone. I can handle Alan."

He looked down into her eyes. "So you think a swift kick is enough to hold off a slime like him." He let out a mirthless chuckle. "You're wrong, Terri. He'll be back. I can guarantee you."

She took a deep breath. "I have less than a week left to go. Then I'll be back in New York, a million miles away from Alan. He's out of my life, Clint." Her voice pleaded with him to relent.

Clint lowered his head, his mouth pursed in contemplation. Then he looked at her again. "If that's the way you want to handle it."

She nodded. "It is. I think it's the best thing to do. This may sound feministic to you, but the last thing I want Alan to think is that I have to have a man come to my rescue. He'll never respect me."

Clint shrugged, still unconvinced. He raised his palms in submission. "All right," he said grudgingly. "All right." But even as he said the words, he knew he couldn't let it rest. He would pay Mr. Martin a visit before he returned to New York.

"Thank you." Gingerly she raised up on tiptoe and brushed his lips with hers. "There's more."

Clint briefly shut his eyes and braced himself.

"I was planning on leaving you," she began slowly. She lowered her eyes when she saw the look of disbelief in his. "Just before I came out here, I came across a news clipping—about you, your wife, and your daughter." She paused and cleared her throat. "I guess I missed it when I looked at the articles weeks ago." She waited for what seemed to be interminable moments, gauging his reaction before she continued.

Clint stood rooted to the spot. He didn't dare interject. He wanted to hear her true feelings without any interference from him.

"I couldn't understand why you didn't tell me something that important. I was hurt and angry and disappointed in you—in us. I convinced myself that if you hid something like that, what else weren't you telling me? Then I realized I hadn't been completely honest with you, either, and just like I had my reasons for hiding from a part of my life, you did, too.

"When I found out that you had a daughter, hundreds of disturbing, buried, and painful thoughts resurfaced. I remembered what it was like always being someone else's child. I didn't believe that I could love a child that wasn't mine. And if I couldn't, how could you and I continue?" She sniffed back her tears, took a breath, and continued. "I was adopted, you see, after my brother and I were separated. He was five and I was seven. After our Nana died, all we had was each other. All I ever wanted, all of my life, was to have a real family, to belong, to have a family of my own. After I was so callously told by my adopted parents that my younger brother, Malcolm, had died, something inside of me died, too. I felt that if we had natural parents, we would have had a chance at life. Not the kind of loneliness and ostracism that I always felt. I believed that we would have been treated differently if we would have had our own parents—and that Malcolm wouldn't have died."

Slowly she crossed the room to stand by the terrace, her misty eyes scanning the lapping waves. Her voice trembled when she next spoke. "I lost my baby about a year ago. I blamed myself and looked at it as another failure in my life."

"I have to believe that there was nothing you could have done, sweetheart. You have to know that, too."

"A part of me does know. It's just so hard to get beyond the hurt sometimes. I had so desperately wanted my own family. Because of my experiences I didn't believe that a child that wasn't your natural child could ever truly be loved. I was sure it would be that way for me, too." Her eyes shimmered with unshed tears as Clint crossed the short space that separated them and gently gathered her in his arms.

He stroked her locks. "And now?" he asked softly.

She looked deeply into his eyes, her own pain and indecision reflected in the obsidian orbs. "I want to try to change those feelings, Clint."

His smile seemed to light up the room. "That's all I need to hear." He ushered her toward the couch and wrapped his arm around her shoulders, his warm breath brushing against her hair. "We will work through this—together. I never meant to keep all this from you, sweetheart. I just never knew how or when to explain. It's been hell on me, too. Since Desiree's death—" he shook his head in shame and regret "—I haven't been able to be a father to Ashley."

"Who takes care of her? Where is she?" she sniffed.

"Ashley lives in England with my sister-in-law, Jillianne. Jill has lived there since her college days. After Desi died and with no family in the States, she stayed. I felt it was the best place for Ashley—to give her some stability."

"But she should be here with you, Clint. You're missing the best parts of her growing up."

"It sounds so simple. I've tried, but every time I look into Ashley's face, I see Desiree, and the guilt is too much for me to handle."

"Guilt? Why guilt? The paper said that it was an accident."

"It's a matter of opinion." Abruptly he got up and began to pace the floor as he spoke. "It was my fault that Desiree died."

Terri's brows grew together in confusion and fear. Her heart began to race. Was this the secret that he withheld?

"We'd had a fight. The same fight we'd been having for months . . . ?

Terri listened as the words poured out, unknown to Clint, exorcising him, relieving him of his self-condemnation.

"Desiree sounded like she was on a path to self-destruction. That wasn't your fault. You couldn't have known that she would take all of those sleeping pills," she added gently as his story drew to conclusion. "You said the doctor was prescribing all kinds of medication, diet pills, antidepressants, stimulants. He's the guilty party."

"I've told myself that hundreds of times. It's never seemed true—" he looked at her "—until now."

Terri stood up, raised her hand, and stroked his cheek. "You have to put it behind you. For your daughter's sake. No one, no one, understands better than I what it feels like to be raised by someone other than your parents. Your daughter was cheated out of her mother. Don't let her be cheated out of her father, too."

He was silent for a long moment. "Will you help me, Terri? Will you stand by me?"

"Clint, I—"

"Come to England with me for Christmas."

Her soft brown eyes widened in trepidation. "Christmas! But Clint, what about—"

"Forget about business. Forget about bills. Forget everything and say that you'll come with me." His voice deepened to a throb. "I need you, Terri. It's as simple as that. I need you, I love you, and I want you with me. Period."

Terri swallowed the knot of joy that lodged in her throat and blinked away the tears that clouded her vision of his beautiful face.

His eyes glided over her face. He caressed her cheek in his hand. "I love you, woman, more than I ever thought I could love anyone. More than I can put into words," he said in a voice so low, so full of awe, it sounded like a prayer.

"And I love you, Clinton Steele." She wound her arms around him, pressing her head against his chest. She listened to the rapid beat of his heart, and hers soared to the heavens. "I'd go with you anywhere," she admitted, "even to England," she added, the excitement of the unknown and the exhilaration of being loved stirring her. "But on one condition."

"Anything, baby. You name it."

Her eyes darkened with desire. "The condition is that we seal it with a kiss." She flashed him a seductive smile.

He stepped closer, his steady gaze warming her by degrees. "Now those are the kind of terms I can agree to without" his lips teased hers "question."

He pulled her solidly into his embrace, his arms locking around her, molding her to his body.

Involuntarily he sighed as the sweet nectar of her tongue glided seductively across his lips, seeking the warm caverns of his mouth.

When had a simple kiss touched her to the very core of her being, she wondered, as she willingly succumbed to the tempting, taunting sensation of Clint's lips. His mouth covered hers, his hot, moist tongue played tantalizing games in her mouth. She shuddered with pent-up longing, unfulfilled passion.

"I missed you, baby," he groaned against her mouth, his large hands stroking her slender waist, gliding down to her hips, cupping her against his rigidity.

She couldn't suppress the sigh of yearning that rose from her throat when she felt his fingers subtly unbutton her skirt and release the zipper, allowing the thin cotton skirt to skim down her bare legs.

Terri's heart quickened with uncertainty. She rarely wore panties when the weather grew warm. It was a secret pleasure that she had. How would Clint respond to her seemingly wanton behavior? But the look of smoldering desire that welled in Clint's eyes instantly quelled all of her fears as his hand glided over the silken, bare flesh, leaving him powerless to resist her a moment longer.

His shuddering groan was intoxicating, and she willingly submitted to his maddening caresses.

Without effort, he swept her up into his arms and carried her through the open bedroom door, gently placing her on the floral quilts. Clint eased alongside of her, his agile fingers stroking and unbuttoning her blouse simultaneously.

Terri's pulse quickened as she watched the fires of arousal dance in Clint's eyes. Her sharp intake of breath was all that could be heard in the torrid air when Clint's eager lips taunted her sizzling exposed skin.

She reached for him with eager, slender fingers that had the ability to make him weak—humble—submissive, like no other hands he had ever known. He gave himself to her as she opened herself to him. They abandoned themselves to the whirl of shuddering ecstasy that they knew would be theirs to share in utter completeness.

"I love you, Clinton Steele," she whispered as their worlds collided.

CHAPTER 19

She felt the warm, steady breathing tickle the wisps of hair on the back of her neck. Terri snuggled closer, contouring her body to mold with Clint's.

He stirred, moaning softly as he slowly rose from the depths of sleep, unwilling to relinquish the magnificent dream of being with Terri again.

She angled closer, commanding his body to stiffen with wanting with each scintillating gyration of her hips, her own desire mounting in intensity as his arousal grew.

Reluctantly Clint's dark, sleep-filled eyes struggled open, only to ignite with yearning realizing that his dream was real—supple flesh and blood—tempting him in the most erotic of ways.

"Mmm," he groaned in her ear, caressing her heated body with long sensuous strokes. "Rule number one, you shouldn't rouse a man out of his sleep like that."

Terri turned over on her side to lie face to face with him. "Why is that?" she whispered against his full lips.

Clint turned her on her back, pinning her body down with his. "Because you never know what he may do to you."

She opened her mouth for a quick retort, but the only sound that was heard was Terri's shuddering moan as Clint made his dream a reality once again.

"Since we're going back to New York together," Clint said, stretching his muscular form and rising from the bed. "It doesn't make sense to use two cars." He reached for his discarded clothing and began to get dressed.

Terri turned on her side and looked up at him through dreamy eyes. "Hmm," she mumbled.

"I'll take my car back to the rental agency and we'll use yours."

"How will you get back?"

"Take a cab." He bent down and pressed his lips to hers. Languidly she raised her arms and wrapped them around his neck.

"I'll hold your place." She flashed him a wicked grin.

Clint slid his hand beneath the sheets and slowly stroked the silky skin. "Oh, you'll do more than that," he taunted. "I promise you."

The evening sun hung low on the horizon, casting a brilliant orange glow across the intimate pastel and white bedroom.

Terri eased out of Clint's embrace and headed for the shower. Turning on the jets full blast, she stepped in, refreshing herself under the pulsing water.

"And rule number two . . . ?

Terri jumped at the sound of Clint's voice. He pulled back the curtain and stepped under the water. "You shouldn't leave me alone in bed." He gave her a quick peck on her shoulder and began lathering her body.

Moments later they emerged, covered in thick terry cloth robes, courtesy of the hotel.

"I'm starved," Terri stated, entering the living room with Clint only paces behind her. "Do you want to go out and get something, or order room service?"

"Either is fine with me. You decide." He rubbed a towel across his damp hair. "So long as we have a chance to talk."

Her heart beat just a bit faster. He's changed his mind about us, she thought frantically. After the pitiful tale of my childhood, he's changed his mind. She stopped in her tracks and turned, causing Clint to collide with her.

"Whoa," he sputtered, catching her by the shoulders before she lost her balance. "You look as if I said a nasty word, or something—worse." A mischievous grin eased across his face.

"No, uh, I mean you said you wanted to talk. About what?"

"Nothing that has to be discussed in the middle of the hallway. And definitely nothing so horrible to cause that look on your face." He rubbed his hair again. "Actually it's a business proposition."

"Business?" Her anxiety slowly diminished.

"Yeah," he grinned, "how unromantic."

"Well, are you going to tell me?" Her curiosity level was at full throttle. She took a seat on the couch. Clint elected to stand.

"I have the opportunity to open a string of bed-and-breakfast inns, actually resorts, on several of the Caribbean islands. There's a developer, Nathanial Carpenter of Mega Development, who's very interested, and I'm going down to Nassau next week to finalize things." He paused.

"And?"

"If all goes well, which I'm sure it will—" he stopped pacing and looked at her "—I'd like you to do the PR work. If you agree, I'll need you to go with me to Nassau to get an idea of what I want and to pitch a campaign to the owners of the land I intend to buy."

Terri remained speechless.

"I know it's short notice, and it's a pretty big job—"

"Pretty big?"

"Well, huge, but I know you can do it. In fact—" he looked at her sheepishly "—I sort of told them that you were part of the deal." His lips rose on one side in a crooked smile.

"Clinton Steele!"

"Don't answer just yet. Think about it. I know it'll be fabulous. It's a dream I've had—"

She felt the excitement in his voice and the caged energy that charged the room as he spoke. Her own creative juices began to flow as ideas flashed through her mind. The Caribbean! The possibilities were endless, and she'd get the chance to visit her homeland—Barbados, which she hadn't returned to since she arrived in the States at the age of eight.

". . . With the right campaign, design team, and location, there's no way that it won't be sensational. All I—"

"I'm sold!" Terri sprang up from the couch, delighting in the look of relief that lit Clint's face. "There are just a few things I have to tie up in New York, and then I'm all yours."

He stepped up to her, his grin warm and inviting. "I hope you mean that in more ways than one."

"Definitely."

He wrapped his arms around her and lifted her off the floor, spinning her around in a circle.

"We're gonna make a winning team, baby. Just you wait and see." He kissed her solidly on the lips. "Oh, and I guess I'm your new roommate until you check out of the hotel. They're all booked up."

Terri giggled and her pulse beat with anticipation.

"Mr. Brathwaite, your offer and your ideas are fantastic," Nathanial Carpenter conceded. He took a sip from his glass of wine. "I must advise you, however, that we have also received a very substantial offer from Hightower Enterprises. His proposal came as a complete package."

Mr. Brathwaite nodded. "I understand that, and I'm sure Hightower would do a wonderful job, but—" he reached into his attache case and pulled out a black leather portfolio"—can Hightower offer you this?"

Expansively he opened the pages and watched with smug satisfaction as Nat Carpenter, one of the world's leading developers, reviewed the pages with awe.

Mr. Brathwaite smiled. This was only the beginning. With a bit more luck and timing the deal was his. They'd never know what hit them.

"These ideas are . . . I can't find the words to describe them," Nat said. He sighed heavily. "However, I must be fair. I'm scheduled to meet with Mr. Steele next week. I feel obliged to at least look at what he has to offer before I make a commitment one way or the other."

"Of course." He reached across the table and slid the portfolio toward him. "I'll be returning to the States tomorrow." He pulled out his business card and handed it to Nat. "Call me." He rose from the table and shook Nat's hand.

"I'll be in touch once the meeting is concluded next week, Mr. Brathwaite."

"I'll be looking forward to hearing from you. And, please, call me Malcolm. I have the feeling we're going to become very good friends. I'm sure that you will also keep in mind our agreement that our meetings are strictly confidential."

"Of course. Don't concern yourself that it would be otherwise."

Malcolm Brathwaite smiled.

CHAPTER 20

"Welcome home, boss lady," Stacy greeted as Terri stepped off the elevator.

Terri eagerly walked into Stacy's warm embrace. "How is everything?" She took Stacy's arm and ushered her toward her office, smiling and waving at her staff as she passed. "Catch me up on all the goings-on—and I have some great news. I'll need your help," she rushed on.

"I see your old enthusiasm is back." Stacy gave Terri a pointed look as they entered Terri's office.

"Believe me, I have every reason to be enthusiastic."

Stacy took her favorite seat by the window. "Don't keep me in suspense. What's the great news?"

Terri turned and faced Stacy, her face illuminated with a grin. "How does a few weeks in the Caribbean sound to you?"

A slow smile of disbelief lifted Stacy's lips and infected her green eyes with astonishment. "What? The Caribbean?" she squealed. "Don't tease me, Terri," she warned, holding one hand to her heart.

Terri's peals of laughter tinkled throughout the room. "Believe me, this is for real!"

"Yes!" Stacy whooped, balling her fingers into a fist and shooting a blow through the air. "Tell me, tell me, when do I get my bikini out of mothballs?"

"I figure just after the holidays. But I'm going down to Nassau in a couple of days to get a better feel for things."

"Lucky you. Are you going to tell me who our benefactor is, or what?"

"Clinton Steele."

"You're kidding?" She looked at Terri with wry suspicion. "You're not kidding. Well, well, Miss Thing, still waters do run deep." She gave Terri one of her naughty-girl looks.

"Don't start, Stacy," Terri warned. "This is business." But even as she said the words, she couldn't keep the grin off her face.

"Yeah, okay, whatever you say. So, what do you need? What's the project?"

Terri sat down behind her desk and pulled out her preliminary notes from her briefcase. Within moments the two women began mapping out a tentative campaign for the resorts.

"This is going to be fabulous, Terri. I can feel it."

"I think so, too. This could be our biggest project to date. If all goes well, Clint is planning on opening connecting bed-and-breakfast inns in England. In other words, a trip would be all inclusive—you stay in one of the Steele resorts in the Caribbean with the second leg of the trip being England, and your accommodations are automatic."

"Does that mean we get to go to merry old England, too?"

"You bet."

"This is getting better by the minute." Stacy checked her watch. "Wow, we've been at it for almost four hours. It's one o'clock already."

Terri got up and stretched. "And I'm starved. Let's take a break."

"Sounds good."

"Oh, Stacy." Terri briefly shut her eyes and pressed her palm to her head in embarrassment. "I didn't mean to overshadow your news about Anita. What's the latest?"

"Right now it looks good. But it's not definite yet. I'm expecting a call with the go ahead sometime this week."

"Well—Powers, Inc., is moving right along. Wouldn't you say?"

"I'd say more than that. We're flying high."

"To think that just a short time ago, we were on the brink of possibly going under." She shuddered slightly, remembering, then shook her head to get rid of the images of Mark. "But," she added quickly, "we should be seeing the fruits of our labor with Viatek Studios before Christmas. They loved everything."

"I knew they would. You may have to think about expanding, Terri, if this pace keeps up. I mean, we're good, you and I, but it may get to a point where we can't handle the load. You especially. You pour your heart and soul into every project."

Terri fingered a stray lock behind her ear and smoothed the red and gold headband that held her hair in place. "I've thought about expanding, Stacy, but to be honest, I like the personal touch we give our clients. I think that's what sets us apart from the other agencies."

"Hmm, you're probably right. Anyway," she shrugged her shoulders and grinned, "whatever works." Stacy gathered her notes. "I'll get on this right after lunch. I should have some preliminaries by morning."

"I'll work on the scheduling and put some feelers out for sponsors."

"Some celebrity faces would be perfect."

"Absolutely." Terri paused for a moment. "I just had a flash."

"What?"

"Check through all of our previous clients and look through their bios. I think the perfect touch would be some celebrities with a Caribbean background. What do you think?"

"I think you're a genius!. I'll have my assistant, Celeste, take care of it."

"I have to get a moment to meet her. I only hope she's half as good as you, Stacy."

"What scares me is that I think she may be better." Stacy's eyes widened in a mock look of fright. "I'll see you later." She walked toward the door, stopped and turned, her face aglow. "Congratulations." She gave Terri the thumbs-up sign and walked out.

"You've been as jittery and edgy as a cat in heat since I walked in this morning, Mel. Is something wrong?" Clint took a stab at his crabmeat salad. He gave Melissa a long questioning look.

Melissa fidgeted with her napkin and shifted in her seat. Her lashes shielded her hazel eyes. "No, I'm, uh, just a little tired I guess." She smiled. "It's been a rough few weeks." Her smile weakened. She cleared her throat. "So, I guess you got Ms. Powers to agree to run the campaign?" She took a sip of her spring water.

"I most certainly did. That's what I wanted to talk with you about." Clint motioned for the waiter to refill their water glasses.

Melissa raised her eyebrow. "Really? The decision and agreement have already been made, haven't they? What is there to talk about?" She put her glass down a bit too hard, spilling some of the contents.

"What do you have against Terri Powers, Mel? What has the woman ever done to you?"

The on-target questions seemed to slap her, catching her off guard. Melissa stiffened, jutting out her chin defiantly. "You're too blind to see what's really going on. All she wants is a piece of the Hightower pie!"

Clint was stunned by her vehemence. "Mel! Don't be absurd. Terri is the president of her own company. One that is doing very well. She doesn't need my money. And she's not the kind of woman who would want it!"

Melissa slapped her napkin on the table. Her nostrils flared with hurt and indignation.

"You don't know her," she hissed, her eyes creasing with anger, thinking of how Mark described her as a money-hungry vulture who would use anyone to get what she wanted.

"And you do?"

What was she doing? She took a shuddering breath, realizing that she was treading a very thin line and losing her cool. Her shoulders slumped in resignation, and she forced calm into her voice. "I have to get back to the office." She rose to leave. Clint clamped his hand down over hers, holding her in place.

"There's something bugging you, Mel." His dark eyes narrowed. "Ever since you took up with that Mark Andrews you've been a different person."

"Don't, Clint." She shook her auburn head vehemently. "Don't you question my personal life. You—" her voice cracked "—of all people."

Clint's grip tightened as he tried to control his mounting temper. His voice dropped to a low, threatening whisper. "When your personal life interferes with business, then that becomes *my* business."

She snatched her hand away, gave him one hard look, and stormed off.

Clint watched her receding back with a mixture of disbelief and foreboding.

Terri checked her watch. She still had some time before Lisa stopped by to meet her for lunch. In the meantime she scanned her appointment book and compared it to the office scheduling for the next four weeks. Before she could make any plans to leave, she had to be sure that everything was covered. She certainly wouldn't feel comfortable leaving Stacy overloaded with work. Even if she did have a top-notch assistant. If everything turned out the way Clint had envisioned, they would be leaving the islands and heading straight for England for the holidays.

Pausing, she tapped the edge of the pen on her teeth. *England.* Just the thought of meeting Clint's daughter made her uneasy. If she could only believe Lisa and Clint. They seemed so positive that everything would work out. She only wished that she could feel the same way without reservation. Clint was the only reason she was putting her emotions on the line. If she didn't feel so deeply for him, the way she did, there was no way that she would be able to go through with it.

She looked at the phone and realized how much she needed to hear his voice, to let him reassure her. Even though they spent every free moment and nearly every night together, it never seemed to be enough. The mere thought of him made her feel warm and desirable. She reached for the phone to dial his number just as it rang.

"Terri Powers."

"Just wanted to let you know that the next time you need to get your point across, you don't have to send 'your boy' out with your messages."

"What? Alan? I don't know what you're talking about. I didn't send—"

"Sure you didn't. But believe me, baby, you won't have to worry about me anymore. I'm out of your life. For good. Just the way you wanted it. Just remember, what goes around comes around." He slammed the phone down in the cradle.

Terri stared at the receiver as though it alone was responsible for the bizarre phone call. What in the world was Alan talking about? "My boy"? Paying him a visit? That was— Oh, no. She didn't want to believe it. It couldn't be. Not after her specific request to stay out of it.

It couldn't have been anyone else but Clint! But when? Her thoughts raced backward to their time together in LA: It had to be during the time he returned the car to the rental agency, she concluded. Her temper rose at an alarming rate. And if it was, he'd have a helluva lot of explaining to do. The nerve!

She pushed herself away from her desk, crossing and uncrossing her arms as she stalked across the floor. She nearly snatched the phone off the receiver when her intercom buzzed.

"Yes!"

"Sorry to disturb you, Ms. Powers, but Mr. Steele is here to see you."

The hairs on the back of her neck bristled. Terri let out a shaky breath. "I'm sorry, Andrea. I didn't mean to snap at you. Have Mr. Steele wait a moment, then send him in."

"Yes, Ms. Powers." Andrea looked across the small reception area and motioned to Clint. He rose from his seat and approached the desk. "Ms. Powers asked me to have you wait a moment. She'll be right with you."

"Oh, she did—did she?" He slipped out of his cashmere coat and draped it across his arm, while Andrea nearly swooned looking at him. He might not be too pleased to have to wait, she thought, but she was loving every minute of it.

Like a caged tiger he traced and retraced his steps in the narrow path he'd cut for himself on the beige carpet. This was the final insult of the day. Not only did he have to put up with Melissa—her attitude and disturbing behavior—now he was being put on hold by his woman. Just how much was a man supposed to take in one day? Then something hit him. He'd had just about enough. What he needed right now was to be in the comforting arms of the woman he loved. And he'd be damned if he'd wait a minute longer.

Before Andrea knew what had happened, Clint swept past her and into Terri's office.

Terri didn't have time to react before Clint pulled her into his arms and kissed her fully on the lips. "Hey, baby—" he breathed against her cheek "—I needed that." He raised his hand to stroke her hair, and she slapped it away.

"Don't touch me," she ordered.

"What? Don't touch you?"

"That's right, you heard me."

Clint took two steps back and looked at her as though she'd gone completely mad. "Is there something you want to tell me, Terri?" He looked ready to explode. "Or do I have to guess?"

She crossed her arms beneath her breasts and stared at him hard. "No, you don't have to guess, Clint, because I'm sure you already know what you've done."

"Done? Listen, now I'm getting pissed. I had a lousy morning, and the last thing I need—"

"I'll tell you what you need," she began, craning her neck back and forth, with both hands placed firmly on her hips as she spoke. "You *need* to stay out of my affairs. When I say something, I mean it, Clint. You *need* to stop thinking that you can walk into my life and take it over. You *need* to stop thinking that you can use scare tactics to settle your problems. That's what you *need!*"

Clint's mouth nearly fell open before he could find the words to lash back at her. He took a threatening step toward her.

"So Mr. Playboy called and told you that he'd been paid a visit." His voice rose. "And you're upset? I find that very interesting. First you didn't want me around when you knew you were going to be with him. Then when he tries to jump your bones, and I take matters into my own hands, you run to his defense! Maybe you *need* to rethink this relationship, Terri," he taunted. "Maybe you *need* to run back down to L.A. and comfort your ex. Because it's obvious that you haven't gotten Alan Martin out of your system."

Without another word, he glared at her and slammed out of the office.

Terri stood in the pounding silence, shaking with anger. Not only did he think he could run her life, she thought, he honestly believed that she was still in love with Alan.

Well, let him, she fumed. She wasn't about to give him any explanations. Not after everything they'd been to each other over the past few months. Hadn't she proven that she loved him? Couldn't he see that?

She turned away from the door just as Lisa bounced into the office, only to be stopped cold by the look of rage that fired Terri's eyes.

"If that's the kind of greeting I'm going to get, I'll leave now," she warned, stepping into the office and placing her purse on the desk. She cautiously approached Terri. "What in the devil is wrong with you? You should be on top of the world instead of looking like you're carrying it on your shoulders." Lisa took a seat and waited.

Terri spun toward Lisa, her red and gold dress fanning out around her. "He thinks I'm some sort of weak, incompetent female who can't take care of herself! I'm no damsel in distress that he has to come and rescue!" She threw her hands up in the air and stomped across the room.

Lisa's smooth face crinkled in confusion. "Honey, what are you talking about?" she asked softly.

"Clint! Who else?"

"Oh, of course. What exactly did he do?" Lisa hid her amusement behind her hand as she listened to Terri's tirade.

Terri huffed as she drew her story to an end. "Can you believe it? How dare he? You just wait until I—"

"Terri, hon." Lisa got up from her seat and stood next to Terri, placing a comforting arm around her shoulders. "I'm sure that Clint didn't intend to make you feel inadequate. You know how men are. He was only looking out for you. And I'm sure that his ego was bruised, too."

Terri pulled on her bottom lip. "Maybe you're right, but I can't have Clint going around running interference every time he thinks I can't handle something. He has to learn to wait for me to ask him. I've had someone manipulating my life for as long as I can remember. I'm not going to fall back into that trap. Not again."

Lisa cleared her throat. "Believe me, I understand how you feel. And on some points you're right. But, Terri, don't you think it's time that you had someone who cares enough about you to put *himself* on the line for a change? Don't you think you deserve that?"

Terri lowered her head. "Maybe," she mumbled. "But I just don't know if I'm ready to let go of everything and put my life, my emotions, and my future into someone else's hands. You can understand that, can't you, Lis?"

"There's going to come a time, whether you want it to or not, when you won't have to ask yourself those questions. Everything will fall into place, and you'll wonder why life wasn't always that way."

Terri gave her a crooked smile. "That from someone who was in love with every male on the college campus," Terri teased. She hugged Lisa to her, then stepped back and held her at arm's length. "But in the meantime," she said, a mischievous grin lifting her lips, "I can't let him think that he can get away with it. Now can I?"

Lisa shook her head and said a silent prayer for Clint. The poor man didn't know what he had gotten himself into.

CHAPTER 21

Clint spent the rest of his afternoon at the health club trying to burn off the anger that had crept into his veins like a poison. He longed for the exhaustion that would make him so numb that he wouldn't dream, wouldn't think, of Terri.

With every stroke of his arms and kick of his legs, in the Olympic-sized pool, he tried to wash away Terri's face. With each slam of the black ball against the wall, he thought of smashing the barriers that had been thrown between them. It seemed that from the beginning, they were doomed to have one obstacle after another erected in their paths. Everything from basic philosophies to old relationships haunted their happiness.

And right now, he thought, as he took his third lap around the track, he didn't know if he had the stamina to deal with them anymore.

Terri. He ran a little faster as the end of the lap approached. She was strong, opinionated, an extraordinary lover, and a woman who could challenge him on every level. That's what he loved about her, he conceded, as he jogged over to the bench, collapsing on the wooden boards. He leaned his head back against the cool tiles and covered his sweat-drenched face with a cotton towel.

Couldn't she see, feel, tell how much he loved her? Maybe he didn't say it often enough, he mused, as he angled his car into the underground garage of his apartment building. But he was not one for words of love. He never had been. He attempted to show how he felt. Unfortunately he usually chose the wrong way to show it. Or worse, not at all. His behavior, compounded with his inability to voice his feelings when a woman needed to be reassured, had contributed to destroying his marriage, and now it seemed to have caused him to lose Terri as well.

Couldn't she understand that he'd taken action because of the way he felt about her? He thought he was showing her how much she mattered to him by setting Alan straight. Hindsight, he thought, the realization raw and painful.

He turned the key in his apartment door and switched on the lights. Empty. He'd grown tired of coming home to an empty apartment. He'd begun to look forward to the end of the work day with nothing but pleasure on the horizon. Terri had been the source of that change. Even his secretary, Pat, had noticed the change in him and commented on his continual sunny disposition. When he'd met Steve for after-dinner drinks the previous week, he'd added his two cents.

"That woman has sure worked her magic on you," Steve had said, tossing down a Budweiser. "Looks like you finally got some sense into that thick head of yours and took my advice."

Clint thought about that now as he entered his empty apartment. He'd spent so many years burying himself in his work at the expense of everyone that was important. Being with Terri was like being reborn. It had taken getting a second chance to make him realize that there was more to life. He wanted Terri's voice, her laughter, her scent to fill all of the empty spaces in his life, not work. But what could he do when the woman he loved was in love with another man?

Clint's heavy sigh filled the room as he kicked off his sneakers and tossed his gym bag and coat on the couch. Through sheer force of habit, he went straight to his answering machine, secretly hoping that there would be a message from Terri. Instead it was an urgent message from Steve—about Mark Andrews.

Frustrated, Terri hung up the phone for the third time that evening. She was tired of listening to Clint's recorded voice and refused to leave a message. She wanted the real thing, especially when she was in the frame of mind to make a truce. She sucked her teeth in annoyance.

Where could he be? She checked the wall clock: 10 P.M. Humph! Obviously he had put their confrontation out of his mind, and the thought that he might be out enjoying himself while she was nursing her injured ego incensed her once again.

Perhaps she was right about him after all. But a small nagging voice inside her head told her that she was wrong. Just as she'd been wrong about him from the beginning. At the moment there was nothing she could do about it, she concluded, stretching out on the couch and taking a sip of fruit juice. Then suddenly she sprang up, nearly spilling the juice in the process. There was something that she could do. And she wasn't about to waste another minute.

Clint's anger had dissolved by degrees after listening to Steve's report. However, his anger was replaced by an unsettling concern that chilled him to the bone.

By rote, he made all of the appropriate turns en route to his destination, maneuvering through the stop and go traffic like the New York pro that he was.

He pulled up in front of the all too familiar apartment building. Just seeing the structure brought back vivid images of ecstasy. Now there was nothing but a dull ache in its place. But he'd face it down, just as he'd faced down all of the other challenges that had come his way.

Constructing an invisible wall of indifference around himself, he strode purposefully forward. He was determined to keep his feelings at bay. This was business. He had to remember that.

Resolved, he walked toward the entrance door just as the first sprinkles of snow began to fall. He pulled up his coat collar and hurried across the street.

Freshly showered and changed, Terri splashed on her favorite scent. She took a quick look in the mirror and was pleased with what she saw. The loose-fitting, lightweight wool pants outfit in a soft emerald green did wonders for her spirits. Pleased, she slipped into her coat, grabbed her purse, and headed for the door.

Once she'd made up her mind, there was no turning back. She had the shortcoming of reacting to situations without looking beyond the surface, especially when it applied to her private life. And it had always cost her. This time the stakes were too high for mistakes. She saw very clearly what she had to lose, and she didn't intend to. Not this time.

She stepped on the elevator and pressed the ground-floor button. She'd remain calm, she thought, knowing how easily her temper flared. She'd listen and try to understand even if she didn't agree. Mentally she ticked off her resolutions and made a silent promise to stick to them. Clint was worth every ounce of crow that she may have to swallow. But still, she thought naughtily, she couldn't let him off too easy.

Quickly she stepped from the elevator and hurried toward the lobby entrance, just as Clint pushed through the glass doors.

He'd come to her. Elation whipped through her. But the shock of seeing Clint coming through the door in no way prepared her for the shock of his chilling detachment.

She stood in front of him, her heart beating with expectation. She looked into his eyes, searching for the familiar warmth and found nothing but a dark emptiness.

"Clint." She said his name hesitantly as though unsure if he would respond.

Clint swallowed hard, inhaling her heady scent, his pulse racing at her nearness. All he wanted to do was take her in his arms and kiss away the tremulous look that hovered around her mouth. But he wouldn't.

"I was just on my way to see you." She smiled up at him.

"Had I known, I could have saved myself a trip." He watched her recoil at his callousness, and a part of him withered inside. He shoved his hands into his coat pockets to keep from wiping away the stricken look on her face.

Her smile slowly evaporated. She cleared her throat, her back grew rigid, and she jutted out her chin, looking him squarely in the eye.

"I see. Well, since you came all this way, you may as well tell me what this is all about."

"We need someplace to talk."

It would be so easy to tell him to come up to her apartment—to settle things between them, but she was just as determined as he to be difficult.

"What's wrong with right here?" she asked coyly. She saw his jaw tighten and knew she had hit the mark.

"Right here is pretty inappropriate, Terri," he uttered in a low rumble. He quickly scanned the lobby, then turned to her, his growing ire blazing in his eyes like hot coals. "Let's go to my car." It was more of an order than a suggestion. But she realized she had left herself no other choice. Then she thought, as she followed his rapid footsteps, the car was even more intimate than her apartment!

As they stepped out onto the sidewalk, they were met by a gust of wind full of bitter cold snow.

Terri opened her mouth to voice her surprise, but she was cut off by an icy blast that filled her lungs.

The swirling mass of white had built in dramatic intensity within a short span of time. Already visibility was limited to only a few feet.

Instinctively Clint grabbed Terri around the waist, pulling her next to him, in a effort to both protect her from the blasts of wind and to keep her from falling. He realized, as soon as their bodies made contact, that what he really wanted was an excuse to have her near him.

"This way," he shouted above the wind, ushering her across the snow-covered street.

With the heat turned on in the car, their chilled bodies quickly warmed, but the block of ice that sat between them remained intact.

Terri was the first to break the awkward silence.

"So, what did you want to talk with me about, Clint?"

He slowly turned his head in her direction. "The only way I can say this is the way it was put to me." He took a deep breath, then plunged ahead. "Terri, there is no such person as Mark Andrews. Before you met him, he didn't exist."

CHAPTER 22

Melissa stared up at the ceiling, unable to sleep. She angled her head toward her bedside clock. Midnight. She hadn't heard from Mark since he'd left her office. Maybe it was just as well. He was scaring her.

Clint had hit the nail on the head when he said she'd changed. She shut her eyes, recalling her outburst with Clint. She'd nearly blown everything. She shuddered. Mark would've been furious.

Mark . . . Clint . . . Mark. . . . Again the two men seemed to merge together. One appeared to slip farther out of her reach with each passing day. And the other she had by default. A man who both thrilled and terrified her. But the thrill was slowly diminishing, and the fear was settling over her like a shroud.

Mark was dangerous. There was a dark side to his past that he merely alluded to. Somehow Terri Powers was at the core.

Melissa rolled onto her side determined to fall asleep just as the shrill of her phone put that determination out of her head.

"Hello?"

"Hey, sugah, it's me." The excitement in his voice vibrated across the wires.

Melissa sat up in the bed, running nervous fingers through her hair. "How did everything go?"

Mark stretched across the queen-sized bed, his smile matching the easy movements of his body. "So far, so good. Has Steele actually convinced Terri to do the PR?"

Melissa squeezed the phone between her fingers. "That's what he told me today."

"Then we'll deal with it. Money talks, and thanks to Terri," he chuckled, "this time I have the capital to hold a very heavy conversation." He laughed uproariously at his own wit.

Melissa waited until his deep rumble subsided before she asked the question that was burning on her tongue. "I don't understand something, Mark. I thought you wanted to hurt Terri. What has pulling the rug out from under Clint have to do with that?"

"Satisfaction, Mel." He closed his eyes and smiled smugly. "The satisfaction of seeing her suffer even at the expense of someone else. When I get at Steele, I get at her. Simple. If she's part of the package, I get to pull the rug out from under both of them."

"But how did you know that she and Clint would—" Her question hung in midair.

Mark laughed. "I know Terri. And I saw the look that Clint had in his eyes the moment I started telling him about her. As much as they may have tried to deny it, I could see they were attracted to each other. The rest was inevitable," he concluded, malice lacing his voice.

"You're in love with her, aren't you?" she accused, the words rushing out before she could stop them.

Mark laughed again, this time a cold malicious laugh that cut through her like honed steel. "What's that song that Tina Turner sings, 'What's love got to do with it'?"

CHAPTER 23

It seemed an eternity before she could grasp the words that hung precariously in the cozy confines of the car. "Ridiculous" was the first word that leaped into her head. This time Clint had gone over the edge, she concluded.

But when she looked into his eyes and saw the sincerity, concern, and conviction floating in their darkness, she knew that he was telling her the truth. And with that realization came a fear that sank to her marrow.

Her voice sounded choked when she tried to get the first words out. "I don't understand. How could he not exist?" A tremor sped up her spine. "Then . . . who is he?"

Clint thought about telling her just how long he'd been investigating Mark, and his reasons for doing so. But knowing Terri and her stalwart attitude—that she wanted no one and nothing to interfere in her life—he had second thoughts. Instead, he gave her his basic reason, but not the fact that his suspicions prompted him to continue in order to protect her. She'd have a fit if she knew; L.A. had taught him that.

"I always do a routine check on anyone I plan to do business with. And when our original deal fell through, I told Steve to call off the inquiry."

Terri's eyes held his, then briefly looked away. There was something that was missing from Clint's explanation. All she could do, however, for the time being, was play along.

"So, if you had Steve call off his investigation, are you telling me that you knew about Mark all along and never said anything to me?"

The question, bordering on accusation, caught him off guard. But he quickly recovered noting the skepticism in her voice.

"Apparently Steve had other thoughts. He decided to pursue it on his own."

"You're saying that this is all routine?"

There was that tone again. "Exactly."

She nodded, seemingly mollified by the explanation. "Well, what *exactly* did Steve find out?"

Clint took a deep breath. "Mark's history goes as far back as a year prior to his employment with you. He has no previous address, bank accounts, school, or family information. Nothing. The trail went cold."

Terri tried to absorb the implications of Clint's story. She shook her head in disbelief. "Why didn't I check him out thoroughly?" she said almost to herself. She chuckled mirthlessly. "I know why," she continued, answering her own question. "I was so anxious to get some of the burden of the business off my shoulders, and, so overwhelmed by the circumstances of my private life, that I was negligent."

"Don't do this, Terri. We all make mistakes in business—"

"I'd been so impressed with him at the interview and with his resume," she continued as if she hadn't heard him, "that I bypassed the usual follow-up. I guess I was wearing my wounds on my sleeve. He probably smelled my vulnerability from miles away," she added in a faraway voice.

"Was he recommended by someone?"

Terri frowned as she thought back. "No. I don't think so. I was running an ad as well as putting feelers out." She shook her head. "Things were just so crazy then." Briefly she shut her eyes against the enormity of what was happening. She had employed someone who had a very strong reason to keep his background a secret. Why? And why had he decided to use her and her business as a backdrop? Clint seemed to be reading her mind.

"He obviously had a reason for singling you out. Combine that with his under-the-table dealings, and you have all of the ingredients for serious trouble. What we need to find out is why he chose you."

"We?" She could feel her heart leap, both with fright and exhilaration.

"Yeah, we." He hesitated a moment, lowered his head, then twisted his body halfway in his seat toward her. "Listen, Terri—" he heaved a sigh "—no matter what you may think of me or the way I handle things, I care about you deeply. And I wouldn't sit back and let anything happen to you."

By this time the pulse was pounding so loudly in her ears, she could barely hear herself respond.

"Do you think I'm in some sort of danger?"

"No," he said a bit too quickly. Then he caught himself. "I'm sure it's nothing that serious. It's probably no more than financial manipulation. For some reason he felt that you were the perfect target."

Terri felt her heart begin to slow to normal at the sound of the reassuring words. Clint believed it was no more than pure greed. That reality was something she could deal with.

"If that's all you think it is, and I do, too," she added, "then why all of the concern? Mark is old news."

"Let's just say it never hurts to be careful. I'd feel a lot better if I knew what this guy's motive was."

Terri nodded. "So now what?"

"Steve is going to keep digging. But in the meantime I want you to keep your eyes and ears open, especially involving any new contracts."

"You think he may try something else?"

"I don't know. But I want you to be prepared if he should."

Terri took a deep breath, pulling her coat securely around her. "Thank you," she said softly. "I appreciate your concern." Self-consciously she turned her head toward the passenger window, locking her gaze on the swirling snow that had engulfed the city.

"I'd better be going," she said, making moves to leave. She turned toward him, then quickly reached for the door lock.

Clint's large hand clasped her shoulder, sending a shock wave of pleasure shooting down to her belly. She sat frozen, afraid to leave, afraid to stay.

Clint's voice was low and penetrating, unlocking her spine. "You'd said you were on your way to see me."

She turned in his direction, and his gaze held her in place. Terri blinked several times to rouse herself from the hypnotic pull of his eyes.

"I—" she swallowed, wishing that the dryness in her mouth would go away "—wanted to . . . ?"

"Yes?"

She inhaled and the words poured out in one breath. "I wanted to apologize for the way I acted, the things I said." She looked deeply into his eyes. "You didn't deserve that."

Clint's full lips curved unconsciously with a tentative smile. And Terri had the overwhelming desire to kiss them tasteless. "Are you saying that I'm not the monstrous, chauvinist pig that you thought I was?"

His caressing smile took the sting away from his words. By degrees she felt the weight that had settled in her soul shift and ascend, leaving her feeling vibrant and alive again.

"I never thought that," she said meekly, a flicker of merriment dancing in her eyes.

"Maybe not in those exact words," he teased, "but pretty damned close."

They both laughed, letting their laughter wash over them, cleansing them, allowing them to enjoy the euphoric release of tension.

Clint's features softened as he soaked in the rhythm of her laughter. Instinctively he reached out to tuck a stray lock behind her ear, stroking her cheek in the process.

They both uttered each other's name in unison.

"You first," Clint offered, tracing her lips with his fingertip.

"So many things have stood in our path, Clint."

He sat straighter in his seat. "I feel the same way."

"And," she continued, "I'd begun to feel that there was no way we would ever be able to work things out."

"And?" His one-word question was full of hope.

"I know I've said this all before, Clint, and maybe you have no reason to believe me, but we can work things out between us. I want us to."

"Why?"

Briefly she looked away. She could feel her heart racing like mad in her chest. "Because I love you, Clint, more than I've been willing to admit to you or myself."

"Terri, I—"

"Please—" she held up her hand "—let me finish before I lose my nerve." She let out a shaky laugh. "I've been so wrapped up in being superwoman and shielding myself from getting involved, I wasn't truly ready to accept you, what you stood for, or the idea that someone actually cared enough about me to stick their neck out."

Her long thick lashes shielded the apprehension that hovered in her eyes. She fumbled with the buttons on her coat to avoid looking at him.

"You're worth it, Terri. You're worth all of that and more. Give me half a chance, baby, and I'll put the world at your feet."

He leaned forward and tilted up her chin, forcing her to look at him. His breath caught in his throat when he saw the shimmering fawn-colored pools that looked at him with such wistfulness.

"Don't you ever forget that. I love you, woman, and it's time that you began to accept just—" he planted a light kiss on her cheek, "—how," then another on her lips, "much."

Her head began to spin, matching the speed and fury of the raging snowstorm. Her body became infused with that old familiar heat that scorched her then turned her insides to liquid fire.

Clint raked his fingers through her hair, letting its sensual texture ripple through him. He groaned against her mouth, pulling her as close as the obtrusive stick shift would allow.

"Come upstairs," she whispered.

* * *

The drapes were drawn back, allowing full view of the storm that had swept across the now silent city. A myriad of stars twinkled between the shimmering white flakes, giving the heavens a mystical aura. But Clint and Terri were oblivious to what stirred around them, immersed only in themselves.

Terri's eyes flickered lovingly across Clint's face as he hovered inches above her. Her nude body glowed with the fire that had been ignited within her by Clint's eager mouth, tempting tongue, and maddening fingertips as he trailed languidly across her form.

She reached for him, stroking him in all the right places, awakening every nerve, every fiber, until his body screamed and he could no longer withstand the denial.

Hours later Terri lay nestled in Clint's arms comforted by the steady beating of his heart. She'd make it work this time, she silently vowed, snuggling closer. Even if it meant getting over her fear of meeting his daughter. That day was drawing closer, and as much as she tried to keep thoughts of Ashley out of her mind, the more difficult it became. She eased out of Clint's embrace. How would she act? Would Ashley like her? She slipped out of the bed. What if she didn't?

Stifling a sigh, she eased into her robe and walked toward the window.

She and Clint had been through so much in such a short span of time. Furtively she looked over her shoulder at Clint's sleeping form. Watching him lying there so peacefully, her waves of apprehension waned.

She resumed her vigil at the window, allowing the purity of the falling snow to embrace her and somehow rid her mind of the unsettling thoughts. She and Clint had a bright future ahead of them. That's what she had to concentrate on. That and their impending trip to the Caribbean.

Just the thought of returning to her homeland filled her with a sense of place, and serenity. Those early days with Nana and her brother, Malcolm, were some of the happiest days of her life.

Yet with those feelings of happiness was a sense of melancholy. How different would her and her brother's life have been if Nana had lived to take care of them?

Thoughts of her brother sparked thoughts of Mark. How different was she from him? Her own identity and sense of being was constructed by her adopted parents. They tried to take away everything that was sacred to her—her heritage, her family, even her way of speaking. They said it was uncultured.

Maybe if—

"What are you in such deep thought about?" Clint stood behind her and wrapped his arms around her waist. He pulled her closer and pressed his face into her hair.

She sighed. "I was just thinking about our trip to the islands."

"Is that all? You were looking mighty serious to be thinking about something so pleasant."

She almost laughed at his uncanny ability to read right through her.

"Well, if you must know, I was thinking about my brother, my grandmother, and wondering how different my life would have been. And—" she turned around to look up into his eyes "—I was thinking how I'm not that much different from Mark."

Clint's brow immediately creased into a frown. "What in the devil are you talking about? There's no way you could compare yourself to him."

"Maybe, maybe not. But I'm not the person I appear to be either. I'm a creation of my adopted parents." She smiled without humor. "Molded to their liking. Powers isn't even my birth name. Sometimes I feel like such a fraud."

He pulled her closer. "Oh, baby, no matter what their motives may have been, you turned out spectacular. Don't ever doubt yourself."

Her eyes sparkled. "You really think so?"

"Are you fishing for compliments, lady?"

"Maybe."

"In that case, yeah, I really think so." He bowed his head, sealing his statement with a warm kiss.

Feeling the warning signs of arousal, he reluctantly broke away. He rubbed her shoulders. "Since we're in the mood for revelations, don't you think I deserve to know the real name of the woman I'm getting ready to take back to bed?"

Terri giggled when he lifted her off the floor and headed for the bed. He tossed her unceremoniously on the cushiony mattress and struck a mock pose of seriousness.

"So are you going to tell me, young lady, or will I have to—" he curled his fingers "—tickle it out of you?"

"No! Please, don't," she squealed. "I'll tell. I swear."

"That's more like it." He eased down beside her and began stroking her hip.

"If you keep that up, you're gonna make me forget the question," she whispered.

"I don't think so, baby." He rolled on top of her. " 'Cause I'm going to ask you again." He parted her thighs with his knee and slipped easily inside of her. She moaned softly as inch by inch he filled the walls.

Ever so slowly he moved within her, stunned again by the intensity that consumed him. His mouth covered hers, drinking in the sweetness of her lips. She played teasing games with her tongue, exploring all of the crevices of his mouth.

Forcing himself to pull away, he looked into her eyes. "Who is it that I'm going to pleasure until she can't take any more?"

Terri draped her hands around Clint's neck and rotated her hips, making him groan.

"My real name," she whispered, not missing a beat, "is Theresa Brathwaite. Terri for short."

CHAPTER 24

Terri scanned her closet, selecting the appropriate clothes and depositing them on her bed, while she balanced her portable phone between her ear and her shoulder.

"How have you been feeling these days, Lisa? I've been so busy lately, I've totally neglected you."

"Of course you've neglected me," she teased. "But seriously, don't be silly, I know things have been hectic for you lately. As for me, I think I'm handling the backaches, swollen feet, and bizarre cravings like a pro."

"I envy you," Terri said wistfully, thinking once again of the child she'd lost.

"Envy me! Girl, you've got to be jokin'. You have it made, Terri. You have your own business, you travel around the world, you're intelligent *and* beautiful."

"Believe me, that's all superficial. What I want is a family of my own, a man who's crazy about me, and I want to know that I have that love and security every day."

Lisa was quiet for a moment, knowing that this was a very touchy area for Terri. "Listen," she said softly, "all of those things will fall in place for you. You have Clint—whom I'm dying to meet. And from everything you've told me, he sounds as if he adores you. If that's true, can family be far behind?"

"Maybe," Terri admitted, not daring to hope.

"When are you heading out to Nassau?"

"The ship departs the day after tomorrow. I hope to be on it," she added, looking at the mess on her bed. "That is, if I ever get packed."

"The *ship* departs! Well, well, packing aside, girlfriend, Clint sure knows how to treat a sister, doesn't he?"

"He certainly does." Terri giggled wickedly. "He certainly does."

"Hey, I have an idea. Why don't you and Clint come by tomorrow night for dinner? Sort of a bon voyage. And of course it'll give me a chance to check out Mr. Wonderful up close and personal."

"Hmm. It's fine with me. I'll check with Clint, but I'm sure he'll go for it. The only thing I have on my agenda for tomorrow is dance class for my students before I leave. That's at five. Then just some last-minute details around here."

"Great. Check with Clint, and let me know in the morning."

"No problem. I need to see you anyway."

Lisa quickly picked up on the vibes. "We'll talk tomorrow."

"I'll give you a call before I try to teach my little proteges. We may not have a chance later."

"One of these days you're gonna turn out a star."

"I sure hope so. I deserve it!"

Both women laughed, recalling the torture that Terri went through to get her community program opened and then the grueling task of organizing an unorganized group of eight-year-olds.

"That's for sure. Well, I have to run. I have a doctor's appointment in about an hour."

"Okay. I'll call you tomorrow."

"Do try to make it. I have something that I'm dying to show you."

"What is it?" Terri's curiosity rose.

"If I told you, it wouldn't be a surprise."

"Come on, Lisa," she whined. "You know how I hate being in suspense."

"Yeah, almost as much as you hate me when I don't tell you my little secrets," she giggled. "Bye."

"Lisa!" But all she heard was the dial tone. "Ya really irk me, girl," she mumbled, slipping into her native dialect. Terri replaced the receiver, then picked it right back up and punched in the numbers to her office. Andrea answered on the first ring.

"Hi, Andrea, it's me."

"Ms. Powers, good morning."

"Are there any messages?"

"No. Nothing urgent."

"Good. I'll be in later this morning. Let Stacy know so that she can be available around two o'clock."

"I'll tell her."

"Thanks. See you later." Terri replaced the receiver, then sucked on her bottom lip. With that out of the way, she could concentrate on her packing and about going home. The thoughts of home brought a smile to her face. Something deep inside told her that this trip was going to be a turning point in her life.

"This is Clinton Steele. I'd like to speak with Mr. Carpenter."

"One moment. I'll see if he's in."

Clint briefly shut his eyes and shook his head. If he had a dime for every practiced line a secretary uttered, he'd never have to work another day in his life. That's why he always made it a policy to tell his secretaries to be up front with people.

The gruff voice with the touch of a British accent cut into his thoughts.

"Clint, good day."

"Nat. I was calling to confirm our appointment for next Friday."

He cleared his throat. "Friday is fine. Contact my office when you arrive. I could have someone meet you if you wish."

"That might be helpful. I'll let you know. I'll also be bringing along Ms. Powers, the woman I spoke with you about."

"That's fine. I'm looking forward to meeting her. I've heard fantastic things."

Pride eased up Clint's throat and brought a smile to his full lips. "I'm sure you won't be disappointed."

"Are you still planning on taking the cruise to tour the islands first?"

"Yes. I feel it will give me a better handle on things before our meeting."

"You'll definitely enjoy the trip."

"I'm sure. We'll speak again Friday morning?"

"Yes. Good day, Clint."

"Good-bye."

Nat Carpenter pursed his thin lips. This whole deal was getting more interesting by the day. Brathwaite wanted in, in a big way. But he seriously doubted that Brathwaite could compete with Hightower Enterprises' capital. But Brathwaite seemed determined. Maybe he had a few surprises up his sleeve. However, for him, money was the operative word. He could give less than a damn about Steele or Brathwaite. He went with the winning team. The team with the cash.

Nat leaned back in his seat, stroking his mustache, and wondered which one of them it would be.

The aftermath of the previous night's snowstorm had brought the bustling city to a virtual crawl.

Terri dreaded the idea of having to navigate from her cozy apartment to her office. A cab was out of the question, and she detested the subway about as much as she detested liver. But if her staff could find a way to get in, so would she. Even if she was forced to creep below ground and take the subway. She visibly shuddered from the thought. It was inhuman.

She took a quick glance at the open suitcase full of outfits for the tropics, then reluctantly turned her sights to the white wonderland that greeted her outside her window.

"Yuk." She turned on her heel and walked toward her open closet.

She took a green and red printed *galá* and wrapped it elaborately around her head. From a satin-covered hanger she removed a fire engine red knit dress that reached just below her knees. There was no way to get around wearing boots, she thought miserably, buttoning the tiny buttons that ran up the front of the dress.

Finished, she marched reluctantly toward the door and jammed her feet into her black, knee-high, leather boots. She grabbed her cream-colored, cashmere coat, her briefcase and keys, and headed out the door.

The subway was more crowded than Terri had anticipated. It seemed as though every body and soul in New York had opted for mass transportation. She took a deep breath and held on to the metal strap, swaying precariously as the train lurched and bucked along its dark underworld journey.

Just one more day, she daydreamed, bringing the sandy beaches, sunshine, and crystal blue water into sharp focus. She heard herself sigh heavily and quickly looked left, then right, to see if anyone was paying attention. Satisfied that no one could care less, she started to fantasize again when her gaze fell upon Mark Andrews, leaning against the train door.

Instantly she felt her pulse escalate, and something distant and familiar swept through her. Instinctively she knew that her feelings had nothing to do with Clint's investigation. It was something deeper. Something that she could vaguely touch. It was the same feeling she'd had when she first met Mark, and sporadically since then. But just as quickly as the sensation had taken hold of her, it disappeared, only to be replaced by cold anger.

They stared at each other above the sea of heads separating them. Mark's gaze was almost gleeful, she realized as a shudder enveloped her, as though he were privy to some secret. She wondered if he actually saw her or was only seeing through her.

Her question was quickly put to rest. The train doors opened and Mark squeezed his way out, but not before he nodded his head in her direction. She felt chilled and it had nothing to do with the weather.

It was several moments before she realized that her heart had slowed to normal. Reluctantly she inhaled deeply of the scents and smells and stepped off the subway at the next stop.

Ten minutes later Terri sat behind her desk, surrounded by all of her familiar things—the plants, artwork, handpicked vases, right down to the gold Cross pen that she kept encased in glass in memory of the first contract she'd signed.

Today everything seemed out of place, disjointed. She knew it had to do with her nerve-wracking interlude with Mark. But she couldn't let that reality immobilize her. There was too much to get done before the end of the day, and thoughts of Mark could not interfere. With steadfast determination she went through the process of outlining her day and the days ahead during her absence.

But as the morning ran into afternoon, that nagging, unsettling sensation would not disappear. She reached for the phone and dialed Clint's office.

Mark returned to his apartment. Terri looked the same, he thought, as he tossed his coat onto the couch and took a seat. Mark pulled the sheaf of papers out of his breast pocket. He smiled. Melissa was very thorough. It was only a matter of time before he had Terri just where he wanted her. Destroyed, ruined, alone. Then when she begged for mercy, he'd tell her. He'd tell her everything.

CHAPTER 25

"Melissa, I've written detailed instructions about what to do with the cable station's stock transfers. I want to be sure that Mr. Anderson gets his rightful share. He gave me a great deal, and I intend to see to it that he's treated fairly. The members of the Board of Directors would love to see that he gets nothing. But I've already put a few bugs in several ears." He smiled. "There shouldn't be any problem."

Melissa sat quietly on the plush sofa, jotting down information that she knew she wouldn't need. She knew Clint's plans and ways of negotiation like the back of her hand. They both knew that she could handle the Board with her eyes closed, mouth taped and hands tied. However, she also knew it made him feel better if he thought she was writing everything down. Besides, it gave her a reason not to have to look at him and possibly reveal the turmoil that boiled beneath her serene exterior.

". . . And," he continued, pacing the floor as he spoke, "tell Pat to give a call to my attorney in London and let him know I'll be in town Christmas week and may need his services on very short notice."

"What about Jillianne and Ashley? Do you want me to have Pat purchase the customary gifts and have them sent?"

Clint heard the sarcasm in her voice but refused to rise to the bait. "No. As a matter of fact, I'll be doing my shopping when I arrive in London. I'm sure I can figure out what a four-year-old girl would like."

Melissa gave a silent sniff of indignation. "Certainly." She slowly rose from her seat. "Is that about it? I'm scheduled to meet with the new clients for the auto dealership in about fifteen minutes."

Clint absently waved his hand, his mind already on the days and nights ahead with Terri. "Sure. That's it for now. Let me know how the meeting turns out. I'd like to—" The ringing of his private line cut him off.

Instinctively Melissa hesitated.

"Hello?"

"Clint, it's me, Terri."

Clint's voice dropped two octaves as it reached across the phone lines to caress her. "Hey, baby. I was just thinking about you."

Melissa stiffened and wished once again that those words of endearment were directed at her. One day they would be, she vowed. If—no, not if—*when* Mark's plan was complete, she would leave Mark and Clint would be hers. She cleared her throat to gain his attention.

Clint looked up, having completely forgotten that Melissa was still in the office. He covered the mouthpiece with his hand. "You can go ahead with your meeting, Mel. I'll check back with you later." He gave her an absent smile and went back to his conversation.

Melissa marched out in a huff, which was lost on Clint.

"You sound upset, babe. What's wrong?"

"Clint, I, uh, saw Mark today."

All of Clint's antennas shot up. "Where?"

"On the subway, of all places," she replied, trying unsuccessfully to make her voice sound light.

"And? Did he say anything, do anything?"

"No. He just . . . just . . . ?

"Just what?"

"He just gave me a very uneasy feeling, Clint. I don't know how to explain it. It was almost as if I were seeing him for the first time, but in a way that was familiar. It's happened before."

"I'm not following you, Terri."

She exhaled an exasperated breath. "I know. I don't understand it myself."

"It's probably just a combination of everything that's happened lately and then seeing him unexpectedly."

"You're probably right," she conceded.

"Try to put it out of your head. We have a beautiful three weeks ahead of us, and I don't want anything to interfere with that."

Terri sighed in agreement. "Anyway," she said trying to sound bright, "my friend, Lisa, has invited us to dinner tonight. Sort of a bon voyage. I told her we would probably make it."

"No problem. I'd like to meet her."

Terri chuckled. "That's the same thing she said about you."

"I wonder why?" he responded, his voice full of sarcasm. "What have you told her about me?"

"Only sweet, wonderful things."

He heard the laughter in her voice. "I bet. So what time is this shindig?"

"I figured that seven would be good. I have a class at five. It shouldn't last more than forty-five minutes."

"I'll pick you up at your apartment."

Her voice lowered. "I'll be waiting. Bye."

Clint felt the old familiar rush race through his veins at the sound of invitation in her voice. The next three weeks were going to be pure heaven.

Smiling, he held the phone in his hand for several long moments after Terri had hung up. The shuffling of papers brought him back to reality. His head snapped in the direction of Melissa, standing like a sentinel in the doorway.

Clint frowned, annoyed that she had stayed to listen to his conversation. He replaced the receiver. "I thought you had a meeting," he said in a tight voice.

Melissa straightened, holding her notes against her racing heart. "I came back. I wanted to be sure that there wasn't anything else."

Clint took a long look at Melissa, then took several steps in her direction. "Is something wrong, Mel? If I didn't know better, I'd think you were sick."

She emitted a nervous chuckle. "I'm fine. I was just thinking about everything that needs taking care of in the next few weeks. That's all."

Clint's eyes creased in concern. His voice held an inquisitive tone. "I have all the confidence in the world in you. I'm sure you'll handle everything the way you always have."

"I'd better be going. I'll see you before you leave, won't I?"

Her question sounded almost like a plea to Clint's ears. But that couldn't be possible, he concluded. "Sure, I'll stop by before I head out this evening."

Melissa nodded and walked out, leaving Clint with mixed feelings of empathy and apprehension.

"Come in. Come in," beamed Lisa. She gave Clint a swift once-over and winked her acceptance to Terri. "Clint, it's so good to finally meet you."

"Just please don't say you've heard so much about me," he chuckled as he shrugged out of his coat.

Lisa slipped a possessive arm around Clint's waist. "I promise," she said sweetly. "Now come on in. Brian is in the kitchen."

Lisa led the way into the living room, and Terri let out a startled expulsion of breath. "Lisa! Not again."

Clint looked at Terri skeptically, then at Lisa.

"Don't mind her," Lisa advised Clint in a stage whisper. "She gets a little spacey every time I redecorate."

"Believe me, sweetheart," Terri said to Clint, "if you had any idea how many times this woman redecorates her house, you would lose it, too."

"Are you just going to complain, or are you going to admire and cringe with jealousy." Lisa hid her bubbling laughter behind her hand.

"She's determined to run me into the poorhouse," Brian stated as he stepped into the room. His eyes sparkled with love for his wife.

The trio turned in his direction. Lisa demurely approached her husband. She hooked her arm through his.

"Clint, this is my husband, Brian." They both walked toward Clint and Terri, with Lisa's blossoming belly leading the way.

Brian extended his hand, which Clint shook. "Good to finally meet you, Clint. I've—"

"Just don't say you've heard so much about him," Lisa cut in.

Brian looked at his wife curiously, while the other three erupted into infectious laughter. Brian shrugged his narrow shoulders, and unable to help himself joined in.

"Dinner was fabulous as usual, Brian," Terri enthused. "One of these days you should teach your wife to cook."

"We all have our strong points," Lisa said, trying to sound hurt. "Brian cooks and—"

"You remodel the house," her husband quickly interjected.

"Very funny. You're giving Clint the wrong idea."

"What idea is that?"

"Actually Lisa gets a great deal from a mutual friend of ours, Tempest Dailey," Terri advised. "We've all known each other for years. She decorated my offices also," she added.

"And you would think that my darling wife was trying to personally ensure Tempest's success," Brian chuckled.

"It's more of a bartering system," Lisa said. "She does the house, and I introduce her to a lot of potential clients through the foundation network."

"Interesting system. If she's half as good as these rooms indicate, I'd definitely like to meet her."

"And her husband, Braxton," Lisa offered. "He's the architect."

Clint's thick eyebrows arched. "Fantastic-sounding team. The next time you speak with them, ask them if they would be interested in a joint project in the Bahamas." Clint dug into his pocket and produced his business card, passing it to Lisa. "Ask one of them to give me a call." He looked at Terri. "Or Terri. She'll be as involved as I will. Besides," he added with a smirk, "maybe if we become chummy, they'll give me the same kind of deal you guys get!"

The table erupted into laughter.

"Speaking of the Bahamas, you two," Lisa asked, "what time are you leaving?" She rose to clear the table. Terri helped.

"We have to fly to Puerto Rico in the morning," Clint said, pushing his chair away from the table. "We have a seven A.M. flight. The ship sails from there."

"We're not taking the traditional tour," Terri added. "Since we need to get to Nassau by Friday, we're going to skip a couple of islands. Nassau is not on this route."

"But you will have time to go to Barbados?" Lisa asked, slowly making her way to the kitchen.

"Definitely." The two women entered the spacious kitchen. "I can't wait," she said wistfully. "I feel that something's awaiting me. Don't ask me what it is. But I feel certain that my life is going to somehow change."

Lisa gave Terri an encouraging hug. "Whatever it is, if it's out there for you, hon, you're sure to find it."

Terri smiled.

"And speaking of finding things. I think you've found yourself a winner this time, girlfriend."

Terri's eyes sparkled. "You really think so?"

"Of course." She nudged Terri in the side. "If I weren't so hooked on Brian, Clint would be just the kind of man I'd go after. Later for friendship! Me and you would just have to stop speakin'."

Terri broke out laughing until tears squeezed out of her eyes. "Belly and all, huh?"

"You got it!"

Terri bent over into another fit of laughter. "Girl, you are crazy."

"Crazy as a fox. So look out!"

Terri was finally able to straighten up. She wiped her eyes and took huge gulps of air, slowly regaining her composure.

"Seriously, Lis—do you think I'm making the right decision?"

"You mean about going to England and meeting his daughter?"

Terri nodded.

Lisa leaned to the side, resting her weight on her left foot, and placed her hand on the protruding hip. "From what I see and from what you've told me, you have a good man, Terri. And with the looks that he was giving you all night, I know he loves you. It's in his eyes. It's in his voice every time he says your name. All you have to do is give it a chance. Give his daughter a chance. Everybody deserves one."

Terri took a deep breath. "I know you're right. It's just that I'm afraid that it'll all blow up in my face. After Alan and the baby . . . I . . . ?

Lisa placed a comforting hand on Terri's shoulder. "That's the chance we all have to take if we're going to try for the ultimate goal. Happiness. You have to decide how much you're willing to sacrifice in order to have it."

Terri absorbed the full impact of Lisa's words. When she looked up, Clint stood in the open doorway. At that moment she knew that the illusive road ahead of them would be filled with more than the simple challenges that relationships are built on. Something much more awaited them in the days and months ahead.

A slight shiver ran up her spine, and she silently prayed that Clint would be able to keep the growing chill at bay.

CHAPTER 26

The apartment intercom buzzed.

"The cab is here," Terri called out to Clint. Within moments he emerged from the bedroom, a suitcase in each hand. He placed them by the door and helped Terri with her coat.

"We won't be needing these for long," Clint whispered against Terri's neck as he draped her scarf across the exposed flesh.

"Hmm. I can't wait," she purred, turning into his arms.

Clint planted a warm kiss on her lips. "Hot days and long sultry nights," he crooned against her warm mouth.

"And if we don't get out of here pronto, we'll be spending those nights looking at falling snow and slush."

"No way." Clint picked up the two large suitcases and a smaller one, while Terri draped the suit bag over her arm. With her free hand she carried the traveling bag that she and Clint would share.

She took a quick look around the apartment. "Do we have everything?"

"As far as I can tell. Do you have your notes?"

Terri nodded. "And you have the preliminary contracts for Mr. Carpenter?"

"Yep."

"Then, that's it. Let's go." Terri flicked off the light and stepped out into the hallway, walking stride for stride with Clint.

* * *

"As I said at our last meeting, Mr. Brathwaite, I can't make a firm commitment until I meet with Mr. Steele on Friday," Nat Carpenter intoned. He blew a puff of smoke into the stale office air.

Malcolm gripped the phone. "I understand. I was just calling to see if there had been any changes," he said in a controlled voice. "You know how to reach me. I'd be very interested in hearing what Steele has to offer."

"I'm sure. Well, I must be going. I have another call," he lied smoothly. "We'll talk soon."

"Of course." Malcolm hung up the phone, his jaw locked in irritation. He had to pull this off. If Steele came up with more money to finance the deal, he'd have to find a way to outbid him. He already knew he could out maneuver Terri in terms of her ad campaign. Hadn't he been taught by the master? He was sure that he could easily make her proposal dismal in comparison to what he had in mind. But he needed more than a winning campaign, even though Steele would think that the campaign was the cause of him losing the account. Which was exactly what he wanted.

He had to put an immediate alternative strategy into motion. If Carpenter went for Steele's proposal, and Steele had the financial backing to pull it off, then he'd have to find another source of financing. And fast. Nothing could be left to chance.

Malcolm leaned back in his chair. Suddenly he sprang up as if hit with a jolt of electricity. A plan was rapidly forming in his mind. He reached for the phone, a malicious smile forming on his lips. Everyone had an Achilles' heel, and he'd just found the one he'd been looking for.

Terri felt her heart thump with excitement as she and Clint cut a path up the gangway and onto the *Christina II.* The magnificent ship was like something out of a Hollywood movie. Mirrored walls, lush greenery, ankle-deep carpet, and crystal chandeliers were only the beginning. Winding staircases led to various levels of the ship, and the passengers were as stunning as the ship itself.

As much as she'd traveled over the years, she'd never been on a cruise. This was an experience she wouldn't soon forget.

"Luxurious" was the word that seemed to repeat itself over and again in her mind. She wanted to ooh and ahh like an out-of-town tourist, but she fought to control the urge. Instead she squeezed closer to Clint, which he didn't mind one bit.

"I take it you like what you see?" he asked, looking down into her sparkling eyes.

"It's fabulous, Clint. I just can't imagine so much splendor being contained on a ship."

"You haven't seen anything yet. Wait until you see some of the salons and the entertainment rooms, not to mention—" he stopped, pulled her into his arms and looked deep into her eyes "—the suite that I selected for us."

The intimate timbre of his voice wrapped around her, and all thoughts of anything other than being with Clint flew from her head.

As Terri stepped from the steamy shower, wrapped from head to ankle in terry cloth, Clint slipped behind her, securing her snugly around the waist.

"Hmm," he breathed into her neck, pulling her closer as he buried his face in the hollow of her shoulder. "Good enough to eat," he groaned, nibbling at her neck.

Bubbling giggles rushed up from her throat and filled the air. She turned fully into his embrace. "Is that a threat or a promise, Mr. Steele?" she taunted.

"Don't tempt me," he warned, deftly loosening the belt from her robe and sliding knowing hands along the silken curves beneath.

"We'll be late for dinner," she whispered against his bare chest.

Clint reluctantly stepped back and held her at arm's length. "Speaking of dinner, I have a surprise for you." His eyes darkened with mischief. "Stand right there. Don't move."

Moments later Clint returned from the bedroom, carrying a large white box tied with a huge red and gold ribbon. His smile invited her to step closer. "I hope you like it," he grinned. "I had it sent directly to the ship," he added, seeing the questioning look on her face. He handed her the box.

Terri eased down on the champagne-colored sofa and gingerly untied the ribbon, periodically taking quick peeks at Clint for any sign of what might be inside.

Then in one swift motion, she tossed the cover aside and whipped open the gold tissue paper. Her quick intake of breath was Clint's first indication that he'd made the right choice.

Slowly he stepped forward as Terri's eyes widened in delight. Inch by inch she withdrew the black velvet that felt like butter beneath her fingertips.

"Clint," she breathed, "this is gorgeous." She stood up and held the floor-length gown in front of her.

"When I saw it, I knew you had to have it."

"How did you know what size to get?" she asked, holding the dress against her and knowing that it would be a perfect fit.

"I took a peek at the tags in your dresses. Then I double-checked with a call to Stacy. Try it on. I want you to wear it tonight when we have dinner at the captain's table."

"The captain's table?"

Clint grinned. "Of course. Did you expect anything less?"

"From you, you darling man, absolutely not." She planted a hot, wet kiss on his lips, hugged the dress to her, and ran off to the bathroom.

Moments later she emerged. This time it was Clint who couldn't believe his eyes.

The gown fit Terri like a second skin, skimming and hugging all of her curves. The off-the-shoulder effect gave the viewer an appetizing look at silken brown shoulders that were encased in black satin with metallic gold edging. All of which did little to hide the tempting valleys that fought for equal attention. The perfectly fitting gown embraced her body like a possessive lover, only giving way at the ankle where it widened into a fishtail—it, too, done in the same satin and gold.

"Baby," Clint whispered reverently, "maybe we should forget dinner." He stepped closer as Terri slowly spun around to give him the full effect of the devastating gown. He caught her in his arms and pressed his lips to her throat, making her whimper. "But then again, I want every man on board to see, and then know, that you're mine. Exclusively," he moaned in her ear.

Terri pressed her hands against his chest. "Always?"

"Definitely. I promise you, there's nothing and no one that could come between us." He covered her mouth with his and silently prayed that he could keep that promise.

CHAPTER 27

Dinner at the captain's table was an event straight off of network television, Terri thought as she savored the steamed mussels drenched in a hot butter and garlic sauce. Intermittently she had the hilarious notion of wanting to call the first mate "Gofer." However, no amount of television viewing could have prepared her for the opulence of life aboard a cruise ship.

The entertainment salons, game rooms, and nightclub were more than enough to keep the passengers completely content. Not to mention the private saunas, exercise rooms, boutiques, and hair salons.

But even with so much to keep the mind and body occupied, Terri could not contain her anticipation of returning home.

As she and Clint strolled along the deck, flashes of sandy beaches and tropical fruits danced along the fringes of her thoughts.

"Hmm," she sighed, looking out across the lapping blue and white waves as they glistened beneath the brilliant full moon.

Clint slid his arm around Terri's narrow, velvet waist. "What are you thinking about?"

"Only that in a matter of days I'll be back home."

The childlike wistfulness of her voice touched him. He eased her closer and hoped that memories of her homeland lived up to her expectations.

"This is really important to you, isn't it?"

"If I could only explain how much." She stopped and turned toward him, her eyes willing him to understand. "It was the only time in my life when I was sure that I," she hesitated, "existed—belonged somewhere—to someone."

A flash of anger rose. It felt as if all of the progress they'd made over the months had vanished. She *did* belong. She belonged to him. But with his next breath he understood that Terri would have to come to terms with that on her own, or it would never be real for her.

He needed to change the subject. "Tell me more about your brother, Malcolm."

Terri's coral-colored lips curved into a smile. "Malcolm. Malcolm was two years younger than me, but we were inseparable. He was always the prankster, and I was the one who was practical and wanted to stay out of trouble. I always felt . . . responsible for Malcolm."

She took a long pausing breath, and Clint began to think that she had come to the end of her story until she spoke again.

"Neither of us remembers our mother, and all we knew about our respective fathers was that neither of them were around." Her laugh was hollow.

"So you were sort of a big sister and a mother to Malcolm."

Terri nodded. "We had Nana, who we adored, but there was just something special about our brother-sister relationship. The day we were separated, after Nana grew so ill," her voice wavered, "I promised him that I would come back for him. That I'd find him." Tears of an unfulfilled promise stung her eyes. She quickly blinked them away. "I'll always remember that day. The way he looked at me . . . his eyes . . . ? She felt a tremor scurry up her spine. "His eyes were like . . . ?

Clint felt her shiver. "What is it? Like what?"

"They were just like—like Mark's eyes." She continued in a rush. "That day—on the subway." She turned and looked up at Clint, disbelief and something resembling fear hovered in the soft brown depths.

"Terri, come on. You couldn't possibly be thinking . . . ?

She briefly shut her eyes against the impossible and shook her head. "It was just so weird. I mean, I know that Mark and Malcolm . . . ? her voice trailed away, "couldn't possibly be the same person. "I would know." Her eyes trailed up to meet Clint's questioning stare. "Wouldn't I?"

Clint braced Terri's shoulders. "You're letting your imagination get the best of you. Now, listen—" he lowered his head and tilted hers upward with the tip of his finger "—your brother Malcolm is dead. You said so yourself. Mark is a whole separate issue. One that you need to put behind you."

"There was always something about Mark that I could never quite place but was still vaguely familiar," Terri went on, ignoring Clint's suggestion. She took a shaky breath. "His accent sounds pure New York. He claimed his roots were here. I never thought otherwise . . . but I guess you're right. Let's just forget it." Even as she forced a smile on her face, she remembered what Clint had discovered about Mark and his nonexistent past. So did Clint.

"That's better. Even though you could improve on that fake smile." He took her hand, and they walked in the direction of their suite. "Dedicate the next few hours to us," he whispered, "and I guarantee that I'll make you forget all about it."

But thoughts of Mark left a shadow over them both.

The next three days were a whirlwind of activities. The first stop was the magnificent island of Aruba, which seemed like two worlds rolled into one. The dramatic desert interior and spectacular blue-water beaches stood in sharp contrast to each other. Terri and Clint did the tour along Palm Beach and Eagle Beach, stopping off at all of the exclusive resorts with their renowned casinos along the way. The highlight of their stopover was the snorkeling that Terri insisted upon. Much to Clint's dismay.

"You look a little green around the gills," Terri teased as they returned to the hotel, laden with their equipment.

Clint tried unsuccessfully to pretend indifference. "I told you I wasn't too thrilled about going snorkeling. I had some paperwork . . . ?

"Oh, mon, let's be for real," she chuckled, slipping into dialect. "You could have told me you couldn't swim, ya know." She covered her widening grin with her wet hand.

He turned a glowering look in her direction. "I'm happy you're so amused." He wiped his face with a mint green towel.

Terri placed a reassuring hand on his bare shoulder. "I'm sorry, baby." She reached up on tiptoe and kissed his cheek. "I would have never guessed that you couldn't . . . ?

"Don't say it, okay? There's always something that a person can't do. I just happen not to be able to . . . swim . . . very well. Is that so horrible?"

"Of course not." Terri fought down the chuckle that bubbled in her throat. "I mean . . . ? she rolled her eyes up toward the air in thought "—I can't drive a stick shift. That should make you feel better, honey." With that last jab at his ego, Terri took off as fast as her feet would take her, barely escaping Clint's grasp.

"You're really asking for it," he yelled, taking off behind her. "You'll be sorry if I catch you!"

Mark walked out of the travel agency office on Fifth Avenue. Swirling snow stung his eyes. He took no notice. A smug, satisfied smile eased across his cocoa-colored face. Wanting to reassure himself, he tapped the breast pocket of his black shearling coat. His ticket was in place. He wasn't taking any chances. He would be able to leave at a moment's notice. Now all he had to do was wait and see what happened on Friday.

He stood on the corner and hailed a cab. An evening with Melissa was just the thing to take the edge off, he mused. Soon he'd be rid of her, too. But in the meantime . . . ?

CHAPTER 28

After a day at sea, the cruise ship pulled into La Guaira, the port for the capital city of Caracas in Venezuela. The temperature at 8 A.M. was a sizzling 98 degrees.

Undaunted by the stifling temperature, which continued to climb, Terri and Clint took the scenic half-hour tour ride inland that led to Caracas where Spanish antiquities were displayed at the *Colonial Art Museum.* Clint purchased several pottery pieces from local shops, and Terri selected a brilliant abstract painting for Lisa and Brian.

Before long the exhausted duo had to return to the ship. And it was on to Barbados.

As the ship rolled gently over the waves, Terri nestled in Clint's arm. He turned on his side, aligning his body with hers.

"I don't think I'll be able to sleep tonight," she whispered in the dark.

Clint placed a soft kiss on the back of her neck. "I know. You've got me so worked up about it, I don't know if I'll be able to sleep either."

Terri laughed softly. "Tomorrow," she sighed. "It's only a few hours away, but it feels like an eternity."

"Before you know it, you'll be setting foot on solid ground." He stroked her hip. "Then I get to see this fabulous place you call home."

Terri was up with the sun and pulling Clint up behind her.

"We still have two hours before we dock, baby," he mumbled. With great effort he stretched and sat up in bed.

"I know, but—" she turned sparkling brown eyes on him "—I just want to be ready."

Clint shook his head in defeat. "At least let me order room service. I know you won't be able to sit still for a meal."

She continued putting clothes into the suitcases. "I couldn't eat a thing. But you go ahead."

Clint pulled himself out of bed and stood beside her. He picked up a freshly starched shirt and hung it in the carrying bag.

Terri turned and looked up into eyes that shone back with quiet understanding. No words were needed.

Two hours later Clint and Terri stood in the port capital of Bridgetown. The bustling town was brimming with activity. Small shops, restaurants, and street merchants all vied for the tourist trade.

The streets were lined with mahogany and cabbage palm trees, providing a cool breeze in the balmy tropical paradise.

"I can't believe it, Clint. I'm finally here."

He hugged her next to him as they eased past a tour group. "Is it anything like what you remember?"

"Yes. Just bigger and more people."

Everywhere they turned, beautiful people in all shades of brown hurried about their activities.

"We'd better head on over to the hotel and get settled," Clint suggested.

"I want to take a ride over to my old neighborhood. I won't be able to rest until I do."

"Can't you at least put your things down first?"

"You go ahead. I'll meet you later. I shouldn't be long."

"Terri—"

"Clint, please try to understand. I know this may seem obsessive, but it's something I have to do." She stroked his arm. "And I need to do it alone."

He nodded. "If that's what you need. I'll see you at the hotel."

"Thank you." She reached up and kissed his lips, then turned to walk in the direction of Holetown, one of the three largest towns on the island. Within moments she was swallowed up in the ebb and flow of bodies, and Clint lost sight of her.

On the next corner, Terri hailed a taxi.

"Where to, lovely miss?" the affable driver asked. He turned and looked over his shoulder at Terri, exhibiting a bright gold-front tooth when he grinned.

"Do you know where Codrington Hill is in Saint Michael?"

"Jon know where every'ting be on our lovely island. He know everybody and," he grinned, "everybody's business, I been told. You name de place, I take you der." He flashed her another gold-tooth grin. "Jon Saint Hill at your service."

Terri laughed. He was the typical island cabbie. And she was quite sure that he was right about his assessment of himself. Maybe he'd even be of some help to her. "You're from Jamaica, aren't you?" Terri quizzed.

"Ah. You notice, eh? But I live 'ere for more years than I can count. I be what you call an island hopper. One foot 'ere, one foot der. And you?"

"I was born here."

"You be raised up on de island?" he asked in disbelief. "You sound pure Yankee."

"True. It's been long, mon, since I been home."

Jon chuckled when he heard the lilting melody of the Bajan tongue. "Yeah, you true Bajan." He winked at her through the rearview mirror. "How long you been gone from home?"

"I moved to the States when I was about eight years old."

"You still have family 'ere?" he asked, taking a sharp right turn with ease.

"No," she answered so softly, Jon wasn't sure he'd heard her. He asked again.

Terri cleared her throat. "No. My family died a long time ago. My grandmother and my . . . my brother."

Jon was silent for a moment. "You come back to reclaim your roots, eh?"

"Something like that."

Jon stole a peek at her through the mirror. Her face held a faraway look, hopeful yet resigned. "What your family name?"

"Brathwaite."

Jon brightened. "For true? I know a Brathwaite. He come maybe once a year to visit. About this time, for true. Some year not at all. He grew up 'ere."

Terri felt her pulse begin to race. She leaned forward in the cab. "He?"

"Yeah. Maybe you two be related," he grinned. "Everybody on de island related one way or de other."

"So I've been told." She grinned at the old wives' tale that everybody with the same last name was somehow related. If it were true, then maybe she really did have some family left. The possibility excited her. "Do you know where this other Brathwaite goes when he visits? Maybe I could track down some family members."

Jon frowned. "He go to a small house down dis next turn. He stand in front of de house and stare. Den he get back in de cab, and I take him to de cemetery outside Saint Michael. He bring a small bundle of flowers, drop dem on a gravesite, and leave. He be a strange one."

"What do you mean?"

"Usually he talk a lot when he first get in me cab, tell me all about life in de States. But when he get back in, he a changed man. Almost evil." Jon gave a slight shudder. "Such a shame. I remember 'im as a boy."

Terri frowned. This Brathwaite didn't sound like anyone she wanted to know. But perhaps he was some distant relation who could shed some light on her family and provide the link that she so desperately sought. She'd have to put her misgivings aside.

"Have you seen him recently, Jon?"

"No. Can't say so, ya know. But, if ya let me know where ya be stayin', I make sure to tell ya, if I should see 'im."

Terri thought about it for a moment. Her first inclination was to deny Jon's request. Her years of living in New York had made her wary of strangers, especially friendly strangers. But this wasn't New York, and if she intended to get the help she needed, she was going to have to trust someone.

"All right," she said finally. She reached in her bag for a pen and paper, quickly jotting down her hotel name and room number.

Clint took a quick inventory of the suite. He was sure that Terri would love it. The sweeping balcony, just off the bedroom, overlooked the beach, which glistened beneath the dazzling island sun. Rows of palms swayed gently against the warm tropic breeze. The sunken living room colored with muted corals, bronzes, soft copper, and rich cream, whispered *comfort.* The adjacent bedroom echoed the same hues and was complemented further with blooming bouquets of island flora and a king-sized canopy bed draped with sheer white netting. Every nuance of the luxurious bedroom invited intimacy.

Clint checked the kitchen. As he'd requested, he found the fridge and cabinets completely stocked.

"Perfect," he smiled, "except for the lady of the house." He took a final look around the suite. Satisfied that everything was in order, he stretched out on the rattan couch and reached for the phone. It had been a while since he'd spoken with Jillianne and even longer since he'd heard his daughter, Ashley's, voice. He wanted to assure them both that everything was still on schedule, and that he'd be bringing a guest home for the holidays.

CHAPTER 29

"Ashley! Ashley, honey. Come down for lunch," Jillianne called. Her tall, toned body moved gracefully through the spacious rooms until she reached the kitchen, where her housekeeper and nanny, Mrs. Hally, was unloading bags of groceries.

"Oh, there you are, Mrs. Hally. Ashley will be down shortly. Please fix her a bowl of soup and a sandwich, would you?"

"Of course, Ms. Jill. Right off."

"Thank you."

Mrs. Hally was instantly caught in the magic of the breathtaking smile that had slowed the hearts of many, before Jill turned to make her way to the living room. She came to a stop in the center of the room, her jet black curls glistening in the afternoon sun. With one hand on her slender hip and the tip of a finger pressed against full, pouty lips, she assessed the space.

Although her field was real estate, specifically selling mansions and large blocks of land which afforded her a lavish life-style, Jillianne always had a knack for decorating. She took every opportunity to practice her talent, with the living room and bedrooms being her favorite sites in the sprawling four-story town house. Very often she would offer decorating suggestions to prospective home owners, and in many cases her ideas helped to cinch the deals.

Today, however, her motivation for change was entirely personal. Clint was coming home, and she wanted everything to be perfect. More than perfect. Just the thought of seeing him, in only a few days, caused waves of desire to run havoc through her stomach. Maybe this time, she thought, he'd come home to her to stay.

Without conscious effort, his face danced before her eyes. Her long-lashed lids drifted close. She envisioned the lips that she longed to claim, the hard muscular frame that promised total satisfaction. She trembled and wrapped her slender arms around her body as if to contain the fire within her. Clint represented everything that was wonderful in a man. He was handsome, sexy, warm, and caring about everyone around him. Not to mention the charisma and power that he exuded in business, which to her was a natural aphrodisiac. What was most appealing about Clinton Steele was the mystery that coated him like a second skin. His elusiveness compelled women to seek him out and attempt to uncover the secrets beneath the picture-perfect exterior.

The ringing phone pulled her out of her romanticizing. Shaking her head, she reached for the phone. "Yes?"

"Hello. May I speak with Jillianne Davis?"

"This is Ms. Davis," Jill exhaled.

"You don't know me, but I'm a very close friend of your brother-in-law, Clint. My name is Mark Andrews."

"I'm sorry, sir, but that line is still busy," intoned the hotel operator. "I could ring your room back when the line is free."

Clint checked his watch. Terri should be back shortly, and they'd planned to do some shopping and then go to dinner.

"That's all right, operator. I'll try back later. Thank you."

How many times had he insisted that Jill get call waiting? Time and again she refused, stating that if the call was that important, they'd either call back or have the operator interrupt. There was nothing more annoying, she'd said, than to have a perfectly lovely conversation interrupted with another call.

He shrugged and made a mental note to call her later.

The cab eased up the dirt road that led to rows of two-story homes. Terri's heart quickened and filled with old memories. "It's just down the road, on the right," she whispered.

Jon's smooth caramel brow creased. "Dis be de place? Dis street?"

Terri nodded, swallowing the lump that sat in her throat. "Yes."

Jon shook his head and turned to look at her. "You *dat* Brathwaite?"

"What do you mean?"

"De family dat I speak of, der was a grandmother who took care of her two grandchildren, a little girl and de same Brathwaite fellow I told ya 'bout."

Terri's pulse quickened.

"What happened?"

"From what I be remembering, de grandmother got very sick, and died. De authorities couldn't find no relatives to take care of de children—dey shipped off to foster homes. De boy stay 'ere on de island. No one know what happen to de girl."

"That's what happened to us," she whispered. "It has to be—"

"But you say your brother died. So it can't be. Dis man far from dead." Jon shook his head. "Maybe I be mistaken. It be so long ago."

Terri leaned forward in her seat. "The man that comes here, the little boy, I mean—has he ever told you his name?"

"Hmm." Jon thought for a moment. "He told me his name one time." Jon scratched his head, while mumbling a string of names.

Terri held her breath.

Jon brightened. "Yes. I be remembering now. He say his name be Malcolm! Yes. Malcolm Brathwaite."

CHAPTER 30

"I don't recall Clint ever mentioning anyone named Mark Andrews," Jill responded, suspicion rising in her tone.

Mark chuckled. "That's Clint for you. You know how busy he is. He probably just forgot." His voice lowered two octaves. "But he's told me *all* about you."

Jillianne felt her heartbeat quicken. "Clint told you about me?" Her spirits soared.

Mark immediately heard the eagerness in her voice, and he pounced on it. "He certainly did. Wonderful things. I told him that you sounded almost too good to be true."

Jill laughed in pure joy.

He reeled her in a little more. "As a matter of fact, he's always telling me how much you mean to him. You're a very important person in his life, Jill."

She could hardly breathe. "What can I do for you, Mr. Andrews?"

"First of all, call me Mark."

"All right." She smiled.

"Well, I just called Clint's office and they told me that he would be away until after the New Year." He chuckled again. "I talked the secretary into telling me that he was coming to England for the holidays. Which is great because I plan to arrive tomorrow morning."

"Really? I'm sure Clint will be happy to see you."

"Yes. I'm sure." Jill mistook the cynicism in his tone for jest. "But I wanted to surprise him. We haven't seen each other in a while, and I was hoping that you could arrange something."

"Of course. I'd love to."

"Great. Why don't I give you a call when I arrive tomorrow? That should give you enough time to think of something."

"More than enough time. Where are you staying?"

"I have reservations at the Savoy."

"You're perfectly welcome to stay here, once Clint arrives," she amended. "I'm sure he would want you to."

"Thanks for the invitation. Let me think about it. But . . . how about if I take you to dinner tomorrow night? We could talk, get to know each other. I want to see if all of the fantastic stories that Clint told me about you are true."

Jill giggled. "That sounds wonderful, but let me think about it."

"I'll call you."

"That sounds fine. Have a safe flight."

"Bye, Jill."

Jill replaced the receiver. A small smile dimpled her cheeks.

Mark merged with the crowd, moving with them toward the departure gate, and boarded the plane to England.

CHAPTER 31

Terri felt her throat constrict. She struggled to breathe as a surge of heat infused her body.

"No." She wanted to scream the single word, but her voice was a mere whisper. Her hand trembled ever so slightly as she wiped away a bead of perspiration that slid slowly down her brow.

Jon glanced in his rearview mirror. "Be ya all right?" He pulled the cab to the side of the road. *Please don't let dis come-lately Bajan woman faint in me car. De wife she never believe another one.* "Can I get ya some'ting? Some water?"

Terri shook her head. Taking a deep breath, she blurted out the question that had been sitting on her tongue. "Can you take me to the gravesite that the man goes to?"

His soft brown eyes held the unspoken question between them. What if she was that same little girl in the story? She was so lovely, with her silky mahogany skin and glistening locks. How could he deny those eyes that held such passion and sorrow?

Jon nodded and turned the cab in the direction of Saint Michael's cemetery.

It was nearly six o'clock. The evening sky was gray. Ominous. Melissa sighed. She'd be alone again tonight, just as she'd been alone every night since the last one spent with Mark. He hadn't called since then. She had no idea where he was or what he was doing. And she had no real desire to find out, not after the things he did to her when they were last together. Mark's lovemaking had taken on a dangerous tone. He was more aggressive, angry, as if he were trying to punish her. She shuddered. Mark was changing day by day, and it frightened her. An uneasy feeling had settled in her stomach days ago, and she couldn't seem to shake it. All she wanted to do was try to put Mark out of her mind. Slowly she rose from her desk, closed her appointment book, and turned toward the window, wondering what Clint and Terri were doing on the sunny island of Barbados.

Her pulse drummed in her ears. Terri had everything! Everything! The resentment ignited in her hazel eyes, turning them almost black. Terri had a thriving business, beauty, brains, and Clint. Melissa's smooth jaw clenched in frustration.

She crossed the room and snatched her coat from the closet. Through habit, she meticulously scanned the office, collected her purse and briefcase, and left.

She stood waiting for the elevator. Maybe she'd take herself to dinner. There was no reason to rush home, and cooking for one was depressing.

Melissa pushed through the revolving doors and was greeted by a blast of bitter cold wind. She pulled her silver fox coat tightly around her slender body and slipped on a pair of dark shades to shield her eyes from the biting wind.

She stepped to the curb, intent on hailing a cab, when she heard her name whip across the windy street.

Turning in the direction of the sound, she caught sight of Steve's midnight blue Lexus angling its way through the rush of pedestrians.

"Melissa!" he shouted again as he pulled to a stop on the opposite side of the street.

Momentarily she had a flash of their brief affair together as she watched him make a U turn and stop in front of her. Steve was a wonderful, caring, considerate man, and a great lover. But he wasn't Clint, and she never gave him a chance to be anyone else. That compounded with his line of work led to the demise of their relationship. At times she still wondered what could have been. She inhaled the shudder of remembrance as she stepped toward the car.

"What brings you uptown? You know Clint is away?"

"Yeah. I know. I had some business up the street. I was on my way home."

"Oh." She smiled slightly and tugged on her coat.

"Want a lift?"

"No, thanks. I can take a cab."

"Come on, Mel. You have plans or something?"

"No."

"So . . . hop in. I'll take you home, and I promise I won't bite."

"I wasn't going home."

"Can I come?" A big grin overtook his features, and Melissa couldn't help laughing. Steve always had the ability to make her laugh, even when she didn't want to. The single memory warmed her ever so slightly.

"Why not?" she said finally. She rounded the car and slipped into the lush leather seat.

"That's better," Steve said. He gave her a private look which she tried to ignore as he maneuvered for a spot in the backed-up lane of traffic.

"How's everything been going?" Steve asked after several awkward moments of silence.

"Not bad."

"You don't sound too sure." He glanced in her direction.

"Let's just say that it's nothing worth talking about."

"Hmm. That good, huh?"

Melissa grinned. "You're rather nosey."

"That's my job. Remember?"

"Very well, actually."

They sat in silence for a few moments before Melissa spoke again. "Are you working on anything interesting?"

Steve thought about his answer, wondering if he should tell her that he'd been investigating Mark and her in the process. He decided against it.

"I was, but the trail, as we say in the business, ran cold."

"That doesn't sound like the Steve I know. You never left a stone unturned." She stared at his profile, reacquainting herself with the full lips, chiseled cheekbones, trim mustache, creamy brown complexion, and the salt and pepper hair.

"Let's put it this way, my client decided not to pursue it any further. So . . . ? He shrugged his shoulders in dismissal.

"You mean Clint?" She waited for a reaction.

"You'd make a pretty good PI yourself," he answered noncommittally.

"Clint told me about the check he'd run on Mark. I should have known he'd have you handle it. That's why you were at the office. Wasn't it?"

He tossed off her question.

"I guess he also told you that you could do better than Mark Andrews with buck teeth and a limp?"

Her head snapped in his direction. Her voice was clipped and precise. "I'll tell you just like I told Clint. My personal life is just that—personal! I don't need him or you telling me whom I should see!"

"All right! Calm down. We—he—I was only concerned about you, Mel." His deep voice softened. "I've always been interested in your happiness. Whatever it was."

Melissa sighed and tugged on her bottom lip with her teeth. "I'm sorry," she said softly. "I didn't mean to snap at you."

"Sure you did," he said without malice. "And you're right. It is your business." He patted her shoulder.

"How about this?" he asked, cutting through two lanes of traffic. "Why don't I treat us to dinner? We can start over, pretend this conversation never happened. I'll even tell you detective stories." He grinned wickedly.

"Steve . . . ?

"Mel . . . ?" His thick eyebrows rose comically.

Melissa shook her head helplessly. "Where to?"

Clint lay sprawled out across the king-sized bed. The barely audible sound of the local jazz station whispered in the background. Clint's eyes drifted close.

Everything was finally coming together, he mused. He had Terri's love, he and his daughter would be together soon, and he was sure that now he could be the father that she deserved. Because of Terri his world had opened. Her revelations about her childhood helped him to see the importance of the parent-child relationship. She was right. Desi's death was not his fault, and in order to be all he could be for both Ashley and Terri, he had to finally let go of the guilt. Now that the doorway to his heart was opened, he was eager to have his daughter enter. He ached when he thought of all the time he'd wasted. But things would be different now. He was different now. He'd bring his daughter home where she belonged. They'd be a family.

To top everything off, he was on the verge of closing the greatest deal of his career. It seemed that since Terri'd entered his life, magic had happened. He felt alive again. He had a real purpose again. Most of all he had someone to share his joys.

A slow smile of contentment eased across his face. His eyes fluttered open. Then, just as quickly as the smile had come, it disappeared when he looked up at the figure that stood above him.

CHAPTER 32

Like a catapult, Clint sprang up in the bed.

"Terri! For chrissake, you scared the hell outta me." It took him a moment to register the devastation on her face.

"What—?" he got up, his eyes rapidly scanning her face, her body "—what is it? What happened?"

She seemed to deflate as she sat on the edge of the bed. Her voice was flat, devoid of the emotion that she felt. "My brother is alive, Clint."

"What are you talking about? You said your brother was dead."

"I know what I said! That's what I was told. That's the horrible, vicious lie I was told!"

He could see that she was on the verge of snapping. "Baby," he said gently, "please—start from the beginning. How do you know?"

Terri took a deep shuddering breath, then began her unbelievable story from the time she'd sat in Jon's cab until she'd stood in front of her grandmother's tombstone. The very same tombstone that Malcolm Brathwaite visited.

Clint shook his lowered head in a combination of disbelief and disgust. How anyone could have been so cruel to a little girl was unthinkable. He put his arm around her, pulling her close.

"What must Malcolm have thought all of these years?" Terri asked, the tear-filled voice registering her pain. "I should be happy that he's alive." She turned toward Clint, her large luminous eyes brimming with tears, "But instead I feel guilt."

"Guilt? Why would you feel guilty?"

"Maybe if I had come home, I—"

"Listen—" he squeezed her shoulder with the pads of his fingers "—there was no reason for you to disbelieve your parents, Terri. If you grew up believing that your brother was dead, why would you come back to look for him?"

She pulled away from his grasp and stood up. "I . . . always had a feeling, a sensation, I don't know what to call it—a gut feeling that he wasn't dead. I would imagine that I saw his face in the men I'd meet. But I never followed my instincts."

"Let's look at this rationally. Even if you had followed your instincts, you still might not have found him."

"But I could have tried! I never tried." The weight of her pent-up tears spilled over her lids, her shoulders shuddered as the silent sobs shook her.

Clint wrapped her in his embrace, pressing her head against his chest.

"It'll be all right," he soothed into her cottony soft hair. "We'll take care of everything when we get back from England."

Terri instantly tore away from him, nearly losing her balance in the process.

"I can't go to England. I won't go. I have to stay here—find out all that I can. I've got to find my brother!"

"Don't be ridiculous, Terri. You can't stay here. What do you think you can accomplish? We have business to take care of." His voice rose in unison with her mounting anxiety. "Your part of the proposal presentation is crucial to clinching this deal. You know that!"

"Deal? I don't give a damn about any deal! Not now. Not when I'm this close!"

"You'd let everything I've worked toward collapse on a whim?"

"A whim?" Her outrage at his insensitivity was complete. Her voice was low, icy cold. "Is that what you call this?"

"Yeah, damnit! A whim. What do you think you can do here? You have no contacts, no leads—you don't even have a picture."

She stared at him hard, a hundred thoughts tumbling through her head at once. The most troubling of which was that their relationship was coming to a devastating end.

"I'm not leaving." She was firm and unrelenting.

"I can't close this deal without you, Terri."

"You'll find a way," she answered coldly. "You always do."

For several moments he stared at her with unbelieving eyes. Then without another word he stormed off into the bedroom. Moments later he returned with his suitcase.

"The room is paid for until the end of the week. After that it's up to you." He strode toward the door, then stopped. His hand clutched the doorknob. He looked at her over his shoulder. "You have our itinerary, if you change your mind." He opened the door.

"I won't." She tossed the two verbal daggers at his departing back.

The only sound in the tension-charged room was the pounding of her heart and the reverberation of the slamming door.

Clint tore along the winding road, barely missing the oncoming traffic. His thoughts were a collage of anger, hurt, disappointment, and confusion. All of which fought for precedence over his emotions.

She was being a fool, he thought, as he made the hairpin turn toward the airport. It wasn't like Terri to think with her heart and not her head. She was always rational and clear in her thinking. He just couldn't understand her now.

His thoughts turned to the resort deal, and his anger flared anew. This was his dream—he wanted her to be a part of it. But she'd rather chase a fantasy instead.

He pulled into the driveway of Avis Car Rental, returned the car, then boarded the shuttle bus to the terminal.

As he stood in line waiting to have his flight changed, he saw her face float before him. He couldn't recall ever seeing anyone so hurt, so desperately wanting. And he'd left her alone at a time when she needed him more than ever. Visions of Desiree and their last night together collided with his vision of Terri. He'd lost Desiree because of his career; his wanting to have it all had been more important than anything else. His selfishness had cost him everything and Desiree her life.

"May I help you, sir?"

His eyes focused on the smiling reservationist behind the counter.

"May I help you?" she asked again.

Clint put his ticket on the counter. What was more important? The question rang through his brain like a thousand church bells, over and again.

The door chime tinkled softly through the sprawling town house.

Jill gave each room a satisfied glance as she passed through, en route to the door.

She pulled open the door and was pleasantly surprised by the handsome figure that stood before her.

"You must be Jill," the smooth voice greeted. "You're even more beautiful than your pictures. I'm Mark."

CHAPTER 33

"Mark, I wasn't expecting you until tomorrow. Please come in."

Mark walked past her into the corridor. He quickly scanned the open, inviting space. "Great place you have," he commented and turned toward her. "Did you have a hand in the design?"

Jill stepped through the foyer to stand next to him. "Decorating is a pet project of mine."

"You have excellent taste." He gave her an appraising look that made her fully aware of her femininity.

"Why, thank you. You can leave your bag here. May I offer you something?"

"No. I'm fine. But I would like to see more of the house. If you don't mind."

"Of course not," she smiled, reveling at every opportunity to display her handiwork, to the exclusion of propriety or safety. "Follow me."

"I'm sorry to show up unannounced," he said, following her into the living room. "But I was able to get an earlier flight. I should have called. I know this is an imposition."

"Don't be ridiculous. It's fine. This gives us more time to work on a surprise for Clint. He should be here by the weekend. He'll be so surprised to see you."

Mark smiled.

"When I called his office, they said he was traveling with a *business associate.*"

"Really? He didn't mention anything to me."

Mark saw an opening. "That's Clint for you. I would think he would have told you about her."

"Her?"

"Yes. Terri Powers. They're a real item."

Jill's spine clenched. "This is the living room," she said in a tight voice, trying to shake off the green monster that nipped hungrily at her heels.

The large room overlooked a magnificent garden and was decorated in a soft floral design. Strategically around the smooth mauve walls were portraits by Picasso, van Gogh, and Rembrandt. Mark quickly assessed the value to be in the millions.

"Through the door on your right is the dining room." She walked in that direction. "Do you know Terri Powers?" she asked trying to sound blasé, and failing, much to Mark's pleasure.

"Very well. Her reputation as a gold digger precedes her," he said, adding salt to the festering wound.

"And you say Clint is involved with her?"

He duly noted the tension in her voice and the possessive way she said Clint's name.

"As involved as any man and woman can get. Beautiful room," he added, pretending to be unconcerned.

She inhaled her fury. "Upstairs are the bedrooms, guest room, and baths," she breathed.

"I'm sure they're just as magnificent."

Her smile was wooden as she turned to face him.

"I can't understand why Clint would get himself involved with that type of woman. It doesn't sound like him." Her statement was more of an accusation than an observation.

Mark shook his head sadly, playing upon her blatant emotions like a master pianist. "Listen, since we're talking like this, I have to tell you, I feel the same way. I tried to talk to him about Terri, but he won't listen. He gets outraged if you say anything against her." He paused, watching her face tense.

"Personally," he continued, "I think it's the worst move Clint could have made. I'm really worried about him."

"There must be something that can be done."

Mark opened the door a bit farther. "Maybe there is. Why don't we go in the living room and talk? I was going to do this alone, but . . . if you're willing to help . . . ?"

Aimlessly Terri paced through the suite, trying to formulate some sort of plan. Maybe Clint was right. How did she think she could find her brother with no way of tracing him?

Jon was her only link, and he hadn't seen Malcolm in months. There had to be a way. Perhaps the foster care agency that placed them could help her.

If she could only remember the name of the agency. She walked into the small reception area of the suite and took the phone book from the wall shelf.

Maybe if she saw the name of the agency, it would come back to her.

She flipped through the book until she found the section that she wanted. Quickly she scanned the names of the foster care agencies with her index finger.

There it was! Little Hearts Foster Care. Her pulse quickened in a mixture of sadness and relief. It was a name that she had long since relegated to the recesses of her mind—one that she had fought hard to forget.

With shaky fingers she dialed the number and waited for what seemed like an eternity before a heavily accented woman answered the phone.

Jill thought long and hard about what Mark had proposed. The plan was dangerous. But if that's what it took to get Clint away from Terri and into her arms, she would do it willingly.

Sighing, she rose from the overstuffed sofa and slowly paced the hardwood floor. Finally she turned to him. "You're sure that no one will be hurt?"

"Of course not. Clint will believe it's all Terri's fault and see her for what she really is. Then she'll be out of his life."

He tugged on the noose that he had slipped around her neck. "I can tell you care a great deal about Clint."

Momentarily she looked stricken, but seeing the concern in Mark's eyes, she nodded in agreement.

His easy, open manner, his way of making her feel that he was in tune with her feelings, left her vulnerable. Without thinking, she opened herself up to him, revealing her deepest feelings.

"I've loved Clint for as long as I can remember," she said wistfully. "When he married my sister, Desiree, I was devastated. Then . . . when she died, I . . . ?

"You thought he would turn to you," Mark said, finishing her sentence.

She smiled weakly, feeling for the first time that she'd found someone who truly understood. "Yes. But he never did. And now that he's finally coming back, I just knew he was coming for me."

Mark rose and stood next to her. Warily he put a comforting arm around her shoulder.

"I'm sure that Clint will finally see things as they truly are," he assured her. "How can he help but know how much you care about him? All he has to do is look in your eyes. He's the one who's been losing out all these years."

"Are you sure that this plan will work?"

"Absolutely. But timing is everything. Remember that. You keep me posted, and I'll walk you through it, step by step."

Jill nodded and prayed that she was doing the right thing.

She escorted Mark to the door. He opened his suitcase and pulled out a thick manila envelope and handed it to her.

"Hold on to these. I'll tell you what to do with them and when. But whatever you do, don't let either of them see it."

Her hand trembled slightly as she took the package and held it to her breasts.

"I'll call you," he said, turning for the door. "You know where to reach me." He stroked her cheek. "Don't look so upset. Everything is going to be fine."

"Why are you doing this?"

"Let's just say that I have a debt that's been owed to me for a long time by Ms. Powers. And—" his lips lightly brushed her cheek "—I love helping beautiful ladies. But . . . if you're having a change of heart . . . just tell me. I'll understand."

Jill's pent-up obsession with Clint blinded her and propelled her forward. "*No!* I . . . I mean no," she said with more calm. "I'll do whatever needs to be done."

CHAPTER 34

"Are you absolutely sure?" Terri insisted.

"Believe me, the records are sealed. There's no way I or anyone can give you that information, miss. I'm sorry."

"Thank you anyway." Terri reluctantly hung up the phone. Her one flicker of hope slowly diminished.

"Now what?" she said out loud just as the doorbell rang.

Frowning, she strode toward the door and pulled it open.

"Clint!"

"Is there room at the inn?" he asked humbly.

A soft smile lifted her full lips. "There's room next to me, if you don't mind sharing."

"Sounds perfect." He stepped across the threshold and pulled her into his hard embrace.

"I'm so sorry, baby," he crooned. "There's no way I could let you go through this alone. My ambition cost me my wife, and I'll be damned if I'll lose you, too."

She eased out of his arms and looked up into his eyes. "Thank you," she whispered. "But you were right." She held his hand and walked to the couch.

"I contacted the foster care agency that placed Malcolm and me."

"And . . . ?"

"They told me the records were sealed."

Clint sat down. "There has to be a way to find him. There are agencies that help people find relatives. I'll make some calls. And I'll get Steve on it right away."

"Whatever you can do, Clint. I'd appreciate it. I know it's going to take a long time. Sometimes these searches can take years. But I just need to know something, for sure."

She slowly got up from the couch. "There's no real point in us staying here any longer. Your appointment in Nassau is tomorrow. I know how important that is to you."

He smiled at her. "Not as important as I thought. We'll do this together, Terri."

"I had a great time, Steve. Thanks," Melissa said.

"So did I." He paused. "I'd like to keep seeing you, Mel," Steve said.

"I think I'd like that, too," she admitted. The realization warmed her.

"I know that we could be good for each other," he rushed on. He searched her face and found acceptance in her eyes.

"Listen, Mel." He lowered his head then quickly looked into those eyes that he could never forget. "I know that things weren't the greatest between us . . . before."

She raised her hand to his chest. "Steve, you don't have to—"

"Yes, I do." He took her hand in his and squeezed it. "At least they weren't great for you. I know how you feel about Clint."

Melissa's eyes widened in surprise. She opened her mouth to refute his statement. Steve cut her off.

"I've always known, Mel. And I know that's the reason why you couldn't love me . . . the way that I love you." He exhaled heavily. "There, I've finally said it."

"Love me?" she whispered. Her brow creased in disbelief. "I didn't . . . I never knew."

"I know." He laughed a self-deprecating laugh and lifted her hand to his lips. "I can keep a secret when I have to. That's my business," he chuckled without humor.

Her eyes searched his face for any sign of deceit but found none. Had she wasted so many days, hours, months of her life wanting someone who would never love her when she had someone who truly did, only a phone call away? She wanted to scream at the injustice of it all. The things that she had done, what her resentment and obsession had driven her to do was frightening.

She shivered. Steve took it that she was cold and put his arm around her shoulders.

Before he could stop himself, his lips found hers and for the first time in longer than he cared to remember, he felt that he'd come home.

But even as she kissed him in return, she knew that revealing her role in Mark's plan could destroy the tiny thread of happiness that was weaving a path to her heart. She couldn't take that chance. Not now.

His mouth slowly released hers. He took a shaky breath and smiled. "Tomorrow?"

"Tomorrow sounds fine."

"I'll call you." He lowered his head and brushed her lips one last time. "Sleep well."

Slowly Melissa closed her apartment door, amazed at how her predictable evening had turned around.

She'd put all of the negativity behind her, she decided. This was a chance for her to start over. She couldn't spend the rest of her life pining over Clint. Maybe in time she would come to truly love Steve the way that he deserved to be loved.

The future was finally looking brighter, and she had no intention of doing anything to jeopardize it.

With a lightness in her step, she kicked off her shoes and practically skipped into her bedroom.

She threw herself across the bed. A satisfied smile illuminated her face, until the ringing phone brought her crashing back to reality. She lifted the receiver.

"Mark!"

"Hey, Mel. Just calling to check on you."

Her heart thudded. "Why haven't I heard from you? Where are you?"

"Whoa. One question at a time. First, I've been busy, real busy. I wanted to see you before I left, but I didn't have time. Things were happening too fast. Now for your second question. I'm in merry ole' England—and, baby, the plan is going even better than I expected." He laughed at his own cunning.

"I'm gonna have it all! And Terri Powers will be finished. Thanks to you."

CHAPTER 35

Jillianne returned to the living room and sat down heavily on the couch. She stared at the thick envelope. What could it possibly contain? Her curiosity burned her fingertips as she stroked the seal.

"Auntie! Auntie!" The sound of her niece's voice startled her, and she shoved the envelope between the cushions of the couch. She hadn't heard the school bus when it pulled up. Mrs. Hally must have let Ashley in.

"In here, Ashley." She put on her best smile as Ashley ran into the room.

"Hi, sweetie. Did you have a good day in school?" She gave Ashley a kiss on her cheek.

"We went to the park today," she said, her dark eyes, so much like her mother's, lighting up with excitement.

"That sounds like fun." Jillianne took Ashley's hand. "Why don't you run upstairs and wash up. I'll tell Mrs. Hally to fix you a snack."

Ashley raced off at her aunt's request, her thick plaited ponytail whipping behind her.

Just as Jill was about to retrieve the envelope, Mrs. Hally entered the room.

"Excuse me, Miss Jill, Mr. and Mrs. Rogers are here to see you. They said they have an appointment."

Jill pressed her palm against her head. She had completely forgotten that she was to show a house to the newlywed couple.

"I'll be right there."

"They do seem a bit anxious, Miss Jill."

Jill shot a glance in the direction of the couch and decided that the envelope would be safe until she returned. She went to meet her clients.

NASSAU

"Do you have everything you need?" Terri asked while applying a stroke of coral-colored lipstick to her mouth.

"Yes!" Clint called from the front room. "Now would you please hurry. I hate being late for meetings. And this Carpenter guy is acting strange. I didn't like the vibrations I got the last time we spoke and I don't want to give him any reason to change his mind."

"I'm ready." Terri emerged from the bathroom, clad in an off-white linen shirtdress, cut in a low vee in the front and trimmed with wide gold buttons. Her long locks were wrapped high atop her head, adding to the length of her slender neck, which was encircled with a thin braided chain of gold.

"Hmm, you look good enough to eat . . . again," he taunted, patting her on her round derriere.

"Not now," she purred seductively. "Later," she teased, pinching his cheek. The soft fragrance of her scent wafted through the air as she passed.

"I'm gonna hold you to that," he tossed back.

She collected her purse and portfolio, which contained the advertising presentation, and strutted toward the door, where she stepped into her shoes. Turning toward Clint, the light of love burned in her eyes.

"You were wonderful last night," she said softly, pulling him by his silk tie to stand in front of her.

"There's plenty more for you later," he answered in a low, intimate voice that tantalized her.

"I can't wait. Now let's go before we never get out of here."

Nat Carpenter reviewed the elaborate proposal that lay before him. The presentation by Terri had been inspiring to say the least, although it rang with familiarity.

He peered at the handsome duo over half-rim glasses. "Very impressive," he stated simply.

"Then we have a deal," Clint said.

Nat held up his hand and tilted his head slightly to the side.

"Not quite."

Clint felt the hairs on the back of his neck begin to tingle.

"What do you mean, not quite?"

"I've been approached by another prospective client. When you and I initially spoke, there were no other offers. However, things have changed."

Clint fought to control his mounting anger. "Exactly what are you saying?"

"What I'm saying is, one, you'll have to come up with a fresher advertising scheme. Second, I'll have to consider your offer under a sealed bid—with the contract, land, and all the rights going to the highest bidder."

Slowly Clint rose from the leather-bound, high-back chair. Terri dared to look up at him and immediately saw the dark, dangerous lights flicker in his eyes. His jaw clenched.

"How much time do we have?" he asked with a calm that alarmed Terri.

"I'd say about five days. I'm expecting a call from your competitor later today. I'd like to close the deal before the holidays." He leaned back in his chair and linked his fingers across his rotund belly.

Clint leaned forward, pressing his palms down on the cherry wood desk.

"I don't know what you're trying to pull, Carpenter, but we had an arrangement. I've had this plan on the burner for months, and you know it!" he shouted.

"There's no point in getting irate, Mr. Steele. Business is business. You're a businessman, and you know how things operate. Get back to me with your best offer, and we'll take it from there."

Nat Carpenter stood up. His imposing presence filled the room. "If there's nothing further." He smiled. "I have another engagement."

Clint threw him one last parting look and snatched the documents from the desk. Terri had to double her step to catch up with him as he tore through the maze of offices to the exit.

"Clint! Clint! What in the world is wrong with you?" Terri cried as she tried to keep up with his blinding pace. But he wouldn't stop until he stood in front of their rented convertible in the parking lot. He briefly shut his eyes and slammed his fist down on the hood. He spun toward her.

"Didn't you hear what went on in there?"

"I did. But that's no reason for you to perform like some thug from the hood. It's not even like you."

He shook his head. His voice lowered. "Don't you see what's happening? My dream, my vision, is slipping away. No one, no one knew about this except you and me."

Terri's jaw tightened, hearing the light touch of doubt in Clint's voice.

He saw her look. "No. I don't think it was you," he assured. He looked away. "But who?"

By degrees she relaxed. "Did it occur to you that Carpenter is out to get as much as he can?"

"It's possible." He heaved a sigh. "Maybe. All I know is, I can't lose this. It's too important to me."

"You won't," she said softly. "I'll get to work on an alternative campaign as soon as we get to England."

He nodded. "I just have to figure how much I need to bid in order to go over the top." He put his arm around her waist and kissed the top of her head. "Thanks."

"Anytime." She stepped out of his embrace and looked up at him. "Now, let's go see your daughter."

Melissa sat behind her desk, reviewing the fiscal reports for the cable stations. This new acquisition was doing extremely well, she thought, pleased with the role she'd played in the negotiations. Clint was destined to be a very rich and powerful man. He had a way of making something out of nothing and turning it into dollars.

The irony was, he never cared about the money. He thrived on the hunt. That was the characteristic that had always appealed to her.

Enough of Clint. She closed the folder. She had to move on. But the memory of the phone call from Mark marred her new vision.

Mark was determined to hurt Terri for some inexplicable reason, at whatever cost, and she knew that it would ultimately hurt Clint as well. Was that why she'd been more than willing to help Mark? What was he going to do with the information that she'd given him?

What she did know was that Mark, too, was a man who thrilled for the hunt. The one difference between him and Clint was that Clint salvaged his prey. Mark destroyed his.

She turned toward the window. Mark was in England now, and Clint and Terri were on their way. A sinking feeling of disaster swept over her. But what could she do to stop it if she didn't know what it was?

CHAPTER 36

After a week of balmy tropical weather, arriving to the chill of England was a physical shock.

Terri snuggled closer to Clint's warmth as the cab sped down the open roadway toward his town house in Lancaster.

"What if she doesn't remember me?" Clint said, speaking more to himself than to Terri.

She turned to him. "How long has it been?"

"Over a year," he said heavily. "I just couldn't bring myself to go back after the last time."

"What happened?"

"Nightmares. Guilt. I couldn't find a way to get through them. Every time I looked at Ash, I saw Desi. So instead of being a loving father, I was a cold stranger, and Ashley felt it. I saw it in her eyes, the hurt, and I wanted to die. I wished that I could have reached out to her and explained, but I couldn't." He turned away from her, not daring to let her see the anguish that burned his eyes.

"Clint," she said gently, "we'll work through this. You have me now. You won't have to handle it alone."

But even as she uttered the reassuring words, she wasn't sure how she was going to deal with the reality of Clint's daughter, when the heartache of her own lost child was still so raw on her emotions. Her own loveless childhood had twisted her sensibilities, and she didn't know how she would overcome her fear of not being able to love a child that was not truly her own.

All she could be sure of was that Clint needed her. She would have to force her misgivings aside and be there for him. But how long would she be able to hide her real feelings?

Jillianne knelt down in front of her niece, and adjusted the wide collar on her blue velvet dress.

"You look beautiful, luv," Jill said with loving pride.

"Thank you, Auntie," Ashley beamed.

"Your daddy will be so happy to see you."

Instantly the smile faded. She crushed herself against her aunt's body, burying her face in Jillianne's neck.

"No, he won't!" she cried. "He hates me."

"Ashley, that's not true, sweetheart. Your daddy loves you very much." She pressed the tiny body against her own, wishing that she could absorb her hurt. Clint's inattention to his daughter was the one fault that Jillianne could not accept, even though she understood. She loved Ashley blindly, so much so that at times she believed the child to be her own.

She understood the difficulty Clint had in dealing with Desiree's death and the prospect of raising a young daughter alone. That's why she took over the rearing of Ashley in the hopes that one day Clint would see how much of a family she and Ashley were, and how much they both needed and loved him.

But Ashley's hurt over her father's indifference toward her made Jillianne's job that much more difficult. And that Terri woman had complicated matters even further.

"If my daddy loves me, why does he stay away?" She looked at her aunt with large bright eyes filled with confusion.

Jill took a deep breath. "Sometimes adults do things that children don't always understand. Sometimes they don't know how to deal with their feelings, and they do strange things. Your daddy doesn't know how to be a daddy yet. That's why you and I have got to help him. Together."

"If we help him to be my daddy, will he stay here forever?"

"That's what we'll hope for. All right, luv?"

"Okay. You really think he'll like my dress?" she asked. Hope filled her voice.

"He'll love it. Just as he loves you. Now . . . give Auntie a big hug, and then you can have some ice cream."

"Yeah!" Ashley quickly threw herself into her aunt's arms and then tore off toward the kitchen in search of Mrs. Hally.

Jillianne smiled at the little figure, then turned her attention to the living room.

A magnificent seven-foot-tall Christmas tree stood majestically in the center of the room. She'd spent the entire previous evening decorating it with antique ornaments of gold and red. The only thing missing was the star on the top. She'd save that honor for Clint.

Satisfied with her handiwork, she walked toward the bar, intent on pouring herself a glass of wine, when she caught a glimpse of the brown envelope sticking out from between the couch cushions.

The doorbell rang.

"Miss Jill, Ashley, he's here," Mrs. Hally called.

Jillianne snatched the envelope from the cushion. Quickly she looked for a safe place to put it just as Clint walked through the archway. She slid the envelope into the small Queen Anne desk drawer.

When she looked up, she saw him. Her world seemed to stand still. She felt breathless and trembling with desire. She remained glued to the spot, afraid that if she moved this magnificent vision would vanish. Her heart beat wildly as she watched him close the distance between them.

"Jill!" He pulled her into his arms, and her head spun. How long had she waited for this moment? She inhaled his scent.

"It's good to see you. You look beautiful," he whispered in her ear.

Before she had a chance to recover, he stepped away. She hadn't even noticed Terri standing in the archway until Clint motioned to her, and the spell was broken.

"Jill, I'd like you to meet Terri Powers. Terri, this is my wonderful sister-in-law, Jillianne Davis."

Terri slipped out of her shoes and stepped fully into the room. Jill was immediately overcome by her regal presence. Even in bare feet, she was tall, statuesque with a crystal clear complexion of smooth mahogany. Her eyes were large, tilting slightly upward at the corners, giving her an exotic look that was both mystifying and intimidating.

As Terri slowly approached, Jillianne could almost visualize the voluptuous curves that defined the smooth-fitting suit of bronze silk.

Jill unconsciously patted her own silken, ebony hair when she looked at the luxurious shoulder-length locks that draped sensuously around the perfect face.

In an instant her jealousy of this woman ignited with a vengeance.

Terri stepped forward. An inviting smile of greeting illuminated her face. She extended her slender hand.

"I've heard so much about you," she said in a low voice edged with an island accent. "It's a pleasure to finally meet you."

Jill reluctantly took the outstretched hand. "I wish I could say the same about you. I mean," she added with a tight smile, "I wish Clint had informed me that he was bringing a guest." Her eyebrow arched as she gave Clint a look that he could not read.

But Terri read it very well, and the realization unnerved her.

Then, at the sound of footsteps, almost in unison, the three turned toward the archway to see Ashley standing next to Mrs. Hally.

Clint looked briefly at Terri, and her smile reassured him. Slowly he knelt down.

"Hi, baby," he said softly.

Step by step she crossed the room until she stood in front of him. She kept her eyes riveted on her patent leather shoes.

"Hi, Daddy," she mumbled.

"Can I get a hug? I missed you so much, Ash."

She looked up at him with such hope in her eyes, and his heart nearly broke. Gently he pulled her to him, and he wasn't sure whose heart was pounding the hardest.

"I missed you, baby," he whispered again. "I'm going to make it up to you. I promise. Things are going to be different from now on."

"Are you going to come here to live?"

Clint glanced up at Terri. "We'll talk about that later." He picked her up, holding her in one arm. "But first I want you to go out into the hallway and open the big box out there. It's a special pre-Christmas present."

Ashley ran into the hallway to see a large box decorated in brillant Christmas colors. Her squeals of delight upon opening her gift rang throughout the large foyer.

"Let me carry it inside for you," Clint said. "It's almost bigger than you!" He brought the huge box into the living room and placed it under the tree, where Ashley immediately finished the job of demolishing the wrappings.

"It's a playhouse, Auntie! A real live playhouse!"

"I see. It's beautiful, luv."

Terri stood on the sidelines, watching the picture-perfect scene unfold.

Clint was kneeling down next to Ashley with Jill close by his side. They had completely forgotten her.

As she watched, images of her own childhood emerged before her. How many Christmases had she sat on the side while her parents showered their own children with beautiful gifts? Even though she received her share of presents, it just wasn't the same. She always felt that she didn't belong, that she wasn't truly loved.

The old hurt and feelings of lonely isolation resurfaced. *She didn't belong here, either.*

Quietly, and unnoticed, she walked out of the room and into the foyer. She sat on the antique, pale peach chaise lounge and waited.

Several moments later Clint emerged and took a seat beside her.

"Baby, you were right about everything," he beamed. Even white teeth reflected against the dark skin. "It's going to work this time. I can feel it."

He's so happy, Terri realized.

She forced herself to smile. "I told you it would. You just had to give it a chance."

He hugged her to him and planted a solid kiss on her forehead. Then his expression changed. "Why are you out here?"

"Oh, I thought that, well, you know . . . family." She cleared her throat and smiled. "You need all the time you can get with your daughter."

"There you two are."

They both turned to see Jill standing in the archway.

"Mrs. Hally has your room ready, Clint. I'm sure you'll want to get settled and freshen up." She gave Terri a cutting glance. "I'll have her get your room ready, Ms. Powers."

"That won't be necessary, Jill. Terri and I will stay together."

Jillianne pouted. "Now, Clint," she said in a stage whisper, "do you really think that would be appropriate? I mean . . . what will Ashley think?"

"You're absolutely right, Jill," Terri responded. "I wouldn't want Ashley's and my relationship to start off on the wrong foot, and please, call me Terri."

Jillianne inhaled and smiled triumphantly. "You see, Clint, Terri feels the same way."

Clint tossed up his hands in defeat. "I know when to quit." He pulled himself up from his seat. "Can I at least take Terri's bags to her room, or is that out of the question?" he taunted with a smile.

Jillianne giggled. "Of course. Don't be silly. As a matter of fact, I'll go up with you and help Terri get settled." She glanced at Terri, smiling sweetly. "That is, if you don't mind?"

"That's just what I need. Thanks." Terri struggled to hold back what she really wanted to say. Jill was being an unnecessary bitch, and it was obvious that she wanted to wedge herself between her and Clint. This trip was going to be even more difficult than she anticipated. Not only did she have a child to get adjusted to, she would have to deal with an overpossessive sister-in-law who was obviously in love with her man.

Clint collected the luggage and climbed the two flights to the bedrooms above. Jill remained close on his heels and Terri followed, keeping her temper in check with each step.

"You know where your room is, Clint," Jill said when they'd reached the landing. "And I think the guest room down the hall will be perfect for Terri." She turned to her. "I'm sure you'll love it."

"I'm sure I will," she smiled, realizing that her jaws were beginning to ache from the plastic smile that she'd carved on her face since her arrival. She peeked over Jillianne's shoulder to see Clint grin and shrug his shoulders in helplessness. Terri wanted to scream.

Jill showed Terri to her room and busied herself fluffing pillows and checking windows.

"Everything seems to be in order. I'll have Mrs. Hally bring you up some fresh towels. Your bath is right through that door."

"Thank you," Terri mumbled.

"If there's anything you need, just ask."

I need you to give me some breathing room, she wanted to say, but instead, "I'm sure everything will be fine."

"Well, then, I'll check on dinner. It should be ready in about a half hour. Will that give you enough time to make yourself presentable?"

Terri's eyes flashed, much to Jill's pleasure.

"Excuse me?"

"I mean, will you have enough time to change? What did you think I meant?"

"It's more than enough time."

"Good. I'll see you at dinner." She turned to leave, then stopped and faced Terri. "By the way, how long have you known Clint?"

"A while. Why?"

"Oh, I was just curious. Clint never mentioned you, and we talk so often, of course." She shrugged her shoulder dismissively. "I could only assume that your relationship was short term."

"You know the old saying about 'assume,' " Terri tossed back with a catty smile.

Jill's nostrils flared. She threw Terri a parting glance and left the room.

Terri sat down hard on the bed and silently prayed that she would be able to endure the next few days.

Dinner passed by relatively uneventful. Terri said very little during dinner, making comments only when necessary and smiling or laughing at the appropriate spots.

With each passing moment she felt more and more isolated. The pain of her youth seemed to overtake her, and she was again the small defenseless child trapped in a loveless home.

Clint focused all of his attention on Ashley, Jill hung on his every word and ignored her completely except to make an insinuating comment, and if she didn't know better she'd swear that Jill's behavior was wearing off on Ashley. Ashley barely said a word to her through the entire meal and responded to her questions about school and her friends in one-word answers. Apparently Clint didn't seem to notice a thing.

General talk about work, school, and the weather dominated the conversation. Ashley said very little, but continually looked at her father as though if she took her eyes off of him he might disappear.

Mercifully dinner concluded. Clint attempted to take Terri's arm.

"When was the last time you tucked your daughter in?" Terri asked.

Clint looked at her curiously. "Why?"

"I think she'd like that a lot. Haven't you seen the way she's been staring at you all night?"

He glanced in Ashley's direction and saw the look of doubt in her eyes.

"Maybe you're right. But what will I say to her?"

Terri tiptoed and kissed his cheek. "You'll think of something." She said her good nights and made a hasty escape to her room, while Clint took Ashley up to bed.

They spent the first few awkward moments in silence as they sat on the edge of the bed. Then Ashley spoke.

"Daddy, why did you bring that lady with you?"

"Terri?"

Ashley nodded.

"She's a very good friend of mine, and I wanted you to get to know her." He lifted the covers and placed Ashley beneath them.

"Why?" She snuggled down until the tip of the floral quilt reached her chin.

"Because I want you to know the people I know, and I want you to like them as much as I do."

"What if I don't like them?"

Clint was momentarily caught off guard. "Why wouldn't you like them?"

"Because."

"Because what, Ash?"

Ashley yawned. "I'm sleepy. Can we talk tomorrow?"

He leaned down and kissed her cheek. "Sure. Sweet dreams, baby."

Slowly Clint rose from the bed and eased out of the door. Why had she asked that question? He shook his head as he walked down the hallway toward his room.

Terri aimlessly sifted through her dresser drawer and selected a nightgown of sea green chiffon. She felt as if a heavy weight held down her spirit after she had struggled for so many years to free it from emotional bondage.

Slowly she walked toward the bathroom, turned on the tub full blast, and filled the rushing waters with a mixture of African oils designed to soothe and relax the body and mind.

Within moments the steamy room was filled with the aromatic scent that rushed to her brain, and she sank into the calming waters.

Where was Clint? she wondered as she lay stretched beneath the cool sheets. The steamy bath had provided her with the relaxation she needed, and the twenty minutes of meditation had put on the final touches. She felt almost like her old self. If only Clint were here with her, everything would be perfect.

Her eyes drifted close, so she had to be dreaming when she thought she saw Clint standing above her.

"Shh," he cautioned. He eased down beside her. "I don't want to wake Ashley, and I'm sure Jill is still awake. Hmm, you smell good." He nuzzled her neck, and she knew this was not a dream.

"Clint," she whispered, "I thought I was dreaming."

"Really? Does this feel like a dream?" His expert fingers caressed her breasts, making the chocolate peaks rise and harden at his command.

Her body moved rhythmically under his touch, her own hands rediscovering the hard muscular body.

"It feels like it's been forever," he groaned, pushing the sheer gown up above her hips. His hungry mouth sought and found hers, his velvet tongue exploring the warm cavern.

Her fingers, her mouth, stroked him, enflamed him until he was sure that he'd go crazy with longing.

"I love you," he moaned in her ear, pulling her to him, joining them.

She cried out with the pleasure of their union, and like a thief in the night, he took what lay open and waiting. And he took until they were both breathlessly satisfied.

"Clint," Terri whispered in the darkness.

"Hmm?" He buried his face deeper into her neck.

"Jillianne doesn't like me."

"Don't be silly," he yawned. "Jill likes everybody."

"I'm not being silly." She snatched her leg from between his and turned on her back. "Didn't you see how she treated me?"

"Terri . . . come on. What did she do, help you unpack, show you to your room? What?"

She sighed in exasperation. "It's hard to explain. I can feel it. The way she looks at me."

"Jill can take some getting used to. But she's good people. You'll see when you get to know her better."

"Maybe. But Ashley acts the same way."

Clint sat up in the bed. "You're being paranoid. Ashley's just a child. Why wouldn't she like you?" But even as he asked the question, his bedside conversation with his daughter came back to him.

"Believe me, Clint, I know what I feel! I'm not imagining things. Did it ever occur to you that maybe they don't want me around because they want you to themselves?"

Clint shut his eyes. "It's probably my fault," he conceded. "I should have prepared them for your arrival."

He turned on his side and draped his arm across her waist. "But I know that once they get to know you, they'll love you just as much as I do."

Terri wasn't too sure about that, not with the looks that Jillianne gave her every chance she got. She was in love with Clint, and Terri posed a threat. And as the old saying went, *hell hath no fury like a woman scorned.* What would Jill's fury be? The thought chilled her.

"Cold?" Clint pulled her closer and kissed her cheek. "Listen, why don't you and I take Ashley into London tomorrow and do some Christmas shopping? That will give the two of you a chance to get to know each other."

"I have to get busy on the ad campaign. Remember? And Christmas is not my holiday. I celebrate *Kwanzaa.*"

"I know, I know. But this is more important. I want Ashley to get adjusted to the idea that you're in my life. Tell her about *Kwanzaa,* and its importance. I'm sure she'll ask you a million questions. It'll give you two something to share."

Terri brightened. "If you think so." She took a breath. "I so want her to like me."

He pulled her into his embrace. "Oh, baby," he soothed. "I know it's hard. But I'm here for you, just like you're here for me. We can do this. You were the one who convinced me how important it was to establish a relationship with my daughter. I'm trying to do that. But I need your help and your support. It'll be all right, I promise."

"Yes, they arrived this afternoon," Jillianne whispered into the phone.

"Right on schedule," Mark said.

"Now what?"

"I'll let you know when to have the package delivered. The timing is important. Is everything else set?"

"Yes."

"So, how do you like Ms. Powers?"

Jill's pulse raced at the sound of her name. "She's everything you said she was," she said, trying to convince herself that her behavior was justified, even though deep inside she knew she'd seen nothing but goodness in Terri, and her genuine love for Clint.

Mark chuckled. "I'll call you tomorrow."

"Maybe it would be better if I called you. You never know when Clint might pick up the phone."

"You're right. Give me a call later in the day. I have to do some sightseeing tomorrow. Then everything will be in place."

"Fine. Good night."

Jill gently replaced the reciever. Was she doing the right thing? Methodically she paced the room, questioning her involvement in this scheme.

But if she was to get Clint away from Terri permanently, she would do whatever needed to be done.

Quietly she eased out of her room with the intention of going to the kitchen when she saw Clint slip out of Terri's bedroom. He turned down the corridor, never noticing her.

Jillianne's conviction was renewed.

CHAPTER 37

Clint met Jill in the den.

"There you are." He walked toward her and gave her a kiss on the cheek. "I was looking for you. After breakfast, Terri and I are going to take Ashley to London for some shopping."

"Oh, I was planning on us all spending the day together."

He held her shoulder and looked into her eyes. "Can we do that tomorrow? This is really important."

Her heart fluttered. "Of course. Enjoy yourselves. I have some clients to see anyway."

"Thanks." He turned to leave, then over his shoulder, "We'll be back in time for dinner."

"Great," she murmured. She crossed the room and sat on the loveseat that overlooked the small pond that ran along the back of the property. She couldn't allow Terri to make any headway with Ashley. It would make things more difficult for her. She quickly ran upstairs to Ashley's room.

"I thought we'd go to Picadilly Square first and have lunch," Clint said to his silent riding companions. "Then we'll have enough strength to shop until it gets dark. How does that sound, Ashley?" He peered at her through the rearview mirror.

"Can I get whatever I want?" she asked in a soft voice.

"Of course. Today is your day."

Ashley took a quick look at Terri. "Then why does she have to go?"

"She? You mean Terri?"

Terri winced.

"Yes."

"Because I want to spend the day with my two favorite girls. And since you're so familiar with London, I thought that you would be the perfect guide for Terri."

"Oh." She sat up straighter in her seat, somewhat appeased.

This wasn't going to be as easy as he thought. He dared to look at Terri and instantly caught the pained look. He reached over and patted her hand. She smiled in response, but he knew her heart wasn't in it. What was he going to do if he couldn't win Ashley over and convince Terri that they could all live together as a family? Was he willing to give up one for the other?

Mark cruised down the back roads of Lancaster, intermittently checking the map he'd purchased at the hotel.

According to the map, the huge fork in the road indicated that a small town was off to the right and woods were to the left. He turned left.

He drove for about a mile down a dirt road shaded almost totally by enormous trees whose bare branches gave the deeply wooded area a sinister feel. If what Jillianne told him was true, he should be coming to his destination shortly. Then he saw it, directly in front of him. He brought the car to a stop. A slow smile crept across his face.

"Perfect."

He reached into his pocket and pulled out the worn, crumpled picture.

He stared at the tiny face, his irrational hatred burning his eyes.

"Soon."

"What do you want to do tonight, Mel?" Steve asked as he sipped his coffee.

"Let's rent a movie and relax. We've been out every night for the past week."

"Yeah, and it's been great!" He pulled her onto his lap and kissed her full on the mouth. "I'm glad you're back in my life, Mel. I didn't think it would ever happen."

She gently stroked his face. Steve had been a dream, a fantasy come true. She couldn't understand why she had forced him out of her life. He was good for her. Somehow she'd always known that, but tried to convince herself that if she waited around long enough Clint would . . .

Clint. Mark. Her conscience attacked her. She should tell Steve what was going on. But if she did, she'd have to also confess to her role. She wasn't ready to risk her first taste of real happiness. Clint was a big boy. He could take care of himself. And anyway, he had Terri to help him. She'd stay out of it.

Eagerly she returned Steve's kiss and pushed thoughts of Clint and Mark to the back of her mind.

Clint, Ashley and Terri exited the cozy café to be met by the chilly December air.

"Listen, you two," Clint said, "I'm going to take a quick peek in the jewelry store and see if I can find something for Aunt Jill. Why don't you both head down to the toy store, and I'll meet you there."

Ashley looked up at Terri, and her warm smile convinced her. "Okay."

Terri took a deep breath and took Ashley's hand. Clint bent down and kissed Terri's lips. "Thanks, babe," he whispered. "I'll see you in about a half hour."

Terri nodded and took Ashley down the street.

"I have a friend with hair like yours," Ashley said in a timid voice.

"You do?" Terri smiled. "Is she as pretty as you are?"

Ashley giggled and nodded her head. "You have nice hands," Ashley commented, gripping Terri's hand tighter.

"And so do you," Terri replied.

"Do you like my daddy?"

"Yes, I do. Very much."

Ashley was quiet for a moment as if she had to digest the information. "My auntie likes him, too."

Terri avoided reading anything into her comment. "Your daddy is a very special man. A lot of people like him."

Everything her aunt had said came rushing out. "I love him. But he doesn't want me. Auntie was going to help Daddy love me—but . . . you want to take my daddy away from me." She was near to tears.

Terri stopped in her tracks and bent down in front of Ashley. Several pedestrians had to detour around them. Terri braced Ashley's shoulders and looked directly into her eyes. She spoke softly and firmly, praying that wisdom would come with every word.

"Ashley, your daddy loves you more than you could ever imagine. He told me. It's just that your daddy has been so busy, he thought it would be best if you stayed with your aunt. But he wants to be a part of your life. He just doesn't know how. It's going to take time. And I would never try to take your daddy away from you."

"Do you like me?"

The question startled her. When she looked at Ashley, the child's eyes were large with wonder and need.

"Yes, I do." And once she said the words, she realized that she really did. A sensation of warmth enveloped her, and she had the overwhelming desire to want to protect Ashley from the world. Instead she hugged her, and the hug she received in return almost brought tears to her eyes.

"Now—" Terri cleared her throat "—let's see how much shopping we can do before your dad finds us. Deal?"

"Deal."

As they exited the enormous toy store, Terri heard her name being called, and her spine stiffened. *It can't be.*

"It seems as if we keep running into each other."

Terri reluctantly turned around to see Alan Martin standing behind her. Her face hardened.

"What are you doing here, Alan?"

"I'm on a job." He glanced at Ashley. "Whose kid?"

"None of your business."

"No need to be nasty." He looked cautiously around. "No bodyguard? Or has Mr. Clinton Steele moved on to greener pastures?"

"That's my daddy," Ashley cried. "Do you know my daddy?"

Alan gave Ashley a lopsided grin. "Let's just say we've met."

Terri took Ashley's hand. "Come on, Ashley." She turned to go.

"Ashley, that's a pretty name."

Ashley grinned up at him. "Thank you."

"I'm sure we'll be seeing each other again, Terri."

"Not if I have anything to do with it."

Terri took off at a rapid pace, pulling Ashley behind her. Ashley had to run to keep up.

"What's wrong, Miss Terri? Is that a bad man? Is he a *stranger?*" She sounded almost excited.

"No, Ashley. Let's find your father." She pushed her way down the crowded street and ran smack into Clint.

"Whoa. What's the rush?"

"The crowd was beginning to get to me. I needed some air. And I think we have plenty of toys."

Clint looked at the two armloads of packages and relieved Terri of them.

"I'd say so." He looked down at Ashley. "There won't be anything left for Santa to bring." He grinned at Ashley. "Did you have a good time, sweetheart?"

Ashley nodded her head vigorously. "We met a stranger, Daddy," she chimed as they moved down the street toward the car.

"A stranger?"

"It was Alan," Terri said.

Clint caught Terri's look. "Alan! What does he have—radar? He didn't try anything, did he?" Visions of Alan and Terri, back in California, raced through his head.

Terri shook her head. "He was just obnoxious."

Clint put his arm around her. "Forget it. Alan isn't worth worrying about."

That's what she kept trying to tell herself.

Jillianne sat at the desk and opened the drawer. The manila envelope was still tucked safely inside. Mark told her that the next day she was to arrange to have the package delivered.

She turned the thick envelope over in her hand. What could it contain that could be so damaging to Terri?

"Auntie! We're back." Ashley raced into the living room just as Jill returned the envelope to its hiding place. Soon enough she would find out.

"Auntie, Miss Terri told me all about *Kwanzaa.* It's very special," she said in her most serious voice. "And we get gifts for seven days!" she squealed. "I think I like *Kwanzaa.*"

"That's very nice, dear," Jill replied, trying to hide her annoyance. She hadn't expected that Terri would have charmed her niece after all she'd told her.

"Why don't you find Mrs. Hally and get yourself a snack?" she told Ashley, who quickly ran off in the direction of the kitchen.

Clint, Terri, and Jill sat together in the living room, while Ashley rattled a nonstop conversation with Mrs. Hally.

"Can I get you something, Terri? Some wine, a drink?"

"No, thank you. I don't drink. But if you have some fruit juice, that would be fine."

Jill looked at her curiously. "I'll check with Mrs. Hally."

Clint eased closer to Terri on the couch. "See, Jill's not so bad."

"She's fine when she's around you, Clint. It's when we're alone that the daggers get thrown."

Jill returned several minutes later with a tall glass of cranberry juice. "This is all we have." She handed the glass to Terri.

"Thank you. This is fine."

"If you'll tell Mrs. Hally what you like, I'm sure she'll stock up." She turned to Clint. "Do you think you'll have some time for your dear sister-in-law this evening?"

"Sure. What did you have in mind?"

"Why don't you let me surprise you." Then to Terri, "You wouldn't mind if I borrowed Clint for a while, would you?"

"No." Terri stood up. "As a matter of fact, I have a ton of work to do." She turned to Clint with an "I told you so" look in her eyes. "I have plenty to keep me occupied. If you'll excuse me, I think I'll get started."

Clint gave Terri's hand a squeeze of reassurance as she passed by.

"I thought we could take a drive, like the old days, and just talk." Jill sat next to Clint, sitting as close as she dared. "How does that sound?"

Clint stretched back in the couch. "Sounds fine. When did you want to leave?"

"In about an hour."

"That'll give me time to get a quick nap. If I remember correctly, your 'drives' turn into major events."

Jill laughed at the memories and tapped Clint playfully on the thigh. "I'll meet you out front in an hour." Her spirit was light as she climbed the stairs. She'd finally have Clint to herself, and she was going to make the most of it.

The sound of laughter nudged Terri out of her sleep. Slowly she opened her eyes and tried to focus. She peered at the wall clock: 3 A.M. She shook her head to clear it and discovered that she'd fallen asleep at her desk, having worked on the ad campaign for hours.

The voices drew nearer. She instantly recognized Clint's deep timbre and Jill's sultry laughter. Had they been out all night? An irrational anger swept through her. Some ride, she fumed, rising from the padded seat. She stretched, trying to get rid of the knots that had formed in her back and neck.

Quietly she crossed the room. She definitely didn't want Clint to think she'd been waiting up for him. Soundlessly she opened her dresser drawer and extracted a nightgown. Moments later she was in bed . . . waiting.

The house grew quiet. Her anger switched to disappointment, then hurt. Clint hadn't even stopped in to say good night! Were they together? Was Jill's obvious attraction to Clint mutual?

The unanswered questions tripped through her mind as she tossed and turned, finally falling into a fitful sleep full of images of Clint and Jill.

"Clint, good morning," Jill greeted upon finding him in the kitchen. "Where's Terri?"

"I guess she decided to sleep late," he mumbled, draining a glass of orange juice.

"I had a wonderful time last night," she practically purred.

Terri stood at the top of the stairs as Jill's suggestive voice floated upward. Her senses heightened while she waited for Clint's response.

"So did I. It's been a long time, Jill."

A long time. What did that mean?

"I know," Jill said softly. Her eyes caressed him. "Will you be here all day?"

"For the most part." He yawned. "Terri and I have some kinks to work out with a deal we're negotiating."

The sound of Terri's name broke the mood. Jill checked her watch. "And I have an appointment in about fifteen minutes. So I'll see you later. Mrs. Hally took Ashley to school. Today is her last day before the holidays."

"What time does she get home?"

"About noon."

"Good. I'd like to spend some time with her."

"She'd like that." She stepped closer. "I'd like it, too." She tiptoed and kissed his cheek.

Terri returned to her room, locked the door, and sat by the window replaying the conversation over and over again in her head.

Had it been more than just a ride around town between them last night? The way Jill sounded, and from Clint's response, it appeared to be. She knew that Clint wouldn't betray her like that. Especially right under her nose. However, her feelings about Jill clouded her judgment. It was Jill that she didn't trust. Jill was not above doing whatever she could to get to Clint. Even though he seemed unaware of her intentions. Or was he?

Clint braced Jill's shoulders and looked squarely at her. He'd been trying to figure out the best time and the best way to tell her. There wasn't any.

"Jill, sit down. There's something I want to tell you."

Jill felt a sense of doom spreading through her as she blindly sat down in the kitchen chair.

"I don't know how to tell you this except straight out. I've been thinking about it for a long time, and now that Terri's in my life, I know it's the right time."

Her heart raced uncontrollably, and she suddenly felt faint.

"I plan to take Ashley back to the States with us after the holidays."

She was sure she couldn't have heard right. That was impossible. Ashley belonged to her. He belonged to her. Her insides twisted. "You can't do that."

Her voice was so soft and flat, Clint wasn't quite sure that she'd spoken. He reached for her hand, and she snatched it away.

"You can't do that," she repeated. Her voice rose and trembled as she spoke. "I raised Ashley. She's like a daughter to me. I did it for you! For you!" She leaped up from the chair. Tears streamed down her face. "How could you do this to me? How could you?"

She went for his face, but not before Clint grabbed her wrists.

"Jillianne—listen to me," he commanded.

She shook her head violently. "No. I won't. You can't do this. I won't let you." She snatched her hands away and raced from the room.

"Jill!" Clint took off after her. He reached her just as she stuck the key in her car door.

He grabbed her by the shoulder and spun her around, pinning her body between his and the car.

From her bedroom window Terri watched in agony as the obviously intimate scene unfolded before her. She turned away, not willing to allow herself to be hurt any further. Now everything that she'd overheard took on real meaning.

"Let go of me, Clint," Jillianne spat.

"We need to talk, Jill. I'm not taking her away from you. She's my daughter. And she needs to know that. You've got to be able to understand that." His voice softened, understanding her hurt and confusion. "I'd never do anything to hurt you, Jill."

"You already have." She tore away and faced him. "You already have."

Clint stepped back and watched her race out of the driveway. He breathed heavily. She'd have to come to terms with it, he thought. Somehow she'd have to learn to deal with it.

With a heavy heart he returned to the house. He needed to talk with Terri.

As Jill raced down the winding road, she contemplated what she was about to do. She never wanted to come back to this house. Not if she had to live in it without Ashley and Clint. Tear-filled eyes glanced at her purse that carried the package. It was worth it.

CHAPTER 38

The light knock at her door broke into her swirling thoughts. It could only be Clint. She wasn't ready to see him now. Her confusion mixed with anger did not bode well for any sort of congenial conversation between them. After what she'd heard and then seen, she didn't know what there was to talk about.

The knock came again. This time the doorknob turned as Clint called her name.

She stood still in the hopes that he would think she was still sleep. Moments later she heard his footsteps descending the stairs.

She couldn't avoid him forever. But at least now she'd have some time to think and sort things out before she confronted him. And confront him she would.

After a long shower, Clint decided to take a ride into the city. Driving always helped to clear his head. Maybe Terri would be up and around when he returned, and Jill would have calmed down enough so that they could have an intelligent conversation.

Anyway, he wanted to select a special gift for Terri for the holidays. Even if she didn't celebrate Christmas, he still wanted her to have something to open on Christmas morning. Something to seal their love and their lives together.

His thoughts warmed when she came to mind. She'd become everything he'd hoped for. He trusted her with his deepest thoughts and desires and truly loved her more than he thought he ever could. He smiled.

He hoped the diamond brooch he'd ordered for Jill would help to ease her feelings of abandonment. Maybe he would ask Jill if she wanted to relocate to the States. He shook his head as he slipped on his coat. He didn't know what else to do. He wanted his daughter with him, and that was final. He, Terri, and Ashley were going to be a family. Jill would have to decide if she wanted to be a part of it.

Clint put his hand on the doorknob just as the bell chimed. He opened the door and was surprised to see a young man from the local courier service.

"I have this package for—" he checked his log "—a Mr. Clinton Steele."

"I'm Clint Steele." Clint reached for the envelope and flipped it over. His brows creased in curiosity. There was no return address.

"Sign here, please."

Clint signed his name. Absently he reached into his pocket and tipped the courier.

He took the envelope and returned to the kitchen. When he began to review the contents, his head began to pound with disbelief. Page after page outlined his plans to buy the property in the Caribbean. Documents that no one had access to except him and Terri.

Every step of the plan, from concept to completion, was contained on the pages. And the most damning evidence of all were the notations of counteroffers and correspondence to Nat Carpenter from *Theresa Brathwaite.* His stomach lurched.

She'd set up a dummy company to run the project and compete with him for the deal. It was Terri all along!

A torrent of emotions ripped through him. How could she do this? Why would she do this? And all along she'd pretended to love him only to benefit herself in the long run. His thoughts swirled back to their initial meeting. Terri practically came out and told him that she disliked him and everything that he stood for. She lied to him when she feigned outrage at the things that had been written about him.

He knew she was ambitious. He knew that her business had been in trouble for a while. How far would she go to reach the top? He sat down heavily in the chair. Something like this he would have expected from someone like Mark Andrews, not Terri. Not Terri.

He'd told her everything about his plan. Everything! And she used that information against him.

His anger and sense of absolute betrayal rose to a point of explosion. Never before had he felt such a bottomless void, bereft of any emotion except to destroy.

He pounded his fist against the butcher block table. If she thought she could get away with it, he'd show her who the real master of the game was.

He stuffed the incriminating contents back into the envelope. As he did he wondered briefly where the information had come from. *What did it matter?* He had it now. That's what was important. He'd find out the source soon enough. In the meantime he wanted her out of his house and out of his life.

Terri checked herself in the mirror. She refused to put off talking with Clint another minute. The anxiety and tension were eating away at her. She had to know, for sure, what was the extent of his relationship with Jill. Did anything happen between them? What were his feelings for Jill, and was he aware of her feelings for him? What was that scene in the courtyard really all about?

If she left the questions unanswered, there would always be a seed of doubt and lack of trust in their relationship.

With that determination made, she left her room in the hopes of finding Clint still at home.

Clint spun around at the sound of a presence behind him.

Terri involuntarily stepped back when she saw the look of pure rage and something bordering on pain hovering in the darkness of his eyes.

She opened her mouth to speak, but Clint quickly cut her off.

"How could you?" he seethed.

Terri's voice rose in bewilderment. "How could I what?"

"Don't play your innocence game with me. I know everything! I know what you've been doing."

"Clint, I don't know what you're talking about." She took a hesitant step toward him.

He instantly held up his hand. "Don't come near me." His voice escalated to a thundering roar, and for the first time, Terri actually felt afraid of the man who stood ominously in front of her.

"You were the one behind this whole competitor's scheme with Carpenter!"

For several unbelievable seconds, Terri couldn't absorb what she was hearing.

Clint equated her silence with guilt, and the bottom went out of his world.

"Have you totally lost your mind?" Terri cried. "I don't know what you think you've discovered, but I don't like the sound of it or what you're implying! If you have something to say, then say it!"

"Here." He tossed the envelope at her. She caught it as it landed against her stomach. "That says it all."

Terri's pulse raced. Her head began to pound as she scanned the pages of notes and correspondence. Her vision clouded over as her own anger spiraled to match his. *This* was the man who claimed to love her?

How could he believe that she would do something like this? Yet everything looked authentic. Everything. To a point where she briefly began to think that she was losing her senses. If she didn't know better, she, too, would believe that these were documents she'd created, and all signed with her birth name. *Theresa Brathwaite.* The implication was unfathomable. Yet Clint believed it.

She looked up at him, pain-filled eyes meeting anguished ones. Maybe this was a sign, she thought, that things would never be right between them. Obstacle after obstacle erected themselves in their paths.

She dropped the documents on the floor. The line was drawn. She straightened her shoulders, drawing herself up to her full height. Her proud chin jutted forward defiantly.

"Think whatever you want, Clint. If you can believe this, then you'll believe anything about me. And that doesn't say very much about this relationship, which has now come to an end."

She spun away and walked purposefully out of the kitchen, willing herself not to crumple under the weight of her hurt.

Clint remained like a stone statue in the heavy silence that followed. Devastation swept through him. Could she be telling the truth? Had he allowed his anger to cloud his judgment and good sense? But when she saw the contents of the envelope, she never flinched. Not once.

He didn't know what to think.

Still, just looking at her left him with nagging doubts. If it wasn't Terri, then who was it? And more importantly how did they get the information and know Terri's birth name?

Clint headed for the door. He was going to find the source of the information. He took a fleeting look up the staircase as he opened the door. *No,* he decided. He wouldn't go to her now. He was sure she wouldn't listen, and she'd have every right. When he came back to her, he wanted to have the information and the name of the person who was out to destroy them.

Melissa sat across the table from Steve and thought about how happy she was. Yet her happiness was not complete. Her conscience gnawed at her. Was their budding relationship strong enough to withstand the secret that she held? Steve might eventually find out her role. Then what?

"You're deep in thought," Steve commented. He took a sip of hot chocolate. "Anything you want to talk about?"

She looked away. Her thoughts raced.

Steve reached across the table and covered her hand with his. "You can tell me, Mel. Whatever it is."

She looked into his warm brown eyes.

"Even if it may change the way you feel about me?"

He sat back in his seat, a look of concern darkened his eyes. Then he leaned forward. "Nothing could change the way I feel about you. What could be so terrible?" He smiled at her encouragingly.

Melissa took a deep breath. She couldn't look into his eyes as she slowly revealed her masochistic relationship with Mark and her involvement in his plan to hurt Terri and Clint in the process.

Hot tears burned her eyes while she mechanically threw her clothing into her suitcase. The door below slammed shut, and moments later she heard the roar of Clint's car tear out of the driveway.

The tears came hard and fast now, the emptiness and hurt almost more than she could stand. Who would do such a thing and why? More importantly, how could Clint believe it under any circumstances? Maybe she should have tried to defend herself, convince him that she didn't . . . wouldn't do anything like that.

It didn't matter, she concluded, slamming the suitcase shut. She and Clint were not meant to be together, and maybe this was for the best.

Terri closed her bedroom door and descended the stairs. She'd have to call a car service to take her to a hotel. At least until she could make arrangements to have her return flight to New York changed. Mrs. Hally should have a number.

Jillianne entered the lobby of the Savoy and approached the reception desk.

"Would you call Mr. Andrews's room, please?"

"Whom shall I say is here, madam?"

"Jillianne Davis."

"One moment."

Jill and Mark sat at a small table in the hotel's exquisite dining room.

"Why do you look so upset?" Mark asked as soon as the waitress was out of earshot. He leaned forward. "Did something go wrong?"

Jill shook her head. "I sent the package. He should have it by now."

"Great. So what's the problem?"

"He wants to take Ashley away."

Mark's jaw clenched. "What do you mean?"

Jill explained what Clint told her.

Mark thought about it for a moment, totally unmoved by Jill's plight. His main concern was the completion of his plan. This little twist only meant that everything would have to be moved up.

He patted her hand. "Don't worry about a thing. By the time this is all over, he'll be so glad to be rid of Terri and have his daughter, he'll do anything you want. We move tonight."

"Tonight?"

"Yes. Now just remember what you have to do. I'll do the rest."

* * *

Steve felt as if his insides were being squeezed shut. He stared at Melissa in astonishment. He would have never imagined that Melissa could be capable of such duplicity. Had her obsession with Clint driven her to such lengths?

"Why, Mel?" he asked in a strained voice. "Why?"

Unable to face him, she looked away. "I was hurt. Confused. Obsessed." She looked at him. "Lonely. I thought if I could help Mark to get Terri out of the picture, I would have Clint. I even went so far as to let Mark be a replacement for Clint. But it never really worked." Her voice cracked. "Then Mark became more and more irrational, more demanding, frightening." Tears slowly fell from her eyes.

Steve rounded the table and knelt down beside her. He lifted her chin with the tip of his finger, forcing her to look at him.

"Whatever you've done can be undone. Now I want you to tell me everything you know."

CHAPTER 39

Clint arrived at the delivery offices of Quic Courier. With little difficulty he found a parking space and moments later stood in front of a very harried dispatcher.

"Yes? What can I do for you, sir?"

Clint started to speak but was cut off by the ringing phone.

"One moment, sir," he said to Clint. He then spat out instructions to the caller, while simultaneously answering another line and putting it on hold. He put his hand over the mouthpiece and spoke to Clint.

"I do apologize, sir. My assistant grew ill and had to leave. I'm the only one here at the moment. I'll be with you shortly." He returned to his conversation.

Clint paced as he watched the stout, middle-aged man move agilely around the small office, fielding phone calls and writing orders. The office of Quic Courier was small but neat. The reception area could hold a maximum of three people and then consider the place crowded. They prided themselves on personalized service, dealing mainly with the local residents and neighborhood businesses. If you wanted something delivered without a lot of hassle and high prices, Quic was the place to go. Clint couldn't remember a time when they weren't around.

Finally, he was finished and turned his attention to Clint.

He exhaled deeply. "So sorry, sir. How can I be of service to you?"

Clint peeked at his name tag. "Mr. Willis, I received this package this morning." He put the envelope on the table. "It didn't have a return address. I want to know who sent it."

"Hmm." Mr. Willis slipped his Benjamin Franklin glasses onto his nose. He shook his head as he looked at the address. "I didn't send this out. Let me check the log."

Mr. Willis ambled down to the end of the long counter and pulled the log book out from the bottom shelf. Quickly he scanned the pages, then checked the office copy of receipts.

He returned to where Clint stood. "The client paid us in cash." He peered up at Clint. "There's no other information."

"Can I see that?" Clint reached for the receipt. "How can you accept something like this without a name?" He handed it back in disgust.

"As long as the delivery is paid for and the mailing address is clear . . . ? He shrugged his shoulders.

"Would you at least remember what the person looked like?"

"As I said, I did not prepare this order. My assistant did. Perhaps she'd remember. If you'd care to pop in tomorrow, she may be able to help you."

Clint sighed heavily. "Thank you. Maybe I will." As his temper began to ebb, he had a strong sensation that he had been very wrong about everything. He turned to leave, wondering what his next move should be. He checked his watch. Ashley would be home shortly, and he wanted to select a gift for Terri. He owed Terri more than a gift, but at least it would pave the way for the groveling that he would have to do in order to get her to listen to the apology that she deserved.

He drove into the heart of London and found the most expensive jewelry shop in the city.

"You'll stay here in the hotel," Mark instructed Jill. "I can't take a chance that you'll cave in and ruin everything." He tossed the balance of his brandy down his throat.

"I can't stay here. They'll wonder where I am."

"That's even better. Clint will be so relieved to see you when you return, he'll be putty in your hands. Now let's go." He rose from his seat and took Jill by the elbow, leading her out of the dining room.

When he reached the door, he stopped short. "Wait," he urged. He pulled Jill back into the dining hall. "Over there." He pointed in the direction of the lobby. "That's Terri."

Jill saw her, too. "What is she doing here?"

"It looks like she's checking in."

They watched the bellhop take her bags onto the elevator.

"This changes things," Mark said. "We'll have to move quicker than planned. I can't afford to run into her in the hotel. And neither can you."

"Do you have Clint's phone number in England?" Steve asked Melissa.

"I have it at the office."

"Is anyone there?"

"Maybe one of the secretaries is still around. I'll call."

Melissa dialed the number to Hightower Enterprises. The phone rang for quite a while before it was finally answered.

"Hightower Enterprises. May I help you?"

Melissa readily recognized the voice of her assistant, Chris. "Hello, Chris. This is Melissa."

"Oh, hello, Ms. Taylor. Is something wrong?"

"I need a favor. Look in my office on my private Rolodex, and get me Mr. Steele's number in London."

"Sure. Hold on."

Melissa put her hand over the mouthpiece and spoke to Steve. "She's going to get it. I just hope that we're in time to stop whatever it is that Mark is planning."

Chris came back on the line. "Ms. Taylor. I have the number."

"Thanks, Chris." Melissa jotted down the number and hung up. She handed the slip of paper to Steve. He took her place at the phone and dialed.

The line was busy and remained busy every time they called for the next hour.

"Maybe there's trouble on the line," Steve concluded, hanging up the phone for the countless time.

"We can try again later," Melissa offered.

Steve nodded.

Clint returned home to find Terri gone. He quizzed Mrs. Hally until she was on the verge of tears, then found himself apologizing by giving her the night off.

He then spent the next hour on the phone trying to track down the cabdriver that had picked up Terri, only to find out that the cabbie was now gone for the day. He hadn't turned in his trip sheet and would not be back on duty for two days. The second hour was spent blasting the airline reservationist and anyone else who came on the line to tell him that they couldn't give out any information on passengers.

And where was Jillianne? he fumed. He paced the expanse of the living room until he finally flopped down on the couch in frustration. He'd really done it this time. He'd let his temper blind him to the truth, and now he'd probably lost Terri for good.

He had to find her. He had to tell her how wrong he was and that together they would find out who was behind trying to ruin them and their relationship.

Clint checked his watch. It was after two o'clock. He frowned. *Where was Ashley?* He didn't even have the name of the bus service that brought her back and forth. *Some father he was.* And he'd been so busy apologizing to Mrs. Hally, he hadn't thought to ask her. Now what?

Once again, he began to pace. His jaw clenched. Something was wrong. He could feel the onset of trouble continue to brew with each passing moment. Terri was gone. Ashley wasn't home as expected, and Jill had torn out of the house in such a state, he couldn't imagine where she might be. And where was his daughter? That unanswered question disturbed him most of all.

Mrs. Hally's phone number had to be around somewhere. He went to the kitchen and checked the list of phone numbers tacked to the cork-board. *Here it is.*

The phone rang endlessly. Annoyed, he placed the phone back in the cradle. He felt completely impotent. There had to be something he could do.

He'd go to the school. Maybe they had some extended activity, and Jill had neglected to mention it. He headed toward the door with one thought on his mind . . . Ashley.

Just as he reached the door, the phone rang. A temporary feeling of relief loosened the frown that had hardened his face.

He grabbed the phone.

"Yes?" he barked into the mouthpiece.

The voice was garbled, barely discernible, as if the voice were electronic. Clint immediately concluded that it must be some sort of crank call and started to hang up until he heard the voice mention Ashley's name.

"What? What did you say about my daughter?"

"I suggest you listen carefully, Mr. Steele. And most importantly do not call the police. We have your daughter, and if you do as we say, nothing will happen to her."

"Who is this, damnit!" He gripped the receiver with such force that his knuckles began to hurt. "If anything happens to my daughter, I'll find you and I'll bury you!"

"No time for idle threats, Mr. Steele. Are you willing to listen, or should I hang up? The choice is yours."

Clint forced himself to breathe as millions of unspeakable atrocities whipped through his head. He pushed calm into his voice. "I'm listening."

"That's better. Now the first thing I want you to do is to contact Nat Carpenter and tell him that you're no longer interested in the resorts in the Caribbean."

"What? Are you out of your mind? What do the resorts have to do with my daughter?"

"You're asking too many questions again, Mr. Steele. I think I'll have to hang up."

The sound of the dial tone buzzed madly in his ear.

Clint slammed down the phone, throwing it to the floor. Blindly he stooped down and picked it up, staring at it as though the ivory instrument were at the root of this vicious joke.

Rage, fear, and shock took over his body and his thoughts. He paced, unable to think clearly. His darkly handsome face was contorted into a mask of fury and pain. He pressed his large fist against his mouth to keep from screaming. Call, damn you!

Dear God, not Ashley. Not Ashley. He slammed his fist against the table. He'd never been a father to her—and now this. He had to make things right. No matter what it took. If those bastards wanted the resorts, they could have them and anything else they wanted. As long as he got Ashley back.

Call! He stared at the phone, willing it to ring. Moments later it did.

Clint snatched up the phone. "Yes?"

"Are you ready to listen now, Mr. Steele?"

He took a deep breath. "Go ahead."

"After you make that call to Mr. Carpenter, I want you to gather your liquid assets. I want two million. In cash. Out of sequence. By tomorrow morning."

Clint was momentarily stunned. "I can't get that kind of money by tomorrow!"

"If you want your daughter, you'll get the money and make the call. I'll call you in the morning and let you know where to drop off the money and pick up your daughter."

"Wait! How do I know you have Ashley? Let me talk to her."

"Why, of course. I thought you'd never ask. Ashley, your daddy wants to talk to you."

"Daddy? Daddy?"

"Ashley, sweetheart. It's me. I'm gonna get you home, baby. Are you all right?"

"I can't see. There's something over my eyes. Daddy, I—" The phone was snatched from her hand.

"That's quite enough. You have plenty to do to keep you busy, Mr. Steele. Expect to hear from me tomorrow."

The phone went dead.

Clint held the phone for countless minutes, trying to digest all that he'd heard. The money he could understand. But why the resorts? Obviously the kidnapper and his competitors were one in the same. Or at the very least his competition had paid someone to do this.

Finally he replaced the phone and went in search of Nat Carpenter's number in the Bahamas. A cruel and chilling thought seeped through his veins as he flipped the pages of his phone book. What if Terri did have something to do with this? But just as quickly he tossed it off. No.

That's what they wanted him to think. Someone else was behind this, and they were determined to ruin them both. But why Terri? Who hated her so much that they would invent such an elaborate scheme to implicate her?

He didn't have time to dwell on that right now. He had to call Carpenter and get in touch with his accountant and his banker immediately. He had to find a way to get the money before tomorrow afternoon.

CHAPTER 40

"What are we going to do now?" Melissa asked Steve.

"We'll wait and try again later."

Melissa swallowed the knot of fear that had settled in her throat. Hesitantly she asked the question that had hovered in her head for hours. "And . . . what about us?"

Steve sighed heavily, stood up, and walked to the other side of the bedroom. He turned and faced her. "I know how I feel about you, Mel. What you did was deplorable, but you still have a conscience. I think the reason you needed to tell me was because of how you're beginning to feel about me. Am I right?"

She nodded, and a flicker of hope lifted her heart.

"Then we can work everything else out. As long as we're honest with each other. Deal?"

Slowly she rose, then ran across the room and into his arms. "Deal," she whispered against his chest.

Steve took a step back and held her at arm's length. "Let's see if we can get Clint on the phone."

Melissa dialed the number again and was overjoyed to hear the familiar ringing sound.

"It's ringing," she said.

The phone was finally picked up.

"Hello?"

"Hello, this is Melissa Taylor."

"Ah, Ms. Taylor, how are you?" answered Mrs. Hally.

"I'm fine. Actually I need to speak to Mr. Steele. Right away."

"I'm sorry, he's not here. He told me I could have the night off, but when I finally arrived home I discovered I'd left my small purse with my house keys. I've just returned to pick them up and found the house empty."

"Do you have any idea where he could be?"

"No, I don't."

"Is Ms. Powers there?"

"Oh, no!" She shook her head vigorously and lowered her voice to a conspiratorial whisper. "She and Mr. Steele had a terrible tiff this morning. She packed her bags. I called a cabbie for her myself."

"What? Do you have any idea where she might be?"

"No, mum. She may be at one of the hotels, or she could have gone to the airport."

"All right. When Mr. Steele comes in, please tell him to call me. It's urgent that I speak with him as soon as possible."

"I certainly will. But you know our Mr. Steele, he does things in his own time."

"I know. Thank you, Mrs. Hally."

Melissa hung up and replayed the conversation to Steve.

"Damn! Everything's coming apart at once." He shook his head. "I'm sure I can track down Terri. I have a few connections in London. Maybe that's what we can do in the meantime. This affects her as much as Clint. I just wonder what the hell happened between them that would make Terri leave."

Melissa wondered, too.

Clint burst through the door, nearly knocking Mrs. Hally over with the sheer force of his entry.

He quickly clasped her shoulders to keep her from tumbling backward.

"Mrs. Hally," he breathed in relief. "Thank God you're here. Please sit down."

He quickly ushered her onto the chaise lounge in the foyer and told her about his conversation with the abductor.

Mrs. Hally made the sign of the cross three times and sent up silent prayers for Ashley's safe return as tears rolled down her cheeks.

Clint put his arm around her trembling shoulder. "We're going to get her back. I promise."

She nodded, putting all her faith in his words.

"I have to go out. But I'll be back as soon as I can. We're not to contact the police in any way. Or tell anyone. Do you understand?"

"Yes, sir," she sniffed.

"Fine. I need you to stay here to answer the phone."

"Of course, Mr. Steele. Anything."

He patted her back. "Thank you." He got up to leave when Mrs. Hally remembered the phone call from Melissa.

"There was a call while you were out." She blew her nose.

Clint's pulse raced. "Who?"

"Ms. Taylor from your office in New York."

His hopes slowly diminished. "Oh. I'll have to try to get back to her." He moved toward the door.

"She said it was very important."

Clint opened the door, then turned around. "Not as important as getting my daughter back safely."

Terri ordered room service but merely picked at the shrimp salad. She lay down the fork and tossed the linen napkin to the side. She pushed herself away from the table and walked toward the window. The city of London spread out beneath her view.

What an ideal place for the perfect romantic interlude, she thought, then laughed derisively. This trip had turned out to be anything but perfect.

She pulled the satin belt of her robe around her waist. How could things have gone so badly? She'd had misgivings about coming, but she never envisioned that the problem would be her and Clint.

Clint. Just the thought of his name made their painful parting resurface with a vengeance. How could he have thought such a thing about her? Did he have so little faith in their relationship that he would allow some vile lie to ruin what they had built?

She'd even begun to care about Ashley and believed that in time she would find it in her heart to truly love her. Their afternoon together had been the turning point. But now . . . ?She turned away from the lights of the darkening city. Tomorrow she'd be back in New York. Once again she would have to reconstruct her life from the rubble of yet another failed liaison.

Sadly she lay across the canopied bed. Maybe happiness was not hers to have, she concluded, as she drifted off into a trouble-filled sleep.

There was a distant, persistent ringing. Slowly Terri floated up from sleep and tried to focus in on her surroundings. Where was she? She squeezed her eyes shut and quickly opened them again. *The hotel.* Then the reason for her being there came rushing back. The ringing continued, and she realized it was the phone.

Clumsily she reached for it as daybreak peeked through the drawn drapes.

"Hello?"

"Terri? Is that you?"

"Who is this?" She was fully alert and sat up in bed.

"It's me, Steve. Clint's friend."

Her heart began to race. *Something happened to Clint.*

"Steve? How did you get this number?"

"I find people for a living."

"Why did you have to find me? Has something happened to Clint?"

"No." He paused. "At least not yet. We've been trying to reach him since yesterday."

"Steve, you're scaring me. Get to the point. And who is we?"

"Melissa and I."

Terri frowned. "Are you going to tell me why you called me at six A.M., or are you going to make me guess?"

Steve exhaled. "This may sound crazy, but Mark Andrews is in England and he's out to get you, and Clint in the process . . . ?

An hour later Terri sat on the edge of her bed, stunned by what she had been told. But after finally digesting the information that Melissa and Steve provided, everything began to make sense. The question now was, What was Mark's next move?

She had to get to Clint. There was no point in calling him and having him not take her call. She'd go to his house.

Why did Mark hate her so much? she wondered as she slipped into a pair of winter white cashmere pants. What had she ever done to him, to anyone, to deserve such loathing? It had to go beyond just firing him. But what?

Maybe now she would finally get to the bottom of everything, she thought, as she closed the door behind her. Hopefully whatever grudge Mark had against her would be settled once and for all.

CHAPTER 41

Clint hadn't slept the entire night. His eyes burned and felt as if sand had been tossed in them. But adrenaline pumped through his veins, giving him the stamina he needed to get through the next few hours.

He stood under the pulsing force of the shower, wishing he could miraculously wash away the nightmare that had become his life.

He hadn't even had a free moment to track down Terri. He needed her strength now more than ever. But she was probably in New York by now, he concluded. When this was over, he was going to get her back. No matter what.

He stood in front of the bedroom mirror and pressed the heels of his palms against his eyes. Ashley had to be all right. She just had to be.

He'd made arrangements the previous afternoon to have all of his holdings transferred into his London account. His banker had made special provisions to have the money delivered by courier yesterday evening. And he'd made the call to Carpenter. He'd done everything that he was told. Now the waiting began.

He stepped out into the hallway just as the phone rang. He ran down the hallway and answered the phone at the top of the stairs.

"Yes?"

"Mr. Steele?"

"It's me."

"Take down these instructions. . . ."

* * *

Clint knocked on Mrs. Hally's door.

"Come in," she answered.

Clint peeked his head in the door. Mrs. Hally approached.

"Mrs. Hally, I'm leaving now. Did Jill come in last night?"

"No, sir."

He didn't have time to worry about Jill's temper tantrum at the moment. She'd come back when she cooled down.

"I'll need you to stay here until I get back. And when I do, I'll have Ashley."

She took his hand in hers. "She'll be fine, Mr. Steele," she said softly.

Clint's lips tightened and he nodded. "Please, you're not to tell anyone." He turned to leave and silently prayed that Mrs. Hally was right.

Terri stood in front of Clint's door. Several times she attempted to ring the bell, but her hand stopped in midair. She didn't want what she had to say to sound like some sort of lame excuse to see him again.

She took a deep breath. This was too important for trivial ego tripping. He'd just have to listen.

She rang the bell. Moments later the door was answered by a very distraught Mrs. Hally.

"Mrs. Hally, are you all right?" Terri looked beyond Mrs. Hally into the foyer for any sign of trouble, then focused back on the middle-aged woman.

Before she knew what she was doing, Mrs. Hally was in tears, blurting out to Terri everything that had transpired since Terri left, right up to Clint's departure.

"Oh, Ms. Powers," she cried, "if anything happens to our little girl . . . ?

Terri hugged the plump body against her own. "Everything will be fine," she assured. Terri stepped back, and holding Mrs. Hally's shoulders, she looked down into her tear-filled eyes. "Where is Clint?"

Mrs. Hally gasped and covered her mouth with her hand. "Oh, heavens, I promised Mr. Steele that I wouldn't tell anyone. He'll be furious."

"That's not important now. I think I know who has Ashley. Where did he go? Did he tell you?"

She shook her head vigorously. "He got the phone call this morning and he left. He wouldn't tell me where."

Terri sighed. "I need to use the phone."

"You mustn't call the authorities. Mr. Steele promised that they wouldn't be contacted. Oh, Ms. Powers, please don't. For Ashley's sake."

"For Ashley's sake we have to tell the police, Mrs. Hally. Or her kidnapper will get away."

Terri walked past Mrs. Hally into the living room and dialed the police.

* * *

Clint pulled up to the enclosed wooded area as instructed. He waited five minutes, then left the car with the suitcase in hand. There was no one around and no sign of Ashley.

He placed the briefcase beneath a large stump at the foot of a small incline and returned to his car. He pulled off and drove directly to the service station two miles away and waited by the pay phone for the call.

"I'm telling you, officer, I know who has Clinton Steele's daughter."

"You have proof, Ms. Powers?" the skeptical constable asked.

"Not exactly. But we have every reason to believe that it's him. You can't ignore this information. Suppose you're wrong?"

Constable Langly looked scornfully at this woman who thought she could tell him how to do his job. How dare this Yankee dred come here and give orders. But good sense overrode his pride. She was right. If there was any validity in what she'd told him, and he ignored it, he'd have hell to pay.

"All right, Ms. Powers. I'll have some of our men cover the airport, bus and train stations. Do you have a picture of this bloke?"

Terri shook her head, then remembered the cover photo of the public relations package that she used for her firm.

"One minute. I think I have something that you can use."

She returned shortly with a copy of the company brochure, complete with a close-up shot of Mark Andrews.

Constable Langly took the brochure, and Terri pointed out Mark. "This'll help."

Terri folded her arms, satisfied that she had done the right thing. She just hoped that she wasn't too late, and that Clint would understand her reasons for going against his wishes.

"We'll contact you as soon as any of this pans out, Ms. Powers. And tell Mr. Steele that we'll do everything we can to get his daughter . . . ?

"You can tell me yourself," Clint stated, striding into the room. His eyes were two dark slits as he glowered at the assemblage of officers in his living room and Terri in the midst of them. He didn't know whether to be happy or furious at seeing her. "What the hell are you all doing here? I said no police!" He threw a murderous look at Mrs. Hally, who nearly collapsed under his unwavering gaze.

"This is not something you can handle alone, Mr. Steele," offered Constable Langly. "We're trained for things like this." Clint opened his mouth to lash out but Terri hurried toward him, and for an instant his guard went down. She stepped into his outstretched arms and welcomed the power of his embrace. She swore she felt him tremble as if he held back the weight of the world. She looked up into his eyes.

"Clint. Oh, Clint, I'm so sorry about Ashley. I called the authorities because I think I know who took her."

He grabbed her by her shoulders, the force of his grip burning into her flesh.

"Who? Who has my daughter?"

Terri quickly explained her conversation with Steve and Melissa.

Clint sank down onto the couch. He shook his head in disbelief. "Why? Why would Melissa do something like this to me?"

"Clint, Melissa is in love with you, or at least she thought she was. Her passing information to Mark was her way of getting back at you for ignoring her. She never imagined that it would come to this."

Clint braced his forehead on his palm. "Unbelievable."

"The person Mark is really after is me. He was the one behind the information you received. He's probably your competitor for the resort deal as well."

"That would make sense. That's why the caller was so insistent I tell Carpenter the deal was off." He raised his head and looked at her. "But what does all of this have to do with you?"

"Mark obviously believes that if he hurts you, he hurts me. If he could implicate me, that would turn you against me."

Clint swallowed. "It almost worked," he admitted. He took her hand in his. "You've got to forgive me, Terri. I was stupid to ever think you would do something like that. I love you. You've got to believe me."

"I love you, too, Clint."

He pulled her into his arms, finding a momentary solace in the warmth of her nearness. "We've got to find my baby, Terri," he groaned in her hair.

"We will. I gave the police a picture of Mark. They're going to be looking for him everywhere."

"Mr. Steele—" Constable Langly stood above him as he sat "—what were your instructions?"

"I was told to drop off the money and then go to a phone booth and wait for the call to tell me where to pick up Ashley. I waited for three hours. The call never came. It never came!" He sprang up from the couch. His thundering voice rose to the rafters of the house.

"When I get that little bastard, I'm going to kill him!"

Terri put a restraining hand on his arm. "Clint," she cautioned.

"We'll get him, Mr. Steele. It's only a matter of time."

"A matter of *time?* My daughter is out there. Do you understand? I don't want *in a matter of time.* I want now!"

Constable Langly nervously cleared his throat. "We'll do the best we can, Mr. Steele." He turned to leave. "We'll call as soon as anything happens, and please try to keep the line free," he said as he strode through the door, followed by three other officers.

Terri tugged Clint's arm, forcing him to acknowledge her. "Clint," she hissed. "They're not here to hurt, they're here to help. And you practically threatening them is not going to make them more cooperative."

Clint clenched his jaw. He jammed his hands in his pockets. "Now what?"

"Now we wait," Terri said.

They both took a seat on the couch, each caught in their own private thoughts. The sound of the front door opening made them both look up.

Clint rose. "Jill."

Jillianne stepped into the living room, surprised to see Terri standing next to Clint. Slowly she approached, and the closer she got, the clearer Clint's face became.

She could see that he'd had little or no sleep. His beautiful black eyes were bloodshot. His usually smooth brow was furrowed with worry. But most of all his spirit, his vibrancy, was missing. And she'd done that. To the man who meant everything to her.

Clint came forward. Pain edged his voice. "Someone's taken Ashley, Jill."

Jill stood stock still.

"Actually we have a pretty good idea who it is," Terri interjected.

Jillianne's pulse began to gallop. She felt hot and cold at once. She couldn't speak. *Please.*

"Mark Andrews," Clint stated. "He used to work for Terri, until she fired him for embezzlement."

This didn't make sense, she thought, confusion clouding her mind. She looked from Clint to Terri and back again. Mark was Clint's friend. He said so. Jillianne began to sway back and forth. What had she done?

Clint hurried to her side and captured her around her waist. "Are you all right?"

Weakly she nodded. "What does he want in exchange for Ashley?"

"That's just it," Clint said. "I did everything he told me. To the letter. But he didn't deliver Ashley."

Jill felt as if a great weight were pressing against her chest. She couldn't breathe. *This wasn't the way it was supposed to be.*

"The police have cut off the airports, bus and train stations, and boats. They're sure to find him," Terri said trying to reassure Jill, who looked as if she were going to faint any minute.

If they found Mark, he was sure to tell everything, including her role in this whole sadistic scheme. And Mark had broken his promise to bring Ashley back. Her baby was out there, probably terrified. Her heart beat faster. She couldn't let her stay there any longer. Maybe if she confessed her participation before Clint was told by the police, he would find a way to forgive her.

Her voice was barely a whisper. "I know where Ashley is."

"What?" Clint couldn't be sure that he'd heard correctly.

"Clint—" she clutched his shirt "—please forgive me. I never thought he wouldn't bring her back. Oh, God!" she cried. Burning tears began to run down her cheeks.

Clint grabbed Jill and started to shake her viciously.

"Clint, don't," Terri cried. Clint ignored her.

"What are you talking about? Tell me. Now. Damnit. Do you hear me?"

Hysterical, Jill rattled on about the initial phone call from Mark, her agreeing to help him to get Terri out of the picture, the delivering of the envelope, and ultimately the plan to take Ashley in order to get the money he needed to cover the costs of the resort deal.

Incredulity swam in his eyes. "How . . . how could you?"

"Clint, I love you. I've always loved you," she cried. "I waited for you all these years, waited for you to get over your loss of Desiree. I waited for you to come home to me. Finally to me. But when you did, you brought her." She threw a scornful glance at Terri. "And then you wanted to take Ashley away." She shook her head, her body seemed to shrink. "I couldn't let you take her. She belongs here with me. I raised her. I love her like my own. I took care of Ashley all these years to show you how much I love you and how happy we three could be together."

"You don't know the meaning of love." Clint pushed her away in disgust. She fell to the floor.

"Clint, please. You've got to understand. I did it for us. So that we could be together like we were meant to be. Terri doesn't deserve you."

Clint stepped forward meanacingly. Jill recoiled. His nostrils flared. "She's more of a woman than you'll ever be, Jill. Now tell me where my daughter is before I hurt you!"

"She's in the old Wedgewood Cottage," she whimpered, cringing in the corner.

The irony of the location hit him like a kick in the gut. The cottage was where Desiree conceived Ashley. Without another word, Clint sprinted toward the door.

"Call the police, Clint," Terri urged.

"No!"

She hurried to his side. "Then at least let me go with you."

Clint clasped Terri's chin in his hand. "I have to do this alone." He pressed his lips fleetingly against hers. "You, most of all, can understand that." He searched her eyes. Terri nodded her agreement, her soft smile of comfort was the beacon he needed. He snatched his coat and scarf from the rack, then turned toward Jill. "Don't be anywhere in my eyesight when I return," he seethed.

Clint drove blindly along the darkened roads, which were slowly being covered with the first layer of snow. He took the route more from memory than from watching for signs, remembering the turns and inclines from traveling to the hideaway in his early years of marriage.

The cottage had been abandoned after Desiree's death, and he'd never had the heart to return. Imagining the condition it must be in, and his daughter there alone, incensed him, made his gut twist with hurt and rage.

His daughter. It was not until these past hours of mental and emotional torture that he finally realized just what fatherhood was all about. It was not sending a check once each month, or making a dutiful phone call. It was being there during the good and bad times. He loved his daughter, he realized with a powerful jolt. He truly loved her, and no matter what it took, he was going to be the father Ashley deserved.

The car's tires spat gravel as Clint sped up the lane that led to the house. The small cottage was enveloped in darkness. A single dull light illuminated the dust-encrusted window. The car ground to a halt. Clint jumped out and ran toward the door, only to discover it chained shut.

Quickly he searched for something to use as leverage to break the chain. Then better judgment took hold. He didn't want to add to Ashley's terror by breaking down the door.

He ran around to the side window. What he saw nearly tore him in two.

Ashley was huddled in the center of the bed, curled in a tiny ball. His throat constricted when he tried to call out to her. All that came from his throat was a grating, guttural cry, like a wounded animal. From deep inside he found the will to bang on the window. Ashley sat up in the bed and turned toward the noise, her eyes wide and glistening with fear.

"Ashley, baby. It's me, Daddy. I'm going to get you out, baby," he yelled. "It's all right."

There was no way he'd waste precious time searching for something to break the chain, when he heard Ashley scream his name over and over again . . . "Daddy, Daddy!"

He'd go in through the window. He tore the plaid scarf from his neck and wrapped it around his fist. Shielding his face with his free hand, he smashed the window. He tore away the rotting wooden frame with his gloved hands, hoisted himself up over the ledge, and crawled through.

The few steps from the window to the bed were the longest and most painful he'd ever taken. He felt as if his feet were being sucked down in quicksand. He kept his eyes glued on his daughter, who remained motionless, continuing to whimper his name as though unwilling to believe that she was moments away from freedom. Her eyes were red and swollen from hours of crying, and she hugged her stuffed dog to her like a lifeline. It was a picture that Clint would never forget.

Then all at once, he had her in his arms. He felt his own heart slam mercilessly in his chest. He stroked her, hugged her, kissed her, crooning her name over and again, trying to silence her sobs that now filled the dusty air.

She clung to him. Her tiny body shook with relief, relishing the comfort and security of her father's embrace.

Her lifted her in his arms and wrapped her in his coat. "Everything's going to be all right, Ashley," he whispered against her hair. "I'm never, ever going to let anything happen to you again. I swear I won't."

"Please don't leave me, Daddy. Please," she cried, clinging tighter to him.

"Never," he said in a strangled voice. "Never again. I've made a lot of mistakes, Ash. Because I was afraid." He hugged her tighter. "I'm not going to be afraid anymore. We're going to work things out. Together. You, me, and Terri."

Cautiously she lifted her head from his chest. Bewilderment and fear mingled in her eyes. "You're going to leave me with Terri?"

"No, sweetheart. We're going to be a family. The three of us." He looked into her eyes. "A real family. And after the holidays we're going to New York to live. Start a brand new life and put all of this behind us."

"Will you be in New York, too?"

His heart shuddered at the hope-filled question. When he looked at her, into the face that so reflected Desiree's, he knew without question that he owed it not only to Ashley, but to Desi, to make the life they'd envisioned for their daughter.

"Of course I'll be there," he assured. "That's what a family is. People who love each other and want to be together. And I want to be with you, Ash, more than you'll ever know."

She buried her face against his chest. "I want to be with you, too, Daddy, and Terri."

Clint cleared his throat. "Then let's get started by getting you out of here."

"What about Auntie Jill?" Ashley asked as they approached the window.

Clint's jaw clenched. "She has to go away," he said in a tight voice. "But I'm sure she'll write to you." He swallowed the knot in his throat and kissed her forehead. "Let's go home."

CHAPTER 42

Terri sat on the edge of Ashley's bed, gently stroking her face as she slept. She'd given her a warm bath, washed her hair, and told her a silly story until she'd finally fallen asleep. As she watched Ashley, her heart filled with a wonderful feeling of warmth. She was so innocent and precious. So deserving of love and stability.

Over these last hours, Terri realized she'd discovered a part of herself that she hadn't thought existed, the part that could love this child as her own. Unquestionably.

The understanding was like being freed from the emotional quicksand that had suffocated her for so many years. Now she could truly look forward to the happiness she and Clint were destined to share together without reservation.

"What are you smiling about?"

Terri jumped at the sound of Clint's voice, nearly waking up Ashley in the process.

Gently she rose from the bed and tiptoed to the door.

"She's finally asleep," she whispered.

"Is that what the smile is for?" he teased. He gathered her in his arms and softly kissed her lips.

"No, silly. I'm finally free," she whispered.

He looked at her quizzically.

"Don't ask. I'll tell you some other time."

Arm in arm they left the room and went downstairs.

"You're great with her, Terri."

"You really think so?"

"You can see that she adores you. You were the one she asked to give her a bath. That has to mean something," he smiled.

Terri laughed. "I suppose it does."

They approached the kitchen and went in.

"Hungry?" Clint asked.

"A little."

"Let me see what we have." He opened the refrigerator.

"Is Jill gone?"

Clint breathed deeply. "Yes. She left about an hour ago," he added, with the slightest bit of pain in his voice. "I decided to take your advice and not press charges. She'll have her conscience to live with. That should be enough punishment."

Terri walked up behind him and wrapped her arms around his waist. "It's going to be all right," she said gently.

He nodded, unable to comment. This whole ordeal had affected him much more than he let on. Every time he thought about Jill being responsible for Ashley's upbringing, and her being so close to going over the edge, he shuddered. What else might Jill have done?

The phone rang.

Terri disengaged herself. "I'll find something," she offered.

Clint crossed the room and picked up the phone.

". . . Fantastic! How long ago?" They found Mark, he mouthed to Terri. Then his whole relieved expression changed. "What? . . . Is he crazy? . . . Why the hell should she? All right, all right. I'll ask her, but I'm not promising anything. That son of a bitch doesn't deserve any consideration." He mumbled his good-byes and hung up.

"What is it?"

Clint turned to face her. "The constable said that Mark asked to see you. Alone."

Nervously Terri sat in the small dimly lit room, waiting for the guards to bring in Mark.

Maybe Clint was right. Maybe she shouldn't have come. What could Mark possibly have to say to her? But her curiosity and determination to have closure in her life propelled her to come.

She sucked on her bottom lip and paced the dingy gray floor, and nearly leaped out of her skin at the sound of the metal door opening.

A strapping guard ushered Mark in. Terri immediately noticed the handcuffs and felt a vague sense of relief.

The guard pushed Mark down in the chair and connected part of the cuff to a metal post at the corner of the table. "I'll be right outside this door if you need me, miss."

Terri nodded.

Mark stared at her with an emptiness that reached out and touched her heart in a way that was eerily familiar. The sensation overwhelmed her. Where had she seen that very same look before?

They sat facing each other for several minutes. Terri finally broke the uneasy silence.

"Why did you want to see me? What could you possibly say to me about what you've done?"

His voice was flat, vacant. "About what I've done? What about what you've done?"

"You're not making sense, Mark. I was always fair and decent to you from the very beginning."

His laugh was hollow. "You still don't know, do you?"

"Listen, if there's something you have to say, then say it. I'm tired of this cat-and-mouse game you're trying to play."

His voice remained without inflection as he slowly poured out the extraordinary story that was their lives.

"You talk about fair and decent. I don't know what that is. I was a little boy who depended on his older sister to keep her promise. I was the little boy who lived day by day, waiting at the window, on the corner, in my bed for my sister to come for me like she promised," he spat, for the first time revealing the traces of his Caribbean accent.

Terri began to feel a tightness in her throat. Her head began to pound. *No. It's not possible.*

Mark looked off and seemed to return to the days of his childhood as he recounted the horrors of his youth. "They beat me," he said softly. "They told me how stupid I was, and that I'd never be anything. They gave me scraps to eat and clothes that never fit. But I knew my sister, whom I loved more than life, was going to come for me."

He looked at her, and the depth of his pain reached out from his eyes and engulfed her. "They told me that I was the bad one, and my sister was the good one. That's why she would always have the best of everything." His voice broke, and his eyes glistened. "But I was a good boy. I was."

He lowered his head and with difficulty reached into his pocket and extracted an old crumpled photograph. For several moments he stared at it.

"This was all I had. It was what kept me going. Until one day I finally understood that my sister wasn't coming back for me. And that I was doomed to a life of hell until I could find a way out. That day I promised myself that when I found her, I would make her pay for leaving me, for breaking her promise." He slid the worn picture across the wooden table.

Through tear-filled eyes Terri could make out the two little faces of the children they'd been so many years ago. She was looking directly into the camera, and her brother, Malcolm, was looking up at her with adoration. She remembered that day as clearly as if it were yesterday.

She looked across the table. "Malcolm . . . ? How long had she wanted to be able to say her brother's name? "I didn't know." Her voice broke, and choking sobs overcame her. "My adopted parents told me you'd died. You have no idea what that did to me." Her body shook with the force of her crying.

He stared at her with disbelief. "They told you I was dead?" His question held the childlike tone of bewilderment.

Terri nodded.

"All the years I've followed you, waited for the perfect time, planned, obsessed—you never even knew I was alive."

Terri slowly got up from her chair to kneel beside him. Tenderly she stroked his face, his shoulders, his hand. "Life has played a vicious joke on us, Malcolm." She swallowed. "But it's not too late. You don't know how I longed for you, thought about you all these years. But I tried to force you to the back of my mind. Our parting was too painful for me to handle. I had my own nightmares to live with. You may have thought that I had a wonderful life, but I didn't. Those people," she choked, "they never truly loved me. They were very civic minded," she said, her voice filled with regret. "In their own way they thought they were doing some good deed for society by taking me in. They took a kind of pleasure in telling all of their friends how sorry they were for me and had adopted me. They gloried in the adulations that they received for doing such a humane thing. I blamed them for my unhappiness for years. I can't any longer. We were both victims, Malcolm. But we don't have to stay victims."

He looked at her, really looked at her, through eyes that were no longer blinded by hate and resentment, and he knew she meant every word.

She leaned over and hugged him. Hugged him with all the love that had been buried, wishing she could erase some of the pain he'd endured.

Their falling tears mixed, blending into one cleansing stream, and they both knew that tomorrow would be brighter.

EPILOGUE

Terri lay nestled in Clint's arms. Their honeymoon cottage hideaway was right off the beach. Several miles away from where his first resort was to be constructed.

The full moon illuminated the cozy bedroom with iridescent, romantic light. Everything was just perfect, Terri thought.

Clint nuzzled her bare breasts. "So how does it feel to be Mrs. Clinton Steele?"

She moved seductively beneath him. "You mean Mrs. Theresa Powers-Steele?"

He kissed her neck. "This women's lib thing is getting to be too much."

Terri giggled and stretched out her left arm to look wonderingly at the flawless diamond that graced her ring finger. Clint had given it to her on Christmas morning, insisting that even though she didn't celebrate Christmas, she had to have something to open. She'd nearly collapsed with shock when she opened the box and saw the dazzling diamond winking at her with a million rays of light.

She sighed with contentment, reliving their beautiful wedding on New Year's Day. Everything was working out. Mrs. Hally had agreed to come with the new family to the States and was busy keeping up with Ashley in the couple's condominium in New York.

As for Malcolm, Clint had reluctantly agreed not to press charges against him, much to Terri's relief. And in a gesture that was so typical of Clint, he'd offered Malcolm a position with his company after he completed his psychological treatments. Malcolm had declined. He wanted a "new life," he'd said, "with no strings attached." He'd returned the ransom money to Clint. And he'd given back all of the money he'd taken from his sister's company, which Terri invested. Malcolm had said he wanted to try his hand at operating a radio station in New Orleans. The money would be there whenever he was ready, Terri'd decided. It was her way of trying to make things up to him.

It would be years before Malcolm would be truly well, but with her love, the support of his new family, and the psychological help he was getting, she felt confident that one day he would be totally free from the demons that had possessed him.

Their budding relationship was slow but steady, and she looked forward to the visits and phone calls and finally getting to know each other.

Jill remained in England, still bitter and resentful of Terri. But she could live with that, Terri thought. She had Clint. Her deep love for her husband allowed her to be forgiving of others. It was she who persuaded Clint to agree that the barrage of letters Jill constantly wrote to Ashley would be given to her over time. Ashley was still unaware of Jill's participation in her abduction, and they wanted to maintain the memory that Ashley had of her aunt.

Melissa had submitted her resignation, but Clint had refused to accept it. He insisted he couldn't run his company without her. She'd decided to stay, and from the looks of things she and Steve were the next ones to jump the broom.

Lisa was getting as big as a house and happier than she'd ever been in her life. Brian was constantly redecorating to satisfy his wife's whims, and she'd recently heard that Alan was getting married. Poor woman. She should warn her.

"What are you thinking about, baby?"

"Oh," she sighed, "just how happy I am. How happy you make me."

Softly he kissed her lips. "Not half as happy as you've made me." Slowly he parted her warm thighs. His strong, knowing hands stroked her hips. "You've given me so much, Terri." He took one nipple in his mouth and suckled, then released it. "You made me believe I could be a father to my child." He took the other nipple and released it. Terri moaned with yearning. "Through you I realized what love and trust really mean."

His tongue played teasing, tantalizing games with hers. "You showed me what true power is, baby," he breathed against her mouth. "The power to forgive. And I'm never going to give you the chance to regret one single moment of our life together."

In one long, slow motion, he joined them. As they became bound together in their love, riding the crest of their undeniable passion for each other, Terri knew that the happiness that had eluded her for so very long was only just beginning . . .